OTHER TITLES BY ELLA DELORIA AVAILABLE
FROM THE UNIVERSITY OF NEBRASKA PRESS

Speaking of Indians

Waterlily

DAKOTA TEXTS

BY

ELLA DELORIA

INTRODUCTION TO THE BISON BOOKS EDITION BY

Raymond J. DeMallie

UNIVERSITY OF NEBRASKA PRESS
LINCOLN AND LONDON

First Nebraska paperback printing: 2006

Library of Congress Cataloging-in-Publication Data
Deloria, Ella Cara.
Dakota texts / Ella Deloria; introduction to the Bison Books edition by
Raymond J. DeMallie.—Bison Books ed.
p. cm.
Dakota and English.
Originally published: New York: G. E. Stechert, 1932, in series: Publica-
tions of the American Ethnological Society; v. 14. With new introd.
ISBN-13: 978-0-8032-6660-5 (pbk.: alk. paper)
ISBN-10: 0-8032-6660-X (pbk.: alk. paper)
1. Dakota literature—Translations into English.   2. Dakota language—
Texts.   3. Teton Indians—Folklore.   I. Title.
PM1024.A2D4   2006
897'.524308—dc22   2005036090

Raymond J. DeMallie

INTRODUCTION TO THE BISON BOOKS EDITION

Ella Deloria's *Dakota Texts*, first published in 1932, is the single most important publication on the oral literature of the Sioux. The sixty-four stories included in the volume were recorded on Rosebud, Standing Rock, and Pine Ridge Reservations from 1927 to 1931. All are told in Lakota, with the exception of one text presented in the Yankton dialect for comparative purposes. Surprisingly, although the Sioux had been the focus of considerable attention from anthropologists and folklorists since the 1880s, Deloria's collection was the first to be published in the native language and today remains the preeminent source for the study of both Lakota language and Lakota narrative. Originally published as number fourteen of the *Publications of the American Ethnological Society*, the volume was soon out of print. In 1974 a library edition was reprinted, and a paperback edition appeared in 1978, but the latter omitted the native language text of the stories. At long last, this Bison Books edition makes *Dakota Texts* widely available in its original bilingual format.

Deloria's book deserves the attention it has gotten from scholars. It has served as the basis for many analytical works in linguistics as well as in cultural and literary studies.[1] The distinctive literary style of Deloria's free English translations distinguishes her volume from most other contemporary American Indian language text collections, which ordinarily presented the content of stories without concern for style.[2] Following the advice of Franz Boas, her mentor, Deloria edited the translations for style and readability, a task that required the translations to reflect the formal or informal tone of the originals as well as a sense of the Lakota syntax. Readability required providing sufficient contextualization for the reader to understand both grammatical obscurities and cultural particulars; rather than litter her translations with bracketed explanatory material, Deloria used footnotes for essential explanations.

Deloria did not have access to sound-recording devices in her fieldwork; she took down stories from dictation. None of her original field notes are known to have survived, and it seems likely that she discarded them after making typewritten copies. A large body of typescript texts that she recorded in Lakota and Dakota (with both literal and free translations) is preserved among Boas's papers in the American Philosophical Society, but they do not include any of the texts published in the present volume.[3] Deloria always expressed regret that financial exigency allowed the printing of word-by-word literal translations for only the first sixteen texts.

Deloria's most explicit statement of her method of recording texts appears in *Dakota Texts* (p. xxv): "The following . . . tales . . . were written down in the original, directly from story-tellers who related them to me." Additional information can be gleaned from her manuscripts and correspondence. Deloria always sought out the oldest and most knowledgeable individuals and took down their words as closely as possible to verbatim. In one instance she noted, "This story was given me by an exceptionally good informant, one who is used to talking through an interpreter and was able to give out his sentences, and wait for my typewriter without losing the trend of thought."[4] Another man was able to give her examples of "mystical speech" (*haḇlóglaka*): "It is beautiful and full of hidden meanings and archaic words. But he goes at a terrific speed, and when I try to get him to slow up so I can record it, he is very unsatisfactory."[5] In a prefatory note to a story recorded in colloquial style in 1937, Deloria explains that she wrote the tale from her memory of various tellings by old men: "In trying to recall it I find that certain set forms have stayed in my mind. . . . But the narrative portions as I have them are only as I can recall them imperfectly, though essentially they are correct."[6] She does not seem to have been concerned, at least in the early years of her story collecting that preceded the publication of this volume, with documenting stories as performances. Her principle goal was to insure that the texts were presented in linguistically correct Lakota and that the stories represented the range of storytelling genres, from traditional myths (*ohúkaká*) to historical tales.

Dakota Texts was the first step in Deloria's project to document as much of Dakota culture as possible. She wanted to demonstrate the overall oneness of the Dakota way of life and to describe the regional differences that made each group distinct. For this purpose she chose the western Sioux, or Tetons—specifically, the Lakotas at Standing Rock Reservation (among whom she grew up)—as the ethnographic baseline and described the other groups in relation to them. She paid particular attention to differences in speech and culture between Standing Rock and the two more southerly Lakota reservations, Rosebud and Pine Ridge. She frequently contrasted the Lakotas with the Yankton Dakotas (her father and mother were both Yanktons and she herself was enrolled on Yankton Reservation) and undertook fieldwork with the eastern Dakotas (Santees) in Minnesota to extend her comparative perspective to all three major Sioux groups. (Deloria ordinarily used the designation "Dakota" in preference to "Sioux," leading to some confusion between three possible meanings of Dakota: as a generic term for all the Sioux; as a specific designation for the eastern or Santee Sioux; and as the tribal self-designation *Dak'óta* used by both the eastern Sioux and the Yankton-Yanktonai Sioux.)

The objective of Deloria's quest was to study Dakota culture and language as abstract entities. To this end, she felt compelled to check her information with one individual after another to insure reliability. She was concerned with normative behavior, the common sense ways in which proper Lakotas should behave, describing deviant behavior as a means of validating the existence of norms. In short, she shared with the anthropologists of her time a Boasian concept of culture, with its emphasis on the collective knowledge of the social group. This is evident throughout her writings, even in her novel, *Waterlily* (1988), which reconstructs nineteenth-century Lakota culture from women's perspectives.

Deloria's ethnographic work focused on two primary subjects: kinship, family, and the maintenance of social order; and religion, particularly as expressed in ceremony. The focus of her studies was the reconstruction of prereservation culture, but she frequently included reservation-era material to demonstrate cultural persistence into the twentieth century. In her fieldwork she recorded texts and conversations in Lakota and Dakota, both for their value as linguistic documentation and for their relevance to her study of culture. In addition, she recorded interviews and observations in English, frequently clarifying and expanding on information in the texts.

Most of Deloria's field studies took place between 1927 and 1939, during which time she single-handedly created one of the largest and most thorough archives of linguistic and cultural information for any American Indian group. As was the case with most of the large-scale projects of Boasian anthropology, little of Deloria's work was published during her lifetime, and although that was disappointing to her, it in no way diminishes the significance of her legacy. How she came to be the ethnographer and linguist of the Sioux is a remarkable story.

Ella Cara Deloria was born January 31, 1889, on Yankton Reservation in South Dakota, the daughter of Mary Sully Bordeaux and Philip J. Deloria, both mixed-blood Yanktons.[7] Her father, son of a

Yankton chief, was one of the first two Dakota men to be ordained as priests in the Episcopal Church, and in 1890 he was given charge of St. Elizabeth's mission church and school near the community of Wakpala, among the Lakotas on Standing Rock Reservation. Ella was raised there, with her younger sister and brother, Susan and Vine. Deloria's childhood memories of the big tipi her mother would put up during the summers, which served as the children's playhouse, and of the families of Chief Gall and other Hunkpapa and Blackfeet Lakotas from the nearby community of Wakpala are warmly recalled in her writings. Her father, as she later wrote, pressed his parishioners to abandon Indian ways as rapidly as possible—perhaps too rapidly, she thought. He advocated using the Episcopal Church, with its rituals and its societies for men and women, as a substitute for the sociability and pageantry of traditional life. His son Vine recalled that Philip Deloria enjoyed dressing in ecclesiastical garb and leading the ritual processions on holy days, participating in the meetings of the Brotherhood of Christian Unity (a sodality he founded with a group of like-minded Dakota men), and joining in the camps held for the annual summer church convocations.

None of this made for a normal childhood. Ella Deloria wrote that she and her siblings were not completely at home in Indian society, where the social restrictions of gender and rules about respect circumscribed the children's play, and where, in the context of the mission school, they were always the minister's children, always called on to "set an example."[8] Then they were sent to boarding school at All Saints in Sioux Falls; Deloria studied there from 1902 to 1910. That year she entered Oberlin College, then enrolled at Columbia Teachers College in 1913, where she received her BS two years later. During her last semester in New York she was introduced to Franz Boas, who was pursuing study of the Dakota language. Boas hired her—it was Deloria's first paying job—to come to his class and work with him and his students on translating portions of the texts written in Lakota by George Bushotter in 1887 and preserved at the Smithsonian Institution. Doing this work provided her first realization that skill in her native language was valued outside Sioux Country. After graduation, Deloria returned to All Saints, where she taught for four years. In 1919 she took a job with the YWCA as health education secretary for Indian schools. In 1923 she returned to teaching, this time as a physical education instructor at Haskell Institute, an Indian school in Lawrence, Kansas.

Boas did not learn where Deloria had gone until the winter of 1926, when a chance meeting between his student Martha Beckwith, who was collecting Dakota folklore, and Philip Deloria once again put Boas in touch with her. In June 1927 Boas took the train to Lawrence to visit her, and to continue their work on the Bushotter translations. While there, they finalized the writing system for Dakota, Boas reinforcing in Deloria's mind the necessity of distinguishing aspirated, unaspirated, and glottalized consonants. (Boas referred to it, writing to Deloria, as "the alphabet as we designed it"; Deloria characterized it as Boas's "new way" of writing, "for comparative study of primitive languages.")[9] Before leaving, Boas drew up a formal agreement to pay Deloria to continue work during the summer. Writing to Episcopal bishop Hugh L. Burleson, her spiritual advisor and temporal benefactor, Deloria explained her work with Boas this way:

> Dr. Boas of Columbia, with whom I did some work in recording Dakota phonetically, when I was in school, came to see me and we worked out some more material. He is most interested in getting the language recorded accurately for future reference in comparative languages of primitive peoples, and wants me to work with him. . . . I am finishing up now some revision of the Bushotter Dakota texts from the Smithsonian Institute. . . . I am very thoroughly convinced that you can not really get at the heart of a people without knowing their language. I think my knowledge of Dakota is a big asset there.[10]

Her letters from Haskell reveal Ella Deloria's strong identity as a Dakota and as an Indian; this identity was fostered by a network of educated Indian friends and acquaintances. While at Haskell she was particularly proud of her accomplishments in writing and staging pageants, modeled in part after tableaux performed by the students at All Saints. In 1928 she copyrighted "The Wohpe Festival," a day-long celebration of traditional Dakota religion for schools and summer camps. It celebrates Indians as children of nature: "The great lesson is taught that life in any form is precious . . . all children, regardless of race, need to learn it at some time during their lives."[11] Loosely based on the Sun Dance, the directions for the festival give invocations, prayers, dances, and ritual movements. The ethnographic material on which the Wohpe Festival is based, however, did not come out of Deloria's personal knowledge. Most of it is taken directly from a Lakota text by George Sword, supplemented by material from James Walker's monograph on the Sun Dance published by the American Museum. Both of these were provided to her by Franz Boas.

Deloria spent the summer of 1927 working for Boas on the Bushotter and Sword text translations, and transcribing some Lakota stories on her own. She enjoyed the linguistic work and continued it during the fall at Haskell. But at age thirty-nine she found teaching physical education to be too exhausting and was looking for another line of work. In November she sent Boas a handwritten letter, written in an exhilarated tone:

> [I] am considering resigning. . . . I have in view two things,—a position in a book company, or church work at home. But of course that is in case you have nothing for me. I am wondering—you once said that for a time you might have me come to live in your home and do work on the Dakota. Would you care to offer me such a thing at this time? I could come the first part of January. . . . I should have to have a salary, and whenever an opportunity came from a high school or organization, to tell Indian customs and demonstrate dances, as used to come when I was in New York, I would like to be able to go. The rest of the time I could give to any work you would want me to do. . . .
>
> P.S. You spoke of a possible fellowship. If that should materialize, I could come back to the Sioux Country in June. I would like that better than teaching gym work any more.[12]

Boas was guardedly optimistic about being able to provide support for Deloria; he proposed a monthly salary of one hundred dollars and for Ella to live with his family. She preferred a higher salary that would allow her independence in New York. On Christmas Day, 1927, she wrote again to Boas, assuring him that she wanted nothing more than to do work with him on the Dakota language. On January 18, 1928, Boas wrote Deloria that he had obtained funds for her to revise the Riggs dictionary of Santee, recording the equivalent Teton forms. Finally, on January 28, Boas was able to guarantee her regular employment for eighteen months on a project to study Dakota psychology—"the habits of action and thought" of children and adults. He wrote, "You will have to know all the details of everyday life as well as of religious attitudes and habits of thought of the people."[13]

Deloria went to New York in February, delaying her trip until her brother Vine could arrive at Yankton Reservation to stay with their father, who had retired from missionary work and whose health was precarious. The two hundred dollars a month Boas ultimately provided allowed Deloria to rent her own lodgings and to bring her sister with her; neither Ella nor Susan ever married and the two would be lifelong companions. At the end of April Deloria wrote to her bishop that she had completed work on the Riggs dictionary, having written the Lakota forms in the margins. Boas's objective was to reorganize the dictionary according to verb stems. She was also teaching two classes, one presumably devoted to Dakota culture and society, the other a linguistics methods class, "where I do not teach but answer questions put to me by the students who are trying to learn methods of getting at a new, primitive language."[14]

During the summer Deloria returned to South Dakota to continue field study. In a letter to Boas, written from Rosebud, she expressed frustration:

> I am getting along all right. There are some discouraging features— one of them, the temperament of some of my informants. It is the old old man or woman who is most valuable, but unfortunately is apt to be vague and indefinite. I do not see how non-Dakota-speaking workers get along as well as they do.[15]

Searching for someone who would talk about traditional religion, Deloria was led to an old medicine man, a diviner, said to be the only man capable of providing the kind of information she needed. As a half brother of her father's, he was also a father to Deloria, but she wrote, "He hates my father because he considers him disloyal to the teachings and practices of their father."[16] Another old man was a possibility, but his son was married to one of Deloria's half sisters, making her his daughter-in-law, and kinship custom forbade direct communication between them. In short, Deloria's status as an insider was a mixed blessing when it came to her fieldwork.

Deloria intended to be back in New York by fall, but her father suffered a stroke, and she went to be with him. Ella continued working for Boas by writing texts, doing interviews, and correcting dictionary cards as he sent them to her, but she stayed with her father on Yankton Reservation. She was to collaborate with the psychologist Otto Klineberg, who sent her questions for investigation. Most comfortable working with the people at Wakpala, Deloria decided to move her ailing father back to Standing Rock (over the bishop's protest) to facilitate her work. She made three trips there during the summer of 1928, then moved her father in the fall.[17]

Deloria was unable to return to New York until the spring or early summer of 1931. She remained there until the summer of 1932, working with Boas on language and organizing her field data; later, she wrote of this visit, "Professor Boas first gave me intensive training in phonetic transcription of the Dakota language in preparation for linguistic recording of texts and analysis of the grammar."[18] During this visit she finalized the manuscript of *Dakota Texts*, which

Boas took to a printer in Germany. By fall Deloria was back in South Dakota.

The pattern of field study with periodic visits to New York continued. By 1932 Ruth Benedict had taken over directing Deloria's work, and the two women came to develop a very close relationship. In 1933 Deloria undertook field study among the Assiniboines in Montana; in 1934 she worked among the Santees in Minnesota; in 1935 she recorded colloquial Lakota for Boas; in 1936 she completed translation of the Bushotter texts; in 1937 and 1938 she continued work on colloquial Lakota, finished the Sword manuscripts, and investigated the authenticity of James Walker's mythological cycles, which had been recorded around the turn of the century at Pine Ridge.

At last, in May 1939, Boas informed Deloria that there was no more money to continue the work. The grammar they had written together was accepted for publication, bringing closure to their long collaboration. Final corrections and proofing continued through 1940. Lacking funds, ill, and facing the specter of world war, in November 1942 Boas wrote to Deloria, who was then in New York, "It will take such a long time before I can get your Dakota manuscripts published that I should feel much safer if I could have the two copies in different places."[19]

Boas died less than a month later. Benedict continued to provide support for Deloria's work when possible and helped her prepare her material on Dakota social·life for publication. With money from the American Philosophical Society, Deloria completed the manuscript in 1947 and sent it to Benedict for reorganization and editing. Benedict completed her work, and Deloria planned to consult with her on the final editing in September 1948. But when Deloria arrived in New York, she learned that Benedict had died unexpectedly. Deloria continued to work on the book, with the aid of a Bollingin Foundation grant, but in 1955 she responded to a plea from the church to return to Wakpala and run St. Elizabeth's, by now reduced to a mission home for Indian children. She remained there until 1958, retiring to the University of South Dakota to continue her linguistic studies. She interviewed elderly Yanktons in support of Yankton land claims and interviewed elders at Cheyenne River in conjunction with the Doris Duke Oral History project. But at the time of her death on February 12, 1971, all of her major works, with the exception of *Dakota Texts*, were left unpublished.

Reading Deloria's volume today, one is struck by the authenticity of the stories. These are not tales retold for western audiences; they follow the structures and devices of Lakota storytelling conventions. In the mythic narrative tradition, Deloria notes, listeners understood the cultural references without explanation. The *ohŭkakŭ* were, she says, a kind of "hang-over" from the traditional past, stories that served as a source of allusion, and she noted that "similes are drawn from them which every intelligent adult is sure to understand" (p. xxv). These myths include double-faced beings, the people-devouring monster Íya, the trickster-creator Iktómi, and a host of mythic motives, many of which are well-known to students of comparative mythology. What is uniquely Lakota, however, is the way the stories are put together, the spin they received that distinguished them from the stories of all other tribes.[20]

A second category of myth Deloria calls "novelistic *ohŭkakŭ.*" These are constructed from traditional elements but highlight the creative genius of the teller; they are not part of the tribal repertoire but are distinctive to particular narrators. This offers a new perspective on the creativity of traditional narrative. Elaine Jahner, the pre-eminent student of Lakota narrative traditions, commented, "I find Deloria's recognition of the original forms of fiction to be of extraordinary literary historical importance because she documents an expanded range of creative expression in communities where narrative continuity and development depended entirely on oral resources."[21]

The remainder of the stories in *Dakota Texts* are tales and legends that are considered true. Some of these were widely told and involve interactions between humans and spirit beings; others represented a particular reservation—Pine Ridge—and concern local events, many of which involve intertribal warfare.

Deloria's texts invite comparison with other collections of Lakota stories. The first extensive collection was composed in Lakota by George Bushotter in 1887 for James Owen Dorsey—some 258 texts (including ninety-five myths and legends) that Deloria herself retranscribed and translated during her years of working with Boas. Bushotter's stories have never been published in their entirety, although translations or synopses of many of them appear in Dorsey's *A Study of Siouan Cults.*[22] Chronologically, the first published collection of Lakota stories was recorded by Clark Wissler from two men at Pine Ridge in 1902. These ten stories were written down in English, apparently as the interpreter translated them, but they seem to have been editorially polished for publication.[23] After reading them, James R. Walker, the government physician at Pine Ridge, told Wissler that he, too, was recording traditional myths, noting that the narratives of "professional" storytellers were much more elaborate than those

Wissler had recorded. Walker collected some of his narratives as written texts in Lakota, while others were taken down in translation. Walker included twenty of these myths and legends in his study of the Oglala Sun Dance. Later, after retiring from Pine Ridge, Walker used these texts as the basis for a novelistic treatment of Lakota mythology. Boas asked Deloria to verify the contents of these stories, but in the 1930s she failed to find narrators who knew the details of such sacred stories. In the absence of original Lakota texts for these narratives, their status remains uncertain, though Jahner studied them closely and argued for their essential authenticity.[24]

Most directly comparable to Deloria's narratives are those recorded in English by Martha Beckwith in 1926, many of which were told by narrators at Pine Ridge who would also later provide stories to Deloria.[25] Beckwith's collection represents an impressively wide range of Lakota oral narratives, most of which were written down from the translations of reservation interpreters. The tales seem to have been minimally reworked for publication, and their style can be profitably compared with Deloria's more polished translations. This collection includes a winter count (annual calendar) documenting the years from 1759 to 1925 and thirty-six additional narratives that include myths, legends, and personal experiences.

Two other collections of Lakota stories bear mentioning for purposes of comparison. In 1916 Marie McLaughlin, also a mixed-blood Sioux, published a collection of thirty-eight myths and legends from Standing Rock, compiled from notes—apparently taken over many years—made from the storytelling of old men and women. These narratives seem more like literary reworkings than direct translations, though the author was concerned with preserving the "timbre" of the stories as reflecting the "texture" of the people's heart and mind.[26] A later collection by the WPA South Dakota Writers' Project includes forty-one short myths and legends greatly simplified and published for children.[27] Nonetheless, many of these stories are versions of narratives recorded by Deloria and others.

Study of Deloria's stories in comparison with other collections will richly repay the effort. For example, in her study of *Dakota Texts*, Elaine Jahner looked beyond the specificities of plot and overt symbolism to identify in the stories four thematic structures based on categories of spatial relations that characterize the narratives: (1) family interrelationships and life in the tipi; (2) the "heroic pattern," emphasizing interrelationships among various spheres of life (e.g., the tipi, the village circle, the four directions); (3) movement away from the center of the village circle, causing destruction of the social group; and (4) the possibilities of life outside the village circle. The symbolic centrality of the circle reflected in the shape of the tipi and the organization of the village circle, repeated in the cycle of days, moons, and winters, in the four directions (winds), and in an individual's life from birth to death, characterizes the distinctive Sioux narrative style. "Sioux narrative," Jahner suggests, "functioned to relate individuals to their social and physical environment." In this way, narratives made sense of the world and storytelling was—and is—an active force in cultural maintenance and adaptation.[28]

In 1967, at the fifteenth annual meeting of the American Society for Ethnohistory, held in Lexington, Kentucky, Ella Deloria presented a talk on Yankton place names that derived from her work in support of Yankton land claims. Her chatty style of delivery, total mastery of the material, and level of excitement at sharing information with the audience set her presentation apart from all the others. As an undergraduate student already committed to a career as an anthropologist, I listened to Miss Deloria with rapt fascination. At the end of her talk she was explaining the significance of the name of the Vermillion River, where the Dakota used to dig *wasé* (Indian paint), but her time was up. "There's so much left to tell," she said, breathlessly, "so invite me back next year, and I'll tell you more!"

Her writings go on telling generation after generation. Whatever the personal costs of a life preoccupied with recording the minutiae of Dakota language and culture, today we are all the richer for it—and enormously grateful.

ACKNOWLEDGMENTS

My perspective on Ella Deloria's work has been shaped by the privilege I enjoyed of conversations with her in 1965 and 1970; by collaborative study with her brother, the late Vine V. Deloria Sr.; and by many years of association with the Deloria family.

NOTES

1. For example, see Jahner 1975; Rice 1989, 1992a, 1992b; Lungstrum 1995.
2. See the discussion in Kroeber 1981.
3. For lists of these manuscripts, see Freeman 1966:119–21; Kendall 1982:37.

4. Deloria 1937b: story 5.

5. Deloria to Boas, October 17, 1932, Boas Collection, American Philosophical Society Library, Philadelphia.

6. Deloria 1937a: story 1.

7. There is confusion concerning her birth year, which is sometimes given as 1888. The fullest biography of Ella Deloria is Murray 1974. See also the essays by Agnes Picotte and Raymond J. DeMallie in Deloria 1988:229–44, and Medicine 2001. For the Deloria family, see Vine Deloria Jr. 1999.

8. Deloria to Bishop Burleson, January 9, 1927, Episcopal Diocese of South Dakota Archives, Center for Western History, Augustana College, Sioux Falls SD; copy in the Dakota Indian Foundation Archives, Chamberlain SD.

9. Boas to Deloria, January 18, 1928, Boas Collection, American Philosophical Society Library, Philadelphia; Deloria to Bishop Burleson, December 16, 1927, Episcopal Diocese of South Dakota Archives, Center for Western History, Augustana College, Sioux Falls SD; copy in the Dakota Indian Foundation Archives, Chamberlain SD.

10. Deloria to Bishop Burleson, August 8, 1927. Episcopal Diocese of South Dakota Archives, Center for Western History, Augustana College, Sioux Falls SD; copy in the Dakota Indian Foundation Archives, Chamberlain SD.

11. Deloria to Bishop Burleson, August 8, 1927, Episcopal Diocese of South Dakota Archives, Sioux Falls SD; copy in the Dakota Indian Foundation Archives, Chamberlain SD.

12. Deloria to Boas, November 28, 1927, Boas Collection, American Philosophical Society Library, Philadelphia.

13. Boas to Deloria, January 28, 1928, Boas Collection, American Philosophical Society Library, Philadelphia.

14. Deloria to Bishop Burleson, April 29, 1928, Episcopal Diocese of South Dakota Archives, Center for Western History, Augustana College, Sioux Falls SD; copy in the Dakota Indian Foundation Archives, Chamberlain SD.

15. Deloria to Boas, August 21, 1928, Boas Collection, American Philosophical Society Library, Philadelphia.

16. Deloria to Boas, August 21, 1928, Boas Collection, American Philosophical Society Library, Philadelphia.

17. Deloria to Boas, October 4, 1929, Boas Collection, American Philosophical Society Library, Philadelphia.

18. Deloria, grant application to the American Philosophical Society, September 1, 1943; copy in Ruth Benedict Collection, Special Collections, Vassar College Library, Poughkeepsie NY.

19. Boas to Deloria, November 23, 1942, Boas Collection, American Philosophical Society Library, Philadelphia.

20. See Jahner 1975.

21. Jahner 1992:171.

22. Dorsey 1894. For biographical information on Bushotter, see DeMallie 2002.
23. Wissler 1907.
24. These stories appear in Walker 1917:164–221. Other versions, together with Walker's novelistic treatment of Lakota mythology, appear in Walker 1983. Jahner discusses Deloria's attempt to verify Walker's narratives and presents her own attempts to do so in Walker 1983:1–40 and Jahner 1992.
25. Deloria provided retranscriptions of Lakota words in these texts for Beckwith to use in her publication.
26. McLaughlin 1916:10.
27. Reese 1941.
28. Jahner 1975:140–230; the quotation is on p. 143.

REFERENCES

Beckwith, Martha Warren
   1930 Mythology of the Oglala Dakota. Journal of American Folk-Lore 43(170):339–442.
Deloria, Ella C.
   1932 Dakota Texts. Publications of the American Ethnological Society 14. New York: G. E. Stechert. Reprinted, New York: AMS Press, 1974.
   [1937a] Dakota Texts in Colloquial Style. Ms. no. X 8a.16. Franz Boas Collection, American Philosophical Society Library, Philadelphia PA.
   [1937b] Old Dakota Legends. Ms. no. X 8a.21. Franz Boas Collection, American Philosophical Society Library, Philadelphia PA.
   1978 Dakota Texts. Agnes Picotte and Paul Pavich, eds. Vermillion SD: Dakota Press.
   1988 Waterlily. Lincoln: University of Nebraska Press.
Deloria, Vine Jr.
   1999 Singing for a Spirit: A Portrait of the Dakota Sioux. Santa Fe NM: Clear Light Publishers.
DeMallie, Raymond J.
   2002 George Bushotter, Teton Sioux, 1864–1892. In American Indian Intellectuals of the Nineteenth and Early Twentieth Centuries. Margot Liberty, ed. Pp. 105–19. Norman: University of Oklahoma Press. Originally published as American Indian Intellectuals, 1976 Proceedings of the American Ethnological Society. St. Paul MN: West Publishing, 1978. Pp. 91–102.
Dorsey, James Owen
   1894 A Study of Siouan Cults. In Eleventh Annual Report of the Bureau of [American] Ethnology. Pp. 351–544. Washington DC.
Freeman, John E.
   1966 A Guide to Manuscripts Relating to the American Indian in the Li-

brary of the American Philosophical Society. American Philosophical Society Memoirs 65. Philadelphia PA.

Jahner, Elaine A.
  1975 Spatial Categories in Sioux Folk Narrative. PhD dissertation, Indi-
        ana University.
  1992 Transitional Narratives and Cultural Continuity. boundary 2: an
        international journal of literature and culture 19(3):148–79 (1492–
        1992: American Indian Persistence and Resurgence. Karl Kroeber,
        ed.). Reprinted as American Indian Persistence and Resurgence.
        Durham NC: Duke University Press, 1994.

Kendall, Daythal
  1982 A Supplement to a Guide to Manuscripts Relating to the American
        Indian in the Library of the American Philosophical Society. *In*
        AmericanPhilosophical Society Memoirs 65S. Philadelphia PA.

Kroeber, Karl, comp. and ed.
  1981 Traditional Literatures of the American Indian: Texts and Inter-
        pretations. Lincoln: University of Nebraska Press.

Lungstrum, Richard W.
  1995 Switch-Reference and the Structure of Lakhota Narrative Dis-
        course. PhD dissertation, University of Pennsylvania.

McLaughlin, Marie L.
  1916 Myths and Legends of the Sioux. Bismarck ND: Bismarck Tribune.

Medicine, Beatrice
  2001 Ella C. Deloria: The Emic Voice. *In* Leaning to Be an Anthropologist
        and Remaining "Native": Selected Writings. Beatrice Medicine with
        Sue-Ellen Jacobs, eds. Pp. 269–88. Urbana and Chicago: University
        of Illinois Press.

Murray, Janette K.
  1974 Ella Deloria: A Biographical Sketch and Literary Analysis. PhD
        dissertation, University of North Dakota.

Reese, Montana Lisle, ed.
  1941 Legends of the Mighty Sioux: Compiled by Workers of the South
        Dakota Writers' Project, Work Projects Administration. Chicago:
        Albert Whitman.

Rice, Julian
  1989 Lakota Storytelling: Black Elk, Ella Deloria, and Frank Fools Crow.
        American University Studies XXI, Regional Studies 3. New York:
        Peter Lang.
  1992a Deer Women and Elk Men: The Lakota Narratives of Ella Deloria.
        Albuquerque: University of New Mexico Press.
  1992b *Narrative Styles in* Dakota Texts. *In* On the Translation of Ameri-
        can Indian Native Literatures. Brian Swan, ed. Pp. 276–92. Wash-
        ington DC: Smithsonian Institution Press.
  1993 *Ella Deloria's* Iron Hawk. Albuquerque: University of New Mexico
        Press.

1994a *Ella Deloria's* The Buffalo People. Albuquerque: University of New Mexico Press.

1994b Two Roads to Leadership: Grandmother's Boy and Last-Born Brother. *In* Coming to Light: Contemporary Translations of Native American Literature. Brian Swan, ed. Pp. 403–22. New York: Random House.

2004 Lakota: Double-Face Tricks a Girl. *In* Voices from Four Directions: Contemporary Translations of the Native Literatures of North America. Brian Swan, ed. Pp. 397–407. Lincoln: University of Nebraska Press.

Walker, James R.

1917 The Sun Dance and Other Ceremonies of the Oglala Division of the Teton Dakota. Anthropological Papers of the American Museum of Natural History 16(2):51–221. New York.

1983 Lakota Myth. Elaine A. Jahner, ed. Lincoln: University of Nebraska Press.

Wissler, Clark

1907 Some Dakota Myths I and II. Journal of American Folk-Lore 20(77): 121–31, 20(78):195–206.

TO

FRANZ BOAS

TABLE OF CONTENTS.

INTRODUCTION.

The following Teton-Dakota tales from the Standing Rock, Pine Ridge and Rosebud reservations in South Dakota, were written down in the original, directly from story-tellers who related them to me. Each tale is accompanied by a free translation which I have tried to keep as simple and close to the Dakota style as possible; and by notes on the grammar and customs. In addition, a literal translation was made for the first sixteen tales.

The stories are arranged according to Dakota categories, in two parts, each of which is further divided into two parts, giving four groups in all. The first part, 1 to 39, contains all those tales which the Dakotas call *ohú'kaką*. When someone wishes to express incredulity, he says *ohú'kaką s'e* — How like an *ohú'kaką!* When a person is talking nonsense, bragging or making wild promises, the people say, *iśe' he' hųka'kąhe lo'!* — That one is merely telling an *ohú'kaką*; don't mind him! These statements indicate, I think, the light in which such tales are regarded. They are intended to amuse and entertain, but not to be believed. All such stories end with the conventional *hehą' yela owi'hąke'*ᵉ — That is all; that is the end. They may be narrated only after sunset.

This part is divided into two groups of which the first, tales 1 to 28, are best known, oftenest repeated, and farthest removed from the events of every day life of the Dakota people. They are the real *ohú'kaką*. To our minds, they are a sort of hang-over, so to speak, from a very, very remote past, from a different age, even from an order of beings different from ourselves. These tales, in which generally some mythological character like Iktomi, Iya, the Crazy Bull, the Witch, or Waziya (the Cold), takes part together with human beings, are part of the common literary stock of the people. Constant allusion is made to them; similes are drawn from them which every intelligent adult is sure to understand. "Like shooting off the sacred arrow," or, "They are dancing with eyes shut, to his singing" one hears repeatedly. "He is playing Iktomi" is understood to mean that a person is posing as a very agreeable fellow, simply to get what he wants. I am not quite certain about tales nos. 13 and 14, tales with animals as principals but without any mythological characters. No. 12, also dealing with animals, belongs here, because all Dakotas know that Coyote is the animal embodiment of Ikto, just as *śiya'ka*, the undesirable husband in 23, the Heart-killer story, is Iktomi as a human being. It seemed more consistent to put 13 and 14 with 12, than anywhere else.

The second group of *ohų́'kaką*, nos. 29 to 39, contains stories not so universally known; at least, they are not referred to in the same way as the real *ohų́'kaką*. These tales are of the novelistic type. The gods have stepped out of the picture; and while miraculous things continue to take place, they are accepted as something that might have been possible, at least a long while ago, among a people not so different from us.

The stories contained in the second part, from no. 40 on to the end, are regarded as true. The conventional *ohų́'kaką* ending disappears and instead, each tale closes with *šk'e''*, it is said; and *keya'pi''*, they say. The first group in this part includes nos. 40 to 54, stories which are accepted as having happened to our people in comparatively recent times, perhaps in the lifetime of the aged narrator's grandfather or great-grandfather. Some of these tales are legends of localities; and while the miraculous still runs through many of them, they are regarded as occurrences that may happen to someone aided by supernatural powers.

The last group, nos. 55 to 64, contain simple accounts of events that took place in the local band, and are told at times to recall the past or to entertain one who has not heard them. Each locality, each band, has its own stories of this nature. These particular ones belong to the Pine Ridge people who told them to me on my first visit in 1931.

Of the rest, nos. 10, 24, 25, 26, 27, 30, 32, 34, 37, 38, 41, 43, 46, 49 and 50 were obtained on the Rosebud reservation, while 31, the Yankton version of 30, is included in the book because it is an example of pure Yankton, and gives us a chance to see wherein it differs from the Teton dialect. All the other tales were recorded on the Standing Rock Reservation from *Hų́'kpap'aya* and Blackfeet informants. The tale no. 27, with its Standing Rock version, 28, is of European origin. How long the Dakotas have had it, I can not say, of course. But I put the two versions into group one, real *ohų́'kaką*, because the mythological Iya is introduced into the tale.

My thanks are due to more persons in the Indian country than I can name. Of especial assistance were Mrs. Andrew Little Moon, Patrick Shields and Joseph W. Plume of Standing Rock; Richard Bergen and *Wam.ni'yom.ni Oȟ'q'k'o* (Fast Whirlwind) of Pine Ridge, and George Schmidt and Dick Claymore of Rosebud. My father, the late Rev. Philip Deloria, supplied the Yankton version of the Deer Woman, and also gave me immeasurable help with the notes on customs and beliefs, throughout the book.

I am most deeply indebted to Dr. Boas, who first made it possible for me to take up this study, and has wisely directed my efforts and patiently corrected my mistakes. Without him, this book could not be.

E. C. D.

SYNOPSES OF TALES.

*Oh*ŭ*′kak*ą Tales.

1. Iktomi and Iya meet and try to overpower each other with magic until Iktomi tricks Iya into visiting a camp where, with the aid of the warriors, Iya is killed. From his body emerge the countless tribes he has eaten, and they repopulate the earth.

2. Iktomi breaks the avoidance rule towards mothers-in-law, by having his wife's mother accompany him to war. They return years later with a host of children and Iktomi is run out of the village.

3. Iktomi falls in love with his own daughter and pretends to be dead; returning later in disguise to marry her.

4. While Iktomi sings, the pheasants dance with eyes shut, and he kills the largest of them. Later, while his fowls are cooking, he is caught fast up in a tree and a wolf coming by eats all his food.

5. Iktomi kills the Deer Boy and roasts him, but wolves come by and eat up the meat. This is the Cree version of 4, which has been introduced into the Standing Rock tales.

6. Iktomi enters a skull to join in the dance of the mice but they run away, leaving him with his head caught.

7. A buffalo carries Iktomi across a stream, by letting him ride inside; and when it forgets to cough him up, Ikto cuts a gash in its side and gets out. He meets the eye-jugglers, mice who teach him their trick. He tries to win and throws his eyes so high that they are caught in a tree. He goes about weeping, in his blindness, until the Chief Spirit restores his sight.

8. Iktomi, dropped into a hollow tree by the hawk whom he has insulted, plays the raccoon and tricks two foolish women into freeing him.

9. The Double-Face posing as a girl's lover lures her away. She escapes by tying his long strands of hair to the tipi poles while he is asleep.

10. Another tale of the Double-Face luring away a young girl. In this one, the obstacles in the way of the girl's escape are varied, and at last a man who refuses her as a wife but accepts her as his daughter, saves her life.

11. The Double-Face, posing as a young woman, comes to live with four brothers as their sister. The last-born sits on the tipi top to guard her and finds that she is not human. The brothers run away from her and an old woman helps them to escape.

12. Coyote, the animal embodiment of Iktomi, meets Bear, the embodiment of Iya the eater, and they challenge each other much as in tale 1. At last the bear is killed, and Coyote plans a sacred feast, in which the rabbit acts as server. The guests run away with the food, leaving Coyote discomfited.

13. Turtle goes alone to war, because his comrades all perish on the way. The enemy-people capture him and want to kill him. Following his advice, they try to drown him. He swims away triumphant.

14. The snake crawls into the meadow-lark's nest. She pretends to be glad and sends one child after another on errands. When they are all gone, she too flies to safety.

15. Boy-Beloved's blanket is stolen by the Crazy Bull. After much difficulty, he recovers it, with the help of friendly animals and birds.

16. The first part of this tale is the same as no. 11; the second part deals with the good sister, whose child, developed from a pebble she swallowed, grows into the hero, Stone Boy. With miraculous power he resurrects his four dead uncles, and accomplishes other feats.

17. Turtle-Moccasin Boy is driven from home by his angry grandmother whose pemmican he has allowed the dog to devour.

18. Turtle-Moccasin Boy encounters Iktomi and together they try some buffalo-magic which fails. In the end they meet and kill Iya, the eater. Same ending as in no. 1.

19. White-Plume Boy frees the tribe from the four men who menace it. He competes with them and wins, thereby earning the right to kill them. Then he travels, and encounters Iktomi disguised as an old woman who steals his plume, and with it, his powers. He is changed into a cur until a kind girl rescues him. He shoots the red fox and the scarlet eagle, and when he smokes, beautiful articles rain from the smoke, so that the tribe is made rich.

20. The rabbit produces Blood-Clot Boy from a blood-clot over which he makes a sweat-bath. The boy frees his rabbit grandfather from the bear, but later he himself is tricked by Iktomi and fastened to a tree. A girl sets him free, and he enters camp and gives the people food, showing up Iktomi who earlier entered in his guise and tried but failed to work that miracle.

21. When the eagle-man who married the Dakota girl was angry he destroyed the entire tribe. But his son, raised by a meadowlark man, restored them, and became their hero.

22. The Boy who lived with his grandmother defies the Cold-Tyrant, and overcomes both him and his wife and children; all but one who escapes by hiding in a hole made by the tent-pole. He it is that produces the cold we now have.

23. Heart-killer is rescued from the beavers by her four brothers, but later is lured away by two women who take her to marry

Tealduck while they marry the Prince, *B.lecʻe'*. Instead, they marry Tealduck. He is assisted by the Iya who cuts off *B.lecʻe''s* head. Heart-killer, with the aid of her pet beaver, escapes.

24. Two friends after much trouble restore the arm to the buffalo man which an enemy tribe cut from him. On their return to their people, they work a miracle, with the help of the grateful buffalo, so that the people have food.

25. Hakela shoots off his brother's sacred arrow, hoping to kill the scarlet bird. But the bird was only a boy-beloved in disguise, who flew home with the arrow in his body. Hakela succeeds after much effort and some trickery to restore the arrow to its place before his brothers return.

26. The favorite daughter eloped with the wrong man, who turns out to be not human. She escapes, after he removes her scalp, and encounters the Feather man whom she marries. Her struggles with the man's wife, who is a bear-woman, end when she overcomes and kills her.

27. *T'aźi'*, the youngest, after many adventures in which men endowed with magic powers assist him, rescues the chief's daughter from the underworld, and marries her. (Borrowed from the European.)

28. The same tale somewhat modified, in which the father of the lost girl is assisted by birds and insects, in finding the blue egg which alone will kill the Iya.

Novelistic *ohų́ kaką* Tales.

29. The Elk man, representing irresistible masculine charm, works havoc with the women of the tribe, and comes to life when the council tries to get rid of him. He is then given up as immortal.

30. A hunter encounters the girl of his choice in a deserted place. She turns out to be a deer, masquerading as the girl, and in her panic to escape, bestows supernatural powers on the man. The deer is the symbol of feminine charm.

31. A Yankton version of the same tale in the Yankton dialect, without elaboration.

32. A woman falls in love with her daughter's husband and causes her daughter to drown. The latter becomes half-fish but is rescued by her husband and brother and the wicked mother is swallowed up by the earth.

33. A hungry woman puts a curse on the stingy hunter who does not share with her. He later meets all the obstacles she predicted for him, but overcomes them all in various ways.

34. A boy-beloved is tempted by his own sister whose identity he discovers too late. He punishes her and she causes him to grow onto a tree. The Thunder man rescued him in exchange for his younger sister. It transpires that the elder sister was born with the deer-spirit. See tale 30.

35. A woman, angered by her failure to tempt her husband's younger brother, drops him into a deep cave. The wolves rescue him, and in exchange, request him to remember them. He goes home and assembles all the fat from a tribal hunt. Then he invites the wolves, after placing his sister-in-law in the midst, and they devour her with the fat.

36. A man who married a buffalo woman is lured to buffalo land in an effort to rescue his son. After many trials, he returns with his family, and then punishes his wife by the same method as in no. 35. The wolves devour her.

37. A skull compels a woman to carry it to camp. She escapes it and reaches home. Next day, the skull has devoured the entire tribe, except the poor boy who lived with his grandmother away from the circle. He shoots at a spherical object in the centre of the camp-sites and breaks it. From within the people pour out and resume life as before.

38. Twin spirits are born, and grow to manhood in spite of every effort to find some excuse for sulking and leaving this world, according to the way of twins, only because their parents practise great care not to offend them.

39. A poor boy with supernatural power, presents food to the chief during a famine, and wins the younger daughter, who is compelled to marry him, since the elder, for whom he asked, rejects him. He turns out to be an elk spirit, (see no. 29). He is the tribe's saviour, supplying buffalo magically whenever the people need food. He is said to have made the first medicine-bundles.

Tales more Recent than *ohų́kaką* Tales

40. A buffalo calf which was of some importance in his own land, poses as a human boy and marries into a starving tribe. Through his buffalo grandfathers, he supplies meat, like a true Dakota son-in-law. His skull is later kept as an object of prayer.

41. A woman is lured away from the tribe and becomes one with a wild herd of horses. She bears a colt, and when captured by the people, she ignores her children and husband, so they turn her loose again.

42. A man who is abused in the tribe prays for revenge and the Fish-god turns him into a huge fish. He circles about the encampment and crushes all the people.

43. A young man, bewitched by the buffalo spirit, drowns in a shallow stream. He is rescued by a holy man, and comes to his senses when gunpowder is exploded in his face.

44. A man tracks down a war-party which stole his wife, but is discovered through his wife's treachery, and his eyes are put out. The owls fit him with a pair of their eyes, advising him never to enter a sweat lodge ceremony. He does so in his old age and the eyes pop, this time for ever.

45. A girl refuses to marry the man who is giving many horses for her, and runs away. She turns into a rock which now stands as a monument at Standing Rock Agency.

46. Two friends compose a song which they agree to use as a signal of distress. When one meets with trouble, the other, on hearing it comes to his aid.

47. When the tribe divides into two hunting parties, it separates a pair of lovers. The girl sickens and dies from longing but is allowed to return by the gods, who are impressed by the devotion of the two. They are commissioned to demonstrate a perfect union to the tribe.

48. A child is sent out into the dark for being naughty, and disappears. He is later found in the hands of a hairy monster who has abused him severely. The people kill the monster, and believe he was the mythical Double-Face.

49. Four warriors eat the flesh of a buffalo, although the one who shot it saw that its tail was a rattle-snake. They turn into snakes, and their people worship them and bring them offerings, as to beings with supernatural power.

50. A woman running away from a cruel husband lives with wolves for a time. They give her supernatural powers. She also collects fat from communal hunts and feeds the wolves.

51. A youth, caught in adultery, is killed by the angered husband who discovers too late that he has killed his nephew. He and his family hide in the wilderness where Crow Indians find them and take them home. Said to be the first instance of Dakotas taking up residence in an alien tribe.

52. Out on a war-path, a man turns against his life-long friend who kills him in self-defence. When he surrenders to the council he is told that his friend was naturally bad; that all knew it, he alone being too loyal to believe it. They set him free.

53. A little bird brings a beautiful horse to a poor couple who could not keep up with the tribal march. The horse sires many fine horses noted for their speed. The owner gains renown and the tribe benefits greatly, until someone tries to kill the horses. Then the blessing stops.

54. Years ago, an old woman and her pack dogs were lost near a lake in Canada. To this day, they say, she and her dogs may be seen roaming about on the island in the lake.

Local Tales

55. A woman sings a death song and then jumps over a cliff and is killed in the very spot where her lover perished some time before.

56. Bear Woman was so named because she killed a bear single-handed, when it knocked her down.

57. A ghost who guards a certain spot, molests a war-party who stop there for the night, until a gun is fired which scares it away.

58. A Dakota and a Crow scout, meeting in a cave to escape the storm, agree to fight each other. They later show such valor that when they die, the rest of the warriors decide to stop fighting and go home. There was glory enough for them all to take home.

59. A Dakota woman, brought up as a Crow, returns to her people and marries the chief's son. Through her knowledge of the Crow language, she is able to disarm a Crow enemy, giving her husband a chance to kill him and win a war honor.

60. A woman discovers in the dark, that the man who comes with meat is not her husband. She kills him in his sleep. Later, her own husband, whom the Crow scout had slain and impersonated, is found near camp.

61. The Gartersnake-Earring-Wearers, a band of the Og.lala, got their name through this amusing incident.

62. A girl who all her life has suffered from the obsession that her doll is human, finally dies from the effects of her imagination.

63. A man who has been getting rich by returning the bodies of slain Crow warriors to their people, is finally apprehended by the cousin of an innocent boy whose death he caused, and is punished.

64. A girl who has sulked for days, is taken on a trip by her brother and sister-in-law. Out in the country, she finds a Crow Indian husband, and her sulking stops.

1. Ikto'mi Conquers the I'ya.

1. Hé′c'eṡ Ikto'mi ka'k'ena tok'e'-ec'a'c'a¹ oma'ni-ya`hą ṡk'e᾽ᵉ.²
2. Paha' wą ka'k'el-iya`hįkta hą'l I'ya ̣i'ṡ-᾿eya'³ ųma' ec'i'yatąhą
hiya'hą c'ąke' Ikto' li'la nihį'ciyį ną — E! ̣ ąpe'tu-le`c'ecaka c'a e'l
mat᾽į'kta hųṡe, — ec'į'-hįg.la ṡk'e᾽ᵉ. 3. Mak'a'-b.lu icu' ną sic'ą'⁴ kį
li'klila kpawi'yakpa ną leya' ṡk'e᾽ᵉ, — Hųhųhê, misų`, nąi'ṡ c'iye`,
(haṡ+, i'ṡ tukte'-ųma` t'oų'kap'api huwo'?) — eya' ṡk'e᾽ᵉ. 4. K'e'yaṡ
I'ya c'uwi' oki'niya c'ą'ṡna Ikto' yace'kcek icu'ⁿᵘ; c'ąke' k'oki'p'eñcį
ną, — Wą, misų`, nąi'ṡ c'iye`, ak'o'wap'a na'ẕį ye'. Mi'ṡ-᾿eya' wac'į'
hą'tąhąṡ yat'a'hena ic'i'cukte lo', — eya' ṡk'e᾽ᵉ. 5. K'e'yaṡ I'ya
ayu'pteṡni yųk'ą' hehą'l ak'e' — Ho, it'o' misų`, nąi'ṡ c'iye` (haṡ+,
i'ṡ tukte'-ųma` t'oų'kap'api c'a!), to'hųwel nit'ų'pi huwo'? — eya'
ṡk'e᾽ᵉ. 6. Yųk'ą' — Eya' mañpi'ya ną mak'a' kį lena' t'oka'-ka`gapi

Literal Translation.

1. And so / Iktọmi / into yonder direction / at random / to travel
he was going, / they say. 2. Hil| / a /,the instant he was about to
reach the top / then / Iya / he too / other (side) / from / he reached the
top / so / Iktomi / very / he was frightened / and / "Ah! / this sort
of day / such / in / I shall die / evidently," / suddenly he thought /
they say. 3. Dust / he took / and / thigh / the / very-very / he polished his own / and / said this / they say / "Well, well, well, / my
younger brother, / — or else / my elder brother, / — (Haṡ! / then /
which of two / we are the elder / I wonder?") / he said / they say.
4. But / Iya / trunk / he breathed into his own / (he breathed
deeply) / then each time / Iktomi / jerking, causing to stagger / he
took him; / so / he feared him very much / and / "Why, / my
younger brother, / or else / my elder brother, / farther off / stand
do! / I too / I so wish / if-then / closer this way, by means of the
mouth / I will take you," / he said / they say. 5. But / Iya / he did
not reply / and so / then / again / "Now / then, / my younger
brother, / or else / my elder brother, / (Haṡ! / then / which of two /
we are the elder / such!) / at what time / were you born?" / he
said / they say. 6. And then / "Well, / sky / and / earth / the / these /

---

¹ tok'e' ec'a'c'a — aimlessly; at random; without serious intent; as a pastime.
² ṡk'e᾽ᵉ — it is said; from ṡk'a. Unless an eye-witness is relating anything in
Dakota, all statements attribute their authority to somebody. Ṡk'a, it is
said, occurs particularly in myths; ke'ya'pi, they say that; abbreviated
to ke', is used in tribal tales, and in war and other stories. In all this material,
ṡk'e᾽ᵉ or ke'ya'pi᾽ⁱ or ke'᾽ᵉ, should close every declarative sentence; though
some informants have omitted it.
³ i'ṡ-᾿eya', sometimes written i'ṡ eya', is best translated "he too; he, as well
as (the person previously mentioned)". Eya' is a word of many uses; and
no direct English equivalent will satisfy.
⁴ sic'ą', the outer side of the thigh, including the seat.

1

k'ų he' ehą' mat'ų'pe lo', — eya' c'ąke' Ikto' i'yog.mus g.lu'zį ną,
— Wą, witko`, mahpi'ya ną mak'a' kį hena' le' miye' waka'ǧe lo'.
....Ohą́, wana' wawe'ksuye cį ec'i'yatąhą, ehą'kec'ų mig.lu'štą ną
hehą'l ta'kula wą ka'l yupsų'psų ihpe'waye c'ų he' le' niye'la ye lo'.
C'a c'iye'mayaye lo', — eya'-oki'yaka ke'ᵉ. 7. — Ho, misų`, le' ta'ku-
oma`yani huwo'? — eya' yųk'ą' — Wą, le'c'iya oya'te wą wic'o't'i
c'a ekta' wic'a'b.le lo'. Hena' wic'a'wag.lutįkta c'a, — eya' šk'e'ᵉ.
8. Yųk'ą' Ikto' — Huhuhê, ak'a'š 'wic'o'wepila ye. Wą, misų`, le'
mi'š-'eya' hena' ekta'¹ wic'a'b.la c'a sak'i'p ųyį'kte lo, — eci'ya š'k'e'ë.
9. Wana' ya'hąpi k'e'yaš I'ya li'la tke' c'ąke' ig.lu'hašni² kį ų
lehi'c'it'a-iyų`k ya'pi ną wana' wic'o't'i kį ik'ą'yela iyų'kapi šk'e'ᵉ.
10. Wana' I'ya ištį'ma c'ąke' Ikto' i' kį e'l ao'kas'į yųk'ą' t'ezi'-mahe'l
oya'te t'epwi'c'aye c'ų hena' oya's'į ho'c'okat'ųt'ųyą oi'yokip'iya
wic'o't'i-wąya'ka šk'e'ᵉ. 11. Mak'a' aką'l ų'pi k'ų he'hą' to'k'el
op'i'ic'iyapi k'ų he'c'ena'ᵃ. K'ii'yąkapi ną haka' ų'pi ną pai'yąkapi

they were first made / the (past) / that / then / I was born," / he
said / so / Iktomi / mouth closed / he held his own / and, / "Why, / you
fool, / sky / and / earth / the / those / this / myself / I made. / ....
Oh, yes, / now / I recall / the / according to / it now appears / I
finished (my work) / and / then / little something / a / aside /
wadded / I cast / the (past) / that / this / it is little you. / So / I am
your elder brother," / to say-he told him. 7. "Now / my younger
brother, / this / for what do you travel?" / he said / and so / "Why, /
over here / people / a / camp / such / to / them-I-go. / Those / them-
mine-I shall eat / therefore," / he said / they say. 8. And then /
Iktomi / "Well, well, well, / no wonder / they are of common
parentage, the little ones! / Why, / my younger brother, / this / I
too / those / to / them-I go / so / together / we shall go," / he said
to him / they say. 9. Now / they were travelling / but / Iya / very /
heavy / therefore / he did not have himself / the / therefore / stopping too often for the night / they travelled / and / now / camp /
the / near it / they lay for the night / it is said. 10. Now / Iya / he
slept / so / Iktomi / mouth / the / there / he looked in / and behold /
inside the stomach / people / he devoured them / the (past) / those /
all / in camp circles / happily / to be encamped he saw / they say.
11. Earth / upon / they lived / the (past) / then / what manner /
they conducted themselves / the (past) / it was still so. / They ran
races / and / hoop-game / they used / and (another game) / they
used / too / he saw / they say. Over there / on the other hand /

---

¹ ekta', to; towards, as something ahead, or removed; wic'a — them; b.la
(from ya), I go. Whereas English says "I go to them" the Dakota says
"to or towards / I-them-go".
² ig.lu'hašni — he does not have himself (literally); an idiom meaning:
"he can not manage his weight; he is too heavy"; ic'i'g.luhašni (with
ic'i — reflexive) would seem a better form. g.luha' (from yuha') to
have one's own; to hold one's own.

ų'pi k'o wąya'ka śk'e'e. Ka'l i'ś yup'i'yela t'ap-ka'psicapi ną kak'i'-
yot'ą i'ś hoa'g.lag.la Miwa'tani-wac'i ahi'yaya śk'e'e. 12. Nakų'
k'ohą' wa'g.li uki'yį ną nakų' wi'c'įska'-wac'i¹ ahi'yaya śk'e'e.
13. T'i'pi-iyo'k'iheya² wą e'l wo'ai k'o' śką'pi ną he'l wic'a'ħcala
kį li'la oi'yokip'iya yąka'pi śk'e'e. Oya'te wic'a'ninika wic'o't'i c'a
I'ya i' kį mahe'l he'c'el t'ąį' śk'e'e. 14. Ikto'mi li'la yuś'i'yayį ną
I'ya to'k'el g.na'yįkta he'cįhą he' iyu'kcą śk'e'e. 15. Kikta' c'ąke'
le'c'el wi'yuga śk'e'e, — Misų`, le'c'el-yau̯'ke cį³ e'ś taku'ħcį k'oya'-
kip'e se'ce lo', — eya' yųk'ą', — Ha'.o, ħla'ħla kaħla'pi kį he'
k'owa'kip'e lo'; ną c'ą'c'ega ap'a'pi kį he' k'owa'kip'e lo'; ną hįhą'
hot'ų'pi kį he' k'owa'kip'e lo'; ną aki'ś'api kį he' k'owa'kip'e lo', —
eya' śk'e'e. 16. Yųk'ą', — Ak'a'ś⁴ wic'o'wepila ye, wą, misų`, mi'ś-
'eya' hena' iyu'ha k'owa'kip'e lo', — eya' śk'e'e. 17. — It'o', misų`,

beautifully / they caused the ball to jump by striking / and / over
in that direction / still another thing / along the camp ring / dancing the Mandan / they went along / they say. 12. Too / meantime /
successful in the chase / they were returning / and / also / Pack-
strap-White-dancing / they went along / they say. 13. Council-tipi /
a / to / carrying food / too / they were actively engaged / and /
there / old men / the / very / pleasantly / they were sitting / it is said. /
People / "as in the good old days when they lived" / they were
camped / such / Iya / mouth / the / inside / in that way / it was
visible / they say. 14. Iktomi / very / he was frightened / and / Iya /
what way / he will trap him / if-then / that / he thought on / they
say. 15. He awoke / so / thus / he questioned him / they say: / "My
younger brother / as thus you exist / the / "eś" / some specific
thing / you fear, / perhaps," / he said / and so / "Yes, / rattles /
they cause to rattle / the / that / I fear; / and / drum / they strike /
the / that / I fear; / and / owls / they hoot / the / that / I fear; / and /
they shout / the / that / I fear," / he said / they say. 16. And then /
"No wonder, / they are of common parentage, the little ones! /
Why, / my younger brother, / I too / those / all / I fear," / he said /
they say. 17. "Supposing / my younger brother, / right here, / sit!

---

¹ They went by, doing the *"wi'c'į-ska'* dance."
² *t'i'pi-iyo'k'iheya* is the official name for the council-tent, among the
Tetons. (The Yankton word is *t'iyo't'ipi*) In reality, there are two words
here, with independent accents. I have seen this translated as "the tipi
next." That would be correct, if the accent fell on *i* — *i'yokiheya* next to
it. But it doesn't. *O'k'ihe*, joint; a joining on; *ya* to cause; *i*, to. The
reference here, I think, is rather to the fact that in enlarging a tent, in
order to accomodate the company who are to sit in it, the poles, and the
sheathings of two or more tipis are added or joined on to each other. "A
tipi made by joining on", is something of the meaning, I think.
³ *le'c'el*, thus; *yau̯'*, you live on; you exist; *ke (ka)*, as it were; some-what;
rather; in a manner of speaking; in a way; *cį (kį)* the. This comprises
an idiom of which no direct English equivalent meaning has been found.
⁴ *ak'a'ś*, (?). This word gives the force of "No wonder!" "Of course,"
"Wouldn't you know it ?" or some such expression, to the sentence.

1*

*le'na yąka' yo'; k'ohą' wic'o't'ita m.nį' ną t'i'pi-oc'o'kaya kį he'
t'iyo'pa kį e'l kai'c'iyopteya iwa'kazo ną waku'kte lo'. Hehą'l ųyį' ną
ihą'ke anų'k oya'te kį t'epya' awi'c'aųkukte*[1] lo'. Ną tukte'-ųma t'oke'ya
t'i'pi-oc'o'kaya kį he'l ųg.li'hųni hą'tąhąṡ he' ųma' kį t'epyį'kte lo',
he' ohi'yįkta c'a, — eya' yųk'ą' I'ya he'c'etula ṡk'e'ᵉ.   18. C'ąke'
he'c'ena Ikto' į'yąk-'ic'ic'iyį ną i't'ap wic'o't'ita ihų'ni ną pą' į'yąka
ṡk'e'ᵉ. — Ho po'+,*[2] waho'ṡi-wahi c'e naḣ'ų' po'+! I'ya wą wak'ą'ḣca
c'a wag.na'yį ną le' wau' we lo'.   19. Ną taku'ku k'oki'p'a he'cįhą
imų'ġa yųk'ą' ḣla'ḣla kį he' e ną c'ą'c'eġa kį he' e ną hįhą' hot'ų'pi
kį he' e ną aki'ṡ'api kį hena'keca k'oki'p'a ke'ye' lo'. C'e yui'naḣni
po', — eya' ṡk'e'ᵉ. 20. — Nakų' iṡtį'ma hą'l i' kį mahe'l wąb.la'ka
yųk'ą' t'ąma'hel wį'kcekce' oya'te-t'ą'ka wic'o't'i ye lo'. Wip'a'-t'oya`
nąi'ṡ wip'a'-sapya` k'o t'io'wa o'ta ye lo', — eya' c'ąke' he'c'ena
ṡica'wac'į ig.lu'wįyeyapi ną Ikto' iha'kap ya'pi ṡk'e'ᵉ. 21. Kai'yuzeya
paha'-ai'napya e'nażį*[3] c'ąke' Ikto' iṡna'la I'ya yąke' c'ų ekta'
k'iyo'ḣpayį ną wana' k'ihų'ni-wai`yehal hįhą'-hot'ų`pi ną c'ą'c'eġa
ap'a'p'a aki'ṡ'api ną natą' e'yaya ṡk'e'ᵉ.   22. I'ya kikta' hiya'yį ną*

Meanwhile / to camp / I shall go / and / middle tipi / the / that /
doorway / the / at / crossing each other / I shall make marks / and /
I will come home. / Then / we (shall) go / and / end / on each side /
people / the / eating / them-we shall come along. / And / which of
two / first / middle-tipi / the / there / we arrive / if-then / that one /
other / the / he shall devour, / that one / he shall be the winner /
therefore," / he said / and / Iya / he considered it all right / they
say. 18. So / immediately / Iktomi / to run-he caused himself / and /
quickly / at camp / he arrived / and / shouting / he ran / they say. /
"Attention! / to bring news-I have arrived / so / hear ye it! / Iya / a/
very supernatural / such / I have deceived him / and / this / I come.
19. And / various things / he fears / if-then / I asked him / and /
rattles / the / that / and / drum / the / that / and / owl / hooting /
the / that / and / shouting / the / that many / he feared / he said.
So / make haste," / he said / they say. 20. "Also / he slept / during /
mouth / the / inside / I saw / and / inside the body / unconcernedly /
vast peoples / they are camped. / (Tipis with) wind-flaps painted
blue / or else / wind-flaps painted black / also / painted tipis /
many," / he said / so / at once / madly / they got ready / and /
Iktomi / following him / they went / they say. 21. Slightly removed
from it / hidden by a hill / they took their stand / so / Iktomi / he
alone / Iya / he sat / the (past) / to / he went down hill / and / now /
judging his probable arrival back there / they hooted-owl / and /
drums / striking / they cheered / and / charging forth / they went /
they say. 22. Iya / he sat up / and / fearfully / head / they turn it

---

[1] *au'*, to bring; *awi'c'au*, to bring them; *awi'c'aųku*, we two bring them;
kta (kte), shall. We two shall bring them. *t'epya'*, to consume; eat up.
The two verbs mean, "We shall proceed, eating them up, as we come."
[2] The plus sign indicates a prolonged shout.
[3] *e'nażį*, another form for *ka'l (he'l) ina'żįpi*, (there) they came to a stand.

nihį́ciya p'a' yuptą́pi s'e yąka' tk'a'š ec'ą́l ao'g.lut'eyapi ną
*ac'ą́kozapi ną kte'pi šk'e*ᵉ. *23. He'c'ųpi ną hehą́l t'ezi'-kah.le'capi*
c'ąke' etą́hą ąpe'tu wą a'taya oya'te-t'ąkt'ą̀ka ig.la'ka ag.li'nap'į ną
wakpa'-iyùkšąyą kį hena' iyo'hiic'iya e't'ipi ną i't'ap htawo'hąpikta
c'a c'et'i'pi c'ąke' to'k'iya kį oya's'į p'e'ta wiya'kpakpayela oi'yoki-
*p'iya yąka'pi šk'e*ᵉ. *24. He'c'ehcį I'ya t'akpe'-ipišni yųk'ą́š oya'te*
*kį lehą́hųniyą (waši'cu k'o'ya) t'epwi'c'ayahikta tk'a'¹ šk'e*ᵉ. *25. I'ya*
kte'pi ną he' ų́' mak'o'c'e kį a'taya lehą́l oya'te owi'c'at'įzi ną tukte'ni
*ok'ą' wani'ce cį he' he'c'etu šk'e*ᵉ. *26. Hetą́hą nake's wic'o'ic'aǧe kį*
*a'wicak'eya hiyu' šk'e*ᵉ. *27. Ho, it'o' wą'cahcį' Ikto' wawa'p'ilaya*
šk'e'. *Ną hetą́hą ak'e' to'k'el iya'yeca c'e'l. 28. Hehą́yela owi'hąke*ᵉ².

from side to side / like / he sat / but indeed / at that instant / they surrounded him / and / swung clubs on him / and / killed him / they say. 23. That they did / and / then / they tore open his abdomen by striking / so / out from it / day / an / entire / people in great numbers / moving camp / they came back out / and / bend of river / the / those / assigning one to each group / they camped / and / soon after / they were going to cook for the evening / such / they built a fire / so / (places) somewhere / the / all / fire / sparklingly / pleasantly / they sat / they say. 24. In that very way / Iya / to attack-they went not / if-then / people / the / even up till now / (White people / included) / he would be eating them up / but / they say. 25. Iya / they killed / and / that / on account of / land / the / entire / today / people / they crowd in it / and / no place / open space / it is lacking / the / that / it is so / they say. 26. From then on / at last / growth of the peoples / the / in earnest / it came / they say. 27. Now / for a wonder' / at least once / Iktomi / he gave cause for gratitude / they say. And / from there / again / which way / he went off / who knows ? 28. There / it ends.

Free Translation.

1. Iktomi[3] was wandering off in a certain direction, walking along at random. 2. Just as he reached the hill-top, Iya,[4] the eater, also

---

[1] *tk'a*, but, is used at the end of a sentence to make the statement a contrary-to-fact clause. *t'epya'*, to cause to be consumed; i. e., to eat up. *(t'e'pa*, to wear away.) *wic'a'*, the plural object pronoun; *t'ep-wi'c'a-ya* to cause them to be worn away; i. e., to eat them up; *hį* (from *hą*, continued action); *kta*, will; *tk'a*, but, contrary to fact; *t'epwi'c'ayahįkta tk'a*, he would have been eating them up (even to this day, etc.).

[2] *hehą'yela owi'hąke*, that is as far as it goes; that is where it ends; that is all. (The conventional ending to all bona fide myths, and legends; the improbable tales, which are generally regarded as not possible at the present time.)

[3] The trickster in Dakota mythology; always visualized as having the appearance of a man. He is out to get the better of others, but generally comes through, the loser. The name is also the word for spider, and some translators and interpreters call him "Spider" in English. The only relation I have found is in a story of spiders coming out of the ashes of the dead Iktomi.

[4] Iya is the Ogre in Dakota mythology. Anyone who eats excessively without ever seeming to have enough is said to be an *i'ya*.

reached it, coming up from the other side; so Ikto was much frightened and, "Ah! So it is on a day like this that I am to die, is it ?" he thought suddenly. 3. He took some earth and polished his thigh vigorously and said, "Well, well, well! my younger brother[1], — or is he my elder brother ? — Haś! (O, the deuce!) which of us is the elder anyway ?" 4. But each time Iya took in his breath he jerked Ikto towards him, with such force that he staggered; he therefore was very much frightened and said, "Now, now, my younger brother, — or my elder, — stand farther off, can't you ? I too have something I can do; I can pull you towards me if I care to !" he said. 5. But Iya did not reply; so then, once more, "Come now, my younger brother, — or is he my elder brother ? — Haś! Which of us is the elder, anyway ? . . . Well, when were you born ?" Ikto asked. 6. Iya answered, "Why, I was born when this earth and this sky were created." Ikto clamped his palm over his mouth, surprised[2]. "So ? Well, you fool, I made the earth and the sky myself! Oh, of course, now, as I recall it, there was a bit of leavings, after I had finished making the earth and sky, which I didn't know what to do with; I therefore rolled it into a wad and tossed it aside. And you grew from that! There isn't any doubt now. I am the elder !" he said. 7. "Now then, little brother, what errand are you on ?" And Iya said, "Over in this direction there is a tribal camp, and I am going there. I shall eat the people, for they are mine." 8. "Well, of all things! Funny, isn't it ? Yet what else can you expect, with brothers ? Why, little brother, that is just the people I am going to; and we shall travel together !" Ikto told Iya. 9. They were now travelling, but Iya could not manage his weight, and they were obliged, therefore, to stop often; but they were now stopping for the night near the encampment. 10. When Iya slept, Ikto ventured to look into his body through his mouth, and saw there all the tribes that Iya had eaten in the past, living on in contentment in their respective tribal circles. 11. Inside Iya, they were living and having their being in exactly the same fashion as when they lived on earth. Races and ȟaka'[3] and paį'yqkapi[3] games were in progress. Yonder, on the other hand, a game of Dakota ball was being played with great skill; while, in another direction, could be seen a group of Miwatani[4]-Society dancers performing their dance around the circle. 12. Meantime, successful hunters were returning with game; and also the White-Pack Strap group[5] were going along,

---

[1] Iktomi always calls everyone his younger brother. In social kinship, when a man seems to have more younger brothers than any other relations, they say he is like Ikto.
[2] A common Dakota gesture to indicate surprise, real or pretended.
[3] ȟaka' and paį'yqkapi are two Dakota group games well described by Ɋ Bushotter in a Manuscript owned by the Bureau of American Ethnology.
[4] Mandan or Miwátani: a men's society among the Dakota.
[5] wi'c'į ska' literally means a white pack strap, and so I have translated it here.

dancing. 13. Another thing else was that women were taking food to the council tipi, and there the old men of the tribe foregathered, with much feasting and the recounting of past glories. Taken all in all, the sight presented a picture of the good old days when the people lived; such Ikto saw inside the Iya's body. 14. Very much frightened, Ikto tried to think out a way to capture the Iya. 15. And when he woke, this is what Ikto said to him, "All appearances to the contrary notwithstanding, there must be something that you fear?" — "Yes; the sound of rattles, and drums, the hooting of owls, and the shouts of men — all these I fear," Iya admitted. 16. So then, "Well, of all things! Just what you would expect, though, of brothers! Why, little brother, those are exactly what I too fear!" Ikto said. 17. He added, "I'd suggest you stay here, little brother, while I go ahead. I will select the center tipi, and mark it with a cross, and then I shall return. Then we two can go together, and, starting at either end, we shall progress towards the center tipi, eating the people as we go. And he who arrives first at that center tipi shall have the right to eat his opponent, as his reward for winning." And Iya thought that a good idea[1]. 18. So Ikto ran hard and soon he arrived shouting, at the tribal camp. "Hear ye, everybody! I have something to tell you, so listen! I have just deceived a very supernaturally powerful Iya, and I have come. 19. And when I questioned him, he admitted that he feared certain things: rattles, and drums, and the hooting of owls, and the shouting of men. So make haste!" he said. 20. "Moreover, while he slept, I looked into his mouth, and inside his body there actually live great tribes of people. Tipis with tops painted blue, and some painted black, — many painted tipis I saw," he said. So immediately the people prepared in frantic haste, and followed Ikto out. 21. At a little distance away, hidden by a hill, they stopped, and allowed Ikto to proceed alone, and after he had disappeared downhill, and it seemed time that he had reached Iya, they charged forth, making all those noises that Iya feared. 22. Iya jumped up and sat with his head turning nervously from side to side, as if someone pulled it about[2]; but they soon surrounded and clubbed him to death. 23. They tore open his body; and then, for one entire day, great tribes of people crawled out of Iya, moving their camps, and settled by groups in the many pleasant bends of the river; and soon they built their fires for cooking the evening meal, and no matter where one looked, one could see the campfires, sparkling like stars, and it was a beautiful sight. 24. Now, if Iya had not been

---

[1] Iya is generally indicated as enormous in bulk and very dull in his mind; he is easily manaqed by Iktomi.

[2] This is a figure of speech in Dakota and graphically expresses a nervous state wherein a person looks about quickly, as a puppet might, if the strings were worked fast. It is difficult to render the exact picture by any English phrase.

destroyed in just that way, he would undoubtedly still be eating people up, White people and all. 25. Iya was killed and that is why the entire country is now so full of people that it is impossible to find any open spaces anymore. 26. From that time on, the expansion of peoples began in earnest, they say. 27. Now, that was one time at least that Ikto must be given credit; he did do a great service to people, and merits thanks for it[1]. And from then on, who knows where Ikto went next?[2] 28. That is all.

2. *Ikto'mi Takes his Mother-in-Law on the Warpath.*

1. Ikto'mi wị'yą wą li'la wị'yą̇ ẇaśte'[3] *yu'za ᶩśk'e'ᵉ. 2. Yųk'ą' to'hųwel ąpe'tu wą e'l ho'c'okata i'' ną g.li' ną ta'ku iyo'kip'iśni s'e ini'la yąkị' ną t'ag̊o'śahą̇*[4] *śk'e'ᵉ. C'ąke' t'awi'cu kị waya'ząkta ke'c'ị' ną awą'yak k'uwaᶯᵃ*[5]. *3. Leye'ᶯᵉ: — To'k'a he'? Ta'ku iyo'nicip'iśni se'ce? — eya' yųk'ą' ayu'pteśni, ta'ku li'la iyo'yake*[6] *s'e yąka'hą-ke'ᵉ. 4. N'ąke' i't'ehąłca yųk'ą', — Hehehe', T'ᶜehi'ya le' wasu'yapi c'a iwa'mayaząkte s'e le'c'eca kị, tok'e naya'h̓'ųśniyelak'a? — eye'ᶯᵉ. 5. T'awi'cu kị he' ta'ku c'a wasu'yapi he'cịhą iyų'g̊a yųk'ą', — Le'c'eya' wic'a'śa iyu'ha k'ų'ku o'p zuya' yewi'c'aśipi c'a t'ehi'ke lo',*

Literal Translation.

1. Ikto'mi / woman / a / very / woman / good / he had for a wife / they say. 2. And / once / day / a / on / to centre of camp circle / he went / and / came home / and / something / he was displeased by / like / quietly / he sat / and / he was spitting / they say. / So / his wife / the / he will be sick / she thought that / and / keeping watch on him / continued to do. 3. She said this: / "What's the matter? / Something / you are displeased by / perhaps?" / she said / and / he replied not / something / very / it bothered him / like / he was sitting / they say. 4. So / a long time later / and then / "Alas! / horribly / this / they have decreed / so / I shall be sick from it / like / it is so / the / can it be / you have not heard, evidently?" / he said. 5. His wife / the / that / what / such / they decreed / if-then / she asked / and then / "This is so, right now, / men / all / their mothers-in-law / with / to war / they are ordered to go / so / it is terrible," /

---

[1] Rarely does Ikto get such thorough praise as here.

[2] Many tales end like this; for nobody can say where Ikto keeps himself until he turns up again wherever and in whatever shape he chooses to accomplish his purposes.

[3] *wị'yą ẇaśte'*, woman / good. When treated as two words, independently accented, this phrase means "To be beautiful". When hyphenated, and accented as one word *wi'yą-ẇaśte`*, with only one main accent, it means "a good woman."

[4] *t'ag̊o'śa*, to spit, as saliva; *t'ag̊e'*, saliva, (with emphasis on its foamy quality); *t'awa'g̊ośa*, I spit; *t'aų'g̊ośa*, we (dual) spit.

[5] *k'uwa'*, to chase; pursue; to treat; Following the verb *awą'yaka*, to guard, it means, "to keep a close watch over."

[6] *iyo'yaka*, to be mentally or spiritually disturbed by something; *i*, by it; *iyo'ya*, to yawn.

— *eya' c'ąke', — Kinaš*[1] *ina'-t'oka`p'a kį kic'i' le' šni*[2]*? — eya'*
yųk'ą' c'įšni ke'ᵉ. 6. C'ąke', — Ho, ec'a`, ina'-i`yok'ihe kį he' i'š
to'k? — eya' yųk'ą' — Ta'kuš he' nahpa'hpake c'u, — eya' ke'ᵉ.
7. C'ąke', — Kinaš ina'-haka`kta kį kic'i' le' šni? — eya' yųk'ą'
Ikto'mi i' p'ahte'hca ke'ᵉ. 8. T'e'hą-ta`keyešni, he'c'el e'š c'į'ka, nake'
ini'la yąka' šk'e'ᵉ. I't'ehą yųk'ą', — h'ąhi'yehcį, c'uwi' oki'niya ną
eye'-kapį s'e, — Hoh̃[3]*! . . . . . . Wą! . . . . Ho'ye*[4]*! — eya' ke'ᵉ.*
9. C'ąke' wana' k'u'ku-haka`kta k'u kic'i' zuya' iya'ya ke'ᵉ. T'oke'ya
ig.lu'wįyeya c'ąke' waka'p'api o'ta yuha'pi ke'ᵉ. 10. Li'la t'e'hą-g.li`-
pišni c'ąke' ec'e'l eš e'wic'aktųžapi yųk'ą' etą' wani'yetu o'ta hą'l
ųg.n'ahąla — Ikto' wana' wakte'-ku' we lo', — eya'pi yųk'ą' šuk-
'a'kąyak paha'-ai`yohpeya ku' c'ąke' c'įca' o'ta c'a a'wiwiyela o'kšą
į'yąkapi šk'e'ᵉ. 11. Yųk'ą', — T'ehątąhą awi'c'awakula c'ąke' Ate'

he said / so. / "In that case / my mother-eldest / the / with / you
go / not ?" / she said / and / he refused, they say. 6. So / "Well, /
then / my mother-next / the / that one / as for her, / what ?" / she
said / and lo / "*Ta'kuš* / that one / she is untidy / the-past," / he
said, they say. 7. So / "In that case, / my mother-youngest / the /
with / you go / not ?" she said / and / Iktomi / mouth / he was
veritably tied / they say. 8. Long he said nothing / that way / indeed /
he wanted / yet now / silent / he sat / they say. / A good while
after / then / very slowly / trunk / he breathed in his own / and /
to say it-loath / like / "The idea! / . . . . Well ? / . . . All right!" / he
said / they say. 9. So / now / his mother-in-law-youngest / the-past /
with / to war-he went off / they say. / First / she got herself ready /
so/ dried and pounded meat / plenty / they had / they say. 10. Very
long-they returned not / so / at last / indeed / they forgot them /
and lo / from it / winters / many / then / unexpectedly / "Ikto / now /
he returns having killed," / they said / and lo / on horse-back /
down-hill / he was coming / so / his children / many / such / running
in ever-altering groups (like chicks) / around him / they ran / they
say. 11. And then / "From far off / I bring the little things / so /

[1] *kinaš*, sometimes contracted to *kįš*, always begins a sentence which offers
a suggestion; "well, in that case —" etc.

[2] When *šni* indicates a direct negative, it is written as a suffix to the verb,
as already mentioned. When it is pronounced independently, it gives the
sentence the force of "Why don't you, or didn't you, do so-and-so ?" Thus:
oma'yanišni, You do not walk about; *oma'yani šni*, Why don't you walk
about ? On occasion, we get a form like this; *oma'yanišni šni*, which means,
"Why don't you not walk ?" or "Why not stay at home ?" that is to say,
"Why not desist from walking ?"

[3] *hoh!* a man's word, indicating his disagreement or adverse attitude toward
the matter in hand.

[4] *ho'ye!* all right; very well! Again a man's word. A woman says, *"ho'na"*
to correspond to *ho'ye*. It indicates being in accord with a suggestion.
nųwe'-ųyįkte', let us go swimming; *ho'na* — all right; let us! (woman
talking). Often these words are used by the promoter of a plan, as a preface
to its suggestion. Thus: *ho'na nųwe'-ųyįkte*, let us go swimming. Reply:
ho'na! Agreed!

ema'kiyape. Heya'pi k'e'yaś wic'a'kte po'! — eya' c'ąke' a'beya
c'e'ya į'yąkapi śk'e'ᵉ. 12. C'ąke' hų'kupi kį iwi'c'akikcu ną wic'a'-
g.luha to'k'i ye'ca nųtk'a'¹ ke'ᵉ. 13. Ikto' wic'o't'i-e'g.na g.licu' c'ąke',
— Ikto' k'ų'ku-g.lu`ze lo'. Tuwe'ni he'c'ųśniwasu'ųyąpi k'ų, k'ica'kse
lo', — eya'pi śk'e'ᵉ. 14. He'c'ena aki'c'ita ap'a'pikta c'a k'uwa'
a'yapi k'e'yaś to'k'eśk'e ḣ'ą' ną nai'c'iśpa śk'e'ᵉ. 15. Hehą'yela
owi'hąke'ᵉ.

Father / they say to me. / They say that / yet / kill them!" / he
said / so / in all directions / crying / they ran / they say. 12. So /
their mother / the / she took her own-them / and / them-having /
she didn't know where to go. / 13. Ikto / camp-into / he returned /
so / "Ikto / he has taken his mother-in-law for wife. / Nobody / to
do that not-we have a rule / the-past, / he has broken it in two," /
they said / they say. 14. At once / camp-police / they were about to
strike him / so / chasing / they took him / but / somehow / he acted /
and / saved himself / they say. 15. There / it ends.

Free Translation.

1. Ikto was married to a very beautiful woman. 2. One day he
returned from the council-tent, appearing to be very sad over
something[2]; he said nothing, but just spat saliva[3] ever so often. So
his wife, sure that he was coming down with some dread sickness,
watched him closely. 3. She said, "What is the matter? Something
is disturbing you, evidently." But he didn't answer; only acting
much upset by something. 4. Finally, after a long while, "Alas,
that they should make such a ruling. Why, it is enough to make
anyone ill; in fact, I feel sick this instant, over it. Haven't you
heard the terrible decree?" he said. 5. When she asked about it,
he told her that every man was bidden to go to war with his mother-
in-law. So his wife suggested that he take her eldest mother. But
that didn't appeal to him[4]. 6. "Well, how about my next mother?"
she said; but he refused to consider her because she was untidy.
7. "In that case, why don't you take my youngest mother?" she

---

[1] *ye'canų tk'a', ye (ya)*, to go; *ca (ka)*, at all; in a way; rather; *nų*, a particle,
denoting almost; on the verge of; *tk'a*, but. With *to'k'i*, where, the phrase
means, "Not knowing where to go; at sea as to which way to turn."

[2] Perhaps Ikto's chief characteristic is that he is an inveterate poser; he has
no conception of sincerity. Anyone who poses in order to make people
believe he has sincere motives when in reality he is working to bring matters
about in his favor is said to *Ikto'-kaǵa* — make, or act Ikto.

[3] The Dakota associate spitting with illness; as a symptom of impending
sickness. "He is growing thinner, and he spits habitually."

[4] He gives a vulgar reason for refusing this one. It was not repeated to this
recorder. This wife had three "mothers." It doesn't come out clearly which
one is her own; perhaps none of these three, who might be sisters or parallel
or cross cousins of her mother, who might be elsewhere. In a close-knit
Dakota clan, it is often difficult to know which the real parents are, for the
sisters, brothers, parallel and cross-cousins all seem to feel as responsible
for a child, as its own parents do.

asked, and her words seemed to clamp Ikto's mouth shut. 8. Long he remained silent, (though that was what he was really hinting for!) and then, finally, he said, very slowly, after a deep sigh, as if he dreaded to consider it (on account of the avoidance[1],) "O, No! .... Well? .... All right!" 9. Now the two started off to war; the mother in-law had prepared carefully for the journey so that they were well supplied with dried meat for the trip. 10. They were gone so long that in time they were completely forgotten. And then, years later, all of a sudden the cry went up, "Ikto is returning from war!" Everybody ran out to see. There was Ikto, riding a horse, and racing downhill towards the tribal camp; and his many children, on foot, ran in ever-shifting groups (like chicks) around him as he came. 11. And he sang out, "I have brought them such a long distance that they (captives) call me father. Even though they do, kill them off!" So they ran crying in fear. 12. Their mother, the former mother-in-law to Ikto, gathered her children about her and ran here and there, trying to find safety for them. 13. When Ikto entered the camp circle, the people shouted, "Ikto has married his own mother-in-law. That is a forbidden relation among our people, but Ikto has broken the regulation." 14. And the camp-police went toward him in order to punish him for his offence against the people. But somehow, it isn't known just in what manner, he slipped away, and saved himself. That is all.

3. Ikto'mi Marries his Daughter.

1. Ikto'mi t'ii'snala k'e'yaś c'ica' o'ta c'ąke' oya'te-t'ą`ka iye'c'el manį'l t'i' śk'e'ᵉ. 2. Hokśi'-t'oka`p'a kį he' wik'o'śkalaka c'a li'la wį'yą waśte'ᵗᵉ. 3. Yųk'ą' ąpe'tu wą e'l Ikto' t'awi'cu kį le'c'el wo'kiya-ke'ᵉ: — *Ho, winų`hca[2], ta'ku wążi' iwa'hoc'iyįkte lo'. He'c'el ų'*

Literal Translation.

1. Iktomi / single-family / yet / children / many / therefore / large nation / like / away from the tribe / he lived / they say. 2. Eldest child / the / that one / young woman / such / very / woman / good. 3. And / day / a / on / Ikto / his wife / the / thus / he talked to her, / "Now, / old woman, / thing / one / I will warn you against. / That

---

[1] There is normally a strict avoidance between a son- or daughter-in-law and the mothers- and fathers-in-law, and a trifle stricter where opposite sexes are involved. But it isn't surprising to find Ikto attempting to break it. He is immoral always. That phrase, in Dakota parlance, which I translate "O, no! ...... Well? ...... All right," with significant pauses between words, is sometimes used to indicate a slow change of attitude, but apart from the implications here.

[2] *winų'hca;* *wi*-female; *nų* grown? cf. *k'oya'nų*, to grow rapidly; said of a child that grows tall fast. *k'oya'*, fast? cf. *k'oya'h'ą*, hurry up! *h'ą*, to act. *hca*, very; indeed. In Santee, *winų'hįca* means a mature woman; among the Yankton and the Teton, *winu'hca* is the familiar term of address by a man to his wife; used also in speaking of her to friends, informally. *winų'-hcala* (diminutive *la* added) means "Old Woman," among the Teton, and Yankton.

wakta′kel yaų′kta c‘a.   4. Lec‘a′la wic‘o′t‘i ki̧ ekta′ wai′ yu̧k‘ą′ hetą′ hą k‘oṡka′laka wą le′l u′kta tk‘a′ he′ mic‘ų′kṡi yu′zi̧kta c‘i̧′ ną ų′ u′kta ṡk‘e′ lo′.   5. C‘a he′ tohą′l hi′ ki̧hą, tok‘e′tuke c’e′yaṡ mic‘ų′kṡi hi̧g.na′yi̧kte lo′. Miye′ tk‘a′ le′ ąpe′tu tukte′ mit‘a′wakta t‘ąi̧′ṡniyą waų′ we lo′. He′c‘el-ami`c’ib.leze lo′.    6. Tohą′l ųg.na′ c‘ąya′le[1] yu̧k‘ą′ c‘oḋi̧′ ṡa′ oya′kaȟloka hą′tąhąṡ he′-ąpe`tu ki̧ mat‘i̧′kte lo′.   7. Wak‘ą′heża o′tapi k’ų t‘eȟi′ya owi′c‘awakiȟ’ąkte lo′.   He′ ų′ le′ iwa′hoc‘iye[2] lo′.   8. Ųg.na′ mat‘a′ hą′l k‘oṡka′laka ki̧ he′ hi′ hą′tąhąṡ wą′cak ta′ku eye′ṡni k‘eṡ mic‘ų′kṡi k‘u′ wo′.   9. He′ e′cuȟci′ṡ t‘ąhą′ku ną hąka′ku wi′wic‘akig.ni̧kte[3].   10. Ho ną mat‘a′ se′hi̧g.le[4] ci̧hą ec‘a′ṡ ṡuȟpa′la ki̧ le′ wążi′ tąye′ȟci̧ lolo′pyi̧ ną yuha′ e′maųpa yo′. Eyaṡ[5] wama′loteteka c‘aṡ sloly′aye c’ų, — eya′ ke’ᵉ.   11. Heya′hi̧ ną yuṡtą′ c‘ąke′ t‘awi′cu ki̧ c‘ąk’i̧′-iya`ya ke’ᵉ. Ekta′ to′to hi̧g.la′hi̧ ną

way / on account of / expecting it, in a way, / you will live / thus. 4. Recently / tribal camp / the / to / I went / and / from there / young man / a / here / he is coming / but / that one / my daughter / he will marry / he wishes / and / therefore / he will come / they say. 5. So, / that one / sometime / he arrives / the-then, / no matter how it is, / yet / my daughter / she shall marry him. / I, / but / this / day / which one / it will be mine / not clear, / I live. / That way I have observed myself. 6. Sometime / by chance / you are hunting firewood / and / pith / red / you break into / if-then / that-day / the / I shall die. 7. Children / they are many, / the-past / dreadfully / I-them-will do. / That / on account of, / this / I warn you. 8. By chance, / I was dead / then / young man / the / that / he came / if-then / at once / anything / saying not / instead / my daughter / give to him. 9. That one, / at least, / his brothers-in-law / and / sisters-in-law / for them he will provide. 10. Now, / and / I die, / it should happen / if-then / then / puppy / the / this / one (of them) / thoroughly / cook till tender / and / having it / lay me out. / Don't you recall, / I am fond of food, / such indeed / you know / the-past" / he said / they say. 11. He was saying these things / and / finished / so / his wife / the / to get wood-she went / they say. / Over there / striking-sounds / kept happening / and / now / after a time / then /

---

[1] *c‘ǫle′;* to gather firewood; *c‘ǫ,* wood; *ole′,* to hunt; search for. Only in this specific use, is the *o-* omitted; that is, when it refers to gathering firewood. We have *ṡųk-’o′le,* to hunt for horses; *pte-o′le,* to round up cattle; *t‘i-o′le,* to hunt for a house, i. e., to go visiting, just for the sake of eating.

[2] *iwa′hoya,* to warn concerning the future; *i,* on account of it; *wa* (?); *ho,* voice (?); *ya,* cause (?); *iwa′howaya,* I warn (him) in regard to; on account of; *waho′ya,* to send for, as a relative, from some distant band.

[3] *wi′wic‘akig.ni̧kte; wa,* things; *ig.ni̧′,* to go after; forage for, as food; to go about to provide; *wic‘a′,* them; *ki,* the dative; *kte (kta);* future. He will provide for them their things (food).

[4] *se′hi̧g.la,* if it should by chance be (that I die).

[5] *eyaṡ,* without any accent, means "as you know; don't you recall ?" (Not to be confused with *eya′ṡ,* which is only *eya′* with the adversative *ṡ* added.)

wana' tohą'tuka yųk'ą' ec'i'yatąhą c'ą' o'ta k'į' g.li' ną heya' ke'ᵉ:
12. — Wic'ahca'¹, sica'ya waho'siwaku we'. Ąpe'hą c'ogi' sa' wą
owa'kahloke' — eya' yųk'ą' he'c'enahci Ikto', — Hą', mat'a'², —
eyi' ną aptą'yą ke'ᵉ. 13. C'ąke' c'ica' k'u iyu'ha o'ksą c'e'ya ų'pi
ke'ᵉ. — Atê, atê,³ — eya'ya c'e'yapi ke'ᵉ. 14. Yųk'ą' hų'kupi k'u i's
wase' g.lub.le'b.lel hina'zi ną c'e'yaya heya' ke'ᵉ, — Wawi'tątąlake
c'u, to'k'el wase' we'cicųlakta huwê',⁴ — eya' yųk'ą' he'c'ena lec'a'las
t'e' c'u, tųwi' ną — Ite' o'ksą⁵, — eyi' ną ak'e' t'a' ke'ᵉ. 15. C'ąke'
c'ica' ki, — Ina', ate' kini'la⁶ ye', — eya'pi yųk'ą' ak'e' p'a-ka's'i ną
— Wą'cala, — eyi' ną ak'e' t'a' ke'ᵉ. 16. C'ąke' wase' ki'cicų ną t'ą-
c'ą' ki a'taya tąyą' ope'm.nit'upi ną sųhpa'la wą lolo'p-k'iyapi ną
c'ąa'g.nakapi ki ekta' e'upapi ke'ᵉ. 17. — C'uks, niya'te ta'ku to'na

from that place / wood / much / carrying on her back / she came
home / and / said / they say, 12. "Old man, / badly / I come home
with news. / Today / pith / red / a / I broke into," / she said / and
then / immediately / Ikto / "Yes; / I die," / he said / and / fell
over / they say. 13. So / his children / the-past / all / around him /
weeping / they continued / it is said / "Father, / father," / saying /
they cried / it is said. 14. And then / their mother / the-past / as for
her, / war-paint / untying her own / she came and stood / and /
weeping / said / they say: / "The dear one, he was so fastidious, /
the-past, / what way / war-paint / I shall apply for him, / I wonder,"
/ she said / and then / at once / having died just now, / the-past / he
opened his eyes / and / "Face / around," / he said / and / again /
he died / they say. 15. So / his children / the / "Mother, / father / he
has come to life, the dear one," / they said / and / again / head-he
raised / and / "Just once," / he said / and / again / he died / they
say. 16. So / war-paint / they applied for him / and / body / the / all
over / carefully / they wrapped it / and / puppy / a / they cooked
till tender / and / funeral-platform / the / there / they laid him / they
say. 17. "My daughter, / your father / things / several / he warned

---

¹ *wic'a'*, male; *hca*, very. See note 2, page 11, for corresponding data regarding the familiar term for wife. This word means *husband*.
² Ikto is generally quoted as doing without all the little particles, enclitics
etc., which color the language, and using the barest skeleton of speech.
An ordinary man would doubless say, *"he'c'el wąla'ka huwo' ? Hųhųhi', he'*
wana' mat'i'kte ci og.na'yą ye lo'; ho'!" "So you found it like that, did you ?
Alas, now my impending death is indicated; very well!" or some such
elaborate statement, even in times of stress.
³ It is characteristic Dakota to address directly the one dead, in the correct
relationship term.
⁴ The same tone inflection as used for a gradual realization, (See *ohą* p. 2,
l. 3) is also used to denote soliloquizing. The wife is wondering, aloud, in
what manner to apply the funeral-paint; not expecting an answer; least
of all, from the dead man.
⁵ See note 2, above.
⁶ *la*, diminutive, sometimes indicates affection; or pity; or tolerance. Thus
si'celaye (The bad one!), much as in English we say of a child, "The little
wretch!"

iwa'homayį ną iya'ya c'a hena' ec'e'l ec'ų'k'ųpikte'. 18. Wana'
išna'la nisų'kala lol-'i'wic'akig.nį k'ų wahpa'niwic'aye', — eya'
ke'ᵉ. 19. Ape'tu wą e'l hįg.na'ku hpa'ye c'ų he'c'iya i' ną i'c'ilowąhį¹
ną g.li' ną heya' ke'ᵉ: — C'ųkš, i't'ap wana' niya'te huhu' kį k'u'ya
oka'lalaya he', — eya' c'ąke' wik'o'škalaka k'ų c'e'ya ke'ᵉ. 20. (Leya
hena' šųhpa'la-huhu` c'a Ikto'mi tąye'la yasmi' ną k'u'l ihpe'ye šą'
slolya'pišni'ⁱ.)² 21. I'tonac'ą yųk'ą' ųg.na' hokši'la-haka`ktala wą
špu'kešni³ yųk'ą' he' e' c'a to'k'iyatąhą g.li' ną heya' ke'ᵉ: — Ina`,
wic'a'ša wą paha'ta na'žįhą c'a ekta' wai' yųk'ą' he' wic'a'woha-hi⁴
k'e'yaš ec'ą'l t'ųką'yįkte c'ų t'a' c'a iyo'kišilya na'žį ke'ye'lo', —

me of, / and / went away, / so / those / accordingly / we shall do.
18. Now, / he alone / your little brothers / he provided food for
them / the-past / he has made them poor," / she said / they say.
19. Day / a / on / her husband / he lay / the-past / there / she went /
and / she was singing death wails / and / returned / and / said /
they say / "Daughter, / already / now / your father / bones / the /
below / scattered about / it stands," / she said / so / young girl /
the-past / she wept / they say. 20. (Actually, / those / puppy-bones /
such / Iktomi / thoroughly / he ate all the meat off / and / down /
he threw / yet / they knew it not.) 21. Some days later, / and /
suddenly / youngest boy / a / wide awake / and / that one / it was /
such / from somewhere / he returned / and / said / they say /
"Mother, / man / a / on the hill / he was standing / so / to / I went /
and then / that one / to be son-in-law-he came / but / at that time /
he was going to have him for a father-in-law / the-past / he is dead /

---

¹ *hą*, to stand, is added to verbs to indicate repeated or continued action, (*hį*
before *ną*); *i'c'ilową*, to sing, (with reflexive *ic'i*,) means to sing a death
dirge. Normally *ic'i'* takes the accent on the second *i*. I think the full form
here is *ii'c'ilową*, to sing regarding one's self. In that case, the first *i* is a
compound, which explains the accent on the first syllable.

² Ever so often, a narrator, in inserting a sentence of an explanatory nature,
will let her voice down perceptibly. I have made such sentences parenthetical, for so they seemed to me in the telling.

³ *špu'kešni* means "to be wide awake; alive to what is going on," often to
the point of being meddlesome. It is reserved to describe children and
young people. *špu-* a monosyllabic stem requiring instrumentals, meaning
"to take off, as something, that comes off easily; to unfasten, as a button;
unhitch, as a team;" *ke* (for *ka*) rather; *šni*, not.

⁴ to be a son-in-law, he comes. *wic'a'*, man; *woha*, (?) This has been translated as meaning "hidden" (from *wo'ha*, a cache) with the idea that a son-
in-law must keep out of the way, because of avoidance rules. But that is not
correct. The word for daughter-in-law is *wi-wo'ha*; sometimes more fully
wi-wa'yuha which throws light on the problem. For *yuha'* is "to follow;
to be attracted to, so that one stays near by;" two horses that like to "run"
together on the prairies where they graze, are said to *yuha'* each other. Two
old women that enjoy each other's company are said to "*iya'kic'iyuha.*"
wic'a'woha-hi, then means, "he came in the capacity of a man who stays
by, on account of an attraction;" *wiwo'ha* would be the equivalent for a
woman who stays near her husband's people "from attraction."

eya'-oya`ka ke'ᵉ. 22. — Iho', cᶜ'ųkš, niya'te ta'ku iwa'homayą ke'p'e'
c'ų he' le e' ye'.   He' nihi'yohi c'a niya'te eye' c'ų og.na'yą wą'cak
hįg.na'yayįkte',   — eya' ke'ᵉ. 23. He'c'ena ina'yąpi kį t'i'pi wą
t'ą'ka it'i'cagį ną t'ima'hel yuc'o'k'ak'aya e'g.le ke'ᵉ. 24. Wic'a'ša-
c'o'la c'ąke' c'ųwį'tku hįg.na't'ųkte cį e'l išna'la ški'ciye cį he'
awa'c'į ną ic'i'kcąpta c'e'ya šk'e'ᵉ. 25. — C'uks, niya'te wawi'tątąlake¹
c'ų, lehą'l ak'e' to'k'eĥcį šką'kta tk'a' ye', ec'ą'mi ną li'la c'ąte' maši'ce'.
Iše' lehą'l ni' ų' yųk'ą's ani'lowąpi² k'o'kta tk'a' ye', — eyį' ną c'e'yaya
wo'waši ec'ų' c'ąke' c'ųwį'tku kį ak'e' o'kiye'ᵉ³. 26. Wana' lol-i'ĥ'ą
yuštą' ną   — Ho', c'įkš, iya'yį ną nit'ą'hą kic'o', — eya' 'cąke'
hokši'lala wą t'oka'-waho`ši-g.li` k'ų he' iya'yį ną — T'ąhą`, ina'
wana' ni'c'oumaši ye lo'. T'ąke' kic'i' yaų'kta c'a, — eya' yųk'ą' —
Ha.o', — eya' ke'ᵉ. 27. — He'c'etu we lo', t'ąhą`. Tk'a' t'o' k'e'yaš
wic'a'woĥa-wahišni s'e li'la c'ąte' maši'ca c'a wac'e'yįkte lo'. Heheĥi,

so / sadly / he stood / he said," / saying-he told / they say. 22. "Now /
/ daughter, / your father / something / he forewarned me / I said /
the-past / that / this one / it is. / That one / he has come for you / so /
your father said it / the past / accordingly / at once / you shall marry
him," / she said / they say. 23. Immediately / they have for a mother /
the / tipi / a / big / she erected / and / inside / making it attractive /
she set it / they say. 24. She was without a man, / so / her daughter /
about to marry / the / that / in / alone / she was active / the / that /
she thought on / and / taking pity on herself / she wept / they say.
25. "Daughter, / your father / he, poor thing, was so proud, / the-
past / now at this time / again / how indeed / he would be working /
but. / I thought it / and / very / heart / I am bad. / Really / now /
alive / he was / if / they would sing over you even, / but," / she said /
and / weeping / work / she did / so / daughter / the / again / she
helped her (to weep). 26. Now, / cooking / she finished / and /
"Now, / son, / go / and / your brother-in-law / invite," / she said,
so / little boy / a / at first brought the news / the-past / that one /
he went / and / "Brother-in-law, / my mother / now / she com-
mands me to invite you. / My elder sister / with / you will live, /
therefore," / he said / and so / "Yes," / he said / they say. 27. "That
is right, / my brother-in-law. / But / then, / nevertheless, / to be a
son-in-law I came not, / as if, / very / heart / I am bad / such / I
must weep. / Alas, / father-in-law / he is dead!" / saying / he wept /

---

¹ *i'tą*, to be proud of; *wa*, things; *tątą*, reduplicated; *la*, indicative of the
  speaker's affection; *ka*, rather; likely to be; somewhat; somtimes *wa* and *i*,
  instead of being separated by *w*, inserted, are contracted, and we get
  wi'tątąka.
² *lową'*, to sing; *a*, over; *ni*, you. In the *hųka'* ceremony, they sing over the
  candidates, waving a particular type of wand, decorated with horse-tail
  hair, in rhythm with the song.
³ *o'kiya*, to assist; aid; help. If a person weeps, and another joins, out of
  sympathy, that one assists the first.

t'ękǫ'[1] *t'e' lo'*, — *eya'ya c'e'ya ke'*ᵉ. *28. He'c'ena c'e'yaya t'i'pi kį e'tkiya u' c'ǫke' k'ųyǫ'pikte c'ų o'kiyį nǫ* — *Wic'a'śa wǫ wawi'tǫtǫka le'l t'i' k'ǫ, e'l ų'śni hǫ'l t'ako'ś-t'ų nǫ oi'yokiśice le'*, — *eya'-c'e'ya ke'*ᵉ. *29. Wana' t'i'pi wǫ lec'a'la-it'i'caǵapi k'ų he'l t'ima' i'yo-taka c'ǫke' it'ǫ'kal wį'yǫ k'ų he' taku'ku o'ta otu'h'q*[2] *ke'*ᵉ. *K'ohǫ' o'kśǫ oya'te kį wic'a'wota ke'*ᵉ. *30. Hokśi'lala k'ų he' t'ǫhǫ'ku kį iha'kap ece'-ų*[3] *yųk'ǫ' ųg.na' hų'ku ekta' g.li' nǫ* — *Ina', t'ǫke' hįg.na'ku kį li'la ate' iye'c'eca ye lo'*, — *eya' c'ǫke' i'yoktekį*[4] *nǫ* — *Niya'te t'a' c'aś wana' huhu' oka'b.lelya yųke' cį, ta'kuhca k'a' c'a!* — *eyį' nǫ t'ǫka'l śkal-śi' k'e'yaś ak'e'śna-g.li nǫ heya'hǫ ke'*ᵉ. *31. Hǫke'ya awa'c'įya c'ǫke' hį'hǫnahcį kikta' nǫ c'ųwį'tku t'i' kį e'l e'yokas'į yųk'ǫ' Ikto'mi he' e' c'a sic'ǫ' zizi'yela*[5] *yųka' c'a wǫya'kį nǫ li'la ito'm.ni ś'e c'ǫze'ka śk'e'*ᵉ. *32.* — *Wahte'śni kį,* — *eya'ya ohų'nicat'a wǫ yuha' t'ima'hel iya'yį nǫ kahu'huǵa śk'e'*ᵉ. *33. Ikto'mi t'o'h'ǫ*

they say. 28. Then / weeping / tipi / the / towards / he came, / so / she will be a mother-in-law / the-past / she helped him (to weep) / and / "Man / a / proud / here / he lived, / the-past. / Here / he is not / just when / he acquires a son-in-law, / and / it is sad," / saying-she wept / they say. 29. Now / tipi / a / recently erected / the-past / there / indoors / he sat down / so / outside of it / woman / the-past / that one / certain things / many / she was giving away / they say. / Meantime / around / people / the / they were eating / they say. 30. Little boy / the-past / that one / his brother-in-law / the / following him / always he was / and then / all at once / his mother / to / he came back / and / "Mother, / my elder sister / her husband / the / very / my father / he looks like him," / he said, / so / she scolded him / and / "Your father / he is dead, / so indeed / now / bones / scattered about / he lies, / the / what-indeed / he means / such!" / she said / and / outside / to play-she ordered him / but / he returned-again and again / and / he kept saying that / they say. 31. At last / he caused her to think of it / so / early in the morning / she arose / and / her daughter / she lived / the / in / she peeped / and / Ikto / that one / it was / such / thighs / yellow-ly / he lay / so / she saw him / and / very / dizzy / like / she became angry / they say. 32. "Worthless one / the," / saying / club / a / carrying / indoors / she went / and / broke him into pieces / they say. 33. Iktomi / deeds of his / bad ones / many / still / people / among / they do /

---

[1] *t'ęka'śi* is the correct term for "my father-in-law," whether in speaking of, or to him. It is characteristic of Íkto to speak as he pleases; here he dispenses with the final syllable and nasalizes the *ǫ*.

[2] *otu'h'ǫ*, the act of giving property away, in the give-away fashion; *otu'ya* or *itu'h'ǫ*, in vain. *h'ǫ*, to act.

[3] *ece'*, plus a verb, and the two accented as one word, means "always, invariably in that manner".

[4] *i'yokteka*, to scold; speak sharply to; to correct, as a child, (and box his ears at the same time); *i*, mouth; *o*, in; *kte*, to kill; *ka*, rather.

[5] *zi*, yellow; *zizi'yela*, literally, "yellow-yellow-ly in appearance."

šikší'ca o'ta nahą'hcį oya'te e'g.na ec'ų'pi kį hena' ųspe'wic'ak'iya šk'e'ᵉ. 34. K'e'yaš e'k'eš tuwe'ni c'ųwį'tku-g.lu'zešni nac'e'ce'ᵉ. Eha'š¹ Ikto' ao'kaǧe'ᵉ². Witko'tkokapi kį ohi'ye lo'³. 35. Hetą' Ikto' to'k'el iya'yeca c'e'l. 36. Hehą'yela owi'hąke'ᵉ.

the / those / he taught them / they say. 34. But / at least / nobody / he marries his daughter not / perhaps. / Too much / Ikto / he over-does. / They are bad / the / he wins. 35. From there / Ikto / whither / he went / who knows ? / 36. There / it ends.

Free Translation.

1. Iktomi was camping outside of the tribal circle as a single family; but because he had so many children, it appeared like a small tribe in itself. 2. His eldest daughter was a very handsome young woman. 3. One day Ikto talked to his wife in this fashion, "Wife⁴, there is something I wish to prepare you for. It is simply so that you may keep it in mind. 4. I have just been to the tribal camp, and while there I learned that a young man is coming soon to see us; but his real reason is he wishes to marry our daughter. 5. When he comes, my daughter shall marry him, no matter what happens. As for me, I do not know from day to day which time will be mine. I have studied myself, and feel I am soon to die. 6. Someday, when you are gathering fire wood, you are going to strike a tree with a red pith. When that happens, I shall die. 7. I worry because there are so many children, and my going will impoverish them. That is why I am talking thus of the future. 8. If, in the event of my death, this young man should come, and ask you, you must without argument give up our daughter. 9. I shall feel easier if I know that he will hunt and provide for his little brothers- and sisters-in-law. 10. Another thing: In case I do die, you know how I love to eat. Take one of these little puppies and cook it until tender, and lay it by me on the burial scaffold." 11. So his wife went to get wood. All day one could hear her ax striking the trees, and after a time she returned with much wood; and said, 12. "Husband, I have bad news. Today I broke open a log and struck red pith." Without a pause, Ikto fell over. "I die⁵!" he murmured. 13. His children all came crying around his body, "O,

---

¹ *eha'š* appearing in a sentence gives the idea "too much."
² *ao'kaǧa*, to overdo; overstep the bounds; go beyond the pale. *a*, on; *o*, in; *ka'ǧa*, to make.
³ This last remark is an editorial comment; the narrator is winding up with his own views on Ikto's behavior. Hence he omits the usual *šk'e'ᵉ*, they say.
⁴ I translate this "wife." In its ordinary use, the word *"winų'hcala"* means an old woman. But without the diminutive ending, it means "very woman." and is the current Santee word for a woman of maturity; Teton and Yankton use it as a direct term of address to one's wife.
⁵ Generally Ikto is quoted, in a voice curiously nasal and twangy, and with a disdain for enclitics and particles.

2

father, father!" they sobbed. 14. Meantime his wife advanced with
her (bag of) face-paints open and said through her tears, "He was
always so fastidious, the dear one. I wish I knew how he would have
liked his face paint applied," and immediately, he who was so
dead, opened his eyes to say, "Around my face, circularly," and
then fell off in death again. 15. His children exclaimed with joy,
"O, mother, he came back to life; our dear father!" and once more
he raised his head to say, "Only once," and was dead again. 16. So
she applied his face paint, and dressed him carefully in the proper
materials, and prepared the puppy as he had instructed her; then
he was laid away on a funeral platform, with the cooked puppy
beside him. 17. "Daughter, your father left certain things to be done,
and we must carry them out carefully. 18. You see, he was all your
little brothers and sisters had to provide food for them, and now
he has forsaken them and they are poor from losing him," she said.
19. One day she visited the burial place, and sang death dirges
there; and said, "Daughter, already now your father's bones lie
scattered below the platform", so the young woman wept. 20. (As
a matter of fact, Iktomi had carefully picked all the meat from the
puppy and left the bones down here; which of course they did not
know.) 21. Some time later, the smallest boy, who was wide-
awake to everything, came home and said, "Mother, a man was
standing on the hill so I went to him and he told me he had come
to be a son-in-law but that the man whose daughter he wanted to
marry had died, so that he was very sorrowful." 22. — "There, that
is just what your father said would happen, daughter. This man
has come for you to make you his wife; so according to your father's
wishes, you shall marry him," the mother said. 23. She went right
out and proceeded to erect a large tipi and to arrange things
attractively inside. 24. She began pitying herself that she, without
a husband's assistance, must prepare for her daughter's wedding;
and she cried, 25. "Daughter, what a pity your father is gone. He
was proud to do things properly. If only he were alive, how hard he
would be working now! That is what I think, and I am sad. If he were
here, he certainly would not rest until he had arranged a *Huka'*
ceremony[1] for you!" talking thus, she worked, weeping; so her
daughter also wept. 26. When she had finished preparing food, she
told the boy to call the young man; so he ran to the hill and said,
"My brother-in-law, my mother orders me to invite you now; you
are to live with my elder sister." And the man said, "Thank you.
27. That is right, brother-in-law. But first I must weep; for who
would ever take me for a bridegroom, seeing I come mourning with a

---

[1] The Dakota text says, "Were your father living, he would no doubt even
arrange for them to sing over you." — "To be sung over" was to undergo
the *huka'* ceremony, and assume all the privileges and obligations it carried.
It was a great honor, indicating the love in which the candidate was held
by her parents or other relative who arranged it.

sad heart. Alas, that my father-in-law is dead!" 28. He approached the tipi wailing aloud[1], so his mother-in-law-to-be joined him in wailing and said, "A proud man once lived here; alas, he is no longer here, and it is sad!" 29. He entered the newly erected tipi and sat down, while all the guests sat outside in a ring, feasting; and his mother-in-law gave away many things. 30. But that little boy, always inquisitive, followed his brother-in-law all around and then returned to his mother, very much troubled. "Mother, you know, sister's husband looks just like father!" he said. His mother boxed his ears and sent him outside, saying, "You shouldn't say that about your father. He is dead and already his bones lie scattered about. What do you mean by talking like that?" So he went out to play. 31. He kept coming back until he made her curious; so much so that she arose early one morning and looked into her daughter's tipi. And there she saw Iktomi lying asleep. His yellow thighs[2] identified him. When she saw what had happened she was dizzy with anger. 32. "The worthless wretch!" she said, snatching up an ax, which she carried into the tipi. She pounded Iktomi with it, breaking all his bones. 33. Iktomi's many bad deeds persist among the people, no doubt, because he first taught them and set the example. 34. But at least nobody marries his own daughter, surely. Right there Iktomi overdid it. He wins in wrong-doing. 35. From there, who knows where Iktomi went? 36. That is all.

4. Ikto'mi Tricks the Pheasants.

1. Ikto'mi ka'k'ena wakpa'la-op'a`ya tok'e' ec'a'ca-oma`nihą yųk'ą' ųg.na' to'k'iyap wac'i'pi naĥ'ų'-ihe'yį ną pat'a'k ina'żį śk'e'⁶. 2. Nų'ǵoptąptą ną wana' ka'tu s'e le'c'eca c'ąke' e'tkiya yį' ną o't'ąiyą ina'żį yųk'ą' hena'keĥcį śiyo'pi c'a yup'i'yela wac'i'pila śk'e'⁶. 3. He'c'ena c'ąma'hel iya'yį ną ina'ĥni c'ą' wą p'eżi'-śaśa` ao'pem.ni

Literal Translation.

1. Iktomi / off yonder / along the creek / without specific purpose he was going about / and / by chance / somewhere / dancing / he heard suddenly / and / stopping short / he stood / they say. 2. He listened / and / now / it was there / like / it seemed so / therefore / towards / he went / and / within sight of it / he stopped / and / every one of all those / pheasants / such / beautifully / they dance / they say. 3. At once / into the wood / he went / and / hurriedly / stick / a / red grass / wrapping about it / he packed it on his back /

---

[1] This is again a pose. The other characters in these Ikto stories are always represented as being "taken in" by Ikto's pretence; and during the telling of a story there are little asides or comments made constantly by the story-teller and hearers, concerning the folly and stupidity of the people who believed in him.

[2] Ikto had yellow thighs, some stories say. I never heard this among the Yankton, but it is current among the Teton.

k'į' ną wic'i'yopteya e'l e'wic'atųweśniħcį hiya'ya śk'e'ᵉ. 4. — Wą, ka'k'iya ka Ikto' wak'į' ną hiya'ye. Ųki'c'opikte lo', — eya'pi ną — Ikto' +! — eya'hąpi k'e'yaś naħ'ų'śni-kųs hiya'ya c'ąke' p'ip'i'ya-kipą`pi yųk'ą' e'na ina'źį c'ąke', — Hena' ta'ku c'a yak'į' huwo'? — eya'pi śk'e'ᵉ. 5. Yųk'ą', — I'śe'[1] lena' olo'wąla c'a wak'į' kį. Le'c'iya wac'i'pikta śk'į' ną waho'mayąpi c'a le' ina'ħni-oma`wani kį, le' ta'ku k'a'pi c'a! — eya' śk'e'ᵉ. 6. — C'iye`, u' ną wąźi'la eśa' ųki'-cahiyayapi ye', — eya'pi yųk'ą', — Hoħ, le' ina'waħni c'eś ep'e' śą', — eyį' ną ak'e' iya'yįkta śk'e'ᵉ. 7. K'e'yaś li'la kitą'pi c'ąke', — Ho po', ec'a, — eyį' ną wo'p'aħta k'ų g.luźu'źu ną olo'wą wąźi'laħcį iki'kcu śk'e'ᵉ. 8. — Ho, le' olo'wą ki wo'wasukiye wą yuha' ye lo', — eya' c'ąke', — To'[2], — eya'pi śk'e'ᵉ. Yųk'ą', — Awa'hiyaye cį ic'ų'hą tuwe'ni yatų'wąpikteśni ye lo', — eya' c'ąke' he'c'etu ke'ya'pi śk'e'ᵉ. 9. Yųk'ą' c'ą'c'eǧa g.luħpį' ną wana' lową' ną iya'p'a c'ąke' śiyo' k'ų iyu'ha sliya' ,wac'i'pi śk'e'ᵉ. Oi'yokip'iya wac'i'pi śk'e'ᵉ, wi'yela k'o'ya. 10. Yųk'ą' le'c'el ahi'yaya śk'e'ᵉ:

and / on, past them / at / them-looking-not-indeed / he went along / they say. 4. "Hey! / Over there / yonder / Ikto / he carries something on his back / and / he goes along by. / Let us call him over," / they said / and / "Ikto!" / they kept saying / but / not to hear-pretending / he went along / so / again and-again-they called to him / and then / where he was / he stopped / so / "Those / what / such / you carry on your back?" / they said / they say. 5. And / "Only just / these / little songs / such / I do carry / the. / Over here / they will.dance / they say / and / sent for me / so / this / in haste-I travel / the, / this / what / they mean / such!" / he said. 6. "Elder brother, / come / and / only one / at least / sing for us, / please," / they said / and / "*Hoħ!* / I am in a hurry / such / I said / yet!" / he said / and / again / he was going on. 7. But / very / they insisted, / therefore / "Well, then," / he said / and / pack / the-past / he undid his own / and / song / only one indeed / he took out his own. 8. "Now, / this / song / the / regulation / a / it carries," / he said / so / "Very well," / they said. / And then / "I sing it / the / during / nobody / they shall not use their eyes," / he said, / so / all / they agreed / they said. 9. And then / drum / he took down his own / and / now / he sang / and / drummed, / so / pheasants / the-(past) / all / (with a characteristic sound as of dancing) / they did dance, they say. / Pleasantly / they danced; / females / included. 10. And / thus / he sang / they say, /

---

[1] *i'śe'*, sometimes pronounced *į'śe'*, begins a sentence in which the speaker wishes to belittle what he is going to mention, "Oh, nothing, just some little old songs that aren't worth much!" "O, I'm just going for a little while." "He is just saying that; he doesn't mean it!" *i'śe'* also expresses "really" in such sentences as: *i'śe' m.ni'kta śk'a' owa'g.lakeśni*, I am really going, but I didn't say so; *i'śe' wica'k'eśni*, (don't worry) he doesn't actually mean it!

[2] *To'*, used by both sexes, surely; certainly; indeed yes; by all means.

Išto'g.mus wac'i' po'!
Išto'g.mus wac'i' po'!
Tuwa' yatų'wąpi kįhą išta' niḣca'pikte lo',
Išto'g.mus wac'i' po'!
11. *He'c'el lową' c'ąke' išto'g.mus wac'i'hąpi yųk'ą' k'ohą' to'na mak'u' t'ąkt'ą'kapi kį hena' kat'a' awi'c'aya šk'e'ᵉ.* 12. *Ųg.na' wąži' tųwą' yųk'ą' wana' o'ta wic'a'kte c'ąke', — Hą'ta po'! Ikto' nica'sota-pikte lo'! — eyį' ną kįyą' k'ig.la' c'ąke' ųma'pi kį iyu'ha iha'kap kįyą' ina'p'api šk'e'ᵉ.* 13. *He'c'ena Ikto' iḣa't'at'a wic'a'kpahi ną, — Wą'ca-tąwa`watešni¹ c'ą'šna ka'k'el eca'mų we! — eya'ya pta'ya p'awi'c'aḣtį ną wic'a'k'į owa'štecaka wąži' ole' ya'hį ną ka'l iyo'tą-oi`yokip'i ną p'eži'-hįkpi`la² c'ąke' e'l c'et'i' šk'e'ᵉ.* 14. *He'c'ų ną šiyo' kį etą' pasnų' e'wic'ag.le ną etą' i'š c'owi'c'ak'į ną e'l špą-a'p'e yąka'hą yųk'ą' iwą'kap c'ą nų'p i'c'icameya hą' c'ąke' t'ate' hiyu' c'ą i'c'icakįzahą šk'e'ᵉ.* 15. *Yųk'ą', — Misų`, he'c'ųpilašni ye'. Ksu'-yeyec'iyapikte, — eya' he c'e'yaš he'c'ena ec'e'cahą šk'e'ᵉ.* 16. *Hąke' ya Ikto' ekta' iya'li ną yųk'i'nųk'ą wic'a'yus-wac'į k'e'yaš ec'ą'l ab.la'-*

Eyes shut / dance ye!
Eyes shut / dance ye!
Whoever / you open your eyes / the-then / eyes / you will be sore. /
Eyes shut / dance ye!
11. That way / he sang, / so / eyes shut / they were dancing / when/ meantime / how many / breast / they were large / the / those / striking dead / them-he took along. 12. By chance / one / opened his eyes / and lo, / now / many / them-he struck dead / therefore / "Take care, / Ikto / you-he will kill off," / he said / and / flying / he went away / so / rest / the / all of them / following him / flying / they went away. 13. At once / Ikto / laughing / them-his-he collect-ed / and / "On a rare occasion / I fare not well / then-regularly / that way / I do," / so saying / together / them-he tied / and / them-packing on his back / pleasant place / a / hunting / he was going / and / yonder / especially-attractive / and / grass-turf / such / at / he built fire. 14. He did that / and / pheasants / the / some / to roast on spits / he set them up / and / some / again / them-he cooked in ashes / and / there / to be done-awaiting / he was sitting / when, lo! / above him / trees / two / rubbing against each other / stood, / so / wind / it came / then / they sqeaked against each other. 15. And so / "My younger brothers, / don't do that, little ones. / You might injure each other," / he kept saying, / but yet / it kept happening. 16. At last / Ikto / to / he climbed / and / pulled apart / them to hold-he aimed / but / just then / it suddenly became calm / so / hand / the /

---

¹ *tąwa`watešni*, I do not eat well; *tą* (from *tąyą'*), well, or satisfactorily; *wa*, things; *wa'ta*, I eat; *šni*, not.
² *p'eži'*, grass; *hįkpi'la*, this means soft, short thick grass, as on a lawn; *hį* means also "fur, the hair on a skin;" *la* is diminutive; *kpi* (?).

*kela-hįg.la c'ąke' nape' kį e'na ana'ǵipa šk'e'ᵉ. 17. — Misų́, misų́,
ama'yuśtąpila ye'. Wac'o'wak'įla c'a ec'e'l p'iwa'kiyįkte, — eye'
c'e'yaś he'c'ena ana'ǵip i'yanica šk'e'ᵉ. 18. Hcehą'l śųk-ma'nitu wą
ka'k'iya tok'i'-hiya'ye¹ c'e'yaś ho'yek'iyį ną, — He'+, naca' wą
le'l wawa'pasnų we lo'+. Ųg.na' t'epma'yak'iyįkte, — eya' šk'e'ᵉ.
19. — Wica'k'e se'ce lo', witko' kį, — ec'į' ną kawį'h hiyu' ną c'et'i'
k'ų he'l i' yųk'ą' yup'i'yela wana' wapa'snų k'ų śpą' c'ąke' e'na
wo'tahį ną iyu'ha t'epya' yuśtą' ną wana' iya'ya šk'e'ᵉ. 20. Yųk'ą'
ak'e' Ikto' c'ąwą'katąhą ho'uyį ną, — Wac'o'wak'įla k'ų e'cuñcį's
omi'yecapta c'e'·š², — eya' c'ąke' ak'e', — Wica'k'e se'ce lo', witko'
kį, — ec'į' ną kawį'h iya'yį ną c'et'i' k'ų e'l i' yųk'ą' śiyo' to'na
mahe'l c'ok'į'-yąka'pi c'ąke' c'aho'ta kį kawa'swas iye'yį ną iwi'c'acu
ną p'iya'-wo'ta šk'e'ᵉ. 21. Ig.lu'śtą ną wana' nake'ś iya'ya hą'l ak'e'
t'ate' hiyu' ną c'ą' k'ų hena' kak'i'nųk'ą iye'ya c'ąke' (Ikto') nape'
iki'kcu ną k'u'ya g.licu' tk'a'ś wana' wac'o'k'į ną wapa'snų k'ų hena'
iyu'ha hena'la šk'e'ᵉ. 22. He'c'el eś wo'teśni c'ąke' loc'į'hca hetą'*

right there / it was pinned. 17. "My younger brothers, / my younger
brothers, / let poor little me go, / please. / I am humbly roasting
something, / so / as it should be / I will reset my own," / he said; /
but / still / pinned to / he remained fast. 18. Just then / wolf / a /
yonder / going about his business / but / he called to him / and /
"Hey, / chieftain / a / here / I am roasting things on spits. / By
accident / you might eat it up for me!" / he said. 19. "He is right /
perhaps / fool / the," / he thought / and / turning / he came / and
he built a fire / the (past) / there / he arrived / and / perfectly / now /
he roasted (meat) on spits / the (past) / cooked, / so / right there /
he ate / and / all / to consume / he finished / and / now / he went
away. 20. And then / again / Ikto / from up-tree / he called / and /
"I roasted (meat) in ashes / the (past) / at least that / you left for
me, / surely," / he said / so / again / "He is right / perhaps, / fool/
the," / he thought / and / turning / he went / and / he built a fire /
the-past / there / he arrived / and / pheasants / several / inside / to
roast-they sat, / so / ashes / the / pawing away / he sent it / them-he
took / and / anew-he ate. 21. He finished his own / and / now / for
sure / he went away / when / again / wind came / and / trees /
the-past / those / forced apart / they went / so / hand / he took out /
his own / and / below / he returned, / but / now / his roastings in
ashes / and / his roasting on spits / the-past / those / all / there was
none. 22. Thus / *eś* / he ate not / therefore / hungry indeed / from

---

¹ *tok'i'* plus an active verb, gives the force of independence of interest and
motives. Here it means the wolf was going along on his own business,
paying not the least attention to Ikto' or his affairs. In other words, if
Ikto' had kept still, there would have been no story.

² *c'e.ś* is a contraction of *c'e'l eś*. Here it means "No doubt." Sometimes it
means "Who shall say ?" "Who knows ?" No direct English equivalent can
suffice.

ya'hą yųk'ą' c'ąku'-og.na' šųk-ma'nitu wą wat'e'pk'iye c'ų he' t'a' hpa'ya c'ąke' e'l ina'žį ną li'la iyo'p'eya šk'e'ᵉ. 23. — Ho', kahą'l eš tukte'ešni¹, tuwa' mik'i'yela ta'ku ec'ų'-wac'į c'ą'šna le'c'el t'e' lo', — eya'ya icu' ną hįye'tąų k'į' ną ya'hą šk'e'ᵉ. 24. Eha'š to'k'el ec'ųkta t'ąį'šni ną hąke'ya owa'štecaka wą e'l ai' ną c'et'i' ną e'l wi'yukcą yąka'hą šk'e'ᵉ. 25. — Ho, it'o' ha' kį le' hąke' t'ewa'šlakį ną hąke' i'š hįmį' ną hąke' owa't'ų nąį'š ta'ku-wayįkta huwó? — eya'hį ną he'c'etuka-k'eš iyu'p'ah yu'zį ną — Ta'ku wašte' k'eš ihą'kyapi kį, — ęya'ya p'e'ta kį c'oka'ya ihpe'ya šk'e'ᵉ. 26. Yųk'ą' ehą'kec'ų šųk-ma'nitu kį t'e'šni hųše p'eta'ǧa ona'b.leb.lel kikta' hiya'yį ną naki'p'a c'ąke' Ikto' iye' eha' yuš'į'yayį ną ig.lu'šnašna na'žį šk'e'ᵉ. 27. Ną hetą'hą Ikto' tok'i'yot'ą iya'yeca c'e'l. Hehą'yela owi'hąke'ᵉ.

there / he was going / and lo / in the road / wolf / a / he ate up his things / the-past / that one / dead / he lay; / therefore / there / he stopped / and / very / he scolded him. 23. "Now, / then / (What did I tell you?) / whoever / near me / something / to do-he tries / then-regularly / thus / he dies," / saying / he took him up / and / on the shoulder / he packed him / and he was going on. 24. *Eha'š* / how / he would do / it was not clear / and / at least / pleasant place / a / to / he took him / and / built a fire / and / there / cogitating / he sat. 25. "Now, / suppose / skin / the / this / piece / I (will) wear about the head / and / piece / next / I (will) wear as a blanket / and / piece / I (will) wear as leggings / — or else / what shall I use it for?" / he was saying / and / "to settle it anyway," / taking him up in a heap / he held him / and / "Something / good / yet / they destroy it / the!" / saying / fire / the / midst / he threw him. 26. And lo, / evidently / wolf / the / he was dead not / perhaps / embers / scattering with the feet / springing up / he hurried / and / ran off, / so / Ikto / he / rather / he was frightened / and / trying to get hold of himself in vain / he stood / they say. 27. And / from there / Ikto / in which direction / he went indeed / "who knows?" / There / it ends.

Free Translation.

1. Iktomi was walking at random along a creek and he heard dancing, so he stopped to listen. 2. He finally located the source of the sound; so he went towards it and stood within sight of the place; and saw that those were all pheasants who were dancing and having a jolly time. 3. Immediately he withdrew into the wood and wrapped some red grass about a piece of wood; this he put on his back, and then walked past without paying the slightest attention to the dancers. 4. "Hey, there goes Ikto. Let's call him over," they said. "Ikto!" they called but he continued as if he hadn't heard;

---

¹ *kahą'l eš tukte'ešni* means, "I told you so!" (with a vengeance!) Word for word, it gives no sense in English.

so they called repeatedly until he stopped; and then they asked,
"What's that you carry on your back ?" 5. — "These ? Why they are
just some silly little songs. There is to be a dance farther up, and
I've been sent for. That's why I am in a rush; now what are they
after[1] ?" he added. 6. "O, elder brother, come over here and sing us
one tiny little song; just one," they said and again he said, "Indeed
not! I've just told you I'm in a hurry. What's the idea ?" and he
walked on. 7. But they were very insistent, so he relented. "Very
well, then," he said, undoing his package and bringing out a single
song. 8. "Now, this song has its special regulation; will you heed it ?"
— "Surely," they said. "All right, then. While I am singing it, nobody
is to open his eyes," Ikto told them; and they said that would be
all right with them. 9. So he got out his drum and began beating
it as he sang; so the birds danced, making a rhythmic noise with
their feet. It was a good sight to watch them dancing; females
included. 10. This is what he said,
"Dance with your eyes closed.
Whoever opens his eye shall get a stye,
Dance with your eyes closed."
11. They danced with their eyes closed and meantime Ikto was
selecting those with the fattest breasts, and killing them in turn.
12. One happened to look, after a while, and seeing many dead,
called out, "Fly for your lives! Ikto will kill you all off!" and with
that, he flew out of the place; so the rest followed him. 13. Iktomi
laughed as he picked up his prey, and, tying the birds into a bunch,
he said to himself, "On those rare times when I am faring poorly,
that's the trick I work!" and he began looking for a pleasant spot;
yonder in the woods was a lovely place where the grass was soft and
thick; he built a fire there. 14. Then he set some of the pheasants
up on spits to cook, and some he covered with ashes to roast; but
while he sat there waiting, two trees in contact overhead kept
making a loud squeaking noise each time there was a gust of wind.
15. So he called up, "Little brothers, please don't do that. Why,
you will injure each other that way!" But the noise persisted.
16. At last Ikto climbed up one of the trees, planning to hold the
two apart, but just when he had his hand between the trees there
was a calm, and he couldn't pull his hand out. 17. "Little brothers,
little brothers, let me go, please. I am cooking something in ashes
and I need to go and attend to it." But his hand continued to be
pinned there. 18. At that moment, a wolf was going by, in the
distance, on his own business; and Ikto called to him, "Hey! I, a

---

[1] In expressing disapproval or disgust or displeasure, it is common to do so
in the presence of the person provoking it, but not addressed to him
directly. If someone fumbles, for example, and tries the patience of another,
that other will, in nine out of ten cases, say, not "What's the matter with
you, anyway!" but "What's the matter with him, anyway!" even though
they might be working side by side at something.

chieftain, am cooking meat on spits here. Get out; I won't have you eating it up for me!" — 19. "The idiot might just happen to be talking sense," the wolf thought; so he turned and came over to find out; there, sure enough, was some meat on spits, just about done, so he sat down and ate it all up and then started to go. 20. From overhead Ikto called again, "At least I hope you have left for me what is cooking in the ashes," he said; so again the wolf thought he might just be talking sense and came back to the fire; and sure enough, there were some birds cooking in the ashes. So he brushed them off, and took them and feasted again. 21. He finished and was going off when at last the wind came up again and the trees separated so that Ikto took his hand away and came down, only to find all his food gone. 22. Thus it happened that he didn't eat after all; and he was going away very hungry; when, as he walked along, he came upon the wolf who had taken all his cooking. He was lying dead directly in his path, so Ikto stopped to scold at the dead animal. 23. "There you are; and that's just what you get. Everybody dies like this who tries to pull something on me!" With that, he lifted the wolf to his shoulder and walked along with him. 24. Puzzling as to the best way to handle that body, he walked till he found another pleasant spot in the wood. There he built a fire and sat beside it to think. 25. "I believe I will use at least a piece of this hide as a head-kerchief; and some of it I shall use for a blanket-robe; a piece will make me some leggings, and — aw shucks, what shall I do with it anyway?" he was saying, and at last he took it in his arms impatiently and said, "It has been done; even very fine things are sometimes discarded!" So he hurled the body into the fire. 26. Now, the wolf wasn't really dead, it appeared, for he sprang up, scattering live coals about, and ran away; so that Ikto was himself so frightened that he repeatedly grasped and let go of himself[1]. 27. From there who knows whither Ikto went? That is all.

5. *Iktomi Kills the Deer-Boy.*

1. *Ak'e's Ikto'-wic'a`sasni*[2] *ki ka'k'ena oma'nihą yuk'ą' t'a'hica-hoksi`la wą ita'zipa, wąhį'kpe k'o' li'la waste'site c'a yuha' yąka'hą c'ąke' e'l ina'zi ke'ᵉ.* 2. *Yuk'ą' Ikto' heya' ke'ᵉ, — Huhuhe', tok'e*

Literal Translation.[3]

1. Again / Iktomi-tricky one / the / off yonder / he was travelling / and / deer-boy / a / bow / arrows / too / very / nice ones / such / having / he was sitting / so / at / he stopped. 2. And / Ikto / he said, /

---

[1] This last is an awkward literal translation of the phrase, "*ig.lu'snasna*" which simply means to act as people do in a panic, when frightened or frantic or highly nervous; crazed.

[2] *wic'a'sa*, man; *sni*, not. As a unit, *wic'a'sasni* means to be tricky; deceptive; crooked in dealings; mischievous, as a child; waggish, as a man or woman.

[3] From here on, the quotative is not always translated.

*misųʹkala le eʹla¹ soʔ Wą́hįʹkpe wašteʹšte yuhaʹla ye loʹ. Pazoʹ yeʹ
tʼoʹ, misųˋ, tąwąʹcʻiciyakįkte, — eyaʹ keʼᵉ. Cʻą́keʹ iʼš-ʼųmake cįʹ², Iktoʹ
iyoʹwikʻiya cʻą́keʹ wą́hįʹkpe ną itaʹzipa kʻu henaʹ kʻoʹ ikiʹcu ną
yuhaʹ yąkįʹ ną ųg.naʹ ohʼąʹ hąʹhą³ sʼe wą́hįʹkpe wą ektaʹ eʹg.le ną
heyaʹ keʼᵉ, 3. — Eʹš toʹk, misųˋ, tokʻaʹš tukteʹl niwąʹkʻala⁴ seʹce.
Wicʻaʹša iyuʹha leʹ tukteʹl wąʹkʻapila kį, — eyaʹ yųkʻąʹ, — Hąʹ,
nawaʹte kį heʹl miʼš mawąʹkʻala kʻų, — eyaʹ keʼᵉ. Heʹcʻena Iktoʹ taʹku
eyeʹšni nawaʹte kį ag.leʹ yuʹzį ną kʻuteʹ cʻą́keʹ tʼaʹ iyaʹya keʼᵉ. 4. Yųkʻąʹ
tʼaʹhca-hokšiʼla kʻų icuʹ ną cʻąoʹwaštecaka oleʹ kʼį omaʹni keʼᵉ; ną
kaʹl tąyąʹ cʻą́keʹ eʹl aiʹ ną pʼaʹtį ną tʼaloʹ kį hąkeʹ cʻeiʹcʼipa keʼᵉ.
5. Icʻųʹhą yąkeʹ cį iwąʹkap cʻąʹ nųʹp tʼateʹ cʻąʹ iyeʹna iʼcʻicakįzahą
cʻą́keʹ Iktoʹ tokʻeʹ ecʻaʹca-lowąˋkta kʻeš onaʹhʼų-šilyapi keʼᵉ. 6. Lowąʹ-
pʼicašni kį ųʹ ešaʹš itʼoʹ ištįʹmįkta cʻa kʻuʹl iyųʹke cʻeʹyaš akʻeʹš kahiʹ-
cahąpi cʻą́keʹ oʹhąketa heyaʹ keʼᵉ: — Misųˋ, iniʹla yąkaʹpila yeʹ.

"Well, of all things, / can it be so / my little brother / this / it is,
little one, ? / arrows / good ones / he has, the little dear. / Let's see
them, / now, / little brother, / better-I will see them for you," / he
said. So / he-just as foolish / the / Ikto / he allowed / so / arrows /
and / bow / the-past / those / also / he took his (another's) / and /
holding them / he sat / and / suddenly / Ohʼąʹ hąʹhą sʼe — as
if in fun / arrow / a / in place / he set it / and / said, / they say,
3. "How about it, / my little brother, / perhaps / somewhere / you
are weak / perhaps. / Men / all / this / somewhere / they are weak /
the," / he said / and then / "Yes, / temples / the / there / I indeed /
I am weak / the-past," / he said. At once / Ikto / thing / saying not /
temple / the / against / he held it / and shot him / so / dead / he
became. 4. And so / deer-boy / the-past / he took up / and / pleasant
spot in the wood / seeking / carrying him on his back / he travelled;
and / there / it was fine; / so / there / he took it / and / butchered it /
and / meat / the / a part / he roasted for himself. 5. Meanwhile / he
sat / the / above / trees / two / wind / whenever-then / each time /
they grated against each other, sqeaking / so / Ikto / for diversion-he
would sing / yet / to hear it-they caused it to be bad. 6. Impossible
to sing / the / therefore / might as well / then / he will sleep / so /
down / he lay / but / again / they caused him to waken / so / at last /
he said, / "My younger brothers, / quiet / sit, little ones. / That you

---

¹ *eʹla*, it is he, the little one. In other words, this is a particle, *e*, indicating
identity, with the suffix *la*, diminutive.
² *iʼš-ųmaʻke cį;* literally, *iš*, as for one; *ųma*, the other one of two; *ka*, in a
manner of speaking; *cį*, the. It means something like this: "Then he, the
other one of a pair." In other words, this second person which comes up
for consideration, is instantly labelled as being exactly as stupid, silly,
ridiculous, as the other just mentioned.
³ *ohʼąʹ hąʹhą*, in fun; to no serious intent; in a trifling manner. *ohʼąʹ*, act;
hąʹhą, (?).
⁴ *wąʹkʻala*, fragile; weak; breakable; delicate; and always takes the diminutive
la.

*He'c'anųpi kį ų' tukte' ehą' ksu'yenic'iyapikte lo', — eya' ke'ᵉ.
7. Le'š ta'ku k'e' ec'i'šni he'c'ena c'ą k'ų kakį'zahąpi c'ąke' hąke'ya
ekta' iya'li ną yuk'i'nųk'ą wic'a'yus-wac'i ȟcehą'l nape' kį ana'ǵipyapi
c'ąke' to'k'a-¹ iki'kcušni ke'ᵉ. C'ąke' c'ąwą'kal yąkį' ną, — Wą, misų',
ama'yuštąpila ye'. Wic'a'šapilašni ye lo'. O'we hą'hąpila š'a k'ų
wana' ak'e'! — eya'yakel wic'a'yaec'eca-wac'i nąšna hehą'l nape'
kį g.luti'tą k'eš suta'ya ana'ǵipa ke'ᵉ. 8. I'yec'ala t'ok'a'la k'eya'
tok'i'-yapi c'aš hiya'yape šą' ho' yewic'ak'iyį ną, — Misų', he'l
ya'pišni yo'. He'l t'alo' c'emi'c'ipe. Ak'e' he'c'ekc'e-yaȟ'ą'pika c'a
t'epma'yak'iyapikte lo', — eya' ke'ᵉ. 9. Wic'a'kic'o iye'c'el heya'
c'ahe'c'e² o'ptaye kį a'taya kawį'ȟ hiyu'pi ną t'alo' k'ų a'škąšni š'e
t'epya' iye'yapi ke'ᵉ; wac'o'k'į k'ų hena' e' ną nakų' špąšni hiye'ye
c'ų iyu'hala. 10. Wana' t'alo' kį a'taya hena'la³ c'a iya'yapi ȟcehą'l
c'ą k'ų hena' k'inų'k'ąkiya iya'ya c'ąke' nape' kį iki'kcu ną k'u'ya
g.li' ke'ᵉ. 11. K'e'yaš wana'š t'alo' kį heki'cinala c'ąke', — Hehehi,*

do / the / on account of / some / time / you will hurt each other," /
he said. 7. Here indeed / something / he means / thinking not / still /
trees / the-past / they continued squeaking, / so / at last / to / he
climbed up / and / pulled apart / them to hold-he tried / just then /
hand / the / they clamped on / so / he couldn't get his own out in
any way. / So / up-tree / he sat / and / "Come now, / my little
brothers, / let me go, poor me, / please. / They are little scamps! /
They make jokes / regularly / the-past / now / again!" / speaking
after this fashion / to win them over-he tried / and regularly / then /
hand / the / he pulled on his own / yet / tightly / it was pinched.
8. Soon after / foxes / some / they were on their own business /
such indeed / they went along / yet / he called to them / and / "My
younger brothers, / there / go not. / There / meat / I am roasting for
myself. / Again / in such ways you are apt to behave, / so / you will
eat them up for me!" / he said. 9. He invited them / like / he said
that; / so of course / pack / the / all / turning / they came / and /
meat / the-past / in no time at all / it seemed / eating up / they
finished / he was roasting / the-past / those / it was / and / also /
uncooked / it lay about / the-past / all of that. 10. Now / meat / the /
all / it was gone / so / they went / just then / trees / the-past / those /
apart / went; / so / hand / the / he took out his / and / below / he
came back. 11. But / now indeed / meat / the / it was gone-to him; /

---

¹ *to'k'a* plus a negative verb, means "not to be able to —". *to'k'a-manišni,* he
can not walk; *to'k'a-wotešni,* he can not eat. Here: Ikto couldn't take his
hand away. (There was no way that he could take his hand away.)
² *c'a-he'c'e* is another word for "and so; and therefore; consequently."
³ *hena',* those   *hena'la,* only those; that is all; its all gone.
  lena', these   *lena'la,* only these; these are all that are left
  kana', those yonder *kana'la,* only those yonder; those yonder are all
                          that are left.
The diminutive *la* gives the sense of a small quantity remaining; but an
added meaning exists in the case of *hena'la,* "that is all; it is all gone."

misų́ tʿalo′ kʿų a′taya tʿepma′kʿiyape lô, — eyį́ ną locʿį́ cʿąke′ tʿo′e′l¹
wo′yute owe′kicʿeyahą škʿeʾᵉ. 12. Cʿe′yahe cʿų ųg.na′ tʿaʿñca pʿa kį
e′na ayu′štąpi cʿa wąya′k ihe′yį ną tʿana′sula mahe′l ų́ kį hena′
cʿįʾᵛ. — Hena′ e′cuñci′š wa′tįkte lo′, — eyį́ ną icu′wacʿį kʿe′yaš
oñlo′ka kį oci′kʿayela cʿąke′ napo′-kipʿišniʾⁱ. 13. He′cʿetu kʿeš, zuze′ca-
icʿicʿągį ną oñlo′ka-ciˋkʿala kʿų he og.na′ mahe′l iya′yį ną he′cʿiya
tʿana′sula iʾm.naicʾiyeʾᵉ. Li′la napį́ ną wašte′ cʿąke′ oñʾąkʿoya
tʿepya′ iye′yeʾᵉ. 14. Wana′ g.lina′pʿįkta yųkʿą́ hušti²! wo′tapi cʿų́
pʿaˊ kį li′la tʿą́ka cʿąke′ oki′pʿišni cʿa to′kʿani-g.licuˋšni cʿąke′ e′na
ñpa′yį ną cʿe′yehą keʾᵉ. Asni′snikiya ho′yeyį ną akʿe′šna cʿe′yahe
cʿe′yaš tuwe′ni nañʾų́šni keʾᵉ. 15. O′hąketa pʿaka′sʾį-wacʿį yųkʿą́
eya′š tʿaʿñcapʿaˊ kį li′la kapʾo′źela cʿąke′ iyo′wasʾįyą naʾźį hiya′yį
ną įˊyąk ya′ yųkʿą́ ųg.na′ ta′ku wą suta′ cʿa e′l iwo′ñtaka keʾᵉ.
16. — Nitu′we huwo′? — eya′-iyųǵa yųkʿą́, — Wazi′ miye′ ye lo′.
Cʿųˊtʿeñika kį he′cʿiya mahe′l ima′cʿaǵe lo′, — eya′ keʾᵉ. 17. Akʿe′

so, / "Well, well, / my younger brothers, / meat / the-past / all /
they-mine-ate up," / he said / and / he was hungry / so / delaying a
while / food / he was crying over his. 12. He was crying / the-past /
suddenly / deer / head / the / still there / they left it, / so / he saw it /
suddenly / and / brains / inside / they were / the / those / he desired.
"Those, / at least / I shall eat," / he said / and / to take-he tried /
but / opening the / it was small / so / hand-it fitted not. 13. Anyway,
/ then / snake / he made himself / and / small opening / the-past /
that / through / inside / he went / and / there / brains / he satisfied
himself with. Very / rich flavor / and / good / so / quickly / eating /
he finished. 14. Now / he would come back out / and then, / too
bad! / eating / on account of / head / the / very / large / so / it fitted
not / so / in no way he came out / so / in there / he lay / and / he
was crying. / Resting ever so often-he called out / and / again / he
wept / but / nobody / heard him not. 15. Finally / to raise his head-
he tried / and / at least / deer-head / the / very / it was light in
weight / so / still with it on / to rise / he proceeded / and / running /
he went / and then / of a sudden / something / a / hard / such / at /
he bumped it. 16. "Who are you?" / saying-he asked / and so /
"Pine / I am. / Difficult forest / the / there / inside I grow," / he

¹ tʿoe′l and tʿowa′š (or itʿo′ kʿe′yaš) both indicate that time is taken, before
doing something important, to do something else first. In the case of tʿoe′l,
the speaker is impatient with the delay; in the second case, he approves, is
sympathetic towards it. If I say, hiyu′kte cʿe′yaš tʿowa′š (or tʿo kʿe′yaš or
itʿo′ kʿe′yaš) wo′teʾᵉ (he is about to start, but first he is eating) I show that
I am in sympathy; it is quite proper for him to take time to eat, before
coming; I approve of the delay; but if I say, hiyu′kte cʿe′yaš tʿoe′l wo′teʾᵉ
(he is about to start, but first he is eating) that tʿoe′l indicates at once that
I am disgusted with him for taking time out; I think it is a needless delay;
I am unsympathetic in regard to his eating.
² hušti′! An expletive, for men only, I think; I have only heard it perhaps
twice. It indicates sudden and unlooked-for disappointment. I believe the h
was omitted once when I heard an old man named Little Bear use the word.

hetą́ i̯'yąki̯ ną ta'ku wą suta' c'a iwo'ħtak ina'ẕi̯ ke'ᵉ. 18. — Ho, ni'ṡ nitu'we huwo'? — eya' yųk'ą', — Wą le' pṡe'ħti̯ miye' ye lo'. C'a m.ni-i'k'iyela ece'-ima'c'aǵe lo', — eya' ke'ᵉ. 19. — Ec'a he'c'etu he'ciħą m.ni-i'k'iyela wau̯' se'ce. lô, — ec'i̯' ħcehą́'l maya' ki̯ nao'spa iye'yi̯' ną ohi̯'ħpaya ke'ᵉ. He'c'i k'u'ya m.ni' huṡe ekta' ohi̯'ħpaya c'ąke' he'c'ena onų'wą u̯' ke'ᵉ. 20. Hetą'hą wakpa' ki̯ op'a'ya nųwą' ya' ke'ᵉ. Yųk'ą' ug.na' waye'-i k'eya' wąya'kapi ną ayu'ta na'ẕi̯pi ke'ᵉ. 21. — Wąya'kapi ye' t'o. Ka ta'ku wą nųwą' hiya'ye ci̯ he' wic'a'ṡa iteke lo', — wąẕi' eya' yųk'ą' wąẕi' i'ṡ, — Hoħ, wą k'e'ya, he' t'a'ħca ye lo'. Miyeṡ he'c'el wąb.la'ke, — eya' ke'ᵉ. 22. Heya'hąpi ki̯ ic'u̯'hą k'iye'la s'e hiya'ya c'ąke', — T'a'ħca, le'c'iya u' ye' yo'! — eya'-hoyek'iyapi ke'ᵉ. 23. To'k'el-kipą̀'pika t'ąi̯'ṡni, itu'ya-heya`pi ke'ᵉ. To'k'eniṡ nawi'c'aħ'u̯ṡni iye'c'el iye' k'a'piṡni s'e hiya'ya ke'ᵉ. He'c'etu k'eṡ m.ni' ki̯ ekta' iyo'psicapi ną e'tkiya nųwą' ya'pi ke'ᵉ. 24. U'-wą- wi'c'ayaka yųk'ą' nap'i̯' ną iyu'weħtakiya to'k'el-oki'hi nųwą' ya' ke'ᵉ. He'c'u̯ ną he'c'iyatąhą maya'-g.liħe`ya ki̯ a'taya i̯'yą k'e'yaṡ hąke'ya m.ni-ma'hel hą' c'ąke' naku̯' tuwa' tu̯we' c'e'yaṡ wąya'ki̯ktesni iye'c'eca ke'ᵉ. Yųk'ą' he'c'etkiya to'k'el-oki'hi nųwą' yi̯' ną ug.na' i̯'yą k'u̯ hel, t'ost'osye`la iwo'to c'ąke' t'a'ħca p'a' k'u̯ a'taya waṡte'yela

---

said. 17. Again / from there / he ran / and / something / a / hard / such / bumping into / he stopped. 18. "Well, / as for you, / who are you?" / he said, / so / "Why / this / ash / I am. / Such / near water / always-I grow," / he said. 19. "In that case, / it is true / if then / near water / I am / perhaps," / he thought / just then / bank / the / with the foot breaking off / he went / and / fell down into / it. / There / below / water / evidently / there / he fell in; / so / at once/ swimming / he continued to be. 20. From there / river / the / with the stream / swimming / he went / and then / unexpectedly / hunters / some / they saw him / and / looking at / they stood. 21. "Look, ye. / That / something / a / swimming / he goes along / the / that / man / very likely," / one / he said; / and so / one / as for him / "Hoħ! / why, / you are wrong; / that one / deer. / I indeed / that way / I see it," / he said. 22. They continued saying that / the / meantime / near by / rather / it went / so / "Deer! / over here / come thou!" / saying-they sent him voice. 23. Why / they called to him / not plain / vainly-they said it. / In no wise / he heard them not / like / him / they meant not / like / he went by. / Anyway then / water / the / into / they jumped / and / towards / swimming / they went. 24. He saw them coming / then / he ran from them / and / towards the opposite shore / as much as he could / swimming / he went. / He did so / and / on that side / precipice / the / all / rock / but / partly / under water / stood / so / also / someone / he was using his eyes / yet / he would not see it / it was so. / And / towards that way / as much as possible / swimming / he went / and / without warning / rock / the-past / there / with a banging sound / he bumped it; / so / deer-head / the-past / entire / thoroughly / he shattered it.

*wob.le′ca ke*ᵉ. *25. He′c′es Ikto′ wana′ ak′e′ nii′c′iyį ną wic′a′śa-
kaȟya o′huta kį ekta′ k′iya′li ną he′l na′źį ke*ᵉ. *Ną e′tkiya ya′pi
c′ąke′ ohi′tiyela nųwą′pi kį iwi′c′aȟat′a śk′e*ᵉ. *Ho′t′ąkaya iwi′c′a-
ȟat′ahį ną oi′wic′aȟaȟa śk′e*ᵉ. *26. C′ąke′ waye′-ipi k′ų Ikto′ wic′a′-
g.naye cį aki′b.lezapi nąś kawį′gapi śk′e*ᵉ. *—Ho, i′ś ektą′ȟcį, he′ktakiya
ųg.la′pikte lo′. Wana′ ak′e′ he′ Ikto′ e′ c′a ųg.na′yąpe lo′. Kawį′ga
po′, — eya′pi ną u′pi k′ų he′c′etkiya ak′e′ nųwą′ k′ig.la′pi śk′e*ᵉ.
*27. Heȟą′yela owi′ȟąke*ᵉ.

25. Thus / Ikto / now / again / he saved himself / and / man-like /
shore / the / to / he climbed back / and / there / he stood. / And /
towards / they went / so / putting forth great effort / they swam /
the / he laughed at them. / Out loud / he was laughing at them / and /
making sport of them. 26. So / hunters / the-past / Ikto / he deceived
them / the / they realized it concerning themselves / and indeed /
they turned back. / "Well, / what's the use, / back / we will go
again. / Now / again / that one / Ikto / is / such / he is tricking us. /
Turn about," / they said / and / they came / the-past / towards that
way / again / swimming / they went back / it is said. 27. There /
it ends.

Free Translation[1].

1. Once again, Iktomi, the trickster, was walking along when he
came upon a deer boy sitting with his beautiful new bow and some
arrows in his hand. 2. "Well, well! If it isn't my little brother! And
what fine weapons he has! Let's see, little brother, I want to
inspect them," he said, so the boy handed them to Ikto, who sat
by him and examined them. After a time, he casually slipped one
of the arrows into place on the bow, as if toying with it, and said,
3. "I suppose you have a weak spot on you, somewhere. Everybody does. Do you?" And so the deer boy answered, "Yes, I guess
my temples are my weakest spot." And forthwith, Iktomi turned
the deer boy's arrow right on him, and shot him through the temple
so that he died instantly. 4. He picked up the dead deer and carried
it to an attractive spot in the wood, where he butchered it and
proceeded to roast a part of the meat. 5. Now, immediately over
his head two trees were in contact, and each time the wind blew,
they came together and rubbed against each other causing a squeaking noise. When Ikto tried to sing for amusement, they annoyed
him so he could not hear himself. 6. Next he tried to sleep, but
again they disturbed him so that he called to them, "Hey, brothers,
can't you keep still? You might hurt each other doing that, some
day!" 7. They paid no attention to him, so finally he climbed one of
the trees and was about to grasp hold of them to keep them apart

---

[1] This story was taken from the Crees who came into the Dakota country and
settled there.

when they came together and pinned his hand in, and held it fast. As he could not get away, he sat in the tree, saying, "Hey, little brothers, don't do this to me! ... O, the little scamps, forever playing jokes! ... Are they at it again!" First he would say something like that, and then try to withdraw his hand; but it was held fast. 8. Presently, soon after, he saw some foxes running by, not far off, evidently headed for some place beyond. But he called to them, and said, "My little brothers, don't go there. That is where I am roasting meat! It is just like you, you mischiefs, to eat it all up for me!" 9. That was like an invitation and the whole pack ran towards the meat and soon had it completely eaten up; both the roasting meat and the raw meat near by. 10. Just then, as they finished and were leaving, the two trees sprang apart and Iktomi was free to take his hand away and to come down. 11. He saw that his roast was all gone, and said, "Alas! My younger brothers have eaten all my meat up." He was so hungry that he had to stop and cry over his loss. 12. Then his eyes fell on the deer head which they had left and at once he thought of the brains still inside. "At least I can have those!" he thought and tried to get them; but the opening into the brain cavity was too small for him. 13. The only thing left was to change himself into a snake, which he did promptly, and then he crawled without effort into the skull, as far as his head, so that he could eat. Plenty of fine, rich, tasty brains were there. He ate them quickly. 14. Then he tried to come back out, but by eating he had grown so that his head was no longer able to fit the opening, and he could not get out. He lay shouting for help again and again, but nobody heard him. 15. He found at last in trying to lift his head that the skull was very light; so he stood up and ran with it on his head till he struck it against something hard. 16. "Who are you?" he asked. "I am Pine, and I grow in the heart of the forest," something replied. 17. Iktomi ran on, and once again he bumped into something. 18. "And who are you?" he asked. "I am Ash, and I grow near the water," was the answer. 19. "Ah! in that case, I must be somewhere near water," he thought; and at that instant his foot slipped over the bank and he fell into the water down below; so he started swimming at once. 20. Down-stream he swam on and on. Soon some hunters saw him in the distance and stood watching. 21. "Hey, look at that, yonder! That thing swimming this way looks like a man!" said one. Another said, "No, I think that is a deer. It appears as such to me." 22. As he went by, nearer the men, they were sure it was a deer. "Deer, come over this way!" they called. 23. Though they were inviting him they might as well not have called, he paid no attention; as if they didn't mean him. The only thing was now for them all to plunge into the river; they started to swim towards him. 24. When he heard them coming he turned and tried to run away from them; he swam hard towards the opposite shore to escape them. Now, on that side, a great rock stood, forming the bank; partly under water so that Ikto could not have seen it even without the deer skull. He made towards it and swam with such terrific force that he suddenly crashed into it with an impact great enough to shatter the deer head to pieces. 25. At once, on thus being freed, Iktomi changed into a man again and crawled up the bank, where he stood. Then he turned to watch the swimmers as they approached, struggling in the water. And he laughed loudly and long at them, making sport of their efforts. 26. So Iktomi deceived the hunters who saw the trick, and turned about in disgust. "O, ps̨haw! What do you say? Let us turn back. Because that is only Iktomi again making fools of us all. Swim back to the shore, where we came from," they said, and all of them headed again for the opposite shore. 27. That is where this legend comes to an end.

6. Ikto'mi and the Buffalo. The Eye-Juggler.

1. Ikto'mi li'la loc'i̯' c'ąke' wo'yute oi'c'ile-oma`nihą s̨k'e'ᵉ. K'e'yas̨ wakpa' wą s̨ma' e'l i̯' ną to'k'a-iyu`weg̨es̨ni c'ąke' o'huta ki̯ e'l c'e'yahą ke'ᵉ. 2. Yųk'ą' t'at'ą'ka wą e'l hi' ną heya' ke'ᵉ, — To'k'a yųk'ą' le' yac'e'yahą huwo'? t'e'hąl wau' k'ų he'hą'ni nac'i̯ĥ'ų we lo', — eya' ke'ᵉ. 3. Yųk'ą', — Hehehi', misų', le' k'owa'katą yewa'- c'ąmi k'e'yas̨ to'k'a-ib.lu`weg̨es̨ni c'a inų'wą-ib.lu't'e c'e'yas̨ m.nii'- t'ąc'ą ki̯ li'la s̨me' lo'. C'a le'c'eya' loc'i̯'pi c'ų' mat'i'kte s'e le'c'eca ye lo'. — eya' ke'ᵉ. 4. T'at'ą'ka ki̯ ų's̨ila ną heya' ke'ᵉ, — Ho, ec'a, le' ib.lu'weg̨ikta c'e c'ąk'a'hu aką'l mayą'ka yo', ac'i̯'yi̯kte, — eya' ke'ᵉ. 5. — Ho'ĥ, wą nit'ą'ka c'a to'k'ani ana'c'iskapes̨ni ki̯hą oma'slohi̯kte lo', — eyi̯' ną wica'las̨ni ke'ᵉ. 6. C'ąke' ak'e's̨, — Ho, he'c'ecakta hą'tąhąs̨ site' e'l oma'yuspi̯ ną miha'kap o'kaĥ u' wo', to'ks̨a' iyu'weĥ

Literal Translation.

1. Iktomi / very / he was hungry / so / food / to hunt for himself-he was travelling / they say. But / river / a / deep / at / he arrived / and / he had no way of crossing / so / shore / the / on / he was crying. 2. And then / buffalo-bull / a / to / he came / and / said: / "Why / and so / this / you are weeping? / far off / I came / the-past / even then / I heard you," / he said. 3. And / "Alas, / my younger brother, / this / across (the river) / I hope to go / but / I have no way of crossing / so / to swim-I tried / but / main-current / the / very / deep. / So / right now / hunger / on account of / I will die / like / it is so," / he said. 4. Bull / the / he took pity on him / and / said: / "Well, / then / this / I am going to cross / so / back / on / me-sit, / I will take you," / he said. 5. "The idea! / why, / you are big, / so / in some way / I do not clamp my legs tightly about you, / the-then / I shall slide off," / he said / and / refused. 6. So / again / "Well, / it is going to be like that / if-then / tail / on / me-hold / and / me-following / floating / come / certainly / across / I shall take

ak'i'ĥpec'iyįkte, — eya' ke'ᵉ. 7. K'e'yaŝ ou'ŝila ŝi'ca ke'ᵉ. — Hoĥ,
wą, misų`, situ'psą iye'yaye cįhą m.niyo'kak'ap iye'mayayįkte lo', —
eya' ke'ᵉ. 8. C'ąke' t'at'ą'ka kį ak'e', — Ec'a p'a' kį aką'l mayą'kį ną
he' kį oko' og.na' he'l mayą'ka yo', — eya' ke'ᵉ. Tk'a'ŝ ak'e' wica'-
laŝni ke'ᵉ. — M.nila'tke cįhą maya'luŝnakte lo', wą, — eya' ke'ᵉ.
9. Hehą'yą wana' t'at'ą'ka k'ų i'waĥtelaŝni ke'ᵉ. — C'aŝ c'į to'k'el
ĥ'ąp'i'ca he? — eya' yųk'ą' Ikto' i'ŝ hehą'l le'c'el eya' ke'ᵉ, — Iye'ŝ,
misų`, nama'pca yo'; ec'a'ŝ iyu'weĥ iya'hųni kįhą hoya'ĥpį ną
ig.le'p hiyu'mayayįkte, — eya' ke'ᵉ. 10. Tąyą' eye' ŝ'e le'c'eca c'ąke'
wana' t'at'ą'ka kį Ikto' napcį' ną iyu'wega ke'ᵉ. Ho, k'e'yaŝ ųma'
ec'i'yatąhą ihų'ni k'ų hehą'l hoĥpį'kte c'ų he' a'tayaŝ e'ktużį ną ka'l
c'ąi'yohązi wą e'l iyų'kį ną he'c'enaĥcį iŝtį'ma ke'ᵉ. 11. T'ezi'-maĥe'l
Ikto'mi c'ąze'kį ną oi'kcapta ų' k'e'yaŝ he'c'ena go'pahą ke'ᵉ. 12. He'-
cetu k'eŝ hohu'-mila wą mig.na'ka c'ąke' iki'kcu ną ų' c'uwi'-hepi'ya
wahų' ną etą'hą g.lina'p'a c'ąke' t'at'ą'ka k'ų ų'ŝtįma t'a' ke'ᵉ.
13. He'c'ų ną, k'iye'la wic'a'g.naŝka-ożu c'ąke' e'l na'żį ną wi'p'i-
ic'iyį ną hetą'hą ya'hą yųk'ą' t'į'toska wą e'l hit'ų'kala k'eya' ŝka'tahąpi ke'ᵉ. 14. Wo'ŝkatela wą oĥ'ą' wo'wiĥaya ecų'hąpila c'ąke' wąwi'-
c'ayak na'żį ke'ᵉ. 15. Ųma' t'o'kt'ok iŝta' wąka'l yeki'yapila ną ak'e'

you," / he said. 7. But / to pity-he was bad. / "The idea, / why, /
my younger brother, / switching the tail / you go / if-then / knocking
into the water / you will send me," / he said. 8. So / bull / the /
again / "Then, / head / the / on / me-sit / and / horns / the / space
between / in / there / me-sit," / he said. But / again / he was unwilling. / "You drink water / if-then / you will drop me, / wą," / he
said. / 9. From then / now / bull / the-past / he was disgusted with
him. / "Well then, / of course / what way / is it possible to do?" /
he said / and then / Ikto / he / next / thus / he said: / "Rather, / my
younger brother, / you swallow me; / later, / across / you arrive /
the-then / you (will) cough / and / vomiting (because of me) / you
will send me forth," / he said. 10. Well / he said / like / it was so /
therefore / now / bull / the / Ikto / he swallowed / and / crossed
(the stream). Now, / but / other (side) / on that side / he arrived /
the-past / then / he was to cough / the-past / that / entirely indeed /
he forgot / and / yonder / shade of a tree / a / at / he lay down /
and / instantly / he slept. 11. Stomach-inside / Iktomi / he was
raging / and / talking angrily / he continued to be / but / still / he
was snoring. 12. To settle the matter, / then / bone-knife / a / he
wore in his belt; / so / he took his own / and / with it / side of the
trunk / he cut a gash / and / from / he came out / so / bull / the-past /
in his sleep / he died.

13. He did that / and / near by / gooseberry thick growth, / so /
there / he stood / and / gorged himself / and / thence / he was going /
when / opening in the forest / a / there / mice / some / they were
playing. 14. Little game / a / "oĥ'ą' wo'wiĥaya" (ingenious) / they
were doing it / so / them-looking at / he stood. 15. One after another /

3

he'ktakiya iki'kcuhǫpi ke'ᵉ. T'ukte'-wǫżi iyo'tǫ wǫka'tuya iṡta' yeki'yįkta he'cįhǫ he' aki'c'iyapi ke'ᵉ. 16. T'ǫkį'yųla wawo'kip'ap'aka c'ǫke' ak'e' e'l yį' nǫ heya' ke'ᵉ, — Misų`, he' wo'ṡkatela kį ųspe'mak'i- yapila ye'; mi'ṡ eya' waṡka'telakte, — eya' ke'ᵉ. 17. Eya' he'c'el- eye`ca c'a ųspe'k'iyapi nǫ — Ho', Ikto`, ni'ṡ hehǫ'tu we lo', — eya'pi c'ǫke' iṡta' nųp'į' wǫka'l yeki'ya ke'ᵉ. 18. K'e'yaṡ iye' ohi'yewac'į li'la eha'ṡ wǫka'tuya yeya' c'ǫke' k'u'takiya ku' kį e'l c'ǫa'letka wǫ ekta'ni ik'o'yaka ke'ᵉ. He'c'eṡ Ikto' wana' iṡta'-c'o`la ke'ᵉ. 19. Hehǫ'l wana' hit'ų'kala k'ų nap'a'pi ke'ᵉ. — Hǫ'ta po'! E'l-ųka`yapikte lo'! — eya'pi nǫ a'beya tok'į'yot'ǫt'ǫ e'yaya ke'ᵉ. 20. Ho hetǫ'hǫ wawǫ'ya- keṡni c'ǫke' ų'ṡiya yut'ǫ't'ǫ iyo'tiye'kiya oma'nihǫ ke'ᵉ. Wac'į' yeye'ṡni kį ų' ka'l i'yotakį nǫ c'e'yahǫ ke'ᵉ. 21. Iṡta' wani'ca c'ǫke' iṡta'm.nihǫ`pi-c'o`la kį ų' ho' ece' ų' c'e'yahǫ ke'ᵉ. 22. Iṡna'la yǫka' ke'c'į' k'ų, tuwa' le'c'eg.lahćį, — Ta'ku le' yak'a' c'a leha'hǫ huwo'? — eci'ya ke'ᵉ. 23. C'ǫke' — Hehehi, misų`, ot'e'hike lo', ta'ku yak'e'. Le' iṡta'-mac'ola c'a wo'yute ye'ṡ to'k'a-iwa`g.niṡni kį ų' wana' aki'h'ǫ- mat'įkte lo', — eya' ke'ᵉ. 24. Leyalaka he' Wana'ġi-It'ǫ`cǫ kį e' c'ǫke', — Ho, ec'a c'ǫ' wǫ yuha' nǫke' cį he' icu' nǫ mak'a' kį yumi'meya ica'ġo e'g.le yo', — eya' ke'ᵉ. 25. Ec'e'l ec'ų' yųk'ǫ' hehǫ'l heya' ke'ᵉ,

eyes / upward / they were sending up their own / and / again / back / they were receiving their own. Which one / most / high / eyes / he will send his / if-then / that / they vied with each other for. 16. Despite his bigness / he was eager to join everything / so / again / to / he went / and / said that, / "My younger brothers, / that / little game / the / teach poor little me, / please; / I / too / I will play it," / he said. 17. Of course, / he said that / so / they taught him / and / "Now, / Ikto / you / next," / they said / so / eyes / both / upward / he sent his own. 18. But / he / to win-aiming / very / too much / high / he sent / so / downward / it returned / the / in / tree-branch / a / up there / it caught. Thus / Ikto / now / eye-without. 19. Then / now / mice / the-past / they ran away. / "Look out, / they will blame us!" / they said / and / in all directions / in various ways / they went. 20. Now, / from then / he could not see, / so / pitifully / feeling his way / suffering extreme agony / he roamed about. / Mind / he sent it not / the / therefore / aside / he sat / and / he was weep- ing. 21. Eyes / he lacked / so / tears / he was without / the / there- fore / voice / only / with / he was crying. 22. All alone / he sat / he thought / the-past / someone / very near him / "What / this / you mean / such / you continue to say this?" / he said to him. 23. So / "Alas, / my younger brother, / it is awful! / what / you mean. / This / I am without eyes / such / food / even / I have no way of getting / the / therefore / now / I shall starve to death," / he said. 24. Come to find out, / that one / Spirit-Chief / the / it was, / so / "Now, / then, / stick / a / holding / you sit / the / that / take it / and / ground / the / circularly / marked / set it," / he said. 25. Accordingly / he did / and then / then / he said: / "Now, / this / you have marked / the /

— *Ho, le iya'kaǧo kį he' it'i'mahetąhą op'i'mic'iye lo. He'c'el yut'ą't'ą oma'ni ną yu's-'iyąkmawac'į yo'. Wanų' eśa' to'kel oma'yaluspe se'hįg.le cįhą yatų'wįkte lo', — eya' ke'ᵉ. 26. C'ąke' ta'ku iyu'ha wi'-ś'oś'oka¹, ak'e' yut'ą't'ą o'iyąkį nąśna t'em.ni'teic'iya c'ą asni'kiyį ną ak'e' ec'ų'hą ke'ᵉ. 27. Ya'm.nic'ą he'c'ų ną ici'topac'ą yųk'ą' Wana'ǧi-It'ą'c'ą kį oyu'spa ke'ᵉ. 28. He'c'ena ak'e' iśta' k'ų hena' ec'e'l k'i'yotakį ną tąyą' wab.le'sya śk'e'ᵉ. Ho hetą'hą ak'e' tok'i'yot'ą wic'a'-g.naye-iya`yeca c'e'ś. Hehą'yela owi'hąke'ᵉ.*

that / inside of it / I have my being. / Therefore / feeling about / walk around / and / try to get hold of me. / By accident / even / somehow you catch me / suppose it should happen, / the-then / you shall see," / he said. 26. So / things / all / he was enthusiastic / again / feeling around / he ran about / and regularly / he made himself perspire / then / he rested / and / again / he was doing it. 27. Three days / he did so / and / fourth day / and then / Spirit-Chief / the / he caught him. 28. At once / again / eyes / the-past / those / as before / they sat back down / and / well / he saw. Now, / from there / again / which way / to trick people-he went / who knows ? / There / it ends.

Free Translation.

1. Iktomi was so hungry that he started out in search of food. But when he came to the bank of a deep river he had no way of crossing; so he sat down to cry. 2. A buffalo-bull came to him and said, "Why do you cry ? I could hear you even while I was still far off." 3. So Iktomi told the buffalo the reason for his tears, saying he tried to swim but the main current was too swift for him, so he gave it up and was now nearly dead from hunger. 4. The bull pitied him and said, "In that case, since I am going over, I will take you if you will sit on my back." 5. "The idea! Why you are so huge that I can't clamp my legs about you to hold on. I'd be sure to slide off," he objected. 6. So again, "Well, then grasp hold of my tail and float after me; I'll get you over, that way," he suggested. 7. But Ikto was difficult to pity. "The idea, younger brother! Why the moment you switched your tail, I should be sprawling in the water," he said. 8. So once more the bull, "Sit on my head, between my horns." But Ikto refused again. "When you bend your neck down to get a drink you may drop me into the river," he said. 9. The bull gave up, disgusted. "Well, then, how can you get over ?" he said, and Ikto offered his plan. "A better way, my younger brother, is for you to swallow me; I will ride inside, and when you get over there, just cough and throw me up," he said. 10. It sounded very feasible, so the bull took Ikto over in that fashion, but unfortunately when he reached the other bank, he forgot to cough; he just went off to a nice shady place and went to sleep. 11. Inside the stomach, Ikto

¹ *iś'ś'oya*, enthusiastically; *wa-i'ś'oś'oka* or *wi'ś'oś'oka* means to be over-enthusiastic; or, at least, a person who readily and very eagerly falls in with every plan that is suggested; not infrequently, to his own undoing.

3*

stormed and raged, but the bull snored on. 12. Finally, Ikto took
his bone knife and slashed an opening in the bull's side, and
stepped out into the world again; so the bull died in his sleep.
13. Having done that, Ikto filled up on the goose-berries that
grew in great profusion near by, and from there he was travelling
when he came to a clearing in the wood. There he saw some mice at
play. 14. It was an ingenious little game they were playing. 15. One
after another sent their eyes upward, and let them fall back into
place again. The contest was to settle who could send his eyes
highest. 16. As big as he was, Ikto was always wanting to get into
things, so he approached them. "My younger brothers, teach me
that little game; I want to play it too," he said. 17. Since he wished
it, they taught him, and, "Now, Ikto, it is your turn," they said, so
he took out both eyes at once and tossed them upward. 18. He tried
to excel, so he sent them ever so high; and when they were coming
back down they caught in a tree and hung there, out of reach. Now
Ikto was totally blind. 19. The mice ran away. "Get away, or he'll be
blaming you!" they said to one another; so they scattered. 20. From
then on, he was pitiful, without his eyes. Suffering all things, he
went feeling his way about. 21. Since he had no eyes, he could have
no "eye-water" (tears), so he used only his voice to cry. 22. He
thought he was alone when someone said, right in his ear, "What
do you mean by crying thus?" 23. So Ikto related his plight to him.
24. Really, though he didn't know at the time, he was talking with
the Spirit-Chief who said, "Take that stick you are holding, and
make a ring on the ground." 25. When he had done so, "Now, you
must remain inside, and go round and round, trying to catch hold
of me, for I shall stay inside too. If by luck you do catch me, your
eyes shall be restored to you." 26. So Ikto, with characteristic
enthusiasm[1], ran swiftly around for a time, trying to get hold of the
Spirit; and then he would be so tired that he had to sit down and
rest awhile. Thus he continued. 27. The third day came and went;
and on the fourth day, the Spirit-Chief was caught. 28. Straightway
Ikto's eyes came back into place and he could see as well as ever.
From there he went off again, doubtless with plans to deceive more
people. But where, nobody knows. That is all.

7. Ikto' and the Raccoon Skin.

1. *Ikto' ka'k'ena i'cimani-ya'hą yųk'ą' le'c'el haki't'ų šk'e'ᵉ.*
2. *Wizi' wą kaza'zapi c'a ot'ų' ną ptehį'paḣpa wą peg.na'kį ną wic'a'²*

Literal Translation.

1. Ikto / in yonder direction / to make a journey-he was going /
and / thus / he was dressed / they say. 2. Smoked-tanned tipi / a /

---

[1] Another salient characteristic of Ikto: to be over-enthusiastic, often
bringing ridicule or punishment on himself by it.
² *wic'a'*, short for *wic'i'te-g.le'ǵa*, both names are used for the raccoon. From
wic'a', human; *ite'*, face; *g.le'ǵa*, striped.

*ha' wą słte'-ao`p‘eya į' šk‘e’ᵉ. 3. T‘așį'ta¹-mi`la wą yuha' ną ita'zipa
wą wą' nu'p k‘o' he'c‘el yuha' šk‘e’ᵉ. 4. Wakpa'la-ci`k²ala wą op‘a'ya
ya'hą yųk‘ą' ųg.na' wakpa' wą ot‘ą'kaya ną šma' c‘a e'l iyo'ħloke
c‘ąke' o'huta kį e'l ina'źį’ⁱ. 5. To'k‘a-iyu`wegešni c‘ąke' e'na i'yotakį
ną c‘e'yahe ħcehą'l ptego'p‘eca wą kįyą' hiya'ya c‘ąke' kipą' ną —
He', misų', huya', misų', — eya' yųk‘ą' — To'k‘a huwo'? — eya'
c‘ąke', — Misų', k‘o'wakatą e'iħpemayela ye' — eya' ke’ᵉ. 6. Yųk‘ą',
i'š-ųmake cį — Ohą' — eyį' ną k‘iye'la paha' wą t‘ą'ka yąka' c‘ąke'
he'c‘iya ai' ną, — Ho, aką'l mayą'ka yo'. Ną suta'ya yu'za yo'.
Oi'nitom.nikte se'ce — eya' yųk‘ą' — To'kša' he' tąyą' makį'kte cį;
p‘ila'mayaye lo', misų` — eya'ya i'yotaka ke’ᵉ. 7. — He'c‘etu we
lo', misų`, hokši'c‘ąlkiyapi c‘ą' he'c‘a le'c‘el wąų'šila ye lo' — eya'ya
ak‘ożal² i'yotaka ke’ᵉ. 8. Wana' ptego'p‘eca kį Ikto' k‘į' kįyą' iya'ya
yųk‘ą' k‘ohą' nażu'te kį ap‘o'šįšį ną ac‘e'żiyąpyąp yąkį' ną wana'
m.ni' kį o'pta ye' c‘ų hehą'l ec‘ą'l ptego' p‘esle'te kį oka't‘apt‘ap
yąka' šk‘e’ᵉ. 9. K’e'yaš zitka'la kį nagi'ta wąg.la'k kįyą' c‘ąke' —
Waħte'šni, wana' ak‘e' le' Ikto' e' ye lô. It‘o' c‘ų'ħ.loka wąźi' ekta' o-*

slashed / such / he wore on his legs / and / fur shed from the buffalo /
a / he placed on his head / and / raccoon / skin / a / tail included /
he wore as a blanket / they say. 3. Buffalo-tail knife / a / he carried /
and / bow / a / arrows / two / also / he carried / they say. 4. Small
creek / a / along / he was going / when / unexpectedly / river / a /
wide / and / deep / such / at / it emptied / so / shore / the / at / he
stopped. 5. He had no way of crossing, / so / right there / he sat down
/ and / he was crying; / just then / hawk / a / flying / it went by, /
so / he called to it / and / "Hey, / my younger brother, / come here, /
my younger brother," / he said / and / "What's the matter?" / he
asked; / so / "My younger brother, / across (the river) / take and
leave me," / he said. 6. And then / he-the other (foolish) one / the /
"All right," / he said / and / near by / hill / a / big / it sat / so / over
there / he took him / and / "Now, / on top / me-sit. / And / tightly /
hold. You will get dizzy by it / perhaps," / he said; / and so then /
"It will be / that / well / I shall sit, / the; / thank you, / my younger
brother," / saying / he sat down. 7. "That is right, / my younger
brother, / Boy-beloved / such / then / thus / he shows pity," /
saying / straddling / he sat down. 8. Now / hawk / the / Ikto /
carrying on his back / flying / he went off / and / meantime / nape
of the neck / the / making faces at / and / sticking out the tongue
at / he sat / and / now / water / over / they went / the-past / then /
just then / hawk / crown of the head / the / making the sign of
contempt at / he sat. 9. But / bird / the / in the shadow / seeing his
own / he flew, / so / "Worthless one, / now / again / this / Ikto / it is.

---

¹ *t‘așį'ta*, is one of the nouns ending in *e*, which change the terminal vowel
to *a*, whenever the classifier *t‘a* (ruminant) is prefixed.

² *ak‘o'żal* and *aka'żal* (used interchangeably) mean "in a straddling position;"
a, on; *k‘o*, (?); *ża'ta*, bifurcated.

b.*lu'śna kê* — *ec'i'c'i̧ ki̧yą' ya' yu̧k'ą' Ikto' og.la'ḣniǧe s'e* — *Ho'*,
he'na k'eś, misu̧`, he'na k'eś, — *eya'ya ną k'ohą' ak'e' oka't'apt'ap*
yąka' yu̧k'ą' ak'e' naǧi'ta wąg.la'ka ke'ᵉ. 10. C'ąke' c'u̧'ḣloka wą
wana' ka'l hą' c'ąke' isą'p e'kawi̧ǧi̧ ną he'ktakiya ku' ną iwą'kap
oḣ'ą'k'oya ig.lu'ptąyą iya'ya c'ąke' Ikto' ekta' mahe'l oka'śicaho-
wa`ya¹ iḣpa'ya ke'ᵉ. 11. He'c'iya mahe'l yąki̧' ną c'e'yahą yu̧k'ą'
wag.nu'ka p'a' śa' wą e'l hi'yotaka c'ąke' — *Misu̧`, he'l omi'caḣlokela*
ye', — *eya' yu̧k'ą' kato'hi̧ ną ki'caḣloka c'ąke' hetą'hą t'ąka'takiya*
e'tu̧wą yąka'hą ke'ᵉ. 12. Ḣcehą'l wi̧'yą nu̧'p c'ąk'i̧'-hiyayapi c'ąke'
— *To'k'eśk'e kana' wic'a'wag.nayi̧kta huwô* — *ec'i̧' ną u̧g.na' olo'wą*
wą yawą'kal e'yaya ke'ᵉ.

13.   *Hi'* — — *ho'! Hi'* — — *ho'!*
         Wic'a'-c'e'pa lél mąke' lo'!

14. *Heya'hą yu̧k'ą' wi̧'yą k'u̧ u̧ma'* — *Mǎ², c'ep'ąśi, wic'a' wą*
he'l yąka' ke'ye' — *eya' c'ąke' hehą'l iyo'tą li'la howa'ya ke'ᵉ.*
15. *Są'p ho't'ąkakiya lową' ną leya' ke'ᵉ:*

Suppose / hollow tree / a / into / I drop him / (ke!)" / thinking /
flying he went / and / Ikto / he sensed the matter concerning himself / like / "Now / right there / will do / my younger brother / right
there / will do," / he said / and / meantime / again / making the sign
of contempt at / he sat / and again / in the shadow / he saw his own.
10. So / hollow tree / a / now / yonder / stood, / therefore / past it /
he made a turn / and / backward / he came returning / and / above
it / quickly / turning his body / he went; / so / Ikto / into / inside /
crying into / he fell. 11. There / inside / he sat / and / he was crying /
and then / woodpecker / head-red / a / to / he came and sat, / so /
"My younger brother, / there / make me a little hole," / he said /
and so / he pecked on at it / and / made him a hole; / so / from there /
towards the outdoors / looking / he was sitting. 12. Just then /
women / two / to get fire wood-they were going by, / so / "In what
way / those / I shall trick them / I wonder, " / he thought / and /
song / a / raising it with his mouth / he took it along.
13.   Hi — — ho! Hi — — Ho!
            Raccoon-fat / here / I sit!

14. He kept saying that / and then / women / the-past / one of
them / "*Mah!* / Cousin, / raccoon / a / there /he sits, / he says," / she
said / so / then / more / very / he cried out. 15. Further / making his
voice loud / he sang / and / said this:

---

¹ *o*, in; *ka*, instrumental prefix; *śica'howaya*, to groan; howl; *howa'ya*, to
groan, *(waho'waya*, I groan) as a sick or injured man; *ho*, voice. The two
words, essentially, mean the same thing; but my feeling is that *howa'ya*
is excusable and rather more dignified than *śica'howaya*.
² *mǎ!* A woman's exclamation. Said with various intonations it means
different things. On suddenly hearing something, as in this case, it is said
with a very short vowel, accompanied by much expulsion of breath.

Wic‘a'-c‘e`pa le'l mąke' lo'!
Wic‘a'-c‘e`pa le'l mąke' lo'!

16. *Yųk‘ą', — he'c‘a ki wahį'yų-waste`pi k’ų, ųko'k’įkte*[1]*, — eya'pi
yųk‘ą' ak‘e', — Oma'kaħloka po', wahį'yų-mawa`ste ye lo', — eya'
ke’ᵉ. 17. C‘ąke' wana' nazų'spe iki'kcupi ną c‘ą' k’ų kaų'kapi yųk‘ą'
wic‘a' ha'-sina` wą į' k’ų he' site' ki*[2] *ohlo'ka wą kaħwi'c‘asi k’ų
hetą'hą pat‘ą'kal hiyu'yį ną ak‘e'sna-yuma`hel icu'hą c‘ąke' ak‘e'
wį'yą ki ųma' heya' ke’ᵉ, 18. — Cep‘ąsi, le'naħci yąke', to'k‘esk‘e
ec‘ų'k’ų kįhą waste'kta huwê, — eya' yųk‘ą' Ikto' — P‘e'ta au'pi ną
oi'zilmayą po'. He'c‘el ece'la wag.li'nap‘įkte, — eya' c‘ąke' he'c‘etulapi*[3]
*ną wana' ųma' g.nį' ną p‘e'ta au' ną ųma' i's e'na awą'yak na'zįkta
ke'ya'pi ke’ᵉ. 19. — Hiya`, nųp‘į' ya' po'. Owe'ki's ųma' ni'cisnipi
k’e'yas ųma' e'cuħci's tąyą' p‘e'ta aya'g.lipikte lo' — eya' yųk‘ą' ak‘e'
he'c‘etulapi ną nųp‘į' iya'yapi c‘ąke' ka'kel ai'sįyą iya'yapi tk‘a's
Ikto' g.lina'p‘į ną c‘aa'nakitą ną he'c‘iyatąhą ahi'yokas’i yąki' ną
iħa't‘ahą sk‘e’ᵉ. 20. — Ta'ku c‘e'wis wį'yą nų'p witko'pi ke, og.na'ye-*

Raccoon-fat / here / I sit!
Raccoon-fat / here / I sit!

16. And then / "That sort / the / to grease skins-they are good /
the-past, / let us dig it," / they said / and / again / "Make a hole
to-me / to grease hides-I am good," / he said. 17. So / now / ax /
they took up their own / and / tree / the-past / they knocked down
and lo! / raccoon-robe / a / he wore as a blanket / the-past / that one /
tail / the / hole / a / he ordered made / the-past / from there / forcing
outside / he sent it forth / and / at intervals-drawn back in / he kept
taking it / so / again / women / the / one of them / said that: 18. "Cousin, / right close here / he sits, / what way / we do / the-then / it will
be good / I wonder?" / she said; / and then / Ikto / "Fire / bring /
and / smoke me out, / that way / only / I will come out," / he said /
so / they agreed / and / now / one of them / (will) go home / and /
fire / (will) bring / and / other one / as for her / right there / guarding/
she will stand, / they said. 19. "No; / both / go. / It might happen /
one of you / it (will) go out for you / yet / other one / at least /
safely / fire / you will bring back," / he said / and / again / they
agreed / and / both / they went; / so / the instant / out of sight /
they went, / but indeed / Ikto / he came back out / and / wood-he
rushed for / and / from there / looking out / he sat / and / was
laughing. 20. "What / how indeed / women / two / they are fools /
(*ke*) / to trick-they are good / and / I / myself / the / I am just about

---

[1] *ųko'k’įkte*, let us dig it; we must dig it out; *ų(k)*, we two; *o*, in; *k’a*, to dig;
kta, future. Sometimes, as here, *kte* is not to be translated as shall or will,
but as, "let us."

[2] *site' ki* is the object of *pat‘ą'kal*, the sixth word farther on.

[3] *he'c‘etu*, it is so; that is right; *la*, to consider; *pi*, they; *he'c‘etulapi*, they
agreed to it; they thought it all right.

wašte`pi nǫ mi's miye' kį mak'i'li[1] ye lo', — eya' ke'ᵉ. 21. Wana' wį'yǫ k'ų nųp'į' p'e'ta yuha'pi nǫ t'em.ni't'ekinįl[2] ku'pi c'ǫke' ig.lu'-š'įš'į nǫ ig.lu'ħlaħlata ke'ᵉ. 22. Ina'žį nǫ t'asį'ta-mi'la k'ų he' ų' ina'ħni wǫsa'k-waksa`ksa hiya'yį nǫ kaži'pžip e'tkiya wic'a'ya ke'ᵉ. 23. — T'ǫkši, ta'ku le' to'k'anųpi huwo'? — eya' yųk'ǫ' oki'yakapi c'ǫke', — O'c'ic'iyapikte lo'. Ec'a's he'c'a kį li'la wi'g.li o'tapi c'a etǫ'hǫ wǫsa'k-ˀisla`ye maya'k'upikte, — eya'ya c'ǫpa'hi škǫ' ke'ᵉ. 24. Wana' a'taya oi'leyapi nǫ c'ǫ' k'ų kab.le'b.lecapi k'e'yaš ta'kunišni yųk'ǫ' Ikto' heya' šk'e'ᵉ: — T'ǫkši`, wic'a' kį li'la wic'a'šapišni k'ų, į'še' p'e'ta hiyo'ilalapi k'ų slolya' he'cįhǫ ka'k'el ai'sįyǫ ila'lapi k'ų he'c'ena tok'i'yot'ǫ iya'ya nac'e'ce lo', — eya'ya ħeya'p k'ina'žį nǫ šina' o'ǧeya[3] wic'a'kat'apt'ap na'žį ke'ᵉ. 25. — It'o' ec'aš ak'e' wǫsa'k-kaska` oma'wanikte, — eyį' nǫ c'ǫa'g.lag.la iħa't'at'a ya'hǫ ke'ᵉ. 26. — Wį'yǫ nų'p a'taya c'aǧu'-iyu`ħpa wani'cape lo'. Lena' tukte'l kių'upilake[4] lo'. Wac'į'ka yųk'ǫ's nųp'į' to'k'ašniyǫ i'nawic'a-

right," / he said. 21. Now / women / the-past / both / fire / they carried / and / nearly sweating to death / they were returning / so / he tickled himself / and / scratched himself, many times. 22. He stood up / and / buffalo-tail knife / the-past / that one / with / hurriedly / cutting sticks for arrows / he went along / and / shaving off the bark / towards / them-he came. 23. "Younger sisters, / what / this / you are doing?" / he said / and then / they told him; / so / "I shall help you, / By-and-by / that sort / the / very / grease / they are much / so / some from it / arrow-oil / you will give me," / saying / picking up wood / he was busy. 24. Now / entirely / they set it afire / and / tree / the-past / they knocked it to pieces / but / there was nothing / and then / Ikto / he said: / "My younger sisters, / raccoons / the / very / they are tricky / the-past. / Really / fire / you went for / the-past / he knew / if-then / the instant / out of sight / you went / the-past / instantly / into some direction / he went perhaps," / saying / farther off / going he stopped / and / robe / through / making the sign of contempt at them / he stood. 25. "Then / in that case, / again / to cut sticks for arrows-I will walk about," / he said / and / along the edge of the wood / laughing / he was going. 26. "Women / two / entirely / lungs / included / they are lacking. / These / somewhere / they must live their lives in *some* way! / I felt

[1] *mak'i'li*, I am quite the clever fellow. This is distinctly colloquial, heard, so far as I know, only among the Standing Rock people, where it was invented, or at least, revived.

[2] *kinįc'a*, almost. This is always used as an enclitic. Both neutral and active verbs may take this ending. Here it is contracted. Almost overcome by perspiring; i. e., utterly fatigued.

[3] *o'ǧe*, a veil; a sheath between any two objects; *o'ǧeya*, screening; hiding; shutting off; literally "using for a veil." (Through his blanket, he made these insulting signs at the women.)

[4] *kių'upilake*, as we might say, "they must live *some* life!" *ki*, dative; *ų*, to be; to exist (reduplicated) *pi*, they; *la*, refers to one who is open to mild ridicule.

waḣmįkta tk'a'[1]. *Tk'a' ak'e'š witko'pi k'e'yaš nima'yąpi c'a it'o'*
eya'š he'c'enakte lo', — *eya'ya ya'hą šk'e'*[e]. *27. Hehą'yela owi'hąke'*[e].

so inclined / if / both / without any trouble / I could take them off
with me / but. / But / again / they are fools / yet / they saved my
life / so / then / enough / it will be all right," / saying / he was going /
they say. 27. There / it ends.

Free Translation.

1. Ikto was starting off on a journey and this is how he was
dressed. 2. He wore leggings made of tanned tipi-hide and slashed
down at the outer seams, and a headdress of buffalo-hair[2]; and he
wore about him a robe of raccoon skin with the tail left attached.
3. He carried a ruminant's tail knife, and a bow with two arrows.
4. He was following a narrow creek which emptied unexpectedly
into a large deep river. Here Ikto came to a stop. 5. Since he could
not cross, he sat down on the shore to bewail his misfortune[3] when
a hawk flew by. So he shouted to him for help. "What's the matter?"
the hawk asked, and on learning that Ikto wished to be transported
to the other bank he agreed to carry him over. 6. Taking Ikto to a
large hill near by, he said, "Now, sit on my back, and hold on
tightly. You might grow dizzy." To which Ikto replied, "Don't
worry about that; I shall be all right. And thank you, younger
brother," he added, getting into his seat. 7. "That's right, younger
brother," he continued, "When one is a child-beloved, it is incum-
bent on him to show kindness[4]." So saying he straddled the bird.
8. Then, just as the bird flew off, Ikto repeatedly wrinkled up his nose[5]
and stuck out his tongue[6] at the back of the bird's neck and as they
flew over the river, he snapped[7] his fingers at the crown of his head.

---

[1] *tk'a*, but. When this ends a verb it gives a contrary-to-fact nature to the
statement.
[2] When buffaloes shed their hair it comes off in large flat pieces and is used
in various ways, generally as part of the religious dress of "buffalo-dream-
ers" or medicine men.
[3] Ikto delights in weeping; he never seems to mind it that it is unmanly to
weep about trivial things; he lacks pride.
[4] He loves to flatter people, and animals, into helping him to accomplish
his ends. There is a sort of "noblesse oblige" to being a child-beloved. But
we have no reason to think this hawk is a child-beloved. Yet almost anyone
would like to be thought one by strangers, and the hawk is willing to play
the rôle, for the pleasure of being called that; and Ikto gets himself carried
across the river.
[5] To wrinkle the nose, that is, work the muscles of the nose up and down
quickly while facing a person is to register disgust at or even hatred for them.
Children do it at each other until corrected, but of course it isn't polite,
and grownups refrain from it, as a general thing.
[6] Sticking out the tongue at a person is another insult and shows that the
person doing it doesn't think much of the person at whom he does it.
[7] Snapping the fingers is still another insult. It is done this way: bend in the
fingers and the thumb, thumb on top. Then quickly extend all the fingers.

9. Now, the bird could see this last, by looking at the shadow they cast on the ground, so he said to himself, "The wretch! Here he is again. Ikto. Well, I'll just find a hollow tree and drop him into it!" It seemed as if Ikto sensed the plan in the hawk's mind, for he said, "Right here will do, younger brother, right here will do!" He wished to be put off at once; but meantime, as he said this, he continued to snap his fingers at the bird, and again the bird saw it in the shadow. 10. So when he sighted a hollow tree below, he flew on past and then making a turn, he swept down toward it. The instant he was directly over the hollow, he gave his body a sudden dip sideways, and sent Ikto howling into the hole. 11. So Ikto sat down inside and cried, and cried. After a while, a redheaded woodpecker came and sat on the tree, so Ikto addressed him. "I say, younger brother, make a little hole here for me, please." And the bird started at once to peck and soon had a hole made through which Ikto could look out upon the world. 12. At that instant, two women went by, on their way to gather firewood; so Ikto tried to decide how to deceive them to his advantage. Suddenly he started to sing.

13.   Hi — — Ho! Hi — — Ho!
            A fat raccoon, here I sit!

14. "Did you hear that, Cousin[1]? He says he is a fat raccoon," one of them said; this encouraged him to try harder. 15. Raising his voice the more, he sang out:
            A fat raccoon, here I sit!
            A fat raccoon, here I sit!

16. Then one of the women said, "O, we must get it out; that kind of fat is so fine for dressing hides[2]!" And Ikto said, "Get me out; I am fine for dressing hides!" 17. So the two women knocked down the tree with their axes and Ikto took the tail to his raccoon robe, and thrust it out through the hole the woodpecker had made for him, and then drew it back in. He repeated this several times, till one of the women said, 18. "Cousin, he is sitting right about here. What's the best thing to do, I wonder?" and again Ikto advised, "Bring fire and smoke me out; in that way only can you get me." They agreed to the suggestion and decided that one of them should go home for fire while the other remained to watch the raccoon.

---

and the thumb towards the object. When done repeatedly, the stress is on the extension of the fingers; the bending is only long enough to snap them out. A Dakota would almost sooner be shot than have fingers snapped at him.

[1] It is courteous always to address your companion by some kinship term whether that be a natural or a social kinship. As a rule, the young people of our days tend to omit it, partly because they do not do it in English; and the older people feel that it is bad form, discourteous. The surest way of gaining an entré into a social group is to determine one's relation-ships promptly, and then not fail to use the proper term with each person. It helps you to "belong" and it shows you to be a bona fide Dakota.

[2] *Wahį́yu*, as I have it in the text, means oil for dressing skins, hides; *wąhį́yu* oil for making arrow heads. See next note.

19. "Don't do that; it is just possible that one's fire may go out; but if so, at least the other's will still be burning." Again they agreed with him, and started for home together, so the moment they went out of sight, Ikto stepped out, and ran for the wood; and sat looking out, laughing. 20. "Were two women ever such fools as these? They are fools, easy to trick; and as for me, well, I'm quite a fellow!" he said. 21. The two returned with fire, sweating to death almost, in their hurry; when he saw them, he tickled and clawed himself with delight. 22. He took out his knife, and hastily cut a few saplings for arrows; whittling these he came towards them. 23. "Well, younger sisters, what are you doing here?" he asked; so they told him. "Let me help. In return, I hope you will give me some of the grease for oiling my arrows[1]. That kind always have plenty of fat," he said, picking up wood for the fire. 24. They had the inside of the tree all burned out; and broke it open, but there was no raccoon. So Ikto consoled them, "Ah, that's a shame. Younger sisters, you know, raccoons are tricky animals. Why, I'd wager anything that since he knew you were both going for fire, he stepped out the moment you went out of sight, and ran away somewhere." He stepped back a little, as he said this, snapping his fingers at them, under his blanket, the while[2]. 25. "Well, I may as well go on cutting my sticks for arrows," he said and started walking along the edge of the wood. 26. "I've heard of people without hearts[3]; these women have even the lungs missing! Where did they grow up, anyway? I could persuade them without the slightest effort to run away with me. Still, why bother? Besides, fools though they are, they did save my life, after all. So I'll just let it pass," he said to himself as he walked along. 27. That is all.

8. Iktomi in a Skull.

1. Ikto'mi ka'k'ena oma'ni-yahą yųk'ą' to'k'iya lową'pi ną aki'š'api c'a naȟ'ų' śk'e'e. C'ąke' ana'ǧoptą na'ži ke'e. 2. He'c'ena li'la i'š-'eya' wac'i'-kinica ną sic'u'ha ki yaśpu'yaya c'ąke' tukte'tu c'a le' oi'yoki-

Literal Translation.

1. Iktomi / in yonder direction / to travel-he was going / and then / some-where / they sing / and / they cheer / such / he heard / they say. 2. Immediately / very / he too / to dance-he longed / and / soles / the / itched / so / where it was / such / this / gaily / they were active /

---

[1] Ikto says he can use some of the raccoon fat to grease his arrows. However, Standing Bear of the Standing Rock Reservation said arrows did not need greasing.

[2] Ikto finds a personal satisfaction in snapping his fingers, under his blanket where the women can't see him.

[3] When anyone does something that shows him to be thoughtless, the Dakota say he has no heart; no sense. Ikto says in Dakota, "Lungs included, these women are missing," which means their hearts, and the adjoining organs too, are gone. Or, they have even less sense than people who have none.

p‘iya šką'pi he'cįhą he' iye'ye-wac‘i ke’ᵉ. 3. Naȟ’ų' na'žį kį ec‘e'l są'p
ho't‘ąka lową'pi ną wac‘i'pi ną aki'š’api yųk‘ą' le'na c‘ąku'-ica`g.la
pte-p‘a' wą še'ca yąka' yųk‘ą' he' it‘i'mahetu c‘a nake'š slolya' ke’ᵉ.
4. T‘ima'hel iyo'yąpyela ižą'žąyąpi ną li'la ok‘i'lita c‘a wąya'ke’ᵉ.
5. C‘ąke' išto'ȟloka kį etą' e'yokas’į yųk‘ą' hena' hit‘ų'kalapi c‘a
wac‘i'pi wą oi'yokip‘i-t‘ąka c‘a ka'ğapi’ⁱ. 6. Ikto' t‘iyo'pa kato'to ną,
— Misų', ų'šimakilapi ną t‘ima' u'-iyo`wįmak‘iyapila ye'. Mi'š-’eya'
wawa'c‘ikte, — eya' ke’ᵉ. 7. — Wą, ece'š c‘iye' kiyu'ğąpi ye', — eya'pi
c‘ąke' wana' laza'tąhą t‘iyo'pa kį kiyu'ğąpi’ⁱ. Yųk‘ą' p‘a' kį t‘oke'ya
pat‘i'ma hiyu'kiye c‘e'yaš hehą'yela oki'hišni ke’ᵉ. Oya't‘ake cį he' ų'.
8. Yųk‘ą' wąži', — Hą'ta po', Ikto' he e' ye lo'! — eya' c‘ąke' tok‘i'-
yot‘ą iyu'ha našlo'k ak‘i'yag.la šk‘e’ᵉ. Ną oi'yokpaza c‘ąke' to'k‘iya
t‘ąį'šni’ⁱ. 9. He'c‘eš Ikto'mi išna'la t‘ap‘a' wą p‘o'štąyį ną he'l
c‘e'yahą ke’ᵉ. 10. C‘ąku'-ica`g.la yąkį' ną tuwa' k‘iye'la hiya'ya-
naȟ’ų` c‘ą' iye'na li'la ho't‘ąka-kiya c‘e'yį ną e'l u'šni są'p iya'yapi
c‘ą'šna ak‘e' naȟma'ȟma-c‘e`ya ke’ᵉ.
11. Ho, akša'ka hetą'hą to'k‘el ȟ'ą nac‘e'ce c‘e'yaš o'takiya nawa'ȟ’ų
c‘ąke' to'k‘etu kį tąslo'lwayešni’ⁱ. 12. Į'yą-t‘ą`ka wą yąka' yųk‘ą' e'l
i' ną, — T‘ųka`šila, le' mi'cašloki ye', — eya' c‘ąke', — Ho, ec‘a
p‘a' kį le'c‘etki'ya ko'skos hiyu'ya yo', — eya'-ayu`pta šk‘e’ᵉ. C‘ąke'

if-then / that / to find-he tried. 3. Listening / he stood / the / as /
more / loud-voice / they sang / and / they danced / and / cheered /
and then / right close / beside the road / buffalo-skull / a / dry / it
sat / and / that one / inside of it / such / at last / he knew. 4. Indoors /
brightly-lighted / they caused it to be lit, / and / very / exciting /
such / he saw. 5. So / eye-hole / the / through / he peeped in / and /
those / mice / such / dance / a / great festival / such / they made.
6. Ikto / door / he rapped on / and / "My younger brothers, / take
pity on me / and / inside / to come-permit poor me, / I too / I will
dance," / he said. 7. "Well, say, / certainly / elder brother / open for
him," / they said; / so / now / in back / door / the / they opened for
him. / And / head / the / first / forcing inside / he sent his in / but /
that far / he could not. 8. And / one / "Look out, / Ikto / that / it
is!" / he said; / so / into some directions / all / rushing / they left /
and / it was dark / so / where / it was not plain. 9. Thus / Iktomi /
all alone / buffalo-head / a / he wore as a headgear / and / there / he
was crying. 10. Road / beside / he sat / and / whoever / near / to
go by — he heard / then / each time / very / causing his voice to be
loud / he cried / and / to (him) / he comes not / past / they went /
then-regularly / again / in low tones-he wept / it is said.
11. Now, / unfortunately, / from here / what way / he did / perhaps / but / in many ways / I hear it / so / it is what way / the / well-I
know not. 12. Rock-big / a / it sat / and / to it / he came / and /
"Grandfather, / this / take it off for me, / please," / he said / so /
"Well, then, / head / the / towards this way / swinging / send it," /
saying-he replied / it is said. So / he did it / and / rock / the / on /

*ec'ų' nǫ į'yǫ kį e'l iya'p'a c'ǫke' t'ap'a' k'ų a'taya kab.le'cį nǫ iye'
p'a kį iyo'was'įyǫ iya'p'a c'ǫke' nata' ksu'yeya šk'e'ᵉ. Ig.la'itom.ni nǫ
to'nac'ǫ owǫ'žikži yǫkį' nǫ g.le'pahǫ šk'e'ᵉ.*
     *13. Ak'e' le'c'el oya'kapi'ⁱ. T'ap'a' kį he' m.niyo'hpǫyešipi c'ǫke'
ec'ų' nǫ m.ni' t'ei'c'iya šk'e'ᵉ.*
     *14. Etǫ' i'š heya'pi'ⁱ: C'et'i' nǫ iwǫ'kap t'ap'a' kį yu'ze-šipi¹
c'ǫke' e'cų'nǫ hug̣.na'h-ic'iya šk'e'ᵉ. 15. He'c'ekc'e ošte'šteya wo'yakapi
kį le' oya'kapi s'a'ᵃ. Hehǫ'yela owi'hǫke'ᵉ.*

he struck / so / skull / the-past / entirely / he smashed it / and /
himself / head / the / along with it / he struck / so / head / he hurt
it, / they say. He made himself dizzy / and / several days / very still /
he sat / and / he was vomiting / they say.
     13. Again / thus / they tell it. / Buffalo-skull / the / that / they told
him to soak in water / so / he did / and / drowned himself / they say.
     14. Some / as for them / they say, / to build a fire / and / over it /
skull / the / to hold it-they ordered him / so / he did / and / he
burned himself up / they say. 15. In such ways / oddly / tale / the /
this / they tell / regularly. / There / it ends.

Free Translation.

     1. Iktomi was off on a trip when he heard singing and shouting and
dancing near by. He stopped to listen. 2. Immediately he wished to
dance too², so much that his soles itched; and he tried hard to
locate the source of the sounds. 3. While he listened, it seemed as
though the dancing and shouting grew louder and louder; and at
last he knew that it came from a dry buffalo skull lying near his
path. 4. He saw that the interior was all cheerfully lighted up, and
inside was great jollity. 5. When he peeped in through one of the eye
socket openings, he saw that the mice were staging a great dance.
6. So Iktomi knocked on the door and said, "My little brothers, take
pity on me and let me enter. I want to dance too." 7. "Aw, let's
open for big brother!" they said, and opened the back door for him.
He thrust his head in and could go no further. 8. Then someone
said, "Look out! It is Iktomi!" and soon they disappeared into the
darkness. 9. Ikto sat down with the skull on his head and began to
weep. 10. He sat by the road and whenever he heard someone going
by, he wept loudly; and when they went on past, then he wept in a
low voice.
     11. Unfortunately, I have heard this story related in various
ways until I can not tell which is the correct version. 12. Some

---

¹ I should expect *yus-ši'pi* here; that is, if *yu'za* is to be used at all. A more
likely word, also meaning, "to hold," is *oyu'spa*, which would fit in here
more naturally. *Oyu'spe-šipi* is what I should say.
² Ikto likes to get into everything; he is always begging to be allowed to
join whatever activity is in progress.

there are who say he ran to a rock and said, "Grandfather, knock this loose from me." So the rock replied, "Very well. Swing your head this way." Whereupon Ikto swung his head so forcefully towards the rock that he shattered the skull to bits, and bruised his head into the bargain. He was dizzy for days and went about vomiting, they say. 13. Others tell it this way. He was told to soak the skull in water to soften it, so it would stretch. He tried that and drowned himself. 14. Still others declare that he was told to build a fire and burn off the skull. He tried it and burned himself. 15. In such odd ways they always tell this story. That is all.

9. Double-Face Tricks the Girl.

1. Oya'te wą t'i'pi yuk'ą' e'l wik'o'škalaka wą wį'yą waste' c'a li'la waste'kilapi šk'e'ᵉ. Wau'šila ną nakú' ksa'pa c'ąke' wic'a'ša kį iyu'ha c'ąti'heyapi ną yu'zapikta c'į'pi k'eš wica'lašni šk'e'ᵉ. 2. Yuk'ą' ug.na' k'oška'laka wą to'k'iyatąhą li'la waste' c'a ahi'oyuspa šk'e'ᵉ. 3. He'c'el e's c'į'šni s'a k'u nake' li'la iyo'kip'i ną hig.na'yįkta ke'ya' šk'e'ᵉ. 4. K'e'yaš huka'ke kį owi'c'akiyakešni, kic'i' iya'yįkta-ig.lu'štą ną nahma'la-ig.lu'wįyeya ną wasna', hą'pa k'o'k'o mig.na'k wakta' yąka' ke'ᵉ. 5. Wana' htai'yakpaza hą'l tuwa' t'ila'zata ho'p'iciya ke'ᵉ. K'e'yaš he'c'el kic'i' g.luštą' c'a, — Tohą'l t'ila'zata ho'p'imiciye[1] cįhą hehą'l hina'p'a yo'; uki'yayįkte, — eya' ke'ᵉ. 6. C'ąke' c'a'pala wą

Literal Translation.

1. People / a / they dwelled / and / there / young woman / a / woman / good / such / very / they-her-their own-regarded good (loved her). / Compassionate / and / also / chaste; / so / men / the / all / coveted her / and / they will marry her / they wanted; / yet / she was unwilling. 2. And then / unexpectedly / young man / a / from some place / very / good / such / coming he paid her court. 3. Thus / indeed / she wanted not / regularly / the-past / at last / very / she was pleased / and / she will marry him / she said. 4. But / her parents / the / she told them not, / with him / to run off-she agreed / and / secretly-she got ready / and / pemmican / moccasins / too / carrying about her waist / waiting-ly she sat. 5. Now / evening-dark / then / someone / behind the tipi / he cleared his throat. But / that way / with him / she settled / therefore / "What time / behind the tipi / I clear my throat / if-then / then / come outside / we shall start off," / he said. 6. So / beaver-little one / a / pet / she had /

---

[1] *ho'p'iciya*, to clear one's throat, often as a signal. I have heard this word with the *c* both medial and glottalized, in the first person, but I do not know what is correct. Literally it means "to repair or set the voice aright;" *ho*, voice; *p'iya'*, to repair; doctor; arrange, etc.; make right; *ci* is from *ki*, dative.

*wani'yąpi yuha' c'a he' iki'kcu ną he'c'ena hina'p'į ną k'oška'laka kį
t'ila'zata p'a'mahel ic'o'ma¹ na'žį c'ąke' kic'i' iya'ya ke'ᵉ. 7. Li'la
ya'pi ną m.ni' wą šma' c'a o'huta kį e'l ihų'nipi yųk'ą' wic'a'ša kį, —
Ho, iwa'nųwįkta c'e, c'ąk'a'hu kį aką'l ima'yotaka yo', — eya'
ke'ᵉ. 8. K'e'yaš wik'o'škalaka kį ec'ų' c'į'šni yųk'ą' he'c'ena wic'a'ša
kį li'la c'ąze' ną, — E'l i'yotaka yo', ep'e' lo'. Ec'a'nųšni kįhą m.ni-
ma'hel ihpe'c'iyįkte, — eya' ke'ᵉ. 9. Li'la k'oki'p'a c'ąke' ec'e'l ec'ų'
ke'ᵉ; ag.na' nųwą'pi ųspe'šni kį he' ų'. 10. Wana' nųwą' ya' c'ąke'
c'ak'a'hu aką'l yąkį' ną nažu'te kį e'l e'tųwą yąka' yųk'ą' he'c'iyatąhą
nakų' ite' šk'e'ᵉ. Le anų'k ite' ewi'c'akiyapi kį he'c'a šk'e'ᵉ. 11. K'o-
ška'laka wą waste'lake c'ų ehą'k'ų he' le e'šni kį nake'š hehą'l slolyį'
ną li'la wahte'lašni ną nakų' hįyą's²-g.la ke'ᵉ. 12. Iyu'weh k'ina'žįpi
ną c'ąma'hel wak'e'ya wą li'la t'ą'ka c'a etą'hą šo'ta izi'tahą yųk'ą' e'l
k'i'pi ke'ᵉ. 13. Yųk'ą' he'c'eg.lala wic'a'ša kį, — Mahwa' ye lo'. C'e
heyo'micile ye', mišti'mįkte, — eya' ke'ᵉ. 14. C'ąke' wahte'lašni ų'
alo'slos hįg.le' c'e'yas k'ąye' hiyų'ka c'a wana' heyo'kicile ną yui'štįma
ke'ᵉ. K'e'yaš mat'a'peh'ą k'eya' li'la cikci'k'apila c'a héyawic'aya*

therefore / that one / she took up her own / and / immediately / she
came out / and / young man / the / behind the house / head-inside /
wearing his blanket / he stood / so / with him / she went. 7. Very /
they went / and / water / a / deep / such / shore / the / at / coming
they stood / and / then / man / the / "Now, / I shall swim across /
back / the / on / me-sit," / he said. 8. But / young woman / the / to
do it / she was not willing / and then / at once / man / the / very /
angry / and / "There / sit. / I say. / You do so not, / if-then / into the
water / I will throw you," / he said. 9. Very / she feared / so / accordingly / she did; / moreover / to swim / she knew not how / the /
that on account of. 10. Now / swimming / he went / so / back / on /
she sat / and / nape of the neck / the / at / looking / sat / and lo! /
on that side / also / face. This / on both sides / face / they are called /
the / that sort. 11. Young man / a / she loved / the-past / it appeared /
that one / this / it was not / the / at last / then / she knew / and /
very / she hated him / and / too / she loathed him. 12. Arriving
across / they stopped / and / in the wood / tent / a / very / large /
such / from / smoke / it was rising / and so / there / they arrived
home. 13. And then / instantly / man / the / "I am sleepy. / So /
hunt lice for me, / I will sleep," / he said. 14. So / she despised him /
on account of / she felt repulsion in waves over her, / but / out in
front / coming he lay / so / now / she hunted lice for him / and /
induced him to sleep. / But / toads / certain type / very / little ones /
such / he had for lice. / So / those / it was / such / hair / the / among /

---

¹ *ico'ma* to wear blanket held tightly around the body, the arms holding
the edges in front of the body. *į* to wear a blanket loosely hanging
from the shoulders.

² *hįyą's* from *hįyą'za*, ugly; unlikeable; *g.la*, to abhor; to feel gagged on
account of something ugly.

c⁽ąke̓ hena̓ e̓ c⁽a p⁽ehı̨̓ kı̨ e̓g.na psi̓l ų̓pi¹ ke̓ᵉ. 15. C⁽ąke̓ i̯̓yą-b.laska̔ nų̓p g.na̓kı̨ ną wązi̓ oyu̓spa c⁽ą̓sna he̓l kasli̓sli-kat̓a̔ ke̓ᵉ, i̯̓yą kı̨ oko̓ og.na̓ e̓wic⁽ag.nakı̨ ną̓sna i̯̓yą kı̨ i̓c⁽iyap⁽a ų̓. 16. Li̓la yui̓ṡtı̨ma c⁽ąke̓ wana̓ kiksu̓yeṡniyą h̓pa̓ye cı̨ hehą̓l p⁽ehı̨̓ kı̨ li̓la hą̓skaska c⁽ąke̓ etą̓ icu̓ ną t⁽oṡu̓ wą ekta̓ e̓iyokaṡkı̨ ną ak⁽e̓ etą̓ t⁽oṡu̓-t⁽okeca wą ekta̓ e̓iyakaṡkı̨ ną he̓c⁽el a̓ya ke̓ᵉ. 17. He̓c⁽el t⁽iyo̓kawı̨h̓ g.lihų̓ni c⁽ąke̓ ikto̓mi-t⁽awo̔kaṡke² s̓e hą̓ c⁽a c⁽oka̓ya wic⁽a̓ṡa kı̨ h̓pa̓ya ke̓ᵉ. 18. He̓c⁽ena c⁽a̓pala k⁽ų he̓ iki̓kcu ną g.licu̓ ke̓ᵉ. I̯̓yąkapi̓ ece̓ ec⁽ų̓ ną wana̓ t⁽i̓k⁽iyela ku̓ yų̓k⁽ą̓ b.le̓ wą ṡma̓ g.lakı̨̓yą h̓pa̓ya c⁽ąke̓ to̓k⁽a-iyu̓weǵeṡni ke̓ᵉ. E̓na i̯̓yotakı̨ ną c⁽e̓yahą ke̓ᵉ. 19. He̓c⁽ena c⁽a̓pala k⁽ų he̓ k⁽ohą̓ c⁽ąya̓ksaksa i̯̓yąkı̨ ną c⁽eya̓kt⁽ųpi wą i̓t⁽ap ka̓h̓ yuṡtą̓ c⁽ąke̓ ali̓ g.licu̓pi ke̓ᵉ. 20. Ų̓ma̓ ec⁽i̯̓yatąhą wana̓ mak⁽a̓ ali̓pi hął tuwa̓ laza̓tąhą pą̓pą u̓ c⁽ąke̓ ekta̓ e̓tųwą yų̓k⁽ą̓ anų̓k ite̓ k⁽ų he̓ e̓ c⁽a nape̓-apa̔haha e̓tkiya i̯̓yąka ke̓ᵉ. 21. O̓huta kı̨ e̓l hina̓zı̨ ną i̓ṡ eya̓ wana̓ c⁽eya̓kt⁽ųpi k⁽ų he̓ ali̓wac⁽ı̨ k⁽e̓yaṡ li̓la oci̓k⁽ayela kı̨ ų̓ iwą̓yak h̓ąhi̓ya u̓ c⁽ąke̓

jumping / they stayed. 15. So / flat stones / two / she had lying by / and / one / she caught / then-regularly / there / mashing it-she killed it / stones / the / space / between / in / she placed them / and regularly / stones / the / she struck one against the other / by means of. 16. Very / she made him sleep / so / now / not remembering concerning himself / he lay / the / then / hair / the / very / long / so / some / she took / and / tipi-pole / a / to / she tied / and / again / some / tipi-pole / different / a / to / she tied / and / that way / she continued. 17. That way / around the room / she came to her starting point / so / spider-its-web / like / it stood / such / in the midst of / man / the / he lay / 18. Immediately / little beaver / the-past / that / she took her own / and / started home. / Running / that kind only / she did / and / now / near home / she was coming / and then / lake / a / deep / across her way / lay / so / she could not cross / Right there / she sat down / and was weeping. 19. At once / beaver / the-past / that one / meantime / cutting trees with his mouth / he ran / and / bridge / a / promptly / making he completed, / so / stepping on it / she came through, on her way home. 20. Other / that side / now / land / she stepped on / then / someone / from behind / shouting / he was coming / so / towards / she looked / and lo / on both sides / face / the-past / that one / it was / such / hand-raising at / towards / he ran. 21. Shore / the / there / he came to a stop / and / he / too / now / bridge / the-past / that / to step on-he tried / but / very / narrow / the / on account of / carefully / slowly / he

---

¹ *psi̓l ų̓pi*; from *psi̓ca*, to jump; *ų̓*, to be; exist; live. They jumped about habitually. This construction is common in Dakota, and denotes continued action, as much as *hą* suffixed to verbs, does; but in this form, the emphasis is on the being; the having existence (while jumping about; weeping; talking etc.).

² *ikto̓mi*, spider; *t⁽a*, its; *wo̓kaṡke*, place of imprisonment; *kaṡka̓*, to tie fast.

k'ohą́' c'a'pala k'ų he' t'ahe'natąhą g.lużu'żu a'yį ną c'oka'ya u'
ḣcehą́'l oka'psakya ·c'ąke' m.ni' t'a' śk'e'ᵉ. 22. He'c'ena wik'o'śkalaka
k'ų c'a'pala kį alo'kiksohį¹ ną li'la į'yąk ece'-ku ną t'iwe'g.na g.licu'
c'ąke' k'o' se'hįg.la śk'e'ᵉ. 23. Hųka'ke kį li'la wi'yuśkįpi ną nake'ś
k'ośka'laka wą anų'k ite' kį e'ekuze c'ų he' yuo'nihąyą k'u'pi c'ąke'
hįg.na'yą śk'e'ᵉ. 24. C'a'pala k'ų he' t'eḣi'lapi ną tąyą' yuha'pila
c'ąke' wic'o't'i kį he' a'taya e'l waų'kaic'ilala² śk'e'ᵉ. 25. Hehą'yela
owi'hąke'ᵉ.

came / so / meantime / little beaver / the-past / that one / from this
side / taking apart his own / he went / and / midway / he was
coming / just then / he caused it to break in, / so / water / he died /
22. Immediately / young woman / the / little beaver / the / she took
her own up in her arms / and / very / running that way always-she
came / and / into camp / she came back / so / wild excitement / like
it became suddenly. 23. Her parents / the / very / they were glad /
and / this time in earnest / young man / a / on both sides / face /
the / to be-he pretended / the-past / that one / with due ceremony /
they gave to him / so / she took him for a husband. 24. Little beaver /
the-past / that one / he was loved / and / comfortably / they kept
the little one / so / tribal camp / the / that / entire / in / he regarded
himself as a privileged little dweller. 25. There / it ends.

Free Translation.

1. In a tribal camp there lived a girl who was very beautiful and
greatly loved. She was kind and also virtuous so that all men
coveted the right to marry her, but she was contrary-minded. 2. Then
one day a young man from somewhere else came to pay her court;
he was very handsome. 3. Whereas formerly she did not want such
attention, now she was pleased, and promised to marry him. 4. But
she didn't confide in her parents that she agreed to go with him,
and she got ready secretly, preparing pemmican and moccasins
too, for the journey; carrying them in her belt she waited for him.
5. In the twilight of evening, someone cleared his throat back of the
tipi. That was the arrangement for a signal. "When I clear my
throat behind the tipi, come out; for we shall go off then," he had
said. 6. She took her pet beaver and went outside and there stood
the young man behind the tipi, his blanket pulled up over his head:
so she went off with him. 7. They travelled fast till they came to a
deep river, and then the man said, "I will swim across; sit on my
back." 8. She didn't care to do that and immediately he became

---

¹ alo'ksohą, to carry in the arms, as a child; or tucked under the arm, as one
might a garment; a, armpit; alo'waksohą I carry in my arms.
² waų'kaic'ilala, to feel important, as a spoiled child might; wa, indefinite;
ų, to be; ka, as it were; rather; ic'i, reflexive; la, to regard; consider; la,
diminutive; waų'kamic'ila I regard my own existence as of general importance.

very angry, saying, "Do it, I tell you. If not, I'll throw you into the water!" 9. Because she feared him greatly, she did as he said; especially since she couldn't swim. 10. As she sat on his back while he swam along, she looked at the back of his head, and on that side, also, there was a face! This man was what is known as Double-face[1]. 11. Now she knew that this was not that handsome young man she loved; and she despised and loathed him. 12. They stood on the farther shore now, and walked from there to a large tipi in the wood, from which smoke was rising. 13. Right away the man said, "I'm sleepy. So put me to sleep by hunting lice in my hair". 14. She hated him so much that her whole body cringed at his nearness, but he lay down before her so she began to hunt his lice, and induced sleep to him. For lice, he used miniature hoptoads which jumped about in his hair. 15. So she took each one she caught, and laying it between two flat stones beside her, she smashed it to death by striking the top stone on the lower one. 16. She had him in such a deep sleep that he lay utterly unconscious; so she took some of his hair which was very long and tied it to one tipi-pole; then she took some more and tied it to the next pole, and thus she continued to do. 17. She completed the circle about the tipi, so that the man lay in the centre of what appeared like a spider-web. 18. Snatching up her pet, the woman proceeded to run away. All she did was to run and when she neared her home, there lay a deep lake across her direction so that she could not go on. She sat down and wept. 19. Immediately, the little beaver ran about, cutting down trees with his teeth, and in no time at all he had a bridge finished so they crossed on it. 20. As they stepped on the ground on the opposite side, someone came shouting from the rear and it was the Double-face who came along, angrily shaking his fist at them. 21. He stopped at the shore, and then he too tried to walk on the bridge, but because it was very narrow he had to walk very slowly, picking his way with care; so the beaver meantime started to undo the bridge at his end. When the Double-face was halfway across, it broke down, dropping the man in the midst of the lake where he drowned. 22. At once the young girl took her pet in her arms and ran hard all the way homeward and soon she entered the camp, to safety; so a great shout went up from the excited people. 23. Her parents were very glad and this time the right young man for whom the Double-face substituted himself, was told he might marry the girl; so it happened. 24. The little beaver was so well-loved and well-treated in that camp that he came finally to consider himself the most privileged citizen in the entire tribe. That is all.

---

[1] The Double-face is generally a malevolent being who harms people. Sometimes he is represented as a woman. When I used to play with my little friends from the camp, on the reservation, if we strayed near the woods, someone was always sure to warn us that the Double-face might get us. Nobody knew what that was, but we were all afraid of it.

10. Double-Face Steals a Virgin.

1. *Oya'te-t'ąka wic'o't'i yųk'ą' e'l wit'ą'snaų wą tuwe'ni oki'hiśni c'a ų' śk'e'ᵉ.* 2. *Li'la wį'yą waśte' ną waka'ħ-wo`hitika¹ c'ąke' tuwe' ki iyu'ha yu'zapikta c'į'pi ną li'la o'kśątąhą ok'i'yapi k'eś owa'śyapi- śni śk'e'ᵉ.* 3. *Yųk'ą' tukte'-hąhe`pika wą e'l ak'e' ai' ną oyu'spapi'ⁱ; wążi' wo'kiyak yuha' na'żi c'a ųma'pi ki ena'na ap'e' ħpa'yapi ħcehą'l ito'kagatąhą k'ośka'laka wą u' ke'ya'pi'ⁱ.* 4. *Ka'k'iya t'e'hąl u' k'e'yaś li'la waśte'm.na hiyu' c'ąke' wį'yą k'ų he' ekta' e'tųwą oi'yanici ną t'iza'ni na'żi oki'hiśni śk'e'ᵉ.* 5. *K'ośka'laka wą wo'kiya- kahe c'ų he' e'l a'tayaś e'wac'iśni, ka'k'iya ka wążi' u' k'ų he'c'i ece'la e'wac'i śk'e'ᵉ.* 6. *Wana' he' k'iye'la u' yųk'ą' eya'-wipat'apila² s'e, p'ehi' hą'skaska c'a kao'b.lel iye'ya u' śk'e'ᵉ.* 7. *Hihų'nikta hą'l k'ośka'laka wą wį'yą ki wo'kiyakahe c'ų he' ħeya'p iya'ya c'ąke' le u' k'ų he' wik'o'śkalaka ki ao'hom.ni iya'yi ną it'o'kap hina'żi śk'e'ᵉ.*

Literal Translation.

1. Large tribe / camped / and / in it / virgin / a / nobody / was able not / such / she lived. 2. Very / woman / good / and / skilled in the arts / so / someones / the / all / they will marry her / they wished / and / very / from all around / they courted her / yet / they nowhere near succeeded / it is said. 3. And then / some night / a / to (her) / again / they went / and / they paid court to her; one / telling her something / detaining her / he stood / then / rest / the / here and there / waiting / they lay about / just then / from the west / young man / a / he approached / they say. 4. Yonder / far off / he came / but / very / fragrance / it reached, / so / woman / the-past / that one / towards / looking / she was held involuntarily / and / calmly / to stand / she was not able. 5. Youth / a / he was telling her some- thing / the-past / that / to (him) / at all / she thought not / towards yonder / there / one / he approached / the-past / there / alone / she thought. 6. Now / that one / near / he was coming / and-then / all porcupine work like / hair / long / such / loosely hanging / so arranged / he approached. 7. He was almost arriving / when / young man / a / woman / the / he was talking to / the-past / that one / aside / he went / so / this one / he was coming / the-past / that one / young woman / the / around her / he went / and / in front of her /

---

¹ *waka'ga*, to make things; in the case of women, to perform the arts and crafts belonging to women; *wo'hitika*, to be greedy; derived meaning, "to be fierce, as in war"; and here, "to be energetic, possessing skill, speed, and the will, for such work".

² *eya'-wipat'apila s'e*, to appear as if all embroidered in porcupine quill work. The commoner form, however, is *wi'pat'api eya'la s'e; wa*, things; *ipa't'a*, to work, as with quills; *pi*, they. As a noun "porcupine quill work." The phrase means the man was so laden with such work that he seemed to be solid embroidery. The same form is used for other things beside porcupine quill work. We might speak of a camp thus: *waka'b.lapi eya'la s'e*, meaning the man is such a good provider that you can't see his home for the racks of jerked beef drying around it.

4*

8. Nǫ heya' śk'e'ᵉ: — Ho, wįyǫ, niśna'la waśte'c'ilaka ų' t'e'hǫtǫhǫ wahi' ye lo'. Ųg.nį'kta c'a c'ihi'yowahi ye lo'. C'a iyo'nicip'i hǫ'tǫhǫś miha'kap hiyu' wo', — eya' śk'e'ᵉ. 9. He'c'eg.lahcį eyį' nǫ k'ig.la' yųk'ǫ' he'c'ena iha'kap iya'ya c'ǫke' wii'yap'e¹ k'ų hena' iyu'ha ina'żįpi nǫ ekta'kiya e'tųwǫ na'żįhǫpi nǫ hǫke'ya kib.le'cahǫpi śk'e'ᵉ. 10. Yųk'ǫ' hǫhe'pi a'taya kic'i' g.la'hį nǫ wana' li'la t'e'hǫl g.la'pi c'ǫke' wį'yǫ k'ų heya' ke'ᵉ: — Yu'², ece'ś iwa'śtela s'e g.la' na, li'la nilu'zahǫ c'a hehǫ'yǫ owa'kihiśni ye'. — 11. Yųk'ǫ', — Hoh³, ini'la k'eś ina'hni ye', ǫ'pawi kį hina'p'įkta c'a skaya' u' kį hehǫ'l ųk'i'hųnikte lo'. C'a ina'wahni ye lo', — eya'ke'ᵉ. 12. C'ǫke' p'ip'i'yab.lihe'ic'iya iha'kap ma'ni yųk'ǫ' wana' ǫ'pao' kį ziya' au' nǫ wi' kį hina'p'įkta c'a skaya' u' kį wale'hǫl k'ośka'laka k'ų he' ayu'ta yųk'ǫ' hǫhe'pi kic'i' g.licu' k'ų he' e'śni śk'e'ᵉ. 13. Wi'pat'api nǫ wic'a'p'ehį nǫ wo'k'oyake k'ų hena' iyu'ha to'k'ah'ǫ⁴ nǫ wic'a'śa kį

he came to a stop. 8. And / said, / "Now, / woman / you alone / I love; / therefore / from far away / I have come. / We shall go home (you and I, we two) / therefore / I have come for you. / So / it is pleasing to you / if-then / after me / come on", / he said. 9. Positively that was all / he said / and / went back / and then / at once / following him / she went / so / they waited on woman / the-past / those / all / they stood up / and / towards (her) / looking / they stood / and / at last / they scattered. 10. And it happened / night / entire / with she was going / and / now / very / far / they were going homeward / so / woman / the-past / she said: / "*Yu!* / *ece'ś* / slow rather like / go homeward / do. / Very / you are fleetfooted / such / no longer / I am not able," 11. And / "*Hoh!* / without words / instead / hurry. / Sun / the / it will be up / so / white-ly / it approaches / the / then / we shall arrive home. / Therefore / I am in a hurry," / he said. 12. So / anew-making herself equal to the requirement / following him / she walked / and then / now / dawn / the / yellow-ly / it grew / and / sun / the / it was about to emerge / so / white-ly / it came / the / about then / young man / the-past / that one / she looked at / and lo / night time / with / she started home / the-past / it was not he. 13. Embroideries in porcupine quills / and / scalp locks / and / decorations / the-past / those / all / they were gone / and / man /

---

¹ *wii'yap'e*, to wait for woman. *wi*, classifier for *wį'yǫ*, woman; *i*, for; *ap'e'*, to await. This refers to the old custom of a young man waiting, perhaps for hours, for the girl to come by, after water or wood, so that he can stop her to court her. Having stopped her, he often has to detain her by holding on to her; and so the term for courting a woman means "to catch hold of a woman," *wio'yuspa*.

² *yu!* Said in a rather high voice, is a woman's exclamation, prefacing a reprimand; or a declaration of disapproval.

³ *hoh!* A man's word, denoting objection; rejection of an idea that has been suggested — before he advances his own suggestion which will be quite different.

⁴ *to'k'ah'ǫ*, it is gone; lost; disappeared; *to'k'amah'ǫ*, I am lost; *to'k'a*, indefinite; what; why; *h'ǫ*, to act.

*ak'o'ketkiya g.le' śą' ahi'tųwą ma'ni s'ele'c'eca śk'e'ᵉ. 14. Anų'k iteⁿᵉ.
— Yâ!¹ — eyį' ną e'na pat'a'k ina'źį yųk'ą' — Ya¹! eyapikaś!
K'ośka'laka waśte'śte hena'la kį iyu'ha oni'c'iyapi tk'a' wawi'p'ini-
c'ila² ną iwi'c'ayaȟaȟa ye lo'. Wį'yą c'ą he'c'a hįg.na't'ų ną t'iyu'ha
kį niśna'la t'o'keca-nig.la'wayelak'a³, — eya' ke'ᵉ. 15. He'c'ena kawį'ȟ
hiyu' ną ųźį'źįtka hu' wą yuha' kasa'ksak ma'ni pasi' ag.nį' ną
wakpa'la-c'ų'śoke wą op'a'ya ya'pi yųk'ą' c'ąma'hel śo'ta izi'ta c'a
e'tkiya pasi' ag.la' śk'e'ᵉ. 16. Yųk'ą' he'l wizi'la wą hą' c'ąke' t'iyo'pa
kį e'l ina'źįpi ną wic'a'śa kį leya' ke'ᵉ, — Ho, t'ima' iya'ya yo', —
eya' c'ąke' t'ima' iya'ya yųk'ą' c'atku'ta wik'o'śkalaka nų'p yąka'pi
śk'e'ᵉ. 17. Ite' ną nape' kį a'l-ʾataya ȟąȟą'pi'ⁱ. — Ho, iya'yį ną o'p
i'yotaka yo', hena' i'ś eya' waȟ'ą'ic'ilahąpi c'a awi'c'awag.li ye, —
eya' c'ąke' o'p i'yotake'ⁿᵉ. 18. T'ic'o'kap c'et'i' hį' ną e'l c'e'ġa og.na'
ta'ku piȟya' ana'g.log.lohą ke'ᵉ. 19. Yųk'ą' etą'hą wic'a'nape wą*

the / looking the other way / he was going / yet / looking this way /
he walked / like / it seemed. 14. One both sides / face. / "*Yah!*" / she
said / and / where she was / stopping short / she stood / and so
then / "*Yah!* / The / idea of saying! / Young men / fine ones / all
there were / the / all / they paid you court / but / you withheld yourself as too good / and / you insulted them thereby. / Woman / such /
customarily / she marries / and / household / she keeps / the / you
alone / you consider yourself different." / he said. 15. Instantly /
turning about / he came / and / wild rose / stalk / a / holding /
striking her / walking / causing to walk ahead / he took her / and /
creek / thickly wooded / a / along / they went / and lo! / in the wood /
smoke / it rose / so / towards / causing her to walk ahead / he took
her homeward. 16. Then / there / little smoke-tanned tipi / a / it
stood / so / doorway / the / at / they stopped / and / man / the / he
said this: / "Now, / inside / go!" / he said; / so / inside / she went /
and lo! / in the honor-place / young women / two / they sat. 17. Faces / and / hands / the / all over / they were covered with sores. /
"Now, / go / and / with them / sit / those / they / too / they were
proud / so / I brought them home," / he said. / So / with them / she
sat. 18. In the centre of the tipi / fire made / it stood / and / there /
kettle / in / something / boiling / it bubbled over (with the characteristic boiling noise). 19. And / out of it / human hand / a / forced

---

¹ *yâ!* Is a woman's exclamation of fear. A man doesn't have one. In the face
of danger, he gives the *ȟna'ȟna* (bearlike utterances) to make himself brave.
² *ip'i'la*, to withhold something from another, as being too good for him.
To consider it such, even in the abstract. That is, a man may take a wife;
and always, the mother or some relative of the girl, may entertain a resent-
ment towards the man, as, in her opinion, being unworthy of the girl.
ip'i'wala, 1st person.
³ *lak'a*, evidently, for. Here it is, "evidently you regard yourself as different;
in a class by yourself"; *t'o'keca*, different; *ni*, you; *g.la*, yourself; *wa
(yawa'*, to count); *ye*, a syllable inserted between the verb, and the enclitic,
lak'a. All verbs ending in *a*, *ą*, *e*, *i*, *į*, take this *ye*. Those ending in *o*, *u*, and
ų, take *we*, instead.

nawą́kal hiyu' šk'e'ᵉ. 20. T'iyo'p-'ik'ąyela winų́ħcala wą yąka' yųk'ą' anų́k ite' kį heci'ya šk'e'ᵉ: — Ųci`, lena' wana' eya's špą' nac'e'ce, mi'caze ye', wik'o'škalaka kį lena' o'p wag.lu'tįkte, — eya' c'ąke' wakši'ca-t'ą`ka wą ożu'la kaze' ke'ᵉ, wahą́pi k'o'ya. 21. Ną anų́k ite' kį wo'k'u c'ąke' wahą́pi-ica`pta wo'ta šk'e'ᵉ. Ig.lu'štą ną hehą́l wik'o'škalaka kį wo'yapte c'ų hena' wic'a'k'u šk'e'ᵉ. 22. Akta'- pišni c'ą ųžį'žįtka hu' k'ų he' ų' ite'-g.lakį'kįyą wic'a'kasaka c'ą wahą́pi ną t'alo' kį hena' yu'tapi šk'e'ᵉ. 23. Ho, wo'l yuštą́pi yųk'ą' hehą́l šai'c'iyį¹ ną ak'e' haya'pi-wašte`šte k'eya' ų' wį'yą wą g.na'ye c'ų hena' k'og.la'ka šk'e'ᵉ. 24. Hehą́l winų́ħcala k'ų he' k'į' ną — Ho, ųci`, ak'e' oma'ni-m.nįkta c'a le wik'o'škalaka wą eha'ke-awa`g.li kį le' p'a'-kaksį' ną ak'e' le'c'eħcį c'eħ-o'żula walo'lopya mi'-g.le yo'. 25. Na ec'a's si' kį hehą́'yą kaksį' ną šupe' kį e'l ai'yakaški ną to'k'el waku'kte cį ec'e'l yug.la'g.la iħpe'ya yo'. Hena' t'oke'ya yu'lyul waku'kte lo'. 26. — Ho, ųci`, ep'e' cį ec'e'ħcį ec'ų' wo'. Wana' m.nį́kte lo', — eyį' ną tok'i'yot'ą iya'ya šk'e'ᵉ. 27. C'ąke' winų́ħcala k'ų he' heye'ᵉ: — T'akoża², wik'o'škalaka wašte'šte le'c'el ece'-awic'ag.li

upward / it came. 20. Near the doorway / old woman / a / she sat / and so / on both sides / face / the / he said to her: / "Grandmother / these / now / enough / cooked / perhaps / ladle out for me / young women / the / these / with / I will eat my own," / he said / so / dish-large / a / full / she dipped it out / soup / included. 21. And / on both sides / face / the / she fed him / so / soup-taken up with it / he ate. / He finished his (meal) / and / then / young women / the / leavings / the / those / them-he gave. 22. They refused it; / then / rosebush / stalk / the-past / that one / with / across the face repeatedly / he whipped them / then / soup / and / meat / the / those / they ate. 23. Now / eating / they finished / then ` then / he dressed himself in finery (he made himself red) / and / again / clothing-fine-ones / some / wearing / woman / a / he tricked / the-past / those / he put on. 24. Then / old woman / the-past / that one / he meant / and / "Now, / grandmother, / again / to walk abroad-I shall go; / so / this / young woman / a / last-I brought / the / this / head-chop off / and / again / in this precise manner / kettle-fully / cooking till tender / have standing for me. 25. And / at that time / foot / the / that far / chop off / and / intestine / the / to it / tie it / and / which way / I shall approach, returning / the / that way / unwinding it out / leave it. Those / first / eating / I shall be returning. 26. Now, / grandmother, / I say it / the / exactly / do it. / Now / I shall go," / he said / and / off somewhere / he went. 27. So / old woman / the-past / that one / she said: / "Grandchildren / young women / fine ones / in this

---

¹ *šai'c'iya*, he makes himself red; this means "to dress oneself carefully," as for some occasion. Probably refers to the essential red face paint.
² Sometimes, these direct address forms of kinship take the weak accent on the second syllable; but occasionally, the accent is shifted to the last; in all cases, whenever great earnestness and importance is attached to the thing about to be imparted.

*nąśna wicʻaʼkte ną̣ wicʻaʼyute'. 28. Cʻa takoʼm.ni ʼniʼś eyaʼ niyuʼl-
wacʻịpe'. Tkʻaʼ, tʻakoʼża, niye' nitʻeʼcape'. Miyeʼś makteʼpi ną̣ toʼkʻel
eye' cʻų̣ ecʻeʼl ecʻaʼmaųpi ną̣ liʼla kʻig.laʼpi' — eyaʼ śkʻeʼᵉ. 29. Hehą̣ʼl
leya śkʻeʼᵉ: — Lecʻiʼyotʻą̣ cʻąmaʼhel cʻąwaʼkakse sʼa kʼų̣ heʼcʻiya
nazų̣ʼspe-ciʼkʼala-mitʻaʼwala kʼų̣ he' mapʻaʼ ną̣ miiʼsto-iśleʼyatą̣hą̣ kị
henaʼ iyaʼyustak ińpeʼyapi ną̣ niyaʼm.nipi kị iyuʼha napʻaʼpiʼ, —
eyaʼ śkʻeʼᵉ. 30. Cʻą̣ke' wanaʼ witʻą̣ʼśnaų̣ wą̣ ehaʼke-ag.liʼpi kʼų̣ he e' cʻa
inaʼżị ną̣ winų̣ʼhcala wą̣ ų̣ʼśiyakel yą̣ke' cʻeʼyaś katʼị' ną̣ waeʼcʻų̣śi kʼų̣
henaʼ ecʻeʼkcʻe ecʻų̣' ną̣ hehą̣ʼl śupe' kị yug.laʼg.la cʻą̣ku' kị eʼtkiya
aʼyị ną̣ ihą̣ʼke kị ekta' winų̣ʼhcala siha' kị ų̣ma' aiʼyakaśkị ną̣ heʼcʻena
liʼla kʻig.laʼpi śkʻeʼᵉ. 31. Tokʻiʼyotʻą̣ g.laʼpikta tʻą̣ịʼśni kʻeʼyaś liʼla
ịʼyą̣kapi; ną̣ ą̣peʼtu kị' aʼtaya g.laʼpi ną̣ awiʼiyayapi śkʻeʼᵉ. 32. Akʻe'
hą̣heʼpi aʼtaya ịʼyą̣kapi ną̣ wanaʼ ą̣ʼpa cʻą̣ke' akʻe' ą̣peʼtu kị he'
aʼtaya ịʼyą̣kapi na akʻe' hą̣heʼpi aʼtaya g.laʼpi ną̣ ayą̣ʼpapi śkʻeʼᵉ.
33. Ho wanaʼ yaʼm.nicʻą̣ yų̣kʻą̣' anų̣ʼk ite' kị kʻihų̣ʼni śkʻeʼᵉ. Śupe'
kị yuʼl ag.nị' ną̣ si' kʼų̣ he eʼl kʻihų̣ʼni ną̣ — Hų̣hų̣he', le' ų̣ci' siʼ-
iyecʻekcʻeca ye lo', — eyaʼ śkʻeʼᵉ. 34. — Itʻo' he' woʼkiksuye b.luhaʼkte,
— eyị' ną̣ yumaʼhel icuⁿᵘ. Hcehą̣ʼl cʻąmaʼhel tuwaʼ cʻą̣kaʼtotohą̣ cʻą̣ke'
ekta' hoʼyeya śkʻeʼᵉ. 35. — Ų̣ci', he' kuʼ ną̣ wanaʼ lenaʼ miʼcaze yeʼ,*

manner / always he brings them home / and then / he kills / and /
eats them. 28. So / no matter what, / you / too / to eat you-he plans. /
But / granddaughters / you / you are new. / I / kill me / and / what
way / he said / the-past / that way / do unto me / and / very / start
homeward," / she said. 29. Then / she said, / "In this direction, / in
the wood / I cut wood / regularly / the-past / over there / my little
ax / the-past / that one / my head / and / my arm-right / the / those /
together / throw it / and / you are three / the / all / run away," / she
said. 30. So / now / virgin / a / last-they brought her / the-past / that
one / it was / such / stood up / and / old woman / a / pitifully / she
sat / yet / she killed her / and / he ordered her to do something /
the-past / those / exactly / she did / and / next / intestines / the /
unwinding / road / the / towards / she took / and / end / the / at /
old woman / foot / the / one of them / she tied to it / and / immediately / very / they started home. 31. Which direction / they will go
home / it was not plain / but / very / they ran. / Day / the / all / they
travelled homeward / and / the sun set on them. 32. Again / night /
entire / they ran / and / now / dawn / so / again / day / the / that
one / entire / they ran. Again / night / entire / they travelled homeward / and / day came on them. 33. So / now / three days / and then /
on both sides / face / the / he got home. / Intestine / the / eating /
he went on homeward / and / foot / the-past / that / to it / he arrived /
and / "Well, well, / this one / grandmother / foot-she resembles," /
he said. 34. "*Ito* / that / momento / I will keep it," / he said / and /
pulling it undercover, / he took it. / Just then / in the wood / someone / was striking on wood / so / towards it / he called. 35. "Grandmother, / that one / come / and / now / these / ladle out for me / I

wawa'ṭịkte, — eya' śk'e'ᵉ. 36. Yụk'ą', — T'akoża', hị'yąka', wana'
co'nala ihe'wakiya c'a wag.lu'śtą ną heħą'l waku'kte', — eya'-ayu`pta
ho'uya śk'e'ᵉ. 37. He'c'ena c'ąze'kị ną — Wą, Ụci`, ina'ħnic'iśi¹ ye
lo'. Ną ina'yaħniśni hą'ṭąhąś t'epc'i'yịkte lo' — eya' yụk'ą' winụ'-
ħcala k'ụ he' ak'e' ho'uya śk'e'ᵉ. 38. — Hị'yąka'², t'ako`ża, wana' le'c'e-
g.lala c'a wag.lu'śtąkte', — eya' c'ąke' he'c'etuk'eś anụ'k ite' kị c'ąya'ta-
kiya yị' ną o't'ąịyą ina'żị yụk'ą' k'ụ'śitku kị tukte'ni ụ'śni, e' e'
isto'-iśle`yatąhą kị e' ną p'a' kị e' ną nazụ'spe-cik'ala wą ụ'la s'a
yụk'ą' hena'la c'ąhu'te kị e'l hiye'ya śk'e'ᵉ. 39. He'c'ena — Waħte'śni
śi'capi kị, ụci' mi'ktepi ną to'k'i ya'pikta c'a! — eyị' ną t'ia'nakitą
ną mi'la-t'ą`ka wą iki'kcu ną he'c'ena oye' ot'a'p wic'a'k'uwa śk'e'ᵉ.
40. Wana' wic'a'kig.legịkte ħcehą'l nụ'p ehą'tą-wic'a`yuha k'ụ hena'os
wana' ma'nipiśni c'ąke' e'na c'ąpa'm.na wą e'l ina'ħmapi c'a eha'ke-
ag.li`pi k'ụ hece'la iyo'pteya g.licu' śk'e'ᵉ. 41. K'e'yaś anụ'k ite' kị
li'la lu'zahą hụśe i't'ap iye'wic'aye'ᵉ. Ho, yụk'ą' wic'a'c'iśni ke'yị' ną
he eha'ke-hi k'ụ hece'la k'uwa' śk'e'ᵉ. 42. Ka wị'yą k'ụ he' haki'kta
yụk'ą' wana' anụ'k ite' k'ụ tohą'yela u' ną leya' ị'yąka śk'e'ᵉ: —

will eat" / he said. 36. And then / "Grandchild, / wait / now / few /
I have remaining / so / I (will) finish mine / and / then / I will come
home," / saying-answering / she called. 37. Instantly / he became
angry / and / "Well say, / grandmother, / I am ordering you to
hurry. / And / you hurry not / if-then / I shall eat you" / he said /
and then / old woman / the-past / that one / again / she called: 38.
"Wait, / grandchild / now / this is all / so / I will finish my own" / she
said / so / without further arugment / on both sides / face / the /
towards the wood / he went / and / in sight / he stopped / and lo /
his grandmother / the / nowhere / she was not / rather / arm-right /
the / it was / and / head / the / it was / and / ax-small / a / she used /
regularly / and / that was all / tree-base / the / there / they lay.
39. At once / "Worthless / bad ones / the, / grandmother / they-
mine-killed / and / where / they will go / such ?" / he said / and /
rushed home / and / knife-large / a / he took his / and / immediately /
track / following / them-he pursued. 40. Now / he will catch up
with them / just then / two / already-they were held / the-past /
those / now / they walked not / so / right there / clump of bushes / a /
in / they hid / so / last-she was brought / the-past / that one alone /
past / she came on homeward. 41. But / on both sides / face / the /
very / he was fleet of foot / evidently, for / quickly / he found them.
Now, / then / he did not want them / he said / and / that one / last-
she came / the-past / that one alone / he chased. 42. That / woman /
the-past / that one / she looked back / and lo / now / on both sides /
face / the-past / only so far / he was coming / and / saying this / he

---

¹ The enclitic *śi*, which occurs so often, indicates a command; *ina'ħni*, to make
haste; *c'i*, I to you; *śi*, command; *śi* alone is not used except to shoo dogs off.
² *hị'yąka'* is a defective verb, occurring only in the imperative, and means
"wait a minute, till I do this first; I'll be right with you —" etc.

*Waħte'śni kį, mak'o'c'e wą nį'śkola ye lo', — eyį' ną mi'la kiyu'-
ptąptą u' c'ąke' wį'yą k'ų c'e'yaya į'yąka śk'e'ᵉ. 43. Ħcehą'l it'o'kap
b.le' wą li'la t'ą'ka yąka' c'ąke' o'huta kį e'l ina'źį yųk'ą' c'oka'ta
ma'za-t'ipi wą hą' c'a wąya'ka śk'e'ᵉ. 44. Yųk'ą' etą'hą wic'a'śa wą
hą'skelaħcaka¹ c'a hina'p'a c'ąke' wį'yą k'ų nihį'ciya kipą'ᑫ. —
Wic'aśa', hiyu' na', ta'ku wą makte'kte', — eya' yųk'ą' —ᵛEc'a
taku'mayayįkta he? — eya' śk'e'ᵉ. 45. C'ąke' — Hįg.na'c'iyįkte', —
eya' yųk'ą' c'į'śni'ⁱ. — Hiya, taku'mayayįkta huwo'? — eya' c'ąke'
wo'wahic'ų tona'keca kį iyu'ha c'aźe'yata śk'e'ᵉ. 46. O'hąketa,
Ate'c'iyįkte', — eya' yųk'ą' — Ha.o, c'ųkś, m.ni' kį ali' hiyu' wo', —
eya' ke'ᵉ. 47. C'ąke' m.ni' kį ali'li į'yąkį ną t'i'pi k'ų ekta' ihų'ni
yųk'ą' hehą'l nake'ś wana' anų'k ite' k'ų m.niyo'huta kį e'l hina'źį ną
to'k'a-hiyu'śni c'ąke' ag.la'g.la oka'śkapi s'e ų śk'e'ᵉ. 48. — Ho, c'ųkś,
t'i'l nį'kta tk'a' wakta' yo'. Wama'k'aśką' to'p wic'a'b.luha ye lo'.
49. T'iyo'pa kį it'ą'anųk ig.mu'-t'ą'ka wą e' ną mat'o' wą kic'i'
ħpa'ye lo'. Ną t'ic'o'kap zuze'ca-t'ą'ka wą ħpa'ye lo'; ną t'ic'a'tku kį
he'l i'ś t'at'ą'ka wą ħpa'ye lo', — eya' śk'e'ᵉ. 50. — C'a t'ima' ila'nįkte
cįhą: Ate' t'ima' hiyu'maśi ye', eya' yo', — eya' śk'e'ᵉ. 51. — Ną
zuze'ca wą ħpa'ye cį ak'o'tąhą, t'at'ą'ka wą ħpa'ye cį it'a'hena, he'l*

ran: / "Worthless / the, / earth / the / only this small," / he said /
and / knife / turning it at her / he approached / so / woman / the-
past / weeping / she ran. 43. Just then / in front of her / lake / a /
very / large / it sat / so / shore / the / there / he stopped / and / lo / in
the middle / iron-house / a / it stood / so / she saw it. 44. And then /
from it / man / a / extremely tall / such / he came out / so / woman /
the-past / frantically / called to him: / "Man, / come / please /
something / a / it will kill me" / she said / and then / "In that case, /
what will you take me for?" / he said. 45. So / "I will marry you," /
she said / and then / he refused / "No, / what will you take me for." /
he said / so / kinships / as many as there are / the / all / she named.
46. At last / "I shall have you for father" / she said / and then /
"Yes; / daughter, / water / the / walking on / come," / he said.
47. So / water / the / walking on / she ran / and / tipi / the-past / at /
she arrived / and then / next / at last / now / on both sides / face / the-
past / edge of the water / the / there / he came to a stop / and /
couldn't come on / so / along (the edge) / fenced in like / he was.
48. "Now, / daughter, / inside / you shall go / but / take care. / Animals / four / I have them. 49. Doorway / the / on either side of / cat-
big / a / it is / and / bear / a / with / they lie. / And / tipi-middle /
snake-big / a / he lies; / and / honorplace / the / there / as for it /
buffalo-bull / a / he lies," / he said. 50. "So / indoors / you enter / the-
then: / My father / inside / he ordered me to come, / say thou," / he
said. 51. "And / snake / a / it lies / the / beyond / bull / a / he lies /

---

¹ *hą'ska*, tall; *ħca*, very. The Santee, in order to express the superlative to a
verb, adds *ħca*, very, *hą'skeħca*, which is all that is needed. But the Teton
inserts the *la* and *ka*, so that we have *laħcaka* added to the verb.

*iyo'ko og.na' i'yotaka yo', — eya' c'ąke' ec'e'kc'e ec'ų śk'e'e. 52. Yųk'ą'
hehą'l leya' śk'e'e· — Ho, tok'e'ħcį nihį'niciye c'e'yaś oma'yut'ąśni
yo', — eya' śk'e'e. 53. Heyį' ną i'ś eya' t'ima' g.licu'ʷ. Ną t'iyo'pa-
ma`za¹ kį ec'e'l iye'ye'e. Ħcehą'l anų'k ite' k'ų to'k'eśk'e hiyu'welak'a
hihų'ni ną t'iyo'pa kį kato'to śk'e'e. 54. — Wic'a`śa śica`, wi'yą kį
he' hiyu'micic'iya yo', — eya' c'ąke' — Hiya`, ak'o' g.la' yo'; mic'ų'kśi
ima'yakiħaħa ye, — eya' yųk'ą' he'c'ena c'ąźe'kį ną mi'la-t'ą'ka wą
yuha' k'ų he' ų' t'iyo'pa kį to'kel-oki`hika ap'į' ną kaśpu' śk'e'e.
55. C'ąke' wic'a'śa wą ma'za-t'ipi ot'i' k'ų he e' c'a leya' śk'e'e: — I-
g.mu`, mat'o`, wį'yeya ħpa'ya po' — eyį' ną wahu'k'eza wą ų' anų'k ite'
kį k'įį' śk'e'e. 56. Yųk'ą' mak'u' ot'į's ap'į' ną kao'tą ihe'ya c'ąke'
ig.mu' ną mat'o' kį kic'i' iya'ħpayapi ną kte'pi śk'e'e. 57. C'ąke'
wic'a'śa k'ų he' anų'k ite' kį yuslo'hą a'yį ną b.la'ye wą e'l e'ųpį ną —
Ho, c'ų`kś, c'ąśe'ca o'ta ag.li't'okśu ną ac'e't'i yo', ną e'l wąya'k na'źį
yo', — eya' śk'e'e. 58. — Ną ta'ku wo'yuha waśte'śte hetą'hą napsi'l
hiyu'kta tk'a' wąźi'ni icu'śni yo', — eya' śk'e'e. 59. — Wąźi' ųg.na'
iya'cu kįhą oya'ħ'ąśųkecakte² lo', — eya śk'e'e. 60. C'ąke' wi'yą k'ų*

the / this side of / there / space to (them) / in / sit" / he said / so /
accordingly / she did. 52. Then / he said this: / "Now / no matter
how / you are frightened / but / do not touch me," / he said. 53. He
said that / and / he too / indoors / he came back in. / And / door-iron /
the / as it should be / he sent it. / Just then / on both sides / face /
the-past / by some means / he must have come on / he arrived / and /
door / the / he made sound by striking. 54. "Man / bad, / woman /
the / that one / send mine out to me" / he said / so / "No, / away /
go back / my daughter / you are insulting my own " / he said / and
then / at once / he was angry / and / knife-big / a / he had / the-past /
that one / with / doorway / the / as hard as possible / he struck it /
and / knocked it loose. 55. So / man / a / iron-house / he lived in /
the-past / that one / it was / such / said this: / "Cat, / bear, / in
readiness / lie"; / he said / and / spear / a / with / on both sides /
face / the / he hurled (something) at him. 56. And lo, / chest / full /
he struck him / and / impaled / he sent it / so / cat / and / bear / the /
with / they fell on him / and / killed him. 57. So / man / the-past /
that one / on both side / face / the / dragging / he took him / and /
meadow / a / there / laid him / and / "Now, / daughter, / dry wood /
plenty / bring here and pile up / and / make a fire over (him) / and /
there / watching / stand" / he said. 58. "And something / possessions /
fine ones / from there / jumping out of its own accord / it will come
out / but / single one / take-not" / he said 59. "by chance / you take /
if-then / you will do a horrible thing." / he said. 60. So / woman / the-

---

¹ *t'iyo'pa-ma`za*, said as one word, with the accent as indicated, means "the
iron of the door," that is, the hardware of any door. But if this house in
the story is of iron, the door is all iron, likewise. It would be more correct,
then, to say, *ma'za-t'iyo'pa*, the door made of iron.
² *Oħ'ą'śųkeca*, to act disastrously. *Oħ'ą*, deed. Compare *śųką'yą*, which means
— ?

wana' ec'e'l ec'ų' yųk'ą' anų'k ite' kį ħug.na'ħ a'ye cį ec'e'l ta'ku wo'yuha waste'ste p'e'ta kį etą'hą napsi'psil hiyu' sk'e'ᵉ, iyu'sla nąi's taku'ku wį'yą-t'awo'yuha he'c'a. 61. Yųk'ą' t'ahį'spa k'eya' ihu'pa yuk'ą' c'as ų' ħąp-ka'ǵeǵepi s'a k'ų he'c'a wą li'la waste' napsi'l hiyu' ną wį'yą kį it'o'kap kawo'slal g.liħą' sk'e'ᵉ. 62. Yųk'ą' atku'ku kį he'c'el es eye'sni k'ų, icu' ną a'-oħlat'e yuma'hel icu' yųk'ą' he'c'ena t'ahį'spa kį mahe'takiya ic'a'p ya' sk'e'ᵉ. 63. Ana'kiħma ų' k'e'yas wana' li'la isi'ca¹ a'ya c'ąke' t'į'kte s'ele'c'eca c'a he'c'etu k'es og.la'ka sk'e'ᵉ: — Ate`, ta'kuni icu'snimayasi k'ų², t'ahį'spa wą iwa'cu c'a wana' ų' mat'į'kte' — eya' sk'e'ᵉ. 64. — Ha'.o, he' wic'a'sa kį nikte'kta c'į' k'e'yas witko'ya oya'ħ'ą c'a he'c'e o'yakiyeħce lo', — eyį' ną mat'o' kį p'ik'i'yesi k'e'yas itu'ya ħna'ħna ohi'tiya ską' nąs i'yakc'ųni ke'ᵉ. 65. C'ąke' heħą'l ig.mu'-t'ąka k'ų he' iyu't'e c'e'yas i's eya's oki'hisni, yųk'ą' heħą'l t'at'ą'ka kį iyu't'į ną ak'e' oki'hisni sk'e'ᵉ. 66. Ho zuze'ca k'ų hece'la oka'ptapi c'ąke' wana' owo't'ąlaħcį iyų'kį ną a' k'ų e'l kiya'p'e ħceħą'l t'at'ą'ka k'ų o'pta iya'yį ną zuze'ca

past / now / accordingly / she did / and then / on both sides / face / the / being consumed by fire / he was becoming / the / along with it / things / possessions / fine ones / fire / the / out of / jumping out / they came / scissors / or else / various things / women's belongings / that sort. 61. And then / awl / some kind / handle / it has / such indeed / with / moccasin-they sew / regularly / the-past / that kind / a / very / fine / jumping out / it came / and / woman / the / in front of / in an upright position / it landed. 62. And then / her father / the / that way / indeed / he said not / the-past / she took it / and / armpit / under / under cover / she took it / and / then / immediately / awl / the / towards the inside / piercing / it went. 63. Keeping it secret as regarded herself / she lived / but / now / very / bad from it / she grew / so / she will die / like it was / therefore / without further delay / she told it. / "Father, / nothing / to take-you ordered me / the-past, / awl / a / I took¹ / so / now / by it / I shall die," / she said. 64. "Very well, / that one / man / the / to kill you / he wished / but / foolishly / you have done / so / that is why / you verily aided him" / he said / and / bear / the / he ordered him to treat her / but / in vain / grunting / bravely / he was busy / but indeed / he failed. 65. So / then / cat-big / the-past / that / he tried / but / he too / he could not. And then / next / buffalo-bull / the / he tried / and / again / he could not. 66. Now, / now, / snake / the-past / that one alone / he Was remaining / so / now / very-straightened-out-ly / he lay down / and / armpit / the-past / there / he put his mouth to it for her / just

---

¹ *ıśi'ca*, to be harmed by; *iwa'śte*, to be benefited by; *i'tokcaśni*, to be unaffected by.

² While *k'ų* generally stands as the past form of the definite article, at times it furnishes the "whereas" in a compound sentence. "Whereas you commanded me to take nothing, I took an awl, and am about to die, as a result."

60   Publications, American Ethnological Society   Vol. XIV

*ki̱ si̱te' ali' c'ạke' c'ạze'-hi̱g.ni̱ nạ wi̱'yạ k'ụ wanụ'-yaḱta̱'ka ke'ᵉ.
67. Yụk'ạ' a' ki̱ li'la po' hiyu'yi̱ nạ naḱle'ca yụk'ạ' etạ'hạ t'ụ-a'op'eya
t'ahi̱'špa k'ụ he' naslu'ta c'ạke' wi̱'yạ ki̱ aki'sni šk'e'ᵉ. 68. Yụk'ạ'
hehạ'l wic'a'ša ki̱ heya' šk'e'ᵉ, — Ho, c'ụ̱'kš, tohạ'-yac'i̱ka le'l ụ' wo'.
Nạ tohạ'l niye' iyo'nicip'i nạ yag.ni̱kta yac'i̱' ki̱hạ oya'ka yo', —
eya' c'ạke' wana' tohạ'tuka wạ li'la t'iya'ta g.la' c'i̱' c'ạke' atku'ku ki̱
oki'yaka šk'e'ᵉ. 69. Yụk'ạ' mat'o' k'ụ e' nạ ig.mu'-t'ạ'ka k'ụ kic'i̱'
ak'i̱'ḱpeyewic'aši šk'e'ᵉ: — T'io't'ại̱yạ e'iḱpeyapi nạ g.licu' po', —
eya' iwa'howic'aya šk'e'ᵉ. 70. Ho, c'ạke' mat'o' nạ ig.mu' kic'i̱' wi̱'yạ
k'ụ wana' ag.la'pi nạ t'io't'ại̱yạ ina'ži̱pi nạ hetạ'hạ wi̱'yạ k'ụ išna'la
g.la'hi̱ nạ t'iwe'g.na k'ig.la' c'ạke' hehạ'l kawi̱'gapi nạ i'š eya' t'iya'takiya k'ig la'pi šk'e'ᵉ. 71. Ho, hehạ'yela owi'hạke'ᵉ.*

then / bull / the-past / across / he went / and / snake / the / tail / he
stepped on / so / he became angry / and / woman / the-past / by
mistake-bit her. 67. And so / armpit / the / very / swelled / it became/
and / broke / and then / from it / along with matter / awl / the-past /
that one / it slipped out / so / woman / the / she recovered. 68. And
then / then / man / the / he said: / "Now, / daughter, / as long as
you like / here / stay. / And / what time / you / it pleases you / and /
to go home / you wish / the-then / tell it," / he said / so / now /
certain time / a / very / to her home / to return / she wanted / so /
her father / the / she told. 69. And so / bear / the-past / it was / and /
cat-big / the-past / with / he ordered them to take her home. /
"Within sight of home / take her / and / return home" / saying /
he directed them. 70. Now, / therefore / bear / and / cat / with /
woman / the-past / now / they were taking her home / and / in sight
of home / they stopped / and / from there / woman / the-past / alone /
she continued going home / and / into camp / she entered / so / then /
they turned about / and / they / too / towards home / they started.
71. Now, / there / it ends.

Free Translation.

1. In a tribal camp there lived a young girl that nobody could get.
2. Very beautiful and skilled in woman's arts[1]. Every man wanted
her and from all sides they courted her but they could not succeed.
3. Then on a certain night, as usual, many came to see her; while
one tried to persuade her, the others lay about on the ground waiting their turn; and during that time, a new young man approached
from the south. 4. While he was still far off, fragrant odors came
from him[2], so this young woman's head was turned his way, and
seemed to remain so, and she could not stand still. 5. She paid no

---

[1] Porcupine work first; then beadwork, and then the ability to make garments, dress hides, paint parfleche bags, and care for all the parts of a
buffalo or deer that could be utilized.
[2] Probably sweet herbs blended and pulverized and mixed with marrow-fat,
boiled, and used as a dressing for the hair.

further attention to the one with her, watching only the one coming. 6. As he neared the place, he seemed all covered with porcupine work, and his beautiful long hair he wore hanging loose. 7. When he had nearly arrived, the young man who had been talking to the girl, withdrew, so he advanced and went past and around her and then stopped, facing her. 8. And he said, "Young woman, you alone I can love, and that is why I have come from so far away. I have come to take you with me. So if you are willing, follow me away," he said. 9. That was all he said, and then he left; and at once the girl went after him; so the suitors all stood up and looked now and then at her, going away; and after a time they scattered to their homes. 10. All night they travelled, the man and girl, and after a long time, she said, "Ah, please, let us not go so fast. I can not keep up the pace, you are so fleet-footed." 11. And he answered, "The idea!¹ Stop talking and hurry; I want to reach home when the sun, about to rise, sends a white light in the sky. That is why I am in a hurry." 12. So she tried to brace herself again and again to the effort, as she followed, and now as the dawn broke, all yellow, and the sun, about to rise, sent on whiteness ahead, she looked at the young man and lo, he was not the one she started with. 13. The embroidered clothing and decorations were gone, and the man, though facing forward, had also a face in the back, and appeared to be walking backwards. 14. The Double-face! "*Yah!*"², she cried, and stopped. "'*Yah*,' did you say? You have spurned the advances of all the fine young men of the tribe who wished to marry you; and have insulted them in doing so. Woman is made to marry and have a home, why should you consider yourself an exception?" he said. 15. He turned and came to her then, and caused her to walk in front of him while he whipped her with rose-bush stalks with every step, along a creek; thus they travelled till they reached a tipi in the wood from which smoke was rising. 16. It was a smoke-tanned tipi; so they stopped outside the door, and the man said, "Now, go in," so she entered, and saw two young women sitting at the honor-place. 17. Their faces and hands were covered with sores. "Sit down with them; they too have been haughty like you, and I have brought them here." So she did as he told her. 18. A fire was going in the centre, and a kettle was on it, bubbling over with loud sounds. 19. And from it, a human hand rose to the surface. 20. Near the door sat an old woman, to whom the Double-face said, "Grandmother, this must be about done; serve me some that I may eat with the young women." She served a big dish full, soup and all. 21. She set it before the Double-face who devoured it, and drank the soup with the meat. Finishing, he offered the rest to the two young

---

¹ *hoh!* is used only by men, and is an exclamation denoting disagreement generally. Best expressed here as "The idea!".

² *yah!* is used only by women, and denotes fear or dread and shocked surprise, at times.

women. 22. When they refused it, he struck them across the face
with the thorny rose-bush stalks so then they ate the meat and soup.
23. Then, when the Double-face finished eating he carefully dressed,
and again donned the beautiful things he wore when he tricked the
girl. 24. He said, "Grandmother, I am going away again, so I want
you to behead the last girl I brought home, and have another meal
like this ready for me. 25. And be sure that you cut off a foot, and
unwind the intestines, and stretch them along the path I return by;
and tie the foot to the end of the intestines. Those first I shall eat
as I return. 26. Now, grandmother, do exactly as I say. I am going
now," and off he went. 27. So the old woman said to the young
women, "Grandchildren, many times before this, he has brought
beautiful girls home and killed and eaten them. 28. Undoubtedly,
he is going to do the same to you. But you are young. Take me,
instead, and do to me as he instructed me to do to you, and run
away." 29. Then she said, "You know the place in the wood where
I always cut firewood. Leave my small ax and my head and right
arm there and the three of you run away," she said. 30. So the virgin
stood up and executed the order, killing the pitiful old woman; and
then she unwound her intestines, and laid them along the path and
then tied the old woman's foot to one end. Then they ran away.
31. Not sure where to go, they still ran hard. All day till sundown.
32. Again all night, and now dawn was coming; and again all that
day they ran. Then they travelled all night, and morning came.
33. They had been going three days when the Doubleface got home.
Taking up the intestine down the path, he continued to eat it as he
approached the tipi. He came to the foot at the end, and said, "How
her feet resemble grandmother's! 34. I think I'll keep that for a
souvenir," he said and tucked it away. Somebody was chopping
wood in the forest, so he called to her. 35. "Grandmother, come
home and serve me this; I am hungry," he said. 36. The answer came
back, "Grandson, wait till I finish the little I still have to do."
37. He got angry right away. "Grandmother, I am telling you to
make haste. If you don't, I'll eat you up!" he said, and the answer
was, 38. "Wait, grandson, it is very little that is left." But without
more talking, the Double-face ran toward the woods, and saw,
instead of his grandmother, her ax and head and right arm at the
foot of a tree. 39. "The wretched beings! Having killed my grandmother, where do they think to escape?" he said and running home
he took up a big knife and started after them. 40. When he was
just about to overtake them, the two whom he had first taken
home, could no longer go on, so they hid in a clump of bushes; and
the last one kept going on. 41. The Double-face was such a good
runner though, that he found them. But he decided that he didn't
care about them, so he continued on his way to bring back the other
girl. 42. She looked back and saw Double-face only a short distance
behind her, running hard and calling to her, "Worthless one, the

world is only so large," as he flashed his knife at her till she ran crying. 43. She came to a lake and stopped at the shore, because it was a very wide lake; and in the centre she saw a house of iron. 44. A man, very tall, came out of the house, so the woman in her panic cried out to him, "Man, come, please; there is something about to kill me!" — "All right; but first, what will you be to me ?" he asked. 45. "I will be your wife," she said, but that did not suit him. "No, try something else," he said so she named over the entire list of kinships between men and women. 46. At last — "You shall be a father to me," she said, and then he was pleased. "Very well; come over, walking on the water," he said. 47. She did so, and as she reached the iron house, the Double-face arrived on the shore she had just left, and having no way to go on, he ran back and forth along the edge. 48. "Be careful about entering, my daughter. I have four animals. 49. On either side of the entrance, lie a big-cat and a bear. And in the centre of the room a snake lies coiled; in the honor-place lies a buffalo-bull. 50. So as you enter, say, 'My father told me to enter,'" he told her. 51. "And sit down in the space back of the snake and this side of the bull," so she did that. 52. Then, "No matter how fearful you are, don't touch me!" he said. 53. He too now entered. And closed the iron door. Then the Doubleface, having got over somehow, arrived at the door, and knocked. 54. "Bad man, send my woman out to me," he said. "No; go away; You insult my daughter", he said, and immediately the man became very angry. He took his great knife and banged it so hard on the door that he knocked the lock loose. 55. So the iron-house dweller said, "Lynx, bear, lie ready," he said and hurled his spear[1] at the Double-face. 56. It happened that he struck him full in the chest and the spear stood impaled in his flesh; so the lynx and bear jumped on him and killed him quickly. 57. The man now dragged the Double-face to a smooth ground and bade his daughter gather much dry wood and build a fire and stand by to watch it burn the body. 58. "When choice articles, as are dear to women, spring out of the fire, don't touch one of them", he said. 59. "If by chance you took even one, then you would bring disaster on yourself," he said. 60. She did as her father had instructed and stood by while the Double-face's body burned; and all manner of desirable things jumped out, scissors and other things that women own. 61. But when an awl, the kind used for sewing moccasins, came out and fell upright into the ground, before her, she was tempted. 62. Contrary to her father's warning, she took it and hid it under her blanket, tucking it under her arm. At once it began to work its way into her flesh, in her armpit. 63. She kept it a secret until it was undermining her health, and she feared she might die; then, risking all, she told it. "Father, though you told me not to take anything, I

---

[1] In Dakota we say "he hurled, or threw at him *with* a spear." In other words, *kʻiⁿ'*, to throw something at, is an intransitive verb.

took an awl; and from it I am about to die," she said. 64. "Very well, my daughter; that man was bent on destroying you but you have foolishly assisted him indeed," he said, and ordered the bear to doctor her. He tried, grunting officiously, but in vain. 65. Then the lynx made a try, but he too failed. Then the buffalo-bull attempted to doctor her; he also failed. 66. Only the snake was left; so he lay down in a straight line, and put his mouth to the wound to suck it out. But at that moment, the bull awkwardly stepped on his tail. This angered him so that he bit the girl accidentally. 67. The armpit began to swell horribly, and then broke, and from it there came the awl, along with pus; so the young woman recovered. 68. Her father then said, "Daughter, when you want to go home, though you are welcome here as long as you like, tell me," so after a time, she longed for home, and told her father so. 69. He therefore detailed the bear and the lynx to see her home. "Escort her to a point within sight of her home, and then return," he told them. 70. So the three started forth, the girl, escorted by the bear and the lynx; and when they were within sight of camp, they paused; and the girl alone went on while they stood watching her. When she entered the tribal circle, they turned about and left for their home. 71. That is all.

11. Double-Face and the Four Brothers.

1. Koška'laka ya'm.ni cʻiye'kicʻiyapi cʻa kaʻl tʻi'pi škʻeʻ. *I'š heʻcʻe waye'-ipi nąšna wao'pika cʻąke' wi'cakiżešniyą tąyą'kel tʻi'pi kʻe'yaš wążi'ni*[1] *tʻawi'cutʻąwacʻipišni škʻeʻ*. *2. Yųkʻą' ąpe'tu wą eʻl wi'yą wą ktaye'tu kcehą'l tʻąkaʻl pʻa'-maheʻl icʻo'ma hina'żį škʻeʻ*. *Wo'tahąpi hą'tu cʻąke' tʻoka'pʻa kį heya' škʻeʻ: — Wą, tʻi'l kicʻo' po'; wo'tįkte lo', — eya' škʻeʻ*. *3. Cʻąke' Hakeʻla ina'pʻį ną tʻima'hel uši' yųkʻą' ini'lahcį hi'yotaka škʻeʻ*. *Wo'kʻupi kʻe'yaš kʻo' ini'lahcį icu' ną wo'ta*

Literal Translation.

1. Young men / three / brothers / such / at a certain place / they lived. (In their own way, without troubling or depending on others) for their part / that way / to hunt-they went / and regularly / they were skilled marksmen / so / lacking nothing / well / they lived / but / not one / to marry-they-thought not. 2. And then / day / a / on / woman / a / evening / just then / outdoors / head-inside / wearing her blanket / she came and stood. / They were eating / it was then / so / eldest / the / he said: / "Come, / indoors / invite her; / She must eat" / he said. 3. So / Hakela / he went out / and / inside / he told her to come / and / very quietly / she came and sat down. / They gave her food / but / too / without a word / she took / and / ate.

---

[1] *wążi'*, one; *wążi'ni*, followed by a negative verb, not one; *wążi' sa'pešni*, one (of them) is not black; *wążi'ni sa'pešni*, not one is black.

šk'e'ᵉ. 4. Tok'a'š waži' hią.na'ye-hi se'ca yųk'ą' t'e'hą-el ų' k'e'yaš
ec'a'c'aš hec'i'yot'ą t'awa'c'išni c'a ab.le'zapi šk'e'ᵉ. Hehą'l nake'š
k'oki'p'api ną, — Le' tok'a'š ųkte'pi-wac'į hi' se'ce lo', — eya'pi
šk'e'ᵉ. 5. Hį'hąna c'ąke' oma'ni-ya`pikta yųk'ą' Hake'la le'c'el
eci'yapi šk'e'ᵉ: — Ho, Hake`la, ąpe'tu a'taya t'ia'kąl yąkį' ną awą'-
yaka yo'. Ną ta'ku to'k'a hą'tąhąš oya'ka yo', — eya'pi šk'e'ᵉ.
6. Wana' c'iye'ku kį iya'yapi tk'a'š op iya'ye-kųzį ną he'ktakiya
g.li' ną t'ošu'-į`kpata yąka'hą ke'ᵉ. Wic'e'škohlo'ka¹ kį etą'hą t'ima'
wa'k'il yąka' ke'ᵉ. 7. Yųk'ą' wana' wį'yą k'ų he' išna'la yąka' ke'c'į'
ną šina' wą wic'a'p'aha² ece' ų' ka'ǧapi c'a g.lub.la'ya ke'ᵉ. 8. Ną
leya' ke'ᵉ, išna'-wo`g.lakį ną, — Eha'ke le'l iyo'micihišni k'e'yaš
to'kša' Hake'la p'ehį' kį eya' šikši'celake c'e'yaš ų' e'l e'wakihųnikte,
— eya' ke'ᵉ. 9. C'ąke' Hake'la t'i-a'kąl nah'ų' yąka' hą'l heya' c'ąke'
li'la nihį'ciyela ną ka'kel c'iye'ku g.li'pi tk'a'š wą'cak owi'c'akiyaka
ke'ᵉ. 10. Ak'e' hį'hąna c'ąke' k'oška'laka kį oma'ni-iya`yapi yųk'ą'
hehą'l wį'yą k'ų wo'g.naka wą g.luškį' ną etą'hą ta'ku k'eya' g.mi-
g.ma'ǧ.ma c'a yuši'šiyela pu'za c'a napo'žula³ icu' ną wahą'pi kį e'l

4. Perhaps / one of them / to marry-she came / maybe, / and then /
long time / there / she stayed / but / at all / in that direction / she
thought not / so / they observed it. / Then / in earnest / they feared
her / and / "This one / perhaps / to kill us-aiming / she has come /
maybe" / they said. 5. Morning / so / to roam abroad-they were
going / and then / Hakela / thus / they said to him: / "Now, /
Hakela / day / entire / on the housetop / sit / and / guard her. /
And / something / happens / if-then / tell" / they said. 6. Now / his
elder brothers / the / they went / but indeed / with them / to go-he
pretended / and / back / he returned / and / tipi-pole tips-at / he
was sitting. / Air-vent / the / through / indoors / looking / he sat.
7. And then / now / alone / she sat / she thought / and / woman / the-
past / that one / robe / a / human hair / only / with / it was made /
such / she spread out her own. 8. And / said this / talking to herself /
and / "Still / here / it-mine-is lacking / but / soon / Hakela / hair / the /
of course / rather poor / but / with it / there / I will complete my
own" / she said. 9. So / Hakela / on the tipi-top / hearing / he sat /
when / she said that / so / very / he was frightened / and / the instant
/ his elder brothers / they returned / but indeed / at once / them-he
told. 10. Again / morning / so / young men / the / to roam abroad-
they left / and then / next / woman / the-past / sack / a / she untied
her own / and / from / things / some / round shape / such / wrinkled /
dry / such / handful / she took / and / soup / the / in / she threw it /

¹ wic'e'ška, the upper front surface of a tipi. wi, woman, as classifier, also
used with reference to parts of the tipi; c'eška', the chest area of the body;
ohlo'ka, hole; an opening. Hence, wic'e'škohloka, that opening at the top of
the tipi, through which the smoke comes out.
² wic'a', human; p'a', head; ha hide; hence, The scalp.
³ nape', hand; ožu'la, full.

oka'la nǫ he'c‛ena waka'ġahǫ¹ ke’ᵉ. 11. Wana' śpǫ' c‛ǫke' wo'tįkta c‛a oi'g.lapta yųk‛ǫ' hena'keñcį wic‛a'śa nakpa' c‛a pusya' yuha' nǫ eya'śna yu'ta śk‛e’ᵉ. 12. He'c‛el ec‛ų' c‛a Hake'la t‛i-a'kątąhǫ wǫya'k yǫka' c‛ǫke' c‛iy'eku g.li'pi k’e'l owi'c‛akiyaka ke’ᵉ. Yųk‛ǫ', — Wana' nau'p‛apikte lo', — eya'pi ke’ᵉ. 13. K’e'yaś t‛oke'ya to'nac‛ǫ wi'k‛ǫ wǫ ǫpe'tu a'l-’ataya iyo'ñpeya g.le'pi ke’ᵉ. Wį'yǫ kį oma'ni-iya'ya c‛ǫ'. 14. Wana' eya'ś t‛e'hǫ-pi'ġa ke'ya'pi nǫ pusya'pi c‛ǫke' to'k‛el-oki'hika p‛ǫp‛ǫ'la ke’ᵉ. Wį'yǫ k’ų g.li' c‛ǫke', — Ho', t‛ǫkśi', c‛ǫk’į'-ya‘ yo', — eya'pi’ⁱ. — C‛ǫ k’eya' c‛oġį' śaśa' k’ų he'c‛a ece' aku' wo', — eya'pi c‛ǫke' wi'k‛ǫ kį icu' nǫ c‛ǫma'hel iya'ye’ᵉ. 15. Ai'nap iya'ya tk‛a'ś he'c‛enañcį ųwe'ya yuha'pi nǫ li'la naki'p‛api śk‛e’ᵉ. 16. C‛ǫke' k‛ohǫ' wį'yǫ k’ų c‛ǫka'ksahe c‛e'yaś c‛oġį' śaśa' kį hena' oka'kseśice s'a c‛ǫke' li'la t‛e'hǫ-śkǫ‘ ke’ᵉ. He'c‛el oñ'ǫ'hikta c‛a he' ų' c‛oġį' śaśa' ece' aku'śipi śk‛e’ᵉ. 17. Wana' ok’į' wǫżi' ka'ġį nǫ k’į' ina'żįkta k‛eś ec‛ǫ'l wi'k‛ǫ kį ka'psakahǫ c‛ǫke' iyo'tiye'kiya ke’ᵉ. 18. T‛iya'takiya e'tųwǫ yųk‛ǫ' wana'ś ot‛i'weta c‛ǫke', — Wañte'śni śi'capi kį, ehǫ'kec‛ų le' ec‛a'kel-uma‘śipe lê. Hį'yakapi'. Itu'ka ye'ś wo'yute t‛epwa'kiye c‛ų̂, — eyį' nǫ wic‛a'k‛uwa ke’ᵉ. 19. Haki'ktakta

and / immediately / she was making something (embroidering). 11. Now / cooked / so / she was about to eat / so / she poured out for herself / and lo / all of that / human / ears / such / dried / she had on hand / and / regularly / she ate. 12. That way / she did / such / Hakela / from on top the tipi / seeing / he sat / so / his elder brothers / they returned / the-in / he told them. And so / "Now, / we shall flee away," / they said. 13. But / first / several days / rope / a / day / entire / boiling / they set it / woman / the / to roam about-she went away / then. 14. Now / at last enough / long-boiled / they said / and / they caused it to dry / so / extremely / it was breakable. / Woman / the-past / she returned / so / "Now, / younger sister, / to get firewood-go" / they said. / Wood / some kind / pith / red / the-past / that sort / only / bring home" / they said / so / rope / the / she took / and / into the woods / she went. 15. Out of sight / she went / but indeed / without delay / provisions / they carried / and / very / they ran away. 16. So / meantime / woman / the-past / she was cutting wood / but / pith / red / the / those / to cut-difficult / regularly / so / very / long-she worked. / Thus / she would be slow / so / that / on account of / pith / red / that sort only / they told her to bring. 17. Now / carrying-load / one / she made / and / carrying it on her back / she would stand up / yet each time / just then / rope / the / it kept breaking / so / she found greatest trouble. 18. Homeward / she looked / and lo / now indeed / abandonned camp / so / "Worthless / bad ones / the, / it is clear now / this / on purpose-they sent me / Just you wait. / Anyway / indeed / food / I have eaten all my own / the-past" / she said / and / chased them. 19. Looking back occasion-

¹ "She was making things." To make things, is to do fancy work, principalling with porcupine quills and beads.

i'yąkahąpi yųk'ą' wana' la'zata paha' wą ai'yohpeya mak'a' śo'ta s'e hiyu' ke'ᵉ. Wana' k'iye'la u' c'ąke' t'oka'p'a kį ųkce'kcela wą icu' ną he'ktakiya kah'o'l yeya' yųk'ą' maka'-b.la'ye kį a'taya ųkce'kcela-hįg.la c'ąke' to'k'ani-hiyu'śni ke'ᵉ. 20. C'ąke' h'ąhi'ya, cąku' iwą'yak-yak oka'wįhwįh-iya'ya u' k'e'yaś k'ohą' ak'e' li'la t'e'hąl ihpe'ya g.licu'pi yųk'ą' o'hąketa są'p hiyu' hųśe ak'e' yu'zanų s'e awi'c'au ke'ᵉ. 21. He' u' t'oka'p'a i'yok'ihe kį he' mi'la wą iki'kcu ną he'ktakiya ihpe'ya yųk'ą' t'ahį'śpa-p'esto'stola ece' mak'a' kį a'taya etą' hina'p'i ną p'eśto'staya hą' ke'ᵉ. 22. Ak'e' he'l o'tohąyą to'k'a-hiyu'śni c'a li'la g.licu'pi k'e'yaś to'k'eśk'ekel ak'e' nai'c'iśpį ną wic'a'kig.legįkta-iteya u' ke'ᵉ. 23. He'c'ena nihį'ciya mak'a' nahta'htakapi yųk'ą' mak'a' kį g.laki'yą nasle'ca c'ąke' sąp hiyu'śni ke'ᵉ. 24. Li'la ku'pi ną wakpa' wą ot'ą'kaya c'a g.laki'yą hpa'ya c'ąke' e'l g.lina'źįpi ną wana' c'op'a'pikta hą'l ec'ą'l winų'hcala wą tok'e'cela-ma'nila c'a c'ą' kį etą'hą hiyu' ną, — T'ako'źa', k'owa'katą e'hpemayąpila ye', — eya' ke'ᵉ. 25. Li'la ina'hnipi ną nakų' nihį'ciyapi k'e'yaś ų'śilapi c'ąke' wąźi' ki'c'į ną iyu'weh ai' yųk'ą' hehą'l heya' ke'ᵉ, — I'śe' le' o'c'iciyapikta tk'a' t'o' k'e'yaś wąų'śiyalapi he'cįhą he' slolwa'yįkta wacį' ye'. 26. C'e k'ig.la'pi', to'kśa' anų'k ite' kį le'l u' kte', — eya'

ally / they were running / and lo / behind them / hill / a / down it / dust / smoke / like ? she came. / Now / near / she came / so / eldest one / the / cactus / a / he took / and / barkward / tossing / he sent it / and lo / prairie / the / entire / cactus-became / so / in no way-she came not. 20. So / slowly / path / considering / rounding here and there going / she approached / but / meantime / again / very / far / leaving behind / they came on / and / at last / past / she came / evidently, for / again / taking hold of them / almost / she-them-brought along. 21. That / on account of / eldest / next to / the / that one / knife / a / he took out his own / and / backward / he tossed it / and lo / sharp-pointed knives / that sort only / land / the / entire / from / they came up / and / bristling with points / stood. 22. Again / there / for a time / she could not get through / so / very / they came on / but / by some means / again / she freed herself / and / as if about to catch up with them / she came on. 23. At once / frightened / ground / they stamped on / and lo / land / the / across / it split open / so / past / she came not. 24. Very / they came on / and / river / a / wide / such / at right angles to their way / it lay / so / there / they stopped, bound for home / and / now / they were going to ford it / when / just then / old woman / a / barely walking / such / wood / the / out of / she came / and / "Grandchildren / across (the river) / take poor me / please," / she said. 25. Very / they were in haste / and / too / they were frightened / but / they took pity on her / so / one / he took her on his back / and / across / he took her / and then / then / she said: / "Really / this / I was going to help you / but / first / you have compassion / if-then / I will know it / I wanted. 26. So / go on home / certainly bye and bye / on both sides / face / the / here /

c'ąke' hetą'hą li'la g.licu'pi śk'e'ᵉ. He'c'ena li'la g.licu'pi yųk'ą' i'tohatuka hą'l wana' i'ś eya' anų'k ite' k'ų m.ni-a'g.lag.la ona'tąyą ų' ke'ᵉ. 27. C'ąke' winų'ħcala kį wį'yeya na'żį ną wana' ka'k'el-inųwįkte cį lehą'l p'e'ta wą wakpa' kį ekta' o'iħpeyelaka c'ą' a'taya ile'śaśa-hįg.nį ną m.ni' k'ų p'e'ta ke'ᵉ. C'ąke' hetą' to'k'a-hiyu'śni kį ų iħpe'ya g.licu'pi ną ni' wic'o't'ita g.li'pi śk'e'ᵉ. Hehą'yela owi'hąke'ᵉ.

will come /" she said / so / from there / very / they started homeward/ At once / very / they started homeward / and lo / some time after-ward / then / now / she / too / on each side / face / the-past / along the water / rushing to and fro / she was. 27. So / old woman / the / ready / she stood / and / just as she started to swim it / the / at this point / fire / a / river / the / towards / she threw in / directly / then / all over / flaming red-it suddenly became / and / water / the-past / fire. / So / from then / no way she came on / the / therefore / leaving her behind / they came homeward / and / alive / to camp / they returned / they say. 28. There / it ends.

Free Translation.

1. Three brothers lived at a certain place. They were skilful hunters, so, without troubling anyone, they would go to hunt; and lived comfortably; but never one of them thought of marrying. 2. Then one evening a woman stood, with her shawl over her head, outside their tipi. They were eating, so the eldest said, "Better ask her in; she must eat."[1] 3. So Hakela, the last born, stepped out and asked her in; she entered without a word, and accepted their food and ate it without saying anything[2]. 4. They thought she might have come to marry one of them; but as time went on and she seemed to have no such designs, they feared her and "Maybe she came to kill us!" they said. 5. One morning, they all went away but said to Hakela[3], "Stay home all day; sit on top of the tipi, and watch her. If anything unusual or suspicious occurs, tell us," they said to him. 6. He pretended to start out with his brothers, but soon returned secretly and took his place on the tipi-pole tips. He could look down through the smoke-vent and see into the whole room. 7. When the woman thought she was alone, she took out a robe, and unfolded it; it was trimmed all over with human hair. 8. And she said, "I still have that little bit to finish. I shall use Hakela's hair, — inferior hair though it is!" 9. When Hakela heard this alarming thing about himself,he was badly frightened, and told his brothers

---

[1] This was good manners. To sit at table, and let a visitor sit by and wait for you to eat, was the absolute height of rudeness; it just was not done.

[2] This sentence is enough to tell us the outcome of the brothers' encounter with this person. She enters and accepts food without any word. She doesn't relate herself to them, and she takes their food without acknowledgment.

[3] The last-born does not count in the general reckoning. Of course there are four brothers; but the story says, three brothers, and the lastborn.

the instant they returned. 10. Again next day the young men went away and this time the woman drew out a bag from which she took some roundish, wrinkled things. She threw a handful into the cooking, and went on with her fancy-work. 11. When it was done, she dished it out to eat it, and every one of those round wrinkled things was a human ear! Evidently she ate such things occasionally. 12. Hakela saw this from his perch on the house-top; so when his brothers returned, he related the happening to them. "Now, we must flee," they said. 13. But first they spent several days boiling some rope to make it tender; this was whenever the woman walked abroad. 14. They decided it had boiled enough, so they dried it and it was exceedingly fragile. Then they said to her, "Younger sister, go for some firewood. Get only the kind of wood with the red pith," they added; so she took the rope and went away. 15. The instant she was out of sight, they took food for the trip and ran away. 16. Meantime the woman was chopping firewood, but as the red pithed wood is the toughest to cut, she was occupied in doing it for a long time. They said red pith, purposely, to delay her. 17. When she had a carrying-load ready, and tried to put it on her back and rise to her feet, the rope kept breaking so that she had a very difficult time. 18. She looked towards home and it was already a deserted place. "The worthless ones! I might have known they would send me out for a purpose. Just you wait! Anyway, I am running out of my special food, so it is just as well." She said, as she started to chase them. 19. Looking back from time to time, they ran, and soon they saw her as she ran down a hill, far behind them. As she neared them, the eldest in desperation tossed cactus behind him, and immediately the world became one continuous cactus bed. She could not come on very well. 20. She was slow, picking her way around the thorns, so meantime they gained considerable ground when again she caught up with them and was immediately behind them. 21. Now the next to the eldest tossed his knife behind him, and the whole land became a mass of knives with their points sticking upward. 22. Again for a time she slowed down, so they gained ground, but she freed herself somehow, and once again she was almost touching them. 23. In despair they stamped on the ground, and instantly it opened in a long slit that kept her back from them. 24. They came on till they reached a river that blocked their way. It was wide. They were about to ford it when an old woman came from the wood, and asked to be taken across. 25. They were in such haste that they could hardly spare the time, and were frantic; and yet they pitied her so one of them took her over on his back. Then she said, "Really I am going to help you; but first I wanted to see how kind you were. 26. Run home now, for as sure as anything that Double-face will come here," she said. So from there they started home again. And then sometime later the Double-face too arrived at the river and ran to and fro along the water's edge.

27. So the old woman stood ready and the instant the Double-face tried to swim across, she threw a fire into the river and at once the entire stream became of mass of burning flames. She could not, of course, get past that. So she gave up; and the young men, now rid of her, returned to camp. That is all.

12. Coyote and Bear.

1. *Yaśle' ka'k'ena ya'hǫ yųk'ǫ' ot'i'weta wǫ e'l mi'la wǫ iye'ic'iyį nǫ yuha' ya'hǫ ke'ᵉ. Ħcehǫ'l paha'-ak'o'tǫhǫ mat'o' wǫ u' c'ǫke' k'oki'p'į nǫ b.loka'skaska nǫ, — E', Hį'hǫnaħcį t'ǫkt'ǫ'ka-b.lowa'kaska! — eya' ke'ᵉ. 2. Yųk'ǫ' mat'o' kį i'ś b.loka'skį nǫ, — E'! Hį'hǫnaħcį cikci'k'ala-b.lowa'kaska! — eya' c'ǫke' hehǫ'l iyo'tǫ yaśle' k'oki'p'į nǫ aya'howaśteśtelowǫ' nǫ, — Tuwa' mit'o'kap hiya'ya c'ǫ'śna he' c'awa'p'ap'a nǫ wau'! — eya' ke'ᵉ. 3. Yųk'ǫ' mat'o' kį i'ś eya' yawǫ'kal e'yayį nǫ, — Tuwa' mit'o'kap hiya'ya c'ǫ he' b.laħu'ħugį nǫ wau'! — eya' ke'ᵉ. K'e'yaś yaśle' naħ'ų'śni-kųs aki'- ś'aś'a nǫ mi'la k'ų he' yuptǫ'ptǫ nǫ mat'o' k'ų he' k'uwa' e'yaya c'ǫke' iye'ś t'ǫ'ka k'e'yaś nap'į' nǫ c'ǫwo'hǫ k'ina'źį ke'ᵉ. 4. — Maci'k'ala c'ǫke' c'ǫwohǫ k'ina'źįpi c'ǫ'śna omi'cit'awa. C'ǫ' pazǫ'zǫ ib.la'm.nį nǫ c'awa'p'ap'a! — yaśle' eya' ke'ᵉ. Heya' yųk'ǫ' mat'o' kį ak'e' nap'į' nǫ m.nic'o'kaya ina'źį ke'ᵉ. 5. C'ǫke', — He'c'el m.nic'o'kaya k'ina'źįpi c'ǫ'śna omi'cit'awa; m.ni' kį e'l kig.nų'k ib.la'm.nį nǫ*

Literal Translation.

1. Coyote / off in yonder direction / he was going / and then / abandoned camp / a / at / knife / a / he found for himself / and / having it / he was going. Just then / hill-other side of / bear / a / he was coming / so / he feared him / and / hiccoughed several times / and / "Ah! / Very early in the morning / large quantities-I hiccough!" / he said. 2. And so / bear / for his part / hiccoughed / and / "Ah! / very early in the morning / little quantities-I hiccough!" / he said / so / then / more than ever / coyote / feared him / and / making high breaking notes with his voice-he sang / and / "Whoever / in front of me / he goes by / then always / that one / I stab and I come!" / he said. 3. And then / bear / the / he too / raising it with his mouth / he sent it / and / "Whoever / in front of me / he goes by / then / that one / I chew to pieces / and / I come!" / he said. But / Coyote / not to hear-pretending / he shouted / and / knife / the-past / that one / flashed it / and / bear / the-past / that one / he chased / so / he indeed / big / yet / he ran away / and / among trees / he came to a stop. 4. "I am little / so / among trees / they stop / then always / it is in a way to be mine. / Trees / in and out through / I go / and / I stab!" / Coyote / he said. / He said that / and so / bear / the / again / he ran away / and / water-midst / he stopped. 5. So / "In that way / in midst of water / they stop / then always / it is in a way to be mine. / Water / the / into / diving / I do go / and / I stab," / he

*c'awa'p'ap'a! — eya' ke*ᵉ. *C'ąke' mat'o' kį ak'e' naki'p'a yųk'ą' wana'*
hehą'yą yaśle' k'oki'p'eśni c'ąke', — Misų`, he' ku' ye'!¹ Wac'į'ka
yųk'ą's ehą'nihci c'ac'i'p'ap'akta tk'a' ye lo'. Į'śe' le' waśka'tį ną
*lep'a'he lo'! — eya' c'ąke' mat'o' k'ų e'l g.li' ke*ᵉ. 6. *He'c'eś hetą'hą*
sak'i'p zuya' ya'pi yųk'ą' maśti'cala wą c'ąku'-g.lakį'yą hiya'ya
*ke*ᵉ. *He'c'ena yaśle', — Wą, maśti`cala, nakpa` hą`skaska, p'ute`*
*hcihci`, ku'wi ye², zuya' ųyą'pi c'a o'yap'akte, — eya' ke*ᵉ. *Yųk'ą'*
*maśti'cala kį i'ś, — K'e'yaś ośte'mayag.la kiś, — eya' ke*ᵉ. 7. *Yųk'ą'*
yaśle' ak'e', — Hųhųhi, o'we hą'hą p'eźi-ho'ta-m.na'la ep'e' c'ų,
he' ta'ku wo'śice wae'p'a c'a! — eya' yųk'ą' og.na'ye-waśte` c'ąke'
*wica'la ną o'p iya'ya ke*ᵉ. 8. *Wana' wi' k'u'ciyela c'ąke' pat'a'kapi*
ną p'eźi'-wo`k'eya wą ka'ġapi ną t'ima' i'yotakapi hcehąl wana' t'o'ka
kį ahi'hųni ną na'źįwic'ayapi³ k'e'yaś mat'o' kį t'iyo'pa ot'į's yąka'hą
*c'ąke' yaśle' heya' ke*ᵉ, 9. — *Wą, misų`, maki'yuk'ą ye'. Miyeśtuka⁴*
*wawa'k'utekte, — eya' ke*ᵉ. *O'kpeśni heya'he c'e'yaś nihą'śni yąka'hą*
ec'e'l t'o'ka kį kak'i'yot'ą e'yaya tk'a's mani'takiya į'yąkapi ną
ai'sįyą i'yotakapi c'ąke' t'o'ka k'ų ak'e' ag.li'hųni k'e'yaś wana'

said. So / bear / the / again / he ran away / and lo / now / no longer /
Coyote / he feared him not / so / "My younger brother, / that one /
come home! / I really wished / if / long ago / I will stab you many
times / but. / *Iśe'* / *le* (The truth of this is) / I play / and / I was
saying that" / he said / so / bear / the-past / to him / returned.
6. Thus / from there / together / to war / they went / and / rabbit /
a / crossing the road / he went by. / At once / Coyote / "Say, / rabbit /
ears / long / muzzle / ragged / come here / to war / we go / so / you
shall join" / he said. Then / rabbit / the / he / "But / you called me
names / the!" / he said. 7. And so / Coyote / again / "Of all things! /
in a jest *(o'we hą'hą)* / sage he smells of / I said / the-past / that / what /
bad thing / I said something / such!" / he said / and / to fool-easy /
so / he believed / and / with them / he went. 8. Now / sun / it was
low / so / they halted / and / grass-shelter / a / they made / and /
indoors / they sat / just then / now / enemy / the / arrived / and /
held them at bay / but / bear / the / doorway / filling / he was sitting /
so / Coyote / he said: 9. "Say, / my younger brother, / make room
for me. / I at least / I will shoot things (or people)," / he said. /
Without pause / he kept saying that / but / unheeding / he was
sitting / until / enemy / the / somewhere / they went / but indeed /
away towards the wilds / they ran / and / out of sight / they sat
down / so / enemy / the-past / again / they returned / but / now /

---

¹ *he*, that one; *ku*, come back; *ye*, please! The conventional form, for calling
someone at a distance, to come home. (During the Messiah movement, the
song with which the people called their dead to return to them was:
"*Ina'*, *he ku ye!*" Mother, that one, come home, please do!).
² *ku'wa'*, Come here! It survives only in the imperative form. And followed
by *ye'*, the terminal *a* becomes an unnasalized *i*, as in all verbs in that form.
³ *na'źįwic'ayapi*, they cause them to stand; that is, they hold them at bay.
⁴ *miye's, miyeśtuk'a*, and (Yankton) *miye'k'e*, I, even though nobody else
acts, I will!

*tuwe'niśni kį ų́ a'beya ak'i'yag.la ke'ᵉ. 10. Yųk'ą́' yaśle' heya' ke'ᵉ:
— It'o' ma'zasu' kį hiyu'ųkiyapikte¹ lo'. Tuwa' nų́p o'ta hiyu'yapi
hą́'tąhąś hena' ohi'yapikta c'a wążi' co'nala hiyu'ye cį he' kte'pi ną
yu'tapikte lo', — eya' yųk'ą́' he'c'etulapi c'ąke' wana' ma'zasu'²
hiyu'kiyahąpi ke'ᵉ. 11. Mat'o' kį iye'ś li'la o'ta-opi c'aś ma'zasu' kį
iśna'la o'ta hiyu'ye c'e'yaś iśto'g.mus yąkį' ną he'c'ųhą c'ąke' k'ohą́'
yaśle' maśtį'cala kį kic'i' ohla't'etąhą awa'manųhąpi ke'ᵉ. 12. Wana'
hena'la yųk'ą́' mat'o' kį iśna'la co'nala yuha' c'ąke kte'pikta ke'ya'pi
yųk'ą́' he'c'etula c'ąke' kte'pi śk'e'ᵉ. Yųk'ą́' yaśle' heya' ke'ᵉ: — Ho,
it'o' wak'ą́'-wowahįkta c'e iya'yį ną ųci' t'ac'e'ġa k'ų he' maka'ku wo',
— eya' ke'ᵉ. 13. C'ąke' maśtį'cala kį psi'psil paha' kį ai'sįyą iya'yį
ną i't'ap c'eħ-zi wą wiya'kpayela ag.li' ke'ᵉ. Yųk'ą́' yaśle' he' e'śni
ke'yį' ną ak'e' yeśi' c'ąke' hehą́'l c'e'ġa wą śa' li'la waśte' ag.li' ke'ᵉ.
Ak'e' he' e'śni ke'yį' ną t'o'keca aku'śi c'ąke' wążi' t'oye'la waśte' c'a
ag.li' ke'ᵉ. 14. He'c'eca k'e'yaś ak'e' he' e'śni ke'ya' c'ąke' ak'e' iya'ya
yųk'ą́' c'e'ġa wą ħuħu'ġahą eya'p ec'a' c'a ag.li' ke'ᵉ. — Ho, wac'į́-
t'ųśni'³, nake'ś he' e ye lo', ka' tį'skoya ani'kpab.laye! — eya' ke'ᵉ.*

nobody / the / therefore / scattering / they went away. 10. Then /
Coyote / he said: / "Suppose / bullets / the / we will send out ours. /
Whichever / two / many / they send out / if-then / those / they shall
win / so / other one / few / he sends out / the / that one / they (shall)
kill / and / eat him" / he said / and / they agreed / so / now / bullets /
they were sending out their own / 11. Bear / the / he indeed / very
/ many times-they shot / so indeed / bullets / the / alone / many /
he sent out / but / eyes shut / he sat / and / was doing that / so /
meantime / Coyote / rabbit / the / with / from underneath / they
were stealing from him. 12. Now / that was all / and lo / bear / the /
he alone / few / he had / so / to kill him / they said / and / all right he
considered / so / they killed him. / And then / Coyote / he said: /
"Now, / I think / sacredly-I will make a cooking / so / go / and /
grandmother / her kettle / the-past / that one / bring to me" / he
said. 13. So / rabbit / the / skipping along / hill / the / hidden by /
he went / and / at once / kettle-yellow / a / shining brightly / he
brought back. And / Coyote / that one / it was not / he said / and /
again / sent him / so / then /kettle / a / red /very / good / he brought.
/ Again / that one / it was not / he said / and / different one / to bring
he ordered / so / one / blue-ly / good / such / he brought. 14. It was
like that / yet / again / that one / it was not /he said /so /again /he
went / and / kettle / a / dented all over / *eya'pec'a'* (it couldn't be
called anything else) / such / he brought home. / "Now / brainless
one! / at last / that one / it is, / yonder / that extensively / you have

---

¹ *hiyu'*, to start coming; *hiyu'ya*, to cause to come forth, or out of. They are
here coughing up their bullets.
² *ma'zasu'*, bullets; *ma'za*, metal; iron; *su*, seed.
³ *wac'į́'*, mind; *t'ų*, to give birth to; to acquire; to have; to wear on one's
person; *śni*, not. Hence, one not wearing a mind; a fool.

15. *Wana' wo'soso iyo'ḣpeyį ną e'yapahaṡi c'ąke' e'yapaha oma'ni
yųk'ą' to'k'iyatąhą kį oya's'į, mat'a'peḣ'ą ye'ṡ k'o' ahi'hųni ke'ᵉ.
16. Hi'pi ną į'yą-b.laska` wą aką'l it'ą'c'ą-e`g.nakapi c'ąke' wana'
wic'a'ṡa ya'tapi-ic'ilaḣcį iṡto'g.muṡ ġu'ġa-yąka`hą tk'a'ṡ ųg.na' wo'he
c'ų he' a'taya ik'i'nicapi ṡk'e'ᵉ. 17. C'ąke', ġu'ġa-yą`ka waṡte`ka,
k'uwa' e'wic'ayayįkta yųk'ą' į'yą kį e'na iya'skapa c'ąke' pą' ų'
k'e'yaṡ ec'e'l a'beya ak'i'yag.la ṡk'e'ᵉ. 18. — Wo'soso mic'i'c'aġe
c'ų̨́! — eya'ya c'e'ya ų' hą'l k'ohą' ųkce'k'iḣa wą wo'soso k'ų yuha'
kįyą' iya'ya c'ąke' wąg.la'kį ną c'e'yahą ke'ᵉ. 19. Ic'ų'hą pi'ṡko k'eya'
okį'yąhąpi c'ąke', — Misų̨́, misų̨́, t'eḣi'ya maka'; ų'ṡimalapi!¹ —
eya'hą ke'ᵉ K'e'yaṡ e'l e'tųweṡni okį'yąhąpi yųk'ą' hehą'l, — Nic'į'ca
c'aże'wic'ab.lata! — eya' ke'ᵉ. 20. Yųk'ą' pi'ṡko k'ų wążi' k'u'ciyela
kįyą' hiyu' ną ų'kce-hįg.la kawą'kal k'ig.nį' ną yaṡle' ka'k'i to'k'iya
kaḣla'ya iḣpe'ya ke'ᵉ. 21. Yųk'ą' (to'k² c'į'ka²,) — Ê, ṡįlye'la, i'ṡ he'c'el
make'la k'ų, tuwa'ṡ ohi'tiya hoksi't'eḣila ka! — eya'ya na'żį hiya'yį
ną he'c'ena ųkce'k'iḣa wą wo'soso kae'yaye c'ų he' iya't'ap ya' ke'yį́*

spread yourself flat!" / he said. 15. Now / meat cut in strips / he set
to boil / and / told him to act as crier / so / calling out / he went
around / and so / from everywhere / the / all / toads / even / also /
they arrived. 16. They came / and / rock-flat / a / on / as chief-they
placed him / so / now / thinking himself an esteemed man (a chief) /
eyes closed / haughty-he was sitting / but indeed / suddenly / his
cooking / the-past / that / entire / they fought over. 17. So / proud-
sitter / good one indeed! / pursuing / he would take them / and
behold! then / rock / the / right there / he was fastened / so /
shouting / he was / but / even so / in all directions / they went
away. 18. "Meat strips / I made for myself / the-past!" / saying /
weeping / he continued / while / meantime / magpie / a / meat-
strips / the-past / holding / flying / he went / so / he saw his
own / and / he was weeping. 19. Meanwhile / nighthawks / some /
they were soaring on high / so / "My little brothers, / in distress / I
sit / Take pity on me!" / he was saying / but at (him) / looking not /
they were soaring / and then / next / "Your children / I call their
names!" / he said. 20. And then / night-hawk / the-past / one / low /
flying / he came / and / suddenly defecating with sound / upward /
he went back / and / Coyote / yonder / somewhere / peeled off / he
fell. 21. And then / what way / he wanted rather! / "Êh! / bad one, /
for my part / that way (i. e., hurting nobody) / I was sitting, poor
me / the-past / who indeed / ardently / he loves his children /
rather!" / saying / standing / he went / and / at once / magpie / a /
meat strip / his-it took away / the-past / that one / following / he

---

¹ *ų'ṡimalapi*, take pity on me. Once again, Ikto' (or Coyote, in the animal
world) talks without the usual particles.
² *to'k c'į'ka*, an idiom, meaning something like, "What, then, did he want?"
to'k, from *to'k'el*, what manner; *c'į*, to desire; *ka*, rather.

nǫ m.ni' wǫ ag.la'g.la ya'hǫ ke'ᵉ. 22. M.ni-ma'hel e'tųwǫ yųk'ǫ'
he'c'iya ųkce'k'iħa k'ų he' yǫkį' nǫ wo'soso wǫ icu' k'ų he' ahi'pazohǫ
c'ǫke' li'la c'aze'kį nǫ kig.nų'k ekta' iya'ya ke'ᵉ. 23. C'ete'ta¹ yut'ǫ't'ǫ
k'e'yaś oni'ya-pte' cela c'ǫke' i't'ap naa'kǫl g.licu' ke'ᵉ. 24. Śehaś-tuk'a,
į'yǫ t'ǫwo'kśǫ² oi'c'ig.nakį nǫ ak'e' kig.nu'k iya'ye c'e'yaś tke' kį ų'
oka'spa c'ǫke' ų'nihǫ' niya'śni-t'į`kta c'a tok'e'cela ħeya'ta g.licu' ke'ᵉ.
25. Yųk'ǫ' leyaś c'a-wǫ'kal yǫkį' nǫ wo'soso kį kiyu'tahe śǫ waśte'yela
t'epyį' nǫ iya'yįkta hǫl yaśle' kai'tųkap³ g.liħpa'yį nǫ wǫk'al e'tųwǫ
yųk'ǫ' wǫya'ka śk'e'ᵉ. 26. Heħǫ'yela owi'ħǫke'ᵒ.

would go / he said / and / water / a / along its shore / he was going.
22. Water-in / he looked / and lo, / in there / magpie / the-past / that
one / he sat / and / meat-strip / a / he took it / the-past / that one /
he held it towards him / so / very / he was angry / and / diving / at /
he went. 23. At the bottom / he felt around / but / breath-short /
so / at once / forced to the top / he came back. 24. This time in
earnest / rocks / around his body / he put on himself / and / again /
diving / he went / but / heavy / the / on account of / he was weighted
down / so / almost / breathing-not-he will die / such / with difficulty /
away (from the water) / he came back. 25. And / all the while / up-
tree / it sat / and / meat-strip / the / his-it was eating / yet / completely / it devoured it / and / was about to go / then / Coyote /
forced backwards / he fell / and / upward / looked / and then / he
saw it / they say. 26. There / it ends.

Free Translation.

1. Coyote⁴ was travelling along when, in a deserted camp, he found
a knife; so he carried it and went on his way. Just then a bear
was coming beyond a hill and Coyote was really afraid of him; so he
hiccoughed⁵ several times and, said, "Ah, very early in the morning
I hiccough for big things." 2. And so the bear also hiccoughed and,
"Ah, very early I hiccough for small things!" he answered. More
than ever the coyote feared him but pretended to be calm by
raising his voice in a falsetto and singing, "Whoever goes across
my path him I stab as I come!" 3. Again the bear replied by also
singing, "Whoever crosses my path, him I chew to pieces, as I

---

¹ *c'ete'*, the bottom of any vessel, barrel, a stream, a lake, anything shaped
with deep sides; *ta*, there; at.
² *t'ǫ*, from *t'ǫc'ǫ'*, body; *o'kśǫ*, around.
³ *itų'kap*, flat on the back; lying looking upward.
⁴ *Yaśle'* or Coyote is the *Ikto'* or trickster in the animal world. In Dakota,
when the trickster is appearing in the same cast with men in a story, and
is in the form of a man, he is *Ikto'*; but he is never Coyote with men as far
as I know; on the other hand, the *Ikto'* spirit is in the form of a coyote
when he is acting only with animals. Sometimes he is *Ikto'* even with
animals, but in that case, he always appears to them in the guise of a man.
⁵ To have hiccoughs is an indication that there is to be meat soon. Coyote
here wants to intimidate the bear by saying he hiccoughs for big things,
meaning he is going to kill and eat the bear.

come!" But Coyote pretending not to hear, gave some war-whoops
and flashed his knife in the sun and started to run at the bear; who,
though the bigger, ran from him, and stopped in a thicket. 4. "I am
small of body so when they run and stop in a thicket, that just suits
me; for I can get in between the trees and stab!" he said. Instantly
then the bear ran off again and stood in the water. 5. So, "When
they run and stop in water, that just suits me; I can then dive in and
stab!" he said. At that, the bear started to run again, but Coyote,
now no longer fearing him, said, "My younger brother, come back
here! Why, if I really meant it I could have stabbed you long ago.
I was only fooling when I said that!" he said; so the bear came back
to him. 6. From there they went to war together; and a rabbit
crossed their path. At once Coyote called out, "Hey there, you
rabbit with the long ears and ragged muzzle, come over here and
go to war with us!" But the rabbit was hurt. "But you called me
names!" he said. 7. Then Coyote again, "The idea, all I said, in full,
was that you smelled of sage; and what is so insulting in that?" he
said. The rabbit was easily soothed, and went with them. 8. The
sun was low, so they halted and made a grass-hut and sat down
inside; at that moment the enemy arrived and held them at bay;
but the bear sat in the doorway, taking up all the space. So Coyote said, 9. "Say, my younger brother, make room for me. I want to
do some fighting." He didn't cease a minute from asking him, but
paying no attention, he sat, until now the enemy ran off in some
direction. So the three made for the hills and hid until the enemy
returned; on finding them gone, they left and went home. 10. Then
Coyote said, "Let us all send out the bullets they used on us,"
and the rest agreed. So they stipulated further that they would kill
the one with the least. And they began to cough up their bullets.
11. Really, bear had the most; but while he sat there coughing up
a pile of shot, he kept his eyes closed and didn't know that from
underneath, the rabbit and coyote were stealing from him. 12. When
they finished, the bear seemed to have less then either of the others,
so they said he had lost; they must kill him. He was quite willing,
so they killed him. Then Coyote decided to make a mystery-
feast, and sent rabbit after "grandmother's kettle." 13. The rabbit
went bounding over a hill and very·soon returned with a yellow
kettle, new and shiny. But Coyote turned it down. That wasn't the
right one; so he went after another and this time he brought a nice
red one. Again that did not suit Coyote, so he came back a third
time with a fine blue one. 14. Even that failed to please Coyote,
so he made a fourth trip and returned with a horribly banged-up
old kettle. "There, idiot, that's it at last; you certainly spread your
ignorance over a great area[1]!" he said. 15. Now he made meat-

---

[1] This is an idiomatic expression and conveys very vividly in Dakota that
one is making a great big fool of oneself. The translation here given is
literal, and lacks the force of the Dakota.

strips[1] for boiling and told him meantime to act as crier and call in
a crowd; which he did, and even toads came as guests. 16. On
arriving they insisted on making Coyote their chief by seating him
on a great flat rock. So he sat there in great style, with his eyes
closed, and a haughty air as became his idea of a chief. Suddenly
the guests fought over the food. 17. So the chief of a few minutes ago,
tried to jump up and pursue them, as they scattered in all directions,
but found himself adhering to the rock. 18. "I did make meat-
strips for myself, alas!" he cried, while a magpie flew off with the
meat in his claws. Seeing it, Coyote wept the more. 19. There were
some night-hawks flying about overhead; so, "My younger brothers,
see how I suffer here; take pity on me!" he kept saying. But they
paid not the slightest attention to him. So he tried again, "I call
upon your children!"[2] he said. 20. Then one nighthawk swept
downward, and as he turned upward again, he broke wind with a
terrific explosion[3], and peeled Coyote off his perch, sending him
sprawling to the ground. 21. Then, changing his tune, Coyote scolded, "Curse him! Here I was, just sitting there, and see what he's
done! Such ardent love as somebody must have for his young!"
So talking, he got to his feet and started off to hunt down the magpie
which stole his meat-strip, and walked along a stream. 22. Down in
the water, he saw the magpie sitting and holding out his meat-
strips to tease him, so he got angry and dived in after him. 23. He
felt around at the bottom but his breath gave out soon, and he was
on top again. 24.This time, really, he loaded himself with rocks and
dived in again but they weighted him down so that he barely got out
before he died for want of breath. 25. All the while, the bird was
in the tree overhead, and was eating the meat-strip up there;
which Coyote saw only after he lost his balance and fell backward,
and glanced up. 26. That is all.

---

[1] Meat strips are made by cutting fresh meat in long pieces, against the
grain, about six inches in length, and perhaps two inches in thickness.
Then with a knife, deep gashes are cut into one side, at regular intervals,
each approximating a mouthful. Meat strips are boiled; especially for a feast,
when knives might be scarce, so that the feasters may bite off suitable
pieces with the least incovenience.

[2] The Dakota, in the old life, set such store by their children, that they were
ready for any sacrifice in the name of their sons or daughters. When a
request was made of a parent, and it was earnestly wished that it be
granted, the one asking it would say, "I call your son's (of your daughter's)
name!" and it was a very unfatherly father indeed who could harden his
heart against that.

[3] A certain type of hawk, generally in evidence just before a thunderstorm,
sweeps down and then makes a sudden turn upwards, with a curious ex-
plosive sound.

13. Turtle.

1. Pʻatkaʼśa kaʼkʻena zuyaʼ yaʼhạ śkʻeʼᵉ. Yụkʻạ́ kʻeʼya wạ eʼl uʼ nạ — CʻiyeꞋ, toʼkʻiya laʼ huwoʼ?, — eyaʼ cʻạke', — Ị́śeʼ leʼ zuyaʼ b.leʼ loʼ, — eyaʼ-ayuꞋpta yụkʻạ́ — Itʻoʼ cʻiyeꞋ, ụyị́ʼkte loʼ, — eyaʼ cʻạkeʼ kicʻíʼ yaʼ śkʻeʼᵉ. 2. Yụkʻạ́ Cʻaȟoʼta¹ g.lakị́ʼyạ hiyaʼyị nạ wạwiʼcʻayaka cʻạkeʼ patʻaʼk inaʼżị keʼᵉ. — Toʼkʻiya laʼpi huwoʼ? — eyaʼ cʻa okiʼyakapi yụkʻạ́ oʼp yịʼkta keʼya keʼᵉ. 3. Wanaʼ yaʼm.ni heʼcʻeś yaʼhạpi kʻụ, zicaʼ wạ ị́ś eyaʼ oʼpʻakta keʼya cʻạkeʼ wanaʼ toʼp zuyaʼ yaʼpi keʼᵉ. 4. Akʻeʼ tʻaleʼźa wạ eʼ nạ susweʼcʻa wạ henaʼos ahiʼopʻapi cʻạkeʼ wanaʼ śaʼkpepi cʻa ipaʼȟlalya, tokʻeʼ ecʻaʼcʻa lowạ́ yaʼhạpi keʼᵉ. 5. Tʻoʼka tʻiʼpi kị ihụ́ʼnipiśni ecʻeʼl wakpaʼla wạ iyuʼwegapi yụkʻạ́ liʼla ȟliȟliʼla cʻạkeʼ kʻeʼya kị kaȟliʼ nạ toʼkʻa-hiyuꞋśni kị ụʼ iȟpeʼya iyaʼyapi keʼ. 6. Heʼcʻeś zaʼptạla hetạ́ʼhạ iyaʼyapi keʼᵉ. Yụkʻạ́ kaʼl itʻuʼhu-cʻạ wạ tʻạʼka hạ́ cʻa oȟlaʼtʻe iyaʼyapi yụkʻạ́ heʼl enaʼna uʼta liʼla oʼta hiyeʼya keʼᵉ. Heʼcʻenaȟciś zicaʼ kị sạʼpʻa yaʼ okiʼhiśni cʻạkeʼ eʼna iȟpeʼyapi nạ hetạ́ʼ iyaʼyapi keʼᵉ. 7. Toʼp wanaʼ zuyaʼ yaʼpi kʻụ, ụg.naʼhạla tʻateʼ-hiyuꞋ yụkʻạ́ Cʻaȟoʼta wob.luʼ iyeʼya keʼᵉ. 8. Kaʼl cʻạȟloʼǧu-ożużu wạ eʼg.na cʻạkuʼyapi yụkʻạ́ eʼl wapʻeʼpʻeka oʼta cʻạkeʼ

Literal Translation.

1. Turtle / in yonder direction / to war / he was going / they say. And / tortoise / a / to (him) / he came / and / "Elder brother / to what place / you go?" / he said / so / "*Íśeʼ* / this / to war / I go" / saying-he replied / and then / "Well / elder brother / we two shall go!" / he said / so / with him / he travelled. 2. And then / Ashes / crossing their path / he went by / and / saw them / so / abruptly / he stopped. "Where / go-you?" / he said / so / they told him / and then / with them / he would go / he said. 3. Now / three / thus / they were going / the-past / squirrel / a / he too / he will join / he said / so / now / four / to war / they were going. 4. Again / bladder / a / it was / and / dragon-fly / a / those two / coming they joined / so / now / they were six / such / in rank formation / for fun / singing / they were going. 5. Enemy / they live / the / they arrived at not / ere / creek / a / they crossed / when lo! / very / muddy / so / tortoise / the / mired / and / no way he came not / the / therefore / leaving him / they went on. 6. Thus / only five / from there / they went on. / And then / yonder place / oak-tree / a / big / stood / such / under / they went / and so / there / here and there / acorns / very / many / they lay about. / Instantly then / squirrel / the / past / to go / he could not / so / right there / they left him / and / from there / they went on. 7. Four / now / to war / they went / the-past / suddenly / wind / blew / then / Ashes / blown / it went. 8. At yonder place / weed-growth / a / through / they took their way / and / there / thistles /

---

¹ Sometimes, in animal tales, the article is omitted, after names of animals; in which case, the noun becomes a proper name. I have capitalized such words in this tale.

T'ale'ža iyu'hleca c'ąke' sni'za ke'ᵉ. 9. Ho, wana' Suswe'c'a P'atka'ša[1]
kic'i'la owi'c'akaptapi ke'ᵉ. Yuk'ą' Suswe'c'a pša'-hig.la c'ąk'a'hu
ig.lu'sluta c'ąke' e'na yuka' ke'ᵉ. 10. P'atka'ša heya' ke'ᵉ, — Ê,
ehą'niš mišna'la wau' šni, — eyį' ną wana' t'o'ka t'i'pi kį e'g.na
iya'ya ke'ᵉ. 11. Yuk'ą' oya'te kį, — Wą, tuwa' le'c'iyatąhą u' we lo',
— eya'pi ną li'la iki'k'opi ke'ᵉ. Icu'pi ną wį'yą kį iyo'tą wašte'lakapi
ną, — Ma'![2] *C'e'wiš-wašte'la ke! Ta'kula huwe'? — eya' o'kšą u'pi*
ke'ᵉ. 12. Ta'kowe'-hi kį iyu'ǵapi c'ąke', — zuya' wahi' ye lo' — eya'
yuk'ą', — ožela'![3] *ta'ku oh'ą' wo'wihaya zuya' hi'la ye'! — eya'pi*
ke'ᵉ, wį'yą kį iyu'ha. 13. — Ma', zuya' hi'la se'ca wą. Ta'ku k'oki'p'ela
huwe'? — eya'pi ke'ᵉ. — P'e'ta k'oya'kip'ela he? — eya'pi yuk'ą', —
Ho'h, he' ta'ku wo'k'okip'eka c'aš, — eya' ke'ᵉ. 14. C'ąke' hetą' ta'ku
wo'k'okipe se'ce cį iyu'ha c'aže'yatapi k'e'yaš hena'š i'tok'ašni ke'ya'
šk'e'ᵉ. Į'še' hena' iyu'ha k'oki'p'e c'e'yaš i'hąl-eya` šk'e'ᵉ. 15. O'hąketa
mnima'hel ihpe'yapikta ke'ya'pi yuk'ą' he'c'ena ite'-naki'hma c'e'ya
u' šk'e'ᵉ. — He'c'a ece'la k'owa'kip'e c'ų, — eyį' ną c'e'ya u' c'ąke'

many / so / Bladder / he was torn by it / so / collapsed. 9. Now / now /
Dragon-fly / Turtle /. only with him / they were left. And then /
Dragon-fly / suddenly sneezing / spinal column / he pulled out his
own / so / right there / he lay. 10. Turtle / said / "Ah / originally
indeed / alone / why didn't I come ?" / he said / and / now / enemy /
they live / the / among / he went. 11. And then / people / the /
"Look / somebody / from this direction / he comes!" / they said /
and / very / they were excited by it. / They took him up / and /
women / the / especially / they liked him / and / "*Mah!* / How
indeed-he is good- the little one ! (Isn't he cute ?) / What little thing
is he / I wonder ?" / saying / around / they were. 12. Why / he came /
the / they asked him / so / "To war / I have come" / he said / and lo /
"*Ożela'!* / what / act / amusing / to war / he has come-the little
one!" / they said / women / the / all. 13. "*Mah!* / to war / he has
come / perhaps / *wą!* / What / he fears / I wonder ?" / they said.
"Fire / do you fear ?" / they said / and / "*Hoh!* / that / what / it is
fearsome indeed / such!" / he said. 14. So / from then / things /
fearful / perhaps / the / all / they named / but / those indeed / he
was not disturbed by / he said. *Íše'* / those / all / he feared / but /
not meaning it-he said it. 15. At last / into water / they would
throw him / they said / and then / at once / face-hiding his own /
crying / he remained. / "That sort / alone / I fear / the-past" / he
said / and / crying / continued to be / so / they took him / and / in the

---

[1] Note see page 77.
[2] *mah!* is an expletive used only by women, much as we say in English, O,
look! The equivalent, used by men, is *wą!* Occasionally a woman will say
wą! but a man never says *mah!*
[3] *ożela'* .. Is an exclamation expressing delight and surprise over something
piquantly interesting. For the most part, it is a woman's word; men use
it rarely.

a'yapi ną m.nic'o'kap iȟpe'yapi šk'e'ᵉ. 16. I̧'yą s'e mahe'l iya'ya c'ąke' kawı̧'ȟ g.licu'pikta yųk'ą' ec'ą'l g.lina'p'į ną aki's'aś'a nųwą' hiya'ya ke'ᵉ. He'c'ena tok'i'yot'ą g.licu' ke'ᵉ. 17. T'iya'ta g.lihų'ni c'ąke' p'atka'śa-oya'te kį wo'wiyuškį ų' wac'i'pi šk'e'ᵉ. 18. Lehą'l tuwa' ta'ku wąži' c'į'ȟca k'eś naȟla'l ų-kų'za c'ą'śna Lak'o'ta kį wo'eye wą eya'pi kį he' le' e'ᵉ: — P'atka'śa c'a m.ni'l a'yapikte s'e, — eya'pi s'a'ᵃ. 19. Hehą'yela owi'ȟąke'ᵉ.

midst of water / they threw him. 16. Stone / like / in / he went / so / turning / they were about to start home / and then / just then / he emerged again / and / giving war-whoops / swimming / he went along. Then / towards somewhere / he started this way homeward. 17. Back home / he came / so / turtle-people / the / joy / with / they danced / they say. 18. Now-a-days / anyone / something / a / he really wants / yet / holding back-he pretends / then regularly / Lakotas / the / (proverb?) saying / a / they say / the / that one / this / it is / "Turtle / such / toward water / they will take him / like" / they say it / regularly. 19. There / it ends.

Free Translation.

1. Turtle was on the warpath. As he travelled he met a tortoise who said, "Elder brother, where are you going?" He answered, "Oh, just to war." And then, "Elder brother, I think I'll go with you," said the tortoise; so the two started off. 2. Ashes was crossing their road; he saw them and stopped short. "Where are you going?" he asked; and on being told, he decided to join them. 3. By now, three warriors were travelling together when a squirrel offered to join too; and four warriors continued on their way. 4. A bladder[1] and a dragon-fly added themselves to the group; and now, six happy warriors marched in rank formation, singing for their own amusement as they journeyed. 5. Long before they reached the enemy territory they were fording a stream. The bottom was so muddy that the tortoise became mired in it; and as he couldn't work himself loose, they left him there. 6. So five went on from that point. Under a great oak-tree many acorns lay scattered about. As they passed under the tree, the squirrel couldn't bring himself to go on, so they left him behind. 7. Four journeyed together, when a gust of wind suddenly swept Ashes away. 8. They had to go through a thick growth of weeds and thistle, and a thorn punctured bladder so that he died down and could not continue on the trip. 9. Only dragon-fly was left with turtle. But he sneezed with such suddenness and force that he blew his entire spinal column out through his nostrils, and was no more. 10. Said turtle to himself, "Fool! Why didn't I come

---

[1] The bladders of ruminants were blown up and allowed to dry; and then used for all sorts of things; like oiled paper for carrying greasy foods. Or children carried them inflated, as white children play with balloons.

alone in the first place ?" Now he entered the enemy camp. 11. And
the people made a great fuss, saying, "Look, someone is coming
from this direction." They took him up, and the women were especially delighted with him. "*Mah!* Isn't he cute ? What sort of
little thing is he ?" they exclaimed as they crowded about him.
12. They asked him his mission. So, "I have come to war," he told
them. "Isn't that just too sweet ? How cunning of him to come to
war!" all the women said. 13. "*Mah!* It is possible he has really come
to war, the dear little thing. Wonder what he fears ?" they said. "Do
you fear fire, little one ?" they said and he replied with a laugh,
"Fire ? What's so fearful about fire anyway ?" 14. From then on
they mentioned many things that he might fear, but he continued
to dismiss them as nothing. As a matter of fact, he feared them all,
but he was saying what he didn't mean. 15. Finally they said they
might throw him into the water and instantly his expression changed.
Hiding his face he began to cry. "That is the only thing I fear!" he
said. So they took him, still crying, and tossed him into the river.
16. Like a rock he disappeared, only to come up again, just as they
turned to go back; he went swimming down stream, giving his war-
whoops of victory. He came on home from there. 17. In turtle-camp
there was great celebration and joy. 18. Today, whenever someone
pretends to hold back from the very thing he wants, the Dakota
saying runs, "Like a turtle about to be thrown into water." 19. That
is all.

14. Meadowlark and the Rattlesnake.

1. *P'eži'-hą`skaska-ožu` wą e'l t'aši'yak-nupala[1] wą waho'ĥpi ki-
g.le'la šk'e'ᵉ. 2. C'įca' kį wana' t'aķi'ķiyąpila[2] k'e'yaš nahą'ĥ'cį ķiyą'pi-
lašni kį wale'hąl ųg.na' o'p yąka'he ĥcehą'l site'ĥla wą u' ną waho'ĥpila
kį oka'wįĥ kaksa' hiyų'ka ke'ᵉ. 3. Li'la t'aši'yak-nupala kį c'ąte'
iya'p'a'ᵃ. Ho, k'e'yaš i'tok'ašni s'e, kiwi'haha ną[3] — Hinǫ́, C'aske'la,*

Literal Translation.

1. Grass-long-growth / a / there / little meadowlark / a / nest / she
had hers placed. 2. Her little ones / the / now / they were large /
but / not yet / they flew not / the / about then / suddenly / with
them / she was sitting / just then / rattlesnake / a / he came / and /
little nest / the / surrounding / coiled / arriving he lay. 3. Very /
meadowlark / the / heart / it beat. / Now / though / it did not bother
her / like / she was pleasant to him / and / "Well well / *C'aske'la* /
your uncle / never indeed / he came / not / the-past / he has come /

---

[1] *t'aši'yak-nų'pa*, a meadow-lark; *t'aši'yaka*, the abomasum; *nų'pa*, two.
[2] *t'ąkt'ą'kapila* would be the usual form. This is another way of reduplicating
t'ą'ka, big. cf. the Yankton *t'ąķi'yąyą*.
[3] The style of stopping abruptly with *ną* (and), and with no preliminary
falling into direct discourse, is characteristic Dakota.

nile'kśi tų'wenihcįś hi'śni k'ų hi' c'a wo'wakihįkte'. 4. C'e'ġa olo'l-ya na¹, — eya' c'ąke' he'c'ena c'įca'-t'okap'ala se'ca wą kįyą' iya'yela ke'ᵉ. He'c'eya'-kįye'la k'e'yaś eya'ś tąyą'kel iya'ya ke'ᵉ. 5. T'e'hą-g.liśni c'ąke' k'ohą' t'aśi'yak-nųpa-wį'yąla kį tok'e' ec'a'ca-wo'g.lakahį ną i'tohątu yųk'ą', — Hinų, c'eh-o'lol-iya'ya wą c'e'wįś t'e'hą-g.li'śni ke'ᵉ, — eyį' ną c'įca'-i'yok'ihe kį c'iye'ku ole'-yeśi ke'ᵉ. 6. C'ąke' he' i'ś-'eya' iya'yį ną ak'e' to'k'i iya'ya t'ąį'śni ke'ᵉ. 7. Ak'e' wąźi' yeśi' c'ąke' iya'ya c'a hake'la kį ece'la e'na yąka' ke'ᵉ. 8. Yųk'ą' wana' hehą'yą site'hla kį ap'e'kapį ną p'ip'i'ya-iyų'ka c'ąke' k'oki'p'į ną heya' ke'ᵉ, — Hake'la, c'įkś, nic'i'ye owi'c'ale-ya'; tok'a'ś nų'nipi se'ce, — eya' c'ąke' i'ś-'eya' iya'ya ke'ᵉ. 9. He'c'el iyu'ha ig.lu'sol-wic'ayela ną hehą'l ųg.na' a'kab.lab.lagį² ną — Ho', he'l hpa'yahą ye'. Tuwe' c'a he' wo'nicihįkta he'cįhą! — eyį' ną i'ś-'eya' tok'i'yot'ą iya'ya c'ąke' zuze'ca wą wo'kihąpiktaic'ila k'ų tąye'la g.na'yąpi śk'e'ᵉ. 10. Hehą'yela owi'hąke'ᵉ.

so / I will cook for him. 4. Kettle / to borrow-go." / she said / so / at once / her eldest child / evidently (the eldest) / a / flying / he went. / His first flight then / but / at least / rather well-he went. 5. Long time-he returned not / so / meantime / meadowlark-little woman / the / for no purpose-she was talking / and / some time later / and then / "Well / kettle-borrowing he went / a / how indeed / long he returns not!" / she said / and / her second child / the / his elder brother / to find-she ordered him. 6. So / that one / he / too / he went / and / again / where / he went / it was not clear. 7. Again / one / she sent / so / he went / so / Hakela (Lastborn) / the / alone / at home / he sat. 8. And then / rattler / the / tired of waiting / and / again and again-he settled down, lying position / so / she feared and / said, / "Lastborn / son / your brothers / to find them-go. It may be / they lost their way / perhaps" / she said / so / he / too / went away. 9. Thus / all / she caused them to eliminate themselves and / then / without warning / she spread her wings / and / "There! / in that place / be lying. / Whoever / such / that one / will cook for you / if then!" / she said / and / she / too / off somewhere / she went away / so / snake / a / they will cook for him-he thought himself / the-past / thoroughly / they tricked him. 10. There / it ends.

Free Translation.

1. Where the tall prairie grass grew thickly a little meadowlark had her nest. 2. Though they were now quite grown, her children had not yet had their flying tests when, without warning, a snake came in and lay down, circling the nest. 3. The bird's heart beat in fear. But, as if not disturbed, she was pleasant to him and, "Well,

---

¹ *na,* is used by women, in giving a mild order; as one would to a child, without saying please, and yet indicating by the tone that no sternness is implied.

² *a,* I think, refers here to the armpits; or the underparts of the wings.

Eldest-Born, here is your uncle who never did pay us a visit before; I want to cook him a meal. 4. Go and borrow a kettle," she said; so the one who was evidently the eldest, flew away. His first flight, he started off very well. 5. As he didn't return for a long time, the meadowlark woman talked small talk for a time and then, "The idea! Where is that kettle-borrower that he stays so long ?" she said; and sent her next child to find his brother. 6. He too went off and stayed away. 7. Again she sent the next in order, leaving only Hakela, the last-born. 8. But by now the rattler was evidently restless, for he changed his position repeatedly; so she feared him, and said, "Hakela, you will have to go and find your brothers; it is possible that they have lost their way;" so he too went off. 9. In that way she sent away all her children; and then all of a sudden she spread her wings, and calling out, "There, keep on waiting; whoever you are expecting to cook you a meal!" off she flew; so the snake, trusting to be honored with a feast, was completely tricked. 10. That is all.

15. Boy-Beloved's Blanket.

1. K'oška'laka wą li'la t'eħi'lapi yųk'ą' he' šina' wą waśte' tąye'ħcį ipa't'api c'a į' ną li'la aho'p'eya¹ wąka'l ece'-otke'kiya šk'e'ᵉ. 2. Yųk'ą' hąhe'pi hą'l tuwa' manu'-eyaya c'ąke' ihi'hąna yųk'ą' ta'kuni otke'śni ki ų' k'oška'laka k'ų c'ąte' ši'ca ke'ᵉ. 3. He'c'ena oki'le-iya'yį ną ya'hą yųk'ą' ig.mų'-t'ąka wą k'uśe'ya na'žį ną, — To'k'iya la' huwo', t'ako'ža? Lec'a'la le'l og.na' nit'a'śina wą ak'i'yag.lape lo'. He' oki'le-la² he'cįhą. 4. K'e'yaš t'ako'ža, ta'ku to'k'a kįhą ana'makitą³ yo', — eya' ke'ᵉ. 5. Hetą'hą ya'hą yųką' hehą'l ptehį'cicila wą ka'l

Literal Translation.

1. Youth / a / very / they loved him / and / that one / blanket / a / fine / perfectly / they embroidered it with quills / such / he wore about his shoulders / and / very / with due respect / up / always he hung his own. 2. And / night / during / someone / stole it away / so / next morning / and / nothing / it hung not / the / therefore / youth / the-past / heart / bad. 3. Immediately / to seek his-he went away / and / was going / when / cat-big / a / in his way / he stood / and / "Whither / you go / grandson ? / Recently / here / through / your blanket / a / they took it home. / That one / you are going after your own / if-then. 4. But / grandson / something / happens / the-then / run to me-yours," / he said. 5. From there / he was going / and then / next / ptehį'cicila / a / yonder / he was sitting / so / to it / he arrived. /

---

¹ aho'p'a, to respect; honor; reverence, be courteous to; a, on.
² la, thou goest.
³ ana'makitą yo', run to me-thine; a, to; natą', to charge; run towards, as in battle; ma, me; ki, dative.

*yąka'hą c'a e'l i' ke'ᵉ. Wat'eślake¹ wą sa'pa c'a p'o'śtą na'żį ną aki'ś'-
ahą ke'ᵉ. 6. I'c'imani k'ų e'l i'laka² c'ą' aya'śtą iye'yį ną heya' ke'ᵉ:
— T'ako`ża, śina' oki'le-le cį e'l ta'ku to'k'a hą'tąhąś ana'makitą yo',
— eya' ke'ᵉ. 7. Ak'e' t'at'ą'ka wą e'l i' yųk'ą' i'ś-'eya' heya' ke'ᵉ: —
T'ako`ża, ta'ku to'k'a kįhą ana'makitą yo', — eya' ke'ᵉ. 8. He'c'eś
wana' ya'hą yųk'ą' c'ąma'hel t'i'pi wą hą' c'a e'l i' ke'ᵉ. O'kśątąhą
c'ąku' kį ok'o'sk'osyela³ yųka' c'a e'l c'ąp'a'ksa⁴-ic'ic'agį ną na'żį
yųk'ą' wik'o'śkalaka wą t'aśi'na k'ų he' į'⁵ ną hina'p'į ną t'e'hą-
ayu`ta na'żį ke'ᵉ. 9. — Tų'hįnaś ka' ka'l he'śni k'ų̇—eya'ya na'żį ną
t'ima' k'ig.la' ke'ᵉ. 10. He'c'ena ak'e' k'ośka'laka k'ų iya'yį ną
c'ąo'kpą-pųpų` kį he'c'a-ic'ic'agį ną iyų'ka ke'ᵉ. 11. C'ąke' ak'e'
hina'p'į ną t'e'hąȟcį'-ayu`ta na'żįhį ną he'c'ena ak'o'ketkiya ya'
tk'a'ś na'żį hiya'yį ną ila'zata hiyu' ną śina' k'ų he' k'i'kta c'a
o'k'iza ke'ᵉ. 12. Gahe' s'e howa'ya tk'a'ś yuślo'k k'i' ną g.log.li'yaku
yųk'ą' t'at'ą'ka-g.naśkįyą wą to'hą kį hihų'ni nų t'ąi'śniyą pą'pi ece'*

Kerchief / a / black / such / wearing as headgear / he stood / and /
he was giving warcries. 6. Traveller / the-past / there / *i'laka c'ą'* —
(the instant he arrived) / stopping / he went / and / said: / "Grandson / blanket / to seek yours-you go / the / in / something / happens /
if-then / run back to me-yours" / he said. 7. Again / buffalo-bull /
a / at / he arrived / and so / he too / he said: / "Grandson / something / it happens / the-then / run to me-yours" / he said. 8. Thus /
now / he was going / when / in the wood / tipi / a / it stood / such /
at / he arrived. / From all directions / paths / the / worn hard and
smooth / they lay / so / there / tree stump-he made himself / and /
stood / and lo / young woman / a / his robe / the-past / that one / she
wore as a blanket / and / came out / and / long-looking at him / she
stood. 9. "Indeed never / that / there / it stood not / the-past" /
saying / she stood / and / indoors / she went back. 10. Immediately /
again / young man / the-past / he went / and / chip-rotted with age /
the / that sort-he made himself / and / lay down. 11. So / again /
she came out / and / very long / looking at him / she stood / and /
then / in the opposite direction (from him) / she went / but / to
stand / he went / and / behind her / he came / and / blanket / the-
past / that one / he was about to snatch from her / so / she fought
him over it. 12. Harsh grating cry / like / she howled / but / snatching it from her / he took it away / and / started back with his own /
and then / buffalo-crazy / a / at what time / the / he will arrive /
nų — (not definite) / in a manner not clear / shouting / only / he
did / so / meantime / very / he came on / and / now / small bird /

¹ *wat'e'ślake*, a crown, fillet; *t'eśla'ka*, to wear around the head.
² *laka* is an enclitic, which, added to any active verb means, "the instant he
　did so and so" Always followed by *c'ą*, then.
³ From *k'o'za*, smooth, worn down hard.
⁴ *c'ą*, tree; *p'a*, head; *ksa*, broken off; hence, *c'ąp'a'ksa*, a stump.
　į, to wear around the shoulders, like a blanket; *hįmį'*, I wear as a blanket;
　hįnį', thou wearest; *į*, he wears; *ųk'į'*, we two wear.

6*

*ec'ų́ c'ąke' k'ohą́ li'la ku' ną wana' ptehį́'cicila k'ų he' ana'kitą ną —
T'ų́ka`sila, ta'ku wą makte'kte¹ lo', — eya' c'ąke' g.lakį́'kįyą kįyą́ ų́
c'a oȟla't'e iya'ya c'ąke' ta'ku kį e'l u' tk'a'š iye' kic'i' ec'ų́ c'a k'ohą́
k'oška'laka k'ų li'la t'e'hąl g.lihų́'ni šk'e'ᵉ. Ak'e' wana' ptehį́'cicila
k'ų to'k'ešk'e yug.na'yelak'a ahi'kig.legį̇́kta c'ąke' nihį́'ciya ku' ną
ig.mu'-t'ą̀ka k'ų he' to'k'i ye'ca nų tk'a'² k'uše'ya ų́ c'ąke' oȟla't'e
g.licu' ną — T'ų́kašila, ta'ku wą makte'kte lo', — eya' c'ąke' he' i'š
hehą́'l t'e'hą kic'i' ec'ų́ šk'e'ᵉ. 13. T'e'hą k'ųhą́ wana' ak'e' ig.mu'-
t'ą̀ka k'ų yug.na'yelak'a kig.le'ȟ-kinil au' c'ąke' ec'ą́l t'at'ą́ka k'ų
he' k'uše'ya na'žį c'a e'l kaslo'hą g.liȟpa'yį ną — T'ų́ka`sila, ta'ku
wą makte'kte lo', — eya' c'ąke' k'uše'ya g.lo'g.lo ų́ ną wana' hihų́'ni
tk'a'š kic'i' ec'ų́ ke'ᵉ. 14. Wį́'yeya na'žį hųše k'iye'la u' k'ų héhą'ni
našlo'k itko'p iya'yį ną t'at'ą́'ka-g.naškį̀'ye c'ų t'ezi'-yuȟle'l iye'ya
c'ąke' t'a šk'e'ᵉ. 15. C'ąke' t'at'ą́'ka wą o'kiye c'ų he'na ta'ku wo'yuha
wašte'šte, mak'a'-t'o, šina'luta k'oko k'u ną hetą́ oya'te t'i'pi kį
ekta' g.li' šk'e'ᵉ. 16. Yųk'ą́ hų́'ku ną atku'ku kį nup'į́ c'e'yapi
c'ų́ išta'g̣ųg̣api ną i'yak'ak'ayela kašla'pi³ ną ų'šiyeȟcį c'ąte' šilya'*

the-past / that one / he ran to, as his own / and / "Grandfather, /
something / a / he will kill me!" / he said / so / to and fro across /
flying / he continued to be / so / underneath / he went / so / thing /
the / at him / it came / but indeed / he / with him / did / so / meanwhile / youth / the-past / very / far / he got on his way home (this
way). Again / now / small bird / the-past / somehow / he must have
missed him for / he was almost catching up with him / so / in terror /
he came on / and / cat-big / the-past / that one / where / to go /
doubtful / but / in the way / he was / so / under him / he came on /
and / "Grandfather / something / a / he will kill me" / he said / so /
that one / he / next / long while / with / he did (struggled). 13. Far /
he got on his way / the-past-then / now / again / cat-big / the-past /
he must have let him slip for / overtaking him-almost / he came on /
so / just then / bull / the-past / that one / in the way / he stood / so /
at him / sliding in / he fell / and / "Grandfather / something / a / he
will kill me" / he said / so / blocking the way / grunting / he came /
and / now / he arrived / but / with him / he did. 14. In readiness /
he stood / evidently for / near / he came / the-past / even then /
rushing forth / meeting him / he went / and / buffalo-bull crazy /
the-past / stomach-tearing open / he sent it / so / it died. 15. So /
buffalo-bull / a / he aided him / the-past / right there / things /
possessions / fine ones / blue-earth / robes scarlet / also / he gave
him / and / from there / tribe / they lived / the / to / he returned.
16. And / his mother / and / his father / the / both / they cried / on
account of / they were blinded / and / very closely / they shaved

---

¹ *makte'kte; ma*, me; *kte*, he kills; *kta*, will, he is about to kill me.
² This construction, verb plus *ka* (or *ca*); and then *nų* and *tk'a*, means, "to
be puzzled about what to do, what to say, where to go, etc."
³ *kašla'*, to cut the hair. *ka*, instrumental; *šla*, bare of growth (hair is understood).

yąka'pi hą'l e'l g.li' ke'ᵉ. 17. C'ąke' maǵa'žu-m.ni ista' ki owi'c'akica-štąhį̨ ną ų' ista' wic'a'kiciyužažahą c'ąke' tųwą'pi śk'e'ᵉ. 18. Nakų' p'a' ki a'l-'ataya slawi'c'akicic'iyį ną wic'a'kicicakca c'ą kahą'skeya ece'-wic'a'kicicasto c'ąke' p'ehį' ki hą'skeskeya e'wic'akiciyustą ną hehą'l ak'e' ehą'ni k'ų he'hą' s'e p'ehį' ki hą'skeskeya wic'a'kicisų ną ista' ki k'o' wable'sye-wic'a'kaǵa śk'e'ᵉ. 19. Hehą'yela owi'hąke'ᵉ.

their heads / and / pitifully / heart / badly / they sat / when / he got home. 17. So / rain-water / eyes / the / he kept pouring in for them / and / with / eyes / he kept washing for them / so / they could see. 18. Also / heads / the / all over in both cases / he caused to be oiled for them / and / he combed their hair / whenever / with a flowing stroke / always he brushed (the hair) for them; / so / hair / the / long-ly / he finished it for them / and / then / again / long ago / the-past / then / like / hair / the / long-ly / he braided for them / and / eyes / the / also / to see clearly he made them / it is said. 19. There / it ends.

Free Translation.

1. Once there lived a young man who was beloved of his parents. They gave him beautiful things, among them a handsome robe. This he treasured so highly that he always kept it carefully hung up on the side of the tipi. 2. One morning it was plain that during the night someone had stolen this robe, for it was gone; the young man was therefore very sad. 3. He started out to find it and soon a wild cat stood in his path. "Where are you going, my grandchild?" it asked the young man. "Perhaps you are going to find your robe which was carried past here. 4. If anything evil befalls you, just run to me, your grandfather!" he said. 5. The boy continued on his way until he met a little buffalo bird on the road. This little bird[1] was standing with his head bound in a black fillet; he was shouting. 6. The instant the traveler reached him, he stopped shouting and said to him, "Grandchild, on this journey in search of your blanket, should danger threaten, make for me at once." 7. Then the boy came to a place were a buffalo-bull was standing in his way. This buffalo-bull also gave him the same promise of protection. So the boy said, "All right." 8. He continued his journey until he reached a tipi in a deep wood. Paths leading there from all directions were worn down smooth and hard. So the boy changed himself into a tree stump, and stood near by. Soon a young woman came out, and she was wearing his lost robe. She left the tipi, and stood staring at the stump, thinking seriously. 9. "Why, that tree stump was never there before, was it?" she said to herself, perplexed; and then she went indoors. 10. Immediately then the young man ran and

---

[1] This little bird has a black spot on the head. It is very tiny and used to ride on the buffaloes. I do not know its English name.

changed himself into a piece of rotted chip and lay down again.
11. Once again, the young woman came outside and stood looking at
the tree bark, and then she started to walk away in the opposite
direction from him. The minute her back was turned, he ran up
behind her and struggled with her over the blanket. 12. In spite of
her screaming and yelling, the young man snatched his blanket
out of her grasp, and began to run; and he heard behind him the
raging utterances of the Mad Bull[1], growling and snorting. But for
all those threatening sounds, the Mad Bull did not catch up with
him at once. So for a long time he ran, until he came to the little
buffalo bird and said to him, "O, Grandfather, help me! there is
something after me to kill me!" The bird flew in readiness, to and
fro across the road, so the young man ducked under him and came
on, leaving the bird, with the confidence that it would protect him.
Meantime, he continued running, farther away all the time, and had
covered considerable distance when the buffalo bird must have
allowed the bull to slip past by accident, for the mad bull was again
hot on his trail. The boy barely reached the wild cat, and called to
him, "Grandfather, help! Something is about to kill me!" Then he
came on, but the wild cat was prepared, so when the crazy bull came
by, he detained him by fighting him for some time. 13. But after
the boy had travelled some more, the crazy bull was on him again.
Evidently the wild cat had not been able to hold him back any longer.
Fortunately, he was even then reaching the buffalo which had
promised to protect him. When the young man was reaching him, he
slid to the ground at his feet, crying, "Grandfather, there is something after me to kill me; help me!" So the buffalo-bull fought him
there. 14. He must have been all set to fight, for the moment the
crazy bull arrived, he rushed madly at him, and in a terrible struggle,
tore open his belly; and so killed him. 15. Then and there, the
young man made offerings to the bull which had saved his life by
winning against his enemy. They were such fine things as blue-
earth, red and blue flannels, and so forth. Then he went home to the
camp of his tribe. 16. But when he arrived there, he found that his
father and mother were both blind from weeping for him; and that
they were in such deep mourning for him that their hair was cropped
closed to their heads, and that they sat looking very forlorn with
their great sorrow. 17. So he poured rain water into their eyes, and
washed their eyes with it until they were able to see. 18. Then he
anointed their hair with oil. And whenever he combed their hair for
them, he always employed very long strokes, which caused the
hair to grow long and longer; and then, once again with their eyes
healed and their hair beautifully long, they lived as of old.
19. That is all.

---

[1] The Mad Buffalo-bull is a bad spirit.

16. Stone-Boy.

1. *K'oška'laka t'o'p t'i'pi yųk'ą' Hake'la c'ą' icu'kta c'a ina'p'į ną
i't'ap ak'e' t'i'l g.licu' ną wį'yą wą t'ąka'l na'žįhą ke'ya' šk'e'°. 2. —
Taku'ųyąpikta huwo'?* — *eya' c'ąke', — T'ąke'ųyąpikte lo', t'ima'hel
kic'o' wo', — eya'pi c'ąke' Hake'la ina'p'į ną, — T'ąke', t'ima'hel u'
wo', — eya' šk'e'°. 3. Tąyą'š c'e'kiye šą' ayu'ptešni ini'lahcį t'ima'hel
hiyu' ną he'na o'p t'i' šk'e'°. 4. Wana' k'oška'laka kį oma'ni-ya'pikta
c'ąke' — Hake'la, awą'yaka yo' — eya'pi ną iya'yapi šk'e'°. 5. Hake'la
he'c'ena ški'bibila-ic'ic'ągį ną t'ic'e'-įkpa kį ekta' yąka' šk'e'°.
6. Yųk'ą' wana' t'e'hąl iya'yapi ke'c'į' kį lehą'l wį'yą k'u he' šina' wą
a'taya wic'a'p'aha kšu'pi c'a g.lub.la'yį ną, — Hake'la p'ehi' šikši'-
cela k'e'yaš huha' k'e'l e'cuhcį iyo'wapat'įkte, — eya' šk'e'°. 7. Heya'-
nah'u' kį he'c'ena c'iye'ku kį e'owic'akiyaka c'ąke' g.li'pi ną wi'k'ą wą
lolo'pyapi ną — Ho, t'ąke', c'ąk'į'-ya yo', — eya'pi šk'e'°. 8. C'ąke'
wį'yą k'u c'ąk'į'-i ną wana' ka'k'el-g.liyahpeyįkta c'ą' iye'na wį'k'ą
kį kapsa'kahą c'ąke' t'e'hą-g.lišni šk'e'°. 9. Ec'e'l wak'į' yuha' k'u
iyu'ha oi'leyapi ną naki'p'api šk'e'°. 10. Wį'yą k'u t'iya'takiya
e'tųwą yų.k'ą' li'la izi'ta c'ąke' šo'ta kį wąya'kį ną g.licu' ną, —*

Literal Translation.

1. Young men / four / they lived / and / Last-born (Hakela) / wood /
to take / therefore / he went out / and / at once / again / indoors / he
returned / and / woman / a / outside / she was standing / he said.
2. "What relation shall we have her for?" / he said / so / "She shall
be our elder sister. / Indoors / invite her" / they said / so / Hakela /
went out / and / "My elder sister, / indoors / come" / he said.
3. Correctly indeed / he addressed her / yet / she replied not; / very
silently / inside / she came / and / there / with them / she lived.
4. Now / young men / the / to walk abroad-they will go / so / "Hakela / guard her" / they said and / they went. 5. Hakela / at once /
ški'bibila (a kind of bird) -he made himself / and / top of tipi-point /
the / there / he sat. 6. And then / now / far / they went / she thought /
the / at this point / woman / the-past / that one / robe / a / entirely /
human hair / they appliqued it / such / she spread out hers / and /
"Hakela / hair / poor quality / yet / limbs / the-in / at least / I will
piece mine out with it" / she said. 7. That she said / he heard / the /
at once / his elder brothers / the / going to them he told. / So / they
returned / and / rope / a / they oiled till tender / and / "There /
elder sister / to get firewood-go" / they said. 8. So / woman / the-
past / to get wood-she went / and / now / that instant she is about
to throw it onto herself / then / each time / rope / the / it kept
breaking / so / long time-she returned not. 9. Thus until / personal
belongings / she had / the-past / all / they set on fire / and / ran
away. 10. Woman / the / homeward / she looked / and lo / very / it
smoked / so / smoke / the / she saw / and / came home / and /

*Waḣte'śni kȋ, t'eḣi'ya oma'yakiḣ'ape'+. To'k'iya la'pikta he'+? —
eya'ya wic'a'k'uwa śk'e'ᵉ. 11. Heyȋ' ną p'e'ta kȋ e'l yuġa'lǵal iye'yȋ
ną ma'za-waha'c'ąka wą e' ną mas-ʼi'hųnicat'a wą he'c'el iki'kcu ną
wic'a'k'uwa c'ąke' li'la ȋ'yąkapi kȋ ų' t'em.ni't'api¹ śk'e'ᵉ. 12. T'oka'-
p'a kȋ, — Misų`, iya'ya po'. Miye' wana' owa'kihiśni ye lo', — eyȋ'
ną e'na k'ina'żȋ śk'e'ᵉ. 13. Wąhȋ'kpe o'ta yuha' c'ąke' ų' he'ktakiya
wȋ'yą kȋ o'takiya o' k'e'yaś a'tayaś i'tok'aśni śk'e'ᵉ. 14. He'c'ena u'
ną p'a' kaksa' awi'c'au ną o'wec'ȋhą wic'a'kte ną eha'ke Hake'la
oka'pta hą'l śki'bibila-ic'ic'aǵȋ ną kȋyą' iya'yȋ ną c'ąwą'kal i'yotaka
śk'e'ᵉ. 15. Yųk'ą' oḣla't'e wȋ'yą k'ų hina'żȋ ną kat'a'pt'apa śk'e'ᵉ.
16. Ec'ą'l ųkce'k'iḣa wą iyo'pteya iya'ya c'ąke' e'l e'tųwą tk'a'ś
Hake'la wi'woṡtake² wą iki'kcu ną iyu'żipa-p'aki`ḣte cȋ e'tulaḣcȋ
k'ute' yųk'ą' yuc'ą'c'ąpi s'e yȋ' ną e'l ihe'yȋ ną kte' śk'e'ᵉ. 17. Hehą'l
Hake'la g.liyo'psicȋ ną mas-i'hųnicat'a wą ų' p'a' wic'a'kaksaksa k'ų
he e' c'a icu' ną ų' c'e'yaya i'ś eha'kela wȋ'yą k'ų kaḣu'ḣuġa śk'e'ᵉ.
18. He'c'ų ną hehą'l t'eki'nil ȋ'yą t'okṡu' ną ini'kaǵȋ ną c'iye'ku kȋ
e'l e't'owic'akṡu śk'e'ᵉ. 19. Yųk'ą' i'yec'ala t'ima' tuwa' c'uwi' oki'niya*

"Worthless ones / the / dreadfully / you have done unto me. /
Where / will you go?" / saying it / she chased them. 11. She said
that / and / fire / the / into / she reached / and / iron-shield / a / it
was / and / iron hatchet / a / such / she took hers / and / pursued
them / so / very / they ran / the / on account of / they were exhausted
/ they say. 12. Eldest / the / "My younger brothers / do you run on. /
As for me / now / I can not" / he said / and / right there / he stopped.
13. Arrows / plenty / he had / therefore / with / backwards / woman /
the / in many places / he shot / but / at all / it made no effect on her.
14. Straightway / she came / and / head / cutting off by striking /
she came on them / and / in line / she killed them / and / last /
Hakela / she had remaining / when / śkibibila-he made himself /
and / flying / he went / and / up-tree / he sat. 15. And then /
underneath / woman / the-past / coming she stood / and / snapped
her fingers in the sign of contempt. 16. Just then / magpie / a / past /
it went / so / at it / she looked / but / Hakela / blunt arrow / a / he
took out his own / and / forelock-tied / the / right there / he shot /
and lo! / quivering / like / it went / and / there / it struck / and /
killed her. 17. Then / Hakela / he jumped down / and / iron-hatchet /
a / with / heads / she chopped theirs / the-past / that it was / such /
he took up / and / with it / weeping / he / last in turn / woman / the /
he broke into bits by striking. 18. He did that / and / then / nearly
dead / rocks / he hauled / and / made a sweatbath / and / his elder
brothers / the / there / he took them all. 19. And then / soon after /
inside / someone / c'uwi' — trunk; oki'niya — to breath into one's
own (i. e., to heave a deep sigh) / and / "This one / who you are /

---

¹ t'em.ni', to perspire; t'a, to die. An idiom, meaning to be worn out from
bodily exertion.
² This is sometimes called mi'woṡtake.

*ną — Le' nitu'we c'a wau̜'śiyala he'cįhą maki'yuǧą yo', — eya' c'ąke'
yuǧą' ną c'iye'ku kį iyu'ha t'iya'ta wic'a'g.lok'i śk'e'ᵉ.
20. Tąyą' u̜'pi yuk'ą' ak'e' wį'yą wą t'ąka'l hina'źį śk'e'ᵉ. 21. Ak'e'
t'ima' kic'o'pi ną ak'e' he' t'ąke'yapikta ke'ya'pi śk'e'ᵉ. 22. — Ho,
Hake'la, t'ima'hel kic'o' wo', — eya'pi c'ąke' ina'p'į ną, — T'ąke',
t'ima' u' wo', — eya' yuk'ą', — Hą', misu̜', — eyį' ną t'ima' hi'
śk'e'ᵉ. 23. Nake'ś he' wį'yą kį li'la waśte' c'ąke' tąyą' o'p u̜' śk'e'ᵉ.
24. Wo'wic'akihį nąśna o'p wo'tį ną wą'źu nąi'ś hą'pa k'o' wic'a'kicagį
ną waka'ħ-wo'hitika śk'e'ᵉ. 25. He'c'el u̜'pi yuk'ą' suka'ku kį oma'ni-
iya'yapi ną t'e'hą-g.lipiśni c'ąke' hąke'ya c'e'ya oma'nihą śk'e'ᵉ.
26. Yuk'ą' į'yą-źąźą'la wą iye'ya c'ąke' iyo'g.nak u̜'hą yuk'ą' oya'ślok
iye'yį ną napca' śk'e'ᵉ. Yuk'ą' hokśi'la wą yuha' c'ąke' t'ąka'l kaħ'o'l
iye'ya yuk'ą' t'ima' į'yąkyąk g.licu' c'a ak'e' ini'hąśni kaħ'o'l iye'ya
yuk'ą' nau̜'kce¹ wą t'ima' g.licu' k'e'yaś ak'e' kaħ'o'l iye'yikta tk'a'ś
hehą'yą yuha'śni² śk'e'ᵉ. 27. K'e'yaś tok'e'cela t'ąka'l iye'ya yuk'ą'
hehą'yą k'ośka'laka wą t'ima'hel g.licu' c'ąke', — T'u̜kį'³ mic'į'kśi*

such / you have pity / if-then / hurry on my account" / it said / so /
he opened / and / his elder brothers / the / all / back home / he brought
back his own.

20. Happily / they lived / and then / again / woman / a / outdoors /
she came and stood. 21. Again / inside / they invited her / and /
again / that one / they would have for an elder sister / they said.
22. "All right / Hakela / inside / invite her" / they said / so / he
went out / and / "My elder sister / indoors / come" / he said / and /
"Very well, / my younger brother" / she said / and / inside / she
arrived. 23. Really this time / that one / woman / the / very / good /
so / pleasantly / with them / she stayed. 24. She would cook for them /
and / with them / ate / and / quiver / or else / moccasins / also / she
made for them / and / to make things-very skilled (she was). 25. In
that way / they lived / and then / her younger brothers / the / to
roam abroad-they went away / and / long time / they returned not ⁱ
so / after a time / weeping / she walked about. 26. And then / stone-
little transparent one / a / she found it / so / placed in the mouth /
she continued to be / and lo! / slipping in by means of the mouth /
she did suddenly / and / swallowed it /. Then / as a result / boy / a /
she had / so / outdoors / tossing / she sent him / and lo! / indoors /
running / he came back / so / again / disregarding that / outdoors /
tossing / she sent him / and lo! / youth / a / indoors / he came back /
but / again / tossing / she would send him / but / from then on / she
held him not. 27. Nevertheless, / barely / outdoors / she sent him /
and lo! / from then on / young man / a / indoors / he returned / so /

---

¹ A rather coarse name for young boys in the early and self-conscious stage
of young manhood; before they acquire dignity. Colloquial; confined to
only some of the Tetons. Its use is now dying out, since boys do not ride
as constantly as before.

² *Yuha'śni*, he can not have it; i. e., it is too heavy for him.

³ *t'u̜ki'* and *tok'i'* are used indifferently, to mean "*would that*," in making a
wish.

ka'k'el yuha' nį', — eya' c'ą ak'e' ec'e'l yuha' šk'e'ᵉ. 28. He'c'eš Į'yą-
hoksi'la hų'ku kic'i' t'i' yųk'ą' ąpe'tu wą e'l heya' šk'e'ᵉ: — Ina`,
to'k'a c'a le' ųki'šnalaĥcį ųt'i' huwo'? — eya' šk'e'ᵉ. 29. C'ąke' wį'yą
k'ų leya' šk'e'ᵉ: — Nile'kši o'p le'l wat'i' k'e'yaš oma'ni-iya`yapi ną
g.li'pišni c'a le' ųki'šnala ųyą'ke', — eya' šk'e'ᵉ. 30. — It'o' ina`,
leksi' ekta' wic'a'm.nįkte lo', — eya' c'ąke' c'e'ya g.loni'ca¹ k'e'yaš
ini'hąšni iya'ya šk'e'ᵉ. 31. Ka'k'ena ya'hą yųk'ą' wizi' wą hą' c'a e'l
ya' yųk'ą' etą'hą winų'ĥcala wą hina'p'į ną — T'ako`ža, t'o'wa'š
t'uc'u'hu ona'miciĥuĥugi ye'. Iyeš nile'kši le' t'uc'u'hu² ona'miciĥu-
ĥugapi nąšna iya'yape, — eya' šk'e'ᵉ. 32. — Waĥte'šni kį, le e' c'a
leksi' wic'a'kte se'ce lô, — ec'į' ną, — Ho, iyų'ka yo', — eya' c'ąke'
k'u'l iyų'ka tk'a'š į'yą c'ąke' tkeye'la naĥu'ĥuga c'a nake',³ — T'ako-
ža', eya'š hena'la ye', — eye' c'e'yaš hehą'l iyo'tą li'lala naĥu'gį ną
nat'a' šk'e'ᵉ. 33. He'c'ų ną t'ima' i' yųk'ą' leksi'tku kį t'iwo'kšą
wic'a'ųpa c'ąke' ini'kagį ną į'yą kį m.ni' aka'štąhą yųk'ą' c'uwi'
oki'niyapi ną, — Le' nitu'we c'a waų'šiyala he'cįhą k'oya'makiĥ'ą
yo', — eya'pi c'ąke' iwi'c'akikcu ną li'la o'p c'ąte' wašte' šk'e'ᵉ.

"Would that / my son / in such a way / he possessed / would that!" /
she said / then / again / accordingly / he had it. 28. Thus / Stone-
Boy / his mother / with / he lived / and then / day / a / on / he said : /
"My mother / why / such / this / we two alone / we live ?" 29. So /
woman / the / said this : / "Your uncles / with / here / I lived / but /
to roam abroad-they went / and / returned not / so / this / we two
alone / we sit" / she said. 30. "I think / my mother / to / them-I
will go" / he said / so / weeping / she withheld her own / but /
disregarding it / he went. 31. Off in yonder direction / he was going /
and lo! / smoke-tanned tipi / a /it stood / such / to / he went / and
then / old woman / a / she came out / and / "Grandchild̥/ a little
while first / ribs / by treading break them for me. They / your
uncles / this / ribs / by treading they broke them for me / and then
regularly / they went" / she said. 32. "Worthless one / the! / this
one / it is / such / my uncles / them-killed / perhaps" / he thought /
and / "All right / lie down" / he said / so / down / she lay / but
indeed / stone / so / heavily / he broke her (ribs) by treading / so /
at last / "Grandchild / enough / that is all" / she said / but / then /
more / very hard / he broke her with his feet / and / killed her by
stepping on. 33. He did so / and / indoors / he went / and lo / his
uncles / the / around the room / she had them lying / so / he made a
sweatlodge / and / stones / the / water / he continued pouring on /
and lo! / they breathed deeply / and / "That one / who you are /
such / you have pity / if-then / hurry for me" / they said / so / he
took out his own / and / very / with them / heart / good. 34. His

---

¹ g.loni'ca, to refuse to give up one's own. From ani'ca, to dispute over.
² t'uc'u'hu or c'ut'u'hu; both used. But the latter generally, when t'a, ruminant, is prefixed. Never t'at'u'cuhu.
³ nake', at last (why not sooner ? why all the delay ?)

*34. Lekśi'tku kį t'iya'ta o'p k'i' c'ąke' hų'ku k'ų sųka'ku wąwi'c'a-
g.lakį ną li'la wi'yuśkį śk'e'e.*
*35. I'tohątuka yųk'ą' leya' śk'e'e: — It'o' mi'ś hehą'l oma'wanikte
lo', — eyį' ną ka'k'ena ya'hą yųk'ą' ptesą'-wik'o'śkalaka k'eya'
o'slohąkic'ųhąpi c'ąke' e'l i' śk'e'e. To'papi śk'e'e. 36. K'e'yaś t'o'wa'ś
e'l i'śnihąni paha'-ai`nap iya'yį ną hokśi'la-ų`śikaic'ic'agį ną hehą'l
e'l i' śk'e'e. 37. Yųk'ą', — Hiyu', Hokśi`la, le' o'slohąųkic'ųpi c'a
o'yap'akte', — eya'pi śk'e'e. 38. Yųk'ą', — Į'+!*[1] *Nitke'pi c'a
og.mi'g.ma nihi'yupi kįhą maya'pat'apikte kįś*[2], *— eya' c'ąke', —
E'ca he'ktatąhą nakį'kte, — eya'pi c'ąke' — Ohą', — eya' śk'e'e.
39. He'c'eś he'ktatąhą yąke'k'iyapi ną iya'yapi yųk'ą' iye' į'yą c'ąke'
og.mi'g.ma hiyu'ic'iyį ną iyu'ha wic'a'kte ną ha' iwi'c'acu ną ag.li'
c'ąke' lekśi'tku kį wą'źuyapi śk'e'e. 40. Ak'e' oma'ni-ya yųk'ą'
t'at'ą'ka-wic'a'ћcala wą hekpa'mahą c'a e'l i' ną — T'ųka`śila,
to'k'eśk'e heya'kpamahą huwo'? — eya' śk'e'e. 41. — Wą, t'ako'źa,
le' Į'yą-hokśi`la hokśi'-c'ąlkiyapi to'p wic'a'kte c'a t'akpe'-ayįkta śk'a'
c'a t'uc'u'hute e'cuћcį' ec'į'c'įkel le' hewa'kpamahe lo', — eya' śk'e'e.
42. — T'ųka`śila, he' tohą'tu kį t'akpe'-ayįkta śk'a' huwo'? — eya'*

uncles / the / at their home / with them / he arrived / so / his mother /
the-past / her younger brothers / she saw them,-hers / and / very /
she was happy.
    35. Sometime later / and then / he said this / "I think /I / next /
I will roam abroad" / he said / and / off in yonder direction / he was
going / when lo / white buffalo-cow young women / some / they were
coasting downhill / so / there / he arrived. /They were four. 36. But /
first / there / he arrived-not then / hill-hidden by / he went / and /
boy-poor / he made himself / and / then / there / he arrived. 37. And /
"Come on / boy / this / we are coasting downhill / so / you shall
take part" / they said. 38. And so / "*Į!* (An expletive, indicative of
whining reluctance, as a child, holding back) / you are heavy / so /
rolling down / you come / the-then / you will crush me the-indeed!" /
he said / so / "In that case, / in the back / you shall sit" / they said /
so / "All right" / he said. 39. Thus / in the back / they caused him
to sit / and / they started off / and so / he himself / stone / so / rolling
down / he sent himself / and / all / he killed them / and / hides /
took them / and / brought them home / so / his uncles / the / they
used them for quivers. 40. Again / to travel-he was going / and lo! /
buffalo-old man / a / horns-he was polishing his own / so / there / he
arrived / and / "Grandfather / how is it / you are horn-polishing?" /
he said. 41. "Why / grandson / this / Stone-Boy / children-beloved /
four / he killed them / so / to attack him-they will go / it is said / so /
rib-end / at least / rather thinking it / this / horn-I polish mine" /
he said. 42. "Grandfather / that / what time / the / to attack him-
they will go / is it said?" / he said / and so / "When / clouds / brown-

---

[1] *į+,* said with a very long drawn-out tone, indicates reluctance. Used by
children, mostly, to show fear or inclination to pull back.
[2] *kįś,* generally concludes a statement of reluctance, started with *į.*

yųk'ą' — Tohą'l mahpi'ya ġiġi'ya kahwo'hwok ahi'yaye cį hehą'tukta šk'e' lo', — eya' šk'e'ᵉ. 43. Yųk'ą' — Wą, witko`, le' Į'yą-hokši`la miye' ye lo', — eyį' ną t'at'ą'ka-wic'a`hcala k'ų kte' ną g.li' ną — Lekši`, mahpi'ya ġiġi'ya kahwo'hwok¹ ahi'yaye cįhą t'akpe'-maupikta šk'e' lo', — eya' c'ąke' c'u'kaške o'hiye to'p c'ąka'škapi ną wana' mahpi'ya kį ġiġi'ya kahwo'hwok ahi'yaye c'ų hehą'l t'at'ąka-oya`te kį a'taya ahi'hųni šk'e'ᵉ. 44. C'ų'kaške-t'oka`heya k'ų he'l ahi'hųni k'e'yaš wic'a'ktepi ną Į'yą-hokši`la hų'ku i'š mi'la wą kiyu'mapi c'a ohla't'etąhą sihu'tk'ą wapsa'k awi'c'aya c'ąke' wana' wašte'ya c'ų'kaške kį o'hiye wążi'la ihe'yapi hcehą'l t'at'ą'ka-wic'a`hcala wą — Ho, heya'ta² g.liġ.la' po', Į'yą-hokši`la nica'sotapikte lo', — eya' c'ąke' ak'i'yag.la šk'e'ᵉ. 45. Hehą'yela owi'hąke'ᵉ.

ly / drifting in the wind / they go by / the / it will be then / it is said" / he said. 43. And then / "Look / you fool / this / Stone-Boy / I am" / he said / and / buffalo-old man / the-past / he killed / and / came home / and / "My uncles / clouds / brown-ly / drifting in the wind / they go by / the-then / to attack me-they will come / it is said" / he said. / So / fences / rows / four / they made fences / and / now / clouds / brown-ly / drifting in the wind / they went by / the / then / buffalo-tribe / the / all / they arrived. 44. Fence-first / the-past / there / they arrived / but / they killed them / and / Stone-Boy / his mother / as for her / knife / a / they sharpened for her / so / underneath from / foot-ligament / snapping apart by cutting / she came on them / so / now / really / fence / row / only one / they had left / just then / buffalo-bull old man / a / "Now, / towards the hills (i. e., away from the fray) / walk along back. / Stone-Boy / he will annihilate you" / he said / so / they all left. / There / it ends.

Free Translation.

1. Four young men lived together. One day, Hakela, (which means "The youngest brother") stepped out to get more firewood, but immediately he reëntered the tipi and said that there was a woman standing outside the door. 2. "How shall she be related to us?"³ he asked; so, "Let's have her for our elder sister. Call her in," they said. So Hakela once more stepped outside and said, "Elder sister, come in." 3. But although he had invited her thus, addressing her courteously, she entered without responding⁴; and there she lived with them. 4. The day came for the young men to walk abroad, so

---

¹ *kahwo'ka*, to be blown by the wind; 1st pers.; *maka'hwoka*.
² *he*, mountains; *yata*, towards; *heya'ta* always means "away from; back, as from the centre of activity."
³ The first thing they think of is a proper social kinship. A formal introduction in white people's etiquette is no more important than the deciding on a proper kinship term. Having that, one may address another, with propriety, among the Dakota; except those who come under the avoidance tabu.
⁴ She should have said, "Yes, my younger brother."

they left Hakela at home to keep an eye on things. 5. Immediately he turned himself into a little bird known as *ŝki'bibila* and flew up to the top of the tipi poles, where he sat watching the woman inside, through the smoke opening. 6. When the woman was certain that the men were far away, she opened out a blanket which she was working on, lining it entirely with human scalps. "Although Hakela's hair isn't so wonderful, it will do to piece out the limbs[1], at least," she said. 7. On hearing this, Hakela flew at once to his brothers and told them what he had heard. So they returned at once and boiled a rawhide rope until it was so tender that it would break very easily. They gave it to the woman, saying, "Elder sister, please go after firewood." 8. So she took the rope, and went out for firewood, but stayed away a very long time because it kept breaking each time she tried to lift a load of faggots onto her back. 9. So the brothers had time to set fire to all her things, and to run away. 10. The woman looked towards the tipi, and saw that the place was smoking and that great puffs of smoke were pouring out. So she ran home, screaming, "The scoundrels! What a dreadful thing you do to me! And where do you think you can go, in order to escape me?" Then she started to chase them. 11. She stopped to thrust her hand into the flames; and drew forth from her burning property an iron shield and an iron hatchet; and ran after the men until they were soon overcome with exhaustion. 12. The eldest stopped, finally. "Go on, my younger brothers, I can go no longer," he said. 13. Drawing out his many arrows he turned and shot at her in various places, as she approached, but he could not kill her. 14. On she came, cutting off the heads of the brothers in turn as she came to them, until Hakela alone was running. He turned into a *ŝki'bibila* again, and flew to the top of a tree. 15. The woman came on until she stopped under his tree, and looking up at him she abused him with angry words and snapped her fingers in hatred at him. 16. Just at that moment, a magpie was flying past her, and she turned to look at it; and while her attention was thus diverted, Hakela took his blunt arrow and aimed it at her forelock which was tied into a tight cluster; and shot an arrow which went vibrating towards that spot, and hit her there; causing her death. 17. Then he jumped back down, and taking the very hatchet which had killed his brothers, he ran weeping to the woman's body, and smashed the head to pieces. 18. Then he labored long to carry rocks, and made a sweat lodge and carried his brothers into it, one by one. 19. Soon after, he heard someone within, sighing deeply; and then, "Whoever you are who are thus kind, open the door for me!" So Hakela opened the door and took out his restored brothers, and they went home.

---

[1] In olden times all robes were of ruminant's hide, tanned and decorated, with designs in porcupine quill work or paint. The skin from the legs was included and decorated; and allowed to form part of the trimming.

20. Once again, the brothers lived in peaceful goodwill; and then another woman came and stood outside the door. 21. Again they invited her in and agreed to have her for an elder sister. 22. "Hakela, ask her in," they said; he did so. "Elder sister, come in," he said; and she replied, "Very well, younger brother," and she entered. 23. This time it was a good woman who came; so the brothers lived happily on, with her. 24. She cooked for them, and ate with them[1] and made moccasins and quivers for them, and was expert in all woman's arts. 25. So they lived, until her brothers failed to return from a trip. After a long wait,·she became alarmed and went crying about. 26. She had found a little transparent pebble which she was carrying in her mouth. One day, while weeping, she chanced to swallow it. The result was that a little boy was born to her. So she tossed him out, from the tipi, and a small boy came running in. Not satisfied, she threw him out again, and this time, a youth came back in; again she tried to throw him out, but now she could not lift him. 27. However, with great effort she managed to threw him out again, and now a young man came back in. So she wished for him, saying, "Would that my son had that!" (enumerating various things, horses, clothes, arms, etc.,) and each time the thing she mentioned came true for him. 28. So Stone Boy lived there with his mother, all alone, until one day he said to her, "Mother, why is it that you and I live here all alone?" 29. So she answered, "Your uncles lived here with me; but they went away on a journey and never returned; that is why we live here all by ourselves." 30. Stone Boy said, "Mother, I shall go after my uncles." So she wept and attempted to dissuade him, but he went in spite of that. 31. On and on he travelled. Then, after a long time, he came to a *wizi*[2] out of which an old woman came to him. "Grandson, please stop a little while, and tread on my ribs. Your uncles do that for me regularly before they go on," she said to him. 32. "The old witch! So she's the cause of my uncles' end!" he thought to himself, and then he said, "Very well, then; lie down." When she did so, he began treading on her ribs, first gently, and then, because he was of stone, he made himself very heavy, and came down so hard on her that she cried for relief, "O, grandson, that's enough!" but he did it all the more until he killed her. 33. Having done this, he entered her tipi, and found her victims; and they were his dead uncles, lying around the room. So he made a sweatbath, and poured

---

[1] This means she ate the same food they did; not actually in company with them, for there is some avoidance also between grown-up brother and sister; although not anything like that between in-laws.

[2] *Wizi'; wi* (woman) is a classifier which is prefixed also to the names of the parts pertaining to a tipi. *zi* means yellow. A *wizi'* is a skin tipi, long used so that it is old and smoke-tanned. Old women who were poor, often took discarded tipis, which were smoke-tanned, and made their shelters by bending willows into dome-shaped frames, and covering them with these. The term *wizi'* is synonymous with an old woman's abode.

water over the hot stones; and the dead breathed deeply as in a sigh and said, "Whoever you are who are so kind, hasten on my behalf." So he took his now-restored uncles out, and all were very glad. 34. He took them home, and made his mother very happy. 35. Sometime later he said, "I think I shall see the world next." So he started off, and was travelling along when he saw some white buffalo[1] young women coasting downhill. There were four of them. 36. But he hid behind a knoll first, long enough to disguise himself as a poor boy; and then he approached them. 37. They called to him, "Come on, boy; we are coasting downhill here and you shall join us." 38. But he pretended to demur. "Aw, I wouldn't take the risk. You're so heavy, you might start rolling down the hill; and then, what would become of me?" he asked. So they said, "That's all right; you shall sit behind." Then he was willing to join them. 39. Now they started down, with the boy on the rear end. But, being of stone, he allowed himself to start rolling down, so he crushed and killed all four of the buffalo girls, and took their hides home; his uncles got new quivers from them. 40. Once again he started to walk, and met an old man, a buffalo-bull, who was polishing his horns. "Grandfather, how does it happen that you are polishing your horns?" the boy asked him. 41. And he answered, "Why, grandson, it is because Stone-Boy has killed four daughters-beloved[1], and there is a warparty going out to get him. I am polishing my horns with a modest hope for at least the end of a rib." — 42. "And have you heard, grandfather, just when it is that this attack is planned?" Stone-Boy asked again. And the old buffalo man told him. "Yes," he said, "It is to be when some clouds, tinged with brown, are blown swiftly across the sky." 43. Then Stone-Boy made himself known. "You old fool! Why I myself am Stone-Boy!" and with that, he killed the buffalo. Then he went home. "Uncles," he said, "An attack is being planned against me on that day when some clouds, tinged with brown, are blown swiftly across the sky." On hearing this, the uncles proceeded at once to construct four fences with a common centre, that is, four fences encircling the safety area. And soon, some clouds, tinged with brown, were blown swiftly across the sky; and the buffalo warparty arrived. 44. They came, but Stone-Boy and his uncles met them at the outermost fence and fought with them; while Stone-Boy's mother, with the knife that her brothers had made very keen for her, watched her opportunities to snap the hoof tendons of the buffaloes, and to incapacitate them in that way. This continued until the buffaloes came to the last fence; but by that time, an old man buffalo heralded to his warriors, "It is enough. Retreat now, before Stone-Boy annihilates us all!" So the remaining buffaloes went away. That is all.

[1] White buffaloes were rare and highly valued. They are symbolic of the boy-beloved and the favorite daughter. A white buffalo-girl in buffalo-land would be undoubtedly a child-beloved. And these were.

17. The Turtle-Moccasin Boy.

1. Once, a boy lived alone with his grandmother. And on a day, when she was out in the wood getting fuel, the boy, who was at home by himself, heard a mouse gnawing at something. But until then, he did not know that his grandmother had any food put away; so now he peered around, and found that it was a very fine cake of pemmican[1] which the mouse was eating. 2. As his grandmother was out for the entire day, the boy kept edging around to where the mouse was gnawing. He was afraid that the mouse might bite him. After a long while, when it seemed as if he would eat the whole cake away, the boy went outdoors and called, shouting, "Grandmother, come home! There is a mouse devouring all your pemmican!" 3. And the old woman called back, "All right, grandson, I'll be there. Meanwhile, corner the mouse, and I shall soon brain it with my ax." After a time, the boy was very hungry. He therefore took a little twig and bent it into an arch, over his hand. This he covered with a small piece of cloth[2] and then he reached into the place where the pemmican lay. And he sang,

---

1. He'c'eŝ hokŝi'lala wą k'ų'ŝitku kic'i'laĥcį t'i' ŝk'e'ᵉ. Yųk'ą' ąpe'tu wą e'l k'ų'ŝitku kį c'ak'į'-iya`ya c'ąke' hokŝi'la kį iŝna'la t'iya'ta yąke' cį ic'ų'hą hit'ų'kala wą ta'ku yak'o'ǵahą c'a naĥ'ų' ke'ᵉ. K'e'yaŝ he' winų'ĥcala kį wo'yute mahe'l yuha' kį hokŝi'la kį heĥą'-hųniyą slolye'ŝni ke'ᵉ. Ho tk'a' wana' le' naĥ'ų' kį ų' wo'le yųk'ą' wasna' wą li'la waŝte' k'ų'ŝitku kį g.na'ka c'a he e' c'a hit'ų'kala kį yu'tahą ke'ᵉ. 2. Ąpe'tu a'taya winų'ĥcala kį e'l yąke'ŝni³ c'ąke' hokŝi'la kį hit'ų'kala wą wo'te c'ų e'l ayu'hel k'uwa' ke'ᵉ. Hit'ų'kala kį yaĥta'kįkta k'oki'p'a ke'ᵉ. Wana' ų'nihą' a'taya t'epye' se'ce c'ų heĥą'l hokŝi'la k'ų t'ąka'l ina'p'į ną, — Ųci', he' ku' wo'. Hit'ų'kala wą le'c'i wasna' kį t'epni'c'iyįkte lo', — eya'-pą ke'ᵉ. 3. Yųk'ą', — Ĥį'yąka', t'ako`ža, to'kŝa' waku'kte'. K'ohą' ana'pta k'uwa', to'kŝa' nazų'spe kį le' ų' waka'ĥuĥugįkte', — eya' ke'ᵉ. T'e'hą c'ąke' wana' hokŝi'la kį li'la loc'į' ke'ᵉ. He'c'etu k'eŝ c'ą'la wą yuktą' yu'zį ną m.niĥu'ha hąke' aka'ĥpį ną wasna' wą yąke' c'ų e'tkiya nape' kį paslo'hą iye'kiyį ną heya'lową` ke'ᵉ:

---

[1] The Dakota make pemmican of dried meat, roasted until brittle. This they pound, after wetting it. The result is a remarkably light fluffy substance that is to the touch somewhat like cotton. Then they take a certain proportion of rich marrow-fat and grease derived from boiling fresh pounded bones. They add pounded dried fruit, generally wild choke cherry, but often June berries (and more latterly, raisins,) and knead the whole together into a hard firm cake that keeps indefinitely. This is a delicacy like a dessert. Because of the grease, it is always kept in a parchment wrapper made of the paunch lining, well dried.

[2] More likely, a piece of young calf or deer skin. Because of the present scarcity of skin, and the abundance of cotton goods, the narrator said cloth.

[3] el, at; to; in a given place; yąka', to sit; e'l yąka', to be at home.

Little mouse, what are you eating there ?
Share it with me, that I too may eat.
Won't you ? Won't you ?
4. He would sing thus, and then withdraw his hand; and each time he found a tiny piece of pemmican which the mouse had broken off into his palm. When he tasted it, he knew what good pemmican this was, and wanted much more of it, so he repeated his song and reached his hand in again and again. 5. Three times he received a small piece from the mouse, and ate it out of his hand. While he was thus engaged, his grandmother's dog entered. Then the boy said to the mouse, "Friend, give me a larger portion. If you do, I promise to share my food with you whenever my grandmother serves me."
6. And the mouse replied thus, "No, my friend, your grandmother simply despises me. Whenever I put up food to keep me and my little ones through the winter, she always comes and digs it all up and eats it." — "What is it that you store away, that my grand-mother takes from you ?" the boy asked. "Why, artichoke[1], and earthbeans[2], and food-roots. These I set away and she steals them all from me. So, my friend, I would suggest that the better way

---

Hit‘ų̀kala he' ta'kula c‘a ya'tela so?
Hąke' mak’u'la ye', mi's eya' wa'telakte,
Ic‘e'; Ic‘e'.
4. *He'c‘esna ahi'yayį ną hehą'l nape' kį yut‘ą'kal iki'kcu c‘ą'sna wasna' hąke' li'la ci'scila og.na' ų' c‘ą' he' hit‘ų'kala kį yaptu'h nape' e'l oki'g.nakela ke’ᵉ. Iyu't‘a yųk‘ą' li'la oyu'l-waste` c‘ąke' ak‘e' etą' c‘į' ną ak‘e'sna lową' ną nape' kį mahe'l iye'kiyahą ke’ᵉ. 5. Ya'm.nia-k‘ig.le³ he'c‘ehcį ec‘ų' ną iye'na wasna' hąke' icu' c‘ą yu'ta ke’ᵉ. He'c‘el he'c‘ųhe hcehą'l sų'kala wą k‘ų'sitku kį yuha' yųk‘ą' he e' c‘a t‘ima'hel hiyu' ke’ᵉ. Yųk‘ą' hoksi'la kį hit‘ų'kala ki k‘į' ną, — K‘ola`, wą, t‘ą'ka s'e mak’u' ye', wą. Ec‘į' he'c‘anų kįhą ųci' wo'mak’u c‘ą oc‘i'-cu'kte⁴, — eya' ke’ᵉ. 6. Yųk‘ą' hit‘ų'kala kį heya' ke’ᵉ: — Hoh, wą k‘ola`, nik‘ų'si to'k‘el-oki`hi wahte'malasni ye lo'. Wani'yetu o'pta mic‘į'ca o'p hena' wa'tįkta c‘a wo'yute e'weg.le c‘ą'sna iyu'haha ok‘į' ną t‘epye' lo', — eya' ke’ᵉ. Yųk‘ą', — he' ta'ku c‘a e'yag.le k‘es t‘epni'c‘iya huwo'? — eya' yųk‘ą', — Wą, k‘ola`, p‘ągi' nąi's mak’a'tom.nica nąi's sįkpą'ka k‘o'k‘o e'wag.le c‘ą'sna mama'kinų we lo'. C‘a k‘ola`, iye's wą'cak e's wasna' kį le' a'taya ag.le'mayak‘iya-*

---

[1] Jerusalem artichoke.
[2] Earth-beans are very rich, meaty and of various sizes. They grow under ground, attached to the root of a certain plant. A quick way of obtaining them, was to find a cache made by field mice in which these beans were stored for the winter in great abundance. It is said that that was how old women always got their supply. Hence, there is supposed to be eternal enmity between mice and old women.
[3] *ak‘ig.le*, literally, set one on top of another; added to any number "so many times in succession."
[4] *k’u*, to give; *ok’u'*, to share with, as a meal; to lend anything.

7

would be for you to let me take this cake of pemmican home!"
7. The boy answered, "Well, then, friend, suppose you fight with
grandmother's dog here. If you win, I shall be glad to deliver this
whole cake to your home." And the mouse accepted the terms.
8. Now the boy drew forth the cake, wrapped in dried paunch lining,
with the mouse still inside, and placed it in the centre of the tipi.
All the while, he held his grandmother's dog fast, but he was
squirming to get away; and the boy thought he was impatient to fight
the mouse. 9. So, on signal, he let him go, and urged him on to the
mouse. "Grab it!" he shouted. So the dog sprang forward and
grabbed the pemmican, and the mouse ran out, and up the boy's
shoulder under his shirt; there he struggled, and clawed and
scratched the boy. The boy screamed. "Grandmother, come home.
A mouse is about to kill me!" he called. 10. At that instant, his
grandmother returned, and on seeing the boy crying, she began to
cry too. By this time the dog was eating up the pemmican. She
noticed it and said, "Grandchild, you were deceiving me. You told me
a mouse was eating the pemmican, didn't you?" and she raised
high her ax and knocked open the dog's skull. 11. "Grandson, I see
it now. You stole that pemmican on purpose. So you may go now,
wherever you please; until you can bring me another *wasna'* as big

---

waśte̊' ye lo', — *eya' ke'ᵉ.* 7. *Yu̧k'a̧' hokśi'la ki̧,* — *Ho, ec'a, k'ola',*
u̧ci' t'aśu̧'ke¹ ki̧ le' kic'i' t'oke'ya kic'i'za yo'. He'c'anu̧ yu̧k'a̧' niye'
ohi'yaya ha̧'ta̧ha̧ś c'a̧te' waśte'ya wasna' ki̧ le' a'taya e'ĥpec'ic'iyi̧kte
lo', — *eya' yu̧k'a̧' hit'u̧'kala ki̧ iyo'wi̧yą śk'e'ᵉ.* 8. *He'c'eś wana'*
hokśi'la k'u̧ wasna' ki̧ wale'ga ope'm.nipi c'a k'aye' ahi'g.naka ke'ᵉ.
Hit'u̧'kala ki̧ he'c'ena mahe'l u̧' c'a̧ke' iyo'was'i̧yą ahi'g.naka ke'ᵉ.
He'c'u̧ ną k'u̧'śitku ki̧ śu̧'kala wą yuha' k'u̧ he' yu's u̧' ke'ᵉ. K'e'yaś
iya'yi̧kteĥci̧² c'a̧ke' e'ś hit'u̧'kala ki̧ k'is-i'naĥni ke'c'i̧' ke'ᵉ. 9. *C'a̧ke'*
wana' ayu'śtą iye'yi̧ ną, — *Iya'ĥpaya yo'!* — *eya' ke'ᵉ. Yu̧k'a̧'*
śu̧'ka ki̧ naślo'k iya'yi̧ ną wasna' ki̧ iya'ĥpaya c'a̧ke' hit'u̧'kala k'u̧
he' etą' g.lina'p'i̧ ną hokśi'la ki̧ hi̧ye'te ou̧'yą i̧'yąki̧ ną t'ao'g.le ki̧
mahe'l iya'yi̧ ną he'c'iya nihi̧'ciya naĥla'ĥlal nak'e'ĥk'eĥ u̧' ke'ᵉ.
He'c'ena hokśi'la k'u̧ t'eb.le'ześni³ ną c'e'ya u̧' ke'ᵉ. — *Ųci', g.licu'*
wo'. Hit'u̧'kala wą makte'kte lo'! — *eya'-c'eya ke'ᵉ.* 10. *Ic'u̧'ha̧*
winu̧'ĥcala k'u̧ g.lihu̧'ni ną t'ima' k'ig.la' yu̧k'a̧' hokśi'la ki̧ c'e'ya u̧'
c'a̧ke' i'ś-'eya' c'e'ya ke'ᵉ. Yu̧k'a̧' wana' śu̧'ka ki̧ wasna' k'u̧ t'epyi̧'kta
ha̧'l wąya'ke'ᵉ. — *T'akoża', maya'g.naye'. Le' hit'u̧'kala wą wasna'*
t'epma'k'iyi̧kta ke'he' c'u̧ — *eyi̧' ną nazu̧'spe wą yuha' k'u̧ he' yuwą'-*
kal iki'kcu ną u̧' śu̧'kala k'u̧ nata' ki̧ kaśle'l ap'a' ke'ᵉ 11. — *T'akoża',*
eha̧'k'u̧ ec'a'kel wasna' ki̧ he' mama'yakinu̧ c'a wana' slolwa'ye'.
C'e ak'o' to'k'i-yac'i̧'ka ya', ną wasna' wążi̧' t'o'keca c'a le' i̧'skokeca

---

¹ This sounds like "her horse." *Śu̧'ka-t'awa* is better, for "her dog."
² *kteĥci̧*, added to any verb of action, means "he was eager to do; eager,
almost past restraint."
³ *t'eb.le'ześni*, to be frantic; wild; *t'a*, dead; *b.le'za*, sane; *śni*, not.

as the one I have lost," she said. The boy replied, "Very well, grand-mother; you will first have to make me some arrows and a bow." So she proceeded to do this at once, and when they were completed, the boy started out to go on a journey.

18. The Turtle-Moccasin Boy, Continued.

1. And so the boy started out on his journey. He had not gone far before he came upon a herd of buffaloes. He lay on a hill, peering over at the herd, and wondering how he could get close enough to shoot them. Just then, the herd ran off as though they were fright-ened, and stopped at a short distance. 2. A man was going towards the buffaloes[1]. He walked past them, and knelt down on a level spot some distance from them. And then, one of the buffaloes, a bull, turned and faced west; and so he stood, apart from the others. I should judge that the bull stood about fifteen paces from the man. He threw himself on the ground and rolled. 3. Then he stood up again, and threw dirt over himself with his hoof, in this manner[2].

---

maka'ku', — eya' ke'ᵉ. Yųk'ą' hokśi'la ki i'ś, — Ho, ec'a, ųci`, ita'zipa ną wąhį'kpe k'o' mi'caġa yo', — eya' c'ąke' ki'cagį ną yuśtą' k'ųhą' hokśi'la ki icu' ną yuha' oma'ni-iya`ya śk'e'ᵉ.

18.

1. *He'c'eś wana' hokśi'la k'ų oma'ni-iya`ya³ śk'e'ᵉ. T'e'hą'l ye'śni ec'e'l pte' opta'ye wą t'ą'ka wąwi'c'ayaka śk'e'ᵉ. Paha' wą aką'l ȟpa'yį ną pte' ki ao'wic'akas'į to'k'el ȟ'ą' kįhą wic'i'k'iyela yį' ną wąźi' o'kta he'cihą he' iyu'kcą śk'e'ᵉ. Ȟcehą'l pte' ki ta'ku naki'cip'api-iteya iya'yapi ną ka'k'i k'ina'źipi śk'e'ᵉ. 2. Wic'a'śa wą e'tkiya wic'a'u ną iyo'pteya iya'yį ną mak'a'-ob.la`ye⁴ wą e'l c'ąkpe'śkama-k'ag.le⁵ ina'źi śk'e'ᵉ. Yųk'ą' t'at'ą'ka wą pte' opta'ye ki etą'hą c'a iśna'la ina'źi ną wiyo'ȟpeyatakiya e'tųwą na'źįhą śk'e'ᵉ. To'ktuke e'yaś pte' ki he' wic'a'śa wą ka c'ąkpe'śkamak'ag.le na'źi ke'p'e' c'ų hetą'hą c'ag.le'pi ake'zaptą ec'e'lya na'źi śk'e'ᵉ. Mak'a'ta iȟpe'ic'iyį ną ica'ptąptąkic'ų śk'e'ᵉ. 3. Hehą'l ina'źi ną si' ų' le'c'el mak'a' ai'g.lalala*

---

[1] This is the same scene, related from another angle, in which Ikto', after much importuning, is changed into a buffalo. The man here was Ikto' before the magic worked. Later, when he tries to work it for the boy and initiate him into the mysteries, he ruins his own magic.

[2] The informant took a handful of sand in his right hand and threw it over his left shoulder; and then some in his left, and threw it over his right shoulder, as he said, "in this manner."

[3] *oma'ni*, to walk; *iya'ya*, he went away. This phrase means, "He went off to spend time abroad, away from home." It was every man's duty to scout always, for enemies or for game. A man who habitually stayed around the home was ridiculed.

[4] Flat land. Any level, or slightly rolling piece of land.

[5] *c'akpe'*, knee; *śka*, (?); *mak'a'*, earth; *ag.le'*, set on; hence, to kneel. Variants are *c'aśke'mak'ag.le*, *c'aśke'k'amag.le*, and *c'aśke'kpamak'ag.le*.

7*

Then he charged straight towards the man who was kneeling down. When the buffalo was close, the man gave a cry of fear and fell to one side, so the bull tore on past him, over the spot where he had been kneeling, saying, "*Hį'!*"[1] as he went by. 4. Once again the man took his kneeling position, and the bull charged him; with the same result. Three times he did this, and the fourth time, the man did not dodge. So the bull caught him with his horn, and behold, *two* buffalo-bulls went on together[2]! 5. Then the entire herd disappeared, and in their place remained the newly-made bull. So the boy went towards him. And the bull said, "Well, my little brother, how are you? As soon as you left your grandmother's tipi, I have known of it. I too have had a hard life; always I have had to be on the lookout for some way to keep me and my young alive. 6. At last I have found a way to have plenty of food always. As long as I live, food will be abundant for me in all parts of the land. So, little brother, since you and your grandmother have had so much hardship, I can put you where you will be as well off as I." 7. And the boy said, "But elder brother, just who are you?" and he replied, "I am the one known as Ikto-the-Rover-All-over-the-World. When it

---

śk'e'ᵉ. Ną hehą'l le wic'a'śa wą c'ąkpe'śkamak'ag.le na'żį k'ų he'tkiya naślo'k iya'ya śk'e'ᵉ. Ihų'nikta hą'l wic'a'śa k'ų c'e'ya iya'yį ną ḱeya'p iḱpe'ic'iya c'ąke' t'at'ą'ka kį iyo'pteya iya'yį ną na'żį-ohe' k'ų he'l — Hį'! — eya'-hįg.la iya'ya śk'e'ᵉ. 4. Ho, ak'e' wic'a'śa k'ų ec'e'l k'iyotaka c'ąke' t'at'ą'ka kį a'tayela e'l ye' c'e'yaś ak'e' ec'e'ḱcį ḱeya'p iḱpe'ic'iya c'ąke' iyo'pteya — Hį'! — eya'-hįg.la iya'yį ną ya'm.niak'ig.le he'c'eḱcį ec'ų' ną ici'topa yųk'ą' wic'a'śa k'ų nap'e'śni c'ąke' t'at'ą'ka kį he' ų' ik'o'yak-yį ną e'yaya yųk'ą' pte' nų'p iya'yapi śk'e'ᵉ. 5. He'c'ena pte' opta'ye k'ų iyu'ha tok'i'yot'ą iya'yapi ną wążi'la e'na na'żį c'ąke' hokśi'la k'ų he' e'tkiya ya' ke'ᵉ. Yųk'ą' t'at'ą'ka k'ų, — Misų`, To'k'el-yau`ka huwo'? Nik'ų'śi t'i'la kį etą'hą yahi'nap'e c'ų hehą'tą slolya' wau' we lo'. Ho, eya' mi'ś-'eya' li'la iyo'tiye'wakiye s'a ye lo'. To'k'el mic'į'ca o'p ni' wau'kte cį he e' c'a o'hįni iwa'g.nį ye lo'. 6. Ho, yųk'ą' ki'tąḱcį' to'k'eśk'e ec'a'mų kįhą o'hįni wo'yute b.luha'kte cį iye'waye lo'. Toha'-wani` kį hehą'yą mak'a' sito'm.niyą tukte'tuke c'e'yaś e'l wo'yute o'ta mi'ciyąkįkte lo'. C'a misų`, yac'į' hą'tąhąś ni'ś-'eya' nik'ų'śi kic'i' iyo'tiye'yakiye s'a k'ų, to'k'el wa'map'i kį iye'hąyą wa'nip'ikta c'a ec'e'l c'ica'gįkte lo', — eya' ke'ᵉ. 7. Yųk'ą' hokśi'la kį heya' ke'ᵉ, — Tk'a, c'iye`, le' nitu'we huwo'? — eya' yųk'ą' uma' kį ayu'ptį ną, — Wą, misų`, Ikto'-Mak'a'-Sito'm.niyą-Oyu'm.ni[3] eya'-c'aże`yatapi kį he' le' miye' ye

---

[1] This word is always said with a great expulsion of breath, just as if about to cough. It generally indicates disappointment over failure after a strained effort. Used by men and women.

[2] Ikto' now becomes a bull, because the magic works under the buffalo-bull's direction.

[3] *oyu'm.ni*, to rove; wander about; roam aimlessly.

becomes necessary for me to turn my face on someone, I can do with
him as I please. So I think it would be wise for us to go together."
8. But Hakela said to him, "Why, big brother, don't you know what
my grandmother thinks of you? She calls you the people's deceiver,
and has warned me about you; that you are not to be trusted. In
case we do go about together, who then shall have this bow and these
arrows?" 9. Ikto replied to this, "My little brother, take Hakela's
moccasins, and to one of them tie the bow and arrows, so that when
your grandmother comes looking for you, she will recognize them."
(For you must know that this boy wore turtle moccasins, and he
alone. Beside him, there was nobody who had such footwear.)[1]
10. "Elder brother, I can never wear these moccasins out, that is
why I prize them so highly; nevertheless, at your command they
shall come off." So saying, he took them off, and tied them to his
bow, and placed them together on the ground. 11. Now Iktomi
said, "Ready, little brother; first you must kneel, facing west, with
your eyes closed[2]. Ah! little brother, whereas, in the past, you have
been poor, from now on you shall always have plenty. Don't fear
me. I shall attack you four times[3]. If you are brave, and do not
dodge, so that I stab my horns into you, you shall become like me,
with the power I have," he said. 12. The boy took the position on
his knees, and the Ikto-bull now charged towards him. But the boy

---

*lo'. C'a tohą'l tuwa' ai'tohewaya c'ą'śna to'k'el wac'ị' ec'e'l wak'u'wa
ye lo'. C'a he'c'e sak'i'p ųyį'kta-iye'c'etu we lo', — eya' ke'ᵉ. 8. K'e'-
yaś Hake'la i'ś heya' ke'ᵉ, — Wą, c'iye`, ųci' li'la wic'a'yag.naye⁴
ś'a ke'yị' ną niye' ų' wi'wahomaye c'ų. Ec'a sak'i'p ųye' cįhą tuwa'
ita'zipa ną wąhị'kpe-mit'a`wa kị lena' yuha'ktelak'a? — eya' ke'ᵉ.
9. Ikto' hehą'l heya' ke'ᵉ, — Ho misų`, Hake'la t'ahą'pe kị hena' icu'
ną sani' e'l ita'zipa ną wąhị'kpe kị hena' ai'yakaśka yo', he'c'el
nik'ų'śi oni'cile-u kịhą hena' iye'kiyįkte lo', — eya' ke'ᵉ. (Ec'ị'
hokśi'la kị le' iśna'la p'atka'śa-hą'pa ohą' śk'e'ᵉ. I't'ok'ąyą tuwe'ni
he'c'a yuha'śni'ᵗ.) 10. Yųk'ą', — C'iye`, tų'weni hą'pa kị lena'
nawa'pota owa'kihiśni c'ake' he' ų' li'la t'ewa'hila ye lo'. K'e'yaś
niye' ehe' cị ų' b.luślo'kịkte lo', — eyị' ną yuślo'kị ną ita'zipa kị e'l
ai'yakaśkị ną wi'taya ka'l e'g.naka ke'ᵉ. 11. — Ho, misų`, ig.lu'wịyeya
yo'. C'ąkpe'śkamak'ag.le wiyo'hpeyatakiya e'tųwą naya'žị ną iśto'g.mus
naya'žịkte lo'. Hųhųhi', misų`, ehą'ni wahpa'nica ini't'e c'ų, letą'hą
wana' o'hịni t'alo' o'ta tohą'l-yac'ị`ka c'ą luha'kte lo'. C'e k'oma'ki-
p'eśni yo'. To'paak'ig.le ac'i'hiyukte lo'. Oni'hitikị ną naya'p'eśni
hą'tąhąś c'ac'i'p'e cịhą wo'waś'ake wą b.luha' kị le' hąke' ni'ś-'eya'
luha'kte lo', — eya' ke'ᵉ. 12. Wana' hokśi'la k'ų cakpe'śkamak'ag.le
ina'žị yųk'ą' Ikto'-t'at'ą`ka k'ų e'l u' ke'ᵉ. K'e'yaś hokśi'la kị c'ąte'-*

---

[1] Turtle moccasins brought speed and good luck to the wearer.
[2] Ikto' always makes a fool of himself.
[3] Almost everything is done four times.
[4] *g.na'yą*, to deceive; trick; also, to persuade; sway by argument.

was very brave, and did not dodge, so he stabbed him with his horn and carried him along. And lo, it was Hakela and Ikto the man who went along together! So the mystery-act was a complete failure. 13. Immediately Ikto became very sad. "Alas, my little brother, why did you come along and spoil my act ?" he cried. Then he wept.

So Hakela put his turtle moccasins back on, picked up his bow and arrows, and started forth towards the west, leaving Ikto. He had not travelled far before he saw a very tall man coming towards him. 14. At that moment, another man, wearing a cap of jackrabbit skin, was meeting him, coming out of the creek. "My little brother, where are you going, all by yourself ?" he asked. "Why, I am going to a great people who live west from here," he answered. Now, this was Ikto again, and he said, "Why, little brother, how odd! That is the tribe I belong to; I just came from there now; so we two shall go home together." As they talked, that tall man I mentioned, was now arriving. So Ikto said, "My younger brother, do you see this man coming ? He's the one known as Double-face. His other name is Iya, the Eater." — 15. "Why does he have that name ?" Hakela wanted to know. So Ikto explained it to him. "It is because he swallows both men and buffaloes whole!" — "In that case, elder brother, he might swallow us. What can we do to save ourselves ?"

---

t'įzela c'ąke' nap'e'śni c'a wą'c'ak he' ic'a'p'į ną k'o e'yaya ke'ᵉ. Yųk'ą' hokśi'la wą, Hake'la e' e c'a, Ikto' kic'i' iya'yapi ke. (Wana' pte' nų'papikta ke'c'į' ną he'c'ų tk'a'ś) wak'ą'-k̇'ą k'ų iye'kicic'etuśni ke'ᵉ. 13. Ikto'mi wo't'ek̇i ak'i'p'a ke'ᵉ. — Hê! Misų`, ta'kok̇cowe'- yau'¹ ną wak'ą'-wak̇'ąkte c'ų maya'kiluśica huwo'? — eyį' ną c'e'yahą ke'ᵉ.

C'ąke' Hake'la p'atka'śa-hą`pa k'ų oki'hį ną ita'zipa wąhį'kpe k'ų k'o' iki'kcu ną he'c'ena wiyo'k̇peyatakiya Ikto'mi ų'yą iya'ya ke'ᵉ. T'e'hąl ye'śni ec'e'l wic'a'śa wą li'la hą'ska c'a t'ahe'nakiya u' ke'ᵉ. 14. Hcehą'l wakpa'la kį etą'hą wic'a'śa wą maśtį'ska ha'-wap'o'śtą² wą ų' ną i'ś-'eya' u' ke'ᵉ. — Misų`, to'k'iya la' huwo', niśna'lak̇cį? — eya' c'ąke' hokśi'la kį, — Wą le'c'i oya'te wą wiyo'k̇peyata wic'o't'i c'a ekta' wic'a'b.le lo', — eya' ke'ᵉ. Iśe' he' wana' ak'e' Ikto' e' c'a u' k'e'yaś. — Wą, misų`, he'c'iyatąhą le' wau' c'a sak'i'p ųg.nį'kte lo', — eya' ke'ᵉ. Hcehą'l wic'a'śa wą hą'ska c'a u' ke'p'e' c'ų he' wana' hihų'ni kte'ᵉ. Yųk'ą', — Misų`, wic'a'śa wą u' kį le' wąla'ka huwo'? He' Anų'k Ite' eya'pi kį e' ye lo'. Nakų'ś I'ya eci'yape lo', — Ikto' eya' ke'ᵉ. 15. C'ąke', — C'iye`, ta'kowé'-heci`yapi he'? — Hake'la eya' yųk'ą' Ikto', — Wą, Misų`, wic'a'śa ną pte' k'o'k'o a'l-'ataya t'epwi'- c'aya c'a he' ų' heci'yape lo', — eya' ke'ᵉ. — He'c'eca hą'tąhąś, c'iye`, ųki'ye k'o' na'ųpcapikte se'ce lo', to'k'eśk'e uk̇'ą' kįhą nių'kic'iyįkta huwo'? — hokśi'la kį eya' ke'ᵉ. Yųk'ą', — Hį'yąka yo', to'k'aśni ye lo',

---

¹ *ta'ku*, what; something; *k̇ca*, indeed; *ole'*, to seek; *ta'kok̇cole'*, or *ta'kuk̇cowe'* means, "Why (in the world)?"

² *wap'o'śtą*, cap; head-gear; *wa*, thing; *p'a*, head; *o'śtą*, to fit into.

the boy asked. Then Ikto, "Just wait, and don't fear, little brother,
for I have power to bewitch anybody that I look at." 16. When the
Iya was about ten paces away, he breathed towards these two, and
when he drew in his breath, they were jerked forcibly towards him.
So Ikto said to him as he came to a stop, "Well, my younger brother,
who are you?" — "Why, I am the one they call, 'They-Camp-
inside-his-Mouth'." the Iya said. "My younger brother, when were
you born?" Ikto questioned him. "Why, I was made when this
earth was made!" the Iya replied. "Oh, yes!" Ikto began, again,
"Now, I do recall it! Why, you must be that wretched thing I made
after I had finished making the earth! That being the case, my
younger brother, you had better stay with your mouth closed. I
also can do this!" And Ikto took some sharp breaths, with each
breath drawing Iya towards him. The Eater now became afraid.
"Please don't, elder brother; I don't wish to die!" So Ikto stopped,
and then he said, "Come, then, let us all tell in turn just what things
we fear. Hakela, you begin."—17. "That is easy. Why, elder brothers,
there is just one thing that I fear; it is my grandmother's ax, which
is the cause of my wandering about in this difficult way. Whenever
my grandmother raises that ax over anything, there's no use
trying to live! Why, only recently, she smashed in the skull of her
favorite puppy! What further fear should I have than that!"
Hakela answered. 18. "Now its my turn," Ikto began eagerly, "Well,
brothers, what I fear you shall learn directly. First of all, I fear

---

*misų`, le' tuwa' ai'tohewaya c'ą wah.mu'ǧe lo', — Ikto' eya' ke'ᵉ.
16. Wic'a'ša kį wana' c'ag.le'pi wikce'm.na-wahe`hąyą u' kį he'hą'ni
niya' c'ą' nųp'į' yace'kcek iwi'c'acu ke'ᵉ. Wana' hina'ʐį kį e'l Ikto', —
Misų`, nitu'we huwo'? — eya' yųk'ą' — Wą, le' Ima'he-Wic'o't'i eci'-
yapi kį he' miye' ye lo', — eya'-ayu`pta ke'ᵉ. Yųk'ą', — Misų`,
to'hųwel le' ini'c'aǧa huwo'? — Ikto' eya' yųk'ą', — Wą, mak'a' kį
le' ka'ǧapi k'ų he'hą' mi's-'eya' maka'ǧape lo', — I'ya kį eya' ke'ᵉ.
He'c'ena, — Ohą̀, wana' nake's we'ksuye lo'! Mak'a' kį le' waka'ǧį
ną wana' mig.lu'štą yųk'ą' hąke' iya'ya c'ąke' ų' ta'kula wą ši'cehca c'a
waka'ǧe c'ų ehą'k'ų he' niye' ye lo'. Hec'etu kį ų', misų`, i'yog.mus
ų' wo'. Mi'š-'eya' le'c'el owa'kihi ye lo, — eyį' ną niya' c'ą iye'na I'ya
kį yati'ktitą ahi'yu ke'ᵉ. C'ąke' k'oki'p'į ną — Ci'ye`, he'c'ųlašni ye'.
Wani'ktehcį ye, — eya' ke'ᵉ. Yųk'ą' Ikto' ayu'štą ną, — Ec'a u'wa
yo', taku'kuk'oų'kip'api kį hena' ųko'g.lakapikte. Hake`la, niye'
nit'o'kahe ye lo', — eya' ke'ᵉ. 17. C'ąke' Hake'la wana' heya' ke'ᵉ, —
Ho, c'iye`, ta'ku wąʐi'la k'owa'kip'e cį he' ųci' t'ana'zųspe k'ų he e' ye
lo'. He' ų' le' iyo'tiye'kiya mak'o'skąl oma'wani ye lo'. Tohą'l ųci'
nazų'spe kį he' ta'ku apa'ha c'ą'šna to'k'el niwa'c'į-p'icašni ye lo'.
Wą lec'a'la šų'kala wąš t'ehi'la se'ca yųk'ą' nata' kao'hpe lo'. Ta'ku
isą'p k'oki'p'e-p'icaka, — eya' ke'ᵉ. 18. — Ho, mi's hehą'tu we lo', —
Ikto' iš'o'š'oyehcį eya' ke'ᵉ. — Ho, misų`, ta'ku k'owa'kip'a c'a
ec'a'lahcį naya'h'ųpikte lo'. It'o' t'oke'yalahcį aki'š'api kį k'owa'-*

the shouting of men; and then, I fear gourd rattles; and whistles, and the hooting of owls; and drums and deer-hoof rattles. Those are the things I fear!" And Eater said, "Thank you, elder brother. Those are the very things that I also fear! If I were to hear the sound of any one of these, I should die on the spot!" — 19. "Well, in that case, we are through with that. Now, I think we shall go to the camp, next; I am very hungry. But you, Iya, my younger brother, you had best remain here until Hakela and I whose mouths are tolerably small, go first and eat; while there, we shall line up all the fat men for your meal!" Ikto said. Iya fell in line with this plan of·Ikto's, and said, "That's just the thing to do, elder brother. When you two return, then we shall all go to the camp together." And he proceeded to lie down for a nap, as they were leaving him. 20. Now, as it happened, these really were Ikto's people, so, as soon as he arrived in camp, he told them about Iya, and about the things he feared. So the people hurriedly collected the whistles, drums, deer-hoof and gourd rattles, and everything else that Iya claimed to be frightened by; and when Hakela and Iktomi returned to Iya, they were accompanied by men of the tribe, each of whom carried one of the articles specified. Ikto and Hakela now placed the men in various parts, out of sight, and then they came to Iya, still asleep, flat on his back. His mouth was wide open so they looked into his oral cavity, and were able to hear down to his stomach. And they could hear sounds of many human voices, from there. 21. Ikto turned to Hakela and said, "Little brother, will you shoot him?" So Hakela

kipʻe lo'; ną hehą'l wag.mu'ha kaḣla'pi kį he e', ną hehą'l hįhą'-hotʻųpi ną cʻą́cʻeġa ną tʻasi'ha kaśla'ślapi kį hena' iyu'haḣcį kʻowa'-kipʻe lo', — eya' keʻᵉ. Heʻcʻena I'ya heya' keʻᵉ, — Pʻila'mayaye lo', Cʻiyeˋ. Mi'ś-ʼeya' hena' eʼḣca cʻaś kʻowa'kipʻe cʻų. Heʼ wążi' nawa'ḣʻų hą'tąhąś wą'cak eʼś eʼna matʼį́kte lo', — eya' keʻᵉ. 19. — Heʻcʻeca heʻcįhą wana' ųg.lu'śtąpe lo'. Cʻa wana' wicʻoʼtʻita ųyą'pikte lo', li'la lowa'cʻį cʻa. Tkʻa', misuˋ, niye' leʻna tʻoʼwaʼś yąka' yo'. Koʻhą' Hakeʼla kicʻiʼ iʼ-ųcikcikʻapilaka cʻa woʼl-ųyą'pi ną ag.na' toʼna cʻeʼpapi kį hena' ųni'cipahipikte¹ lo', — Ikto' I'ya heʻcʻel oki'yaka keʻᵉ. I'ya heʻcʻetula cʻąke' — Ho, heʼ og.na'kte lo'. Yag.li'pi kįhą ecʻaʼś iyu'ha akʻe' wicʻoʼtʻita ųyą'pikte lo', — eyį' ną iśtį'ma cʻąke' iya'yapi keʻᵉ. 20. Heʻcʻeya' hena' Ikto' tʻao'yate cʻąke' kaʼkʻel-ihų'ni-pilaka tkʻa' heʻcʻena le I'ya taku'ku kʻoki'pʻa keʼye' cʻų hena' iyu'ha wi'taya m.nayą'pi ną wana' Ikto' Hakeʼla kicʻiʼ g.licu'pikta yųkʻą' wicʻaʼśa toʼna hena' yuha' wicʻiʼhakap ya'pi keʻᵉ. Cʻąke' ai'sįyą ena'nakiya hena' eʼwicʻag.lepi ną iśna'la I'ya ḣpa'ye cį ekta' g.li'pi yųkʻą' itų'kap nai'capyeya' iśtį'ma keʻᵉ. Iʼ kį ekta' eʼyokasʼįpi ną tʻezi' kį iya'g.leya wąya'kapi yųkʻą' heʻcʻiyatąhą wicʻaʼho li'la tʻąį' keʻᵉ. 21. Cʻąke' Ikto' Hakeʼla kʻį' ną, — Misųˋ, niye' kʻute' yo', —

¹ pahi', to gather; collect; pick up; assemble.

set one of his arrows, and shot Iya, who immediately sat bolt upright. Then Ikto took out his war-club and said, "You disobedient sleepyhead, you!" and he made him stand and marched him straight towards the men who had come out with them, and were hiding close by. And Iya said, "Why, elder brother, you may as well know now that if I ever die, it must be through fire, and nothing else. But if anything pops out of the fire, and is picked up, that person who takes it shall surely die. Now, the reason for it is that I have killed many men. And he who picks up something that comes out of my fire, will show thereby that he likes the same sort of things I do; and that is why he too shall die." That was the way he talked, as they walked behind him, and caused him to enter the deep ravine of the creek. 22. Now they were attacked on all sides. With rattles, and drums and shouting, and owl-hooting sounds, and whistles, they came upon the three, but Iya tried to run away; however, they caught him and struck him many times with their axes and war-clubs, and broke all his bones, and killed him. Then they placed a pile of wood over him to burn him. As he was burning, all the nicest things imaginable, popped out of the fire, but as Ikto had already instructed the people about them, nobody took anything, lest he should die instantly. 23. Before they killed Iya in this fashion, he had eaten many people. It was only after he was killed that people began to multiply greatly. Previously, no sooner would the people

---

eya' c‘a he'c‘e wąhį'kpe k'ų wąźi' ekta' e'g.le ną k‘ute' yųk‘ą' he'c‘ena I'ya kikta' i'yotaka ke'ᵉ. C‘ąke' Ikto' c‘ąĥpi' wą iki'kcu ną, — Waĥte`sni si`ca, wana'yaĥ'ųsni-iteya nisti'mahe lo'! — eyį' ną yuna'źįk‘iyį ną pasi' a'ya ke'ᵉ; wic‘a'sa k‘eya' ina'ĥma-yąka`pi k'ų he'c‘etkiya. Yųk‘ą' I'ya heya' ke'ᵉ, — Wą, c‘iye`, to'hųweni mat'į'kte sni, tohą' p‘e'ta ų'pisni kį hehą'. Śk‘a į'se' c‘ig.na'ye lo'. Ho tk‘a' tohą'l ile'mayąpi kįhą p‘e'ta kį etą'ĥą taku'ĥcį napsi'l hiyu' hą'tąĥąs tuwa' he' icu' kįhą i'ś-'eya' t'į'kte lo'. Wic‘a'śa o'ta wic‘a'wakte kį he' ų'. C‘a tuwa' ta'ku miye' etą'ĥą napsi'l iya'ye cį he' icu' hą'tąĥąs he' ta'ku waste'walake cį hena' i'ś-'eya' waśte'laka c‘a he' ų' t'į'kte lo', — heya'ya ia'a¹ yį' ną ec‘e'l wakpa'la-mahe`l iya'yapi ke'ᵉ. 22. T‘o'k‘iyatąĥą kį oya'ś'į wana' awi'c‘ahiyupi ke'ᵉ. Ĥla'ĥla ną c‘ą'c‘eǵa ną aki'ś'api ną hįĥą'-hot‘ų'pi ną waya'źopi k‘o'k‘o ų' awi'c‘ahiyupi c‘ąke' I'ya iya'ye-wac‘į tk‘a'ś oyu'spapi ną e'na ohų'nicat‘a ną c‘ąĥpi' k‘o'k‘o ki'ciųpi ną kaĥu'ĥuǵapi śk‘e'ᵉ. C‘ą wi'taya e'g.nakapi ną e'l ile'yapi'ⁱ. C‘ąke' wana' li'la ile' yųk‘ą' p‘e'ta kį etą'ĥą wo'yuha iĥą'keya-waśte`ste kį iyu'ha napsi'psil hiyu' k‘e'yaś Ikto' wąźi'la ye'ś icu'sni-wic‘aśi ną e'yapaha-wic‘aśi c‘ąke' tuwa' wąźi' icu' kįhą wą'cag.na t'į'kte lo' eya'-e'yapaha`pi'ⁱ. 23. I'ya le'c‘el kte'pisni k'ų he'hą' li'la oya'te o'ta t‘epwi'c‘aya śk‘e'ᵉ. Įse' kte'pi k'ų hetą'ĥą nake's oya'te kį ig.lu'otapi'ⁱ. He' it‘o'kap ka'k‘el wana' oya'te kį wic‘o'ta a'yapi

---

¹ In Teton, *iya'*, is "to speak." But in the reduplicated form, the *y* disappears; *ia'a.*

begin to grow in great numbers than he would come by, and eat
large hordes of them. In this way he kept the race of men down.
24. Then Hakela and Ikto went back to the camp, and this is the way
Ikto introduced Hakela, to the people. "Now, all cause for fear is
removed. This boy who comes to you is a famous one. He is the
wearer of the turtle moccasins. In future, this is the man you may
look to for aid. By means of the bow and arrows which he carries,
you shall eat. And by means of them, too, the tribe's children shall
live to reach maturity. This boy has brought you the bow and
arrows!" In this manner Ikto introduced Hakela. 25. Now, therefore, it is said that the Lakota people have always depended on the
bow and arrows in order to procure food, and so to live to grow up;
and thus they keep the race alive. That is all.

19. White-Plume Boy.

1. A certain man, when his son was born, took him in his arms
and planted a white plume in the crown of his head, naming him
"White-Plume." Then, wishing to hasten his growth, he threw him
outdoors several times, and each time he reëntered the tipi, somewhat bigger than before, until finally, all on the same day, he attained
the stature of a man. 2. Then the father said, "Oh, would that my
son had such and such things!" and it all happened, so that the

---

*c'ą́'śna I'ya e'l hiyu' ną paha'hayela t'epwi'c'ayį ną he' ų' oya'te kį
o'hįni co'napila śk'e'ᵉ. 24. Hake'la wana' Ikto' kic'i' wic'o't'ita k'i' ną
le'c'ųs'e¹ Ikto' Hake'la ų wo'g.laka śk'e'ᵉ, — Ho, wana' letą'hą
wo'k'okip'e wani'cįkte lo'. Hokśi'la kį le' oc'a'ś-t'ųke lo'. Le' P'atka'śa-
Hą̀'pa Ohą́' eci'yapi kį e' ye lo'. C'a t'oka'takiya le' wac'į'yayapikte cį
e' ye lo'. Ita'zipa wą wąhį'kpe k'o' iya'yustak yuha' kį hena' e' c'a ų'
waya'tapikte lo'. Ną hena' ų' oya'te c'įca'pi kį ic'a'ġapikte lo'.
Hokśi'la kį le' wana' ita'zipa, wąhį'kpe k'o' nica'hipe lo'! — Ikto'
eya' oya'te kį owi'c'akiyaka śk'e'ᵉ. 25. He' ų' etą'hą Lak'o'ta-oya'te kį
tohą'tą kį ita'zipa ną wąhį'kpe kį hena' wo'wac'iyeyapi ną ų' wo'yute
icu'pi ną ig.lu'otapi ną nii'c'iyapi śk'e'ᵉ. 26. Hehą'yela owi'hąke'ᵉ.*

19.

*1. Wic'a'śa wą c'įca' wą ki'cit'ųpi yųk'ą' iki'kcu ną p'esle'te kį
e'l wa'c'įhį wą pasla'tį ną — Wa'c'įhį Ska' — eya'-c'aśki't'ų² śk'e'ᵉ.
He'c'ų ną to'na-t'ąka'l kah²o'l iye'ya c'ą iye'na są'p ic'a'ġa c'ąke'
o'hąketa k'ośka'laka wą li'la wic'a'śa waśte' c'a ąpe'tu-hąke'yela
yuha' ke'ᵉ. 2. He'c'ų ną, — Tok'i³ mic'į'kśi ka'k'el ną ka'k'el yuha'
nį', — eya' c'ą iye'c'etu c'ąke' li'la tąyą wak'o'yakį ną nakų' wayu'ha*

---

¹ *le'c'ų s'e*, like doing this; hence: *thus.*
² *c'aśki't'ų*, he names his own; *c'aże'*, name.
³ *tok'i'*, and *t'ųkį'*, both are used for making a wish. "Would that." Generally,
in such a wish, the particle *nį* is placed at the end.

youth possessed handsome apparel and fine things. Then the father talked thus to his son, "These people are in great distress, my son. Four men are abusing them severely. So if there is something you can do, do it." 3. Just as he had said, four men stood outside their tipi the next morning, and called, "White-Plume, we have come to challenge you to a race. Come on out;" to which he answered, "All right." Four men waited for him, and one was painted red, and one was blue and one was white and one was black. 4. And the one who had used red for his paint contended with him first; they ran towards a distant tree, and climbed it; and on getting down, the instant they were landing to run back, the red painted man tossed something out, and it was cattail fuzz. Suddenly the entire meadow became a mass of cattail fuzz which tangled itself into White-Plume's feather. This delayed him long, while he tried to untangle his feather, so that the red-paint man had a good head start. Even so, when White-Plume boy was through, he ran so swiftly that he got home first. 5. And four wooden clubs belonging to the four men, and painted in their respective colors, lay at the base; so White-Plume took up the red club and with it he struck and killed his opponent. So only three men went home. Next morning, the three came again and challenged him to a race. So he went out and raced with the man painted blue. The race included climbing a distant tree, and then coming down, and returning to the home base. But

---

šk'e'ᵉ. Yųk'ą' hehą'l atku'ku kį le'c'el c'įca' kį wo'kiyake'ᵉ, — Le' oya'te kį t'ehi'ya ų'pe lo', c'į̀'kš. Wic'a'ša to'p li'la šica'ya wic'a'k'u-wape lo'. C'e ų' to'k'el yah'ą'-oya`kihi hą'tąhąš ec'ų' wo', — eya' ke'ᵉ. 3. Wana' he'c'el eye' c'ų, hị'hąna yųk'ą' wic'a'ša to'p t'ąka'l hina'žipi ną heya'pi ke'ᵉ, — Wa`c'įhį Ska`, k'ig.le'la-ųhi'pe lo'; hina'p'i ye', — eya'pi c'ąke', — Ha'.o, — eyį' ną ina'p'a yųk'ą' wic'a'ša to'papi c'a wąži' šai'c'iyį ną wąži' t'oi'c'iyį ną wąži' sąi'c'iyį ną wąži' sap-'i'c'iya ke'ᵉ. 4. Yųk'ą' šai'c'iye cų he' t'oke'ya kic'i' į'yąke c'e'yaš c'ą' wą ana'tąpi ną ali' į'yąkapi ną ka'k'el-huk'u'l g.licu'pikta yųk'ą' wic'a'ša-šai'c'iye c'ų he' ta'ku kala' iye'ya c'ąke' Wa'c'įhį Ska' e'l e'tųwą yųk'ą' hįtką' k'ų he'c'a ke'ᵉ. C'ąke b.la'ye kį a'taya he'c'a-ožu`-hig.nį ną wap'e'g.nake-t'a`wa k'ų he' a'taya kai'yapehąhą ke'ᵉ. C'ąke' t'e'hąhcį he'l g.lug.la' ną ak'e' g.licu' ną wic'a'ša šaic'iye c'ų he' ahi'k'ap'a g.lihų'ni ke'ᵉ. 5. Yųk'ą' c'ąksa' to'p he'l kig.na'kapi ną wąži' ša' c'a he' le wic'a'ša wą k'ap'e' c'ų he' t'a'wa c'ąke' icu' ną ų' kat'a' ke'ᵉ. He' ų' ya'm.nila k'ig.la'pi ke'ᵉ. Ak'e' ihį'hąna yųk'ą' ya'-m.ni k'ų hena' t'ąka'l hina'žipi ną k'įį'yąk-ap'e`pi¹ ke'ya'pi ke'ᵉ. C'ąke' ina'p'į ną wana' t'oi'c'iye c'ų he' i'š hehą'l kic'i' iya'yį ną c'ą' wą ekta' ihų'nipi ną ali'pi ke'ᵉ. K'u'l g.licu'pi ną he'c'ena t'i-a'nakitąpi-kta wą og.na'yą he' į'yąkapi ke'ᵉ. K'e'yaš wana' k'u'takiya ku'pi k'ų

---

¹ *ap'e*, to challenge, (when placed after an active verb); also, to invite another to participate in some activity.

as they were coming down the tree, the man who was painted blue
threw something out. It was cockle-burs and at once the whole
place was filled with bur-bearing weeds. 6. They clung to the head-
ornament and made it necessary for White-Plume to stop and
rid himself of them. Even so, he was so fleet of foot that he got
home first, and taking up the man's blue club he struck and killed
him with it. So only two men went home. 7. The third morning the
two remaining opponents came and this time it was the man
painted white who raced with the boy. And he tossed something
about which proved to be choke-cherry stalks. These caught in the
white plume, and it took the boy a long time to remove them, while
the other man started back, and was almost reaching the goal. But
now White-Plume had freed himself, and because his speed was
equal to being carried by the wind[1], he soon caught up with and
passed the man. The whitened club lay at the goal; so he took it
and killed the owner with it. 8. Now only one man remained. The
man who blackened himself came, carrying his black club with
him. He placed it at the goal, and started to compete with White-
Plume Boy. As they were descending from the tree, he tossed
something out; it was crab-apple stalks full of thorns which caught
in the boy's headdress, for they suddenly filled the place. 9. He was

---

lehą'l t'oi'c'iye c'ų he' ta'ku kala' iye'ya c'ąke' Wa'c'ihị Ska' e'l e'tųwą
yųk'ą' hena'kehcị wina'wizi[2] c'ąke' mak'a' kị a'taya wina'wizi-ożu`-
hịg.la ke'ᵉ. 6. Wap'e'g.nake[3] k'ų a'taya ik'o'yaka c'ąke' t'o'e'l he'na
na'żị ną kpahi'hị ną g.luśtą' kị e'l nake'ś g.licu' ke'ᵉ. Ho, he'c'eca
k'e'yaś li'la lu'zahą c'ąke' ag.li'k'ap'ị ną c'ąksa' wą t'oya'pi c'a
oi'yaye kị e'l kig.na'ka tk'a'ś he' icu' ną ų' kat'a' ke'ᵉ. C'ąke' nų'plala
k'ig.la'pi'ⁱ. 7. Ici'yam.ni-hị`hąna yųk'ą' nų'papi k'ų hena'yos ak'e'
hi'pi c'ąke' hehą'l sąi'c'iye c'ų he' kic'i' ị'yąka ke'ᵉ. Yųk'ą' he' i's c'ą'
k'ų he' iya'lipi ną wana' huk'u'takiya ku'pi hą'l ta'ku kah'o'l iye'ya
c'ąke' Wa'c'ihị Ska' wąya'ka yųk'ą' hena'kehcị c'ąp'a'-hu c'ąke'
wa'c'ihị wą p'eg.na'ke c'ų he' a'taya kai'yapehą iya'ye cị ų' he'na
he'l t'e'hąhcị g.lue'c'etuwac'ị śką'hị ną wana' k'ohą' wic'a'śa-są k'ų
he' g.lihų'nikta hą'l nake'ś Wa'c'ihị Ska' g.licu' k'e'yaś kahwo'ka
c'ąke' ila'zatąhą ag.li'kig.lega ke'ᵉ. He'c'eś ak'e' he'l c'ą' wą sąyą'pi ki-
g.na'ka c'ąke' icu' ną ų' kat'a' ke'ᵉ. 8. Ho, eha'ke-hị`hąna yųk'ą' wążi'la
oka'pta c'a he' hi' ke'ᵉ. Wic'a'śa wą sap-'i'c'iyị ną c'ąksa' wą a'taya
sapya'pi c'a g.luha' hi' ke'ᵉ. E'na e'kig.nakị ną wana' Wa'c'ihị Ska'
kic'i' iya'yị ną c'ą' wą ali'pi ke'p'e' c'ų he' ak'e' kic'i' ali' ke'ᵉ. Wana'
k'u'takiya ku'pi ną mak'a'ta g.liyo'psicapikta hą'l ta'ku kala' iye'ya
c'a Wa'c'ihị Ska' e'l e'tųwą yųk'ą' hena'kehcị t'apsą' hu'-p'esto`stola
k'ų he'c'a c'ąke' mak'o'c'e kị a'taya he'c'a-ożu`-hịg.la ke'ᵉ. 9. Wa'c'ihị

---

[1] This is an awkward translation of a very terse expression meaning "to be
swift, as a runner".

[2] wina'wizi, cockleburs; wi, woman; nawi'zi, to be jealous (?).

[3] wap'e'g.nake, head-ornament; wa, thing; p'e, head; g.na'ka, to place; to
have put away; aside.

obliged to take time out to rid his plume of the thorns, so that the blackened man was almost home. But now the boy was through, and starting home. Soon he was nearly touching the blackened man, as he ran. Now he passed him and arrived first at the goal, where he stood with the black club, ready to kill the owner when he got in. From that time, the tribe was free from the oppression of the four tyrants.

10. Then one day the boy said, "I have decided to go on a journey." — "Alas, my son," his father protested, "though I am aware that you are a man and should travel, still, I am troubled; for on your way you are going to encounter a tricky woman." But the boy didn't hesitate to start, on account of this warning. 11. He was travelling westward when he saw a woman, walking along, carrying something in her arms. "Ah! Undoubtedly this is what my father was speaking of," he thought, and tried to go around, so as to avoid meeting the woman. But she got in his path, and offered to rid him of lice[1]. The boy was insulted. "Say, what do you think I am that I should have lice?" he said to her, "I'm no orphan!" And he tried to go on, but she persisted. 12. By some unexplained method she induced him to yield, so that he lay down to have her

k'u he' a'taya ik'o'yaka c'ąke' e'na t'o'e'l g.lušpu'hį ną wana' wic'a'ša-sa'pa k'u he' g.lihu'nikta hą'l nake'š Wa'c'įhį Ska' g.licu' ke'ᵉ. K'e'yaš li'la ila'zata yu'za-nu s'e ku' ną ec'e'l k'ap'a' g.lihu'ni ke'ᵉ. C'ąke' he'l c'ą' sapya'pi wą e'kig.nakį ną iya'ya tk'a'š he' iki'cu ną u' kat'a' ke'ᵉ. C'ąke' hetą'hą oya'te kį tuwe'ni nagi' yewi'c'ayešni c'a oka'b.laya u'pi ke'ᵉ.

10. Yuk'ą' ąpe'tu wą e'l, — It'o' oma'ni-m.nįkte, — eya' ke'ᵉ. C'ąke' atku'ku kį iyo'k'išni ną, — Hehehi', c'įkš, eya' wini'c'a c'a oma'yanikte cį he'c'etu tk'a' aksa'ka he'l k'uše'ya wį'yą wą wic'a'šašni c'a u' k'u, — eya' ke'ᵉ. K'e'yaš a'tayaš i'tok'ašni he'c'ena iya'ya ke'ᵉ. 11. Wiyo'hpeyatakiya ya'hą yuk'ą' wį'yą wą ta'ku yuha' ną ya'hą ke'ᵉ. C'ąke', — Eh! Ta'ku wą ate' iwa'homaye c'u he' le e' se'ce lo', — ec'į' ną t'ą'kaya ao'hom.niwac'į ke'ᵉ. Ho, tk'a'š wį'yą k'u k'uše'ya na'žį ną heyo'kicilektehcį ke'ᵉ. — Ho'h, tase' wama'b.lenicaka c'a'š heyo'mapuze ca! — eyį' ną he'c'ena iya'yįkte c'e'yaš li'la oka'kišya ke'ᵉ. 12. Hąke'ya to'k'ešk'e h'ą' ną g.na'yelak'a iyo'wįyą iyu'ka

---

[1] A self-respecting Dakota dreads lice as much as anyone else. Not only are lice indicative of uncleanliness, but of lack of social standing, as well. Only the lower classes and orphans, and those for whom nobody was directly responsible, had them. People dreaded visits from such persons. They talk about anyone who has them, behind his back. Lice, when they invade a home that has up to that point maintained a stand against them, are believed to be forerunners of impending death. They say that long ago, a man whose son died, sat with his son's head on his lap, as he wept over him for a long while. At last, he sat quiet, watching the boy's face, when something moved from the corner of his eye, and a louse worked itself through the flesh and came out. Ever since that story got around, the belief has persisted that lice come from the dead, from the graves, to warn of another death.

look in his hair. She pulled his hair apart here and there hurriedly
and jerked out the white plume, leaving behind a poor whimpering
puppy, affected with itch. The helpless animal sought out a sunny
spot and lay there all day. 13. Of course it was Ikto again, masquerading as a woman. He now set the white plume in his hair, and
entered the tribal circle in the role of a boy-beloved[1]. So he was
promptly presented with a wife and established in a tipi, in the
rôle of son-in-law[2]. It happened that the woman was a favorite
child, in her own right, so the two had their tent inside the camp
circle. 14. And his wife said, "Each morning a red fox runs by, and
everyone tries to shoot him, but nobody succeeds in hitting him." It
was morning and the camp was in an uproar. "There he is again, the
red fox," the wife said. And Ikto replied with a command. "Prop
up the door flaps so they will stay," he said, and his wife, thinking

---

*c'ąke' wana' heyo'kicile ke'ᵉ. P'ehį' kį yugą'gą ahi'yayį ną wą'cak
wap'e'g.nake k'ų he' yušlo'k icu' yųk'ą' šų'kala wą hakte'la c'a howa'ya
ų' c'ąke' ihpe'ya iya'ya ke'ᵉ. Šika ų'šiyehcį oma'šte wą e'l ąpe'tu
a'taya hpa'yela ke'ᵉ. 13. K'ohą' wana' ak'e' Ikto' he e' c'ąke' wa'c'įhį
wą manų' k'ų he' p'eg.na'kį ną iye' hokši'-c'ąlki'yapi-kahya wic'o't'ita
i' c'ąke' wą'cak wį'yą k'u'pi c'a wic'a'woha-e't'i ke'ᵉ. Wį'yą wą i'š
eya' he' t'ehi'la-yuha'pi yųk'ą' he e' c'a yu'zį ną kic'i' c'oka'p e't'i
ke'ᵉ. 14. Yųk'ą' wį'yą kį leya' ke'ᵉ, — Hį'hąna c'ą'šna šugi'la wą le'
og.na' hiya'ya c'ą' k'ute'pi k'eš tuwe'ni o' oki'hišni k'ų, — eya' ke'ᵉ.
Wana' hį'hąna c'ąke' ta'ku hmu' š'e iki'k'opi yųk'ą', — Iho', ak'e'
wana' he hiya'ye', — wį'yą kį eya' ke'ᵉ. He'c'ena, — T'iyo'pa kį*

---

[1] To be a boy-beloved was a great honor, and carried with it heavy obligations. The parents who wished to declare their child beloved must first
give many presents away in the child's name; then they must always be
foremost in doing kind deeds to the poor and needy, in the child's honor.
In return, the entire tribe set great store on such a child. It did not eventually
make him a chief — only his personal record after he grew up could decide
that, — but it insured him the deference and recognition of the people,
and their affection for him, as for one on whose account many people had
benefited. Girls could be beloved too. The term *hokši'-c'ąlki'yapi* is:
hokši', child; *c'ąl*, contracted from *c'ąte'*, heart; *ki*, sign of the possessive,
their own; *ya*, to cause or use for; *pi*, they; literally, "a child which they
use for their heart."

[2] If a young couple is living near the bride's parents, the husband, as son-in-
law, must always be on the alert to serve, and foresee and do what needs
to be done without being asked. He must bring home game, and if there is
fighting to be done, he must be in the van, protecting not only his wife but
all her people. He must adhere strictly to the avoidance rule towards his
wife's parents; and always be on guard too, to do things right; for his
joking relatives — his wife's brothers and parallel and cross cousins, and
also her sisters, — are watching for a slip on his part so they can laugh at him.
The situation is reversed, when the couple is spending time with the man's
parents. Then the young wife, as daughter-in-law, needs to be exemplary in
every particular, for not only the husband's brothers and sisters and cousins,
but also the neighbors, are going to notice promptly if she fails in any detail.
On the whole, it is a trying rôle.

how he would doubtless shoot from where he sat, hastened to do
his bidding. Instead, just as the fox passed within his range, he
pretended to fumble, and said, "Hard luck! the limbs of my robe
struck my bow!" and he didn't shoot. 15. Again his wife said,
"Now and then, a very scarlet bird goes flying past here, and they
all try to shoot it but nobody ever hits it." After a while, the camp
was in an uproar again and the wife said, "There now, they are
shouting because it is flying by." And Ikto said, "Adjust the poles
of the smoke vent so that the opening is clear." Thinking how her
husband was about to succeed where others had failed, she hastily
adjusted the poles and then came in and sat down to wait. But
instead of shooting the scarlet bird when it flew overhead, he
evidently had cut nicks in his bow-string, because it snapped just
as he placed an arrow. By way of apology he said, "Hard luck! I've
broken my bow-string!" and he did not shoot. 16. Then he said,
"Have your father send a crier around. I am about to smoke." So
a crier made the announcement and soon the tipi was filled with a
waiting crowd. He now said, "Each time I puff out smoke from
this tobacco, be ready to kill something[1]." So they sat in tense
readiness, but nothing magical happened. At last the men took
their departure, heavy-hearted from disappointment. 17. During
all this, a poor girl who lived alone with her mother, in a tipi outside

apa'ǧąyą e'g.le, — eya' c'a t'awi'cu kį ec'e'l e'g.le yųk'ą' i'yokakįyą
hiya'ya c'aš t'i'tąhą k'ute'kte se'ce c'ų, ec'ą'l, — Hį'! Šina'-huha`²
iya'wakip'a, — eya'-hįg.la o'šni šk'e'ᵉ. 15. Ak'e' t'awi'cu kį heya'
ke'ᵉ, — Le'l og.na' eya'šna zitka'la wą lu'ta c'a kįyą' hiya'ya c'ą'
k'ute'pi k'eš tuwe'ni o'šni k'ų, — eya' yųk'ą' wana' ta'ku iki'k'opi
c'ąke' wi'yą ki' heya' ke'ᵉ. — Iho', wana' he kįyą' hiya'yelak'a aki'-
š'ape', — eya' ke'ᵉ. Yųk'ą' — Wip'i'paha³ kį paza'm.ni e'g.le, — eya'
ke'ᵉ. C'ąke' otu'ḣciyakel⁴ hįg.na'ku wao'kta-ic'ila ec'e'kc'e wip'i'paha
kį e'g.le ną wakta' yąka' ke'ᵉ. Yųk'ą' leya wic'e'ška kį og.na' k'ute'kte
se'ce c'ų, ec'ą'l ita'zipa-ik'ą' kį waki'hųhų ną he' yąke'lak'a! — Hį',
Ita'zipa-ik'ą` wag.la'psaka, — eya' ke'ᵉ. He'c'eš ųma'ni o'šni ke'ᵉ.
16. Hehą'l Ikto' heya' ke'ᵉ, — Niya'te e'yapahawic'ašikte lo'. C'ąnų'-
mųpįkta c'a, — eya' c'ąke' e'yapahapi yųk'ą' t'i' ot'į's ahi'yotaka
ke'ᵉ. — Ho, c'ąli' b.lab.lu'kta c'e taku'l kat'e'wac'į po', — eya' c'ąke'
itu'ḣcį wį'yeya yąka'pi k'e'yaš ta'kuni hiḣpa'yešni šk'e'ᵉ. C'ąke'
wic'a'ša kį iyu'ha c'ąl-e'c'ecapišni šk'e'ᵉ. 17. Ic'ų'hą wic'į'cala ųšikala
wą hų'ku kic'i'šnala hoḣe'yatąhą⁵ t'i'pi c'ąke' manį'l c'ąk'į'-i yųk'ą'

---

[1] Another instance of Ikto' playing the supernaturally gifted man's part,
and failing.

[2] *šina'*, blanket; robe; *huha'*, the limbs (parts of the leg-skin of the animal).

[3] *wip'a'*, the large flaps that control the smoke, over the tipi; *i*, by means of;
paha', pushed upwards.

[4] *otu'*, or *itu'*, in vain. *ḣcį*, very; *yakel*, rather; rather in vain.

[5] *hoḣe'yatąhą*, on the rear side of the circle. All tipis face in, normally, with
their rear sides out; *ho*, classifier for camp-circle.

the camp-circle[1], went into the woods to gather fuel for their fire. There she found the little helpless dog and was moved by pity. "You poor little dog, how you must suffer!" she said, pulling up quantities of sage-brush to make him a softer bed. But the dog spoke to her, "You are kind; but even better than to make me a bed here would be to take me home." So she took him up in her blanket and carried him home. 18. She laid him down and went outside; but when she reëntered the tipi, she found instead a very handsome young man sitting in the place of honor[2]. He said to her, "Go now to Ikto who resides in the tipi within the camp circle and ask him to return to me the head-ornament which he took from me." So the girl stood outside Ikto's tipi and said, "Ikto, I have come for that head-ornament, on behalf of its owner." 19. Immediately he began, "Hand it out; hand it out; for it is his." She took the plume and carried it home. At once the people derided Ikto with shouts and jeers, and chased him out towards the wild places and left him still going. "Oh, but what's the use?" they said, "It is Ikto. He'll be turning up again, by and by." 20. Once more the red fox ran by; and it was White-Plume's arrow which pierced and killed him. And the next morning, when the scarlet bird soared overhead, it was White-Plume's arrow which brought it down, piercing its heart. They took the scarlet bird and set it up at the very topmost point

śu̧'kala k'u̧ he' ata'yi̧ nǫ — Ų́śikâ, c'e'wi̧ṡ-śu̧'kala wǫ iyo'tiye'kiyela kê, — eya'ya p'eżi'-ho̧'ta yuśla'śla nǫ owi̧'ṡ-kicat'u̧ yu̧k'ą' śu̧'kala ki̧ heya' ke'ᵉ, — Wic'i̧'cala, akṡa'-wau̧śiyalaka, ama'g.la yo', — eya' c'ąke' he'c'ena śina' og.na' yuha' nǫ t'iya'ta ak'i' ke'ᵉ. 18. T'ima' e'g.naki̧ nǫ ina'p'i̧ nǫ ak'e' t'ima'hel k'ig.la' yu̧k'ą' k'ośka'laka wǫ li'la ową'yak-waśte' c'a t'ic'a'tku e'l yąka' ke'ᵉ. — Ho', Ikto' le c'oka'p t'i' ki̧ e'l yi̧' nǫ wap'e'g.nake wǫ maki'u̧ ki̧ he' mi'c'uśi yo', — eya' c'ąke' wic'i̧'cala ki̧ ekta' i' nǫ t'iyo'pa e'l ina'żi̧ nǫ heya' ke'ᵉ, — Ikto', Wap'e'g.nake wǫ wic'a'kicihiyowahi ye', — eya' ke'ᵉ. 19. Yu̧k'ą', — Iye'kicic'iya, Iye'kicic'iya, t'a'wa c'e, — eya'ya yąka' c'ąke' wap'e'g.nake ki̧ iye'k'iyapi c'a ag.li' ke'ᵉ. He'c'ena oya'te ki̧ Ikto' aṡ'a'pi nǫ mani'takiya a'yapi nǫ t'e'hąl e'yuśtąpi ke'ᵉ. — To'kṡa' ak'e' u'kte lo'; He' Ikto' e'śnika c'aṡ, — eya'pi śk'e'ᵉ. 20. Nake'ṡ ak'e' śu̧gi'la k'u̧ he' hiya'ya tk'a'ṡ Wa'c'į̧hi̧ Śka' ipa'hna o' ke'ᵉ; nǫ ak'e' ihi̧'hąna yu̧k'ą' zitka'la wǫ lu'ta c'a wąką'l oki̧'yą u̧' tk'a'ṡ c'ąte' ki̧ g.laki̧'yą o' śk'e'ᵉ. C'ąke' t'ic'e' ki̧ e'l śaye'la otke'yapi śk'e'ᵉ.

---

[1] The average member of the tribe, able to play his full part in its maintenance and protection, and in the social events, has a right to the camp circle. Those unable to fulfil these requirements, generally old couples, widows, and the familiar old woman with her grandson, withdraw voluntarily from the camp circle and live back of it; while the newly-weds of the higher ranking families, who have a certain social standing because of their benevolence and generosity, live, for a limited time, inside the circle, generally in front of their parents' tipi.

[2] The place of honor is the space in the centre, back of the central fire. So that a guest of honor, when seated, faces the doorway.

of White-Plume's tipi. 21. "Now I shall smoke. Ask them to come in," he said, so the men crowded into the tipi. "I shall send out four puffs of smoke, so try to kill them[1] all," he instructed. They sat in readiness and the instant the tobacco smoke came out of his mouth, birds of every sort filled the room; so the men worked hard to kill them all. Finally even blankets, red ones and blue ones and brown ones and black ones, also fell, and then guns and fine possessions came down. And that was the beginning of such things in the tribe, they say. 22. White-Plume took for his wife the girl who was so humble but so kind-hearted, and the tribe caused them to live in a tipi inside the camp circle and held them in highest esteem and affection, they say. That is all.

20. Blood-Clot Boy.

1. A rabbit lived happily until a bear and his young came and took possession of his home, driving him out. So he was obliged to dwell in a makeshift hut near by. 2. And each morning the bear stood outside his door and said, "You Rabbit with the ragged muzzle, come out. Your buffalo-surround is full." Then Rabbit came out with his magic arrow and, with one shot, sent it piercing through

21. Hehą'l, — Ho', canų'mupįkta c'e t'i'l uwi'c'aśi po', — eya' c'ąke' t'i' ot'į's ahi'yotaka śk'e'°. Yųk'ą', — Le' c'ąli' kį to'pa-b.lab.lu'kta c'a iyu'ha wic'a'kat'ewac'į po', — eya' c'ąke' wį'yeya yąka'pi yųk'ą' ka'k'el c'ąli'-śo'ta kį yab.lu'b.lu kį he'c'el zitka'la oc'a'ze iyu'ha okį'yąpi c'ąke' wic'a'kat'a a'yapi kį ec'e'l śina' oo'wa-śa' nąi'ś t'o' nąi'ś ǧi', sa'pa, k'o'k'o kaħpa'pi ną hąke'ya ma'zawak'ą² ną wo'yuha k'o'k'o kaħpa'pi śk'e'°. Hetą' nake'ś oya'te kį wo'yuha waśte'śte yuha'pi śk'e'°. 22. Wa'c'įhį Ska' wic'į'calala wą ų'śike c'e'yaś są'p-waų'śila k'ų he' yu'zį ną kic'i' ho'c'okap t'iwi'c'ak'iyapi ną li'la. t'ewi'c'aħilapi śk'e'°. Hehą'yela owi'hąke'°.

20.

1. Maśtį'ska wą tąyą's t'i'la yųk'ą' e'l mat'o' wą c'įca' o'p to'k'iya-tąhą hi' ną t'ąka'l iye'yį ną iye' t'o'he kį e'l et'i śk'e'°. C'ąke' maśtį'-skala kį k'iye'la tokį'ś p'iya'-kit'i śk'e'°. 2. Yųk'ą' ohį'hąni kį iyo'hila mat'o' kį t'ąka'l hina'zį nąśna, — Maśtį'cala, p'ute'-ħciħci'la, hina'p'i³ ye'. Nit'a'wonase hiyo't'įze lo', — eya' c'ą hina'p'į ną wą'-wak'ą wą yuha' c'ąke' ų pte' to'na i'c'ipasisa wic'a'o śk'e'°. Waśte'ya wic'a'o

---

[1] This is the mysterious power that Ikto' tried to imitate — the White-Plume boy can bring down valuable things just by smoking and sending the puffs of smoke upward.
[2] *ma'za*, iron; *wak'ą'*, mysterious; holy; sacred; hence a gun. Often, *ma'zak'ą;* rarely, *maśk'ą'*.
[3] *hina'p'a*, come outside; *ina'p'a*, to go outside (the speaker being outside, in the first case; and inside in the second.) We have also, *g.lina'p'a;* and *k'ina'p'a*, to come out again, to go out again.

8

each buffalo in turn till all were killed[1]. Then the bear would rush up with his young, and take all the meat home. 3. They never gave the rabbit any meat, and the result was that he was now very thin. Once again they were cutting up the meat; so he came and stood to one side, but before he even asked for a piece, they ordered him off, so he turned to leave. Somewhat removed from the scene was a blood clot on the ground. So, as he went over it, he pretended to stumble, and picked it up, thrusting it under his belt. 4. And the bear called out, "Hey, there, you worthless wretch, you aren't taking anything, are you ?" So the rabbit answered, "No, I only stagger because I am weak from hunger." Then he came home. Immediately he made a sweat-bath over the blood clot. He was busy pouring water over the hot stones when someone within heaved a deep sigh, and then said, "Whoever you are who are thus kind, open the door for me." So he opened the door, and a young man, red (from the heat), stepped outside. Rabbit was very happy. 5. "Oh, would that my grandson had such and such things," he would say, and instantly they would appear, so that all in the same day, he had everything desirable. Everything he wished for him was his. But Rabbit couldn't offer him food, for he had none. Then Blood-Clot Boy said, "Grandfather, how is it that you starve while a rich man lives near by ?" So Rabbit related everything to him. 6. "Alas, grandson, what do you mean ? Why, the fact is that it is I who shoot

c‘ą hehą'l mat‘o' kį c‘įca' o'p e'l hiyu'pi nąśna t‘alo' kį a'taya icu'pi ną ak‘i'yag.lapi śke‘‘. 3. To'hįni hąke' k‘u'piśni kį ų' wana' li'la t‘ama'-heca ke‘‘. Yųk‘ą' ak‘e' wap‘a'tapi c‘a e'l ina'żį k‘e'yaś wo'laśnihą kiśi'capi c‘ąke' kawįʼħ g.licu'kta yųk‘ą' kai'yuzeya he'l weyo't‘a wą yąka' c‘ąke' ahi'cahe-kųzį ną yuma'hel icu' ke‘‘. 4. Yųk‘ą' mat‘o' kį, — Wą, wahte‘śni śi'ca, ta'ku iya'cu se'ce lo', — eya' c‘ąke', — Hiya`, į'śe' wana' li'la loc‘į'pi ų' mahų'keśni c‘a maka'cekceke lo', — eyį' ną he'c‘ena t‘iya'takiya g.licu' ke‘‘. G.li' ną he'c‘ena weyo't‘a kį he' ini'kicaǧa ke‘‘. M.ni' aka'śtą ohi'tiya śką' yųk‘ą' ųg.na' tuwa' t‘ima‘ c‘uwi' oki'niya ną hehą'l, — He' nitu'we c‘a wąų'śiyala he'cįhą t‘iyo'pa maki'yuǧą yo', — eya' ke‘‘. C‘ąke' t‘iyo'pa kiyu'ǧą yųk‘ą' k‘ośka'laka wą śaye'la hina'p‘a c‘ąke' maśtį'śkala k‘ų li'la wi'yuśkį ke‘‘. 5. — Tok‘i mit‘a'koża ka'k‘el ną ka'k‘el yuha' ni', — eya' c‘ą'śna iye'c‘etu c‘ąke' ąpe'tu-hąke`yela ta'ku waśte' kį iyu'ha yuha' śk‘e‘‘. Ta'ku kikų' k‘ų iyu'ha. K‘e'yaś maśtį'cala ta'kuni yu'teśni c‘ąke' to'k‘a-wo`k‘uśni ke‘‘. Yųk‘ą' We‘-Hokśi`la leya' ke‘‘, — T‘ųka`śila, ta'kole' wic‘a'śa wą waśe'ca c‘a ik‘i'yela yat‘i' ną k‘ohą' aki'ħ'ą-yąų' he? — eya' c‘ąke' to'k‘el mat‘o' kį k‘uwa' k‘ų hena' iyo'kawįħ oki'yaka ke‘‘. 6. — Hehehe‘, t‘ako'ża, ta'ku yak‘e' lo'. Wą k‘e'ya, miye'ħca c‘a pte' kį hena' wic‘a'wao we lo'. Tk‘a' waśte'ya wic‘a'o b.luśtą' c‘ą'śna

---

[1] The arrow hits one buffalo, goes through him into the next, and through him into another, and travels like that without stopping until all the buffaloes are down.

all the game, and then when I am through, the bear comes with his young and they take the meat all away. They always call me by saying, 'Say, you Rabbit with the ragged muzzle, come out; your surround is full.' So I come out, and do the shooting for them." On hearing this, Blood-Clot Boy was very angry. He took a piece of ash and burned it here and there, and made a club, and sat ready with it. 7. As usual, the bear stood outside very early in the morning and, "Hey, you Rabbit with the ragged muzzle, come on out; your surround is full," he said, so he answered as his grandson had taught him, *"Hoħ!* Get out, what are you talking about ? I suppose you'll be claiming all the meat again!"[1] And he didn't come out. The angry bear came in, thinking to force him out, but Blood-Clot Boy was ready for him, and killed him with one blow of his club. 8. Then he sent his grandfather to the bear's wife, telling him what to say. He said, "Bear sends for extra help." And the wife called out, "Is that so ? How many is he carrying ?" — "He is carrying two buffaloes." — "That's funny. I never knew him to carry so few!" 9. So the rabbit tried again. "He is carrying three buffaloes," he said. "How funny. He used to carry more than that," she said. So Rabbit said, "He is carrying four buffaloes." And this time the wife said, "It that so ? Well, wait, then." And she started to come out

mat‘o' c‘įca' o'p hiyu' nąšna a'taya e'yaye lo'. Wą, maštį`cala, p‘ute`- ħcihci`la, hina'p‘i ye'. Nit‘a'wonase hiyo't‘įze, ema'kiya ece' ye lo', — eya' ke‘e. He'c‘el naħ‘ų' ną li'la c‘aze' šk‘e‘e. Ną pse'ħtį wą ǧuǧu'yį ną c‘ąksa' wą ka'ǧį ną wį'yeya yuha' yąka' ke‘e. 7. Wana', he'c‘eca kte c‘ų, hį'hąniħcį mat‘o' kį t‘ąka'l hina'žį ną, — Maštį`cala P‘ute`- ħcihci`la, hina'p‘i ye'. Nit‘a'wonase wą hiyo't‘įze, — eya' c‘ąke' eya' t‘ako'žakpaku kį he'c‘el eye'si kį ų', — Hoħ, ak‘o' g.li' ye', ta'kuħca yak‘e'. Ak‘e' c‘į t‘alo' kį iyu'ha aya'kšiziįkte², — *eyį' ną hina'p‘ešni ke‘e. Yųk‘ą' mat‘o' kį i'šikc‘į ina'p‘ek‘iyewac‘į t‘ima'hel hiyu' tk‘a'š, We'-Hokši'la t‘iyo'p-²ik‘i yela na'žį c‘ąke' c‘ąksa' k‘ų he' ų' kat‘a' iħpe'ya ke‘e. 8. Hehą'l t‘ųka'šitkula kį mat‘o' t‘awi'cu kį ekta' yesi' ną le'c‘el eye'ši ke‘e, — Mat‘o' wag.la'm.na waho'kiye lo', — eye'ši c‘ąke' iya'yį ną mat‘o' kį t‘i' kį e'l it‘ą'kal ina'žį ną, — Mat‘o' wa- g.la'm.na waho'kiye lo', — eya' ke‘e. Yųk‘ą' t‘awi'cu kį t‘ima'hetąhą ho'uyį ną, — Hinų, to'na k‘į' he? — eya' c‘ąke' — Pte' nų'p k‘į' ye lo', — eya' yųk‘ą', — Tuk‘i, tų'weniš hena'lašni, o'taš k‘į' s'a k‘ų, — eya' ke‘e. 9. C‘ąke' hehą'l, — Pte' ya'm.ni k‘į' ye lo', — eya' yųk‘ą', — Hinų, o'taš k‘į' s'a k‘ų, — eya' ke‘e. C‘ąke' ak‘e', — Pte' to'p k‘į' ye lo', — eya' yųk‘ą' hehą'l nake', — Hinų, hį'yąka', — eyį' ną hina'-*

---

[1] The rabbit dares to be haughty only because he has the Blood-Clot Boy behind him. That is a common pattern in Dakota stories.

² *akši'ža,* to withhold, and refuse to surrender. *a,* on; *kši'ža,* bent, clamped on. There is a year-count, "*P‘ut‘į'hį-ska' waa'kšiža*" (from *p‘ute',* snout, *hį,* hairs) and refers to the time when General Harney (*Put‘į'hį-ska* White-Whiskers) held the people as prisoners near the Black Hills.

of the tipi but Blood-Clot Boy was ready for her and the moment her head appeared, he struck her with a resounding blow and killed her. 10. Then he entered the bear's home, and found all the bear children sitting in a circle, eating their meal. So he said to them, "Now, if anyone here has been kind to my grandfather, let him say, I," and they all yelled, "I." And then one said, "Do they think that, simply by saying the word 'I,' they will be spared? He who was kind to your grandfather sits over here!" he said. And in the corner they saw him sitting, the very youngest little bear wearing his very brown coat. 11. The rabbit spoke up, "Grandson, he speaks true. Ever so often, he dragged a piece of meat over to me, and pushed it with his snout into my hut." So Blood-Clot Boy said, "In that case, step outside; you shall live." After he had gone out, the boy killed all the other cubs. The rabbit now moved into his old home and as he still had his magic arrow, he provided meat in abundance so that the three, including the little bear, lived without want.

12. And then one day Blood-Clot Boy declared his plans. "Grandfather, in what direction do the people live?" he asked; so he told him they lived in the west. Then he said he planned to go there on a visit. The rabbit advised against it vigorously. "No, grandson, I dread it for you. Something very deceptive lives on the way." But

---

p'į́kta tk'a'š We'-Hokši̇̀la t'ą́ka'l hina'žį̇ hų́še'ca, ka'k'el p'a' pat'ą́kal iye'kiye cį̇ he'c'ena aką́l t'osye'la ap'į̇' ną kat'a' šk'e'ᵉ. 10. T'ᶜima' iya'ya yų́k'ą̇' mat'o' c'į̇ca'la kį̇ yumi'meya yą̇ka'pi ną̇ wo'tahą̇pi ke'ᵉ. C'ą̇ke', — Ho, tuwa' t'ų̇ka'šila u̇'šiyalapi he'cį̇hą̇, miye', eya' po', — eya' yų́k'ą̇' iyu'ha, — Miye', miye', miye', — eya'pi c'ą̇ke' k̇mu' s'e le'c'eca ke'ᵉ. Hehą́'l wą̇ži', — Miye' eya'pi yų́k'ą̇' wic'a'nikta nų̇c'a'š, u̇'šila wą̇ le'c'iš mą̇ke' šą̇'! — eya' yų́k'ą̇' oka'k̇mi wą̇ ekta' mat'o' c'į̇ca'la-hakȧ'ktala wą̇ ġiye'k̇cį̇ yą̇ke'la ke'ᵉ. 11. Maštį̇'skala k'ų̇, — T'akȯ'ža, he' wica'k'e lo'. Tohą́'tu c'ą̇'šna t'asi'c'oġį̇¹ wą̇ži' t'ima' yaslo'hą̇ iye'mak'iyela ye lo', — eya' c'ą̇ke', — Ho, ina'p'a yo', yani'kte, — eya' c'ą̇ke' ina'p'a c'a ų̇ma'pi kį̇ iyu'hak̇cį̇ wic'a'kat'a šk'e'ᵉ. Hetą́' maštį̇'cala k'ų̇ ehą́'ni t'i' k'ų̇ he'l p'iya'-kit'i ną̇ wą̇'- wak'ą̇ k'ų̇ he'c'ena g.luha' c'ą̇ke' ak'e' li'la waše'ca c'a We'-Hokši̇̀la e' ną̇ mat'o'-hakė'lala k'ų̇ hena' wic'a'g.luha t'i' šk'e'ᵉ.

12. Ų̇g.na' We'-Hokši̇̀la ową́ži u̇' kį̇ iwa'tuk'a ną̇ — T'ų̇kȧ'šila, le' tok'i̇'yot'ą̇ oya'te wic'o't'i he? — eya' c'ą̇ke', — Wiyo'k̇peyata oya'te wic'o't'i ye lo', — eya' yų́k'ą̇' — It'o' ekta' i'c'imani-m.nįkte², — eya' c'ą̇ke' maštį̇'skala kį̇ li'la iyo'k'išni ke'ᵉ. — Hiyȧ', t'akȯ'ža, t'awa't'el- c'ic'iyešni ye lo'. He'l k'uše'ya ta'ku wą̇ li'la wic'a'šašni c'a u̇' k'ų̇, —

---

¹ *t'asi'c'oġį̇* is a piece of meat in the lower leg of the ruminant. It is full of sinew, and a most undesirable part of the meat. Here it is meant to indicate "better than nothing".

² *i'c'imani*, to go, as on an extended trip, to another tribe, or band.

that made him all the more eager to be off, and he started. 13. He hadn't gone far before he saw a man shooting at something. "Ah! This must be what grandfather warned me of as not to be trusted," he thought, and tried to go around him, but he called, "My younger brother, come over here and shoot this for me before you go." — "Impossible! I am on a rush trip, I haven't time to loiter and shoot your game for you!" he said. 14. But he begged so earnestly that he persuaded the boy to turn and come back to him. The boy sent an arrow which pierced the bird; and then he started to go on. But he called again, "That's a fine arrow, younger brother; who would discard it this way?" He shouted back, "Well then, take it and own it," and would go on, but, "My younger brother, please climb the tree and get it for me," he pleaded; so, as the best way to get rid of him, the boy came and prepared to climb the tree. 15. But the man said again, "My younger brother, you better take off your clothes. They are very beautiful; it would be a pity to tear them on the branches." With that he persuaded the boy further, until he removed all his clothes and started to climb the tree in his naked state. He got the arrow and was coming down when he heard the one below saying something under his breath. "Are you saying something?" he called out. "I just said, Hurry down, brother!" he answered. 16. So, "Oh, all right!" he called and continued down. Then, just as he was about to step to the ground, the man called in a

eye' c'e'yaṡ hehą'l iyo'tą kitą' ną hąke'ya iya'ya ke'ᵉ. 13. T'e'hą ye'ṡni ec'e'l wic'a'ṡa wą ta'ku k'ute'hą c'a e'l ya' c'ąke', — Ĕh! t'ųka'ṡila ta'ku wą wic'a'ṡaṡni ke'ye' c'ų he' le e' se'ce lo', — ec'i̧' ną i't'ehąyą ao'hom.niwac'i̧ yųk'ą', — Misų̀, u'wi ye', t'o'wa'ṡ ka' miye'cio ną hehą'l ila'nikte¹ lo', — eya' c'ąke', — Ho'ĥ, ina'ĥni le'- oma'wani ki, tase' le' wac'i'ciokta c'a waų' ka, — eya' ke'ᵉ. 14. Ho, k'e'yaṡ li'la ų'ṡiṡi-ia` c'ąke' kawi'ĥ-g.licu' ną ipa'ĥna ihe'ya zitka'la wą kio' ną he'c'ena iya'ya ke'ᵉ. Yųk'ą' ak'e' kipą' ną, — Wą, misų̀, wąhi̧'kpe wą waṡte' k'ų, tuwa'ṡ he' iĥpe'ye ca, — eya' c'ąke' e'tųwą yųk'ą' wąhi̧'kpe k'ų he' zitka'la ki ik'o'yak c'ąwą'kal i'yanica ke'ᵉ. — Ec'a icu' ną yuha' yo', — eyi̧' ną iya'yikte c'e'yaṡ, — Misų̀, ų'ṡimayala k'ų, iya'li ną ima'kicu ye', — eya' c'ąke' he'cetu k'eṡ, wana' c'ą' ki iya'likte c'a u' ke'ᵉ. 15. Yųk'ą' ak'e' heya' ke'ᵉ, — Misų̀, t'o'wa'ṡ haya'pi ki hena' g.luṡlo'ka yo'. Li'la waṡte'ṡte k'ų, c'ąi'nici- yupsakikte lo', — eya' ke'ᵉ. Ak'e' g.na'yą c'ąke' haya'ke waṡte'ṡte k'oya'ka c'a iyu'ha g.luṡlo'ki ną hac'o'c'ola c'ąi'yali ke'ᵉ. Wana' wąhi̧'kpe ki icu' ną k'u'takiya ku' ki lehą'l naĥma'ĥmala ta'keyaya na'ži̧ c'a naĥ'ų' c'ąke', — Tok'e ta'kehe so? — eya' yųk'ą', — I̧'ṡe' misų̀ k'u'ya ku' ye', k'oyą', ep'e' c'ų, — —eya' ke'ᵉ. 16. C'ąke', — Ohą', — eyi̧' ną he'c'ena ku' ną wana' mak'a'ta g.lihų'nikta hą'l,

---

¹ ila'la becomes ila'ni̧ before kta, because l cannot stand before i̧. "You shall go."

great voice, "Stick to the tree!" And at once Blood-Clot Boy became
glued to the tree. It was Ikto who had thus deceived him, and now
he hurriedly dressed himself in the boy's finery and flung his old
garments at him saying, "There, Blood-Clot Boy, put those on!"
Then he went towards the village. 17. In that village was a young
woman, the eldest child of her parents, and greatly loved by them.
"She-dwells-within-the-Circle" was what her name meant. He was
going to her. As soon as he entered the tribal camp, the cry went
up, "Blood-Clot Boy comes on a journey, and C'oka'p T'i'wį is the
one he comes for!" The parents immediately gave their daughter
to him and placed their tipi within the circle. So Ikto, all in a day,
settled into the rôle of the son-in-law. 18. The next morning he
proceeded to demonstrate his supernatural powers. "Let all the
young men remove the hair from a buffalo-hide and scatter it
about in the bend of the river, beyond the hill." It was done accordingly. Next day he told them to send scouts to see the result. They
went; but came back to report that nothing had happened. 19. Now,
C'oka'p T'i'wį had a young sister who stayed around her tipi. She
didn't like her around, and ordered her off each time, saying, "Go
on away! I don't want her to even look upon my husband!"
Finally the girl went crying into the woods and gathered firewood.
There she came upon a youth, very handsome, stuck fast to a tree.
He said to her, "Young girl, if you have pity, free me from this tree.
Ikto has dealt thus badly with me and gone into camp leaving me to

ho'ništo[1], — Iya'skapa! — eya' yųk'ą' he'c'ena We'-Hokši`la c'ą' kį
e'na iya'skapa c'ąke' ehą'k'ų Ikto' he e' c'a ina'ħni t'aha'yake kį
iyu'ha ec'e'k'ce ų' ną iye' šikši'ca ų' k'ų hena' e'na našlo'k iħpe'yį ną,
— We'-Hokši`la, niye' hena' ų' wo', — eya' aka'ħ'ol iye'yį ną wic'o't'i-
takiya iya'ya šk'e'ᵉ. 17. Wik'o'škalaka wą t'oka'p'a-yuhapi c'ąke'
li'la t'eħi'lapi c'a, — C'oka'p T'i'wį, — eci'yapi yųk'ą' he e' c'a e'l
ya' ke'ᵉ. Ka'k'el-hoc'o'ka kį ihų'ni kį he'c'ena oya'te kį, — We'-
Hokši`la C'oka'p T'i'wį ai'c'imani-hi ye lo'! — eya' e'yapahapi
šk'e'ᵉ. C'ąke' hųka'ke kį wą'cak k'u'pi ną c'oka'p t'iwi'c'ak'iyapi
c'ąke' waste'ka c'a he'l ąpe'tu-hąke`yela wic'a'woħa-et'i šk'e'ᵉ. 18.
Yųk'ą' ihį'hąna kį e'l wą'cak wana' wak'ą'kta c'a, — Ho, k'oška'laka
kį šina'hišma wąži' yušla'pi ną paha'-ak'o'tąhą kaħmi' kį he'l ena'na
hį' kį yuo'b.lecapikte lo', — eya' c'ąke' ec'ų'pi šk'e'ᵉ. Ihį'hąna
yųk'ą' ekta' yewi'c'aši c'ąke' ekta' i'pi k'e'yaš ta'kunišni šk'e'ᵉ.
19. K'e'yaš C'oka'p T'i'wį t'ąka'kula wą e't'i kį e'l ya' c'ą, — Ak'o'
ya' na, wic'a'ša ama'kiyutakta tk'a', — eyą'hą c'ąke' c'e'ya oma'nihį
ną manį'l c'ąk'į'-i yųk'ą' he'c'iya k'oška'laka wą li'la wic'a'ša
waste' c'a c'ąa'iyaskap na'žįhą c'ąke' e'l i' yųk'ą', — Wic'į'cala,
wau'šiyala he'cįhą maka'ħlaya yo'. Ikto' le' t'eħi'ya oma'kiħ'ą ną

[1] ho, voice; nį'sko, this big; į'sko, as big as; kį'sko (ka' į'sko), as big as that
   yonder; hį'sko (he' į'sko), as big as that near you; nį'sko (le' į'sko), as big
   as this; tį'sko (ta'ku į'sko), as big as what?

my fate." So the girl took her ax and peeled the man off from the
tree; and then, sharing her blanket with him, she took him home.
20. And then he said, "Now, go to the one who is living inside the
circle and bring my clothes to me; Ikto has worn them long enough."
So the girl stood at the door of her sister's tipi and said, "Ikto, you
have worn certain clothes long enough; I have come after them for
their owner." But her sister said, "Go away. I don't want you to
look upon my husband!" But all the while Ikto repeated without a
pause, "Hand them out, hand them out[1]." At last then, the young
woman realized that Ikto himself had duped her; so she began to
cry. 21. Now Blood-Clot Boy put on his own clothes and sat looking
very handsome, and said, "Let all the young men remove the hair
from a buffalo-hide and scatter it about in the bend of the river
beyond the hill." They did so; and the next morning when they
went to see, the bend was packed with buffalo, so the people had
a real killing, for this young man had true supernatural power.
22. That evening everyone took part of his killing to the council
tent where men sat about and feasted and talked; and they say all
Ikto took was a shoulder-piece[2]; it was all he managed to secure
(from some hunter). Soon after, Blood-Clot Boy announced that he
was going home, taking with him the girl who saved him. So they

---

wic'o't'itakiya ų'yą ima'yaye lo — eya' c'ąke' nązų'spe ų k'oska'laka
ki kakla'yi ną kic'i' sina' o'wąžila-g.lowį ną t'iya'ta ak'i' sk'e'e.
20. Yųk'ą' heya' ke'e, — Ho, c'oka'p t'i' ki he' e'l yį' ną haya'ke
k'eya' eya's t'e'hą Ikto' maki'ų c'e mi'cicaku wo', — eya' c'ąke'
wic'į'cala ki c'uwe'ku t'i'-t'iyopa ki e'l ina'žį ną, — Ikto`, haya'ke
k'eya' eya's t'e'hą-wic'ayecių c'a hena' hiyo'wahi ye', — eya' yųk'ą'
c'uwe'ku ki wana' ak'e', — Ak'o' yą' na, wic'a'sa ama'kiyutakta
tk'a', — eye' c'e'yas k'ohą' Ikto' yapsa'kesni,[3] — Iye'kicic'iya;
iye'kicic'iya, — eya'ya yąka' c'ąke' nake's hehą'l wik'o'skalaka k'ų
Ikto' g.na'ye cį wąg.la'ki ną c'e'ya ų' sk'e'e. 21. Wana' We'-Hoksi'la
haya'ke ec'e'kc'e kic'ų' ną kopya'kel yąki' ną heya' sk'e'e, — Ho,
k'oska'laka ki sina'hisma wąži' yusla'pi ną paha'-ak'otąhą kakmi'
ki he'l ena'na hi' ki yuo'b.lecapikte lo', — eya' c'ąke' ec'ų'pi ną
ihi'hąna c'a ekta' i'pi yųk'ą' iyestuk'a wak'ą' c'ąke' kakmi' ki a'taya
pte' hiyo't'iza c'a a'wicak'ehą'-wana`sapi sk'e'e. 22. He'-ktaye`tu ki
t'iyo't'ipi ki e'l wo'yute ai'pi ną wic'a'sa wo'g.lakapi yųk'ą' Ikto' e'l
i' ną ta'ku eya'kci t'a'b.lo wą ece'la ai' sk'e'e. He'c'eg.lakci ok'ini c'a.
I'yec'ala We'-Hoksi'la g.ni'kte ke'yi' ną wic'į'cala wą niye' c'ų he'

---

[1] Ikto' always uses the barest skeleton of speech; omitting all the little
words, particles and enclitics.

[2] While the others took choice cuts because they had entire animals at their
disposal, all Ikto had was a shoulder-piece, all that he could secure by
begging *(o ki'ni).*

[3] *yapsa'ka*, to snap off, as a thread, with the mouth, or teeth; *yapsa'kesni*
without snapping off with the mouth, means to say something over and
over again without pause.

made preparations. And the once-proud elder sister who had been so mean to her younger sister, now rejected Ikto and went following the girl and her young husband. 23. They in turn ordered her back, but she did not have any ears[1]. And so they came on until they neared Blood-Clot Boy's home. The little bear who was sitting on a hilltop saw them. He had been sitting there alone, viewing the country round about. He started up, evidently having seen them, and disappeared downhill in the other direction. Breathlessly he arrived home and said, "Grandson is now returning; but he brings a woman home." 24. Immediately the rabbit, very happy, ran hopping out to meet them; and taking his grandson on his back[2] he carried him the remainder of the way. The little bear also came to meet them, and he took the daughter-in-law on his back; but she was so heavy (for him) that he could not lift her entirely off the ground; so her feet dragged on behind. As for the proud elder sister, nobody took any notice of her, so she came along behind them, and lived with them there. They kept her to take out the ashes for them. 25. That is all.

21. The Eagle Boy.

1. An unknown man entered the tribal camp and married a Dakota girl with whom he lived inside the circle. But he never ate

kicʻi' g.nį́kta cʻa ig.lu'wįyeyapi yųkʻą' hokśi'-tʻokapʻa wą waȟ'ą'ic'ila ną tʻąka'kula kį kiśi'cahe c'ų nake' Ikto' hehą́yą hįg.na'yą cʻį̇ sni ną wicʻi̇'hakap cʻe'ya ya' śkʻe'ᵉ. 23. I'ṡ eha'kela kiśi'capi kʻe'yaṡ nų́ǵe wanį̇'l ya'hį ną ecʻe'l wana' We'-Hokśi̇'la tʻi' kį ikʻi̇'yela g.la'pi ke'ᵉ. O'tʻąiyą wana' g.la'pi yųkʻą' matʻo' cʻica'lala kʻų he' iṡna'la paha'ta o'kśąkśą e'tųwą yąka'he ȟcehą̇'tu cʻąke' wąwi'cʻayaka hųṡe na'żį hiya'yį ną akʻo'ketkiya a'iyoȟpeya mahe'l kʻig.la' ke'ᵉ. Niya'ṡniṡni kʻihų̇'ni ną, — Wana' mitʻa'koża ku' tkʻa' wį̇'yą wą aku' we lo', — eya' ke'ᵉ. 24. He'cʻena Maśtį̇'skala li'la wi'yuṡkį ną psi'psil itko'p wicʻa'yį ną tʻako'żakpaku kį ki'c'į̇ ną g.log.la' ke'ᵉ. Cʻąke' matʻo'la kʻų i̇'ṡ-'eya' tʻako'ṡku kį ki'c'į̇ ną iha'kap g.le' c'e'yaṡ yuha'ṡni cʻąke' wikʻo'ṡkalaka kį si' kį makʻi̇'cagogoyela ag.la'pi ṡkʻe'ᵉ. Cʻuwe'ku wą waȟ'ą'ic'ila tkʻa' kʻų he' tuwe'ni e'l e'tųweṡni cʻąke' iye'cʻįka wicʻi̇'-hakap i' cʻa cʻaȟo'l-iȟpeya yuha'pi ṡkʻe'ᵉ. 25. Hehą́yela owi'hąke'ᵉ.

21.

1. Oya'te wą tʻi̇'pi yųkʻą' e'l wicʻa'ṡa tuwe' tʻąį̇'ṡni wą hių'³ ną hąke'ya lakʻo'ta-wį̇`yą wą yu'zį ną kicʻi' cʻoka'p tʻi' ṡkʻe'ᵉ. Kʻe'yaṡ to'hįni

---

[1] This is an idiom. To have no ears is to be disobedient.
[2] This is a very great compliment — to be carried on the back. I am told that, before a hųka' ceremony, the candidates who sit in readiness, in their tipis, are taken up and carried across the camp on the backs of those officially sent out to bring them.
[3] hių', to come here to live; hi, to arrive here; ų, to exist.

carelessly; he required that at each mealtime a special dish should
be prepared for him of some strange food he brought with him. It
was known as *psit'o'*. 2. The wife had a little brother who was very
curious about this food and often stayed around when it was being
served. One day when he happened to be alone in the tipi, the dish
was prepared, and set aside. So he took his forefinger and pushed it
into the centre of the food, and then tasted what adhered to his
finger. And the hole he made in this way did not come together,
but remained constant. 3. When the man returned he was furious.
"Who is it who dares do this to me?" he cried, so his wife tried to
smooth things over. "It was only my little brother, who is a mere
child and doesn't understand," she said. But he was the more
angry. "Bring your brother to me," he ordered. The wife ran out
to her mother's tipi and said, 4. "Mother, he has asked for my little
brother; but don't give him up." So the strange man sulked and
went off somewhere. Ikto happened to be staying there; so he
promptly ran around the camp circle, playing the herald. "Everybody take heed. Put on your moccasins front end backwards[1], and
run for your lives. Soon the eagle-tribe will arrive to annihilate you
all." So the people obeyed him and ran away. 5. Only the eagle-

---

tok'į's-wo`tesni, iye' ta'ku k'eya' g.luha' hi' c'a hena' ece' owo'te-
iyo`hila kiyu'żapi c'ą'sna yu'ta sk'e'ᵉ. Hena' psi't'o eci'yapi kį he'c'a
ke'ya'pi'ⁱ. 2. Yųk'ą' ąpe'tu wą e'l t'awi'cu kį he' sųka'kula wą hoksi'la-
ci`k'ala c'a li'la wo'żapi kį he' ayu'hel k'uwa' s'a yųk'ą' isna'la
yąka' hą'l e'l ahi'g.lepi c'ąke' wae'pazo² kį ų' wo'żapi kį c'oka'yelakci
palo'p e'g.le ną yazo'ka ke'ᵉ. K'e'yas he c'oka'ya oĥlo'ka wą i'ĥąl-
ka`ģe c'ų he' he'c'ena ec'e'l k'ig.le'sni ĥlokya' oi'yanica ke'ᵉ. 3. Ec'e'l
wana' wic'a'sa k'ų t'ima' g.licu' ną li'la c'ąze'ka ke'ᵉ. — He' tuwe' c'a
le'c'el oma'kiĥ'ą huwo'? — eya' c'ąke' t'awi'cu kį, — Į'se' he' misų'-
kala ta'kuni slolye'lasni c'a he'cų kį, etą'hąs he' wak'ą'heża kį, —
eya'ya iye'naye-wac'i k'e'yas ec'ą'l, — Nisų'kala maka'u wo', —
eya' c'ąke' ina'p'i ną hų'ku t'i'pi kį ekta' i' ke'ᵉ. 4. Ną leya' ke'ᵉ, —
Ina`, misų'kala la'³ k'e'yas k'u'pisni', — eya' c'ąke' wic'a'sa k'ų
wac'į'k'o⁴-ina`p'i ną tok'i'yot'ą iya'ya ke'ᵉ. He'c'ena Ikto' e'l ų' c'ąke'
t'ąni's howo'kawiĥ e'yapaha į'yąkį ną, — Ho po', hą'pa he'ktakikiya
oki'hąpi ną li'la nap'a' po'. Wąb.li'-oya'te kį zuya' ahi'hųni ną
nica'sotapikte lo', — eya' c'ąke' oya'te kį ec'e'l ec'ų'pi ną ica'k'oyela
nap'e'-iya`yapi ke'ᵉ. 5. Wį'yą wą wąb.li'-hig.na`ye c'ų hece'la

---

[1] The informant suggested that Ikto' told them this so that the tracks
  pointing in the opposite direction from where the people were hiding would
  mislead the pursuers.
² *wae'pazo*, the first or forefinger; *wa*, things; *e'pazo*, to point out, in the
  distance.
³ *la*, as an independent verb, to ask for, beg, demand; *wala'; ųla'* I, we beg.
⁴ *wac'į'k'o*, to sulk for a long time; acting indifferent to everything; not
  eating; losing all interest in life, because someone has hurt your feelings;
  wac'į', mind; disposition; *k'o*, fast, quick, (?) cf. *k'oya'ĥ'ą*, to hurry;
  k'oya'nų, to grow up tall very fast.

man's wife did not run away but hid in a hollow tree, where they
failed to find her. Her name was Scarlet Hair Woman. As she sat
in the tree weeping, Ikto, carrying her little brother on his back,
walked directly below her, scolding him and saying, "Now see what
you have done! You have brought death on an entire tribe." She
was so unhappy that she cried even harder and dropped a tear
on her little brother as he went by. 6. While she was sitting there,
a tiny man came from somewhere; he was a little meadowlark.
"Well, well, granddaughter, how sad to see you weeping! Come
with me to my home," he said, so she accompanied him to his home.
7. She lived there a while, and then her child, a boy, was born.
So the little meadowlark man took up his new grandson and threw
him outside once, and he came in a fair-sized boy. Several times
he did this, and each time he returned larger than before and in-
creasingly handsome. When at last he came in, a full grown young
man, the meadowlark said, "Would that my grandson had such
and such things!" And each wish came true; so that in a day he
acquired clothes and arrows and bows, and went out to hunt.
8. He was a good hunter, and went out often; but whenever he was
away, his mother would wail in grief. At last he asked her, "Mother,
why do you weep so much?" And she replied, "Son, the eagle-

---

*nap'e'śni, e' e' c'ų'ħloka wą ekta' ina'ħma-iyotaka c'ąke' iye'yapiśni
śk'e'ᵉ. He' P'ehį'-Lu'tawį eci'yapi śk'e'ᵉ. Yųk'ą' he'c'el c'ąwą'kal
yąkį' ną c'e'yahe c'ų, ųg.na' oħla't'elaħcį Ikto'mi he e' c'a sųka'kula
k'ų he' ki'c'į ną iyo'p'eya hiya'ya ke'ᵉ. Leya'ya ke'ᵉ, — Niye'ħca
c'a le' wo'śil-yakaǵe¹ lo', oya'te-t'ą'ka t'ewi'c'ayaye lo', — eya'ya
k'į' hiya'ya c'ąke' wį'yą k'ų ista' kį etą'ħą ista'm.niħąpi wą sųka'kula
kį ahį'ħpaya śk'e'ᵉ. 6. He'c'ena c'ąwą'kal yąka'hą yųk'ą' to'k'iyatąhą
wic'a'śala wą e'l hi'la yųk'ą' he' t'aśi'yak-nųpala śk'e'ᵉ. — Hųhųhe',
t'ako`źa, oi'yokiśilya yac'e'yahe lo'; u' wo', ųg.nį'kte', — eya' c'ąke'
kic'i' t'iya'ta k'i' ke'ᵉ. 7. Hel ų'hą yųk'ą' i'yec'ala hokśi'-ksuyį² ną
hokśi'lala wą yuha' ke'ᵉ. C'ąke' t'aśi'yak-nųpa-wic'a'śala k'ų he'
t'ako'źakpaku kį iki'kcu ną t'ąka'l iye'ya yųk'ą' hokśi'la wą hą'ska
t'ima' g.licu' ke'ᵉ. To'na-t'ąkal iye'ya³ c'ą iye'na są'p t'ą'ka a'ya
ke'ᵉ, nakų' są'p ową'yak-waśte` ke'ᵉ. Wana' k'ośka'laka-į'skokeca
kį hehą'l t'aśi'yak-nųpala k'ų he', — Tok'i' t'ako'źa ka'k'el ną ka'k'el
yuha' nį', — eya' c'ą iye'c'etu c'ąke' ąpe'tu-hąke`yela⁴ ta'ku wo'k'o-
yake nąi'ś wąhį'kpe, ita'zipa k'o' yuha' ną waye'-iya`ya ke'ᵉ. 8. Wana'
li'la wao'ka c'ąke' ak'e' iya'ya c'ą'śna iye'na hų'ku kį c'e'yahą yųk'ą'
to'hųwel, — Ina`, to'k'a yųk'ą' yac'e'ye s'a huwo'? — eya' c'ąke'*

---

¹ *wo'śil-kaǵa*, to be the cause of trouble; *wa*, things; *o*, in; *śil*, from *śi'ca*,
bad; *ka'ǵa*, to make.
² *hokśi'-ksuya*, to be in travail, as childbirth; *hokśi'*, child; *ksuya* (?); cf.
kiksu'ya, to remember; *ksu'yeya*, to cause hurt to.
³ *to'na-t'ąkal iye'ya c'a*, as often as he sent him out.
⁴ *hąke'*, a part of; piece of; *ąpe'tu-hąke`yela*, before the day was over; during
a piece of the day.

people came down and killed your grandfather and grandmother
and all the great tribe to which I belonged. That leaves just you and
me alone in the world. That is why I weep. As for your uncle, they
took him alive somewhere." 9. And he said, "Mother, I am going
to find my uncle." And he left home. As he neared the encampment
of the Eagle Tribe, he entered a river-bed, and as it was winter, he
slid along on the ice, all the way, towards the camp. That day all
the men were playing on the ice and Ikto who was taking part there
as everywhere, called out, "A son of Scarlet Hair Woman is coming
down the river on the ice!" They jeered at him and called him a liar.
10. At that instant the youth came round a bend; so Ikto was
vindicated. "There! What did I tell you?" he said. So all of them
began to shout, "*Psit‘o'*-Eater's son has come!" And the eagle-man
who always ate *psit‘o'*-bulbs[1], came out of his tipi and said, "My
son, my son," and led him in. 11. And there sat his uncle, like a
pitiable captive, on the opposite side of the tipi, never once raising
his head. The minute he beheld him the boy was very angry within.
His father was just then setting before him a dish of his strange

---

*oki'yaka ke’ᵉ. — C‘įkš, nit‘ų'kašila, nik‘ų'ši k‘o wąb.li' wic‘a'ktepi
ną naku' oya'te-i‘ą`ka wą ema'tąhą yųk‘ą' k‘o' a'taya wic‘a'ktepi c‘a
ų'šiyehci ųki'šnala ųk‘ų' kį le' ų' eya'šna wac‘e'ye'. Nile'kši i'š
to'k‘iyap niya'k‘e² ak‘i'yag.la pe', — eya' ke’ᵉ. 9. Yųk‘ą', — It‘o',
ina`, lekši' oki'le-m.nį`kte lo', — eyį' ną he'c‘ena iya'ya ke’ᵉ. Wana'
wąb.li'-oya`te kį wic‘o't‘i c‘ąke' ik‘i'yela ya' c‘a wakpa'la wą ekta'
mahe'l iya'yį ną wani'yetu c‘ąke' c‘ah-o'p‘aya c‘ah-ka'zozo ya' ke’ᵉ.
He'-ąpe`tu kį wi‘ca' kį iyu'ha c‘a'ga kį ekta' ška'tahąpi yųk‘ą' wana'
ak‘e' Ikto' ekta' o'p‘a hųše'ca leya' ke’ᵉ, — P‘ehį'-Lu`tawį³ c‘įca' wą
c‘ah-o'p‘aya u' we lo', — eya' c‘ąke' i'yoktepi ną owe' wak‘ą'k‘ą
ig.nų'pi ke’ᵉ. 10. Hcehą'l yuksą'yą wą ao'hom.ni t‘ąį'yą hiyu' c‘ąke',
— Iho’ᵒ, heš u' kį, — eya' c‘ąke' nake' iyu'ha, — Pšit‘o'la Yu'ta
c‘įca' wą hi' ye lo', — eya' e'yapahapi ke’ᵉ. Yųk‘ą' wąb.li'-wic‘a`ša
wą wo'žapi ece' yu'te c‘ų he e' c‘a hina'p‘į ną, — Mic‘į'kši, mic‘į'kši,
— eya'ya t‘ima' yu's g.lok‘i'yag.la ke’ᵉ. 11. Yųk‘ą' t‘ima' lekši'tkula
k‘ų šika⁴ waya'ka š`e t‘isą'p‘atąhą p‘a icu'šni' yąka' c‘a wąya'kį ną
he'c‘ena t‘ąma'hel c‘ąze'hca ke’ᵉ. Ec‘ą'l atku'ku kį wo'žapi-wak‘ą` k‘ų*

---

[1] *psit‘o'* means beads, such as are used in beadwork. But the first meaning,
now largely out of use, is a certain plant that grew in small ponds, and had
a root like an onion. It was a delicious food, when boiled and mashed.
[2] *niya'k‘e*, in a live state; *ni*, to live; to have life; *wani'*, I live; *ya*, in that
manner; *k‘e*, (?).
[3] *wį*, a suffix meaning "woman", which is added to all proper names (not
always the nicknames.)
[4] *šika*, pitiful one! This word has no accent, and can stand or be omitted
without affecting the sense. It is something of an aside, by the person
telling the story, to stir pity in the hearers for a character in the tale.

food, but the youth defied him by taking his forefinger[1] and
thrusting it into the centre and then stirring it all around. His
father could say nothing. 12. Then he slid the dish over to his uncle.
"Uncle, you eat that!" he said; so he did. Then the youth took a
weasel which he had killed and brought with him; and threw it to
Ikto[2] who had come and sat down in the doorway, saying, "Ikto,
skin that for me!" 13. Immediately, glad of the excuse, he rushed
out of the tipi, saying, "They have a good knife yonder," and
started off. He ran eagerly around the camp circle crying out, "On
this day there is to be a battle!" And he returned without a knife.
"*Hiˀⁱ!* Didn't I tell you to skin that?" the youth said, and glared
at Ikto who was frightened and tried to run out. But he ordered
him to sit down next to the uncle, and then took out his arrows.
14. He shot his father dead first, and then all who sat in the room.
Next he went around Ikto who was crying in fear, and killed all the
people who were outside. Then he took his uncle, and caused Ikto to
carry him on his back; and they started homeward. When they
arrived, they allowed the brother and sister to meet, and the little

---

*etą' ahi'kig.le tkʻaʻṡ wae'pazo ų' cʻoka'ya paȟli' ihe'yį ną a'taya
ica'hi cʻąke' atku'ku kį tokʻa'-yąkeṡni³ ṡkʻeˀᵉ. 12. Heʻcʻų ną hehą'l
lekṡi'tkula kʻų he' wo'źapi kį paslo'hą iyeʻkʻiyį ną — Lekṡi', niye'
hena' yu'ta yo', — eya' cʻąke' yu'ta ṡkʻeˀᵉ. Hitʻų'kasą wą kte' ną
yuha' i' cʻąke' Ikto' tʻiyo'pa eʻl hi'yotaka cʻa iȟpeʻkʻiyį ną — Ikto`, he'
ha' mi'ciyuzi ye', — eya' keˀᵉ. 13. Heʻcʻena Ikto', ta'ku iyo'wal-ye
ca⁴, ina'pʻį ną, — Tʻo'waʻṡ kaʻl mi'la-pʻe wą yuha'pi cʻa, — eya'ya
yuha' iya'ya keˀᵉ. Heʻcʻena howo'kawiȟ ṡica'wacʻį į'yąkį ną leya'
e'yapaha keˀᵉ, — Ąpe'tu tʻahe'na okiʻcʻizekte lo', — eya' į'yąkį ną
mi'la cʻola g.li' cʻąke', — Hiˀⁱ! hitʻų'kasą wąṡ ha' yus-cʻiʻṡi kʻų, —
eyį' ną cʻąze'ka-ayu`ta cʻąke' iya'ye-wacʻį tkʻaʻṡ lekṡi'tkula wą yąke'
cʻų heʻl isa'kʻip i'yotak-kʻiyį ną hehą'l wąhį'kpe iki'kcu keˀᵉ. 14.
Atku'ku kį tʻoke'ya katʻi'ye'yį⁵ ną hehą'l tʻi ożu'la yąka'pi kį iyu'ha
wicʻa'kte ṡkʻeˀᵉ. Hehą'l Ikto' cʻe'ya ų' tkʻaʻṡ ao'hom.ni iya'yį ną
tʻąka'l oya'te ų'pi kį hena' iyu'ha nakų' wicʻa'kte ṡkʻeˀᵉ. Hehą'l
Lekṡi'tkula kʻų iki'kcu ną Ikto' kʻikʻi'yį ną heʻcʻeṡ kʻig.la'pi keˀᵉ.
Kʻihų'nipi ną tʻąke'ku wąg.la'k-kʻiyapi cʻąke' kʻoṡka'lakala kʻų li'la*

---

[1] The boy defies his father by doing to his special food exactly what his
little uncle did in childish ignorance, thereby incurring his displeasure and
causing him to destroy the entire tribe.
[2] Ikto comes and goes as he pleases — never especially welcome, never given
the place of honor unless he comes in in the guise of some boy-beloved;
yet never ordered away. They generally tolerate him, and he sleeps in the
doorway, and sits in the beggar's place.
³ *tokʻa'-yąkeṡni*, he could hardly sit still; he was restless, as he sat there;
tokʻa', with accent on the second syllable, occurs only in this construction.
⁴ This phrase, rather parenthetical, says, "glad of an opportunity, only
too eager for an excuse."
⁵ *katʻi'ye'ya (katʻa'*, to kill by striking; *iye'ya*, he sent), to shoot and kill;
katʻa' iye'ya, as two words, he promptly killed it by striking.

young man was so happy, they say. This time they really skinned the weasel and dried and pulverized the meat and then sprinkled it all over the camp which had been deserted by the tribe. 15. That night they heard dogs barking there; but they refrained from visiting it; and on the second night, they heard young men cheering and shouting. Another night came and then by that time all that tribe which had been annihilated, were restored to life. So the following morning, some men came from there and took Scarlet Hair Woman and her son and also the little meadowlark man back with them. And from that time on, that tribe lived. That is all.

22. The Hero Overcomes the Cold.

1. There was a great tribal camp, and in the centre lived a man with many children. Whenever the people had a killing, he would go there with his children, and the people would leave their meat and run away in fear. And his children would take it all home. 2. This practice had continued so long that the entire tribe was now starving. But even the important men of the camp feared to object, so the tribe was in a sad state. Now there was a little orphan boy who with his grandmother lived in an old smoke-tanned tipi, back of the circle. He said, 3. "Grandmother, go to the tipi within the

---

wi'yuśki ke'ᵉ. Hit'ų'kasą k'ų he' nake'ś ha' yu'zapi ną t'alo' ki pusya'pi ną kpąye'lahci kap'a'pi ną ot'i'wota[1] *ki a'taya oka'lapi ke'ᵉ. 15. He'-hąhe'pi ki ekta' śuk-wa'p'a c'a nah'ų'pi k'e'yaś ekta' ya'piśni ec'e'l ak'e' inų'pa-hąhe'pi yųk'ą' ekta' k'ośka'laka aki'ś'aś'api ke'ᵉ. Ak'e' hąhe'pi yųk'ą' oya'te k'ų hena' iyu'hala p'iya'-kini'pi ną ihį'hąna ki e'l etą' hi'pi ną P'ehį'-Lu`tawį c'ica' ną suka'kula k'ų hena'os, ną t'aśi'yak-nupa-wic'a`śala k'ų k'o' iyu'ha awi'c'ak'ipi ną hetą' nake'ś oya'te ki c'ąlwa'śteya ų'pi śk'e'ᵉ. Hehą'yela owi'hąke'ᵉ.*

22.

1. Oya'te-t'ą`ka wic'o't'i yųk'ą' e'l wic'a'śa wą c'ica' o'ta c'a c'oka'p t'i' śk'e'ᵉ. Tohą'l oya'te ki wana'sapi c'ą c'ica' o'p e'l ina'źį nąśna t'alo' ki iyu'haha ų'yą nap'e'wic'ayi nąśna icu' śk'e'ᵉ. 2. He'c'ųhą c'ąke' wana' oya'te ki a'taya wic'a'akih'ą k'e'yaś wic'a'śa t'ąki'kiyą e'g.na ų'pi ki iyu'ha k'oki'p'api ų' ta'keyapiśni c'ąke' li'la ośi'lya wic'o't'i śk'e'ᵉ. Yųk'ą' hokśi'lala wą wab.le'nica[2] *c'a k'ų'śitku kic'i'- śnala t'ihe'yata wizi' wą ot'i'pi yųk'ą' he' e c'a leya' ke'ᵉ, 3. — Ųci`,*

---

[1] *ot'i'wota;* and *ot'i'weta,* are both used to indicate a site where once people lived. An abandoned house, the site of a home; or a circle of camp-fires indicating a former camp; *o,* in; *t'i,* to live; *o'ta,* many (?). If this is correct the word must have referred originally to the abandoned site of a tribal encampment.

[2] *wab.le'nica,* an orphan; *ni'ca,* to lack.

circle where that man lives, and say, 'My grandchild is hungry and
bids me come here'." So the old woman answered, "What! Why,
that's out of the question, Grandchild! Even the finest people get
no results when they appeal to him for food. What am I, that he
should not kick me out!" There was another hunt and a great
killing; and the boy said, "Well, then, grandmother, I shall go to him
myself!" The old woman did not place any hope in him, evidently,
for she laughed and said, "Really ?"[1]. 4. But he went to the butchering ground, and there he saw the mean man and his children frighten-
ing away the people. But the boy stood his ground, so the tyrant
frowned on him and said, "Get out of here!" The boy replied, "Do
you think that you alone can cause the destruction of so large a
tribe ?" So the people said, "Look! He who-lives-with-his-
grandmother is standing his ground!" 5. But the mean man said,
"Keep still and get away. If you don't, I shall point my finger at
you!" (The people said whenever he pointed his finger at anyone,
that person died at once.) But the boy replied, "All right. Point

---

*c'oka'ta le wic'a'śa wą t'i' kį he'l t'iyo'le-yį[2] ną heya' yo': Mit'a'koźa
loc'į' c'a uma'śi ye', eya' yo', — eye'[e]. C'ąke' winų'ħcala kį, — Takû[3],
t'eħi'yaś ta'kehe, t'ako`źa. Wic'a'śa-waśte`pika ye's wo'lapi kį
nawi'c'aħ'ųśni k'ų, ta'ku lema'c'ecaś t'ąka'l hiyu'mayeśni ka, — eya'
ayu'pte'[e]. K'e'yaś ak'e' wana'sapi yųk'ą', — Ho, ec'a, ųci`, miye'c'įka
k'eś e'l m.nį'kte lo', — eya' yųk'ą' k'ų'śitkula k'ų, we'c'eyeśni hųśe, —
Ece's tuwa' ak'a'kśa'[4], — eyį' ną iħa't'a śk'e'[e]. 4. Tk'a's wana'sapi
kį e'l wana' ak'e' wic'a'śa-śi`ca k'ų he' c'įca' o'p u' kį e'l iyu'ha nap'a'pi
k'e'yaś ową'źila iśna'la na'źį yųk'ą' e'l ite'-yuk'o`kiya[5] u' ną heya'
śk'e'[e], — Ak'o' g.la' yo', — eye' c'e'yaś, — Le' niśna'laka c'a oya'te
wą yuci'k'a ś'e t'ewi'c'ayayįkte lo', — eya' ayu'pta śk'e'[e]. C'ąke'
oya'te kį, — K'ų'śitku Kic'i' T'i'la nap'e'śni ye lo', — eya'pi śk'e'[e].
5. K'ey'aś ec'ą'l wic'a'śa-śica k'ų he', — Ini'la k'eś ħeya'p iya'ya yo'.
Eha's nape' ac'i'pazokte lo', — eya' śk'e'[e]. (He'c'ų c'ą' wą'cak tuwa'*

---

[1] "Really ?" is the rather flat translation of an idiomatic phrase, showing
lack of confidence in another's undertaking, or statement.

[2] *t'iyo'le-ya*, to go visiting, with the express purpose of getting something to
eat; not for social reasons; *t'i*, house; *ole'*, to seek; *ya*, to go. A visitor who
habitually "seeks house" is ridiculed, and dreaded. The social visitor, who
comes to see his friends, and incidentally accepts a meal offered as a mark
of his host's hospitality, and is ready at any time to return the courtesy,
is not said to "seek house," but *t'it'o'k'ą-ya`; t'i*, house; *t'ok'a'l*, some-
where else; *ya*, to go; hence, to go to a different house, as a visitor. Old
people are generally tolerated, and expected to "seek house," and are
treated kindly, anyway. It is their prerogative; assuming that in their day,
they were kind to the aged.

[3] *ta'kû*, something. Spoken with a rise and fall of voice, is an expression of
distress; as we might say, "Help!" without expecting it from any quarter.

[4] *ak'a'kśa* is abbreviated from *ak'a'ka eśa'; ak'a'ka*, "one who is 'the limit'."
tuwa' ak'a'kśa is an idiomatic expression, the meaning of which is untrans-
latable in English.

[5] *'ite'-yuk'o'kiya*, to frown; *ite'*, face; *yuk'o'*, (?); *kiya*, to cause one's own.

your finger at me. And then I will point mine at you in turn. It's no trick to point a finger!" 6. So the man pointed first one of his fingers and then another, at the boy, but he did not die. Then the boy said, "Now it is my turn to point my finger at you!" And the instant he pointed a finger, the man died on the spot. On seeing this, his wife and his many children ran in fear in all directions. Then the people ran to the drying-racks thus abandoned, and scrambled for meat. 7. "Now, grandmother, ask that a crier be sent around to tell the people to heat water." This was done by all the people who used every single vessel available; so meantime the tyrant's wife and children ran for refuge into all the holes in the ground that they could find. Vapor issued from the various holes where they hid. The people ran with the hot water and poured it down all their hiding places, killing them where they lay. Only one hole remained un-touched when the hot water gave out, just as they were going to pour it there; thus, that one child was not killed. And they say that is how it happens that we occasionally have cold weather. That is all.

23. Heart-Killer.

1. Four young men lived together; and Hakela, the lastborn, who stepped out to get firewood, came back in again and said, "There is a young woman standing outside. What shall we call her?" So his

---

apa'ha kį he' t'a' šk'e'ᵉ.) Tk'a'š hokši'la k'ų, — Ho' wo', nape' ama'-pazo wo'. To'kša' mi'š eha'kela nape' aci'pazokte lo', he ta'k wo'ec'ųka c'a¹, — eya' ke'ᵉ. 6. C'ąke' wic'a'ša k'ų nape' wąži' it'o'kt'ok² hokši'la kį apa'zohe c'e'yaš a'tayaš t'e'šni šk'e'ᵉ. Hehą'l — Ho, mi'š hehą'l ac'i'pazokte lo', — eyį' ną ka'k'el-nape' apa'zo tk'a'š he'c'ena t'a' iya'ya ke'ᵉ. C'ąke' t'awi'cu ną c'įca' k'ų a'beya naki'p'api šk'e'ᵉ. Hehą'l oya'te kį wo'c'ąkšu ik'i'nicapi šk'e'ᵉ. 7. Yųk'ą', — Ho, ųcį', e'yapaha-wic'aši ną oya'te kį a'taya m.nik'a'lye-wic'aši po', — eya' ke'ᵉ. C'ąke' oya'te kį ta'ku škokpa' yuha'pi kį iyu'ha ožu'kžula m.ni-k'a'lyapi c'ąke' wic'a'ša-šica k'ų he' t'awi'cu ną c'įca' kį iyu'ha mak'o'ĥloka ekta'kta ona'kip'api c'a oĥe'yųkyųk hiyu' k'eyaš iya'za oka'štą hiya'yapi šk'e'ᵉ. C'ąke' ekta'ktani ot'a'pi ną eha'ke wąži'la oĥlo'ka wą mahe'l iya'ya c'a m.nik'a'ta kį aka'štą iye'yapikte c'e'yaš ec'ą'l m.ni' kį hena'la c'ąke' he' he'c'ena ni' ų' šk'e'ᵉ. C'a he' ų' le osni' š'a kį he' he'c'eca šk'e'ᵉ. Hehą'yela oẃi'hąke'ᵉ.

23.

1. K'oška'laka to'p t'i'pi yųk'ą' Hake'la c'ą' icu'kta c'a ina'p'į ną i't'ap ak'e' t'i'l g.licu' ną, — Wik'o'škalaka wą t'ąka'l hina'žį ye lo'. Taku'ųyąpikta huwo'? — eya' ke'ᵉ. C'ąke' c'iye'ku kį, — T'ąke'ųyą-

---

¹ *he ta'ku*, that something; *wo'ec'ųka*, a trick; "that's easy; there's nothing to that!" is the sense.

² *wąži' it'o'kt'ok*, one after the other; *t'o'keca* is here reduplicated; meaning "different."

brothers said, "Let us call her our elder sister. Ask her in, Hakela," they said. 2. Hakela asked her in and she replied, "Thank you, younger brother,"[1] and entered the tipi. From that day she lived there; a fine girl, as well as a beautiful one, industrious and skilled in the things women do. She made beautiful clothes for her brothers, and when they brought home meat, she took care of it all so that they were never without food. 3. One day all her brothers went away and she was staying alone when she saw a very pretty feather blown along, so she tried to get it but it kept eluding her, leading her on and on, till she was in the dense woods. There near the water, was a hole to which the feather led her. 4. Then certain somethings pulled her into the hole. They were beavers which lived there. So when her brothers got home, they went weeping through the woods looking for their sister, in vain. And then, the one next to the youngest who felt especially sad and walked along a stream hunting her, thought he saw something out of the corner of his eye, so he took a better look at it. And behold! there was his sister, lying face upward, and beavers were draining their hot fish on her face! For a long time they must have been doing this, for by now her face was a mass of sores. 5. He hurried home and told the eldest brother who went angrily to the scene and said, "You worthless, no-account beings, can it be that out of your number, someone was kind to my sister? If so, say, 'I'." The room was filled with, "I, I, I" and when the noise

---

pikte lo'. T'ima'hel kic'o' wo', — eya'pi ke'ᵉ. 2. Hake'la ak'e' ina'p'į ną, — T'ąke`, t'ima'hel u' wo', — eya' yųk'ą' — Hą', misų`, — eyį' ną t'ima' hi'yotaka ke'ᵉ. Hetą' kic'i' t'i'pi k'e'yas li'la waste' ną nakų' wį'yą waste' ną b.lihe'cakį ną nakų' waka'ȟ-wo`hitika ke'ᵉ. Sųka'ku kį haya'pi li'la waste'ste wic'a'kcagį ną t'alo' ag.li'pi kį a'l-'ataya tąyą' kab.la' c'ąke' tų'weni aki'ȟ'ąpisni sk'e'ᵉ. 3. To'hųwel sųka'ku kį iyu'ha to'k'iya iya'yapi c'ąke' isna'la yąka' yųk'ą' wi'yaka wą waste'laȟcaka c'a k'iye'la kaȟwo'ȟwok hiya'ya c'ąke' icu'kta c'ą ak'o'wap'a i'yotaka c'ą he'c'el k'uwa' a'yahį ną ec'e'l c'ąo't'eȟika kį ekta' m.ni-a'g.lag.la oȟlo'ka wą hą' c'ąke' he'c'iya ak'i' ke'ᵉ. 4. Yųk'ą' ta'ku k'eya' yuma'hel icu'pi ke'ᵉ. Hena' c'a'papi c'a he'l t'i'pi'ⁱ. Wana' t'iya'ta sųka'ku kį g.li'pi ną c'e'yaya c'qwe'g.na oki'leȟąpi k'e'yas iye'yapisni ke'ᵉ. Yųk'ą' haka'kta i'yok'ihe kį he' iyo'tą wo't'eȟi ak'i'p'a ną m.nia'g.lag.la t'ąke'ku oki'leȟą yųk'ą' ta'ku ai'stec'elya wąya'ke s'e le'c'eca c'a p'iya'-wąya`ka ke'ᵉ. Yųk'ą' t'ąke'ku k'ų he e' c'a itų'kap ų'papi ną hogą'-k'a'ta ite' ayu'zehąpi ke'ᵉ. He'c'ųpi s'a iteyakel wana' a'taya spą' ų' ȟąȟą' ke'ᵉ. 5. Li'la g.licu' ną c'iye'ku-t'oka`p'a kį oki'yaka c'ąke' c'ąze'ka-iya`yį ną, — Waȟte'sni si'ca kį, tuwa' t'ąke' ų'siyalapi he'ci miye' eya' po', — eye'laka c'ą, — Miye' Miye', Miye'! — ȟmu' s'e eya'pi ke'ᵉ. Yųk'ą' eha'-

---

[1] Of course Hakela said, "Come in, elder sister." And the woman's reply tells us at the very outset that here is introduced a character that will be good.

subsided, a meek small voice said, "Of what good for them to say, 'I' ? The one with the right to say it is I, sitting in the corner;" and the girl said, "My elder brother, he is speaking the truth. When they drain their hot fish on my face, he always drops a small piece of food into my mouth; that is how I keep alive." — 6. "Very well; come outside. You shall live," the elder brother said; so the little beaver went outdoors, and the man killed all the rest. Then he took his sister and the little beaver home, and everything went well again.

7. Once when Heart-killer, (that's what they say she was called,) made a fire away from home and was tanning hides, her beaver-pet was picking chips for her fire. After a time, Hakela came out, and said, "Elder sister, come home now; it is time to eat." So they started for their tipi, but Beaver stayed behind and walked about, singing something; so they listened and heard, "My elder brothers, the best of our family, they have annihilated; and only I, with my inferior hide, am left. I wear red leaves for mittens!" — 8. "Hey, come along, will you ? You too must take food. What do you think you are doing ?" said Hakela to him, and he called back that he was singing a death-song[1].

---

kekċį, — Miye' eya'pi k'e'yaṡ wic'a'ni nųc'aṡ, miye' wąṡ le'c'i make' ṡą', — eya' yųk'ą' wik'o'ṡkalaka k'u, — Misų`, he' wica'k'e'; Hoǧą' kį ama'yuzepi c'ą'sna hąke' iyo'g.nakmak'iya u' ni' mąke', — eya' ke'ᵉ. 6. C'ąke' suka'ku kį, — Ho', ec'a hina'p'a yo'; yani'kte, — eya' c'ąke' ina'p'a c'a uma'pi kį iyu'hala wic'a'kte ną hece'la g.log.li'pi ną hetą'hą tąyą' t'i'pi ke'ᵉ.

7. To'hųwel C'ąkte'wį[2] (eya' he'c'el c'aże' ṡka'[3] c'a,) manį'l c'et'i' ną t'aha' kpąyą'hą c'ąke' C'a'pala c'ąo'kpą kipa'hihela yųk'ą' suka'ku- haka`ktala kį he' ekta' i' ną — T'ąke`, wana' ku' wo', waya'tįkte, — eya' ke'ᵉ. C'ąke' g.licu' k'e'yaṡ C'a'pala ku'sni ekta'ni ta'ku-lową' oma'nihą c'ąke' ana'ǧoptąpi yųk'ą', — C'iye' o'waṡteka[4] wic'a'ka- sotapi ną miye' hį'ṡica oma'kaptape. Wakpe'-ṡaṡa` napį'kpa-waye, — eya'hą ke'ᵉ. 8. C'ąke', — Wą, k'oyą' ku' ye'. Niye' k'o' waya'tįkte. Ta'kukca le' yak'e', — eya' yųk'ą', — Wą, t'o' e'yaṡ mi'c'ilowąla ye lo' — eya' ke'ᵉ.

---

[1] The regular dirge which men, and sometimes women, sing, rather than wail; it generally breaks down into actual wailing, at least with women and old men. It is a dismal yet beautiful sound, loaded with feeling.

[2] *c'ąkte'wį*, heart-she-kills; *c'ąte'*, heart; *kte*, to kill; *wį*, the feminine ending to proper names. *c'ąte'*, contracted, is *c'ąl;* but the "*l*" is dropped, because the next syllable begins with a cluster of two consonants and Dakota avoids clusters of more than two consonants in a word unit.

[3] *ṡk'eᵉ*, the usual sentence ending in myths, and meaning, "it is said", may also occur in a sentence, as here. It is *ṡk'a*, unless it is syntactically placed so that its terminal *a* must change to *e*.

[4] *o'waṡteka*, the better parts, the more desirable, of a piece. Here it means "the best of the Beaver family are killed; I, alone, (the ugly duckling, as it were,) must remain behind."

9

Once more the woman was tanning hides when two women came from somewhere and said, "Heart-killer, come with us. We are going to marry *B.lecʻeʻ¹*, and you must marry Teal-duck². " So she said, "Why? I'm perfectly happy and well off at home, why should I leave my brothers and go away?" 9. They kept teasing her. Then, after a while, seeming to give up, they walked away; but at a distance they turned and called back, "Well, then, just for that, we will take this along," and they showed her her beaver-pet. So she ran after them, begging it back, but they carried it away; she followed them little by little, until they were too far away for her to find her way home; then they surrendered her pet to her. 10. They were now stopping beside a deep stream. And across the river was a tribal camp. So, "We have come to marry *B.lecʻeʻ*, and this one has come to marry Teal-duck!" they called; and, almost at once, a white boat started over. As it neared them, a man, spitting out white beads, came; so they saw him. "There, now, the one coming is Teal-duck; you shall marry him," they said, so Heart-killer was very unhappy and wept as she stood, but there being no way out, like lying down to die³, she entered and went off with him. 11. Just then a blue boat started coming, and the man in it was spitting out blue beads. The two women entered his boat and went off with him.

Akʻeʻ wįʼyą kį wakpąʼyąhe ȟcehąʼl toʼkʻiyatąhą wįʼyą nųʼp eʼl iʼpi ną, — Cʻąkteʻwį, iyaʼya na, B.lecʻeʻ hįg.naʼye-ųyąpi cʻa niʼs Śiyaʻka hįg.naʼyayįkte, — eyaʼhąpi cʻąkeʼ, — Yuʼ, leʼ taʼku woʼsice wau̧ʼ cʻa, taʼkoweʼ misų̧ʼ iȟpeʼya iwiʼcʻab.lam.nįkta he? — eyaʼ keʼᵉ. 9. Heʼcʻena okaʼkisyahąpi ną wanaʼ iʼyakcʻų̧nipi cʻas kʻig.laʼpi seʼca yųkʻą̧ʼ g.lekų̧ʼzapi hų̧se, kawįʼȟ kʻinaʼżįpi ną hoʼuyapi keʼᵉ. — Ho, ecʻa, ehaʼkal eʼs⁴ leʼ ų̧kaʼg.lapikteʼ, — eyaʼpi ną Cʻaʼpala aloʼksohą̧ yuhaʼpi cʻąkeʼ pazoʼzopi ną heʼcʻena kʻig.laʼpi keʼᵉ. Cʻąkeʼ wicʻiʼhakap iʼyąkį ną yuwaʼsaka sʼe kicʻaʼ yaʼhe cʻeʼyas tų̧ʼweni kicʻuʼpiktesni keʼyaʼpi cʻąkeʼ heʼcʻel yaʼhį ną tʻeʼhąl ihų̧ʼnipi yų̧kʻą̧ʼ hehą̧ʼl nakeʼs kicʻuʼpi keʼᵉ. Kʻeʼyas wanaʼs kawįʼȟ-pʻicasni keʼᵉ. 10. Wanaʼs heʼcʻe- g.la m.niʼ wą liʼla sma̧ʼ cʻa icaʼg.la inaʼżįpi keʼᵉ. Yųkʻą̧ʼ iyuʼweȟ wi- cʻoʼtʻi cʻąkeʼ, — B.lecʻeʻ hįg.naʼye-ųhiʼpi ną leʼ iʼs Śiyaʻka hįg.naʼye-hiʼ yeʼ! — eyaʼ pą̧ʼpi yų̧kʻą̧ʼ tʼą̧niʼs waʼta-ska wą uʼ keʼᵉ. Kʻiyeʼla uʼ yų̧kʻą̧ʼ wicʻaʼsa wą psitʻoʼ-skaska itʻaʼsos uʼ cʻa wąyaʼkapi keʼᵉ. Cʻąkeʼ, — Ihoʼ, uʼ kį heʼ Śiyaʻka eʼ yeʼ; heʼ kicʻiʼ yag.nįʼkte cį eʼ yeʼ, — eyaʼpi cʻąkeʼ liʼla iyoʼkipʻisni ną cʻeʼyaya naʼżį kʻeʼyas toʼkʻel ȟą̧- pʻiʼcasni kį uʼ otʼeʼ iyų̧ʼk eʼl iʼyotakį ną kicʻiʼ g.laʼ keʼᵉ. 11. Ecʻą̧ʼl akʻeʼ waʼta wą uʼ yų̧kʻą̧ʼ heʼ iʼs tʼo, ną, wicʻaʼsa wą og.naʼ yą̧keʼ cį heʼ iʼs

---

¹ This is a Boy-Beloved.
² Undoubtedly this is Ikto' in human guise. The characters are identical.
³ When one enters into something in which death is very possible, this phrase is used and means "to lie down as in death."
⁴ *ehaʼkal eś*, in that case; (you brought it on your self). It is very idiomatic, admitting of no fair rendering into English.

As a matter of fact, it was *B.lec'e'* who brought the white boat and
Teal-duck the blue one; but they, in ignorance, went with him.
12. It was evening, and a man came and said, "*B.lec'e'* is to dance;
so you are to come," and Teal-duck tried to confuse the matter as if
not hearing, and said, "Yes, yes, I am to dance." When the man left,
Teal-duck told his wives, "Don't come. Whoever looks on, gets a sty
on the eye; therefore nobody ever looks on." He feared they might
recognize him. 13. But after he had gone they followed him there
and saw him lying on the ground, and *B.lec'e'* dancing on his back.
They returned, very angry, and one made a bag of flying ants, and
one a bag of wasps, and those two bags they laid on either side of
Teal-duck's sleeping place as if they themselves were sleeping there;
and ran away. Some time in the night, Teal-duck returned and,
"Ouch, ouch, I've worn myself out dancing," he said as he crawled
into bed. 14. Just then, one pricked him. So, "Little jealous ones, lie
still, will you?" But, just then, the other stung him. So, "Well, well!
This one is certainly stinging me!" so saying, he turned over, but that
moment, like a great roaring, they all came at him; so, "*Ya! Ya!*"[1]

---

pśit'o'-t'ot'o it'a'śośoś[2] *u' ke'ᵉ. Yųk'ą' he' i'ś wį'yą nų'papi kį kic'i'
i'yotakapi ną k'ig.la'pi ke'ᵉ. Leyalaka wa'ta-ska ahi' k'ų he' B.lec'e'
e' ną, t'o' ahi' k'ų he' Śiya'ka e' yeśą' slolya'piśni c'ąke' Śiya'ka e'ha'*[3]
*kic'i' k'i'pi ke'ᵉ. 12. Htaye'tu yųk'ą' wic'a'śa wą e'l i' ną, — B.lec'e'
wac'i'kta c'a yau'kte lo', — eci'ya yųk'ą' Śiya'ka nah'ų'śni-kųskųs, —
Hą', hą', wawa'c'ikta, — eya' ke'ᵉ. K'ig.la' yųk'ą' t'awi'cu kį wic'ą'k'į
ną, — U'piśni yo'. Tuwa' wawą'yaka c'ą iśta' kį hca' c'a tuwe'ni
wawą'yakeśni ye lo', — eya' ke'ᵉ. He' iye'kiyapikta-k'oki̇'p'į ną heye'ᵉ
13. Tk'a'ś iya'ya c'ąke' iya't'ap ekta' i'pi yųk'ą' k'u'l ų'papi ną nite'
kį aką'l B.lec'e' wac'i'hą ke'ᵉ. He'c'ena li'la c'ąze'ka-g.licu'pi ną ųma'
t'ażu'śka-kįyą̇'pi k'ų he'c'a ożu'wic'at'ų ną ųma' i'ś wic'a'yażipa
ożu'wic'at'ų ną hena'os Śiya'ka hpa'yįkte cį it'ą'anųk*[4] *iye'pi s'e
e'g.nakapi ną g.licu'pi ke'ᵉ. Hąwa'tohąl wana' Śiya'ka g.lihų'ni ną, —
Yų̇, yų̇, wac'i'pi c'ų' nami'c'it'e lo', — eya'ya g.liyų'ka ke'ᵉ. 14. Ec'ą'l
ųma' pażi'pa c'ąke, — Nawi'zila, ową'żi hpa'yapi ye', — eye' c'e'yaś
ec'ą'l ųma' iyo'tą li'la pażi'pa c'ąke', — Huhųhê, le' li'la mapa'żipe
lô, — eyi' ną ųma' ec'e'tkiya ikpa'ptą tk'a'ś ec'a'l hmu' s'e ahi'yu*

---

[1] *Ya!* as indicated elsewhere in these notes is a woman's exclamation of fear.
Men do not use it because it is unmanly, but Ikto' has no pride.

[2] *t'ago'śa* and *t'aśo'śa* both mean "to spit"; *t'ago'śa*, I think, is the better
form, for saliva is *t'aǵe';* I have heard it reduplicated both as *t'aǵo'śaśa*,
and *t'aśo'śośa*.

[3] *e'ha'* is a word introduced into a sentence to show that not the deserving
one, or the one expected, but an unworthy, or different one, reaps the
benefits; or takes the blame. It is an indication of blame or praise, good
or evil, going to the wrong person.

[4] *it'ą'anųk*, on each side of the body; *t'ą*, body, from *t'ąc'ą';* *anų'k*, on each
side, from *anų'k'atąhą*.

he cried, and ran to the deserted places[1], weeping. 15. There came
an Iya to him, "Why are you crying ?" he asked; and he lied to
him, "*B.lecʻe'* has stolen my wife," he said. "Well, then, go home and
bring me a white knife whetted until it is very keen." So off Teal-
duck went, and soon returned with the knife, whetted until it was
flexible from thinness. 16. It was night; so Heart-killer and her
husband lay sleeping when all at once she felt something wet, and
it wakened her. "Get up, something around here is wet," she said,
but she could not rouse her husband; and there he lay, his head
severed from his body, swimming in blood. This she was not aware
of at first. Immediately she jumped up, weeping; and the next day,
he was laid away and the people moved to another camp-ground;
but she stayed behind, weeping. 17. As she wept, she heard a voice;
and as she listened, she happened to see Iya come up over a distant
hill, and run toward her. So she ran with her little beaver, from the
Iya. They came to the deep stream already mentioned, and paused
there while Beaver hurriedly built a bridge over which they crossed
to safety. At once he proceeded to undo it, so they came on and that
night they saw Iya up in the moon which was sailing high in the
sky, and in his hand he held the head of *B.lecʻe'*. The reason was
that he had no way of crossing the stream. 18. At once Heart-killer
and her beaver travelled homeward; and after a long time they

*cʻąke', — Yâ, Yâ, — eyaʻya nakiʻpʻį ną manįʻl cʻeʻya omaʻni śkʻeʻᵉ.
15. Yųkʻą' Iʻya wą eʻl hi' ną — Taʻkole' yacʻeʻyahą huwo'? — eyaʻ-
iyųˋ ga yųkʻą' owe' wakʻąkʻą ną — Le' B.lecʻe' wįʻyą makʻi' cʻa
lepʻaʻhe lo', — eyaʻ keʻᵉ. Yųkʻą', — Ho', ecʻa' g.nį' ną miʻska wązi'
pʻeya' yumį' ną makaʻu wo', — eya' cʻąke' tʻiyaʻta kʻi' ną miʻla wą
gągąyela yumį' ną kai' keʻᵉ. 16. Hąheʻpi cʻąke' Cʻąkteʻwį hįg.naʻku
kicʻi' iśtįʻma yųkʻą' ųg.na' taʻku wą liʻla spaʻye sʻe oyuʻtʻą cʻąke'
ogųˋgį ną, — Kikta', leʻl taʻku wą liʻla spaʻye', — eyį' ną B.lecʻe'
yųhiʻlwacʻį yųkʻą' heʻś pʻa waksaʻpi cʻaś weoʻkab.laya hpaʻye śą
slolyeʻśniʻⁱ. Heʻcʻena cʻeʻya kikta' hiyaʻyį ną hįʻhąna cʻa cʻąʻg.nakapi
ną oyaʻte kį hetą' ig.laʻka iyaʻyapi cʻąke' eʻna cʻeʻyahą keʻᵉ. 17. Cʻeʻ-
yahe cʻų ųg.na' taʻku hoʻnahʻų cʻąke' anaʻgoptą yųkʻą' tʻeʻhąl pahaʻ wą
ekta' Iʻya hinaʻpʻį ną tʻaheʻnakiya u' cʻąke' liʻla Cʻaʻpala kicʻi' napʻe-
g.licuˋ keʻᵉ. M.ni' wą śma' keʻpʻe' cʻų heʻl akʻe' g.linaʻźįpi ną Cʻaʻpala
inaʻhni cʻeyaʻktʻųpi wą kaʻga cʻa ali' g.liyuʻweǵa keʻᵉ. Heʻcʻena akʻe'
iyaʻtap yużuʻźu cʻąke' heʻcʻena g.licuʻpi ną ahąʻhepįpi yųkʻą' wi' kį
wanaʻ wąkaʻtuya hiyaʻya yųkʻą' ekta' hįg.naʻku pʻa' kʻų he' e' cʻa
Iʻya yuha' inaʻźį śkʻeʻᵉ. M.ni' kį eʻl toʻkʻani-hiyuʻśni kį he' ų'.
18. Heʻcʻena Cʻąkteʻwį Cʻaʻpala kicʻi' ku' ną tʻeʻhą yųkʻą' sųkaʻku
tʻiʻpi kį ekta' g.lihųʻni cʻąke' liʻla wiʻyuśkįpi śkʻeʻᵉ. Hetąʻhą nakeʻś*

---

[1] The word *manįʻl* is diffucult to render into English in a single word. The
open country, away from the center where the tribal camp activities were
in continual progress. It might be far, out of range of the camp; or only a
few hundred feet away from the rear of the tipis all of which face in.

arrived at her brothers' home, where they were very happy to see her. From that time, she never went anywhere again but lived with her brothers. The young men kept closer watch of their sister now; so that never again so terrible a thing could come to her. 19. That is all.

24. Two Men Rescue a Buffalo-Man's Arm.

1. In the tribe lived two fine young men who were held in highest esteem by the people, because they were to be chiefs some day. And then, one of them went away and did not return, so the entire tribe looked for him, weeping, but he was really lost. 2. After some time, the other said, "I next will look for my friend." He travelled all day and towards evening he saw a woman standing on a distant hill, her blanket whipping about her in the wind; so he came to her. She was a very beautiful maiden. She invited him to go home with her, which he did. 3. On entering the tipi, he saw an enormous man lying in the place of honor. And he had only one arm. That man was very disheveled as to his hair. "Well, why is it that your father lies there like that?" he asked; and the woman replied, "Why, he went to visit a tribe away off yonder and there they cut off his arm. He came back here with great difficulty; and from that time, he just

---

to'k'iyani ye'śni suka'ku o'p t'i' ke'ᵉ. K'ośka'laka ki nake'ś li'la t'ąke'ku awą'g.lakapi c'ąke' inu'pa he'c'el ta'ku ot'e'hika ak'ip'aśni śk'e'ᵉ. 19. Hehą'yela owi'hąke'ᵉ.

24.

1. Oya'te e'l k'ośka'laka nu'p li'la waśte'śte u'pi c'ąke' hena' t'oka'ta it'ą'c'ą-wic'ak'iyapikte ci u' yuo'nihąyą wic'a'yuhapi śk'e'ᵉ. Yuk'ą' ug.na' uma' to'k'iya iya'yi ną he'c'enahci g.li'śni c'ąke' oya'te ki a'taya c'e'ya ole'pi k'e'yaś he'c'eya-tok'a'h'ą śk'e'ᵉ. 2. T'e'hą yuk'ą' hehą'l uma' ki, — Mi'ś hehą'l k'ola' owa'kilekte lo', — eyi' ną iya'ya śk'e'ᵉ. Ąpe'tu wą a'taya ma'ni ną wana' htaye'tu hcehą'l wi'yą wą paha'-aką'l śina' kam.ni'm.niyela[1] na'źihą c'ąke' e'l ihu'ni śk'e'ᵉ. He' wik'o'śkalaka c'a li'la wi'yą waśte' śk'e'ᵉ. Yuk'ą' g.le-a'p'e c'ąke' kic'i' k'i' śk'e'ᵉ. 3. T'ima'hel iya'yapi yuk'ą' t'ic'a'tku ki e'l wic'a'śa wą li'la t'ą'ka isto' sani' wani'ca c'a hpa'ya śk'e'ᵉ. He' tuwe' ki ģą'lahcaka[2] śk'e'ᵉ. C'ąke', — Huhuhe', to'k'a c'a le' niya'te le'c'el hpa'ya huwo'? — eya' yuk'ą' wi'yą k'u i'ś heya' śk'e'ᵉ, — Ka'k'iya oya'te wą t'i'pi c'a ekta' ate' i' yuk'ą' isto' waksa'pi c'a iyo'tiye'kiya

---

[1] *kam.ni'm.niyela*, an adverb, meaning "moving continuously, whipped about by the wind."

[2] *ģą*, to be with untidy hair; uncombed, not smooth. Smoothly arranged hair is a mark of neatness; the modern "wind-blown" bob, and all curly, shaggy, ungoverned hair, would be *ģą*, indicative of shiftlessness; *lahcaka*, explained before, is the Teton enclitic, added to verbs to indicate the superlative.

lies here like this." 4. Next she said, "It was rather recently that a
young man came here and went on, offering to bring his arm back
to him. But he has not returned yet. That is what he is waiting for."
So now he knew that it was his lost friend who was out to find the
arm. At once he started forth and at evening he climbed to the
top of a hill, from which he could see an encampment down below.
5. In the centre was a great crowd; and of course, at the tipis, also,
there were women busy at their duties. He sat looking down on the
scene, when a man went heralding something around the circle.
Unfortunately, he spoke a foreign tongue, so the young man did not
understand, but at once everyone rushed back to the centre. There
they gathered and built a fire around a central pole, and suddenly
from time to time they would give war-cries and then dance for
long periods. 6. When it was dark, he went near, and entered the
crowd, where he stood as one of the spectators. And there lay his
lost friend, tied to the top of the pole, and above him hung a
buffalo's forearm[1]! Whenever his friend groaned in agony, then
they danced the harder and shouted the louder. 7. So he turned
himself into a mouse, and climbed up to his friend, on the pole, and
whispered in his ear: "Friend, is it you ?"[2] And the reply was, "Yes,
friend, it is I, but I lie here suffering, tied fast to the pole." So he

g.lihŭ'ni ną hehą'tą le'c'el le' ħpa'yahe cį, — eya' śk'e'ᵉ. 4. Ak'e'ś
heya' śk'e'ᵉ, — Lec'a'la s'eś le'l k'ośka'laka wą hi' ną ate' isto'
ki'cihiyoyįkta ke'yį' ną iya'ya ye'ś lehą'-g.liśni c'aś le' ap'e' yųka'he
cį, — wik'o'śkalaka k'ų eya' śk'e'ᵉ. He'c'eś wana' t'ak'o'laku wą
to'k'aħ'ą k'ų he' e' c'a slolya' c'ąke' he'c'ena ekta'kiya iya'yį ną wana'
ħtaye'tu hą'l paha' wą e'l iya'hą yųk'ą' ak'o'tąhą wic'o't'i-t'ą'ka
śk'e'ᵉ. 5. Ho'c'okata li'la owi'c'ota ną eya' t'iya'ta nakų' wį'yą k'o
op'i'ic'iyapi śk'e'ᵉ. Ekta'kiya e'tųwą yąka'he ħcehą'l wic'a'śa wą
howo'kawįħ ta'ku e'yapaha hiya'ye c'e'yaś t'ok-'i'a c'ąke' ta'ku k'a'
t'ąį'śni yųk'ą' ak'e' ina'ħni oya's'į ho'c'okatakiya ya'pi śk'e'ᵉ. E'-
m.niciyį ną c'ąwa'k'ą wą o'kśą c'et'i'pi ną ųg.na'hąhąla aki's'api ną
t'e'hąhą wac'i'pi c'a wąya'ka śk'e'ᵉ. 6. Wana' o'yiokpaza c'ąke' hehą'l
ik'ą'yela yį' ną wic'e'g.na na'źį yųk'ą' leya t'ak'o'laku wą oki'le-hi
k'ų he' e' c'a wąka'l iya'kaśka ų'papi ną iwą'kap t'at'ą'ka isto' wą
otke'yapi śk'e'ᵉ. Tohą'l t'ak'o'laku kį c'ąyą'ka c'ą'śna hehą'tu c'a
li'klila wac'i'pi ną aki's'api śk'e'ᵉ. 7. He'c'ena hit'ų'kala-ic'ic'ągį ną
c'ąwa'k'ą kį ekta' iya'li ną t'ak'o'laku nų'ge kį e'l e'oźi[3] ną heya'
śk'e'ᵉ: — K'ola`, he' niye' huwo'? — eya' yųk'ą', — Ha'.o, k'ola`, le'
miye' tk'a' t'eħi'ya iya'kaśka mųke'[4] lo', — eya' c'ąke', — Ho,

---

[1] The first indication that the young woman and her father were not human
beings but buffalo people.
[2] A formal phrase on meeting.
[3] oźi', to whisper into the ear; to "pull wires;" o, in; cf. źiźi'-lową`, to hum
a tune, between the teeth.
[4] mųka', I lie; nųka', thou liest; yųka', he lies.

asked, "Friend, at what times do they dance long?" and he said it was each time he groaned in agony. 8. "In that case, groan now, using all the breath you can muster; that will make them dance long and shout wildly and meantime we can get away," he said. So he gave out a prolonged groan, and while the people shouted and danced with all their might, they came down in the confusion, and took the buffalo-arm with them. (One thing I did not remember. When the victim told his friend he was tied fast, the latter, being a mouse with sharp teeth, quickly freed him by biting all the ropes apart. That is what I forgot.) 9. The young rescuer was very weary, and his legs gave out, so he fell from time to time, but ignoring his feelings, he threw the buffalo-arm over his shoulder, and carried his friend a fair distance from the scene. Then he ran back and climbed to his friend's place, and gave one last long groan. The dancing and shouting took on new vigor and was apparently going to occupy the people for some time. So he came down and at once started to where his friend was waiting for him. 10. They travelled hard and came to the buffalo-man's tipi and threw his arm down before him. And he said, "Alas, my sons-in-law, even I!"[1] They proceeded to put the arm back in place, and glued it on with gumbo-mud; so there lay the buffalo-man, wearing one rather smoke tanned arm.

k'ola`, tohą'tu c'ą t'e'hą-wac'i`pi huwo'? — eya' yųk'ą' tohą'l c'ąyą'ka c'ą hehą'tu ke'ya' śk'e'ᵉ. 8. C'ąke', — Ec'a to'hąyą oni'ya-nihą'ske c'a c'ąyą'ka yo', he'c'el li'la wac'i'pi ną i'yakiś'api kįhą k'ohą' ųki'yayįkte lo', — eya' śk'e'ᵉ. C'ąke' t'e'hąħcį c'ąyą'ka c'a oya'te kį aki'ś'api ną a'wicak'eya² wac'i'pi tk'a'ś ic'i'g.nuniyą k'u'l g.licu'pi ną t'at'ą'ka isto' k'ų he' k'o' yuha' nap'a'pi śk'e'ᵉ. (Wąźi' we'ksuyeśni ye lo'. Iya'kaśka yųka' ke'ye' c'ų he'hą' hit'ų'kala c'ąke' hi' p'e' c'aś wą'cag.na wi'k'ą kį yapsa'psaki ną kiyu'śka śk'e' śą e'wektuźe lo'.) 9. K'ośka'laka kį li'la watu'k'a ną hu'staka c'ąke' ħilħi'cahą ħpa'ye c'e'yaś ini'hąśni t'i'sto k'ų he' hįye'tauyą k'į' ną e'kta'wap'aya ag.li'ħpewic'ayį ną t'o'wa'ś he'ktakiya ak'e' į'yąka śk'e'ᵉ. T'ak'o'laku t'o'he k'ų he'c'iya iya'li ną t'e'hąħcį, — Yų'! — eya' c'ąke' ak'e' p'ip'i'ya-wac'i'pi ną aki'ś'api c'ąke' k'ohą' huk'u'l g.licú ną he'c'ena g.licu' ną t'ak'o'laka yąke' c'ų ekta' g.lihų'ni śk'e'ᵉ. 10. Hetą' li'la ku'pi ną t'at'ą'ka-wic'a`śa k'ų he' t'i' kį e'l g.li'pi ną isto' k'ų it'o'kap iħpe'kicic'iyapi yųk'ą', — Hųhųhe', t'ako'ś, miye'ka ye'ś! — eya' śk'e'ᵉ. He'c'ena isto' k'ų he' ec'e'l o'kicistąpi ną k'ąǧi'-t'ame³ ų' iya'skap-kicic'iyapi c'ake' isto' sani' ziye'ħcį kic'ų' śk'e'ᵉ. 11. Hetą'

---

[1] The meaning here is, "Alas, that it should come to this, that even I must bow to necessity; must accept assistance." The buffalo-spirit is one of the most potent.
² a'wicak'eya', honestly; truthfully; seriously; certainly; wica'k'a, to be true; tell the truth; be sincere; k'a, to mean.
³ k'ąǧi'-t'ame, gumbo; the sticky kind of mud that clings like glue; k'ąǧi', crow.

11. From there they were starting home, and their wife[1] wished to go with them; but they left her behind, and came on to their own people. And they found the father of one of them utterly blind, sitting pathetically alone, on a hill. 12. So the one whose own father he was, said to him, "Father, here we are; we have returned." But the old man said, "Alas, alas! You are somebody trying to make sport of me by what you say. My son is gone from me; and therefore I sit here, wailing; yet you speak as one without pity," he said. 13. So, "Father, I am not deceiving you," he said; and he brought some water and washed his eyes over and over again; and finally he could see. So very happily they all returned to camp. But the people were without food. So the young men said, "Now then, here is our chance to serve. It was for just such times as this that we went to so much trouble[2]. Send around a crier to tell everyone to collect buffalo-chips." So the father himself acted as crier. 14. At once all the people worked with a will, collecting the dried buffalo-manure that lay about; and piled the chips together in a great

---

g.licu'pikta yųk'ą' t'awi'cupi k'ų he' u'ktehcį tk'a'ś ihpe'ya g.licu'pi ną oya'te t'i'pi kį ekta' g.lihų'nipi yųk'ą' k'oska'laka kį ųma' atku'ku kį ista'-ġuġa c'a paha' wą aką'l ųśiyehcį yąka'he hcehą'l e'l g.li'pi śk'e'ᵉ. 12. C'ąke' ųma' ate'yehce c'ų he e' c'a, — Ate`, lena' ųki'yepi c'a ųg.li'pe lo', — eya' yųk'ą' wic'a'hcala kį heya' śk'e'ᵉ, —Hehehį+[3], tuwa' mag.na'yewac'į ta'kehape lo'. Mic'i'kśi to'k'el ima'kiyąya c'aś le' ho' mawa'k'ąhe śą ec'ą'l wau'śiyalapiśni ta'kehape lo', — eya' śk'e'ᵉ. 13. C'ąke', — Ate`, c'ig.na'yeśni ye lo', — eyį' ną m.ni' ak'i' ną u' ista' ki'ciyużażahą yųk'ą' hąke'ya tųwą' c'ąke' c'ąl-wa'śteya wic'o'tata kic'i' g.li'pi śk'e'ᵉ. K'e'yaś oya'te kį li'la wic'a'akih'ą c'ąke' k'oska'laka k'ų leya'pi śk'e'ᵉ, — Iho', he'c'a u'ś i'ųksapapi[4] k'ų, e'yapahapi ną to'k'el oki'hi oya'te kį a'taya t'at'ų'kce pahi'-wic'aśi po', — eya'pi c'ąke' atku'kupila k'ų e'yapaha śk'e'ᵉ. 14. Wą'-cag.na oya'te kį a'taya iwa'litaya[5] t'at'ų'kce pahi'pi ną apa'ha wą e'l e't'okśupi[6] yųk'ą' hehą'l kah'o'l iye'ye-wic'aśipi c'ąke' mani'taki-

---

[1] Evidently the girl had married each young man when he came; and now she has two husbands. Forbidden in Dakota society, but then "this is just a legend," as the narrators always say when events are at too great variance with actual life. A man may take two or more wives if he does his duty to support them equally; but women may not have more than one husband at a time.

[2] Since they risked their lives to assist a buffalo-man, they had every reason to expect help from him, and got it.

[3] *hehehį+!* When this word for "alas, alack," etc., is said with a long final vowel, and with a rise and fall of the voice, as indicated, it is a mingling of surprise, grief, hurt, and every other emotion but joy.

[4] *i'ksapa*, to give a good deal of time to; to be bothered with; to take pains with. Distinguished from *iksa'pa*, which means to be made wise by (experience); *ksa'pa*, to be wise; a neutral verb in Teton. But I have heard my father, a Yankton, say *waksa'pa*, making an active verb out of it.

[5] *wali'taka*, to be faithful.

[6] *t'okśu'*, to carry in loads to a given place, in transferring anything; *kśu'*, to pile up.

stack. Then the young men gave orders for everyone to take some of them and toss them in all directions. So they flung them about, some far from the camp. Next day they sent scouts to see the place where they had done this, according to the young men's advice. And as soon as the young scouts got on top of the hill where they could see what was beyond, they rode to and fro[1], the signal that buffalo were sighted. So the people all hurried after them. And there they found a herd of buffalo in a close group. They had a great killing that day, and the people were happy and well-provisioned once again. That is all.

25. The Sacred Arrow.

1. Four young men lived together. And they all went on a journey, leaving the very youngest of all, their little brother, at home. As he sat inside the tipi, he chanced to look out in time to see a beautiful bird, scarlet all over, as it perched on a tree near by. 2. So he thought, "*Huhuhe'!*[2] How beautiful! As scarlet as nothing scarlet ever was

kiya yeya'pi śk'e'ᵉ. Ihį'haṇa yuk'ą' he'c'el eya' c'ąke' tuwe'ya wic'a'kaǵapi ną iya'yewic'ayapi śk'e'ᵉ. Yuk'ą' ka'k'el paha' kį iya'-haṗi ną he'c'ena yuksą'ksą į'yąkapi c'ąke' oya'te kį a'taya e'tkiya iya'yapi śk'e'ᵉ. Yuk'ą' pte' opta'ye wą paha'-ak'o'tąhą hiyo't'įza c'ąke' wana'sapi-t'ą`ka ną ak'e' oya'te kį oi'yokip'iya waśe'capi śk'e'ᵉ. Hehą'yela owi'hąke'ᵉ.

25.

1. K'ośka'laka to'p ka'l t'i'pi śk'e'ᵉ. Yuk'ą' iyu'ha oma'ni -iya`yapi ną suka'kapila wą haka'ktalahca c'a ece'la e'na ayu'śtąpila śk'e'ᵉ. C'ąke' t'ima' yąka'hą yuk'ą' ug.na' e'yokas'į hcehą'l le'c'eg.la t'i'k'iyela zitka'la wą a'taya lu'ta c'a to'k'el-oki`hika³ ową'yak-waśte` c'ą-a'letka wą e'l hi'yotaka śk'e'ᵉ. 2. C'ąke', — Huhuhê, c'e'wiś⁴-waśte` ke. Ta'ku lu'ta iye'c'ecaśni ye lo'. It'o' c'iye' wic'a'wakio kê⁵, — ec'į'

---

[1] When scouts rode ahead to look about, if they suddenly ran their horses back and forth, sideways, within sight of camp, the people knew there were buffaloes beyond the hill.

[2] *Huhi', huhuhi',* and *huhuhe',* (women may use only the first of these or *hinu'*) are all expressions of admiration, wonder, surprise, and often caution. The shades of meaning are brought out by the tone of voice, accents, the amount of breath allowed to escape, and the length of vowels. In addition, men speak this word with individual style, so that there is wide latitude in its use. The same is true of *hehi'!* *hehehe',* and *hehehi'* which indicate regret, remorse, failure and the like.

[3] *to'k'el-oki`hi,* as much as able, i. e., as much as possible; *ka* is added for emphasis, sometimes.

[4] *c'e'wiś,* followed by a verb and terminal *ke* has the force of "how very"; *c'e'wiś-waśte` ke!* how very beautiful it is! *c'e'wiś wo'waśi ec'ų' ke!* how very energetically he labors!

[5] *kê,* at the end of a soliloquy, indicates that the subject is toying with an idea of doing something. "What if I should do so and so ?"

before[1]! I must shoot it for my elder brothers." And because the
bird's skin would so add to the beauty of his brothers' quivers, he
tried repeatedly to shoot it, but missed every time. After he had
shot off all his arrows in vain, he took down his eldest brother's
sacred arrow which he had left at home, and with it, he hit the bird.
Unfortunately, the bird flew away, carrying off the sacred arrow
still piercing its body. 3. Hakela (Last-born) was scared; how he
ought to act was not plain. He knew he should get a severe scolding,
if his brothers were to return now. "It is a terrible thing I have
done!" he thought, as he hurriedly put on his turtle moccasins[2] and
started out in the direction the bird had taken. After a long distance,
he reached a tribal encampment. Behind the circle of tipis, there
was a young girl being courted[3]. So he stepped up to her and, "I
guess nothing has gone by here," he said. And she, "No[4]. Boy-
Beloved did go by with a sacred arrow in his side." 4. He hastened on

---

*ną wą'žu e'l iya'g.laškapikta-waste`ka c'ąke' k'ute'he c'e'yaš a'tayaš
o'šni ke'ᵉ. E'ce'l wąhį'kpe g.luso'ta c'ąke' c'iye'ku-t'oka`p'a kį wą'-
wak'ą wą yuha' yųk'ą' he' e'na yąka' c'ąke' icu' ną ų' ak'e' k'ute'
yųk'ą' ic'ų'hąhcį o' k'e'yaš he'c'ena zitka'la kį apa'⁵ kįyą' k'ig.la'
šk'e'ᵉ. 3. C'ąke' Hake'la nihį'ciya to'k'el h'ą'kta t'ąį'šni'ⁱ. C'iye'ku
kį ec'ą'l g.lihų'nipi hą'tąhąš li'la iyo'p'eyapikta slolki'ya c'ąke' he'
ų'. — T'ᵉehi'ya owa'h'ą ye lo'! — eya'ya p'atka'ša-ha`pa wą yuha'
c'ąke' oki'hį ną kįyą' k'ig.le' c'ų e'tkiya iya'ya ke'ᵉ. T'e'hąl ihų'ni
yųk'ą' ki'tąhcį' oya'te wą wic'o't'ⁱ c'a e'l i'ⁱ. Hola'zata he'l wik'o'škala-
laka wą oyu'spahąpi c'ąke' e'l ina'žį ną, — Ta'kuni le'l og.na'
iya'yešni se'ce, — eya' yųk'ą', — Hiya`, le'l og.na'hokši'-c'ąlki`yapi
wą'-wak'ą' wą apa' k'ig.le' c'ų⁶, — eya' ke'ᵉ. 4. C'ąke' iyo'pteya iya'yį*

---

[1] "It is not like some thing scarlet" means, "it surpasses everything that
tries to be scarlet."   [2] For speed and luck.
[3] It was a common thing to see young men and women courting at dusk here
and there, back of the tipis, all along the way from the woods or river where
the girls went to gather kindling wood or to draw water for the night. If
a girl did not wish to be detained, and tried to run, she was caught and held.
If she was ill, or seriously objected to the man, he could tell soon enough
and leave her; but it was unmaidenly to be easily stopped, and almost all
girls feigned to oppose being detained. The term "*wio'yuspa*", to catch
hold of woman, is derived from this custom, and has come to mean courting.
This word is not used among the Yankton. Their word is *wio'k'iya*, to woo
a woman by talking.
[4] Here we should expect "yes", but the Dakota says "no," and the idea
is, "No, what you say is not so; rather it is this way: Boy-Beloved did go
by". This peculiarity has caused more grief to Dakota children learning
English in school than perhaps any other. When a child is naughty, the
White teacher says, after punishing him perhaps, "You won't do it any
more, will you?" And the Dakota child, with his meagre knowledge of
English, says "yes, (what you say is right; I won't do it anymore)."
[5] *apa'* (an adverb) impaled in; as an arrow; with, as some article; "caught
with the goods" *(apa' iye'yapi)*.
[6] Often in direct quotations, the past article, *k'ų*, is used to conclude the
sentence, although the one quoted does not use it. It is good Teton style.

and reached the second encampment. Here likewise, a young girl was being courted back of the tipi-circle, so he asked her the same thing and she replied, "Boy-Beloved did go by, with a sacred arrow piercing him." So he asked how far his tribal camp was, and the girl told him, "You keep right on, and you will reach a tribal camp; but that is not it[1]. Once again you will come to a camp; the second one. And that will be it." 5. So he continued till he came to a camp; but as that was not the right place, he continued until he reached the second camp; but before he arrived, he met an old man with a bundle on his back, cutting across the meadow. "Grandfather, where are you going?" he asked; and the reply was, "Why, grandson, I am going to treat a Boy-Beloved who returned home with a sacred arrow in his side." — "Where does he live?" 6. The old man said, "See that big tipi across the camp-circle? That is his home. When I near it, I sing out, 'To doctor have I come! *Kiki²*, Rattle-in-the-horn!' That is the signal for all the people to shut their doors so that I may approach the Boy's tipi unseen, and do my work." —

ną wic'o't'i ici'nųpa kį ekta' ihų'ni ke'ᵉ. Ak'e' he'l ec'e'ħcį wik'o'śka-laka wą hola'zata oyu'spahąpi c'ąke' e'l i' ną iyų'ġa yųk'ą', — hokśi'-c'ąlki`yapi wą le'l og.na' wą'-wak'ą' wą apa' k'ig.le' c'ų, — eya' ke'ᵉ. C'ąke' ak'e' iyų'ġį ną, — He' letą'ħą tohą'yą t'i' he? — eya' yųk'ą', — Le' he'c'ena nį'³ ną wic'o't'i wą e'l iya'hųnikta tk'a' he⁴ e'-śni'ⁱ; nake'ś inų'pa-wic'o't'i wą e'l yai' kįhą hee'kte', — eya' ke'ᵉ. 5. C'ąke' yį' ną wana' wic'o't'i wą e'l ihų'ni k'e'yaś he e'śni c'ąke' he'c'ena yį' ną ak'e' wic'o't'i-inų'pa kį e'l ye' ħcehą'l wic'a'ħcala wą wak'į' ną b.la'ye o'pta ya'hą c'ąke' e'l i'tkok'ip'a ke'ᵉ. — T'ųka`śila, to'k'iya la' huwo'? — eya' yųk'ą' leya' ke'ᵉ, — T'ako'źa, le' hokśi'-c'ąlki`yapi wą wą'-wak'ą wą apa' g.li' c'a p'ik'i'ye-b.le lo', — eya' c'ąke', — Tukte'l he' t'i' huwo'? — eya' ke'ᵉ. 6. Yųk'ą' wic'a'ħcala kį i'ś, — Ka hosą'p'ata t'i'pi wą t'ą'ka he' cį he'tu we lo'. C'a ik'ą'yela b.la' c'ą'śna, wap'i'ya hibu' we', kiki heyo'ħla' ! ep'a' c'ą oya'te kį t'iyo'pa kį iyu'hala ec'e'l iye'kiyapi c'ą e'l wai' ną p'iwa'k'iye lo', — eya' ke'ᵉ. Yųk'ą', — T'ųka`śila, tukte'-p'eźu'ta c'a nų' so? — eya'

---

[1] This is characteristic Dakota. Mrs. Frank Fiske, of Fort Yates, N. D., who has a Dakota grandmother, pointed out to me that when a Dakota woman tells you the road somewhere, she doesn't say, "Go until you come to the third road branching off to the left;" rather, she will say, "You will go on for a while, and soon there will be a road branching off to the left; but that's not it. Farther on, there will be another; but that's not it. Soon after, there will be a third; and that's it!" I tested it out and found she was right in every instance in which I questioned an old-time Dakota who had never learned English.

[2] I do not know whether the *k* should be medial, aspirate or glottal.

[3] *nį*, you go; from *ya*, to go. *b.la*, I go; *la*, you go. When the *a* becomes *į* before *ną*, the *l* changes to *n*. *l* before *į* is impossible.

[4] *he' e; le e'; e' e';* are accented in various ways, at various times, for sometimes the demonstrative is stressed, and at other times the verb of identity, *e* is stressed.

"Grandfather, which medicine do you use ?" he asked; so the old man showed it to him. At once Hakela killed the old man and continued on his way, carrying the bundle on his back. 7. "To doctor, I am come! *Kiki*, Rattle-in-the-horn!" he began to sing. And the people said, "There's the medicine-man coming again!" and in haste they all closed their doorways. So he went into Boy-Beloved's tipi where they greeted him with deference. 8. All but Iktomi, the trickster. Sitting in the doorway he kept saying, "This is not the doctor,"[1] until the others rebuked him sharply and told him to go off somewhere, lest he anger the doctor and make him refuse to treat the patient. 9. When Hakela, disguised as the old man, had finished treating the Boy-Beloved, he said to him, "Grandson, I would stop here for the night. I am old now, and I do get very tired. Tomorrow I shall go back home." So the Boy ordered a sleeping-place to be made for him. 10. When everyone was certain to be asleep, Hakela quietly put on his magic moccasins and then took down the sacred arrow from its hanging-place; and stepping on the middle of the Boy-Beloved's abdomen, and then scratching Ikto with his foot (for Ikto must have returned in the night; he was now asleep by the doorway[2],) he left the encampment. So Ikto sprang

---

c'ąke' oki'yaka ke'ᵉ. He'c'ena wic'a'ħcala kį kat'į' ną t'awo'p'iye kį k'į' ną e'l ya' ke'ᵉ. 7. — Wap'i'ya hibu' we', kiki, heyo'ħla'! — eya'ya u' c'ąke' oya'te kį, — Iho', wap'i'ye c'ų he e'³ c'a ak'e' wana' u' we lo'⁴, — eya'pi ną ina'ħniħni t'iyo'pa ec'e'l iye'kiyapi c'ąke' hokši'-c'ąlki`yapi t'i' kį e'l i' c'a kini'hąyą k'uwa'pi ke'ᵉ. 8. Ikto' ece'la, t'iyo'pa o'śtą yąkį' ną, — Wap'i'ya k'ų he' le e'śni'ⁱ — eya'he c'e'yaś ųma'pi kį heya'hį ną wap'i'ya kį yaśi'g.lakta⁵-ik'o`p'api ų' i'yoktekte-kapi ną t'ąka'l iya'yeśipi c'ąke' ina'p'a ke'ᵉ. 9. C'ąke' wana' Hake'la wic'a'ħcala-ic'ic'agį ną wap'i'yahį ną g.luśtą' yųk'ą' hehą'l heya' ke'ᵉ, — T'ako`ża, le'na k'eś mųkį'kte lo'. Wana' wima'c'aħca c'ąke' li'klila wama'tuk'a c'a. Ec'a'ś hį'hąna kįhą hehą'l wag.nį'kte, — eya' c'ąke' e'na owį'ś-p'ik'iyapi⁶ c'a iyų'ka ke'ᵉ. 10. Wana' waśte'ya wic'i'śtįma tk'a'ś wa'ħwakiyeħcį hąpo'kihąhį ną wą'-wak'ą k'ų he' wąka'l otka' c'ąke' icu' ną t'ao'pi k'ų he' t'ezi'-c'oka`ya ali' ną iyo'-k'iheya Ikto' to'k'iyatąhą g.liyų'ka hųśe t'iyo'pa o'śtą ħpa'ya c'ąke' naħla'l⁷-hįg.la k'ina'p'a c'ąke' kikta' hiya'yį ną, — Mak'a' wana'ś⁸

---

[1] Ikto' is never taken seriously when he is speaking the truth.
[2] Ikto' never has the place of honor.
[3] See note 4, page 139,
[4] *lo* indicates that only men here are being quoted.
[5] *ya*, with the mouth; *śig.la'*, to resent; *kta*, will; *k'oki'p'api*, they feared; hence, "they were fearful lest he should make him angry." This is translated by one verb in the future tense, and the second verb in the present.
[6] *owį'ża*, bed; quilts; *p'iya'*, to arrange; lay, as a pallet, on the ground, (for a bed); *k'i*, for him.
[7] *-ħlata*, to grip; claw; *na*, with the foot; hence, with the toe nails.
[8] *mak'a' wana'ś*, an idiom, giving the idea of "what did I say ? I told you so, long before."

up, and, "Ah, didn't I say this wasn't the doctor!" he said, running
hither and yon, waking everybody. They began to chase Hakela.
11. But of course he wore his turtle moccasins. Nothing could
catch him, that was plain from the outset. Only a black horse
almost caught up with him, but was obliged to give up the chase.
So he came to the second encampment, and from there, too, they
began to chase him. They could not rival his magic speed, — none
of them, except a buckskin horse which continued after him when
all the rest had dropped out. His rider could almost reach out and
touch him, when the buckskin was obliged to give up. 12. When
Hakela reached the last encampment, the people pursued him with
zeal, and because he was now fatigued, it looked hopeless for him.
Yet again they fell back one at a time, until only a bay was flying
after him. Almost upon him, as one might exclaim, *"wiś, wi!"*[1] he
suddenly fell back and Hakela went on in safety. 13. Thus did he
barely save himself and with effort did he reach home ahead of his
brothers. He had rescued the sacred arrow, and once more it was
hanging on its accustomed pole. His brothers returned, all ignorant
of what had taken place, and everything went smoothly. From
that time on, Hakela began to reverence the sacred arrow. That is
all.

---

*wapʻi'ya wą he e'śni cʻeś epʻe' cʼ*ǫ, — *eya' wayu'ḣil ahi'yaya cʻąke'*
heʻc'ena iyu'ha kikta'pi nǫ Hake'la kʻuwa'pi śkʻeʼᵉ. 11. Kʼe'yaś
pʻatka'śa-hą`pa ohą' cʻąke' ehą'tą na'żį oki'hiśniyą au'pi nǫ śųk-sa'pa
wą ece'la kig.le'ġa nų śʼe ahi'yuśtą cʻąke' hetą'hą ku' nǫ akʻe' wicʻo'tʻi
wą eʼl g.li' yųkʻą' hetą'hą akʻe' kʻuwa'pi keʼᵉ. Kʼe'yaś a'tayaś owa'ś-
ya'piśni cʻąke' wążi'kżila kawi'ġapi nǫ śųk-hįʼżi wą ece'la yu'za nų śʼe
au' kʼe'yaś iʼś eya' hąke'ya iʼyakcʻųni śkʻeʼᵉ. 12. Heʻc'el ku' nǫ wana'
wicʻo'tʻi-ehaʻke kʼų heʼl og.na' g.licu' yųkʻą' hetą'hą akʻe' kʻuwa'pi nǫ
a'wicakʻeya'-ahiʼyupi nǫ wana' tʻem.ni' cʻąke' śehąś tukʻa[2] *ahi'oyu-*
spapikte śʼe leʻc'eca keʼᵉ. Kʼe'yaś akʻe' hąke'ya wążi'kżila iʼyakcʻųnipi
nǫ ehaʻke śųkhįʼśa wą leʻcʻeg.lahcį, — Wiʼś, wi[3]*! — eya'pi śʼe ahi'yuśtą*
nǫ kawi'ġa śkʻeʼᵉ. 13. Heʻc'eś ki'tąhcį' nai'c'iśpį nǫ tokʻe'cela cʻiye'ku
g.lihų'nipiśnihą kʻi' keʼᵉ. Heʻc'ena wą'-wakʻą kʼų he' tąyą' akʻi' nǫ
ecʻe'l akʻe' cʻiye'ku kį otke'kicicʻiya[4] *keʼᵉ. Cʻąke' g.li'pi kʼe'yaś ta'kuni*
oslo'lyeśnihcį g.li'pi nǫ hetą'hą iyu'ha tąyą' ųʼpi śkʻeʼᵉ. Hetą' nakeʼś
Hake'la wą'-wakʻą kį oho'la śkʻeʼᵉ. Hehą'yela owi'hąkeʼᵉ.

---

[1] *wiʼś wi'*, *eye'-pʻika* is an idiomatic expression meaning "in a manner
that warrants saying *wiʼś, wi'!*" which is equivalent to "whew!" in
English, when an accident is just avoided; like a near-wreck; or an arrow
just scales the surface of something it would be a tragedy to hit.

[2] *śehąś tukʻa*, an idiom; "this time, really; for sure, this time."

[3] *wiʼś wi!* see note 1 on this page.

[4] *otka'*, to hang; *o*, in; *tke*, it is heavy. I have heard old people say *tka*,
instead of *tke*, for heavy; i. e., using it as a verb that does not change *a* to *e;*
kici, second dative.

26. The Feather Man.

1. In a tribal camp lived an only daughter who was greatly loved by her parents, and one day a man came from somewhere and wanted very much to marry her. So they asked around to know who he was, but nobody knew about him. Even so, the girl was very deeply in love with him, and had promised to marry him, and had agreed to run off with him during the night. She lay ready, listening for him, so the instant he came, she went outside and started off with him secretly. 2. And he took her to a house of wood; but as they entered the room, she looked at the man and knew that it was not the handsome youth to whom she had promised herself. This was another man, and he had some beautiful girls imprisoned there. 3. On one side of the room were some girls with their legs missing; and on the other side, girls with their hair and scalp all removed. He said to her, "Choose which side you wish to join." So she said, "Those which have no hair I wish to join." So he told her to sit on that side. 4. Then he made a sweat-bath and said, "The new-comer is to hand me my stones." So when she leaned over, head foremost, to push the stones into the sweat-lodge, he reached out and caught hold of her hair, pulling off her entire scalp. Immediately the woman ran crying round and round over the meadow; and she saw a

1. *Oya'te t'i'pi ki e'l wik'o'škalaka wą ece'la yuha'pi ną li'la t'eĥi'lapi yųk'ą' wic'a'ša wą to'k'iyatąhą ahi'oyuspi ną li'la¹ yu'zįkta c'į' šk'e'ᵉ. C'ąke' oya'te hetą'hą se'ca c'a hųka'ke ki ig.ni'pi k'e'yaš a'tayaš tuwe' t'ąį'šni šk'e'ᵉ. He'c'eca k'e'yaš wana' li'la wį'yą ki iyo'kip'i ną wica'kicila² ną hąhe'pi wą e'l kic'i' iya'yįkta-ig.lu'štą ną wana' wi'yeya ĥpa'ya hą'l k'oška'laka ki hi' c'ąke' he'c'enaĥci ki'ci' k'ig.la' šk'e'ᵉ. 2. Yųk'ą' c'ą't'ipi wą e'l ak'i' k'e'yaš t'ima' iya'yapi k'ų ic'ų'hą ayu'ta yųk'ą' wic'a'ša wą oyu'spahą c'ąke' wica'kicila k'ų he' e'šni šk'e'ᵉ. Le' t'o'keca c'a wik'o'škalaka wį'yą wašte'šte o'ta t'i'pi ki he'l wic'a'g.naka šk'e'ᵉ. 3. T'isą'p'atąhą yąka'pi ki hena' oya's'į hu' ksa'pi ną ųma' ec'i'yatąhą yąka'pi ki hena' i'š p'ehį' wani'capi šk'e'ᵉ. Yųk'ą', — Ho, to'k'iyatąhą o'yap'akta he'cįhą og.la'ka yo', — eya' c'ąke', — Ka p'ehį' wani'capi ki he'c'iyatąhą, — eya' c'ąke' o'p i'yotak-ši šk'e'ᵉ. 4. He'c'ų ną hehą'l ini'kagį ną, — Ho, lec'a'la-hi ki he' į'yą t'ima' hiyu'micic'iyįkte lo, — eya' c'ąke' wana' ka'k'el į'yą wą pat'i'ma iye'yįkta c'a p'ama'g.le-iya`ya yųk'ą' nape' hiyu'yį ną p'ehį' ki a'taya yušlo'k icu' šk'e'ᵉ. He'c'ena wį'yą k'ų c'e'ya yukšą'kšą p'ehį'-c'ola į'yąka yųk'ą' ka'l wi'yaka wą li'la wašte'*

¹ I should say, *yu'zįkta li'la c'į'*, to marry her, very, he wished.
² *wica'la*, to believe; with *kici* inserted, it always refers to the acceptance of a suit, in courtship; *wica*, must mean "right"; Cf. *wica'k'a*, to be honest; sincere, etc. in which *k'a*, is "to mean"; *wica'la*, to believe; *la*, to regard; hence, to regard or consider as right; to be persuaded; to accept one's proposal.

beautiful feather in the grass. As she stooped to get it, it blew off, so she caught up with it and tried again to pick it up. And someone said, "Then you will drop blood on me!"[1] It was a Feather-man who spoke, and now he took her home with him. 5. They came to a stream and he said, "Now, dive in here and stay in as long as you can hold your breath." She did so, and on emerging, she saw that her hair had grown somewhat. Again she dived in and stayed a long time, and this time her hair had reached her waistline, so the man dressed it[2] becomingly for her, and they went on from there. 6. "That will do. Now, I must tell you that I am married, but to a terrible woman[3]. Therefore, first of all, I want you to go to yonder bend in the river, and run about crying, as though in distress. And when a man comes to you, say to him, 'Grandfather, two days from now, I shall come here, expecting food. Tell the people!' 7. Those are mice-people and you shall appeal to them for earth-beans. And to-morrow, she will come to ask you to play on a swing with her. The woman I am married to, will say this. In that case, take the swing that is painted brown," he said. 8. So the woman followed the

---

yąka' c'ąke' icu'kta k'eṡ ec'ą'l kaȟwo'k iya'yahą c'a ak'e' e'kig.leǵį ną icų'kta yųk'ą', — Hehą'l we' ama'yaluṡ'ekte⁴ lo', — eya' yųk'ą' he wi'yaka-wic'a`ṡa c'ąke' hetą' kic'i' k'ig.la' ṡk'e'ᵉ. 5. M.ni' wą e'l k'ihų'-nipi yųk'ą', — Ho, le'l kig.nu'k iya'yį ną tohą'yą oni'ya-nihą`ṡke cį hehą'yą m.nima'hel ų' wo', — eya' c'ąke' ec'ų' ną g.lina'p'a yųk'ą' p'ehį' kį tohą'yąkel uya'⁵ ṡk'e'ᵉ. Ak'e' mahe'l iya'yį ną t'e'hą-ų yųk'ą' p'ehį' kį oi'p'iyake kį hehą'yą c'ąke' wic'a`ṡa kį yup'i'yela ki'cisų ną kic'i' g.la' ṡk'e'ᵉ. 6. — Ho, eya'ṡ he'c'etu we lo'. Ho, eya' wį'yą wą b.lu'ze e'yaṡ li'la ṡi'ca c'a ka'k'iya kaȟmi' kį he'c'iya c'e'ya yuksą'ksą į'yąka yo'. Ną wic'a`ṡa wą e'l niu'kta c'a he' le'c'el eya'kiyįkte lo', T'ųka`ṡila, letą' nų'pac'ą kįhą t'iyo'le-wau`kte'; oya'te kį owi'c'aki-yaka', ehį'kte lo', — eya' ṡk'e'ᵉ. 7. — Hena' hit'ų'kala-oya'tepi c'a e'l mak'a'tom.nica it'i'yole-ni`kte lo'. Ną hį'hąna kįhą ho'hotela ų-a'ni-p'epikte lo'. Wį'yą wą b.lu'ze cį he e' c'a heyį'kte lo'. He'c'etu kįhą ho'hotela wą ǵiya'pi c'a he' icu' wo', — eya'-iwa`hoya ṡk'e'ᵉ. 8. C'ąke'

---

[1] The woman's head was bleeding from the area where the scalp had been torn off.
[2] It was a mark of the affection and pride a husband had for his wife to anoint her hair and braid it for her. They didn't always have time for this, nor was it expected as a regular practice. But it was an occasional act of appreciation on the part of the man. Only men who were consistently gentle, might do this — a man who sometimes scolded or whipped his wife, and then attempted to dress her hair was ridiculed.
[3] The Feather-man is now the husband of the rescued girl, and the ex-wife is her opponent in all these contests.
[4] *ṡ'e*, to drip, as water, drop by drop; *yuṡ'e'*, to cause to drip; *a*, on; *ma*, me; *ya*, thou; *kte*, will or shall; or might.
[5] *uya'*, to grow, as in length; said of tress, grass, hair. Cf. *ic'a'ga*, to grow in all ways; to develop.

instructions. And the next morning the bad woman stood outside her door and said, "*Ma!* Come out and let us swing." So she went out but as they were starting, the Feather-man interfered, and a beautiful feather fluttered in the wind before them. 9. The woman took time out to run after the feather, and meantime she called, "The swing colored brown is mine!" But the young woman, not heeding the feather, ran on and reached the swings, and sat down in the brown one. Swinging herself several times, she jumped back down and started homeward; and soon arrived. Sometime after that, the other one came panting in and the people jeered at her. 10. Next morning she came again and said, "Let us go to find earth-beans." So she came out, and ran crying towards the bend in the river. And that Mouse-man whom she addressed earlier as grand-father, started to announce around the camp, "Now my grand-child comes for food. Make haste!" 11. From all quarters, the mice brought fine large earth-beans, and piled them before her. So she took them home; and a long while afterwards, the other woman came home, all covered with sweat from her efforts, and the people laughed at her. 12. Again next morning she stood outside and said, "Come on out, let us go digging." So she went out and took a badger that her husband had brought to her. Going to the hillside, she lay down with it and threw a blanket over herself and it; and the

---

wi'yą k'ų ec'e'kc'e ec'ų' ną wana' hi'hąna yųk'ą' wi'yą wą t'ąka'l hina'żį ną, — Ma', hina'p'a na, ho'hotela-ųki'c'ųkte, — eya' c'ąke', — Ohą', — eyį' ną ina'p'a yųk'ą' kic'i' iya'ya tk'a's wi'yaka-wic'a'śa k'ų he' e'l hiyu' c'ąke' wi'yaka wą waśte'lahcaka c'a wic'i't'okap kahwo'-hwok iya'ya śk'e'e. 9. Yųk'ą' wi'yą k'ų t'o'wa's wi'yaka kį iha'kap i'yąka ke'e, icu'wac'įhcį. Ną k'ohą', — Ho'hotela-ġiya'pi kį he' mit'a'wa ye'+ — eya' pą' ų' tk'a's iyeśtuk'a wi'yaka kį e'l e'tųweśni į'yąkį ną ihų'ni śk'e'e. He'c'ena ho'hotela-ġiya'pi k'ų he' og.na' i'yotakį ną to'nakel ho'hotela kic'ų' ną k'iyo'psicį ną ak'e' k'ig.nį' ną k'ihų'ni yųk'ą' i't'ehąhca hą'l nake's wi'yą k'ų he' t'em.ni' t'eye'la g.lihų'ni tk'a's oya'te kį aś'a'pi śk'e'e. 10. Ak'e' ihi'hąna yųk'ą' t'ąka'l hina'żį ną heya' śk'e'e, — Ma', hina'p'a na, It'i'g.ni-ųyį'kte, — eya' c'ąke' hina'p'į ną eyaś kahmi' wą ep'e' c'ų he'c'etkiya c'e'ya į'yąka śk'e'e. C'ąke' wic'a'śa wą t'ųka'śila eya'-c'ekiye[1] c'ų he' e'yapaha ną, — Ho, wana' mit'a'koża t'iyo'le-u we lo'! Ina'hni po'+! — eya' śk'e'e. 11. He' ų' o'kśątąhą om.ni'ca waśte'śte t'ąkt'ą'ka ece' ahi't'okśupi c'ąke' k'į g.licu' ną t'iya'ta g.lihų'ni ną etą' i't'ehąhca yųk'ą' wi'yą-ųma' ų he' t'em.ni' t'eye'la i'ś-'eya' g.lihų'ni c'ake' oya'te kį aś'a'pi śk'e'e. 12. Ak'e' ihi'hąna yųk'ą' t'ąka'l hina'żį ną — Ma', hina'p'a na, mak'a[2] ok'e'-ųyį'kte, — eya' c'ąk'e ina'p'į ną hig.na'ku kį hoka' wą kag.li' c'ąke' g.luha' į'yąkį ną paha'-hepi'ya śina' aka'hpa iyų'ka

---

[1] *c'e'kiya*, to pray to; also, to address by kinship term; cf. *c'e'ya*, to cry; weep; to wail.
[2] Uncertain whether this was meant for *mak'a'*, earth, or *maka'*, skunk.

badger dug with a humming sound, so she followed in the tunnel it thus made; and came out an the other end; and still the other woman was not in sight. So the people laughed at her. "She is always doing that; don't let her escape," they said. 13. So the young woman took a club and stood ready. So first a bear cub came out, but she killed it with a blow; and then, after that, the woman, its mother, as it were[1], came out, so she killed her also. And from then on, everything went well for them. That is all.

27. *T'aži''s Adventures.*

1. In a certain large village the chief's daughter was very beautiful, they say. But one day she disappeared, so the father said, "Whoever finds my daughter, him I shall allow to marry her." So all the eligible men were looking for her. But as yet nobody had found her. 2. Out from the tribal camp lived a man with five sons[2]. These five went out in turn to look for her but they all returned without suc-

yuk'ą' ħmuye'la[3] mak'a' ok'a' a'ya c'ąke' iha'kap yį' ną ųma ec'i'ya-tąhą g.lina'p'api k'e'yaš wį'yą-ųma` k'ų to'k'i iya'ya t'ąį'šni c'ąke' oya'te kį aš'a'pi ną, — He'c'ų š'a ke c'ų niya'ye ci lo', — eya'pi šk'e'ᵉ. 13. C'ąke' c'ąksa' wą icu' ną wi'yeya na'ži yuk'ą' tohą'l wana' mat'o' c'įca'la wą hina'p'a tk'a'š kat'a' iħpe'yį[4] ną eha'kela hų'kuke cį hina'p'a c'ąke' ak'e' he' kte' ną hetą'hą nake'š c'ąl-wa'šteya ų'pi šk'e'ᵉ. Hehą'yela owi'ħąke'ᵉ.

27.

1. Ot'ų'we wą t'ą'ka ka'l hą' šk'e'ᵉ. Yųk'ą he'l wic'a'ša-it'ą'c'ą kį he' c'ųwį'tku wą li'la wį'yą wašte' c'a ų' šk'e'ᵉ. Yųk'ą' ąpe'tu wą e'l ųg.na'hąla wik'o'škalaka kį he' t'ąį'šni[5] c'ąke' atku'ku kį heya' šk'e'ᵉ, — Tuwa' mic'ų'kši iye'ya hą'tąhąš he' yu'zįkta c'a wak'u'kte lo', — eya' c'ąke' k'oška'laka t'ąšna'[6] ų' kį hena' iyu'ha li'la ole'pi šk'e'ᵉ. K'e'yaš nahą'ħcį tuwe'ni iye'yešni šk'e'ᵉ. 2. Wic'a'ša wą manį'l c'įca' za'ptą c'a t'i' šk'e'ᵉ. C'ąke' k'oška'laka za'ptą kį hena' iyo'hi

---

[1] Since a bear cub first came out, and then the woman, the implication is that the woman was really a bear posing as a human being, but now her cub shows her up.

[2] The man had six sons, by actual count. But *T'aži'*, the lastborn, is hardly considered as a separate being, until he distinguishes himself where the rest failed.

[3] *ħmu*, a humming, droning, sound, as of machinery in constant motion; a drill; a mill; the hum of telegraph lines in the wind; an approaching storm of wind and hail.

[4] *iħpe'ya*, to throw away; to abandon, when following a verb of action, indicates that the act was accomplished quickly, and dismissed.

[5] *t'ąį'šni*, to be lost; not visible; *t'ąį'*, to show; to be manifest. *mat'ą'įšni; nit'ą'įšni; ųt'ą'įšni* I, thou, we are not visible; we are lost.

[6] *t'ąšna'*, single; *t'ą*, body; *šna*, alone. Hence an unmarried person is said to *t'ąšna'-ų*, with single body he lives. *šna* is always in combination. *išna'*, he alone; *mišna'*, I alone. Mostly it takes the diminutive *la; mišna'la.*

cess. And there was a lastborn son named *T'aẑi'* (Buffalo-calf) who
remained at home. He said to his father, "Father, I shall try next
to recover the lost woman." His father forbade him. "No, even your
elder brothers have not found her; then how will you, who are the
youngest, have any luck?" the father said. 3. The boy went off,
defying his father; and after journeying for a while he reached a
creek along whose banks tall trees stood in groups. There he came
upon a Dakota standing like this, — the hand shading the eyes, as
the man looked up into the sky. So the boy said, "The idea! Why
do you stand looking upward like that?" and the Dakota replied,
"I'm just watching that bird that is flying around up there. I intended to shoot it, but waited for you to get here first." *T'aẑi'* said,
"Do it now, then; I am here." The man placed his arrow and with
great power he sent it directly upward. 4. Then he said, "Now, it is
going to take some time. Suppose we sit down there meanwhile."
So they sat down in the shade of a tree. They sat smoking for a time
when, all of a sudden, a tiny blue bird fell before them, the arrow
piercing his body. 5. *T'aẑi'* marvelled. "My, my! how truly well you
shot it," he said, and the Dakota said, "Why not? Seeing my name
is *Waṭ'ạ'yeyela?* (He sends his arrow well)." So *T'aẑi'* told him his

waẑi'kẑila iya'yapi k'eŝ iyo'hila c'ok'a'-g.li`pi[1] *ŝk'e'ᵉ. Yuk'ạ' Hake'la
wạ T'aẑi' eci'yapi c'a t'iya'ta yạke'la yuk'ạ' he e' c'a atku'ku kị e'l i'
nạ, — Ate`, it'o' mi'ŝ hehạ'l wị'yạ kị he' ole'-m.nị`kte lo', — eya'
c'ạke' atku'ku kị li'la iyo'k'iŝni nạ, — Hiya`, nic'i'ye e'pika ye'ŝ
iye'yapiŝni k'ụ, ŝehạ'l e'ŝ le' hani'kakta kị, ta'ku oya'kihiktelak'a, —
eya' ke'ᵉ. 3. K'e'yaŝ he'c'enaŝ atku'ku kị nah'ụ'ŝni iya'yị nạ wana'
tohạ'yạ ya'hạ yuk'ạ' wakpa'la-ag.la`g.la c'ạ-o'ẑuẑu kị e'g.na lak'o'ta
wạ le'c'eħcị, iŝta' kị nape'-ao`hạzikiya wạka'takiya e'tụwạ na'ẑịhạ c'a
e'l ihụ'ni ke'ᵉ. Nạ leya' ke'ᵉ, — Huhe', le' to'k'el wạka'takiya e'tụwạ
naya'ẑịhe so? — eya' yuk'ạ' lak'o'ta kị i'ŝ, — Ị'ŝe' ka'k'iya wạka'ta
zitka'la wạ okị'yạhạ c'a wak'u'tekte c'e'yaŝ t'o' k'e'yaŝ yahi' kịhạ
ec'a'mụkta c'a le' ac'i'pe-nawa`ẑịhe lo', — eya' c'ạke', — Ho, ec'a,
wana' wahi' ye', k'ute' yo', — eya' yuk'ạ' wạhị'kpe wạ ekta' e'g.le
nạ wạka'takiya to'k'el-oki`hika yeya' ke'ᵉ. 4. He'c'ụ nạ heya' ke'ᵉ, —
Ho, t'e'hạkta c'a k'ohạ' le'l ap'e' ụyạ'kịkte lo', — eyị' nạ c'ạ-i'yohạzi
wạ e'l i'yotaka c'ạke' T'aẑi' i'ŝ-'eya' e'l i'yotakị nạ kic'i' o'tohạyạ
c'ạnụ'pahạ yuk'ạ' ụg.na'hạla wic'i't'okap zitka'la wạ t'o' c'a li'la
ci'scilala c'a wạhị'kpe k'ụ he' apa' g.liħpa'ya ke'ᵉ. 5. C'ạke' T'aẑi'
ŝtela'*[2] *nạ, — Huhi', a'wicak'eya'-tạyạ` yao' we lo', — eya' yuk'ạ'
lak'o'ta k'ụ heya' ke'ᵉ, — Tô, c'ị' le' Wạtạ'yeyela ema'ciyapi kị, —*

---

[1] *c'ok'a',* without. This word with a verb to return, as *g.li, k'i; g.lihụ'ni;
k'ihụ'ni,* means "to return unsuccessful, from a venture."
[2] *ŝte,* good; wonderful; unusual; odd; *la,* to consider; regard; hence, *ŝtela',*
to admire. Cf. *waŝte',* something good, beautiful, desirable; *oŝte'ka,* to be
peculiar; *oŝte'-g.la,* to call bad names at people; i. e., mention unkindly
their physical defects; or some blot on their reputation.

name and also something about his quest. And the man said, "In that case, I will go with you." So the two men started off together. 6. They travelled until they went up a hill where great rocks lay about. On the hillside they found a man lying down with large rocks tied on to his legs. *T'aži'* addressed him, "Of all things! Why do you lie here like this ?" And he said, "O, nothing. I am just going to chase that jackrabbit yonder, but I am too swift for it. That is why I tied these rocks on, — to retard my speed. I was waiting till you came, before chasing it." — "Well, we are here now, chase it!" they said and scared the jackrabbit from its lair, so it sprang up and ran away. But the man followed every way it went and very soon he caught it. 7. The others expressed their admiration of him, and *T'aži'* said, "*Huhi'*[1], how quickly you caught it!" — "Certainly; and why not, seeing I am called *Lu'zahela* (Fleet-footed one)," he said. So *T'aži'* and *Wąt'ą'yeyela* each told his name and something of their quest. And he wished to join them; from there, three men went on. 8. Soon they came to a large lake and walked along its edge, where they came upon a man lying on the shore. *T'aži'* said, "Why are you lying here ?" and the other replied, "Well, I am going to drink this lake dry, but first I was waiting for you to get here." — 9. "Then go ahead; we're here now," they said; so he started immediately to drink. Lying flat on his belly, with his mouth

---

eya' ke'ᵉ. C'ąke' T'aži' i's-'eya' c'aže'-oki'yaki ną nakų' to'k'el ų oma'ni ki oki'yaka ke'ᵉ. Yųk'ą', — Ec'a' ųyi'kte lo', — eya' c'ąke' wana' nų'p ya'pi šk'e'ᵉ. 6. He'c'eš sak'i'p ya'hąpi ną paha' wą a'taya i'yą t'ąki'kiyą-ožu` c'a e'l iya'hąpi yųk'ą' hepi'ya wic'a'ša wą ħpa'yahą ke'ᵉ. I'yą' t'ąki'kiyą nų'p hu' ki ai'yag.laški ną ħpa'ya c'ąke' T'aži', — Huhuhi, to'k'a c'a le'c'el nųka' huwo'? — eya' yųk'ą', — I'še' mašti'ska ki ka' wak'u'wakte c'e'yaš ece'š malu'zahą c'a he'ų' lena' i'yą ki hu' ki awa'g.luskite lo'. Yahi'pi kiħą hehą'l wak'u'wakta c'a le' ac'i'p'epe lo', — eya' c'ąke' — Ho ec'a, wana' ųhi'pe k'uwa' yo', — eya'pi ną mašti'ska ki ħap-ki'cic'iyapi c'ąke' yukšą'kšą i'yąke c'e'yaš ec'e'ħci wic'a'ša k'ų i'yąki ną e'oyuspa ke'ᵉ. 7. He'c'ena ųma'pi ki li'la štela'pi ną T'aži' heya' ke'ᵉ, — Huhi, ta'ku c'e'wiš oħ'ą'k'oya olu'spe ce, — eya' yųk'ą' — Tô, eca c'į' le' Lu'zahela ema'ciyapi ki, — eya' ke'ᵉ. C'ąke' T'aži' Wątą'yeyela kic'i' c'aže'- oki`yakapi ną to'k'iya ya'pi ki k'o' oki'yakapi yųk'ą' o'p yį'kta ke'ya' c'ąke' hetą'hą wana' ya'm.ni ya'pi ke'ᵉ. 8. Yųk'ą' b.le' wą t'ą'ka ag.la'g.la ma'nipi k'ų wic'a'ša wą o'huta ki e'l ħpa'yahą c'ąke' kai'yap iħą'pi ke'ᵉ. C'ąke' T'aži', — Ta'kowe' le'c'el nųka'hą huwo'? — eya'- iyų'ga yųk'ą' i's ųma' ki leya' ke'ᵉ, — Wą, le' b.le' ki b.laħe'pikta tk'a' t'o'wa'š ac'i'p'epi c'a le'c'el mųka'he lo', — eya' ke'ᵉ. 9. Yųk'ą' ųma'pi ki, — Ho, ec'a, yaħe'pa yo', wana' le ųhi'pe', — eya'pi c'ąke'

---

[1] *huhi'!* is an exclamation, generally of surprise and wonderment. Women may use it too, but their own word is *hinų!* and that, the men never use.

10*

on the water, he drank and drank until the lake was dry. As the
water lowered, countless fish, not knowing where to go, jumped and
floundered in the centre of the lake. He finished drinking, and the
rest praised him, "My! How thoroughly you have drunk the lake
up!" they said, and he replied: "Of course, am I not the one they
call *B.leya'ḣepela* (The Lake-drinker)?" 10. The others felt called
upon to tell their names too, and then they told something of their
quest; so he decided to go with them. As the four went along, they
came to some tall mountains and while crossing them, they found
a man sitting on the side of the mountain. *T'aẓi'* spoke to him.
"What are you sitting here for?" The man replied, "I was going to
view the country from here, but these mountains blocked my view;
so I am going to throw them out of the way. I will do it now, for I
was waiting for you to get here." — 11. "In that case, do it; for we
are here now," they answered him. Immediately, while they stood
watching, he pulled up his sleeves and then thrust his arms, as far
as the place-for-tapping-the vein[1], into the ground. And then, with
no effort at all, he threw the whole mountain over. 12. "Goodness,
but you're strong!" they said. "Sure; I ought to be. I've earned the
name *Ḣepa'ptąyela* (Mountains-he throws over)!" So they told him

---

*he'c'enaḣcį b.laska'ḣpaya iyų'kį ną m.ni' kį yatką'hį ną iyu'ha
yaḣe'pa ke'ᵉ. Yaḣe'p a'ye cį ec'e'l hogą' kį tukte'ni ya'pišni c'ąke'
napsi'psil yei'c'iyapi ke'ᵉ. Ig lu'štą c'ąke' ųma'pi kį štela'pi ną, —
Huḣî, c'e'wįš a'tayaḣcį laḣe'pe lo', — eya'pi yųk'ą' — To', eca c'į'
le' B.leya'ḣepela ema'ciyapi kį, — eya' ke'ᵉ. 10. C'ąke' ųma'pi kį
i'š-'eya' c'aże'-oki'yakapi ną ta'ku ų' oma'nipi kį k'o' oki'yakapi
yųk'ą' o'p yį'kta ke'ya' c'ąke' wana' to'p sak'į'p ya'ḣapi ke'ᵉ. Ḣe'
k'eya' wąka'lkatuya c'a e'g.na ya'ḣapi kį ic'ų'hą wic'a'ša wą hepi'ya
yąka'hą c'ąke' e'l į'pi ną T'aẓi' heya' ke'ᵉ, — To'k'a c'a le'c'el nąka'hą
huwo'? — eya' yųk'ą', — Į'še' wa'wak'itakta k'eš ḣe' kį lena' k'uše'ya
hą' c'ąke' paptą'ptąyą iḣpe'wayįkta tk'a' t'o k'e'yaš ac'į'p'epi c'a
le'c'el make' lo', — eya' ke'ᵉ. 11. Yųk'ą', — Ho ec'a wana' ec'ų' ye',
wana' le ųhi'pe', — eya'pi ke'ᵉ. Yųk'ą' wąya'k na'żįpi kį ic'ų'hą
isto' yui'coḣcoḣ iki'kcu ną ok'ą'kakpe² kį heḣą'hąyą ḣe' kį maḣe'l³
paḣli' e'g.le ke'ᵉ. Ḣe'c'ų ną to'k'ašniyą ḣe' kį a'taya paptą'yą iḣpe'ya
ke'ᵉ. 12. C'ąke', — Huḣuḣê, li'la wani'š'ake lo', — eya'pi yųk'ą', —
Tô, eca c'į' le' Ḣepa'ptąyela ema'ciyapi kį, — eya' ke'ᵉ. C'ąke' i'š-*

---

[1] The place-for-tapping is on the inner side of the elbow joint. They tapped
in other places too, sometimes, but this name refers always to the place on
the arm.

[2] *ok'ą'kakpe*, where the vein is tapped, in the bend of the elbow; for bleeding,
as a healing device; *o*, in; *k'ą*, vein, sinew; *ka*, by striking; *kpa*, to be
broken, put out, as an eye; as a container, like an inflated bladder, paper
bag; ruminant's stomach, with contents.

[3] *maḣe'takiya*, towards the inward part, is preferable here; *maḣe'l* sounds
here as though the man put his arms clear into the inside of the mountain;
he only reached towards it.

their names and where they were going, and he joined them, making five who travelled together. As they went on from there, they came upon a man lying on his side, with his ear pressed firmly to the ground. 13. But before they had questioned him he said, "Ah! Here you are! I already know where you are going. A woman has disappeared and you are hunting for her. Well, she is far off yonder; but to reach her, you must first encounter some difficult things." So *T'aži'* said, "Well then, *Mak'a'-Nų̀ǵeya*, (He uses the ground for an ear.) will you take us?" At once he stood up and went with them. 14. They walked in silence for a time, and then he said, "First of all, an old woman lives ahead here. Now, she always challenges men to drink whisky; and when she wins, she kills her opponent." As they expected, they arrived at a hut, and an aged woman came out. "Well, well! My grandchildren! How good of you to come. Now, whenever anyone comes, I like to enter a little contest with him to see who can drink the most whisky." The others said, "Go to it, *B.leya'ȟepela!*" 15. So he entered a tipi with

---

eya' c'aže'-okì`yakapi ną to'k'iya ya'pi kį k'o' oki'yakapi yųk'ą i'š-'eya' yį'kte ke'ya' c'ąke' wana' za'ptą ya'pi ke'ᵉ. He'c'eš ya'hąpi k'ų ka'l wic'a'sa wą t'ąo'b.lec'aya mak'a' kį ekta' nų'ǵe i'pasliya¹ ȟpa'yahą c'ąke' e'l ina'žįpi ke'ᵉ. 13. Wi'yųǵapišnihą iye' t'oke'ya, — Ȅȟ'ᵉ! lena' to'k'i la'pi kį ehą'tą -slolwa'ye lo'. Wį'yą wą to'k'aȟ'ą k'ų he' oya'lepikta ke'ha'pi ną oma'yanipe lo'. Ho', wi'yą kį he' ka'k'iya t'e'hąl ų' tk'a' k'ųše'ya ta'ku ot'e'ȟika o'ta ye lo', — eya' c'ąke' T'aži', heya' ke'ᵉ, — Ec'a Mak'a'-Nų'ǵeya, ųka'ya po', — eya' c'ąke' he'c'ena ina'žį ną o'p ya' ke'ᵉ. 14. O'tohąyą² ini'la ya'pi ną hehą'l heya' ke'ᵉ, — Ho, t'oke'ya winų'ȟcala wą t'i' c'a e'l ųki'pikte lo'. Tk'a' he' winų'ȟcala kį li'la waya'tką-awic'aye³ š'a ye lo', na', tuwa' kte'la c'ą he'c'eya'-kte ye lo', — eya' ke'ᵉ. He'c'ecakte c'ų, wana' t'i'pi wą e'l ihų'nipi yųk'ą' etą'hą winų'ȟcala wą hina'p'į ną, — Hinų', t'ako'ža, tąyą' yahi' pe'. Tuwa' hi' c'ą'šna waya'tką-ab.lela⁴ ye', — eya' c'ąke', — Ho' wo', B.leya'ȟepela, b.lihe'ic'iya⁵ yo', — eya'pi ke'ᵉ. 15. C'ąke' wana' winų'ȟcala kį kic'i' t'ių'ma wą ekta' iya'yapi'

---

¹ *i*, against (the earth); *pa*, by pushing; *sli*, crushed or in very close contact; *ya*, in that manner. To flatten one's nose against the window, as a child, in looking out, would be *ipa'sliya* (an adverb).
² *tohą'yą*, some time, or some distance; *o'tohąyą*, or *oto'hąyą*, in or during some time or distance, "For some time, they walked in silence ...."
³ *a'ya*, to take, following a verb to act, means "to contend with, to rival another in a contest of doing (whatever the verb says)" *waya'tką*, to drink; *aya*, she contends with him in —; *wic'a*, plural object.
⁴ *a'b.lela*, I take him, I contend with him; *a'ya* becomes *ab.la* in the first person. The *la* suffix often indicates a bid for sympathy. She wants her hearers to think kindly and tolerantly towards her little program of vieing for honors in drinking; even if the penalty is death.
⁵ *b.lihe'ca*, to be industrious; energetic; full of life; ready for action habitually; *b.lihe'ic'iya*, to cause oneself to be so; *b.lihe'ic'iya yo'*, is the usual exhortation to muster courage to meet a critical situation calling for nerve, and quick action.

the old woman, and there he saw countless kegs of whisky, placed
in rows, and on top of each other. But he objected. *"Hoh'!* This
isn't anywhere near enough! Now, yonder lies a big lake. Let's
drink that up instead." But the old woman refused. In that case,
you take first turn," he said. Immediately the old woman began
drinking whisky, and when she had consumed four kegs of it, she
stopped. So *B.leya'ĥepela* started in, and without the slightest difficulty, he drank every bit up. 16. Straightway they killed the old
woman, according to the terms; and continued on their way.
Mak'a'-Nṵ'ǵeya then said, "Nearby lives another old woman. Now,
her custom is to invite men to run against her in a race. And she
always kills the unsuccessful opponent." Soon after this, they
arrived at the hut, and an old woman came out. "Well, well,
grandchildren! How fine that you are here. I like to arrange for a
little race with my visitors, grandchildren!"[1] she told them, so the
men said, "Brace up, and run with her, *Lu'zahela!"* 17. So he and
the old woman agreed to run around a large lake which was near by.
They stood up together and were off. From the outset, they ran
like something blown along by the wind, and disappeared around a

---

*yṵk'ą' he'c'iya m.ni' wak'ą' kį k'oka' og.na' ĥ'ṵ'hiye-p'icaśniyą hą'
ke'ᵉ, i'c'iyag.laskiskil. K'e'yaś B.leya'ĥepela, — Ho'ĥ, le' ta'ku-
otaka c'a, ṵka'yuśtą ną ka'k'iya b.le' wą t'ą'ka yąka' c'a he' e'ś
ṵya'ĥepįkte lo', — eya' yṵk'ą' winṵ'ĥcala kį wica'laśni c'ąke', —
Ec'a niye' t'oke'ya yatką' yo', — eya' ke'ᵉ. He'c'ena winṵ'ĥcala k'ṵ
wana' m.ni' wak'ą' yatką'hį ną k'oka' to'p yaĥe'pa yṵk'ą' heĥą'yela
i'yakic'ṵni² ke'ᵉ. C'ąke' heĥą'l B.leya'ĥepela m.ni' wak'ą' yatkį' ną
k'oka' yawa'p'icaśni kį iyu'haĥcį yaĥe'pa ke'ᵉ. 16. He'c'ena winṵ'-
ĥcala k'ṵ kte'pi ną hetą'hą iya'yapi ke'ᵉ. Yṵk'ą' ak'e' Mak'a' Nṵ'ǵeya-
e' c'a leya' ke'ᵉ, — Le'l k'iye'la winṵ'ĥcala wą t'i' c'a e'l ṵki'pikte lo'.
He' i'ś k'ii'yąk-awic'aye s'a ye lo'. Ną tuwa' kte'la c'ą' he'c'eya'-kte
ye lo', — eya' ke'ᵉ. I'yec'ala t'i'pi wą e'l ihṵ'nipi yṵk'ą' wana'
winṵ'ĥcala wą hina'p'į ną heya' ke'ᵉ, — Hinų, t'ako'ża tąyą' hi'pe
lê, Tuwa' hi' c'ą'śna k'ij'yąk-ab.le', t'ako'ża, — eya' c'ąke', — Ho',
Lu'zahela, b.liĥe'ic'iya yo', — eya'pi ke'ᵉ. 17. B.le' wą t'ą'ka yąka'
yṵk'ą' he' o'kihom.nipikta ke'ya'pi ną wana' iya'yapi ke'ᵉ. Nṵp'į'
ina'żįpi ną wana' iya'yapi ke'ᵉ. Etą'hą na'żį,³ kaĥwo'ke cį le'c'el
i'yąkapi ną yukśą'yą wą ai'sįyą iya'yapi ke'ᵉ. K'e'yaś heĥą'huniyą⁴*

---

[1] Old people in stories always call everyone else grandchild. In real life they
generally wait to establish a relationship; because so many kinship terms
are possible in Dakota, regardless of disparity in ages.

[2] *i'yakic'ṵni,* to give up the struggle; to find something or someone unattainable, after repeated trying; *i'yawec'ṵni; i'yaṵkic'ṵni* I, we give up. Very
often the *kic'* is contracted to *kc'* in the dual, and plural first person; and
the third person, singular and plural.

[3] *etą'hą,* from; out of; *na'żį,* to stand. These two words together mean
"from the start, from the very outset."

[4] *heĥą'hunįyą,* all that while; *heĥą',* during that time; *ihṵ'nįyą,* reaching to it.

bend. But all the while, *Makʻaʼ-Nų̀ǧeya* lay with his ear to the ground. 18. Now he sat up. "The old woman is shouting something as she runs, for she is going to be defeated. She is shouting to *Luʼzahela*, offering to rid him of lice!" Then he lay down again and listened to the ground. At length he sat up. "And so *Luʼzahela* has stopped, ... and now, the old woman has caught up with him, ... and they have sat down to hunt lice! It is her way of putting him to sleep; now she is continuing the race alone!" he announced. "Terrible! *Wątą́ʼyeyela*, here's your chance to show what you can do!" they said. 19. So he who never missed a shot, took out a blunt arrow, and set it to his bow, and shot at *Luʼzahela*, asleep in the far distance. His arrow struck *Luʼzahela* right in the middle of his forehead, and woke him so that he sprang to his feet and began running; now the old woman ran crying, but he reached her and passed her and got home first. Because the old woman lost, they killed her there, and went on. 20. Again *Makʻaʼ-Nų̀ǧeya* spoke, "Now, the next one that lives nearby is a white man who likes to try his strength against another's. And when the other fails, he kills him." Soon after this information, they reached an iron house from which a white man came out. "Ah! Friends, It is good of you to come! Whoever comes tries his strength in a contest with me, customarily,"

Makʻaʼ-Nų̀ǧeya kʻuʼl nų́ǧoptą ȟpaʼya keʼᵉ. 18. Wanaʼ woslaʼl iʼyotaki ną, — Winų́ȟcala wą kʻapʻaʻpikta cʻa pą́ į́yąke loʼ; Luʼzahela heyoʼkicilekta¹ keʼya pą́ į́yąke loʼ; — eyį́ ną akʻe iyų́kį ną nų̀ǧoptą ȟpaʼyį ną hehą́l iʼyotak hiyaʼyį ną, — Cʻa wanaʼ Luʼzahela eʼna ina̤ʼżį ye loʼ; wanaʼ winų́ȟcala kį kig.leʼǧį ną heyoʼkicile-iʼyotake loʼ; wanaʼ yuiʼstįmį ną hetą́ȟą išnaʼla g licuʼ we loʼ! — eyaʼ keʼᵉ. Cʻąkeʼ, — Otʻeʼȟike loʼ, Wątą́ʼyeyela, b.liheʼicʻiya yoʼ, — eyaʼpi keʼᵉ. 19. Cʻąkeʼ Wątą́ʼyeyela wiʼwoštake wą ikiʼkcu ną itaʼzipa eʼl ikʻoʼyakyį ną Luʼzahela kʻuteʼ keʼᵉ. Kaʼktoʼkʻiyaš ȟpaʼye cʻeʼyaš kʻuteʼ ną pʻaȟteʼ²- cʻokaʼya oʼ ną woȟiʼca³ cʻąkeʼ naʼżį hiyaʼyį ną liʼla g.licuʼ ną winų́- ȟcala kʻų cʻeʼyaya į́yąka tkʻaʼš kʻapʻaʼ-g.licuʼ ną iyeʼ tʻokeʼya g.liȟų́ʼni keʼᵉ. Heʼcʻeš winų́ȟcala kʻų kteʼpila⁴ kį heʼų eʼna katʼaʼpi⁵ ną hetą́ȟą akʻe iyaʼyapi keʼᵉ. 20. Hetą́ȟą akʻe yaʼpi yųkʻą́, — Ho, leʼl iʼš wašiʼcu wą tʻiʼ ye loʼ. Heʼ iʼš wašʼaʼka-awicʻayį našna tuwaʼ kteʼla cʻą heʼcʻeyaʼ-kte ye loʼ, — eyaʼ keʼᵉ. Iʼyecʻala tʻiʼpi wą maʼza cʻa eʼl iʼpi yųkʻą́ etą́ wašiʼcu wą hinaʼpʻį ną heyaʼ keʼᵉ, — Ho, kʻolaʼ, tą́yą́ yahiʼpe loʼ. Tuwaʼ hiʼpi cʻą́šna wašʼaʼka-awicʻab.le šʼa ye loʼ, — eyaʼ

---

¹ *heyoʼkicilekta*, she will hunt lice for him; *heʼya*, lice; *oleʼ*, to hunt; *kici*, sign of the second dative.
² *pʻaȟteʼ*, the space on the brow, directly above the bridge of the nose. *pʻa*, head; *ȟteʼ*, (from *ȟta?*).
³ *woȟiʼca*, to waken, by striking with a point; in this case, by the arrow; *wo*, instrumental; *ȟica*, to waken (always requires a prefix.)
⁴ *kteʼpila*, to win over; to conquer; defeat; *kte*, to kill; *pi*, plural sign; *la*, the diminutive; *kteʼla* always means to defeat; not actually to kill.
⁵ *katʼaʼpi*, they killed her; *ka*, instrumental; *tʻa*, to be dead.

he said. 21. So the visitors said to the one who could overturn mountains, "Now, *Ħepa'ptạyela*, here is your chance!" Now the white man suggested that they try lifting the iron house in which he lived. So they told him to try it first. Whereupon he forced his arms, up to the elbow, under the house; and then raised it a good height, and set it down again. Then *Ħepa'ptạyela* put his two hands under the base, and took the entire house and tossed it aside like nothing. So they killed the white man, seeing he was defeated, and then continued on. 22. Again *Mak'a'-Nụ`ģeya* said, "Now we are coming to a Dakota who likes to try his skill with bow and arrows. And when he wins, he kills his opponent." After a little while, they came to the home of the Dakota. He came to meet them as they approached, saying, "*Hụhi'!* How good of you to come. When I have a visitor, I like to stage a little shooting contest, as a diversion." 23. The men said, "Very well; if that is the case, we have brought our marksman, *Wạtạ'yeyela*, who will compete with you." They set up a target and invited their host to try first. So he sent an arrow, but it fell far short of the mark. *Wạtạ'yeyela* tried next, and hit the target in the very centre, and was the winner. So they killed the Dakota and went on. 24. They sat down to rest, and *Mak'a'-Nụ`ģeya* said, "Now, over there is a lake. Round in shape, very blue, into which we shall dive; and inside is another country at which we shall arrive. Down

ke'ᵉ. 21. C'ạke', — Ho', Ħe-Pa'ptạyela, b.lihe'ic'iya yo', — eya'pi ke'ᵉ. Wana' wasi'cu k'ụ he' t'i'pi wạ ma'za ot'i' k'ụ he' yuwạ'kal icu'-iyu'tapikte ke'ya' c'ạke' t'oke'ya ec'ụ'sipi c'a ispa' kị hehạ'yạ pao'-ħlat'e iye'yị nạ t'i'pi k'ụ tohạ'yạkel yuwạ'kal icu' nạ ak'e' k'u'ya e'g.le ke'ᵉ. Hehạ'l Ħe-Pa'ptạyela i's nape'-nụp'ị pao'ħlat'e iye'yị nạ t'i'pi k'ụ a'taya ta'kunilasni s'e manị'l iye'ya ke'ᵉ. He'c'es wasi'cu k'ụ kte'pila kị ụ' he'c'eya'-ktepi nạ hetạ'hạ ya'pi ke'ᵉ. 22. Yụk'ạ' ak'e' Mak'a'-Nụ`ģeya e' c'a, — Ho', le'l i's lak'o'ta wạ c'ạ' k'ute'-awic'aye s'a c'a t'i' ye lo'; nạ ohi'ya c'ạ'sna ụma' kị kte' ye lo', — eya' ke'ᵉ. Tohạ'tu yụk'ạ' wana' Lak'o'ta wạ t'i' c'a e'l i'pi ke'ᵉ. K'iye'la ya'pi kị he'hạ'ni itko'p hina'p'ị nạ — Hụhụhê, k'ola`pila¹, tạyạ' yahi'pe lo'. Tuwa' e'l mahi' c'ạ'sna ima'ģaģayakel kic'i' c'ạ' k'ute'-awec'iye lo'. — eya' ke'ᵉ. 23. C'ạke' ụma'pi kị, — Ho, he'c'etu he'cịhạ Wạtạ'yeyela le' ụg.lu'hapi c'a kic'i' ec'a'nụkte lo', — eya' ke'ᵉ. Wana' wasa'p-g.lepi² nạ Lak'o'ta kị t'oke'ya iyu't'esipi c'ạke' wạhị'kpe wạ yeye' c'e'yas it'a'henaħcị iħpa'ya ke'ᵉ. Hehạ'l Wạtạ'yeyela i's iyu't'ị nạ c'oka'yelaħcị o' c'ạke' ohi'ya ke'ᵉ. He'c'es Lak'o'ta k'ụ kte'pi nạ hetạ'hạ ak'e' ya'pi ke'ᵉ. 24. Ka'l asni'kiya-i`yotakapi yụk'ạ' Mak'a'-Nụ`ģeya leya' ke'ᵉ, — Ho, le'c'iya le'l b.le' wạ yạka' c'a e'l ụyạ'pikte lo'. T'oye'la mime'ya yạka' c'a ekta' kig.nụ'k ụki'yayapi kịhạ mahe'l

----

¹ *k'ola`pila*, comrades; "pals"; partners (a vocative only); *k'ola'*, friend; *pi*, plural; *la*, indicating affection. This is the usual term of address, among warriors.

² *wasa'p-g.lepi*, a target; goal; *wa*, thing; *sa'pa*, black; *g.le*, to set up.

there stands a great tipi and within it sits the woman we seek. But
she lives with a very bad man; so of course we can't all go there
directly. This side of the tipi, there is a clump of trees where we shall
wait while *T'aži'* goes on alone." 25. They came to the blue lake,
and dived in and landed in a beautiful country. They walked until
they came to a clump of trees on a slope, and there they sat down,
and *T'aži'* went on alone. He arrived at the tipi; and a woman sat
inside. He was lucky, for the bad man was away. She looked at him.
"Go back home. I live with a man so cruel that were he to return
now, he would kill you at once." 26. So, "My, how awfully fearful
he must be! Surely there must be something somewhere by which
he will die!" And she said, "Well, yes, I suppose so; but he has
never mentioned it." — "Why don't you ask him, when he returns?"
he said, and then went away. When the man returned, his wife said,
"As I sat here all alone, an idea came to me that frightened me.
Though on the surface it doesn't seem so, I wonder if there is
something by which you could die?" The man became very angry.

---

*mak'o'ce wą t'o'keca c'a ekta' ųki'pikte lo'. Yųk'ą' he'c'i t'i'pi wą
t'ą'ka hą' c'a he' t'ima'hel wi'yą wą ųko'lepi ki he' yąke' lo'. Tk'a'
wic'a'ša wą li'la ši'ca c'a kic'i' ų' c'ąke' iyu'ha e'l ųyą'piktešni,
it'a'hena c'ąpa'm.na wą e'l ųyą'kapi ną T'aži' ece'la e'l yi'kte lo' —
eya' ke'ᵉ. 25. Wana' m.ni' wą t'oye'la yąka' c'ąke' e'l kig.nų'k iya'yapi
ną mahe'l mak'o'ce wą li'la owa'štecaka c'a ekta' i'pi ke'ᵉ. He'c'ena
ya'hąpi ną c'ąhų'naptąyą¹ wą e'l ihų'nipi, yųk'ą' he'na yąka'pi
c'ąke' T'aži' ece'la hetą' iya'ya ke'ᵉ. T'i'pi k'ų e'l i' yųk'ą' wi'yą k'ų
išna'la yąka' hą'l i' c'ąke' wa'p'i² ke'ᵉ. Yųk'ą' wąya'ki ną, — G.la'³
ye', wic'a'ša wą li'la ši'ca kic'i' wau' c'a g.li' kihą nikte'kte', — eya'
ke'ᵉ. 26. C'ąke' — Ic'e'wiš-wok'okip'eka nac'e'ce; taku'hci i'š-'eya'
ų' t'i'kta wą ki'ciyąka nac'e'ce lo'. — eya' yųk'ą', — Hą'; eya' c'į'
taku'hci yuk'ą' nac'e'ce c'e'yaš to'hini og.la'kešni ki, — eya' ke'ᵉ.
C'ąke', — It'o'⁴ g.li' kihą iyų'ǧi ye' t'o⁴, — eya' ke'ᵉ. Ną k'ig.la'
yųk'ą' oha'kap wic'a'ša ki g.li' c'ąke' t'awi'cu ki leya' ke'ᵉ, — Mišna'la
maka' yųk'ą' ta'ku wą awa'c'ąmi ną wak'o'wakip'e'. Le'c'el-yaų'ke
ci, taku'hci ų nit'i'kta wą yuk'e' se'ce, — eya' yųk'ą' li'la c'ąze'ki ną,*

---

¹ *c'ąhų'naptąyą,* a hill-side, especially a cliff, covered with trees, or bushes.
c'ą, wood; *ħe,* butte; hill; *ų,* (?); *naptą'yą,* to turn, of its own accord, on
its side, like a boat.
² *wa'p'i,* to have good luck; *wa'p'išni,* to be unlucky; *wa,* things; *p'i,* good;
agreeable; pleasant; right; *wa'map'i,* I am lucky.
³ *g.la' ye',* in imperative form (used by women); said as one might say,
You better go; I advise you to go. I think it best for you to go; for your
own good, etc; *g.la'yo',* (used by men). It differs from *g.li' ye',* in that
g.li' ye' is a definite request, the result of which will benefit the speaker.
In this case, *g.la' ye',* it is for the good of the one ordered; *g.li ye'* is used
also by men.
⁴ *it'o'* — *t'o* beginning and ending the sentence, mean, "I dare you to" etc.;
or, "Just do so and so, and see what comes of it."

"What an extraordinary way you talk! *T'aźi'* evidently has been here. Say so, if he has come!" So she answered, "Nobody has been here; I only said it because I grew frightened at what might happen to me if you should die," she said. Then he said, "Well, yes, there is only one thing that could cause my death, and I'll tell you what it is. This side of the lake which is the entrance to this land, is a clump of trees. Somewhere among the trees is a hole, lined entirely with metal. Down there lies a rabbit. And inside the rabbit is a dove. Inside the dove is a blue egg, — an egg blue as though it couldn't be blue enough[1]. If anyone were to get that egg and break it on my forehead, then I should die. But that is impossible. Therefore I say I can not die." 27. Again, soon after, he went away; and then *T'aźi'* came; so she told him what she had heard. He hurried away, and ran and ran to his friends to tell them, but when he arrived they were all busy, looking for the hole. In all directions they were walking, head downward. So he said, "Well, of all things! Here I come, important with news, and you already know what it is!" What happened was that *Mak'a'-Nų̇'ġeya* had been listening

---

— *Hab.le'b.leś-²takehe lo';* *T'aźi' le'l hi' iteke'ᵉ. Hi' he'cįhą oya'ka yo', — eya' c'ąke', — Hiya', tuwe'ni hi'śni ye'; į'śe' hąk'o'wakip'į ną hepe' cį, — eya' yųk'ą', — Hą, eya' ta'ku wąźi'lahcį u' mat'a' oki'hi kį he' oc'i'ciyakįkte lo'. Le m.ni' wą etą' ot'i'mahiyu' kį it'a'hena c'a-o'źu kį he'l ohlo'ka wą hą' tk'a' he' a'taya mahe'tąhą ma'za ye lo'. He'c'i mahe'l maśtį'ska wą hpa'yį ną maśtį'ska kį ima'hel wakį'yela³ wa ų' we lo'. Ną he' ima'hel wi'tka wą t'o'-i'm.naśni⁴ c'a ų' we lo'. He' wi'tka kį tuwa' au' ną p'ahte' kį le'l ama'kahuġa hą'tąhąś ece'la mat'į'kte lo'. K'e'yaś tuwa'ś he' iye'ya oki'hi ka. He' ų' tų'weni mat'a' oki'hiśni ke'pe' lo', — eya' ke'ᵉ. 27. I'yec'ala ak'e' oma'ni-iya'ya hą'l T'aźi' hi' c'ąke' ec'e'l oki'yaka ke'ᵉ. He'c'ena li'la k'iġ ni' ną t'ak'o'- laku owi'c'akiyakįkta c'a į'yąkapi ece' ec'ų' ną wana' ekta' k'ihų'ni yųk'ą' t'ąni'ś ohlo'ka wą mahe'l ma'za ke'ye' c'ų he' ole'hąpi c'a a'beya p'ama'g.le wo'lepi ke'ᵉ. C'ąke', — Huhuhe', waho'śikumic'i- lala⁵ k'ų, t'ąni'ś slolya'pi k'e'yaś, — eya' yųk'ą' leyalaka ehą'niś*

---

[1] A literal translation of an idiom which again suffers in the process. When we want to emphasize the extreme intensity of anything we say, "as if it couldn't be — enough."

[2] *hąb.le'b.leś*, as an adverb, *(hąb.le'*, to seek a vision,) means, "how extraordinary! how, as in a vision! How, as if in the dream world, how unreal." In actual use *hab.le'b.leś* is just an adverb used to describe an act, of which the motive seems odd, without any conscious reference to visions.

[3] *wakį'yela*, a dove; pigeon; *wakį'yą*, thunder; *wa*, being, or thing; *kįyą'*, to fly. Hence, a dove is a little winged being; thunder, as an unseen creature, is *the* winged being.

[4] *i'm.na*, to be satisfied; filled; full, as after a meal. *t'o'-i'm.naśni*, means "it was as blue as could be; not satisfied with its blueness, it would be still bluer, were that possible."

[5] *waho'śikumic'ilala k'ų*, and I was thinking of myself as *the* bearer of news; *wa*, thing; *hośi*, to carry news; *ku*, to be returning; *mic'i*, I, myself, reflexive; *la*, to consider, regard; *la*, diminutive, in this case, to arouse sympathy for himself.

with his ear to the ground, and had told the others what the bad man had said. 28. They quickly found the hole, and stood around it. "Now, *Ĥepa'ptąyela*, do your utmost!" so he knotted his fist and, starting at the base, he advanced toward the opening, striking the hole, and stopping it up by forcing the metal together. With each blow, the rabbit moved backward, coming toward the top. "Now, *Lu'zahela*, get set; for you must chase him when he appears," they said. So he stood ready and the instant the rabbit came out, he darted away, but *Lu'zahela* ran after him, and promptly caught him. 29. Again they stood around the rabbit, about to tear open his abdomen. "Ready, *Wątą'yeyela*, shoot with all your skill!" they said. So the instant the dove was free it flew off, but he set a blunt arrow to his bow, and, without any effort, broke the bird's wing and brought it down. So they took it and tore open its body and found the blue egg which they gave to *T'aźi'*. 30. So he ran with it to the bad man's tipi, and it happened he was lying asleep inside, just at the time. So he approached him directly and broke the egg over his forehead; whereupon he died straightway. Then he said to the woman, "Now, make haste, for I have come after you!" so she started off with him, not even waiting to take anything with her. 31. They arrived at the clump of trees where *T'aźi'*'s friends were waiting for him, and from

wana' Mak'a'-Nų̇ġeya naĥ'ų̇' ną owi'c'akiyaka c'aṡ ehą̇tą-slolya`pi ṡk'e'ᵉ. 28. I't'ap oĥlo'ka kį iye'yapi c'ąke' o'kṡą ina'źipi ke'ᵉ. Ną, — Ho', Ĥe-pa`ptąyela, b.liĥe'ic'iya yo', — eya'pi c'ąke' nape'p'eca g.lu'zį ną ma'za kį wą'ka'takiya¹ ica'b.laska² au' c'a są̇'p ec'e'l maṡtį'ska kį ų̇źiĥekta wąka'takiya u' ke'ᵉ. C'ąke', — Ho', Lu'zahela³, wį'yeya na'źį yo'; yak'u'wakte, — eya' c'ąke' wi'yeya na'źį ną wana' ka'kel-hina`p'į ną li'la nap'a' tk'a'ṡ iha'kap yukṡą'kṡą į'yąkį ną wą'cak oyu'spa ke'ᵉ. 29. Ak'e' o'kṡą ina'źipi ną t'ezi'-yuĥle`capikta c'ąke', — Ho', Wątą' yeyela, wakta'ya na'źį yo'; yak'u'tekte, — eya'pi c'a ka'k'el t'ezi'-yuĥ.le'capi kį he'c'ena wakį'yela wą kįyą' iya'ya tk'a'ṡ wi'woṡtake wą ų' to'k'aṡniyą o' ną ĥupa'hu wowe'ġa c'ąke' icu'pi ną t'ezi'-yuĥle`capi yųk'ą' mahe'l wi'tka-t'o wą ų' c'ąke' he' icu'pi ną T'aźi' k'u'pi ṡk'e'ᵉ. 30. C'ąke' yuha' į'yąkį ną t'i'pi-t'ą`ka k'ų he' ekta' ihų̇'ni yųk'ą' ec'ą'tulaĥcį wic'a'ṡa-ṡi`ca k'ų iṡtį'ma c'ąke' t'ima' iya'yį ną a'tayela yį' ną wi'tka k'ų he' p'aĥte' kį aka'ĥuġa yųk'ą' he'c'ena t'a' iya'ya⁴ ke'ᵉ. C'ąke', — Ho', wįyą`, ina'ĥni yo'; le' c'iĥi'yowahi ye, — eya' c'ąke' wį'yą k'ų he'c'ena wai'kikcuṡni kic'i' g.licu' ke'ᵉ. 31. C'ą-o'źu wą e'l t'ak'o'laku yąka'pi k'ų he'c'iya kic'i' g.li' c'ąke' hetą'ĥą iyu'hala g.licu'pi ke'ᵉ. M.ni' wą t'oye'la⁵

---

¹ *wąka'tkiya* is the usual form; in an upward direction.
² *ica'b.laska*, to cause to cave in, collapse, by striking, so that the two resulting sides of the tube are in contact. *i*, against; *ca (ka)*, by striking; *b.laska'*, flat.
³ *luzahą*, to be fleet of foot; to be a swift runner.
⁴ *t'a' iya'ya*, to die quickly; to be promptly dead. To denote the dispatch with which a thing takes place, this construction is generally used.
⁵ *t'oye'la*, blue-ly; an adverb meaning "appearing very blue"; *t'o*, blue; *ya*, in that manner; *la*, (?).

that point they all started for home. They came out through the lake of blue water, and reëntered this land. After a time, without warning, *Mak'a'-Nǔ`ǵeyala* lay down. "Now, right about here I generally abide, so I shall remain here," he said; so the rest came on without him. And as they were going through the mountains, *Hepa'ptǫyela* refused to travel any farther, so they came on without him. 32. As they walked along the shore of a lake, *B.leya'ĥepela* threw himself down on the ground, and said he would stay there. "Now, my friends, go on from here; I like to live around here, and I shall remain." So from there they came on. When they passed through the country where there were great rocks, *Lu'zahela* declared that was his habitat; and sat down. So they left him there. When they sat down to rest by the creek, in the wood that lined its banks, *Wǫtǫ'yeyela* preferred to remain there. 33. So *T'aži'*, the last-born, in whom nobody placed any confidence, was the one, out of all who tried, who brought home the woman whom they had given up. So the people were glad; and the chief, true to his promise, gave his daughter to *T'aži'*, and they were married. That is all.

28. The Blue Egg.

1. In the very long ago, there was a family with a daughter who was an only child.[1] One day she disappeared. Everywhere, weeping,

───

yǫke' c'ŭ he' og.na' g.lina'p'api nǫ wana' mak'a' akǫ'l ak'e' g.la'pi ke'ᵉ. Yŭk'ǫ' ŭg.na' Mak'a'-Nǔ`ǵeya ka'l g.liyŭ'kį nǫ — Ho', wale'hǫl ece'-op'i`mic'iya c'a le'na waŭ'kte lo', — eya' c'ǫke' he'c'ena g.licu'pi yŭk'ǫ' ĥe-e'g.na ku'pi hǫ'l ak'e' Ĥe-Pa'ptǫyela e'na ig.lo'nica c'ǫke' he'c'ena ŭ'yǫ g.licu'pi ke'ᵉ. 32. B.le' wǫ ag.la'g.la ku'pi yŭk'ǫ' o'huta kį e'l B.leya'ĥepela k'iyŭ'kį nǫ heya' ke'ᵉ, — Ho', k'ola`, iya'ya po'; miye' le'l ŭ'-iyomakip'i c'a le'na waŭ'kte lo', — eya' c'ǫke' hetǫ' ku'pi ke'ᵉ. Į'yǫ t'ǫkį'kįyǫ-ožu` wǫ e'l ku'pi yŭk'ǫ' Lu'zahela he' t'ama'k'oc'e ke'yį' nǫ e'na i'yotaka c'ǫke' iyo'pteya g.licu'pi ke'ᵉ. Cǫ-a'g.la-g.la wakpa'la wǫ ica'g.la asni'kiya-g.li`yotakapi nǫ wana' ak'e' ku'pikta yŭk'ǫ' Wǫtǫ'yeyela e'na ŭ'kta ke'ya' ke'ᵉ. 33. Ho, c'ǫke' T'aži' hokši'-haka`kta c'aš we'c'eyapilašni k'ŭ iye' eha' wi'yǫ wǫ i'yakc'ŭnipi yŭk'ǫ' ag.li' c'ǫke' oya'te kį wi'yuškįpi nǫ wic'a'ša-it'ǫ`c'ǫ kį he'c'el ehǫ'ni eya' c'ǫke' wi'yǫ kį k'u'pi c'a yu'za šk'e'ᵉ. Hehǫ'yela owi'hǫke'ᵉ.

28.

1. *Li'la ehǫ'ni k'ŭ he'hǫ' t'iwa'he wǫ e'l wic'į'cala wǫ ece'la yuha'pi šk'e'ᵉ. Yŭk'ǫ' ǫpe'tu wǫ e'l to'k'iya iya'ya t'ǫį'šni to'k'aĥ'ǫ šk'e'ᵉ.*

───

[1] "Only child" implies a probability of beloved-hood. But sometimes people will lavish everything on an only child, and indulge it with a selfish affection, — selfish in that the tribe does not benefit. In that case, it is no honor to the child. When a parent says, "I love my child", the answer, either expressed or not, is, "Well, prove it then." To prove it is to do good in the child's name, to other people.

they hunted for her but failed to find her, so that they were very sorrowful; especially her father, who went weeping from house to house, seeking her. 2. But nothing came of it; so at last he said, "It is now a certainty that my daughter is gone forever; or someone has secretly killed her." So all the relatives went into mourning. The man was especially affected, and would roam about in the hills, having his fill of weeping. 3. And out there he met a little ant. It said, "Of course I don't give much promise of being useful, but I will go along with you." So the man and the ant went on. Soon after, they met a fly. He said, "Of course I am not worth taking seriously, but I will go with you." So three went from there. 4. As they travelled, they met an eagle who also offered to join them, so four went on together. 5. A hawk added himself to the group, so now five went on their way to find the girl, who, for all they knew, might be dead already. After a while, the ant, seeing how much faster the hawk could go, said, "I am so slow, I think I will go on ahead," and he went on. 6. He came upon a bark-hut in the woods. So he scaled the wall and got on top and looked into the room

C'e'ya tukte'tu kį iyu'ha ole'pi k'e'yaś iye'yapiśni c'ąke' wo't'eĥi iyu'ha ak'i'p'api'ⁱ. Atku'ku kį iyo'tą t'ii'yaza¹ c'e'ya oki'le śk'e'ᵉ. 2. K'e'yaś ta'ku ka'ǵapi t'ąį'śni c'ąke' ḣąke'ya, — Wana' eĥą'kec'ų mic'ų'kśi he'c'eya'-t'ąį'śni ye lo'; nąį'ś tuwa' naĥma'-mi'kte ye lo', — eya' c'ąke' t'i'takuye kį iyu'ha waśi'g.lapi² śk'e'ᵉ. Wic'a'śa k'ų iyo'tą wo't'eĥi ak'i'p'a ną iśna'śnala³ ĥe-e'g.na c'e'ya-im.naic'iya śk'e'ᵉ. 3. Yųk'ą' he'c'iya t'ażu'śkala⁴ wą ata'ya śk'e'ᵉ. Yųk'ą' heya' śk'e'ᵉ, — Ho, eya' wo'wamac'įyekta-iteya wau'śni k'e'yaś it'o' uyį'kte lo', — eya' ke'ᵉ. C'ąke' hetą' kic'i' iya'yeᵉ. Yųk'ą' i'yec'ala t'iĥmų'ga wą ata'yapi'ⁱ. He' i'ś-'eya', — Ho, eya' we'c'eye⁵-map'icakeśni k'e'yaś wau'kte lo', — eya' c'ąke' wana' ya'm.ni ya'ĥąpi'ⁱ. 4. He'c'el ya'ĥąpi k'ų ųg.na' wąb.li' wą ata'yapi yųk'ą' he i'ś-'eya' u'kta ke'ya' c'ąke' wana' to'p hetą'ĥą ya'ĥąpi'ⁱ. 5. C'etą' wą ak'e' o'p'akta ke'ya' c'ąke' wana' za'ptą-kaska` wic'į'calala k'ų wana'ś t'e' se'ce c'e'yaś ole'-yapi'ⁱ. Tohą'yą ya'pi yųk'ą' t'ażu'śkala kį c'etą' kį to'k'el oĥ'ą'k'o kį ab.le'zį ną heye'ᵉ, — It'o' ece'ś li'la maĥ'ą'ĥi c'a t'oke'ya m.ni'kte lo' —eyį, ną iya'ya ke'ᵉ. 6. C'ąma'hel ya'ĥą yųk'ą' ųg.na' t'i'pila wą c'ąha'⁶ ece' ų' ka'ǵapi c'a e'l ihų'ni'ⁱ. C'ąke' t'it'a'hepiya⁷ iya'li yį' ną t'ia'kąl

---

¹ *t'ii'yaza,* from house to house, in running order, missing none. *t'i,* home; cf. *oya'za,* to string, as beads, so that they are in a long row.
² *waśi'g.lapi;* literally, they resent something, is idiomatic for "they go into mourning."
³ *iśna'la,* he alone; *iśna'śnala,* each one by himself.
⁴ *t'ażu'śka,* an ant; cf. *wab.lu'śka,* insects; *g.naśka',* frogs; *g.nųg.nų'śka,* grasshopper.
⁵ *we'c'eya,* to respect, as being of importance; of worth; *we'c'ewaya,* I respect him.
⁶ *c'ąha',* tree bark; *ha,* the skin, outer covering.
⁷ *t'i,* house; *t'a,* its; *hepi'ya,* perpendicular; hence, wall.

through the smoke-vent; and there he saw the lost girl. The poor child cried without stopping and a horribly ugly man with a tattoo on his forehead, sat by, guarding her. 7. He seemed very angry over something. As for the girl, she must have wept continuously since coming there, for her eyes were so swollen that they were not visible. They say it was that one called Iya (The Ogre) who stole the girl. So the ant entered the room and climbed to the girl's ear and whispered, "Tell me in what way it is possible to cause the death of this supernaturally powerful Iya." And she said, "Very well. Among these montains somewhere is a rabbit that is scarlet all over. And inside its belly is a blue egg. If anyone brought that blue egg and broke it on that tattoo mark on his forehead, he would die instantly." 8. The ant left immediately and related this to the fly. He in turn told the eagle who passed the information on to the hawk. So in all directions they looked for the scarlet rabbit. As they expected, they now sighted it. So the eagle swept down low and tried with a sudden turn to soar upward with the rabbit in his claws, — but he missed his hold and failed. The hawk came on after him in the same manner and he succeeded in picking it up. 9. The moment Iya was aware that the rabbit was caught, he went into a very rapid decline and was dying; but they hastened to tear open

---

ihų́ni nǫ śo'ta-oi`yaye[1] *kį etą'hǫ t'ima'hetakiya e'yokas'į yųk'ą' wic'į'calala wǫ ole'pi k'ų he'c'iya t'ima' yąka'he'*ᵉ. *C'e'yahela nǫ k'ohǫ' wic'a'śa wǫ li'la owǫ'yak-śica c'a p'aĥte' kį e'l aki't'o yųk'ą' he' wic'į'cala kį awą'yak yąke'*ᵉ. 7. *Li'la ta'ku iyo'kip'iśni'*ⁱ. *Wic'į'-cala kį i'ś tohą'tą he'l i' kį hehą'tą c'e'ya hųśe iśta' kį naa't'ąiśniśniyą po'*ᵉ. *I'ya eci'yapi kį he e' c'a wic'į'cala kį manų' śk'e'*ᵉ. *C'ąke' t'ażu'śkala kį t'ima' iya'yį nǫ wic'į'cala nų'ge kį e'l e'oźi nǫ heye'*ᵉ, — *I'ya-wak'ą'*[2] *kį le' to'k'el ĥmuĥ-p'i'ca he'cįhą oya'ka yo'; to'k'el t'į'kte cį slolya'ya he'cįhą,* — *eya' c'ąke',* — *Hą'. Le ĥe' kį e'g.na tukte'l maśtį'cala wǫ lu'ta c'a ų' we'. Nǫ he' ima'hel wi'tka wǫ t'o' c'a yąke'. Ho, wi'tka-t'o kį he' tuwa' iye'yį nǫ aki't'o kį he'l c'oka'ya aka'ĥuga hą'tąhąś t'į'kta ke'ye',* — *eya' ke'*ᵉ. 8. *He'c'ena t'ażu'śkala k'ų t'ąka'l g.licu' nǫ t'iĥmų'ga*[3] *kį e'okiyaka ke'*ᵉ. *C'ąke' t'iĥmų'ga kį iya'yį nǫ wąb.li kį oki'yaka c'ąke' są'm-iyo`pteya c'etą' kį oki'yaka ke'*ᵉ. *He'c'ena a'beya maśtį'cala-lu'ta wǫ eye' c'ų he' ole'pi c'a iya'yapi yųk'ą' he'c'ecakte c'ų, wana' wąya'kapi'*ⁱ. *C'ąke' wąb.li' kį kas'a' u' nǫ k'u'ciyelaĥcį kįyą' iya'yį nǫ icu'-wac'į k'e'yaś yug.na'yą ke'*ᵉ. *Iye'c'eĥcį c'etą' kį iha'kap hiyu' nǫ iyeśtuk'a oyu'spį nǫ yuha' kawą'kal k'ig.la' ke'*ᵉ. 9. *Ka'k'el I'ya kį wana' maśtį'cala kį oyu'spapi kį slolya' yųk'ą' he'c'ena waya'zą nǫ ĥ'ąye' c'e'yaś iya'yapi nǫ*

---

[1] *śo'ta-oi`yaye*, smoke-hole; *śo'ta*, smoke; *o*, in; *iya'ya*, it goes out, or away.
[2] *wak'ą'* here means "one with supernatural power;" without reference to its good or bad quality.
[3] *t'i*, house; *ĥmų'ga*, to poison; bewitch; harm with supernatural power; *t'i-ĥmų'ga*, the house fly.

the rabbit and on finding the egg, they ran to Iya's house with it. 10. It was the Eagle and the hawk who did this. Then they gave the egg to the fly who flew in with it and, as Iya was dying, he broke it on his forehead. So Iya then was truly dead. So the lost girl was restored to her father who took her and went back home. That is all.

29. The Elk Man.

1. Originally, they say, this legend belonged to the Pawnee but it is not known just when it came to the Dakota. However, the Dakota now own it also.

Among the people, there was a man who could attract any woman. Women who held themselves dear and lived as if unattainable, easily fell where he was concerned, and those very ones would one day find themselves disgraced by having gone off with him[1]. 2. For this reason, he was greatly dreaded. At last the chiefs met in council and discussed possible ways of getting rid of him. The best plan seemed to be to find the brother of this man, a self-respecting

---

mašti̜'cala ki̜ t'ezi'-yuh̤.le`capi na̜ wi'tka-t'o k'u̜ iye'yapi c'ake' yuha' I'ya t'i' ki̜ ekta' i'pi ke'ᵉ. 10. Wa̜b.li' ki̜ e' c'a C'eta̜' kic'i' le' he'c'u̜ šk'e'ᵉ. T'ih̤mu̜'ga wi'tka ki̜ k'u'pi c'ake' yuha' ki̜ya̜' yi̜' na̜ wana'š t'a au' k'e'yaš he'c'ena aki't'o k'u̜ aka'tu̜lah̤ci̜ aka'h̤uga ke'ᵉ. C'ake' I'ya heha̜'l a'wicakeya t'a' ke'ᵉ. C'ake' wic'i̜'cala wa̜ t'a̜i̜'šni k'u̜ he' atku'ku ki̜ iki'kcu na̜ t'iya'ta g.lok'i' šk'e'ᵉ. Heha̜'yela owi'h̤ake'ᵉ.

29.

1. Le'-wic'owoyake ki̜ li'la eha̜'ni k'u̜ he' eha̜' P'ala'ni t'a'wapi k'e'yaš to'h̤u̜wetuka c'a Lak'o'tata ;hi' t'a̜i̜'šni šk'e'ᵉ. Ho, k'e'yaš leha̜'l wana' Lak'o'ta k'o' t'a'wapi šk'e'ᵉ.

Oya'te t'i̜'pi ki̜ e'g.na k'oška'laka wa̜ li'la wio'wašakya² c'a u̜' šk'e'ᵉ. Wi̜'ya̜ wa̜ži' ot'e'h̤i-ic'ila³ na̜ oo'kihi-p'icašniya̜ u̜' s'e le'c'eca c'a̜ e'lah̤ci̜ tu̜'weni i'nah̤mi̜ na̜i'š mani̜'l e'ih̤peya šk'e'ᵉ. 2. He' u̜' to'k'el-oki`hi wo'k'okip'e-yawa`pi šk'e'ᵉ. O'ha̜keta wic'a'ša it'a̜'c'a̜ ki̜ iyu'ha m.niciyapi na̜ to'k'el k'oška'laka ki̜ he' kte'pikta he'ci̜ha̜ he' iwo'-g.lakapi šk'e'ᵉ. Wana' hec'i'yot'a̜ ta̜y a̜' ke'c'i̜'pi c'ake' k'oška'laka wa̜ wayu'šice s'a k'u̜ he' c'iye'ku wa̜ iyeštuk'a wic'a'ša-wašte`ka c'a

---

[1] The most respectable marriage was the result of an open barter. That showed the high regard the man had for the girl. To run away with a man was not so respectable, because it showed that a girl was willing to take too much of a risk with her reputation which would cling to her for ever. In the case of a maiden running away, the matter was allowed to pass, provided the man thought enough of her to retain her as his wife. And it was altogether forgiven in instances where a girl had no home, no parents, or, worse yet, a step-mother. But when a married woman ran off with another man, she had absolutely lost her standing. This man apparently could influence anybody to go with him.

² *waša'kala*, cheap;

³ *ot'e'h̤i*, dear; priceless; hard of access; *i'cila*, to regard oneself.

member of the tribe, and talk with him. 3. "Come, now, it is becoming a source of worry to the whole tribe that your brother is spoiling everything, and you must grant us your permission to do away with him. Later we will give you horses, a home and a beautiful woman for a wife," they said to him. 4. "How could I ? Were not we two nursed at the same breast ? How then could I sell my own ?" thus he mused many days with a sad heart. Even so, he grew weary of their repeated asking, and at last he was tempted by their offers; so, without more delay, he assented. 5. And then they said, "Let us kill him at the next *ḱaka'*-game, now that at last the brother is willing." And the object of these designs knew what was about to take place. When the date drew near for the next *ḱaka'*-game, he outdid even himself, by eloping with all the remaining women with good reputations; and ruined their names. 6. Then one day he sharpened a knife to a keen thin blade, and took it to his youngest sister-in-law[1] and said to her, "Now, sister-in-law, they are planning to kill me at the next *ḱaka'*-game. So be on hand, and the instant I am killed, rush up, stopping for nothing, and say, 'This one used to

---

i'š-'eya' oya'te e'g.na ų' c'ąke' he' kic'o'-ag-li`pi šk'e'ᵉ. 3. — Ho' wo', le' nisų'kala wą wayu'šica ų' kį wana' oya'te kį wic'i'yokip'išni c'a it'o' ųkte'pikta c'e iyo'wįųk'iya po'. Ec'a'š sų'kak'ą' ną t'i'pi ną wi'yą wąži' wašte' c'a he'c'el ųni'c'upikte, — eya'pi šk'e'ᵉ. 4. Yųk'ą', — Tuwa' ak'a'keša', he' kic'i' ma'ma²-wąži`la awa'zį k'ų. To'k'ešk'e wi'yop'ewayįkta huwô? — ec'į' ąpe'tu o'ta c'ąte' ši'ca ų' šk'e'ᵉ. He'c'etu k'e'yaš p'ip'i'ya iyų'ǵahąpi kį hąke'ya iwa'tuk'a ną nakų' hąke'ya iyu'tąyąpi c'ąke' he'c'etu k'eš iyo'wįyą šk'e'ᵉ. 5. Yųk'ą', — Ho' po', tok'į's eše's³ iyo'wįyą c'e, ḱaka' ų'pi kįhą ųkte'pikte lo', — eya'-g.luštąpi yųk'ą' k'oška'laka wą c'ąta'g.lepi k'ų he' slolki'ya šk'e'ᵉ. Wana' ḱaka' ų'pikta ik'ą'yela ya'pi k'ų lehą'l eha'keke i'-m.naic'iya wii'naḱmapi ece' ec'ų' ną wį'yą eha'ke hena'la wašte'wic'a-k'iyapi yųk'ą' iyu'ha c'aže' wic'a'yušica šk'e'ᵉ. 6. He'c'ų ną ąpe'tu wą e'l, mi'la wą tąye'ḱcį ǵąǵą'yela yumį' ną hąka'ku-haka`kta wą e'l i' ną k'u' ną heya' šk'e'ᵉ, — Ho' wo', hąka`, le' ḱaka' ų'pi kįhą e'l makte'pikta-ao`kiyape lo'. C'e awą'yak na'žį ną ka'k'el-makte`pi kįhą he'c'ena ta'kuni ap'e'šni⁴ hiyu' ną, — Le' mi'š-'eya' šica'ya mak'u'wa s'a k'ų̌! — eyį' ną p'a' wama'ksį ną tsto'-išle'yatą kį he'

---

[1] This is a younger sister or cousin of one of his wives. But since he was so foot-loose, and changed women so rapidly, the chances are that this was the younger sister of his brother's wife; or of a sister's husband.

[2] *ma'ma*, the breasts; human milk.

[3] *tokį's eše's*, an idiom, "luckily enough; almost too good to be true." As here, "luckily enough, he has consented, so why delay the killing ?"

[4] *ta'kuni*, nothing; *ap'e'šni*, awaiting not. This phrase is in the nature of an adverb. *ta'ku*, something; *ni* added, indicates that the sentence is to be negative, ending with *šni;* *ta'kuni* does not mean "nothing;" the sense of negation is only hinted at by *ni*, but not completed until *šni* is introduced.

abuse me too¹!' and cut off my head, and sever my right arm at the
shoulder-joint. 7. Then run with the head and arm to the thick wood
and leave them there," he said. The day came for the *ḣaka'*-game,
and the young girl, though she dreaded to carry out the order, still
felt she should, since he had asked her. She therefore concealed the
knife under her blanket and went to the game, pretending to be a
spectator of it. 8. And now, her brother-in-law, handsomely ap-
pareled, came to look on, but as soon as he stopped, someone shot him
from behind so that he died. Then his sister-in-law ran and exclaim-
ing, "This one used to abuse me too!" she cut off his head and arm.
9. She ran with them to the thick wood, while the people dug a hole
into which they threw the body, and made a fire over it. Then they
declared the country polluted, and moved away. 10. It was now
evening, and the tribe was making camp. But the brother who sold
his own, not having received any of the favors promised him, went
and pitched his tipi, pitifully, at the end of the camp². And then,
that evening, someone approached along the way the tribe had
come. 11. Ever so often he would say, "*U+*!" A long elk-call³.
He came to the brother's tipi and was the one they had killed and

---

*nakų' hiye'te-o'k'ihe ki he'l owa'mapsų' wo. 7. He'c'ų nq yuha'
i'yqki nq c'qo't'eḣika ki ekta' e'iḣpemayq yo', — eya' śk'e'ᵉ. Wana'
ḣaka' u'pikta c'qke' wik'o'śkalaka k'ų li'la t'awa't'elyeśni k'e'yaś eya'
he'c'el-waśipika c'qke' mi'la k'ų he' śina'-mahe'l yuha' nq wawq'yak-
kųs na'źi śk'e'ᵉ. 8. Yųk'q' wana' śic'e'cu⁴ k'ų he' tqye'laḣci ig.lu'źi nq
e'l u' tk'a'ś hina'źi k'ų ag.na' tuwa' laza'tqhq kat'i'ye'ya śk'e'ᵉ. Yųk'q'
hqka'ku k'ų i'yqk iya'yi nq, — Le' mi'ś-'eya' śica'yela mak'u'wa s'a
k'ǫ́! — eyi' nq t'ahu' ki hehq'yq waksi' nq isto'-iśle'yatq nakų' waksa'
śk'e'ᵉ. 9. He'c'ena yuha' c'qo't'eḣika ki ekta' mahe'l iya'ya c'qke'
oya'te ki oḣlo'ka wq k'a'pi nq ekta' k'ośka'laka ki oi'ḣpeyapi nq
ac'e't'ipi śk'e'ᵉ. He'c'ųpi nq hehq'l mak'o'c'e ki wana' śi'ca ke'ya'pi
nq etq'hq ig.la'ka iya'yapi śk'e'ᵉ. 10. Wana' ḣtaye'tu c'qke' e't'ipi
k'e'yaś k'ośka'laka wq sųka'ku wi'yop'ekiye c'ų he' ta'ku k'u'pikta
ke'ya'pi k'ų waźi'ni ye'ś ec'ų'piśni c'qke' t'ii'hqke wq e'l ų'śiyeḣci
e't'i śk'e'ᵉ. Yųk'q' he'-ḣtaye'tu ki c'qku' og.na' ig.la'ka hi'pi k'ų
he'c'el tuwa' u'hq śk'e'ᵉ. 11. Ak'e'śnaśna U+! eya' heḣa'ka-aki'ś'aś'a
u'hq śk'e'ᵉ. Wana' c'iye'ku t'i' k'ų he'l i yųk'q' hi'hqna kte'pi nq*

---

¹ Probably not; that is why he picked her out. She was so young and
insignificant that she was not worth his while; but he was kind toward
her, as an important person might be towards someone obviously not his
equal. He merely teaches her to say that, by way of an excuse to cut the
body up.
² This, I believe, means the end of a sector occupied by a single band;
where it joins on to that of the next.
³ The elk-spirit is the emblem of irresistible masculine charm. A man who
has it attracts all women to him, without any effort on his part.
⁴ *śic'e'*, brother-in-law; *ku*, hers, becomes *cu* after the *e*.

11

cut up that morning; and yet he entered, whole and well. Not at all
angry, he said to his brother, "Now where are the horses, tipi and
woman that they have given you ? Wasn't that why you sold me ?"
he said. 12. And the elder brother wept and said, "Alas, my younger
brother, they gave me nothing!" — "In that case, go to the council
tent and say, 'My brother sends me to claim the things you promised
me!' and see if they don't give them to you," he said. 13. So he went
to the council tent and said what his brother had advised. But they
answered, "*Hoħ!* How could he, when we have just killed and
burned him up ?" He answered, "My brother sits in my tipi, at this
instant. Come and see for yourselves." So they went to his tipi and
were awe-struck to see him sitting there. Immediately they became
very agreeable, because of their fear, and proceeded to give all the
fine things they had promised to the brother and then had withheld
from him; and they said no more about the matter. 14. But things
grew even worse after that. He fascinated all the women so much
that there was not a good woman left in that tribe. And then it was
clear that the young man was really an elk, and so it was beyond
their power to subdue him by killing him; neither could they put a
stop to his attraction for women. They finally gave in and said no
more. That is all.

---

waksa'ksapi k'ų he e' c'a to'kcaśni[1] *t'ima' hi'yotakį ną a'tayaś c'ąze'-
keśni ec'ą'l leya' śk'e'ᵉ, — Ho, tukte' wana' śųkak'ą', t'i'pi ną wį'yą
k'o' nic'u'pi huwo'? He'c'a yac'į' naś le' wi'yop'emayaye c'ų, — eya'
śk'e'ᵉ. 12. Yųk'ą' c'iye'ku kį c'e'yahį ną, — Hehehe', misų', ta'kuni
mak'u'piśni ye lo', — eya' c'ąke', — Ho', wo', ec'a, t'iyo't'ipi'*[2] *kį e'l
yį' ną leya' yo', Wama'yak'upikta ke'ha'pi k'ų hena' wana' misų'
g.liyo'u-maśi` ye lo', eya' yo', to'kśa' nic'u'pikte, — eya' śk'e'ᵉ.
13. C'ąke' wana' e'l i' ną eye'śi k'ų ec'e'l eya' yųk'ą', — Hoħ, le'ś he'
ųkte'pi ną ile'ųyąpi k'ų! — eya'pi tk'a'ś, — Wat'i' kį e'l misų' yąka'
c'e ų'pi ną wąya'ka po', — eya' c'ąke' ekta' i'pi ną wąya'kapi ną li'la
yuś'į'yayapi śk'e'ᵉ. He'c'ena k'oki'p'api kį ų' li'la waśte'-hįg.lapi*[3] *ną
c'iye'ku ta'ku oki'yakapi k'ų hena' iyu'ha k'u'pi ną hehą'yela e'l
ho'yeyapiśni śk'e'ᵉ. 14. K'e'yaś hehą'l iyo'tą wiyu'ha śką'pi kį
ok'i'lita c'ąke' wį'yą kį iyu'ha wic'a'yuśica śk'e'ᵉ. Yųk'ą' ehą'kec'ų
he' k'ośka'laka kį heħa'ka c'aś kte'pi oki'hipiśni ną nakų' wį'yą
iyu'tąwic'aye ų he' nat'a'kapikta oki'hipiśni c'ąke' hehą'yela ta'keya-
piśni śk'e'ᵉ. Hehą'yela owi'hąke'ᵉ·*

---

[1] *to'k'eca*, it is someway; there is something the matter with it; *to'kcaśni*, all
   right.
[2] *t'iyo't'ipi*, council-tent (the Yankton form). The usual Teton form is
   t'i'pi-iyo'k'iheya, the lodge, pieced together; added to, by other tipis.
[3] They suddenly become good; they change their attitude, suddenly, for
   diplomatic reasons.

30. The Deer Woman.

1. Once, a man was walking, away from camp, but as evening was now coming on, he turned homeward and was going through a wood when he met a woman. And it chanced to be a very beautiful woman whom he had been asking for, and offering presents; but he had been rejected repeatedly. And even the girl herself had not looked at him with favor. And here she was. 2. But she turned out to be very agreeable, so he talked pleasantly with her. He thought it was plain that she was after all kindly disposed towards him, so he was happy as he talked, and all the more he wished to have her for his wife. She was wearing a beautiful robe, tan in color; and the man carried a thongrope, coiled about his arm. So he took an end of his rope, and playfully, without her realizing it, ran it through some of the holes[1] in the limbs of her robe, as he talked. 3. Thus they stood when, of a sudden, a woman with a dog emerged from the wood and walked along towards them. The instant the dog saw this young woman, he barked and ran towards her, and she was frantic, and struggled to get away quickly. But now it was clear that she was not a woman but a deer[2], and in the joint of the

---

1. Wic‘a'śa wą mani'l oma'ni-i ną wana' ħtaye'tu a'ya c‘ąke' t‘iya'takiya ku' yųk‘ą' c‘ąma'hel ųg.na'hąla wi'yą wą ata'ya śk‘e’ᵉ. Yųk‘ą' he' wi'yą ki li'la wi'yą waśte' c‘ąke' c‘i'³ ną op‘e't‘ųhą ye'ś k‘u'pisni ną wik‘o'śkalaka ki iye' ye'ś nakų' e‘cą'kikeśni⁴ yųk‘ą' he' e' śk‘e’ᵉ. 2. Li'la waśte'caka c‘ąke' tąyą'kel kic‘i' wo'g.laka śk‘e’ᵉ. Ehą'kec‘ų li'la tąyą' c‘ąte' kiyu'za-iteka c‘ąke' c‘ąl-wa'śteya wo'kiyaki ną hehą'l iyo'tą li'la yu'zikta c‘i' śk‘e’ᵉ. Śina' wą ǵiya'pi⁵ c‘a waśte' i' c‘ąke' wic‘a' ki wi'k‘ą sų'pi wą kaksa' yuha' c‘a ihą'ke ki ų' śina' huhá'-oħlo`ka ki og.na' oya'za ną k‘ohą' wo'kiyakahą c‘ąke' ab.le'ześni śk‘e’ᵉ. 3. He'c‘el yu'ś na'źi ną k‘ohą' wo'kiyakahą yųk‘ą' ųg.ną'hąla wi'yą wą śų'ka wą kic‘i' c‘ąya'tąhą g.lina'p‘api ną t‘ahe'nakiya u'pi śk‘e’ᵉ. Śų'ka ki ka'k‘el-wik‘o'śkalaka ki wąya'ke c‘ų he'c‘ena p‘a'p‘a hiyu' yųk‘ą' nihi'ciya k‘ig.le'-wac‘i li'la k‘oki'p‘a-iteya ig.lu'titą śk‘e’ᵉ. K’e'yaś ehą'k‘ų t‘aħca c‘ąke' iśpa' ki e'l wic‘a'śa ki t‘awi'k‘ą

---

[1] The old-time robes always had holes all around, made by the pegs with which the skin was staked down taut on the ground during the process of dressing. Sometimes these were worked with beads or quills, like button-holes, to add to the beauty and value of the robe.

[2] Just as the elk-spirit stands for masculine charm, so the deer-spirit represents the enticing woman. A man who allowed himself to be ensnared too deeply, died; but those who did not go so far, came through, albeit with difficulty.

[3] *c‘i*, to want, desire; when a man is said to *c‘i* a woman, it means he signifies his wish openly, by asking for her, and offering presents.

[4] *ec‘ą'ki*, to think seriously of. Always negative; *ec‘ą'kiśni*, to not take seriously.

[5] *ǵiya'pi*, a browned robe. It must have been painted brown. Because if it were tanned by smoking over burning bark, the usual treatment for hide for everyday use, the word is *ziya'pi*, they make it yellow.

foreleg[1] the man's rope was twisted into a knot and held her fast.
4. The man knew at once that he had been tricked, and in his anger, he
drew his hatchet from his belt, and would have struck her on the head,
but the deer threw herself here and there to avoid being hit so that
he struck out wildly every way without hitting her. It was a female
of the wood-deer known as the black-tail. 5. At last she spoke again,
as a woman. "That's enough; come on and let me go now. Wait and
see, for I shall give you many powers." The man replied, "Doubtless
you will be sincere in that too!" and he released her, so that she ran
back toward the wood, like one flying. The young man became
dizzy, and without knowing just how, he got home; and he vomited
at intervals. 6. Ever so often when the spell came over him more
than usual, he would whistle like a deer and make as if to run off,
like a wild animal; so the people all felt badly, and were especially
saddened when they recalled what a fine young member he used to
be, in the tribe. 7. At last they made a sweatlodge for him, and
purified him, and that seemed to help him; so then they exploded
some gun-powder in his face and he really came to his right mind, it
seemed. So he recovered. But as long as he lived, he alone, by some
mysterious luck, always brought home the finest horses from war.
The people explained it by saying that the deer-woman who
promised him many powers in exchange for her release must have
kept her word. That is all.

---

*k'ų yuo'siyą ik'o'yaka c'ąke' to'k'ani-iya`yeśni śk'e'ᵉ. 4. He'c'ena
wic'a'śa k'ų g.na'yąpi kį ų' c'ąze'ka nazų'spe wą mig.na'ka² c'ąke'
iki'kcu ną ų' nata'-aką`l ap'e'-wac'į k'e'yaś t'a'ħca kį ena'na iħpe'ic'iya
c'ąke' kaśna'śna ahi'yaya śk'e'ᵉ. T'a'ħca-wi'yela c'a le sįte'-sapela
ewi'c'akiyapi k'eya' c'ąma'hel ų'pi k'ų he'c'a śk'e'ᵉ. 5. Yųk'ą' hąke'ya
ak'e' wį'yą-ių'³ ną heya' śk'e'ᵉ, — Iho', eya'ś wana' ama'yuśtą na;
to'kśa' wic'o'ħ'ą o'ta c'ic'ú'kte, — eya' c'ąke', — Ak'e'ś wica'yak'įkta
c'e'l eś! — wic'a'śa kį eya'⁴ kiyu'śka yųk'ą' c'ąya'takiya kiyę' s'e
k'ig.la' śk'e'ᵉ. He'c'ena k'ośka'laka k'ų ito'm.nim.ni ną to'k'el hetą'
g.la' t'ąį'śni t'iya'ta k'i' ną g.le'pahą śk'e'ᵉ. 6. Tohą'tu c'ą iyo'tą
to'k'eca-au' nąśna t'a'ħca-żo ną nap'į'ktehci c'ąke' oya'te kį li'la c'ąte'
śi'capi ną k'ośka'laka-waśte` tk'a' k'ų he' ų' iyo'tą iyo'kiśicapi
śk'e'ᵉ. 7. O'hąketa ini'kicagapi ną he' owa'śte s'e le'c'eca c'ąke' hehą'l
ak'e' c'aħli' k'eya' ite' ona'p'opyapi yųk'ą' hehą'l nake'ś wac'į'ksape s'e
le'c'eca ną aki'sni śk'e'ᵉ. K'e'yaś to'hą'-ni kį hehą'yą zuya'pi c'ą'śna
iśna'la śų'kak'ą' o'ta awi'c'ag.li s'a śk'e'ᵉ, to'k'eśk'e ec'ų' t'ąį'śni.
C'ąke' he' t'a'ħca-wį`yą wą wic'o'ħ'ą o'ta k'u'kta ke'yį' ną kiyu'śkapi
c'į' k'ų he' hena' oki'hik'iya ke'ya'pi śk'e'ᵉ. Hehą'yela owi'hąke'ᵉ.*

---

[1] This is the tendon that stands out conspicuously in the foreleg in the
elbow joint.

² *mig.na'ka*, to wear about the body; as in the belt; *g.na'ka*, to place. Perhaps
from *mi*, knife, because a knife in its scabbard, was worn on the belt.

³ *wį'yą*, woman; *ia'*, to talk; that is, to speak according to the style for women.

⁴ This should be reduplicated; *eya'ya*, so saying.

31. The Deer Woman.

1. A man went hunting and shot two deer. He carefully cut up the meat and caused his horse to carry it; and now, when the sun was low, he was coming home. He sat down to rest on the edge of a cliff when a woman approached, walking along the cliff. 2. She arrived and stood beside the man, but he sat without speaking. So at last she sat down by him and said, "Don't you recognize me? Why are you so quiet?" And she also settled down, and let her feet hang over the bank. 3. But the man was sad in his heart. "How does it happen that this girl, usually so well guarded that it is impossible to get near her, is out in these wild parts by herself?"

Yankton Version, in Yankton Dialect.[1]

1. *Wicʻaʼśa wą wayeʼi kʼa*[2] *tʻaʼħca nuʼm wicʻaʼo keʼyaʼpiʼ*[i]. *Tąyeʼna wicʻaʼpʻate cʼa*[2] *tʻadoʼ ki tʻaśuʼke kʼikʻiʼye cʻa wanaʼ wiʼ kʻuʼciyena cʻąkʻeʼ*[3] *tiyaʼtakiya kuʼyąka*[4] *keʼyaʼpiʼ*[i5]. *Mayaʼ wą apʻaʼżeżeyena asniʼkiya-iʼyotaka ukʻąʼ*[6] *akʻoʼtąhą wiʼyą wą mayaʼ-akdàʼkda tʻaheʼnakiya uʼyąka e wąyaʼk yąkaʼ keʼyaʼpiʼ*[i]. 2. *Wanaʼ hihųʼni kʻa wicʻaʼśa ki isaʼkʻip hinaʼżi kʻeʼyaś iniʼna yąkaʼ ukʻąʼ*[6] *hąkeʼya kicʻiʼ iʼyotake cʻa — Tokʻe iyeʼmayakiyeśni se*[7]? *Toʼkʻa ukʻąʼ iniʼna*[8] *nąkaʼ he? — eyeʼ cʻa iʼś iyaʼ*[9] *mayaʼ ki eʼd huʼ ġeʼġeya iʼyotaka keʼyaʼpiʼ*[i]. 3. *Ho, Kʼeʼyaś wicʻaʼśa ki cʻąte-maheʼd*[10] *iyoʼkpʻiśni*[11] *kʼa, — Toʼkʻetkʻe*[12] *deʼś akaʼp yeʼśni-awąʼyakapi cʻaś kʻiyeʼna yepʻiʼcaśni kʼu deʼcʻed iśnaʼna maniʼn omaʼni huwoʼ? — ecʼiʼcʼi yąkaʼ keʼyaʼpiʼ*[i].

---

[1] The Yankton style in both oratory and story-telling is markedly vigorous, plain and terse, as compared with the Teton which is flowery, and often weakened by padding and needless romancing.

[2] *ną*, and, is always *kʼa*, in Yankton. It becomes *cʼa*, on occasion, following the rule of change from *kʼ* to *cʼ* after *e* and *i*.

[3] *cʻąke*, therefore; in Yankton *cʻąkʻe*, with the aspirate *kʻ*.

[4] Wherever we find *hą*, to stand, added to verbs, in Teton, to express continued action, in Yankton, *yąkaʼ*, to sit, is used. We have then, the rather contradictory, *naʼżi yąka*, He was standing, literally "he stands sitting." In Teton, *ħpaʼyahe*, he was lying down; is literally "he stands lying."

[5] Wherever we have *śkʻe*, it is said, the Yankton has *keʼyaʼpi*, they say that. The Yankton consider the word *śkʻe*, too indefinite; They consider it a gossip-help, useful because the authority for the gossip is vague to the point of lacking entirely.

[6] *yukʻąʼ*, and then, and so, and behold, then, etc., is *ukʻąʼ* in Yankton.

[7] *so*, the sign of a question in Teton, is *se* in Yankton.

[8] *iniʼla*, without speaking, is *iniʼna*. Here the *l* corresponds to an *n*, not to a *d; la*, diminutive, corresponds to Yankton *na;* but *la*, to regard, and *la*, to ask for, correspond to *da*.

[9] *iʼś eyaʼ*, translated by me as "he, also", is *iʼś iyaʼ*, in Yankton.

[10] *maheʼl* corresponds to *maheʼd*, not to *maheʼn*.

[11] *kipʻiʼ* corresponds to *kpʻiʼ; kicʻiʼ*, with, to *kcʻiʼ*. Contractions of this kind are frequent.

[12] *toʼkʻeśkʻe*, somehow, corresponds to *toʼkʻetkʻe*, in Yankton.

4. Stealthily he looked at her from the corner of his eye and saw that she wore many rings on her fingers, several on each finger; then he glanced at the shadow she cast, and it was not a woman's outline, but a deer's, with the long ears in constant motion. So he thought, "Ah! This is no woman. This is one of those things which they say can trick and mislead men. All right! But try and fool me!" he thought as he quietly felt for his gun. The deer knew it at once, and sprang up and ran like something hurled forth[1], and disappeared in the woods; and its form was that of a deer. 5. It entered the wood causing the leaves to rustle, and almost at once, it looked out at him and called, "I give those rings to you!" So the man looked where the deer-woman had sat, and there, shaped like rings, lay a pile of tendrils from the grape-vine. That is all.

32. A Woman Kills her Daughter.

1. A woman had two children, a boy and a young woman. And a young man came from somewhere and married the girl, so the four lived together. 2. As they lived there, in the same tipi, the woman became enamoured of her son-in-law[2] and because she wanted him

---

4. *I'naȟma s'e kdakį'yą ayu'ta ųk'ą' wį'yą kį napsi'oȟdi o'ta napi'yohina ų' e abde'ze c'a heha'n nagi' kį ekta' e'tųwą ųk'ą' he' wį'yąsni, t'a'ȟca e nakpa' yuho'm.nim.nipi s'e yąka' ke'ya'pi'ⁱ. C'ąk'e', — Eh! De' wį'yąsni yedô. De' ta'ku k'eya' wic'a'śa kna'yąpi s'a ke'ya'pi k'ų he'c'a ye do'. Ho, k'e'yaś tośtoś maya'knaye ca! — ec'į' ma'za-wak'ą' iki'kcu ųk'ą' wį'yą ki sdodye' s'e na'żį hiya'ye c'a kaȟ'o'na³ iye'yapi kį de'c'ed c'ąya'takiya k'ikda' ųk'ą' t'a'ȟca ke'ya'pi'ⁱ. 5. C'ąma'hed waȟpe' yusna'pi kį he'c'ed iya'ye c'a i't'ap ak'e' ec'i'yatąhą ahi'yokas'į k'a heya' ke'ya'pi'ⁱ, — Napsi'oȟdi kį hena' c'ic'u'we'+! — eya' c'ąk'e' wic'a'śa kį e'd e'tųwą ųk'ą' yąke' cik'ų⁴ he'd napsi'oȟdi se'kse c'ąwi'yuwi hu' paha'yena hiye'ya ke'ya'pi'ⁱ. Hehą'yena oi'ȟąke'ᵉ⁵.*

32.

1. *W'įyą wą c'ica' nų'pa śk'e'ᵉ. Ųma' hokśi'la ną ųma' wik'o'śkalaka śk'e'ᵉ. Yųk'ą' k'ośka'laka wą to'k'iyatąhą hi' ną wik'o'śkalaka kį yu'za c'ąke' he'na to'p wi'taya t'i'pi śk'e'ᵉ. 2. He'c'el o'wążila t'i'pi k'ų, wį'yą kį hąke'ya t'ako'śku kį aki'scu⁶ ną li'la iye' hįg.na'yįkta*

---

[1] This takes only one Dakota word to give the picture of a thing moving faster than running or flying, — as something thrown.
[2] This is a disgrace; an indecency. Evidently it was one-sided.
[3] *kaȟ'o'l*, flying through the air, thrown corresponds to *kaȟ'o'na*.
[4] *k'ų*, the past-article, is always *cik'ų* after *e, į*.
[5] Yankton is characterized by a bolder use of vowels in succession, without the insertion of *y*'s and *w*'s, for smoothness.
[6] *scu*, to be self-conscious; "fussed", affected by the presence of one of the opposite sex; *ascu'*, to feel so towards one; *ki*, her own (son-in-law.)

for herself she planned to kill her daughter. She was on the constant lookout for a good way to do away with her. 3. Whenever the son-in-law was in the tipi, she became very silly in her actions, and hardly knew what to do with herself, and couldn't sit quiet. One day when the man was away, she said to her daughter, "Let us go swinging," so the girl replied, "How silly! We are not children!" and she laughed. 4. But she said again, "Daughter, I am always unhappy, and I really wish to swing, just to amuse myself a little." So then the girl consented and together they went to the water. It was deep and along its edge stood a tree with a large branch arching over the stream. And on it were two swings already tied. 5. So she caused her daughter to take the one farther over the water, and took the outside one for herself; and now they swung themselves and at once the girl's rope broke, landing her in the deep stream where she was drowned. 6. It came out later that the crafty woman had previously set those swings and had hacked the rope in one of them so that it would break at once; for what was there about it to make it strong? 7. Immediately she who was so eager to swing, ran home; and as there was nobody around, she hurriedly dressed herself in her

---

c'į' ki ų' śica'ya wi'yukcą śk'e'ᵉ. C'ųwį'tku ki to'k'el kte'kta he'cįhą he' ak'i'l ece'-ų śk'e'ᵉ. 3. Tohą'l wic'a'woña ki t'ima'hel yąka' c'ą' li'la oñ'ą'-witko`tkoki ną to'k'el ñ'ą'ka nų tk'a', ną t'iza'ni yąke'śni śk'e'ᵉ. Yuk'ą' ąpe'tu wą wic'a'śa ki e'l yąke'śni hą'l c'ųwį'tku ki k'į' ną, — Ho'na, c'ųkś, ho'hotela-ųki'c'ųkte, — eya' c'ąke', — Tuk'i' ece'ś ta'ku-hoų`kśika c'a! — eyį' ną iña't'a ke'ᵉ. 4. K'e'yaś, — C'ųkś, li'la iyo'kiśilya ece'-waų c'a ima'ĝaĝaic'iya ho'hotela we'c'ų wac'į' ye', — eya' c'ąke' hehą'l nake'ś iyo'wįyą c'ąke' m.niya'ta¹ kic'i' i' śk'e'ᵉ. Yuk'ą' m.ni' śme' cį ag.la'g.la c'ą' wą ic'a'ĝį ną ale'tka wą t'ą'ka c'a m.ni' ki e'tkiya apa'kįyą hą' yuk'ą' he'l ho'hotela nų'p ehą'tą-oka`śka hą' śk'e'ᵉ. 5. C'ąke' c'ųwį'tku ki iye' m.ni' ki ec'i'yatąhą yąke'k'iyį ną i'ś ųma' t'ąka'tąhąke cį he'l og.na' yąkį' ną wana' yei'c'iyapi yuk'ą' wik'o'śkalaka t'aho'hotela k'ų he' m.ni' ki ekta' oka'psak iya'ya c'ąke' iyo'was'įyą m.ni' t'a' śk'e'ᵉ. 6. Leyalaka wi'yą-wic'a'śaśni k'ų he' e' c'a ehą'ni hena' he'c'el oka'śka e'g.le ną c'ųwį'tku yąkį'kte ų² he'c'iyatąhą wi'k'ą ki wahų'hų c'ąke' he ų' wą'cag.na kapsa'ka śk'e'ᵉ, ec'į' ta'ku ų' suta'kta wani'ca c'ąke' he' ų'. 7. He'c'ena ho'hotela kic'ų'kteñcį-waśte`ka t'iya'takiya į'yąk g.licu' ną tuwe'ni yąke'śni

---

¹ *m.niya'ta*, to the water; *ta* added to any noun, means "to or at that place where it is." But with nouns of one syllable, *ya* is inserted before the *ta*. With longer words, the *ya* is omitted. *b.leya'ta*, to the lake; *m.niya'ta*, to the water; *c'ąya'ta*, to the wood; but *wakpa'ta*, to the river; *paha'ta*, to the hill.

² The Teton strives for smoothness, always. Very often, when *k'* must be changed to *c'*, or often *k'* itself, is omitted, as here. Here *ų* appears to mean, "therefore"; but it means, *k'ų*, the-aforesaid. Likewise, *e'yaś*, from *k'e'yaś* or *c'e'yaś*, could be confused with another word, *eya'ś*, but for the accent.

daughter's clothes; and because there was great resemblance between them, she applied her face paints just like her daughter's. 8. She was sitting in her daughter's place, and was busy at some task when her son-in-law returned. Just then the baby began to cry; so the man said, "What is the need of allowing him to cry? Why don't you nurse him?" And with that he glanced at her and at once he knew it was not his wife who was sitting there. 9. "Where has my wife gone?" he thought, and a great sense of worry came over him. But of course he could not question her, because she was his mother-in-law[1]. And she said, "I have nursed him, and still he cries; what next can I do?" and then, addressing her boy, though it was her own son, she said, "My younger brother, carry your nephew on your back; I must cook some food, yet he detains me." So the boy took the baby on his back, and walked along the bank, crying. 10. "Elder sister, come back to us! My nephew is crying," he was wailing, when his sister appeared, visible from the waistline up. She lay on the shore and said, "Bring him here, little brother, that I may nurse him. Mother has done a dreadful thing to me and now it is too late for any hope. Who is that man anyway? If she wants him so, how much better, had she told me; gladly I would have turned him over to her! but alas, I am now a fish from my waist down."

---

c'ǫke' ina'hni c'ųwį'tku t'aha'yake kį ec'e'kc'e ų' nǫ li'la iye'kic'eca c'ǫke' ee' s'e wase' k'o' ki'cų' nǫ yǫka' šk'e'ᵉ. 8. He'c'el c'ųwį'tku t'o'he kį o'štǫ yǫkį' nǫ wae'c'ųhe hcehǫ'l t'ako'šku kį g.li' šk'e'ᵉ. Ec'ǫ'l hokši'calala wǫ yuha'pi yųk'ǫ' he' c'e'yahǫ c'ǫke' wic'a'ša kį, — Wǫ' azį'k'iyi ye', to'k'el le' luc'e'yahe! — eyį' nǫ ka'k'el-ayu'ta yųk'ǫ' he'c'ena t'awi'cu k'ų he' ešni c'a iye'ekiya šk'e'ᵉ. 9. — Wį'yǫ mit'a'wa k'ų to'k'i iya'ya huwô? — ec'į' iyo'kišil-hįg.le e'yaš k'ųyǫ' c'ǫke' iyų'h-kapį ke'ᵉ. Yųk'ǫ', — Ec'į' le' azį'wak'iya ye'š he'c'ena c'e'yahe cį, šehǫ' to'k'el owa'k'uwakteklak'a²! — eyį' nǫ hokši'la k'ų he' k'į' nǫ, he'š c'įca' k'e'yaš, — Misų`, nit'ų'škala ki'c'į oma'ni ye', wi'yohpewayįkta³ tk'a' leya'he, — eyį' nǫ hokši'la k'ų wak'ǫ'hežala kį k'įk'i'ya c'ǫke' t'ųška'ku kic'i' maya'-ag.la`g.la c'e'ya oma'nipila šk'e'ᵉ. 10. — T'ǫke`, he' ku' ye', mit'ų'škala c'e'ye lo'! — eya'hǫ yųk'ǫ' m.ni' kį etǫ'hǫ t'ǫke'ku k'ų he' c'uwi'-yuksa`la t'ąį'yǫ hiyų'kį nǫ — Misų`, au', azį'wak'iyįkte, Ina' t'ehi'ya oma'kih'ǫ c'a wana' to'k'el h'ǫma'p'icašni ye'. Wic'a'ša kį he' tuwe'ka c'a! C'ǫti'heya⁴ he'cįhǫ owo't'ǫla k'eš og.la'ke šni, wak'u'kta tk'a'; wana' le' nite'hepi kį hehǫ'yǫ hoǧǫ'-ima`c'aǵe', — eya' c'ǫke' hokši'la k'ų p'ip'i'ya-c'e'ya

---

[1] He observes the avoidance which requires that he say nothing to her directly. His wife would be his medium for communication with her; but of course she was missing.

[2] lak'a, how then (shall I handle him?)

[3] iyo'hpeya, to cook (meat) by boiling; wa, things; meat, generally understood.

[4] c'ǫte', heart; ihe'ya, to reach to; hence, to covet; to want very keenly.

At this, the little brother cried harder than ever. 11. The baby, now
satisfied, was asleep. "Now, brother, stand here with your back to
me; I want to help you to take him on your back," she said; so he
turned and stood with his back to her while she placed the infant
there and arranged the blanket about him. Then, the moment she
finished, the boy turned about quickly; but already his sister had
disappeared; and all he saw was the tail of a fish as it vanished
under the water. 12. The next day, when the child cried and the
woman could not quiet him, she caused the boy to take him out
again. So he walked along the bank, singing, "Elder sister, my little
nephew is crying!" And she called out, "Bring him here, little
brother!" And she lay on the shore and fed him and when he slept,
the boy took him home. 13. And then the woman who was in love
with her son-in-law, went off somewhere, so the man questioned
his young brother-in-law like this, "Brother-in-law, where has your
sister gone?" So the boy told him how his mother had cut into a
rope and then made a swing and caused her to fall into the water.
14. And also how once in a while his sister would come to the shore
to feed the baby. So the man said, "The next time your little
nephew cries, take him and say what it is that brings your sister to
the shore." So when the child began to whimper again, he took him
along the bank and called to his sister. 15. Meantime the man had
transformed himself into a tree stump, and stood near by; so when

šk'e'ᵉ. *11. Wana' wak'ą'hežala kį azį' ig.lu'štą ną ištį'ma c'ąke', —
Ho, misų`, ak'o'ketkiya e'tųwą le'l hina'žį', k'įc'i'c'iyįkte, — eya' c'a
e'cų' ną šina kį ec'e'l iye'kicic'iya c'ąke' ka'k'el oħ'ą'k'oya ig.lu'hom.ni
k'e'yaš wana'š t'ąke'ku k'ų hoǧą' c'a sįtu'pi¹ ece'la t'ąį'yą m.nima'hel
k'ig.la' šk'e'ᵉ. 12. Ihį'hąna yųk'ą' ak'e' wak'ą'heža k'ų c'e'yahą c'ąke'
wį'yą kį yua'sniktehcį k'e'yaš i'yakc'uni c'ąke' ak'e' hok'si'la k'ų he'
k'įk'i'ya šk'e'ᵉ. C'ąke' maya'ag.la`g.la — T'ąke`, mit'ų'škala c'e'ye
lo', — eya' oma'nihą yųk'ą' — Misų`, au', — eyį' ną ak'e' o'huta
kį ekta' hiyų'kį ną azį'k'iyį ną kai'štima c'ąke' t'iya'ta ag.li' šk'e'ᵉ.
13. Yųk'ą' wį'yą wą t'ako'šku aki'scu k'ų he' to'k'iya iya'ya c'ąke'
wic'a'ša kį t'ąhą'kula kį le'c'el wi'yųǧa šk'e'ᵉ, — T'ąhą`, nit'ą'ke le'
to'k'iya iya'ya huwo'? — eya' c'ąke' to'k'ešk'e hų'ku kį wi'k'ą wą
wakų'lkųtį ną ų' ho'hotela ki'caška c'ąke' oka'psakį ną m.nima'hel
iya'ye ų he' oki'yaka šk'e'ᵉ. 14. Nakų' tohą'lšna heya'ta hiyų'kį ną
oų'papila² kį azį'k'iye ų hena' oya'ka yųk'ą' wic'a'ša kį leya' šk'e'ᵉ, —
Ho, t'ąhą`, ak'e' nit'ų'škala c'e'ye cįhą icu' ną to'k'el eha' c'ą'šna
nit'ą'ke u' he'cįhą ec'e'l eya' yo', — eci'ya c'ąke' wana' ak'e' hokši'cala
k'ų c'į'ktakta³ tk'a'š he'c'ena ki'c'į ną maya'ag.la`g.la t'ąke'ku
ho'yeki'ya oma'ni šk'e'ᵉ. 15. K'ohą' wic'a'ša k'ų he' c'ąp'a'ksa-ic'ic'aǧį*

¹ sįtu'pi, tail, as of a fish; tailfeathers of a bird; sįte', tail; ųpi', skirts.
² oų'papila, an infant, still of the age to be bound in wrappings. o, in; ųpa,
to lay in a horizontal position; la, diminutive.
³ c'į'ktakta, to whine; whimper; fret, as a child.

his wife came and lay exposed, only as far as her waist, out of the
water, and took her baby in her arms, she suddenly saw it there.
16. "Little brother, that tree stump was never there before, was it?"
she asked, and he said, "*Hoh!* Of course, sister, that has always been
there; you just never noticed it before!" She said, "All right, then,"
and proceeded to feed her baby, and as she replaced him on the
boy's back, and arranged the blanket about him, the man rushed
forward and with a single stroke, severed her body from the fish.
17. The body curved and jumped like a fish, but they managed to
get it home where they made a sweat-bath and restored the young
wife to her former self. Next day, the man was going to hunt; so he
said to her, "I shall bring meat and pile it in a heap beyond the hill;
and when I call for assistance, bring your mother with you." 18. Accordingly in due time, he called out, "Come and meet me!" So she
said, "Mother, that one wishes someone to meet him and help
carry the meat; let us go!" And the mother agreed all too eagerly;
so they went. 19. They divided the meat and each one took a pack on
her back. When they were starting home the man said to his wife,
whispering in her ear, secretly, "Stay near me all the time," so she
said she would. "And when I make a mark on the ground, step over
it quickly." So the woman kept closely behind her husband. 20. He

nǫ m.niyo'huta kị ik'i'yela na'žị c'ǫke' wana' wị'yǫ k'ų nite'hepi kị'
hehǫ'yela t'ǫį'yǫ hiyų'kị nǫ wana' hokši'cala kị iki'kcukte ħcehǫ`l
wǫya'ka šk'e'ᵉ. 16. He'c'ena, — Misų`, tų'weniš c'ǫp'a'ksa kị he'
ka'l he'šni k'ų, — eya' c'ǫke', — Hoħ, t'ǫke`, eyaš he' tohǫ'hųniyǫ kị
he'l he' ų, i'še' aya'b.lezešni nac'e'ce lo', — eya' yųk'ǫ' — Ohǫ`, misų`,
— eyị' nǫ he'c'ena wak'ǫ'heža kị azị'kic'iyị nǫ wana' ak'e' sųka'kula
k'ų k'ịki'yị, nǫ šina' ec'e'l aka'ħpa tk'a'š ec'ǫ'l wic'ǫ'ša wǫ c'ǫp'a'ksa-
ic'ic'ǫje ų he' hiyu' nǫ nite'hepi kị hehǫ'yǫ kaksa' iħpe'ya c'ǫke'
hogǫ' š'e ško'škopa¹ šk'e'ᵉ. 17. Ško'škope e'yaš² ag.li'yakupi nǫ
t'iya'ta ini'kicagapi nǫ g.lue'c'etupi šk'e'ᵉ. Ihị'hǫna yųk'ǫ' wic'a'ša
kị waye'-yịkta c'ǫke' it'o'kap leya' šk'e'ᵉ, — Ho, paha' kị ka'ai'nap
t'alo' ag.li't'owakšu nǫ o'kpe-mau` po' ep'e' cịhǫ ec'a'š nihų' kic'i'
hiyu' wo', — eya' šk'e'ᵉ. 18. C'ǫke' wana' he'c'ecakte c'ų, paha'-ai`nap
hina'žị nǫ, — O'kpe-mau` po'+! — eya'-pǫ c'ǫke', — Ina`, ka' o'kpe-
ya`pi c'ị' nǫ pǫ'hǫ c'a ekta' ųyị'kte', — eya' yųk'ǫ' iš'o'š'oyeħcị
iyo'wịyǫ c'ǫke' kic'i' i' šk'e'ᵉ. 19. Wana' t'alo' k'inų'k'ǫ³ k'ị'pi nǫ
t'iya'takiya g.licu'pikta yųk'ǫ' wic'a'ša kị naħma'la t'awi'cu kị oži'
nǫ leya' šk'e'ᵉ, — Mik'i'yela ece'-ku wo', — eya' c'ǫke' wị'yǫ kị, hǫ',
eya' šk'e'ᵉ. — Nǫ mak'a' kị tukte'l iwa'kago hǫ'tǫhǫš oħ'ǫ'k'oya apsi'l
hiyu' wo', — eya' c'ǫke' wana' wị`yǫ k'ų hịg.na'ku kị ila'zatalaħcị

---

¹ *ško'pa*, to be curved; to have a bend in it. *škoško'pa*, neutral reduplication;
ško'škopa to bend, actively from side to side, as a fish out of water.
² *c'e'yaš* becomes *e'yaš*.
³ *k'inų'k'ǫ*, each one of two; *k'i*, into two parts; *nų*, from *nų'pa*, two (?);
k'ǫ (?).

was carrying a staff in his hand. With it he suddenly made a mark on the ground and started forward quickly, so his wife followed directly behind, and jumped over the line. Then the crafty older woman came along, and as she was about to step over the line, the ground separated right over the line, so she disappered into the abyss, as if someone had dropped her down. 21. At once the ground came together once more. So from that time on, that old woman who was in love with her own son-in-law, was never seen again by anyone; neither she nor the pack of meat she carried. That is all.

33. The Stingy Hunter.

1. A man went hunting and while he was cutting up his game, a woman came and stood by; but he continued without paying any attention to her. He piled his meat in a heap, in one place; and when he had finished, he took it all up and was leaving, when the woman, who evidently stood there because she was hungry, and now realized that he was not sharing anything with her, called to him thus, "No matter where you go, you shall encounter *T'ašų'ke O'tawį*. (She-who-Owns-Many-Horses); and you shall encounter *C'ap'ų'ka T'ą'ka* (Big Mosquito); and *Wihu'powį* (Woman-with-Swollen-Legs); and *Wip'e'ȟlokewį* (She-with-the-Hole-in-her-Crown); and *Išpa' T'ahį'špa*[1] (Elbow-Awl)." 2. The man went on from

---

ku' šk'e'ᵉ. 20. Yųk'ą' c'ą' wą yuha' c'ąke' ųg.na'hąla ų' mak'a' kį e'l ica'ǵo iye'yį ną li'la g.licu' tk'a'š t'awi'cu kį iha'kap oȟ'ą'k'oya i'š-'eya' apsi'l iya'ya šk'e'ᵉ. Yųk'ą' wį'yą wą wic'a'šašni k'ų he' wana' i'š eha'kela e'l g.licu'kta tk'a'š ic'ų'hą oi'caǵo kį og.na'laȟcį mak'a' kį k'ina'ksa c'ąke' ekta' mahe'l oyu'šnapi s'e iya'ya šk'e'ᵉ. 21. He'c'ena ak'e' mak'a' kį ec'e'l nao'k'iyut'a c'ąke' het'ąhą winų'ȟcala wą t'ako'šku aki'scu k'ų he' e c'a t'alo'-k'įka c'a tų'weni tuwe'ni inų'pa wąya'kešni šk'e'ᵉ. Hehą'yela owi'hąke'ᵉ.

33.

1. Wic'a'ša wą wana'se-i ną wap'a'tahą yųk'ą' wį'yą wą e'l hina'žį k'e'yaš a'tayaš ayu'tašni šką'hą šk'e'ᵉ. Ka'k'iya ak'i'kšuhį ną wana' ig.lu'štą yųk'ą' iyu'ha iki'kcu ną wana' k'ig.ni'kta c'ąke' wį'yą k'ų he'c'eya' loc'į' kį ų' ayu'hel na'žįhą hųše ok'u'šni yųk'ą' leya'-ho'yeya ke'ᵉ, — To'k'i le' c'e'yaš T'ašų'ke O'tawį aya'k'ip'akte'; ną C'ap'ų'ka T'ą'ka aya'k'ip'akte'; ną Wihu'powį[2] aya'k'ip'akte'; ną Wip'e'ȟlokewį[2] aya'k'ip'akte'; ną Išpa'-T'ahį`špa aya'k'ip'akte', — eya' ke'ᵉ.

---

[1] *T'ahį'špa* is the name for the awl which women used in sewing with sinew thread. *t'a* is the classifier for ruminant.

[2] *wi*, woman; *hu*, legs; *po*, swollen; *wį*, woman. It is noteworthy, that *wi*, the classifier for woman, used as a prefix, is never nasalized; but always is, when a suffix, to indicate a proper name.

there; and as he travelled, he heard someone on the other side of a hill calling, "Wey! Wey! Wey!" So he thought, "That must be the owner of many horses that I just heard about!" and hurriedly he made up as a feeble old man, and with effort supporting himself on a staff, he continued on to meet her. Sure enough, it was a woman who owned all kinds of animals. She caused them to walk by twos in a long line, and a bear and a buffalo bull were leading. 3. On seeing the old man, they rushed after him but their owner called out to them, "Yû!¹ When someone appears pitiful, the proper thing is to think kindly toward him," she corrected them, so they turned sharply about. The woman advanced and came near enough to see the poor old man. She was going in the opposite direction from the man, so just as she passed him she said, "Back there, in the rear, come the two last ones. Kill them and eat them, wherever you stop tonight." So he thanked her and went on. 4. So the animals continued passing him, and last of all a skunk and a porcupine came along; but those he killed quickly and stopped for the night under the trees where he roasted them; and from there he travelled on until he saw something large, and brown, on a driftlog. So he stopped

---

2. He'c'enaś wic'a'śa k'ų g.la'hį ną̥ paha' wą ak'o'tą̥hą tuwa' to'k'iya — we', we',² — eya'hą c'ą̥ke', — Ě·'! Le' T'aśų'ke O'tawį eye' c'ų e e' se'ce lo', — ec'į̥' ną ina'hni wic'a'hcala-ic'i'c'agį̥ ną tok'e'cela sak-ye'kit'ų iya'hą ke'ᵉ. He'c'ecakte c'ų, wį'yą wą ta'ku-wama'k'aśką' oc'a'że kį iyu'hala nų'pnųp ma'nik'iya awi'c'au c'ą̥ke' mat'o' wą t'at'ą̥'ka wą kic'i' t'oka'heya u' ke'ᵉ. 3. Wic'a'hcala kį wąya'kapi ną e'tkiya naślo'k hiyu'pi yųk'ą' wį'yą wą wic'a'yuha k'ų he' heya' ke'ᵉ, — Yû, ta'ku ų'śika c'ą̥'śna Ųśika' ec'ą̥'kįp kųk'ą'³! — eya' c'ą̥ke' kawį̥'h hna'hna k'ig.la'pi ke'ᵉ. C'ą̥ke' wį'yą kį e'l u' ną ų'śiyehcį sakye'kit'ų kį wąya'ka ke'ᵉ. Wį'yą kį wama'k'aśką' o'p wana' są̥p iya'yįkta hą̥'l iś-eya' wic'a'śa kį iyo'pteya iya'yįkta hą̥'l wį'yą ki' leya' ke'ᵉ, — Ho, laza'ta eha'kehcį nų'p u'pe'. Hena' wic'a'kat'į̥ ną tukte'l inų'ke cįhą wic'a'yuta', — eya' c'ą̥ke' p'iki'la ną iya'ya ke'ᵉ. 4. He'c'eś wama'k'aśką' kį e'yayahį̥ ną eha'kehcį maka' wą p'ahį̥' wą kic'i' u'pi tk'a'ś kat'a' ihpe'wic'ayį̥ ną c'ą̥-o'waśtecaka wą e'l iyų'kį̥ ną he'l c'ewi'c'aųpį̥ ną hetą̥'hą ak'e' ya'hą yųk'ą' c'į̥'coǧa⁴ wą e'l ta'ku

---

¹ "Yu!" with the u held long, is indicative of disapproval of a thing; that the speaker sees a wrong to be righted; it prefaces many statements of correction. Not to be confused with "yų!" which is an utterance of bodily discomfort, like pain or extreme weariness. The former is a woman's word only; the latter is used by both sexes.

² we! we!, a sort of call, to direct and drive dogs, in the old days.

³ kųk'ą', after a correction, means, "the correct, or the polite, or the kind way of doing such and such a thing is so-and-so, (but you don't observe it!)" This parenthetical part, is the idea conveyed by kųk'ą'. — Sometimes final i is dropped, in the pluralization, pi, as in the word before kųk'ą'.

⁴ c'į̥'coǧa, logs that have drifted with the stream, and finally been washed ashore; c'ą̥, wood; i'coǧa, to drift to, or against something.

and looked at it. 5. He crept up to it, and it was a mosquito asleep. He thought: "Ah! This is what she meant by Big Mosquito," and as it was sound asleep he gave its nose a twist and pulled it off and took it with him. Then he met a badger and the badger said, "Well, grandchild, I am not of much use, but you might take me along!" So he took him, and travelled on until he came to a stone in the road. 6. The stone said the same thing that the badger did, so he picked it up and went on with it also. The sun was low when he came to an old smoked tipi where an old woman lived. She invited him in, saying, "Well, my grandson who never came before, has come; for once." She cooked some earth-beans very appetizingly for him, and set them before him, and said, "Now, grandson, you better rest. You must be very tired." And she arranged his bed. 7. When he was reclining on his bed, he heard the old woman saying, "*Yų! Yų!*" as if in great pain; so he peeped at her through a hole in his blanket and she was scratching her leg and causing it to swell; already it was enormous. "Ah! This is Swollen-Legs-Woman of whom that woman spoke. She may be planning to kill me with that enormous leg," he thought. So he took the proboscis of the mosquito and with it he punctured the leg. "The worthless wretch! That he should kill me!"[1] she exclaimed, and died. 8. The man went on from there and

wą li'la t'ą'ka ǵiye'la ħpa'ya c'ąke' e'l ina'źį ke'ᵉ. *5. K'iye'la ana'slal a'ya yųk'ą' he' c'ap'ų'ka c'a istį'mahą c'ąke' lec'į' ke*'ᵉ, — *Ëh! C'ap'ų'ka T'ą'ka eye' c'ų le' e' ye lo'!* — *ecį' ną li'la istį'ma c'ąke' p'a'*² *kį yupe'm.ni yuksa' icu' ną hetą'hą ya'hą yųk'ą' ħoka' wą ak'i'p'a ke*'ᵉ. *Yųk'ą' heya' ke*'ᵉ, — *Wą, t'ako`źa, ta'ku wo'wamac'į-yesni k'e'yas mayu'ha ya' yo',* — *eya' c'ąke' icu' ną yuha' ya'hą yųk'ą' c'ąku'-og.na į'yą wą yąka' c'a e'l ina'źį ke*'ᵉ. *6. He' i's-'eya' ec'e'ħcį eya' c'ąke' ak'e' he' icu' ną yuha' ya'hą ke*'ᵉ. *Wi' k'u'ciyela yąka' hą'l wizi'la wą e'l ihų'ni yųk'ą' he' winų'ħcala wą t'i' ke*'ᵉ. *T'ima' kic'o' ną* — *Hinų, mit'a'koźa to'hįnis hi'sni k'ų wą'caħcį' hi' ye lê,*³ — *eyį' ną yup'i'ya mak'a'tom.nica ohį' ną wo'k'u c'ąke' wo'tahą yų-k'ą' heya' ke*'ᵉ, — *Ho, t'ako`źa, wana' istį'ma'. Li'la wani'tuk'a nac'e'ce',* — *eyį' ną e'upa ke*'ᵉ. *7. Wana' k'u'l ħpa'yahą yųk'ą' ųg.na' winų'ħcala kį* — *Yų, yų,* — *eya'hą c'ąke' sina' e'l oħlo'ka wą etą' e'yokas'į yųk'ą' winų'ħcala k'ų he e' c'a hu' kį g.luk'e'ǵahį ną wana' nį'skot'ąka g.lupo' ke*'ᵉ. — *Ëh! Wihu'powį eye' c'ų le e' ye lô. Hį'sko-t'ąka ų' maka't'įkte se'ce,* — *ec'į' ną c'ap'ų'ka-t'ąka wą p'asu' kį yuksa' yuha' k'ų he' ų' kaħle'l ap'a' c'ąke'* — *Waħte'sni kį, iye' eha' makte' ye lê'!* — *eyį' ną t'a' ke*'ᵉ. *8. Hetą'hą ak'e' wic'a'sa k'ų ya'hį ną*

---

[1] "When, all the while, I was the one to do the killing!" is implied, in that word *e'ha'; e'ha'* is a sign of "tables turned".

² *p'a* (head) is often used to indicate the nose *(p'asu');* *p'a*, head; *su*, seed; chief element.

³ *ye' lê!* When a woman, in a rhetorical sentence, makes an observation, she is likely to end it with *ye' lê!* the voice falling over the last vowel, indicative of realization; *ye lô*, is a man's equivalent.

came to another smoked tipi where another old woman lived. "Well, for once my grandson is coming, he who never came before!" she said, hurriedly setting a kettle on, and then she was busy at something; so he ventured to peep around to see. And the old woman had a hole in her head (fontanelle), and out of it she was extracting brains and dropping them into the kettle. 9. So he took out that stone he brought with him, and set it in the fire to heat; and was sitting by when the cooking was done and placed before him in a dish. But he caused his badger to eat it in his stead and then threw the hot stone into the hole in the old woman's head. "The worthless one! That he should kill me!" she cried, and writhed and kicked until she was dead. That was the one with the hole in her head that he was destined to meet. 10. From there he went on and came to another tipi like the two he had visited, but in this one there lived two old women who were blind. They sat on opposite sides of the tipi. He stood watching but they did not know it as they sat all unconscious of his presence. They each had a kettle of earth-beans cooking on the fire and sat waiting for them to be ready. 11. The food smelled so appetizing that he wanted it very much. So he took the kettle of one, and ate the contents and replaced it empty. Again he ate the contents of the other, and arranged the kettles on the fire as they had been before. But they did not know a thing about this. 12. Finally one of them said, "I think mine must be done," and set her kettle aside and then, "*Ma!* It appears you have eaten my beans up!" And the other said, "*Yu!* Why should I, when I have some cooking, for myself. That reminds me, I must see how

---

wizi'la wą hą' c'a e'l i' yųk'ą' winų'hcala wą e'l yąka' ke'ᵉ. — Hinų́, mit'a'koża wą'cahcį' hi' ye lê', Tų'hįnis hi'sni k'ų́, — eyį' ną ina'hni c'e'ġa wą k'alya' e'g.le ną ta'ku to'k'ųhą c'ąke' ao'kakį yųk'ą' p'esle'te kį e'l p'o'wiwila kį he'c'ena ohlo'kya hą' c'ąke' etą'hą nasų'la hąke' iki'kcu nąsna c'e'ġa kį ekta' iyo'hpeya ke'ᵉ. 9. He'c'eg.la į'yą wą yuha' hi' k'ų he' k'alki'yį ną yąka'hą yųk'ą' wana' wo'hąhe c'ų he' śpą c'ąke' waksi'ca og.na' e'kig.le tk'a'ś hoka' k'ų he' t'epye'k'iyį ną he'c'enaś į'yą-k'a'ta k'ų he' p'esle'te-ohlo'ka kį e'l oi'hpeya c'ąke', — Wahte'sni kį, iye' eha' makte' ye le', — eyį' ną natį'tį hpa'yį ną t'a' śk'eᵉ. Ho he' Wip'e'hlokewį eye' c'ų he e' śk'eᵉ. 10. Hetą' ak'e' ya'hą yųk'ą' wizi' wą e'l winų'hcala-ista'ġuġa nų'p t'i'pi c'a e'l i' keᵉ. T'ia'nųk yąka'hąpi keᵉ. Wąwi'c'ayak na'żįhe c'e'yaś a'tayaś slolye'śnihcį yąka'hąpi keᵉ. C'eh nų'p wo'hąpi c'ąke' wąya'ka yųk'ą' mak'a'tom.nica c'a k'inų'k'ą ohą' g.le'pi ną śpą-a'p'e yąka'hąpi keᵉ. 11. Li'la waste'm.na hiyu' kį ų' c'į'lahcaka c'ąke' c'eġa kį ųma' icu' ną t'epyį' ną ak'e' ųma' t'epyį' ną c'e'ġa kį ha ece'kce p'e'ta kį e'l e'wi- c'a-kicig.le keᵉ. K'e'yaś ta'ku oslo'lyeśnihcį yąka'hąpi'ᶦ. 12. O'hąketa ųma' — It'o' wana' mi'cisṗą se'ca c'a, — eyį' ną heya'ta c'e'ġa k'ų iki'kcu ną hehą'l — Ma'! t'epma'yak'iye se'ce le', — eya' yųk'ą' ųma' kį i'ś, — Yu', mi'ś-'eya' le' etą' iyo'hpemic'iye cį, he ta'kole'.

mine is coming." So she set her kettle aside and was about to take out the contents when she discovered the food was gone. "*Yu!* It is you have eaten my beans!" she said. 13. At once the other said, "Or maybe someone has come; take your cane, and start from where you are to feel along, and I will start from here." So they rose with their canes, and starting at the door and working around, they felt around for a possible visitor, with their sticks. In the centre rear they came upon each other and one began, "So it is you, who have eaten our food!" and she began to club the other. But the other one accused her in turn and struck her, and then they fought each other. Finally they resorted to knives and stabbed each other so that they both died. So the man left and went on from there. That is all.

34. Incest.

1. There was a tribal camp. And in it lived a young man who was the only son of his parents, and was greatly loved; so they had him live by himself in a special tipi in the manner of a boy-beloved[1]. He

---

It'o', heye'ca tk'a'², *wana' wag.lu'tįkte, — eyį' ną i'š-'eya' c'e'gá t'awa kį iki'kcukta tk'a'š ta'kuni ų'šni c'ąke' — Yû, t'epma'k'iyį ną heye' le', — eya' ke'ᵉ. 13. He'c'ena ųma' k'ų heya' ke'ᵉ, — Ma, i'š eša' tuwa' hį se'ca c'e, he'c'iyatąhą sakye' ų' pat'ą't'ą au' mi'š-'eya' le'c'iyatąhą a'm.nįkte, — eya' c'ąke' wana' nųp'į' ina'žįpi ną sakye' ko'skos tiwo'kšą hiya'yapi yųk'ą' ehą'-kic'i'ipi ną ųma' — ehą'k'ų le' niye' c'a wat'e'pyaye še'ce', — eyą'-hįg.la c'a-ko's iye'yį ną i'š-'eya' ųma' kį — yû, iye'š iye' yesą', — eya'-hįg.la itko'p ap'a' c'ąke' he'c'ena kic'i'zapi šk'e'ᵉ. O'hąketa mi'la iki'kcupi ną c'aki'c'i-p'ap'api ną kic'i'ktepi šk'e'ᵉ. C'ąke' wic'a'ša k'ų he' hetą'hą iya'ya šk'e'ᵉ. Hehą'yela owi'hąke'ᵉ.*

34.

1. *Oya'te wą t'i'pi šk'e'ᵉ. Yųk'ą' e'l k'oška'laka wą ece'la wic'a' yuha'pi c'ąke' li'la t'ehi'lapi c'a išna'la wak'e'ya wą og.na' hokši'-c'ąlki'yapi-t'i³ šk'e'ᵉ. Yųk'ą' t'ąkši'tku nų'pa⁴ c'a hena' i'š hųka'ke⁵*

---

[1] Boys-beloved always, and girls-beloved often, after they were grown, were allowed separate tipis for privacy.

[2] *heye'ca tk'a'*; *heya'*, to say; *ka*, rather; *heye'ca*, he said it just to be saying; *tk'a*, but. The whole means, "by the way, or "that reminds me."

[3] To live in the manner of a child-beloved; that is, with all due ceremony; possibly in a separate, decorated tipi, where the poor may always find welcome and food.

[4] His sisters, they were two. When two is used as a neutral verb, as here, it is *nų'pa*. When used as an adjective, modifying a noun, it is always *nų'p.*

[5] *hųka'ke*, parents. cf. *hųka'*, the relationship established in the *hųka'* ceremony. Also, *hųka'yapi*, They have for a relative, is the formal way of addressing the Sun in prayer.

had two younger sisters who lived with their parents.The entire tribe
loved this young man, and the plan was to make him a chief some
day. 2. And it happened that one night as he lay sleeping, a woman
entered his tipi and lay down beside his bed. This she did to tempt
him. But of course it was dark, so he could not tell what woman it
was. In the morning he did not tell his father; he simply said,
"Father this evening I want you to set a dish of red face paint near
my bed." — "What does he mean?" the father thought, but was
reluctant to ask him[1]. 3. The next night, the woman entered again
and bothered him, so he secretly dipped his hand in the paint and
applied it over her dress as thoroughly as he could. The next
morning he said, "Father, I wish all the women in camp to engage
in a shinny game." — "What does my son mean?" he thought, but
he was reluctant to ask him; so he went without a word to the
council tent where he told the boy-beloved's wish. Immediately a
shinny game was arranged for the women. 4. But he could not tell
whether the woman who visited him nightly was in the game or not;
because she could change her clothing for other before taking part.
Again she came, (the next night), so this time he covered her entire
face with the paint, and sent her out. Next day he ordered another
shinny game, and it was arranged through the council tent. In

---

*o'p lehą'yak t'i'pi śk'e'ᵉ. K'oska'laka kị le' oya'te kị a'taya waste'la-
kapi ną t'oka'ta wic'a'sa-it'ą'c'ą ka'gapikta c'a ayu'hel ų'pi śk'e'ᵉ.
2. Yųk'ą' hąhe'pi c'a istį'ma-ḣpaʾ ya hą'l wị'yą wą t'ima' naḣma'laḣcị
hiyu' ną t'o'yuke kị ica'g.lalaḣcị iyų'ka ke'ᵉ. He' nagi' yeya'² c'a
he'c'ų'ᵛ. K'e'yaś ec'į' oi'yokpaza c'ąke' k'oska'laka kị he' tuwa'-
wị'yą kị iye'kiyeśni'ⁱ. Hị'hąna c'ąke' atku'ku kị oki'yakeśni ikce'
leye'ᵉ, — Ateʾ, ḣtaye'tu kịhą mit'o'yuke¹ kị ik'i'yela wase' etą' e'-
g.naka yo', — eya' c'ąke', — To'k'a c'a heya' huwô? — ec'į' k'e'yaś
iyų'ḣ-kapị'ⁱ. 3. Ak'e' hąhe'pi yųk'ą' wị'yą wą t'ima' hiyu' ną ak'e'
nagi' yeya' c'ąke' naḣma'laḣcị wase' k'ų he' nape' ig.lu't'ąt'ą ną
wị'yą kị t'awo'k'oyake kị waste'yela a'taya iyu't'ąt'ą ną ayu'stą'ᵠ.
Hị'hąna c'ąke' heye'ᵉ, — Ateʾ, it'o' wị'yą wic'o't'i e'l ų'pi kị iyu'haḣcị
t'ap-ka'psicapikte lo', — eya' c'ąke' — Mic'į'kśi to'k'el k'a' huwô? —
ec'į' k'e'yaś iyų'ḣ-kapị c'ąke' a'inila t'iyo't'ipi kị e'l e'oyaka c'ąke'
wana' wị'yą t'apka'psil-wic'aśipi śk'e'ᵉ. 4. K'e'yaś wị'yą k'ų he' e'l
o'p'a he'cịhą slolye'śni'ⁱ; ec'į' haya'ke t'o'keca kic'ų' ną śka'te cị ų'.
Ak'e' hąhe'pi yųk'ą' wị'yą k'ų he' hi' c'ąke' śehąstuk'a it'e' kị a'taya
wase' iyų' ną k'ig.le'-ye'ᵉ. Ihị'hąna c'ąke' t'ap-ka'psil-wic'aśi ną*

---

[1] When a son or daughter has arrived at years of discretion the father and
mother fall very naturally into a subordinate place, willingly, proudly,
for having raised such a son or daughter. The dominating parent, that
wants to hold the reins forever, is generally missing among the Dakota.

[2] *nagi'*, spirit; ghost; *yeya'*, to send; *nagi' yeya'*, to bother, as a child will
its elders. Also, as an importunate person may keep hammering at a
request; or as a man or woman trying to arouse the passions of one of the
opposite sex.

time, all the women assembled in the centre of the enclosure¹, and
now they ran. 5. Out of all the players there was one who unbraided
her hair and left it hanging loosely about her face. As she played,
with her face thus hidden, he studied her to make sure, and it
shocked him to realize that she was the elder of his own two younger
sisters! Her face was as if dipped in blood². That is why she hid it
as she played. It came over him then that one of his own sisters was
tempting him, and he was filled with anger and shame. 6. As he
was retiring he said, "Father, get an iron rod and heat it thoroughly,
and wait near the tipi. When I clear my throat³, slide it in to me."
Why he should request this was not at all clear, but the father did
what his son commanded. And now, once again the woman entered
and came and lay down beside his bed. But that instant, he cleared
his throat, and his father, who sat immediately outside the tipi,
slid the heated iron in to him, under the base of the tipi. With
the iron he branded the woman's face all over, and then sent her
out. Now that he was aware that this was his own sister he was
very much ashamed, and angry. 7. After she left he slept; and on
waking, he felt something move under him, so he looked down and
saw that he was standing attached, as if glued, to a tree which was

---

*t'iyo't'ipi ki' etą'hą ie'yapahapi ke'ᵉ. He'c'ena wį'yą ki iyu'hala
ho'c'okata e'nazi̧ ną wana' i̧'yąkapiᵖⁱ. 5. Yųk'ą' ska'tapi ki etą'
wązi'la p'ehi̧' g.lukca' ną kao'b.lel iye'ya ska'ta c'ąke'tą-a'b.les-wac'i̧
yųk'ą' wic'a'yus²i̧yaye⁴ s'e iye' t'ąksi'tku ųma' t'oka'p'a k'ų he e''ᵉ.
Ite' ki a'taya we' opu'tkąpi⁵ s'e le'c'eca c'ąke' heų' ite'-naki'hma
ska'te'ᵉ. Hehą'l nake's iye' t'ąksi'tku ki ųma' c'a e'l hi' nąsna nagi'
yeya'he ci̧ he' aki'b.lezi̧ ną li'la c'aze'ki̧ ną iste'ce'ᵉ. 6. Wana' i̧yų'kapi-
kte c'ąke', — Ate', it'o' ma'za wązi' tąye'la k'alyi̧' ną yuha' wihu'ta-
ica'g.la yąki̧' ną tohą'l ho'p'imiciye ci̧hą hiyu'mak'iya yo', — eye''ᵉ.
Ta'kowe'-heya' t'ąi̧'sni k'e'yas ec'ų'si ki ec'e'l ec'ų''ᵛ. Yųk'ą' wana'
ak'e' wi̧'yą wą t'i̧'l hiyu' ną t'o'yuke ki ica'g.la hiyų'ka tk'a's he'c'ena
ho'p'iciya c'ąke' atku'ku k'ų wihu'ta ki etą' ma'za-k'ata wą hiyu'k'iya
c'a icu' ną ų' wi̧'yą ki ite' a'taya waste'yela gugu'yi̧ ną k'ig.le'ye'ᵉ.
Wana' he' t'ąksi'tku ki e' c'a slolye' ci̧ hehą'yą li'la iste'ci̧ ną c'ąze'ke'ᵉ.
7. He' i'yec'ala isti̧'mi̧ ną ogų'ga yų-k'ą' hpa'ye c'ų ohla't'e⁶ ta'ku wą
skąska' s'e le'c'eca c'ąke' k'u'tkiya e'tųwą yųk'ą' c'ą' wą ai'yaskap*

---

¹ In a large tribal encampment, the land enclosed by the circle was ample
  for these games.
² A simile, commonly heard, to describe redness.
³ Clearing the throat is a very common device for attracting attention and
  giving signals. But it involves loss of dignity, in adults. One who is given
  to it too much is suspected of having a secret affair.
⁴ *yus²i̧' yaya*, to be frightened; *yus²i̧' yeya*, to frighten another; *mayu's²i̧yaya*,
  I am frightened; *yus²i̧yewaya*, I frighten another.
⁵ *opu'tką*, to dip into a liquid; *o*, in; *pu*, an obsolete prefix, by pressure. See
  Int. Journ. Am. Ling. VII, p. 114; *tką*, (?), perhaps "to spread, gradually,
  as by capillary attraction."
⁶ *ohla't'e*, underneath.

12

rapidly growing taller; of course, since he was part of the tree, he
was rising higher all the time, too. 8. Until now he was rising out
of the tipi through the smoke-vent. So the people below took down
the tipi in haste. Then the tree grew even faster, elevating the young
man higher and higher. The people were frightened by the miracle,
and because of fear they moved away and disappeared from the
scene. Only the good little sister of the young man stayed at the
base of the tree and wept. 9. It did not disturb her that the people
had left her behind, and as she stood weeping, suddenly, from the
wood near by, the wicked sister looked out, and called tauntingly,
"There's someone loves her brother very much; but I have caused
him to grow onto the tree!" And the young man called down to his
good sister, "Reply this to her, little sister, 'There is someone who
tempted her own brother, but he caused her face to be branded
with a hot iron!'" So the girl called back as her brother had taught
her, and straightway the one in the wood called back, "O, that's
the thing I resent!" and a deer[1] ran back into the wood amid rustling
leaves. 10. From then on, the girl who was very weary, slept, until
a man came from somewhere, and said, "Young girl, roast this for

---

*ną'žį ną c'ą' kį he' li'la oh'ąk'oya wąka'takiya ic'a'h a'ya c'ąke'
ik'o'yak i's-'eya' są'p wąka'takiya ya' śk'e'ᵉ. 8. Hąke'ya wana'
wic'e'śka kį papta' iya'yįkta c'a wak'e'ya kį kahpa'pi yųk'ą' hehą'l
iyo'tą oh'ą'k'oya ic'a'h a'ya c'ąke' iyo'was'įyą k'ośka'laka k'ų li'la
wąka'takiya ya' śk'e'ᵉ. Oya'te kį li'la wi'k'op'api ną ini'hąpi ų i-
g.la'kapi ną t'ok'ą'l iya'yapi śk'e'ᵉ. C'ąke' t'ąksi'tku ųma' haka'kta wą
ksa'pela k'ų hece'la c'ą-hu'te kį e'l na'žį ną c'e'yahą śk'e'ᵉ. 9. Ihpe'ya
iya'yapi k'e'yaś ini'hąsni e'na na'žį ną c'e'yahą yųk'ą' ųg.na'hąla
c'ąma'hetąhą c'ᵘuwe'ku wą witko'tkoke c'ų he' ahi'yokas'į² ną —
Tuwa' t'ib.lo'ku t'ehi'la tk'a'ś c'ą' au'yewaye!³ — eya'-ho'uya ke'ᵉ.
Yųk'ą' k'ośka'laka wą wąka'l na'žį k'ų he' heya' ke'ᵉ, — T'ąkś'i,
ni's-'eya' leya' yo', Tuwa' t'ib.lo'ku nagi' yeki'ya tk'a'ś ite' kį ma'za-
k'ata įpa'mamaye: eya' yo', — eya' ke'ᵉ. C'ąke' wic'į'cala wą
wae'yeśipi k'ų he' ec'e'l eya' yųk'ą' he'c'ena, — He' wo't'ehi-wakila⁴
k'ų, — eyį' ną t'a'hca wą c'ąma'hel wahpe' yusna'pi s'e k'ig.la'
śk'e'ᵉ. 10. Hehą' wana' wic'į'cala kį watu'k'a c'ąke' iśti'mahą yųk'ą'
to'k'iyatąhą wic'a'śa wą e'l hina'žį ną, — Wic'į'cala, le' nit'i'b.lo*

---

[1] All unknown to the family in which this daughter had been reared, she
had the deer spirit, described under Page 163, note 2. It was only now
demonstrating itself.

[2] *ahi'yokas'į*, to look out of, with the speaker on the outside; *s'į*, to crane the
neck.

[3] I cause him to grow on to a tree; *uya'*, to grow tall; a neutral verb. *uma'ya;
ųku'ya*, I, we grow tall; *wa*, I; *ya*, to cause.

[4] *-wakila*, I consider it (mine); *wo't'ehi-wakila*, I hold that as a bitter painful
thing to me. (The death of a favorite, will cause one to say these very
words in reference to it. That means that the loss is not mitigated by time.)

your brother," and he threw her a piece of deer meat. So she rose
and cooked it and tossed it up to her brother, though by now he
stood very high. Her brother ate it. 11. Then the man said to her,
"Now, I have something for you to decide. If it pleases you that
we two shall live together, I can cause your brother to come down."
So she told her brother what the man had said to her; and the
brother said, "Do it, sister; I want to come down; I am so thirsty."
12. So the girl consented[1] to become the wife of the stranger, and he
said, "In that case, lie down under here." She did so, and he covered
her with a blanket, and pegged down the four corners so securely
that she was imprisoned underneath. Thus it was that she did not
see how her husband worked his magic, and was unable to tell it.
13. He was actually a Thunder man, though they did not know at
first. For the Thunder man opened his eyes, (lightning), and repeatedly he roared (thunder), and the tree was split in two, and fell
broken to the ground so that the young man stepped off. Then the
man took out the tipi-base pegs and removed the blanket, and
helped the girl to her feet. So she greeted her brother. 14. Because
he was thunder he killed many buffaloes, and with his bare hands
he ground the meat and bones[2], and made a cake of pemmican

c‘eki'pa yo', — eyi' ną t‘a'ĥca-t‘alo` wą hiĥpe'k‘iya c‘ąke' ina'ži ną
c‘eu'pi ną wąka'tuya na'ži k‘e'yaš ekta' iĥpe'k‘iya c‘ąke' yu'ta
šk‘e⁾ᵉ. 11. Hehą'l wic‘a'ša k‘u heya' ke⁾ᵉ, — Ho, it‘o' wi'g.lukcą yo',
ųk‘ų'kta c‘a iyo'nicip‘i kiĥą nit‘i'b.lo k‘u'l kuwa'k‘iyįkte lo', — eya'
c‘ąke' wic‘į'cala ki t‘ib.lo'ku ki ec‘e'l oki'yaka yųk‘ą' — T‘ąkš'i,
hig.na'yą yo'; i'mapuza³ c‘a k‘u'ya waku'kte lo', eya' ke⁾ᵉ. 12. C‘ąke'
wic‘į'cala ki iyo'wįyi ną wic‘a'ša ki ec‘e'l oki'yaka yųk‘ą' heya' ke⁾ᵉ, —
Ec‘a le'l oĥla't‘e iyų'ka yo', — eya' c‘ąke' ec‘ų' yųk‘ą' šina' wą icu'
ną oi'se to'pa ki oya's‘į suta'ya oka'tą c‘ąke' og.li'cu-šilya` ĥpa'ya ke⁾ᵉ.
He'c‘el u hig.na'ku to'k‘el ec‘ų' ki wąya'kešni c‘ąke' oya'ka oki'hišni
šk‘e⁾ᵉ. 13. Yųk‘ą' leyalaka, he' waki'yą-wic‘a'ša hųše'ca wak‘į'yą
tųwą'-hig.ni` ną i'yak‘ig.leg.le waki'yą hot‘ų'⁴ yųk‘ą' c‘ą' k‘ų
nasle'sleci ną kawe'ĥ g.liĥpa'ya c‘ąke' k‘oška'laka k‘u he' g.licu'
šk‘e⁾ᵉ. Hehą'l nake's wihį'paspe⁵ k‘ų hena' yužų' ną šina' ki ĥeya'p
icu' ną wic‘į'cala k‘ų he' yuna'žik‘iya ke⁾ᵉ. C‘ąke' t‘ib.lo'ku ki wą-
g.la'ka ke⁾ᵉ. 14. Waki'yą c‘ąke' pte' o'ta wic‘a'kte ną napi'yų⁶ t‘alo' ną
hohu' ki kap‘i' ną wasna' wą ka'ği ną t‘ahą'ku ki k‘u ke⁾ᵉ. — Ho,

[1] A girl's regard for her brother was such that she would marry anyone
(other things being equal) who could benefit the brother.
[2] He ground the bones to extract the rich oils which are the essential part
for this delicacy.
[3] *i*, mouth; *pu'za*, to be dry; hence to be thirsty.
[4] *hot‘ų'*, to bleat; neigh; crow; hoot; in short, to give forth a characteristic
utterance, according to nature; *ho*, voice; *t‘ų*, to have on; wear; acquire;
give birth to.
[5] *wi*, prefix used to express "women" and "part of tipi." *wihį'paspe*, the
pegs that hold down the tipi, all around the base.
[6] *napi'yų*, with hands; with the bare hands; without instruments or cover.

which he handed to his brother-in-law. "Now, go to your tribe, and invite them back to this camp-site they have abandoned," he said. So he went to his people and called them together. Then he gave every one a piece of the pemmican, in very small amounts. 15. He was distributing it in that manner when a very greedy woman who was in the company complained at the smallness of her share, and threw it all into her mouth at once. Then she chewed; but it gradually increased in amount until finally her mouth could not hold it all; and she was choking on it. So they took a knife, and cut out piece by piece until she was relieved. 16. Despite the smallness of the cake, the quantity continued to increase, until they were able to fill many containers with it. Then the young man invited the people to their old camp ground. So they followed him back, and on their arrival, they found at each individual site, great quantities of meat, jerked, and drying on poles. "That is our camp-site!" was heard on all sides as families identified their places and proceeded to set up their homes again; and they were very well provisioned. 17. From then on, that people no longer knew want, they say. Then the Thunder-man told his wife this, "Now, young girl, you whose love for your brother was so big that you consented to be my wife for his sake, I am going home. It is enough, for I have now given you aid." And so he went away, somewhere, wherever it is that the thunders abide. That is all.

---

nit'a'oyate kį ekta' wic'a'yį ną ot'i'weta kį le'c'i kuwi'c'aśi yo', — eya' c'ąke' iya'yį ną oya'te kį wi'taya wic'a'kic'o c'ąke' ahi'yotaka ke'ᵉ. Yųk'ą' iyo'hilaḣcį wasna' kį hąke' ta'ku wo'kitąḣcį yuśpa' wic'a'k'u ke'ᵉ. 15. He'c'el kpam.ni' ahi'yaya yųk'ą' wį'yą wą li'la wo'hitika c'a e'l o'p'a c'ąke' ci'k'ala k'u'pi ke'yį' ną a'taya iyo'kaḣ'ol iye'ya ke'ᵉ. He'c'ų ną yat'e' c'e'yaś są'p o'ta a'yį ną hąke'ga i' kį oki'p'iśni ną wana' katkį'kta c'ąke' mi'la icu'pi ną wasna' kį waksa'- ksa iki'cicupi śk'e'ᵉ. 16. Wasna' kį ci'k'ala selya są'p t'ą'ka a'ya c'ąke' wakśi'ca li'la o'ta i'yoźuyapi śk'e'ᵉ. Heḣą'l t'iya'ta kuwi'c'aśi c'ąke' iha'kap g.la'pi ną ot'i'weta k'ų he'l k'i'pi yųk'ą' eḣą'ni t'i'pi tk'a' k'ų he'c'ekc'e t'alo' kab.la'pi waśte'śte wo'c'ąkśu ożu'kżula otka' c'ąke' — Ka'l ųt'i'pi k'ų, — eya'ya ec'e'kc'e k'i'yotakapi ną li'la waśe'capi śk'e'ᵉ. 17. Hetą'hą oya'te kį he' wi'c'ak'iżeśni ų'pi śk'e'ᵉ. Yųk'ą' heḣą'l wakį'yą-wic'a`śa k'ų he' t'awi'cu kį k'į' ną heya' śk'e'ᵉ, — Howo', wic'į'cala, nit'i'b.lo a'wicak'eya'-t'ey`aḣila ų' hig.na'mayayįkta ye'ś k'o' iyo'wįyaye c'ų, wana' wag.nį'kte lo'. Eya'ś wana' o'c'iciya c'a, — eyį' ną to'k'i wakį'yą t'i'pelak'a he'c'etkiya k'ig.la' śk'e'ᵉ. Heḣą'yela owi'ḣąke'ᵉ.

35. *The Wicked Sister-in-Law.*

1. A young man lived in the son-in-law rôle, and kept his younger brother, a boy, with him. And whenever the latter remained at home with his sister-in-law, she tried to tempt him, so at length the boy said to her, "*Hoħ!* You are my brother's wife; how can I do what will bring disgrace to my brother?" So saying, he resisted her, but she continued to try. 2. At last the woman resented the fact that the boy ignored her, and caused a badger to dig the ground, directly under her brother-in-law's bed in the tipi. Then she made up his bed over the hole. So when the boy came in, he went and sat down on it, but fell through into the pit. But his relatives were not alarmed by his disappearance. "He has probably gone off on a little trip. It is a common trick with boys of his age. He will be turning up one day," they said, and dismissed the matter. 3. And then the camp was moved, so he was left behind in that pit. Presently a pack of wolves came to go over the camp site for leavings, and as they hunted around, a wolf with an ugly tawny coat, stood listening, and said, "Hey, come here, all of you. There is a human being crying somewhere here." So they all listened, and sure enough, someone was crying underground. 4. A deep pit stood near, and that was where it was, so one of the wolves jumped in

---

1. K'oska'laka wą wic'a'woħa-t'i ną e'l sųka'ku wą g.luha' yųk'ą tohą'l hokši'la kį he' ħąka'ku kic'i'snala yąka' c'ą'sna wį'yą kį iye'[1] *eha' nagi' yeya'hą c'ąke' hokši'la kį leya' ke'ᵉ, — Hoħ, le' c'iye' kic'i' yau' we lo', to'k'esk'e c'iye' oho'walasni iye'c'el wae'c'amųkta he? — eyį' ną c'į'sni k'es li'la iyu'tąye-wac'į k'uwa' sk'e'ᵉ. 2. O'ħąketa wį'yą kį e'l e'tųwąpisni kį he' siki'g.la ų' sic'e'cu t'o'wąke kį e'l mak'a' kį mahe'tuya ħoka' wą ok'e'k'iya ke'ᵉ. Aką'l owį'st'ų ną tąyą' e'g.le c'ąke' wana' hokši'la kį g.li' ną t'o'wąke kį e'l i'yotakįkta yųk'ą' kama'hel t'ąį'sniyela iya'ya ke'ᵉ. K'e'yas t'i'takuye kį, — Ho į'se' to'k'iyap oma'ni-iya`ye lo'. He'c'a wą he'c'ekc'e-ħ'ąpika c'a ųg.na'hąla iya'ye lo'. To'kša' g.li'kte cį, — eya'pi ną iwa'tok'iyapisni ke'ᵉ. 3. Ec'ą'l oi'g.lake c'ąke' ų'yą tok'i'yot'ą iya'yapi yųk'ą' sųk-ma'nitu*[2] *kį ot'i'weta e'l wo'kile-hi`pi yųk'ą' wąži' ħi'zi-sica c'a nų'goptąptą na'žįhį ną, — He', ku'wapi ye' t'o. Wic'a'ša aką'tula*[3] *wą le'l tukte'l ho't'ąį ye lo', — eya' c'a ana'goptąpi yųk'ą' tuwa' mak'a'-mahe'l c'e'yahą ke'ᵉ. 4. Oħlo'ka wą mahe'tuya c'a hą' yųk'ą' he'tu c'ąke' sųk-ma'nitu kį wąži' ekta' iya'yį ną i't'ap wic'a'ša wą yap'a'*[4] *ag.li'-*

---

[1] *iye' e'ha'*, she, rather than —; *e'ha'*, as explained before, indicates that the wrong person, does something. Here, evidently, she is doing what is regarded rather as a man's part.
[2] *sų'ka*, dog; *mani'tu*, in the wild, uninhabited country. A wolf, or a coyote.
[3] *wic'a'ša aką'tula*, human being. In legends, the animals always speak of man in this way. *wic'a'ša*, man; *aką'tu*, on top; *la*, diminutive.
[4] *yap'a'*, to hold in the mouth, between the jaws, without actually biting.

and dragged out a man, holding him with his teeth. They all came
around, and also got hold of him, and carried him to the chief of the
pack. And he said, "Call White Wolf hither; and Little White Wolf;
and Crazy Wolf; and Hollow Flanks; and Big Bellied Wolf; and
Black Wolf. Call them all here." So in time they all arrived. And
one was very white and one was a whitish mixture; and one was
mad, or so he acted; and one was very thin, and one had a huge
belly; and one was entirely black, and he was a beauty, the most
handsome of them all. 5. Now these constituted a court, and the
chief of the pack who first called them together now asked them
what they should do with this man. And Crazy Wolf said, "Why,
he is ours; let us eat him!" White Wolf said, "No; on the contrary,
let us let him live." The rest took sides, and tied; but the chief
favored the suggestion of White Wolf, so the decision to let the
man live carried. 6. Then off they went, with much ado; and soon
after, having evidently had a killing, they returned with plenty of
meat. Then the chief, who could speak the human language, said,
"Now, grandchild, lie under cover while your grandfathers eat. Take
warning; don't look at them." So the boy lay under a blanket.
7. But when he heard a great humming noise, he thought, "I wonder
just how they eat," and looked through a tiny hole in his blanket.
But at that moment, they sent a piece of bone flying his way, and
it struck his eye, and put it out. "Grandfather, they have sent a

---

nap'į ną t'ąka'l yaslo'hą g.lihpe'ya ke'ᵉ. He'c'ena ak'i'ptą-yap'a`pi
ną šųk-ma'nitu-it'ą`c'ą kį ekta' kak'i'pi yųk'ą' heya' ke'ᵉ, — Wą,
Šų'ka Ska' hiyo'yapi ną, Šų'ka Hįska'la hiyo'ya po'; ną nakų'
Šų'ka-Witko` hiyo'ya po'; ną T'ac'u'wi Ok'a' kic'o' po'. Šų'ka Niǧe'
T'ą'ka kic'o'pi ną Šųk-ma'nitu Sa'pa nakų'; ho, hena'keca le'l awi'c'a-
ku po', — eya' c'ąke' iyu'ha hi'pi ke'ᵉ. Yųk'ą' wąži' li'la ska' ną
wąži' i'š hįksa'yakel ec'e'ca ną wąži' g.naški'ye s'e op'i'ic'iyį ną
wąži' li'la t'ama'heca ną wąži' niǧe' t'ą'kapi c'į'la ną wąži' a'taya
sa'pa c'a he' ihą'keya ową'yak-wašte` šk'e'ᵉ. 5. Ho, hena'keca waya'su-
iyotakapi ną šųk-ma'nitu-it'ą`c'ą wą t'oka' ekta' wic'a'yuwitaye
c'ų he' iwi'c'ayųǧa ke'ᵉ, wic'a'ša kį he' to'k'el ok'u'wapikta he'cįhą.
Yųk'ą' Šų'ka Witko`, — Wą, ųg.lu'tapikte lo', — eya' šk'e'ᵉ. Šų'ka
Ska' i'š, — Hiya`, eya'š it'o' ni' ų'kte lo', —. eya' ke'ᵉ. Nų'pakiya
he'c'el eya'pi ną ųma'ma iye'pi k'e'yaš it'ą'c'ą k'ų he' ni' ų'kta
ke'ya'pi kį he'c'iyatąhą wawo'kiya c'ąke' he'c'el-yuštą`pi šk'e'ᵉ.
6. He'c'ena to'k'etkiya bu'-wic'ahįg.nį ną i't'ap wana'sapelak'a t'alo'
osų'kyela ag.li'pi yųk'ą' hehą'l nake'š it'a'c'ą kį wic'a'ša aką'tu-ia`
hųše'ca, — Ho, t'ako`ža, nit'ų'kašila wo'tapikta c'e mahe'l hpa'ya yo'.
Ųg.na' awi'c'aluta kį lo', — eya' c'ąke' šina' p'a' ag.la'hpa iyų'ka
ke'ᵉ. 7. Ho, k'e'yaš hmuye'la šką'pi c'ąke' hąke'ya, — It'o' to'k'ešk'e
wotapi ka, — ec'į' ną ohlo'ka wą ci'k'ayela hą' c'a etą'hą ao'wic'akas'į
tk'a'š ec'a'l huhu' wą yapsi'l yeya'pi ną išta kį kahle'l ic'a'p'api
c'ąke' kakpa'pi šk'e'ᵉ. He'c'ena, — T'ų'ka`šila, išta' oma'yapsicapi

bone jumping into my eye, and I can not see!" he said, so the chief replied, "Alas, grandson, didn't I warn you in good time not to look out ?" 8. Then he turned to the pack. "Make haste on behalf of our grandchild," he said; so they went off somewhere, and brought him a pair of jack rabbit eyes. But they did not fit; they stood out too prominently; next they tried fox eyes on him, and they fitted perfectly. 9. So he remained there with the wolves, utterly safe and content, until one day the chief said to him, "Now, grandson, you are to go home. But do not forget how hungry your grandfathers get at times. When you get home, make haste on their account." So the boy started home. As he neared his tribal camp, he saw someone sitting on a hill all by himself; so he came to him. It was his poor father, an old man. 10. But he was blind from weeping. So he said, "Who are you who come from somewhere ?" — "Why, father, it is I who have returned." — "Alas, alas, whoever you are, you have no pity. You are doubtless misleading me for fun. Don't you know this, that my son disappeared suddenly, I have lost him as in death and am now blind through much weeping as here I sit," he said. 11. But the boy took his father by the hand and led him to a pool of rain water and poured some of it into his eyes, and washed them for him. "Now, father, dive in and lie with the water covering your face," he said. The father did so, and recovered his sight. So together they returned to the camp. The old man advanced shouting, "My son has returned!" and the camp was

c̔a watų́weśni ye lo̔', — eya' c̔e̓ya ų' c̔ą́ke' — Hehehe', t̔ako̓ža, mak̔a̓' wana̓ś ahi̓yokas̓įśni-c̔iśi k̔ų, — eya' śk̔e̓ᵉ. 8. Heḣą̔l ųma̓́- śųk-ma̓nitupi kį wic̔a̓k̔į ną, — T̔ako̓ža k̔oya̓kiḣ̔ą po̔', — eya' c̔ą́ke' a̓beya iya̓yapi ną maśtį̓ska iśta̓' wą kag.li̓pi c̔ą́ke' o̓kiciśtą k̔e̓yaś kip̔i̓śni, aze̓zeyakel otka̓' c̔ą́ke' heḣą̔l t̔ok̔a̓la iśta̓' wą kag.li̓pi yųk̔ą́' he̓' nake̓ś tąyą́' kip̔i̓' śk̔e̓ᵉ. 9. C̔ą́ke' e̓na śųk-ma̓nitu o̓p tąyą́' ų́ḣį ną t̔e̓ḣą yųk̔ą́' heḣą̔l it̔ą́c̔ą k̔ų he̓' el i̓' ną, — Ho, t̔ako̓ža, wana̓' yag.nį̓kte lo̔'. Tk̔a̓' nit̔ų́kaśila li̓klila loc̔į̓pi c̔aś slolya̓ye lo̔'. Yak̔i̓' kiḣą̓ wic̔a̓kiyuinaḣni yo̔', — eya' ke̓ᵉ. C̔ą́ke' he̓c̔ena k̔ig.la̓' ke̓ᵉ. T̔i̓k̔iyela g.la̓' yųk̔ą́' tuwa̓' paha̓'-akąl iśna̓- laḣcį yąka̓ḣą c̔ą́ke' e̓l k̔iḣų̓ni yųk̔ą́' atku̓kula wą wic̔a̓ḣcala k̔ų he̓' e̓' ke̓ᵉ. 10. K̔e̓yaś c̔e̓yapi c̔ų' iśta̓'-ǧųgala c̔ą́ke', — Tuwa̓' to̔k̔iyatąḣą yau' huwo̓'? — eya' ke̓ᵉ. — Wą, ate̓, le̓' miye̓' c̔a wag.li̓' ye lo̔', — eya̓'-ayu̓pta yųk̔ą́' — Heḣi̓', tuwa̓' wau̓śiyalaśni ye lo̔'. Maya̓g.naye-wac̔ą́ni̔[1] se̓ce lo̔'. K̔e̓ya wą, le̓' mic̔į̓kśi ųg.na̓ḣąla ot̔e̓' wag.nu̓ni c̔a le̓' wac̔e̓yeca c̔ų' iśta̓'maǧųga c̔a le̓c̔el maka̓he lo̔', — eya' ke̓ᵉ. 11. Yųk̔ą́' hokśi̓la k̔ų he̓' atku̓ku nape̓' e̓l yu̓žį ną maǧa̓žu-m.ni wą e̓l yu̓s ai̓' ną m.ni̓ kį ų' iśta̓' ki̓ciyuža- žaḣą ke̓ᵉ. Heḣą̔l heya̓' ke̓ᵉ, — Ho, ate̓, kig.nų̓kį ną ite̓' kį m.ni̓- g.na̓kya ḣpa̓'ya yo̔', — eya' c̔a ec̔ų́' yųk̔ą́' tųwą̓' śk̔e̓ᵉ. C̔ą́ke' kic̔i̓' wic̔o̓t̔ita k̔i̓' ną — Mic̔į̓kśi g.li̓' ye lo̔', — eya̓'-ho̓yeya g.la̓' c̔ą́ke'

---

[1] From *ec̔į́*, to think.

in an uproar. 12. Even his sister-in-law, "Oh, my brother-in-law has returned!" she said, playing the Iktomi[1]. And now there was a chase, and the boy asked that fat be collected for him; so they collected and heaped up a great amount some distance away. He stood by it and called, "I want my sister-in-law to come to my assistance!" — "Certainly!" she said and ran to him. "Brother-in-law, lift this up for me," she said, but he stood apart and called, "Now!" And from all sides all the wolves in the world, apparently, sprang forward suddenly, and scrambled for the fat and, in the confusion, they tore the woman to pieces and devoured her also. She tempted her brother and when he resisted her, she caused him great trouble, and she in turn received this treatment, they say. That is all.

36. The Man who Married a Buffalo Woman.

1. A man, with a tattoo mark on his forehead, had two wives; and one was a corn woman the other a buffalo woman. And the corn woman first gave birth to a child. It was a boy, with a tattoo mark on his forhead, exactly like his father's. The buffalo woman then had a son but he had no such mark. So, when the two wives quarrelled, the corn woman threw this fact up to the buffalo woman who resented it and went home to her people. 2. Of course the man

---

oya'te kį ħmu' s'e le'c'eca ke'ᵉ. 12. Hąka'ku k'ų he' k'o', — Śic'e' g.li' ye lê, — eya' ikto'mi-ka`ǵa² ke'ᵉ. Wana' wana'sapi yųk'ą' waśį' m.naye'-wic'aśi c'ąke' m.nak'i'yapi ną kai'yuzeya e'kicalapi yųk'ą' ekta' ina'żį ną, — Hąka' o'kpe-mau`kte lo', — eya' c'ąke', — To'ś, eyį' ną ekta' į'yąk ihų'ni ną, — Śic'e`, e'miciyaku ye', — eya' tk'a'ś ec'ą'l i't'ehąyą k'ina'żį ną, — Ho'! — eya'-pą yųk'ą' śųkma'nitu hena'la mak'a' aką'l ų'pi kį iyu'ha ųg.na'hąla ahi'hųni ną ħmu' s'e waśį' ik'i'nicapi ną wį'yą k'ų he' k'o' ic'i'g.nuniyą t'epya'pi śk'e'ᵉ. Śic'e'cu naǵi' yeki'yį ną wica'laśni yųk'ą' t'eħi'ya oki'ħ'ą k'ų i'ś eha'kela he'c'el ak'i'p'a śk'e'ᵉ. Hehą'yela owi'hąke'ᵉ.

36.

1. K'ośka'laka wą p'aħte' e'l aki't'o c'a wi'yą nų'p wic'a'yuza yųk'ą' ųma' wag.me'za-wį`yą ną ųma' i'ś pte'-wį`yą śk'e'ᵉ. Yųk'ą' wag.me'za-wį`yą k'ų he' t'oke'ya hokśi'yuha śk'e'ᵉ. Yųk'ą' hokśi'la c'a atku'ku aki't'o k'ų ec'e'ħcį aki't'o śk'e'ᵉ. Pte'-wį'yą kį i'ś eha'kela hośki'yuha yųk'ą' i'ś-eya' hokśi'la k'e'yaś p'aħte' e'l aki't'ośni c'ąke' wį'yą kį aho'yekc'iyapi³ ną pte'-wį'yą k'ų wac'į'k'o-k'ig.la` śk'e'ᵉ.

---

[1] Anyone who poses, pretending to be very cordial and agreeable, with an ulterior motive, is said to play the Iktomi.

² ka'ǵa, to create, to act as; to impersonate; hence, ikto'mi-kaǵa, to act very agreeable, and suave, and likeable, for a purpose; to be insincere.

³ aho'yeya, to quarrel; a, on; ho, voice; yeya', to send.

followed, because his son had been taken away. In the evening he came upon their camp for the night, which was very far from the place from which they had started. He stood outside, without saying anything, and his wife said, "Well, isn't it enough that he took so long to get here? Why then does he not come in?"[1] So he entered and picked up his son who was playing beside the fire, opposite the family-side of the tipi[2]. All night he tried to lie awake, but he must have fallen asleep, for when he woke he was alone. 3. Springing to his feet, he followed them again, and after a long journey he reached the camp where they were stopping for the night. Again he waited outside; and again his wife said, "Well, isn't it enough that he took so long to get here? Why then does he not come in?" So he went in. This time he grasped his wife's blanket tightly, thinking to lie awake holding it all night; but he must have dosed again; for at dawn he found himself alone on the camp-site. 4. Again he followed them. And as he was reaching their camp, his son ran to meet him. "Father, my mother says that tomorrow we must travel over a dry country; so take note of my tracks. In the tracks made by my left foot there will be water; drink it when you

---

2. Wic'a'ša kị c'įca' wą ki'cak'iyag.lapi c'ąke' iha'kap ya' šk'e'ᵉ. T'e'hąl ak'i't'ipi c'ąke' ktaye'tu hą'l e'l ihų'ni ną ini'lahci t'ąka'l na'žįhą yųk'ą' t'awi'cu kị, — Tuk'i' nakų'-ec'ala hi'ka c'a, t'ima' ų šni, — eya' c'ąke' t'ima' iya'ya yųk'ą' t'isą'p'atąhą³ c'įca' k'ų ška'tahą c'ąke' iki'kcu šk'e'ᵉ. Hąhe'pi a'taya kikta' kpa'yahe s'e le'c'eca k'ų tų'weni istị'ma hųše ikpe'ya k'ig.la'pi c'ąke' ot'i'weta kị e'l ayą'pa šk'e'ᵉ. 3. Na'žį hiya'yị ną ak'e' wic'i'hakap ya'hị ną li'la t'e'hąl ak'i't'ipi c'ąke' ekta' ihų'ni ną ak'e' t'ąka'l ina'žį yųk'ą', — Tuk'i', nakų'-ec'ala hi'ka c'a, t'ima' u' šni, — t'awi'cu kị eya' c'ąke' t'i'l i' šk'e'ᵉ. Šehąstuk'a t'awi'cu t'aši'na kị e'l yu's kikta' kpa'yewac'į yųk'ą' ak'e'š tų'weni istị'ma c'ąke' ą'pao' yųk'ą' ot'i'weta e'l išna'la ayą'pa šk'e'ᵉ. 4. Ak'e' wic'i'hakap ya'hą šk'e'ᵉ. Ną wana' ak'i't'ipi kị e'l ihų'nikta yųk'ą' c'įca' k'ų itko'p u' ną, — Ate', hị'hąna kị m.ni' wani'ca wą o'pta ųg.la'pikta ina' ke'ya' c'e oye' ama'tųwą yo'. Mi'oye-c'atka`yatąhą kị m.ni' og.na' hị'kta c'e i'nipuza c'ą' atų'wą yo',

---

[1] See note 1, page 24.

[2] The family side of the tipi extends from the right of the door to the beginning of the central area or place of honor already described, when one stands in the door, looking in. In other words, it is the right hand side of the tipi. The opposite side referred to here, would be the corresponding section on the left hand side. It is where relatives sit, and uninvited but welcome guests who come rather too often for it to be an event, and casual callers. The place of honor is for special, distinguished guests, for whom extensive preparations have been made; while the space to the left of the doorway, immediately inside, is where old people sit, and those coming to "seek house", with the definite and only purpose to get something to eat.

[3] *t'isą'p'atąhą*, on the opposite side of the tipi. This always means the left hand side of the tipi as one enters; or across from the family-section.

are thirsty," he said. Next morning when he awoke they were
gone again, so he followed them. 5. Just as his son had promised, his
left tracks were filled with water which he drank whenever he was
thirsty, throughout the day. When at last he reached their camp,
he stopped outside again, and his wife said, "Well, isn't it enough
that he took so long to get here? Why then does he not come in?"
So he entered. Again his son talked to him secretly. "Father, my
mother says we are to cross a wide body of water tomorrow. So
arrange what you can, for yourself." 6. Seriously this time he tried
to keep awake, yet he must have slept, for once more they were gone
when he awoke. When he came to the water over which the boy and
his mother had already gone, he changed himself into a feather and
was blown across by the wind, without any difficulty. About to
arrive at the camp, he sat down on a hilltop first to look around,
and saw a great tribe in camp below. And his son came to him, and
played about, near him. 7. "Father, be patient. I have four mothers[1],
all exactly alike; but the one who will come to you last will be my
own mother; and when you arrive down there, my grandmother
will open the door for you; you better arrange something for yourself there," he said. 8. "And I have four mothers, but they are very
much alike; so take warning. If you do not claim my mother, my
grandmother says she will kill you. So look very sharply; for I will
place a little blade of grass on my own mother's head, to the left

---

— eya' śk'e'ᵉ. Ihį'hąna c'a kikta' yųk'ą' wana'ś ak'e' ehą'ni tok'i'yot'ą
iya'yapi c'ąke' wic'i'hakap ya'hą śk'e'ᵉ. 5. C'įca' kį eye' c'ų ec'e'ħcį
oye'-c'atka`yatąhą kį hena' m.ni' ożu'la hą' c'ąke' m.ni' c'į' c'ą'śna
yatkį' ną ak'e' ya' śk'e'ᵉ. Ak'i't'ipi kį e'l ihų'ni k'e'yaś ak'e' t'ąka'l
na'żįhą yųk'ą', — Tuk'i`, nakų'-ec'ala hi'ka c'a t'ima' u' śni, —
t'awi'cu kį eya' c'ąke' t'ima' i' śk'e'ᵉ. Ak'e' c'įca' kį naħma'-wokiyakį
ną heya' śk'e'ᵉ, — Ate`, hį'hąna kįhą m.ni' wą li'la ot'ą'kaya c'a
o'pta ųk'i'yag.lapikta ina' ke'ye' lo'. C'e e'l to'k'el ħ'ą-wa'c'į yo', —
eya' śk'e'ᵉ. 6. Śehąśtuk'a kikta' ħpa'ye se'ca yųk'ą' wana'ś ak'e' iśtį'ma
hųśe tų'weni tok'i'yot'ą k'ig.la'pi śk'e'ᵉ. Wana' m.ni' wą k'e' c'ų he'
o'pta k'ig.la'pi c'ąke' e'l i' ną wa'c'įhį-ic'ic'aǵį nąś to'k'aśniyą o'pta
iya'ya śk'e'ᵉ, kaħwo'ħwok. Wana' t'i-i'hųnikta c'a t'owa'ś paha' wą
e'l i'yotaka yųk'ą' oħla't'e oya'te wic'o't'ilaħcaka c'ąke' e'l e'tųwą
yąka'hą śk'e'ᵉ. Yųk'ą' c'įca' kį ekta' hi' ną o'kśą śka'tahį ną heya'
śk'e'ᵉ, 7. — Ate`, wac'į' t'ą'ka² yo'. Ina' to'papi k'e'yaś iyu'ha
a'k'iyec'ecapi c'a wążi' eha'ke-hikte cį he' ina' e'e c'e wac'į' t'ą'ka yo'.
Ną yai' kįhą ųci' t'iyo'pa nici'yuǵąkta c'e he'l to'k'eśk'e ħ'ą'ka yo' —
eya' ke'ᵉ. 8. — Ną ina' to'papi kį hena' iyu'ha li'la a'k'iyec'ecapi c'e
wakta' yo'. Ina' iye'kcuśni kįhą ųci' nikte'kta ke'ye' lo'. C'a li'la
tąyą' ab.le'za yo'. Ina' p'eyo'zą-c'atka`yatąhą p'eżi' wążi' e'wa-

---

[1] The calf-boy's three aunts, sisters of his mother, are also called his mothers,
    in the Dakota kinship scheme.
    wac'į' t'ą'ka, big mind. To have patience.

of the parting of her hair," he said. "Very well," the man said, and
was sitting when one, who might well be his wife, came to him and
said, "Well, isn't it enough that he was so slow in coming? Why does
he linger here? Why is he sitting thus?" she said and then turning
she went home; so the man almost sprang to his feet and yet he
didn't, when he recalled his son's warning; so he sat still. 9. Again
a second one came, and she seemed to be his wife this time. She
stood by and said, "I invite him, and he sits on; better come now,"
and she went back. So he almost stood up; but his son's words came
to him and saved him. Again one came, the third one, and, "Well,
the idea! I've invited him; what is he waiting for? Come now, for
you must eat!" He almost stood up but his son's words kept him
down. "That would not be according to my son's warning," he
thought. 10. The fourth one came. "I come four times and still he
sits on; why? Come now, and eat," she said, and her very words
brought him to his feet. When he arrived at the doorway, an old
woman came out and said, "I'll be the one to open for the son-in-
law," so she opened a heavy door made of stone; but the man
transformed himself into a feather and the wind took him in.
11. Indoors sat four young women, each in her respective bed-space[1],
but it was hard to tell which one was his wife; so he stood a minute,
studying them, and one had a small blade of grass in her hair, at
the left of the parting; so he sat down beside her; and the old woman
laughed maliciously. "*He, yo!* Of course; isn't that his wife? Then

*g.nakįkte lo', — eya' šk'e'ᵉ. — Ha'.o, — wic'a'ša kį eyį' nąš yąka'he
c'ų wana' t'awi'cu kį e'e se'ca u' ną — Nakų'-ec'ala hi'ka c'a, tuk'į`
u-wa'c'įšni, le' ta'kuħcowe'-yąka` c'a, — eyį' ną kawį'ħ iya'ya
c'ąke' ina'žįkte są' ak'e'š cįca' kį ta'keye c'ų he' kiksu'ya ihe'yį ną
ową'žila yąka' šk'e'ᵉ. 9. Ak'e' wąži' u' k'e'yaš t'awi'cu kį hee' s'e
lece'c'a šk'e'ᵉ. Hina'žį ną, — We'c'o kį to'k'el yąka' c'a, wana' u' we'
ma, — eyį' ną k'ig.la' c'ąke' ina'žį nų s'e ak'e' c'įca' oi'ye k'ų kiksu'yį
ną e'na yąka' šk'e'ᵉ. Ak'e' iya'm.ni kį u' ną, — Huħî, we'c'o kį, ta'ku
ap'e' c'a. U' we', waya'tįkte, — eya' c'ąke' ina'žįħcįkte są' c'įca' oi'ye
k'ų ų' e'na yąka' šk'e'ᵉ. — Mic'į'kši he'c'el eš eye'šni k'ų, — ec'į'
šk'e'ᵉ. 10. Ak'e' ito'pa wą u' ną, — Wana' to'pa-wahi` kį to'k'el yąka'
c'a. U' we', waya'tįkte, — eya' tk'a'š yana'žį iye'yeħca šk'e'ᵉ. T'iyo'pa
e'l ihų'ni yųk'ą' winų'ħcala wą e'l u' ną, — It'o' wic'a'woħa kį
t'iyo'pa waki'yuğąkte, — eyį' ną t'iyo'pa kį į'yą c'ąke' yuğą' tk'a'š
wa'c'įħį-ic'ic'ağį ną kaħwo'ħwok t'ima' hiyu' šk'e'ᵉ. 11. T'ima'
wik'o'škalaka to'p t'o'wąkepi k'e'yaš tukte'-wąži t'awi'cu t'ąį'šni
c'ąke' awi'c'ab.les na'žįhą yųk'ą' wąži' p'eyo'zą-c'atka`yatąhą p'eži'
wą yąka' c'ąke' he' į'yap'e į'yotaka yųk'ą' winų'ħcala kį, — Hê yô! toš,*

---

[1] In a Dakota lodge, the space reserved for each grown-up member of the
family was as much respected as a room in a house occupied by an individual. Up against the rear, piled up in neat array, were the belongings of
that person, in beaded saddle-bags, (so-called), rawhide cases, and latterly,
in leather suit cases.

why should he not claim her ?" she said. Again his son spoke to him. "Father, tomorrow the boys are all to run a race; and if you don't claim me there, my grandmother says she will kill you," he said. "But watch carefully for me; I shall be on the west end, and before I come to a stop, I will buck and jump a few times; and when we come to a stop, I will keep stamping my foot on the ground." — "Very well," the father answered. 12. The boys were now assembled to run and they were all tawny-yellow calves. And from the time they started home, the one on the west end kicked up his heels playfully as he ran, so the man stood watching him; and when they stopped, he kept stamping his foot on the ground. The father saw all this, but stood for a minute pretending to look for him; and then, forcing an opening, he went and claimed his son. The crafty old grandmother laughed, "*He, yo!* Why not? Isn't that his child?" 13. Again the son said, "Father, the boys are to run again tomorrow. If you don't single me out of the group, and claim me, my grandmother says she will kill you. But when I come to a stop, I will stand turning my ears first this way, and that, so watch for me." So morning came and some calves of a trifle darker coat were running, but his son was among them. When they ran and came to a stop, one of them stood with his ears moving continually; so he pretended to be looking for him, and then went and took him. "*He,*

t'awi'culaka wą́s iki'kcuŝni ka! — eya' ŝk'e'ᵉ. Ak'e' c'įca' kį heya' ŝk'e'ᵉ, — Ate, hį'hąna kįhą hokŝi'la k'įy'yąkapikta c'a ima'yaki-kcuŝni hą'tąhąŝ ųci' nikte'kta ke'ye' lo, — eya' ŝk'e'ᵉ. — K'e'yaŝ wiyo'hpeyatąhą ihą'keya eha'keke nite' wąka'lkal yewa'kiyį ną wag.li'nażį ną mak'a' nato'to nawa'żįkta c'e tąyą' ama'k'ita yo', — eya'cąke' — Ha'.o, — eya' ŝk'e'ᵉ. 12. Wana' hokŝi'la k'įy'yąka-pikta c'a m.nawi'c'ayapi k'e'yaŝ ptec'į'cala-żi'la kį he'c'a ece' e'wic'a-g.lepi ną wana' ka'k'el g.licu'pi k'e'yaŝ wą'cak wiyo'hpeyatąhą ŝka'ŝkal nite' wąka'lkal yeki'ya į'yąko' c'ąke' awą'yak au' yųk'ą' ka'l g.linażį ną si' kį mak'a' nakita'htak na'żį c'ąke' eya' he' wąya'ke c'e'yaŝ t'o'wa'ŝ awi'c'atuwe-kųs na'żį ną hehą'l wica'yuokoko¹ yį' ną e'ikikcu c'ąke', — Hê yô! Toŝ, c'įca'laka wą́s, iki'kcuŝni ka! — winų'hcala kį eya' ŝk'e'ᵉ. 13. Ak'e' c'įca' kį heya' ŝk'e'ᵉ, — Ate', ak'e' hį'hąna kįhą hokŝi'la į'yąkapikta ŝk'e' lo'. C'a ima'yakikcuŝni kįhą ųci' nikte'kta ke'ye' lo'. K'e'yaŝ wag.li'nażį kįhą nakpa' g.luho'm.nim.ni² nawa'-żįkta c'e ama'k'ita yo', — eya' c'ąke' wana' ak'e' hį'hąna yųk'ą' hehą'l ptehį'cala ki'tąla-hįsapapila kį he'c'a ece'hcį k'įy'yąkapi yųk'ą' e'l o'pa hųŝe wana' ak'e' g.lina'żįpi k'uhą' wążi' nakpa' kį' g.luptą'ptąhą³ ŝk'e'ᵉ. Ak'i'ta-kųs na'żį ną hehą'l iya'yį ną e'ikikcu

---

¹ *wic'a'yukoko*, making spaces between them; that is, threading his way, in and out, in the crowd; *wic'a*, them; *yu* with the hands; *oko'*, a space, between two objects.

² *yuho'm.nim.ni*, to turn round and round.

³ *yuptą'ptą*, to turn a long object, in such a way that now one long side is exposed, and now another, as one might turn a sword.

yo! And why not ? Isn't that his son, why shouldn't he claim him ?" the old woman cackled. 14. The child said now, "My grandmother is going to challenge you to race with her tomorrow; so see what you can do for yourself in the matter;" and in the morning she came. "I shall race with the son-in-law," she said; and a (? some sort of buffalo) started off, its tail swinging as if being kicked to one side with each step. But he made himself into a feather and was carried along by the wind and first reached the tree they were to climb; so she ran, calling, "Wait a bit; I haven't sat down yet[1]." But at that moment, the thunder crashed very low, and knocked her off, and struck her repeatedly, so the people cheered, "She is always doing tricks like that; don't you spare her!" She fell, broken in many pieces. So they immediately broke camp and returned to the (man's) tribe. 15. And when the man saw his father he said, "Father, make an announcement during the chase. Tell them I want the fat." So, soon two young men took a rawhide around, collecting fat for him. When it was piled high at a certain place, he called for his wife to come to his aid. 16. He must have been planning this, for he took his wife, and oiled her hair and combed and braided it care-

---

c'ąke', — Hê yô! Toś, c'įca'laka wąś, iki'kcuśni ka! — winų'ħcala k'ų eya' śk'e'ᵉ. 14. Ak'e' c'įca' ki leya' śk'e'ᵉ, — Hį'hąna kiħą ųci' k'ię'yąk-aniukta c'e to'k'eśk'e ħ'ą'ka yo', — eya' c'ąke' hį'hąna yųk'ą', — Wic'a'woħą ki kic'i' k'iwa'įm.nakikte', — eya'ya ną ptet'a'maka wą site' nak'a'p yeki'ye s'e iya'ya tk'a'ś iye' wa'c'įhį c'ąke' kaħwo'k iya'yį ną c'ą' wą ali'pi k'e'yaś iye' t'oke'ya ali' į'yąka² c'ąke', — Hį'yąka', nahą'ħcį i'b.lotakeśni ye'+! — eya'ya tk'a'ś wakį'yą³ wą k'u'ciyela iyo'ħuħuǵahe s'e hiyu' ną oka'ħpį ną iyo'k'iheheya e'l iye'ya c'ąke' oya'te ki aś'a'pi ną, — He'c'ų s'a ke c'ų, niya'ye ci lo'! — eya'pi śk'e'ᵉ. Oka'weħweǵa c'ąke' he'c'ena ig.la'kapi ną wic'o't'ita g.liħų'nipi śk'e'ᵉ. 15. Yųk'ą' k'ośka'laka ki atku'ku wąg.la'ki ną heya' śk'e'ᵉ, — Ate`, wana'sapi ki le'l iye'yapaha yo'. Waśį' ki hena' m.nama'k'iyapikte lo', — eya' c'ąke' wana' k'ośka'laka nų'p t'aha'saka⁴ wą yuha' hiya'yapi ną waśį' m.nak'i'- yapi śk'e'ᵉ. Wana' paha'yela m.nayą'pi ki hehą'l t'awi'cu ki wa'- g.lam.na⁵ waho'kiya śk'e'ᵉ. 16. He'c'ųwac'iyelak'a, yį'kte c'ų he'hą' t'awi'cu ki tąye'la ki'cisų ną nata' slaki'cic'iyi ną wase' k'o' ki'cicų

---

[1] Most of these races, at least in legends, involve some obstacle. The runners either circle around a lake or hill, or climb a tree and sit on it a moment before returning.

² *į'yąka*, to run, is very irregular; *waį'm.nąka*, I run; *yaį'nąka*, thou runnest; *ųk'į'yąka*, we two run. It takes two subjects.

³ *wakį'yą*, thunder; a flying being. The buffalo and thunder are traditional enemies.

⁴ *t'aha'saka*, rawhide, after it is allowed to dry stiff. *t'a*, ruminant; *ha*, skin; *sa'ka*, to be stiff, as leather that has become wet, and dried out.

⁵ *wa'g.lam.na* This word has to do with assistance on the return trip. I know a man whose Dakota name was *Mat'o' Ig.la'm.na*, and it meant "A bear that suddenly turns about to charge."

fully, and applied her face paints for her. When she came to aid him, he said, "Now, carry this on your back, meantime (there is something else I must do)." And as he walked away she called, "Well can't he stop long enough to help me with it?" But he said, "Do it the best you can; I am going yonder a moment." And he turned from her, and stood looking into the distance. 17. "Now, then!" he called and the wolves came from everywhere, just how they came was not plain, and they scrambled madly for the fat, and in the confusion they tore at the woman who had caused her husband agony, and they do say that sounds of a buffalo, grunting as in a struggle, were heard. She was soon reduced to bones. She tried various means to conquer her husband, but he saved himself; yet now, when she was put to a single struggle, she could do nothing, they say. That is all.

37. The Rolling Skull.

1. Four women, on a journey, were passing a burial scaffold near the road when one of them who liked to joke said in fun, "*Hųhi'*, Here lies the one I had for a sister-in-law!"[1] By accident, she was really speaking to a woman, for it was a woman who lay dead

---

śk'e'ᵉ. Wana' hi' c'ąke', — Ho, lena' k'į' yo', it'o' k'e'yaś,[2] — eyį' ną ka'k'ena ya' c'ąke', — Tok'e k'įmi'cic'iye śni, — eya' tk'a'ś, — Hiya', niye'c'įka k'eś kic'į' yo', t'o'wa'ś ka'l m.ni'kte, — eyį' ną ak'o'ketkiya e'tųwą na'żį śk'e'ᵉ. 17. — Ho' po'+! — eya'-ho'yeya c'ąke' śųkma'nitu kį to'k'iyatąhą t'ąį'śni hiyu'pi ną waśį' k'ų ik'i'nicapi ną wi'yą wą wayu'kakiże c'ų he' k'o' o'ġeya ik'i'nicapi yųk'ą' pte' wą yag.lo'g.lopi ną a'taya huhu' e'ce' ihpe'yapi śk'e'ᵉ. Iye'ś wic'a'śa kį he' o'takiya k'uwa'pe'ś[3] nai'c'iśpe c'e'yaś iye' wą'cakiyela k'e'yaś nii'c'iya oki'hiśni śk'e'ᵉ. Hehą'yela owi'hąke'ᵉ.

37.

1. *Wį'yą to'p ka'k'ena i'c'imani-ya`hąpi yųk'ą' wic'a'ag.nakapi wą iyo'pteya oc'ą'ku c'ąke' og.na' iya'yapi hą'l wążi' o'we hą'hą s'a yųk'ą' he' e c'a ak'e' heya' ke'ᵉ, — Hinų, le' śce'p'qwayela[4] k'ų le'c'el le'l hpa'yahe lê! — eya' yųk'ą' leyalaka he' wį'yą c'aś hpa'ye śą*

---

[1] Sister-in-law is a joking relation. The woman here is pretending to plague a sister-in-law because she is obliged to be dead. "To think she is so worsted that she lies like this," is the meaning.

[2] *It'o'*, and *t'o k'e'yaś* and *t'o'wa'ś* are all words with which a sentence, uncompleted in sense, may stop. It is as though one might say, "I am going to read, but first —" It is a sort of murmured excuse for delaying.

[3] *pe'ś*, contracted from *pi ye'ś* hence the accent. *pi*, plural sign; *yeś*, yet.

[4] *śce'p'qwayela k'ų*, she was my sister-in-law. *la* indicates a joking or flippant attitude, which is correct between two women bearing the *śce'p'ą* relation to each other. A *śce'p'ą* is the wife of a brother, or a cousin (parallel or cross); and the sister or female cousin of one's husband.

there. 2. After travelling far, as night was coming on they built a grass shelter and lay down to rest; but before they were asleep, they heard, coming in the direction they themselves had come, some one who was wailing. Gradually that one was talking, so they listened carefully as they lay, and it said, "Four women came this way, and one of them is my sister-in-law[1]!" They were greatly frightened, and kept still, trying to hide by so doing. The new-comer walked about the shelter saying, "Sister-in-law, open for me, wherever the door is." 3. The others were thoroughly disgusted with the one (who had been joking), for always talking such stupid nonsense, so they said, "You first claimed her as your sister-in-law. Open for her!" and when the voice came from the doorway, they sneaked out from the rear of the hut, and ran away. 4. There was nothing else to do, so the woman left alone opened the door, and a human skull, dried and blanched, with the eye-sockets like caves of blackness, rolled into the room. "Now, sister-in-law, carry me on your back; we shall go to camp," she said. So, much as she feared it, she was obliged to take the skull on her back; and they started towards camp. Suddenly something ran before them, knocking off the dew (from the grass) as it ran, so the woman said, "Sister-in-law, I would like to eat that which ran, knocking off the dew." And the skull said, "Very well, then, set me down." So she

---

*a'tayelaĥcį heya' ke*ᵉ*. 2. T'e'hąl ihų'nipi hą'l wana' oi'yokpaza c'ąke' p'eži'-wok'eya wą ka'ǧapi ną e'l iyų'kapi yųk'ą' isti'mapisni ec'e'l tuwa' u'pi k'ų he'c'iyatąhą c'e'ya u' ke*ᵉ*. Hąke'ya ia'a u' c'ąke' ana'ǧoptąpi yųk'ą' leya' u' ke*ᵉ*, — Wį'yą to'p le'c'etkiya hiyu'pi c'a he' wąži' sce'p'ąwaye' ! — eya'ya u' c'ąke' li'la k'oki'p'api ną ini'la ina'ĥma-ĥpa`yapi k'e'yas wana's hihų'ni ną t'iwo'ksą, — Scep'ą`, tukte'l t'iyo'pa he'cįhą maki'yuǧąlaka'!*² — eya'hą ke*ᵉ*. 3. C'ąke' ųma'pi kį li'la wae'yayake c'ų he' i'waĥtelapisni*³ ną — Niye' he' t'oka' ekta' sce'p'ąyaya ke'ha' c'a niya't'ap hi' ye'. Kiyu'ǧą ye', — eya'pi ną t'iyo'pata ho't'ąįį tk'a's t'ic'a'tkutąhą ipa'pta ina'p'api ną li'la naki'p'api ke*ᵉ*. 4. Wana' to'k'el ĥ'ąp'i'casni c'ąke' he'c'etu k'es kiyu'ǧą yųk'ą' wic'a'nata-se`ca wą ista' okpa'kpasyela t'iyo'kag.mi-g.ma hiyu' ke*ᵉ*. Ną — Iho', scep'ą`, mi'c'į', oya'te t'i'pita ųg.nį'kte', — eya' c'ąke' li'la k'oki'p'e c'e'yas ki'c'į ną wana' g.la'pi ke*ᵉ*. Yųk'ą' ųg.na' ta'ku wą wic'i't'okap c'u-na'k'ąk'ą*⁴ iya'ya c'ąke', — Scep'ą`, he ta'ku wą c'u-na'k'ąk'ą iya'ye cį he' wa'tįkte', — eya' yųk'ą' wic'a'nata k'ų, — Ho, ec'a mayu'ĥpa', — eya' c'ąke' yuĥpą' c'a tok'i'yot'ą iya'ya*

---

[1] Like a true Dakota, the ghost claims kinship promptly.

[2] *laka*, attached to a request or command, means, "make some attempt at least to do it for me."

[3] *waĥte'lasni*, to hate; to dislike (out-and-out). But *i'waĥtelasni*, to be disgusted with someone, on account of some specific reason; but to like him otherwise.

[4] *c'u*, dew; *na*, with the feet; *k'ą*, falls off in drops, or little round things; as berries, dewdrops, even ripe wheat.

did, and the skull went off somewhere and returned with a wood-deer; so the woman melted the fat and poured it, together with the marrow-oil, into the paunch of the deer; carrying this, they went on. 5. As they journeyed, something again went before them, knocking off the dew; so again the woman said, "Sister-in-law, I wish to eat that thing." — "Well, then, set me down," the skull replied; when she did so, it ran off somewhere and returned with a buffalo. There was much fat to it, so the woman poured great quantities into the buffalo paunch, and they continued on their way. 6. Again something went before them, leaving its tracks; "Sister-in-law, I wish to eat that," the woman said; "Well, then, set me down," the skull replied; it went off somewhere; this time however, the woman did not wait but started home. 7. She had covered a long distance, when the skull came rolling behind her, shouting, "You have done dreadfully to me. Where do you think you can go ?" So the woman ran, crying, but it came faster and was almost under her feet; so in desperation she threw the deer-paunch down and burst it open, causing the oil to spread over a wide area on the ground. The skull stopped to lap it up, and was so busy there that the woman came on, and gained a great distance. 8. A long time after, the skull came on again and was almost under the woman's feet when she threw down the buffalo paunch, breaking it and pouring the oil over the ground. So the skull remained to lick the grease and take bites in the paunch. And during that time the woman reached camp. As she related her experiences the people in fear kept a sharp lookout but as nothing seemed to be coming, they

---

yuk'ą' c'ą'-t'aħca wą ag.li' c'ąke' śį' kį śloyį' ną huhu'-wig.li` kį k'o'ya niǧe' kį el oka'śtą ną yuha' iya'yapi ke'ᵉ. 5. Ak'e' ya'hąpi hą'l ta'ku wą c'u-na'k'ąk'ą oye' iya'ya c'ąke' — ścep'ą`, he' ta'ku kį wa'tįkte' — eya' yuk'ą' ak'e' — Ec'a mayu'ħpa', — eya' c'ąke' yuħpa' c'a tok'i'yot'ą iya'ya yuk'ą' pte' wą ag.li' ke'ᵉ. Wi'g.li o'ta c'ąke' paha'yela niǧe' kį e'l oka'śtą ną ak'e' ya'pi ke'ᵉ. 6. Yuk'ą' ta'ku wą ak'e' oye' iya'ya c'ąke' — ścep'ą`, he' wa'tįkte', — eya' c'ąke', — Ec'a mayu'ħpa', — eya' c'a yuħpa' yuk'ą' tok'i'yot'ą iya'ya tk'a'ś i'ś-'eya' he'c'ena iya'kip'eśni li'la k'ig.la' ke'ᵉ. 7. T'e'hąl g.la' hą'l ug.na' laza'tąhą pag.mi'yąyąpi s'e iha'kap u' ną — T'eħi'ya oma'ya-kiħ'ą ye'! To'k'iya nį'kta¹ he'? — eya'ya į'yąka c'ąke c'e'ya naki'p'e c'e'yaś wana' oħla't'e hihų'nikta c'ąke' he'c'etu k'eś t'a'ħca niǧe' k'u he' aka'p'op ap'a' yuk'ą' mak'a' kį ka' tį'skoya o'kab.laya ya' c'ąke' he'na wic'a'nata k'u he' sli'pahį ną u'śni c'ąke' k'ohą' g.licu' ną li'la t'e'hąl g.li' ke'ᵉ. 8. I't'ehą yuk'ą' ak'e' u' c'ąke' wana' oħla'te hihų'ni-kta hą'l pte' niǧe' k'u he' aka'ħlel ap'a' yuk'ą' mak'a' kį a'taya aka'śtą c'ąke' e'na yaśpa' sli'pahą c'a ec'e'l wį'yą k'u oya'te t'i'pi kį ekta' g.lihų'ni ke'ᵉ. Oya'ka c'ąke' nihį'ciya o'kśą e'tuwą u'pi k'e'yaś ta'kuniśni ną ec'e'l wana' wic'i'yuka ke'ᵉ. Wana' hąhe'pi-wic'i`śtįma

---

¹ *la kta*, you will go, becomes *nįkta*, *l* becoming *n* before *į*.

went to bed. While they slept at night, the entire tribe disappeared. 9. The next morning, only one old woman and her grandson, who lived a little distance from the circle, found themselves on the scene. "Grandson, wake up; the entire tribe has gone away," she said, so the boy arose and took some pointed arrows he had, and went to see in which direction the tracks would lead. 10. And there, in the centre of the deserted camp, he found something white and spherical, so he stood aiming at it, and then sent his arrow piercing it; and lo, they say that out of it all the people came back, pouring out, as if belched forth. The people were restored, and went back to their camp-sites to take up life again; and from then on, they made the boy chief, because he had saved the tribe; and caused him and his grandmother to live within the circle, and they loved them. That is all.

38. The Twin-Spirits.

1. Two twin-spirits walked around the camp circle looking for a place to go. They would practically decide on a certain tipi, and then, one of them would see something about it that didn't just suit his fancy, and they would go on past. Yonder stood a white tipi, evidently new, placed somewhat inside the circle. They looked in, just by the way, and saw a handsome young couple sitting inside.

yųk'ą́ k'ohą́ oya'te ki̧ a'tayeĥci̧ to'k'aĥ'ąpi ke'ᵉ. 9. Hi̧'hąna yųk'ą́ winų'ĥcala wą t'ako'żakpaku kic'i'la mani̧'lwap'aya¹ t'i̧' yųk'ą́ hece'la e'na t'i'la ke'ᵉ. C'ąke' — T'akoża', kikta', oya'te ki̧ a'taya to'k'i̧ e'yaye', — eya' c'ąke' hoksi'la k'ų ina'żi̧ ną wąhi̧'kpe kap'e'stopi k'eya' yuha' c'ąke' g.luha' i̧'yąki̧ ną to'k'etkiya oye' e'yaye se'ca c'a atų'wą ke'ᵉ. 10. Yųk'ą́ ot'i̧'weta-c'oka`ya ta'ku wą g.mig.me'ya skaye'la yąka' c'ąke' apa'ha na'żi̧ ną ipa'ĥna o' yųk'ą́ oya'te ki̧ etą'ĥą ag.li'nap'i̧ ną g.le'papi s'e hiyu'pi ke'ᵉ. Ak'e' oya'te ki̧ ec'e'l k'ig.la'pi ną to'k'el t'i'pi tk'a' k'ų ec'e'kc'e ak'i̧'t'ipi ną hetą' hoksi'la wą niwi'c'aye c'ų he' it'ą'c'ąk'iyapi ną k'ų'sitku kic'i̧' ho'c'okata t'iwi'c'ak'iyapi ną li'la t'ewi'c'aĥilapi śk'e'ᵉ. Hehą'yela owi'ĥąke'ᵉ.

38.

1. C'ekpa'² nų'p hoa'g.lag.la tukte'l ya'pikta-ak'i̧'l oma'nihąpi śk'e'ᵉ. Wana' tukte'l tąyą' se'ca k'eś ec'ą'l ųma' e'l takų'l iyo'kip'iśni c'ą' iyo'pteya iya'yahąpi śk'e'ᵉ. Yųk'ą́ ka'l c'oka'p t'i'pi wą t'ą'ka skaye'la hą' yųk'ą́ t'e'ca-iteyakel ec'e'ca c'ąke' tok'e' ec'a'c'a e'l e'yokas'i̧pi yųk'ą́ t'ima' wik'o'śkalaka wą k'ośka'laka wą kic'i̧' yąka'pi k'e'yaś nųp'i̧' li'la ową'yak-waśte`pi śk'e'ᵉ. 2. Hec'e'ya wi̧'yą ki̧ he'

¹ *wap'aya*, added to an adverb of place, means "somewhat more"; farther off; nearer; more towards etc.
² *c'ekpa'*, twins; the navel. Term of address between two friends that like each other's company for the fun, and joking they can have. It is not so dignified as *k'ola'*, friend.

2. The woman was a bride that had been brought there recently. It seemed like a good place to stop, so the twins stood and conferred about it in the doorway, but those within neither saw nor heard them. Both the twins were named *Ža'ta* (two-pronged or bifurcated.) One was Big *Ža'ta*, and the other was Little *Ža'ta*. And Little *Ža'ta* said, "There's no use talking, — this is where we go." So the other agreed with him, and they entered, and were soon sitting within their mother. 3. They waited patiently and were very good until the time drew near for them to come out; and then they acted outrageously. They were arguing over which one should come out first; because whoever came out first would be the elder. So they sat inside, holding onto each other, and refused to stir until it grew very serious with their mother who was almost dying; so the people ran frantically about to find medicine for her; but all the while these two were acting in this way. 4. The minute the woman drank the medicine, a snake entered the room where the two *Ža'ta* sat, and coiled himself there; Big *Ža'ta* who saw him first nudged Little *Ža'ta* so he also looked, — and then they were struck stiff with fear. Just as they both looked at the snake, he stuck out his tongue at them again and again, so those fine[1] disputers gave up,

yu'zapi nǫ ag li'pi c'a he'l yǫka'pi šk'e'ᵉ. He'l tǫyǫ' s'e le'c'eca c'ǫke' t'iyo'pa kį e'l c'ekpa' kį na'žįpi nǫ wa'k'iyapi k'e'yaš t'ima' yǫka'pi kį a'tayaš wǫwi'c'ayakapišni nǫ nawi'c'aȟ'ųpišni šk'e'ᵉ. C'ekpa' kį nup'į' Ža'ta ewi'c'akiyapi šk'e'ᵉ; uma' Ža'ta-T'ǫka eci'yapi nǫ ųma' i'š Ža'ta-Cik'ala eci'yapi šk'e'ᵉ. Yųk'ǫ' Ža'ta-Cik'ala e' c'a leya' šk'e'ᵉ — Iho', Žata`, tok'e'tuke c'e'yaš le'l ųyi'kte lo', — eya' c'ǫke' ųma' kį i'š-eya' he'c'etula kį ų' t'ima' iya'yapi nǫ hų'kupikte cį t'ǫma'hel² i'yotakapi šk'e'ᵉ. 3. T'e'hǫ ye'š tǫyǫ' waa'p'e yǫka'hǫpi k'ų wana' hina'p'apikta-iye`hǫtu ȟcehǫ'l wa'k'inicapi nǫ ta'k t'ą̇'- pišni³ šk'e'ᵉ. Tukte'-ųma` t'oke'ya hina'p'įkta he'cįhǫ he' ak'i'nicapi šk'e'ᵉ; nųp'į' t'oka'p'apikteȟcį⁴ kį ų'. He'c'eš ekta'ni yu's kic'i'yǫka- hǫpi nǫ t'e'hǫ-hiyu'pišni c'ǫke' ų'nihǫ' hų'kupi k'ų t'į'kta c'a šica'- wac'į p'ežu'ta iki'g.nipi k'e'yaš owo' hį'sko he'c'ųhǫpi šk'e'ᵉ. 4. Yųk'ǫ' wana' ka'k'el-p'ežu'ta kį yatkǫ' yųk'ǫ' he'c'ena zuze'ca wǫ Ža'ta yǫka'pi k'ų he'c'iya hiyu' nǫ t'iyo'kakša hiyų'ka c'ǫke' Ža'ta-T'aka t'oke'ya wǫya'kį nǫ Ža'ta-Cik'ala pani' c'ǫke' i'š-'eya' wǫya'kį nǫ t'ǫsa'k t'a'pi⁵ šk'e'ᵉ. Nųp'į' zuze'ca kį ayu'tapi ȟcehǫ'l c'eži'yǫpyǫp

---

[1] When a person seems engaged in an activity with serious intent, and then for some slight disturbance, gives up, they say "*wašte'ka.*" *Wašte'*, good; fine; *ka*, rather, in a manner of speaking, sort of; and sometimes, as here, ironically meaning the opposite; "no good; he is a fine one!"

[2] *t'ǫma'hel*, within; inside the body; *t'ǫ*, body, from *t'ǫc'ǫ'*.

[3] *ta'k t'ą̇'šni*, it is not plain what he is. This is an idiom, amounting to, "he is just no good! You can't do a thing with him!" Said generally of a wilful child; or an unreasonable person; *ta'k* from *ta'ku*, something.

[4] *t'oka'p'a*, elder; or eldest. *t'oka'*, first; *p'a*, head. *kteȟcį*, added to a verb, means "to want very much, almost beyond restraint."

[5] *t'ǫsa'k t'a*, "to be scared stiff." Literally, to die, with the body stiff.

at last. "Watch out!" they yelled, and they came out, tumbling
over each other in such confusion that they never did know which
was the elder after all. 5. Now they were lying all bound up, in the
Dakota fashion, and their father came in to speak to them. "Well,
my sons, since you have come to me, in spite of my humble station,
see to it that you do not grieve me. Live content, and be kind to
each other. For I shall love you both with the same degree of love."
6. They were wrapped in the conventional beaded cradles; which
were exactly alike. And they were each caused to rest their heads
on a pillow made after the style then in use, with porcupine work in
many, fine parallel lines, running lengthwise on the top. When
nobody was with the babies, they would converse, small as they
were. Once again, when their mother had gone out, and they were
lying all alone, they rolled over on their stomachs, and hurriedly
counted the rows of embroidery on their pillows. 7. But they found
that they were just alike. Then one said, "Well, *Ža'ta*, I guess when
your father[1] said, that time, that he would love us both, without
preference, he really meant it; for they have caused us to own
pillows of equal[2] value." It was Little *Ža'ta* who made this remark.
Once again they were alone when a dog entered the tipi and dived into

*hiyu'ya c'ąke' wa'k'inicapi-waśte`ka nake' — hą'ta[3] yo'! — eya'-hįg.la
i'c'ipahaha hiyu'pi ną ehaś tukte' uma' t'oka'heya kį slolya'piśni
śk'e'e. 5. Wana' owi'c'aupapi ną ĥpa'yapi yuk'ą' ate'yapi kį t'ima'
hiyu' ną wąwi'c'ag.lakį ną leya' śk'e'e, — Ho, eya' c'į`kś, u'maśika
tk'a' e'l maya'hipi c'a ųg.na' maya'luc'ąte śi'capi kį lo'. Ową'żila
u'śikic'ilaya u' po'. Nup'į' a'k'iyec'el t'ec'i'ĥilape lo', — eya'·śk'e'e.
6. P'o'śtą[4] u' owi'c'aupapi k'e'yaś nup'į' a'k'iyec'eca śk'e'e. Ną
ehą'ni ipa'hį k'eya' ĝuhe'ya ipa't'api c'a he'c'a k'inų'k'ą ipa'ĥiwi-
c'ak'iyapi śk'e'e. Yuk'ą' tohą'l tuwe'ni t'ima' yąke'śni c'ą'śna hį'śko-
pila k'e'yaś wo'g.lakahąpi śk'e'e. Ak'e' hų'kupi kį t'ąka'l iya'ya
c'ąke' iśna'la ĥpa'yapi yuk'ą' paptą'yą iĥpe'ic'iyapi ną k'inų'k'ą
ipa'hi kį to'na-ipa't'api he'cįhą hena' ina'ĥni-g.lawa`pi śk'e'e.
7. K'e'yaś nup'į' a'k'iyenakecaĥcį o'hiye kį yuka' śk'e'e. Yuk'ą', —
Żata`, ehą'k'ų niya'te[5] a'k'iyecel t'eu'ĥilapikta ke'ye' u he'c'eya'-
heye`lak'a ipa'hį kį e'l p'ahį' a'k'iyenaknakeca[6] yuha'uk'iyape lo', —
Ża'ta-Cik'aka eci'yapi kį e' c'a eya' śk'e'e. Ak'e' iśna'la ĥpa'yapi
ĥcehą'l śų'ka wą t'i'l hiyu' ną wo'kap'e wą yub.le'l waka'p'api ożu'la*

[1] The twin-spirits say "your father" and "your mother" when speaking to
each other, concerning their common parent.
[2] They are always suspicious; looking for a slight indication that one of
them is being discriminated against. They want to find something as an
excuse for going away again, by dying.
[3] *hą'ta yo'!* "watch out! get away (for your own safety.)"
[4] *p'o'śtą*, beaded cradles into which infants were strapped.
[5] Your father. Instead of saying "father," or "our father," a twin is reputed
to say this, when speaking to his twin-brother of their common father.
[6] *a'k'iyenakeca*, the same, as to number. This generally reduplicates as
ak'i'yenakelkeca; rather than in the form used here.

13*

a rawhide container[1] which lay open, full of pounded meat. 8. When
this happened, Big Ža'ta saw it first and said, "Hey, Ža'ta, hit that
dog, for your mother; it will eat up all her food." Little Ža'ta
replied, "Hoħ! Do it yourself. You are closer to it." So Big Ža'ta
sprang up, and with a stick he struck the dog many times, and sent
it howling out of the room. 9. Their mother ran in, but by then the
twin had jumped back into his bed, so she called, "Mother, there's
nobody here, yet that dog howled so!" Forthwith, the twins' grandmother came in saying, "It might be a snake; and right here, where
my grandchildren are lying, too!" and she looked all about but
there was no snake. 10. Again, when their mother was going out for
a little while, she did not realize that the fire in the centre was
smoldering; so, after a time, the wind changed, blowing directly in,
and blew up the smoke which so filled the room that the twins were
almost suffocated. They could hardly breathe, so they crawled in
back of the screens or backrests, behind the beds, and thrust their
heads outside, under the tipi, between the pegs. Thus they lay,
bodies indoors and heads outside, and chatted contentedly, when
their mother returned; but they stayed there, not hearing her come
in. 11. So she said, "Well, well, did my poor little sons almost choke
to death from the smoke!" and she took them up while the grandmother busily rearranged the poles outside which hoisted up the

yąka' yųk'ą' iya'ħpaya šk'e'ᵉ. 8. Yųk'ą' Ža'ta-T'ąka t'oke'ya wąya'kį
ną, — Wą, Žata`, nihų'² aki'cip'a yo'. Wat'e'pk'iyįkte lo', — eya'
šk'e'ᵉ. Yųk'ą' Ža'ta-Cik'aka, — Hoħ, niye's ec'a'nų šni; niye's
ik'i'yela nųke' cį, — eya' c'ąke' Ža'ta-T'ąka ina'žį ną c'ą' wą ų'
sų'ka k'ų kab.lo'b.lo ną kaši'cahowaya k'ig.le'ya šk'e'ᵉ. 9. C'ąke'
hų'kupi k'ų t'ima' g.licu' k'e'yaš wana' ehą'ni oyų'keta k'iyų'ka
c'ąke', — Ina`, tuwe'nišni šk'a³ he'c'eħcį howa'ye', — eya' c'ąke'
c'ekpa' kį k'ų'šitkupi kį hiyu' ną, — Zuze'ca se'ce le', mit'a'koža le'l
ħpa'yapi k'ų, — eyį' ną a'taya ole'pi k'e'yaš ta'kunišni šk'e'ᵉ.
10. Ak'e' hų'kupi kį to'k'i iya'ya yųk'ą' p'e'ta kį oi'zitahe šą' he'c'ena
iya'ya c'ąke' t'ate'-kaho'm.ni ną t'iyo'pa kį a'tayela uya' c'ąke'
t'iyo'šota ną c'ekpa' k'ų ošo'ta-t'apikte s'e le'c'eca šk'e'ᵉ. Li'la oni'ya-
ši'capi c'ąke' uħna'ħ-kaška'pi kį ila'zata wihu'ta kį etą'hą p'a'
pat'ą'kal iye'ya ħpa'yapi ną wo'g.lakahąpi hą'l hų'kupi kį t'ima'
g.licu' k'e'yaš naħ'ų'šni he'c'el ħpa'yahąpi šk'e'ᵉ. 11. Yųk'ą', —
Hinų', ųšika mic'į'kši to'hįni ošo'tamakit'apila tk'a' ye le'! — eyį'
ną iwi'c'akikcu c'ąke' k'ohą' k'ų'šitkupi kį wip'a' kį ec'e'kc'e ipa'ha

[1] This was generally made of the hide from the head of the buffalo, leaving
the head and face part intact. It was then shaped like a large pan, and
used for pounding the meat for pemmican. The eye and nostril holes were
sewed up.
[2] nihų', your mother. See note 5, page 195.
[3] šk'a, yet; but. This has the same force as k'e'yaš.

wind-flaps of the tipi. So, very soon, the smoke cleared away and
once more breathing was possible. In such a way, always, as one
might say, "*Ahą'!*"[1], they guarded the children, so that they both
grew up, and were very handsome youths. But they had one
disadvantage — they smelled of porcupine[2], like white men.
12. Now, in the land from which they came, there was a good
remedy for this, and the boys knew it. So at the next buffalo hunt,
when there was meat in abundance, they went to their mother and
said to her, "Mother, please give us the fat from two ruminant
intestines." She said, "Why sons, what do you want with it?"
and they told her. "O, nothing much. We just wish to doctor
ourselves," they replied. 13. So she gave them the fat, peeling it off
from the intestines, and with it they went away from camp. Where
there was nobody, they built a fire and piled wood on it; and when
that died down, they threw the fat over the live coals so that it
smoked profusely. They sat one on either side of the fire, causing
the smoke to play over them, and then that odor they had was
killed. That is all.

---

*e'g.le śk'e'e; c'ąke' ec'a'lahci śo'ta ki kaska' iya'yi ną ak'e' t'ima'hel
oni'ya-waśte' śk'e'e. He'c'el i'żehą — Ahą'! — eya'pi s'e ece'-wic'a'yuhapi c'ąke' nup'i' ic'a'ġapi ną wana' k'ośka'lakapi k'e'yaś li'la
ową'yak-waśte'śtepi śk'e'e. Akśa'ka li'la waśi'cu s'e p'ahi'-m.napi
śk'e'e. 12. Yuk'ą' mak'o'c'e wą ec'i'yatąhą hi'pi k'u he'c'i p'eżu'ta
wą he' ta'ku ki owa'śte-slolya'pi c'ąke' wana'sapi ną t'alo' o'ta hą'l
hu'kupi ki el i'pi ną leya'pi śk'e'e, — Ina', t'aśu'pa-waśi' nu'p
uk'u'pi ye', — eya'pi c'ąke', — C'iks, hena' to'k'anupikta he'? —
eya' yuk'ą', Ża'ta-Cik'ala ayu'pti ną, — I'śe' ap'i'ukic'iyapikte lo',
— eya' śk'e'e. 13. C'ąke' wana' he'c'a-waśi k'eya'-wawi'c'akihlayi ną
wic'a'k'u c'ąke' yuha' mani'l i'pi śk'e'e. T'uwe'ni u'śni wą ekta'
c'et'i'pi ną o'ta el au'pi ną wana' iya'sni tk'a'ś hehą'l waśi' k'u hena'
el au'pi c'ąke' li'la izi'ta śk'e'e. C'ąke' p'e'ta ki anu'k yąka'pi ną
azi'l-'ic'iyahąpi yuk'ą' p'ahi'-m.napi k'u he' aki'snipi śk'e'e. Hehą'-
yela owi'hąke'e.*

---

[1] "*Ahą'!*" is equivalent to "Watch it!" "Careful!" or any similar warning.
Used by both sexes.
[2] The full-blood Dakotas as a group are remarkably free from the odor of
perspiration of the armpits. The contrast between them and White people,
and even Dakotas with a White strain, is so striking that they call, in
common speech, "*a' ozi'*" anyone with white blood, whether they individually give out that odor or not; *a*, armpit; *o*, in; *zi* yellow. The odor is
singularly repulsive to Dakotas. Of course there is a more dignified term
for Dakotas with a White strain: *Waśi'cu-C'ica'*, Children of the White
people. They call this odor the porcupine smell.

39. The Boy with Buffalo Power.

1. An old woman lived alone with her grandchild. The people were in winter camp[1] along the creek, and these two lived near by. It was a winter of famine so they kept alive by the old woman picking wild rose berries and making a stew of them[2]. 2. To add to the misery of lack of food, it snowed steadily for ten days and the very deep snow was terrible. And the boy said to his grandmother, "Grandmother, make me a hoop of rawhide, and when you finish it, then a bow and some arrows; and when you finish those, paint them carefully with red clay paint[3]." 3. So the old woman said, "What a request at such a time as this!" Then she thought, "Well, he must have some reason; else he would not ask this; I better just do as he orders." So she took a bag of smoke-tanned rawhide, and soaked it and made the hoop; then she made a bow and arrows, and painted them red. 4. Then she said, "Now, grandson, I have made the things as you wished them," and he said, "Very well, grandmother. Now, take all your knives and sharpen them and then sweep away the snow from the doorway, leaving a clear path." —

---

1. Winų'ĥcala wą t'ako'żakpaku kic'i'la t'i' śk'e'ᵉ. Wakpa'la wą op'a'ya oya'te kį wani't'ipi c'ąke' ik'i'yela kaĥmi' wą ekta' c'ąma'hel heni'yos t'i'pi śk'e'ᵉ. Yųk'ą' wani'yetu kį he' li'la wic'a'akiĥ'ą c'ąke' winų'ĥcala kį ųżį'żįtka yuża' c'ą yu'tapi ną ece'la ų' ni' yąka'pi śk'e'ᵉ. 2. Wo'yute wani'ce cį ic'ų'hą wikce'm.nac'ą ica'm.na ną waśma' c'ąke' ot'e'ĥika śk'e'ᵉ. Yųk'ą' hokśi'la k'ų he' k'ų'śitku kį leci'ya śk'e'ᵉ, — Ųci`, t'ahu'ka-c'ąg.le'śka wążi' mi'caga yo', ną he' luśtą' kįhą hehą'l ita'zipa wążi' wąhį'kpe k'o'ya mi'caga yo', ną hena' luśtą' kįhą tąye'ĥcį śaya' yo', — eya' śk'e'ᵉ. 3. C'ąke', — Tulá, t'ako'ża, waśma'-ot'e'ĥi k'ų ec'ą'l! — eye' śą ak'e', — Eya' to'k'aye-lak'a'ś t'ako'ża he'c'el wama'śi kį, it'o' we'cagįkte, — ec'į' ną wizi'p'ą wą ĥpąyį' ną t'ahu'ka-c'ąg.le'śka wą kiyu'śtą, ną hehą'l ita'zipa wą, wąhį'kpe k'o' he'c'el yuśtą' ną hena' tąye'la śaya' śk'e'ᵉ. 4. He'c'ų ną, — Ho', t'ako'ża, wana' iyu'ha ec'e'l b.luśtą' ye' — eya' yųk'ą', — Ho, he'c'etu we lo', ųci`, — eya' śk'e'ᵉ. Ak'e'ś, — Ho, ųci`, mi'la to'na luha' he'cįhą hena' iyu'ha g.lumį' ną hehą'l t'iyo'pa kį e'l og.na' ot'ą'kaya kahį'l e'g.le yo', — eya' c'ąke', — Takú, mahų'keśni[4] kų,

---

[1] A winter camp is made by first staking the tipi down to stay for the winter; then inserting a lining of skin around the inside, between the tent and the poles. This is generally about five feet high, and insures added warmth. Then a shelter is set up by interlacing willows, set into the ground, all around the tipi except in front. The space around, inside this shelter, is circular, of course, and about eight or ten feet in width.

[2] Wild rose berries are a common food, disdained except during famines. It is considered one of the humblest of foods.

[3] Red clay paint denotes that a thing is being set apart, consecrated, for religious use.

[4] hų'keśni, to be weak; feeble; slow, as in running.

"Of all things, grandson, I haven't the energy for that!" but he said, "No, grandmother; only do as I ask." 5. So she swept the snow and left a clear path in the doorway and then the boy stood up with his bow and arrows and said, "Grandmother, say, 'Grandson, there goes a fat buffalo!' and roll the hoop towards me." So she did it, and as the boy stood ready, he shot the hoop when it rolled toward him from his grandmother's hand; and a buffalo staggered and fell dead. 6. So the old woman went eagerly at the task of cutting it up and soon had it all cared for. Then the boy said, "Do the same thing again, grandmother." So once again, "Grandson, there goes a fat buffalo!" she said as she rolled the hoop toward the boy, and again the boy shot through it. 7. And a buffalo went staggering forward and fell dead. So once more the old woman took care of all the meat and finished cutting it for drying. Just as I have described it, this was done four times, and then the boy was satisfied. Then he said, "Now grandmother, take some pemmican[1] and dried meat on your back in a pack, and carry it to that chief who has the two daughters, and say: '*Oma'wahitų*[2], my grandson bids me bring this food'. Slide it inside the tipi and come away." 8. So the grandmother took the food as instructed, and

---

tⁱako`ža, — eya' yųkⁱą' — Hiya`, ųciˋ, ini'la kⁱeṡ ecⁱe'l ecⁱų' wo', — eya' ayu'pta ṡkⁱeᵉ. 5. Cⁱąke' tⁱiyo'pa o'ṡtą kahį'l yuṡtą' yųkⁱą' hokṡi'la kį wąhį'kpe g.luha' ina'žį ną, — Ho, ųciˋ, leya' yo': Tⁱako`ža, pte' wą cⁱe'peȟca cⁱa he g.le', eyį' ną tⁱahu'ka-cⁱąg.leˋṡka kį pacⁱą'-g.leya hiyu'ya yo', —eya' cⁱąke' eⁱce'l eya'-hįg.la pacⁱą'g.leya hiyu'ya yųkⁱą' hokṡi'la kⁱų wąhį'kpe g.luha' wį'yeya na'žį cⁱąke' g.lakį'yą³ o' keᵉ. Heⁱcⁱena pte' wą kⁱiȟpa'yį ną tⁱa' ṡkⁱeᵉ. 6. Cⁱąke' winų'ȟcala kⁱų pⁱa'l iyą'kį ną kab.la' ną a'taya yuṡtą' ṡkⁱeᵉ. Yųkⁱą' akⁱe' hokṡi'la kⁱų, — Ho, ųciˋ, akⁱe' ecⁱe'ȟcį ecⁱų' wo', — eya' cⁱąke' akⁱe' — Ho, tⁱako`ža, pte' wą cⁱe'pa cⁱa he g.le', — eya'-hįg.la cⁱąg.le'ṡka kⁱų he' pacⁱą'g.leya hiyu'ya yųkⁱą' akⁱe' hokṡi'la kⁱų g.lakį'yą o' ṡkⁱeᵉ. 7. O yųkⁱą' pte' wą kace'kcek yį' ną hąke'ya tⁱa' g.liȟpa'ya ṡkⁱeᵉ. Cⁱąke' akⁱe' winų'ȟcala kⁱų tⁱalo' kⁱicⁱą'yąpi ece' ecⁱų' ną a'taya yuṡtą' ṡkⁱeᵉ. To'pa-akⁱig.le ob.la'ke cį leⁱcⁱų s'e ecⁱų'pi ną wana' pte' to'p wicⁱa'o yųkⁱą' hehą'l ayu'ṡtą ṡkⁱeᵉ. Yųkⁱą' hehą'l hokṡi'la kį heya' ṡkⁱeᵉ, — Ho, ųciˋ, wasna' ną pa'pa kⁱo' kⁱį' ną wicⁱo'tⁱita wicⁱa'ṡa itⁱą'cⁱą wą cⁱųwį'tku nų'pa cⁱa tⁱi' kį he' e'l yį' ną leⁱcⁱel eya' yo', Omaˋwahitⁱų, lena' mitⁱa'koža au'maṡi cⁱa awa'u we', eya' yo'. Ną patⁱi'ma iye'yį ną g.licu' wo', — eya' ṡkⁱeᵉ. 8. Cⁱąke' ecⁱe'kcⁱe kⁱį' ną

---

[1] Pemmican, already described, is the choicest food to take to another and is a mark of honor to be either the donor or the recipient.

[2] This is a term of direct address, used regardless of sex, between the parents, aunts, uncles and grandparents of a person, when speaking either of or to that person's spouse's parents, uncles, aunts and grandparents.

[3] *g.lakį'yą*, across; at right angles to the direction in which a person is going; in this case, the arrow pierces the body horizontally.

carried the pack on her back, and in spite of the deep snow which
made walking difficult, she went to the tipi specified; and saying
what her grandson had advised her to say, she pushed the food into
the tipi, and went home. They were too surprised to speak, but when
they looked out they saw the old woman who lived down the bend
with her grandson, just as she walked away. 9. At once men and
women from here and there were invited in and when they ate the
food which had been brought, they marvelled. "How in the world..!"
they said. When the old woman got home, the boy said, "Now
grandmother, do again just what you did according to my instructions." So the old woman carried more pemmican and the choicest
of dried meat to the chief's home, where the two daughters lived,
and said, "*Oma'wahitu̥*, my grandson bids me bring this food." And
she pushed it into the tipi; they took it and asked, "How did you
come by this, that you can bring it ?" So the old woman said, "Next
time I come, I shall tell why I do this." 10. She said to her grandson,
"They questioned me in such a manner, and this is how I replied."
So, "In that case, grandmother, take more food and repeat what
you have been doing. And you shall say, 'My grandson wished to
marry your elder daughter; that is why he bids me bring this food'."
11. So, once more she carried pemmican and dried meat in great
abundance, walking with difficulty through the deep snow; and

*wana' wašma' c'a oo'mani-t'eħi`ke c'e'yaš ya'hi̥ nḁ t'i'pi wḁ k'e' c'u̥
e'l t'iyo'pa paǧḁ' nḁ, — Oma`wahit'u̥, mit'a'koža lena' au'maši c'a
awa'u we'! — eyi̥' nḁ wo'yute wani`ce c'u̥ ec'ḁ'l wasna' nḁ pa'pa k'o'
ec'a'šni s'e pat'i'mahel iye'yi̥ nḁ k'ig.la' šk'e'ᵉ. Eha's yuš'i̥'yayapi
u̥' ta'keyapišni k'e'yaš t'ḁka'takiya e'tu̥wḁpi yu̥k'ḁ' wana' winu̥'-
ħcalala¹ wḁ kaħmi'ta t'ako'žakpaku kic'i'la t'i'la yu̥k'ḁ' he e' c'a
ak'o'kiya g.la'hḁ šk'e'ᵉ. 9. Wḁ'cag.na wic'a'ša nḁ wi̥'yḁ k'o' ena'na
wic'a'kic'opi c'ḁke' wo'yute k'eya' ahi'pi k'u̥ hena' yu'tapi nḁ li'la
ini'hḁpi šk'e'ᵉ. — To'k'ešk'e! — eya'hḁpi šk'e'ᵉ. T'iya'ta k'i' yu̥k'ḁ'
hokši'la ki̥ heya' šk'e'ᵉ, — Ho, u̥ci`, ak'e' to'k'ešk'e ec'u̥'c'iši k'u̥
he'c'eħci̥ ec'u̥' wo', — eya' c'ḁke' winu̥'ħcala k'u̥ wasna'· nḁ pa'pa-
wašte`ħca k'o'ya k'i̥' nḁ wic'a'ša it'ḁ'c'ḁ wḁ c'u̥wi̥'tku nu̥'pa k'u̥ he'
t'i' ki̥ ekta' i' nḁ, — Oma`wahit'u̥, mit'a'koža lena' au'maši ye',
eyi̥' nḁ wo'yute ki̥ pat'i'mahel iye'ya c'ḁke' icu'pi nḁ —Lena' to'k'ešk'e
luha'pi nḁ le'c'anu̥hḁ he? — eya'pi yu̥k'ḁ', — To'kša' inu̥'pa-wahi̥'
ki̥hḁ ta'k'ole'-le`c'amu̥he ci̥ naya'ħ'u̥pikte', — eyi̥' nḁ k'ig.la' šk'e'ᵉ.
10. T'iya'ta k'i' nḁ t'ako'žakpaku ki̥ oki'yaka šk'e'ᵉ, — T'ako`ža,
ka'k'el wi'mayu̥ǵapi c'ḁke' mi'š le'c'el ep'e', — eyi̥' nḁ oki'yaka
yu̥k'ḁ', — Ho, ec'a, u̥ci`, ak'e' iye'c'el ec'u̥' wo'. Nḁ ini'yu̥ǵapi ki̥hḁ
lehi̥'kte lo': Mit'a'koža nic'u̥'wi̥tkupi-t'oka`p'a ki̥ he' yu'zi̥kta c'i̥' nḁ
he'c'u̥maši ye', ehi̥'kte lo', — eya' šk'e'ᵉ. 11. C'ḁke' k'u̥'šitkula k'u̥*

---

¹ *winu̥'ħcala*, old woman; the added *la* is a bid for the sympathy of the
hearers. If a witch were under discussion, we should never have it.

when she pushed the food into the tipi they asked her the reason; so she said what her grandson had instructed her to say. They replied, "Wait till we think this through and you shall hear." So she went home and, "What did they say, grandmother ?" he asked. 12. So she said, "Grandson, this;" and she related what they had said. Then, soon after, at his request she took more food. As she was pushing the food in, they invited her to enter, so she went in and sat down, and the man said, "Now, tell this, 'My daughter shall marry the young man who has been giving us food.'" At once the young woman broke out in anger: "Not *me!* It is I who loathe One-who-Lives-with-his-Grandmother[1]! 13. "Younger sister, do you marry him!" So the girl cried and objected, but they decided that the younger daughter should marry the boy. They placed a tipi within the camp circle, and invited the boy there and when he came, he took his wife first to the little old shelter of smoke-tanned tipiskin which had been his home. 14. And back home, the elder one kept saying, "I wonder how she who married One-who-Lives-with-his-Grandmother and went off with him, is getting on!" And she would laugh ironically. But, they say, the young girl who had

wana' ak'e' pa'pa ną wasna' k'o' ośų'kye k'į' ną wayu'hli[2] ya'hį ną wic'a'śa it'ą'c'ą wą t'i' k'ų he'c'iya i' ną wo'yute ai' k'ų hena' pat'i'ma iye'ya yųk'ą' iyų'ġapi c'ąke' to'k'el eye'śi k'ų ec'e'hcį eya' śk'e'ᵉ. Yųk'ą', — Ho, to'kśa' wae'he cį le' ų' to'k'el wi'ųyukcąpi kį naya'k'ųkte lo', — eya'pi c'ąke' he'c'ena g.licu' ną t'iya'ta g.li' yųk'ą', — Ųci`, ta'keyapi huwo'? — eya' śk'e'ᵉ, hokśi'la kį. 12. C'ąke', — T'ako`źa, leya'pe', — eyį' ną ta'keyapi k'ų hena' oki'yaka yųk'ą' he'c'etula ke'yį' ną ak'e' i'yec'ala wo'ayeśi c'ąke' wasna' pa'pa k'o' ai' śk'e'ᵉ. T'ima' wo'yute kį iye'ya yųk'ą' kic'o'pi c'ąke' t'ima' iya'yį ną i'yotaka yųk'ą' — Ho', oya'ka yo'. Mic'ų'kśi k'ośka'laka wą wo'ųk'upi kį he' hįg.na'yįkte lo', — wic'a'śa it'ą'c'ą kį eya' yųk'ą' wik'o'śkalaka kį — E'ktą'ś miye'lahcį[3], miye'ś K'ų'śitku-Kic'i'-T'i'la wahte'walaśni k'ų. 13. Mit'ą`, niye'ś kic'i' ų' we'! — eya' c'ąke' li'la t'ąka'ku kį wica'laśni ną c'e'ya ų' k'e'yaś haka'kta kį he' hįg.na'yįkta ke'ya'-yuśtą`pi śk'e'ᵉ. T'i'pi wą c'oka'p it'i'caġapi ną hokśi'la k'ų he' e'l kic'o'pi c'ąke' wana' ekta' hi' ną t'awi'cu kį kic'i' wizi'la wą ot'i' k'ų he'c'iya t'oke'ya k'i'pi śk'e'ᵉ. 14. Yųk'ą' t'iya'ta t'oka'p'a k'ų he' e' c'a — K'ų'śitku-Kic'i'-T'i'la hįg.na'yį ną to'k'iya iya'ye c'ų lehą'l to'k'eśk'e yąka'he cį — eyį' nąśna iha't'ahą śk'e'ᵉ. K'e'yaś

---

[1] This is generally a name of derision, which becomes one of honor, or is discarded later, for a grander name, because of some deed meriting the change.

[2] *wa,* snow; *yu,* with the hands; *hli,* anything the consistency of which is such that it falls away. This means she fell from time to time in the snow, and helped herself up, with her hands. *kahli',* would be, to be mired in deep snow.

[3] *miye',* I. *lahcį,* added, gives the force, "Why me, of all people ?"

married, was very kind to her husband, and showed him respect. And after four days had past, the couple were sent for, that the boy might come to his wife's people to live in the *rôle* of son-in-law. They were to live in the tipi placed within the circle. 15. And the man said, "Go home alone, and wait for me; I shall be there sometime during the night." So the girl went home alone. And her elder sister greeted her with sarcasm, "Why doesn't she stay away and keep on living in her *rôle* of daughter-in-law; who wants them here that she should bring One-who-Lives-with-his-Grandmother here?" 16. Her mother said, "Why do you keep talking like that? Don't be saying this against your sister's marriage." But she answered, "My younger sister's husband sickens me!" and she pretended to vomit. 17. It was night, so the wife lay in her tipi awaiting the coming of her husband, and towards dawn she heard, throughout the camp, a whistle like that of the elk, one from each of the four directions; and as she lay listening, soon someone entered; and when she looked at him, she saw a very handsome man, with a very sweet odor about him, and as he started towards the place of honor, she looked again, and saw an elk, with its horns branching out and filling the center of the tipi. 18. Again he turned into a man; and then she saw that One-who-Lives-with-his-Grandmother had transformed himself; and when morning came, she found herself with

wiha'kaktala[1] *wą hįg.na't'ų k'ų he' li'la wic'a'śa aho'kip'ela śk'e'ᵉ. Yųk'ą' wana' to'pac'ą c'ąke' i'ś hehą'l wic'a'śa kį wic'a'woħa-ukta wą og.na' wic'a'hiyoipi śk'e'ᵉ. C'oka'p t'i'pi wą e'g.lepi kį he'tu c'a. 15. Yųk'ą' wic'a'śa kį leya' śk'e'ᵉ, — Niśna'la ekta' g.nį' ną ec'a'ś hąhe'pi t'ahe'na wai'kta c'e iya'makip'e yo', — eya' c'ąke' iśna'la k'i' śk'e'ᵉ. K'i' yųk'ą' c'uwe'ku k'ų, — Ekta'ni k'eś wiwo'ħa-ų śni, K'ų'śitku-Kic'i-T'i'la le'l wic'a'woħa-aku we! — eya'ya li'la ikca'pta śk'e'ᵉ. 16. C'ąke' hų'ku k'ų, — Ta'ku le' yak'a' c'a! Nit'ą'-kala hįg.na't'ų kį e'l ho'yeyeśniye', — eya' yųk'ą', — Mit'ą' hįg.na'kula kį li'la wag.la'ħce! — eyį' ną g.le'g.lep-kųza śk'e'ᵉ. 17. Wana' hąhe'pi c'ąke' wį'yą kį hįg.na'ku g.li'kta-aki'p'e ħpa'yahą yųk'ą' ą'pao'-ec'i'yatąhą wic'o't'i kį e'g.na t'ati'ye to'pa kį iyo'hila ekta' heħa'k-t'aśi'yot'ąka wą yaźo'pi c'a naħ'ų' ħpa'yahą yųk'ą' i'yec'ala tuwa' t'ima'hel hiyu' c'ąke' ayu'ta yųk'ą' k'ośka'laka wą li'la waśte'-m.na ną ową'yak-waśte' c'a t'ima' hiyu' ną c'atku' kį ekta' hiyu' c'ąke' i'naħma s'e p'iya'-ayu'ta yųk'ą' t'ic'o'ka kį e'l heħa'ka wą ona'ħa s'e na'źį c'a wąya'ka śk'e'ᵉ. 18. Ak'e' kiwi'c'aśa-ikce'ka yųk'ą' k'ų'śitku kic'i' t'i' k'ų he' e c'a ig.lu't'okeca c'a wic'a'śa wa iħą'keya' ową'yak-waśte' kic'i' ayą'pa*[2] *śk'e'ᵉ. He'c'eś i'pi'lap'ika*[3] *ec'ą'kipi k'ų eha'ś*

---

[1] *haka'kta*, youngest; *la*, again a bid for sympathy; for being youngest is not such an honorable rank, yet, according to the narrator, we must like this girl for her obedience to her parents.

[2] *ayą'pa*, it becomes day over him, is the Dakota way of saying, "daylight found him".

[3] *ip'i'la*, to withhold, as too good for one. *ip'i'lap'ika*, of such kind as to be considered too good for him.

a very handsome young man. So, though people thought at first
that he was not good enough for her, yet here he was, a most
attractive man, with whom the younger daughter met the dawn.
As the sun was rising, the father himself stood outside the tipi and
said[1], "Now, daughter, if you are up, your mother has finished
cooking that my son-in-law may eat. So come!" 19. What really
took place was that they prepared the food and the mother said,
"Take this to your brother-in-law that he may eat," but the elder
sister refused to take the food, saying, "I am not living so that I may
take food to One-who-Lives-with-his-Grandmother!" and she did
not stir, until her father had to come himself. 20. So the last-born
girl came out and entered her mother's tipi and said, "Mother, last
night towards dawn the boy I married came into the tipi, and a
very handsome and sweeting-smelling man walked toward the place of
honor, so I looked stealthily at him and he was an elk whose antlers
filled the centre of the tipi, and again he was a man. And this
morning he is a transformed man, and I have the handsomest husband in the world." 21. The moment she spoke, "*It'o'*[2]," the elder
sister murmured and rushed out, and entered her sister's tipi where

wic'a'ṡa wą ḣopya'kel wiha'kakta k'ų kic'i' ayą'pa ṡk'e'ᵉ. Wana' wi'
u' yųk'ą' atku'kula kį iye' iyų'k'ala t'ąka'l hina'ži ną, — Ho, c'ų`kṡ,
wana' ye'kta he'cįhą mit'a'koṡ wo'tįkta c'a nihų' wo'hą yuṡtą' ye,
hiyu' wo', — eya' ṡk'e'ᵉ. 19. Leyalaka he' t'oka'p'a kį k'a'pi ną, —
Niṡi'c'e wo'tįkte, lena' kaa'ya'[3], — eya'pi yųk'ą', —Tase' le' k'ų'ṡitku
kic'i' t'i'la wąži' wo'wakam.nįkta c'a wau' ka c'aṡ! — eyį' ną ini'hąṡni
yąka'hą c'ąke' he' u' wic'a'ḣcala kį iye' iyų'k'ala hi' ṡk'e'ᵉ. 20. C'ąke'
wiha'kakta k'ų hina'p'į ną hų'ku t'i'pi kį t'ima' iya'yį ną leya' ṡk'e'ᵉ,
— Ina`, hokṡi'la wą hįg.na'waye c'ų hąhe'pi a'pao'-wahe'hal t'i'l
hiyu' yųk'ą' k'oṡka'laka wą ową'yak-waṡte` ną ec'e'ya waṡte'm.na c'a
c'atku'takiya u' c'ąke' i'naḣma ṡ'e ab.lu'ta yųk'ą' t'ic'o'ka kį ožu'la
heḣa'ka wą ona'ḣa ṡ'e na'žį ną ak'e' wic'a'ṡa ye'. Yųk'ą' ą'pao' kį e'l
ig.lu't'okeca c'a k'oṡka'laka wą ihą'keya waṡte' hįg.na'waye', — eya'
ṡk'e'ᵉ. 21. Ka'k'el heye' c'ų he'c'eg.la, — It'o', — c'uwe'ku kį eyį' ną

---

[1] This scene is very characteristic. The father or mother would never enter
but call softly, outside the door, to their daughter and speak of their son-
in-law with highest respect; but not directly to him. Normally, it is the
sister-in-law's place to enter, and indulge in banter and small talk while
the brother-in-law and sister eat the food she brings; because she and he
are in joking relation.

[2] *it'o'* I have translated as, "I think I'll do so and so", or "I guess I'll go
there", etc. and that is close enough, when *it'o'* begins a sentence that is
completed. But when said alone, generally under the breath, it is a sort of
murmured apology for making a sudden move. It is employed to assure
those present that there is nothing important the matter. "I'll just step
out a moment."

[3] *au'*, to bring here; *kau'*, to bring here to someone; but *a'ya*, to take there;
.*kaa'ya*, to take there for someone. In other words, no contraction occurs
in the latter case.

the handsome young man sat; suddenly changing her attitude, she
sat down beside the one she had despised only recently, and clasp-
ing him about his neck, she would not give him up. So the younger
sister, who, having married him properly, had prior right, stood
outside, restless[1]. 22. The father said, "No, daughter, come away.
That is your younger sister's husband. Why, he is the one you
rejected when he wanted you!" And the mother added her words,
but still she sat and would not release the man. 23. This young man
later demonstrated that he was very powerful in a supernatural way.
When things looked hopeless, and the people were dying for want
of food, this is what he said, "Take all the fur robes you have, and
remove all the hair, and scatter it as extensively as you can, back,
away from camp. Do not go there for four days." 24. They did so,
and on the fourth day, they sent scouts to look around, and they
found the prairies crowded with buffaloes. When they reported this
at home, and the people prepared to go out for a hunt, he said,
"See that nobody brings home the heads, the four feet and the tail
of any animal." They observed this order. 25. The tribe named him
Sacred Boy. And whenever the people were suffering from want,
and appealed to him, he helped them. Because of this, he was
highly esteemed. He was the first, too, they say, who made the

ina'p‘į ną t‘ąka'ku t‘i' kį ekta' iya'ya yųk‘ą' k‘ośka'laka wą ħopya'kel
yąka' c‘ąke' na'k e'ś he' waħte'laśni yuk‘ą' nake' isa'k‘ip i'yotakį ną
p‘o'skil yu's akśi'źa c‘ąke' t‘ąka'ku k‘ų iye'ś he' otą'-ħig.naye c‘ų
e'ha' t‘ąka'l ona'tąyą¹ ų' śk‘e‘ᵉ. 22. C‘ąke' atku'kula kį, — Hiya`,
c‘ų`kś, ħeya'p ec‘ų' wo'. Nit‘ą'kala he' ħig.na'ku we lo'. He'ś nila' ye'ś
waħte'yalaśni k‘ų, — eyį' ną hų'ku kį naku' ta'keyayake c‘e'yaś
ini'ħąśni akśi'ś ų' śk‘e‘ᵉ. 23. Ho, yųk‘ą' hokśi'la kį he' li'la wak‘ą'
c‘a ikpa'zo śk‘e‘ᵉ. Oya'te kį wic‘a'akiħ'ą c‘ąke' li'la oi'yokiśica ħą'tu
yųk‘ą' le'c‘el eya' śk‘e‘ᵉ, — Ho, pte-hį'śma to'na luha'pi he'cįhą hena'
hį' kį wasmi'smipi ną ħeya'ta tohą'yą-oya'kihipi oka'la oma'ni po'.
To'pac‘ą tuwe'ni ekta' la'pikteśni ye lo'. — eya' śk‘e‘ᵉ. 24. Wana'
ec‘ų'pi ną ito'pac‘ą k‘ų hą' ekta' tųwe'ya² k‘eya' iya'ħąpi yųk‘ą'
b.la'ye kį a'taya ok‘ą'śniyą pte' hiyo't‘įza śk‘e‘ᵉ. Hośi'g.lipi³ c‘ąke'
oya'te kį a'taya wana'se-yapikta yųk‘ą' le'c‘el eya' śk‘e‘ᵉ, — It‘o'
ptep‘a' ną siha' to'pa kį hena' t‘asį'ta kį k‘o'ya tuwe'ni aya'kupi-
kteśni ye lo', — eya' c‘ąke' naħ'ų'pi śk‘e‘ᵉ. 25. Hokśi'la-wak‘ą eya'-
c‘ażeyatapi ną tohą'l oya'te kį ta'ku ica'kiżapi ną ic‘e'kiyapi c‘ą'śna
iye'c‘el yue'c‘etu keya'pi‘ⁱ. He'c‘eca c‘ąke' li'la yuo'niħąpi śk‘e‘ᵉ.
Nakų' wo't‘awe ka'ġapi ną ų' oki'c‘ize ec‘ų'pi kį he' iye' t‘oka' ka'ġa

---

[1] Ona'tąyą, the word used in the text, carries with it the idea of restlessness
to the extent of pacing the floor, or rushing to and fro, as a caged beast.
Never still a moment, because of tense anxiety.

[2] tųwe'ya, to scout; to be a scout. tųwą', to open the eyes; look about; ya,
to go.

[3] hośi'', to carry news; g.lipi, they return. They came back to report.

medicine-bundles with which the people went to war. In many ways, this one who used to be called One-who-Lives-with-his-Grandmother demonstrated his supernatural ability. That is all.

40. A Pawnee Story of Aid Given by the Buffalo.

1. A few Pawnees were camped, away from the tribal centre, while a big famine was on. Away from this small camp, the little girls used to play out where the ground was bare of growth[1]. Though there was nobody about, suddenly there came a boy from somewhere. In his hand he had a piece of meat which the other children coveted very much. 2. They told the smallest girl to live with him[2], so she did, and in the evening, he said, "Go home now; for I too shall go." And he ran off. Three times in succession he did this, — coming to them at their play, and then in the evening sending them home, and going off himself. 3. On the fourth day, he brought a piece of fat with the meat, so the little girl who was his playmate secretly cut a piece off, and took it home. "Father, a boy comes from somewhere carrying a piece of meat; then we roast it and eat it as we play; and the last time he brought this piece of fat also."

śk'e'ᵉ. O'takiya K'ṷ'śitku-Kic'i'-T'i'la eci'yapi tk'a' k'ṷ eha'ś wo'wap'et'okya³ wo'wayup'ike⁴ yuha' śk'e'ᵉ. Hehą'yela owi'hąke'ᵉ.

40.

1. P'ala'ni co'nala ḣeya'ta t'i'pi k'e'yaś li'la wic'a'akiḣ'ą śk'e'ᵉ. Yṷk'ą' wic'i'cala to'nakel manį'l mak'o'śla⁵ wą ekta' śka't hąpi śk'e'ᵉ. Tuwe'niś ṷ'śni k'ṷ, ṷg.na' to'k'iyatąhą t'ąį'śniyą hokśi'la wą e'l wic'a'i śk'e'ᵉ. Napo'g.na t'alo' hąke' ec'a'śni s'e yuha' i' c'ąke' ṷma'-wak'aheża kį li'la as'į'pi⁶ śk'e'ᵉ. 2. Wic'i'cala kį wążi' c'i'k'ala c'a he' kic'i' t'iśi'pi c'ąke' kic'i' t'i' yṷk'ą' wana' ḣtaye'tu c'ąke', — Ho, wana' g.la' po'; mi'ś-'eya' wag.nį'kte lo', — eyį' ną mani'takiya į'yąk k'ig.la' śk'e'ᵉ. Ya'm.ni-ak'ig.le he'c'eḣcį śka'tapi kį ekta'śna i' ną ḣtaye'tu c'ą g.licu'wic'ayį ną i'ś mani'takiya ece'-k'ig.la śke'ᵉ. 3. Ito'pa-i yṷk'ą' t'alo' wą waśį' wą iya'yustak yuha' ak'e' i' c'ąke' wic'i'cala wą kic'i' t'iśi'pi k'ṷ he e' c'a hąke' naḣma'la yuksį' ną yuha' t'iya'ta k'i' ną — Ate`, hokśi'la wą to'k'iyatąhą eya'śna t'alo' yuha' hi' c'ą c'eṷ'k'ṷpapi ną yu'l ṷśka'tapi yṷk'ą' ak'e' waśį' kį le'

---

[1] Children, liked to play in those spots on the ground which were as smooth as a floor, and without a single blade of vegetation, because they then were sure no snakes or insects were around. Besides, such places are always circular, like a tipi, and well adapted to all kinds of games.

[2] When you are on the same side with another, in a game, you "live" with that person. He is your team mate, as against your opponents.

[3] *wa'p'et'okeca*, a sign; symbol; something with an inner significance.

[4] *wayu'p'ika*, to be skilled in.

[5] *mak'a'*, ground; *o*, in; *śla*, a bare spot; bereft of hair or grass or any sort of growth.

[6] *as'į'*, to want something very much that another is enjoying; especially food. *a*, on; *s'į*, to crane the neck.

she told her father. 4. "At what time does he leave to go home?"
he asked; so the daughter replied, "In the evening when it begins to
grow dark, he says: 'Go home, now,' and he too goes away." Then
the man instructed his daughter in this manner, "When he prepares
again to go home, say, 'Come home with me; haven't I married
you already?' and hold fast to him," he said. So they were at play;
he came and played with them, and in the evening he was about to
go; so she said what her father had instructed her to say. 5. And
she pulled him along home, but each time he tried to resist and
struggle, they heard a calf grunt, so it was awkward for him to
pull back too much; and thus the girl got him home. As they neared
the tipi, he relaxed, and then said, "Well then, tell them to burn
incense indoors. Then only will I come in," he said. So the girl went
in and said, 6. "Father he says he will only come in, if incense is
burnt," she said. So at once the father burned incense of sage and
cedar, in the place of honor, and there he laid gifts, scarlet flannel and
a piece of shell in the form of a disk, suitable for a necklace pendant.
7. Then the boy entered and sat in the seat of honor. He was willing
to remain now, and spend the night. In the morning he said, "Now
that I have taken this girl for my wife, I am going home." So they stood
watching as he came out of the tipi, and when he was receding into

---

k'o' yuha' hi' k'ų, — eya' śk'e⁾ᵉ. 4. — Tohą'l ece'-g.la huwo'? — eya'-
iyų̈'ga c'ąke' c'ųwįtku kį leya' śk'e⁾ᵉ, — Wana' ḣtaye'tu-iya`kpaza
c'ą, Ho, wana' g.la' po', eyį' nąśna i'ś-'eya' k'ig.le' c'ų, — eya' śk'e⁾ᵉ.
Yųk'ą' wic'a'śa kį le'c'el wic'į'cala kį iwa'hoya śk'e⁾ᵉ, — Ho, ak'e'
g.nį'kte cįhą leya' yo', He'c'eg.la c'aś hįg.na'c'iye, u' na, ųg.nį'kte,
eyį' ną yu's ų' wo', — eya' śk'e⁾ᵉ. C'ąke' wana' ak'e' śka'tapi yųk'ą'
e'l hi' ną o'p śka'tahį ną ḣtaye'tu c'ąke' g.nį'kta tk'a'ś yu's ų' ną
atku'ku wae'yeśi k'ų he'c'el eya' śk'e⁾ᵉ. 5. Heyį' ną yuce'kcek ag.la'
c'ą ig.lu'titą ną śkį'ciyįkta¹ k'eś iye'na ptehį'cala wą g.lo'g.lo c'ąke'
to'k'ani-śkį`ciyeśni ec'e'l t'iya'ta ak'i' śk'e⁾ᵉ. T'i'k'iyela g.la'pi
yųk'ą' hehą'l iyo'wįyą yį' ną heya' śk'e⁾ᵉ, — Ho, ec'a², t'ima' wazi'l-
yewic'aśi yo'. He'c'eca kįhą t'i'l wau'kte, — eya' c'ąke' wic'į'cala kį
t'ima' k'i' ną leya' śk'e⁾ᵉ, 6. — Ate`, wazi'lyapi hą'tąhąś ece'la u'kta
ke'ye', — eya' c'ąke' he'c'ena atku'ku kį c'ąc'ą' s'e³ wazi'lyį ną t'ic'a'tku
kį e'l p'eźi'-ḣota ną ḣąte' k'o' zilyį' ną yąkį'kte cį e'l a'taya p'eźi'-
ḣota owį'źapi ną he'l śina'-lu`ta, k'ąpe'ska-wana`p'į k'o' e'g.nakapi
śk'e⁾ᵉ. 7. Hehą'l hokśi'la k'ų t'ima' hiyu' ną c'atku'ta i'yotaka śk'e⁾ᵉ.
Hetą'hą wana' iyo'wįyą e'na ų' ną e'na ayą'pi śk'e⁾ᵉ. Ną hį'hąna
yųk'ą', — Ho, wana' le' b.lu'za c'a wag.nį'kte lo', — eya' c'ąke'
awą'yak na'źįpi kį ic'ų'hą k'ina'p'į ną g.la' yųk'ą' ptehį'cala we'tu-

---

¹ śkį, from śką, to move.
² ec'a, in that case, if we are to follow your lead, then —; it indicates a sort
of giving in, with a proviso.
³ c'ąc'ą', to shake, quake, move rapidly all over. c'ąc'ą' s'e is a way of expressing energetic and rushed preparation.

the distance, they saw a buffalo-calf, the kind born in the spring of
the year; it was loping along as it rounded a hill and disappeared.
There was a buffalo-cow who was lame in one foot and could not
walk, at the time the herd was moving north; so they left her
behind; and there she stayed. 8. In the spring, she had a calf and it
was this buffalo-boy. When he reached his mother, she said, "Well,
son, I have already heard how you have taken a wife. Now, therefore, you must go to seek out your father." Then she rolled on the
ground, and made a wallow[1], and, "Now, roll there," she said. So he
did it, and stood up, suddenly grown into a buffalo with polished
horns, the kind that are the fleetest runners. 9. The reason she
wanted him to find his father was that he had married into a people
that needed food badly. So the buffalo boy started northward.
After a time, he came to an old man buffalo who spoke thus to him,
"Grandson, I stand here, knowing you seek your father. Now and
then, you will find treachery in man; therefore, stand here facing
me. Of course I am no longer what I used to be, but I want you to
take some of my power along." Then he breathed into the boy's
mouth. "Now go; you will know your father's tipi by the drum
which is always sounding[2]." 10. So the boy went on and soon, without

wic'a't'upi k'u he'c'a wą i'catonauk[3] paha' wą ai'nap k'ig.la' śk'e'ᵉ.
Yuk'ą' he' pte' wą sihu'śte c'a to'k'a-ma'niśni hą'l wana' pte' opta'ye
ki wazi'yatakiya ag.le' c'e'yaś ihpe'ya ak'i'yag.la c'ąke' e'na ų'
śk'e'ᵉ. 8. Ną we'tu yuk'ą' c'ica't'ų c'a he' ptehti'cala-hokśi'la ki e' e
śk'e'ᵉ. Wana' hų'ku ki e'l k'i' yuk'ą' pte' ki, — Ho, c'ikś, eya' le'
t'awi cuyat'ų c'a nah'ų' mąke'. C'a niya'te oki'le-nikte', — eyi' ną
ica'ptąptąkic'ų ną ptema'k'okawaze[4] wą t'ą'ka c'a ka'gi ną, — Ho,
he'l ica'ptąptąkic'ų', — eya' śk'e'ᵉ. C'ąke' ec'ų' yuk'ą' he' śluślu'ta
wą, hena' ihą'keya lu'zahąpi k'ų he'c'a c'a ina'zi śk'e'ᵉ. 9. Ta'kowe'
atku'ku oki'le-yeśi k'ų he' oya'te wą wic'a'akih'ą c'a e'l e't'awicut'ų
ki he' ų' heya' śk'e'ᵉ. C'ąke' wana' wazi'yatakiya iya'ya śk'e'ᵉ.
Tohą'yą ya'hi ną t'at'ą'ka-wic'a'hcala wą na'zihą c'ąke' e'l ihų'ni
śk'e'ᵉ. He' ka'k'el eci'ya śk'e'ᵉ, — T'ako'za, le' niya'te oki'le-la c'a
slolya' wau' we lo'. Ųg.na'hąśna wic'a'śa aką'tula wic'o'wic'aśaśni
c'e le'l ahi'tuwą hina'zi yo. Eya' wana' oh'ą' ema'c'etusni[5] tk'a
miyo'h'ą wązi' yuha' ni'kte lo', — eya' śk'e'ᵉ. Heyi' ną i' oni'yaya
ną, — Ho, tukte'l niya'te t'i' ki he'l c'ąc'ega wą ho't'ąiiyą yąki'kte
lo', — eya' śk'e'ᵉ. 10. C'ąke' hetą'hą wana' ak'e' ya'hi ną oya'te wą

---

[1] These buffalo wallows are found on the prairies, and are called *pte-
o'wac'i*, buffalo dance-place.
[2] This is a magic drum, always sounding without hands to strike it.
[3] *i'cato*, to run in a certain way. *nau'ka*, to gallop; the combination means to
lope along, at an easy speed.
[4] *pte-o'wac'i*, where the buffaloes dance, is the usual term for this word,
meaning a buffalo-wallow. But the word in the text seems to be more
descriptive of the wallowing; *mak'a'* ground; *oka'waze* to wallow in.
[5] *oh'ą'*, actions; *ema'c'etuśni*, I am not as I should be; I am not what I once
was; I am no longer up to the mark. Old people often say this.

any warning, he came upon a great camp of human beings; but, recalling his grandfather's gift, he blew out his breath vigorously and straightway a heavy fog filled the land, so that you could not see this far from you. (Gesture here, indicating perhaps two feet from the speaker.) So he went past the camp in perfect safety. Soon after, he reached the encampment of the buffalo people; and met an old man buffalo, wearing white shells on a necklace; he was walking across the camp-circle. 11. He said, "Grandson, your father knows you are coming. Yonder, where the drum is singing, is your father's house." At once he called out, "Looking[1]-Bull's son has come!" so the people were in clamorous excitement while the boy's father approached him and led him into his tipi. 12. Then the buffalo-bulls said this, "Now, grandson, there will be one day, and the next after that, I[2] shall arrive. I crave red flannel and blue flannel and eagle feathers and blue-earth paint, so tell them that," they said. "And on the third day and on the fourth day the buffalo-people will arrive there," they said. So the boy started home at once, and stopped at his mother's abode, and then came home to his wife, saying, "Tomorrow, my grandfathers will arrive." 13. So the people were very happy, and they placed a tipi inside the camp circle for the son-in-law, and with great enthusiasm they entered into the work of collecting red flannel, feathers and blue-earth; and shell necklaces. They filled that tipi with all conceivable goods of the very best kind, and they were happy in that they were soon to eat

---

t'ą́ka wic'o't'i c'a kai'yap ihą' tk'a's t'ųka'śitku wae'ye c'ų he' o-g.na'yą niya'ya yųk'ą' p'o' wą le'c'eg.lala iyo'wot'ąiśni c'ąke' iyo'pteya iya'ya śk'e'ᵉ. Hetą'hą i'yec'ala pte'-oya'te kį wic'o't'i c'a e'l ihų'ni yųk'ą' pte'wic'a'hcala wą t'uki'-skaska` k'eya' owį' ną howo'pta hiya'ya hą'l e'l ihų'ni śk'e'ᵉ. 11. Yųk'ą', — Ho, t'ako`ża, yau' c'a niya'te slolye' lo'. Ka k'i ka c'ą'c'eǵa wą ho't'ąi kį he'l niya'te t'i' ye lo', — eya' śk'e'ᵉ. He'c'ena ho'yeyį ną, — T'at'ą'ka Wa'k'ita c'įca' wą hi' ye lo'! — eya' c'ąke' oya'te kį k'o'wic'ahig.nį ną atku'ku k'ų ec'i'yatąhą u' ną yu's ag.nį' ną t'ima' ak'i'yag.la śk'e'ᵉ. 12. Hehą'l t'at'ą'ka-wic'a'hca kį hena' leya'pi śk'e'ᵉ, — Ho, t'ako`ża, le' wą'cac'ą ną inų'pac'ą kį hehą'l wai'kte lo'. Śina'-lu`ta ną śina'-t'o ną wąb.li' ųpi' ną mak'a't'o kį hena' c'ąto'wakpani c'e oya'ka yo', — eya'pi śk'e'ᵉ. — Ną iya'm.nic'ą ną ito'pac'ą kįhą pte'-oya`te kį e'hųnikte lo'` — eya'pi śk'e'ᵉ. C'ąke' hokśi'la k'ų wą'cak g.licu' ną hų'ku yąke' cį e'l g.li' ną hetą'hą t'awi'cu kį ekta' g.li' ną, — Hį'hąna kįhą t'ųka'śila ahi'hųnikte lo', — eya' śk'e'ᵉ. 13. C'ąke' oya'te kį wi'yuśkįpi ną wic'a'woħa kį t'i'pi wą c'oka'p it'i'kicaǵapi ną śina'-lu`ta ną wi'yaka ną p'ąke'ska ną mak'a't'o k'o' m.nayą' ohi'tiyela śk'ą'pi śk'e'ᵉ. Wo'yuha waśte' kį iyu'ha t'i'pi kį' e'l t'iyo'kśupi ną ec'a'la wo'tapikte

---

[1] The correct meaning is, "Bull that looks around; scouts."

[2] A spokesman speaking for a great group, generally says "I", as for each one, individually.

again. 14. When morning came, the buffalo bulls came right in among the tipis in the camp[1], so they killed them and in each case they tore off a strip of red flannel and tied it on the horns and sprinkled blue-earth over the body before cutting it up; and the people were very rich in food then. Meantime, they dug in the hill and made caches into which they threw even the buffalo-hoofs and covered them over with earth until needed. 15. All this, while the son-in-law was sitting in his tipi; and when the people finished caring for all the meat, he said, "Now I am going home. It is enough now, for you have killed all my people." So his wife and his mother- and father-in-law all tried to detain him and wept, yet they could not dissuade him. 16. "No matter what, I am now going home. But as long as you live, you may depend on me. When a small herd coming from the west is sighted, look for one with shiny polished horns; that will be I. Kill me and cut off my head down as far as the widest span of the chest. And whenever you need help, tell me," he said. 17. Then he left; and now, when the sun was low, a small herd was returning from the west, and among them was one buffalo with shiny horns. As he ran, the horns flashed in the sun like signal-mirrors; so they concentrated on him and killed him. 18. They all assembled over his body, and wailed as for the dead; and then they

ci ų' k'oye'hą[2] wi'yuškįpi šk'e'ᵉ. 14. Wana' ihį'hana yųk'ą' t'at'ą'ka kį t'iwo'hąhą ahi'yu c'ąke' wic'a'ktepi c'ą šina'-lu`ta hąke' yuĥle'l he' kį e'l ai'yawic'akaškapi ną mak'a't'o awi'c'akalalapi ną hehą'l wic'a'p'atapi ną li'la wawi'c'aśeca šk'e'ᵉ. K'ohą' paha' kį ok'a'pi ną wo'ĥa-mak'at'ipi ka'ǧapi ną t'asi'ha ye'š k'o' iĥpe'yeśni iyu'ha e'l okšu'pi ną aka't'api šk'e'ᵉ. 15. Yųk'ą' wic'a'woĥa k'ų he' t'ima' yąka'hį ną wana' wap'a'l yušta'pi k'ų hehą'l heya' šk'e'ᵉ, — Ho, wana' wag.nį'kte lo', eya'š wana' mit'o'yate kį oya'š'į wic'a'yaktepi c'a, — eya' c'ąke' t'awi'cu ną k'ų'ku ną t'ųką'ku k'ų k'o' iyu'ha c'e'ya g.loni'capi k'e'yaš a'tayaš g.na'yąpiśni[3] šk'e'ᵉ. 16. — Tako'm.ni wana' wag.nį'kte lo. Tk'a' tohą'-yani`pi kį hehą'yą wac'į'mayayapi-kte lo'. Tohą'l wiyo'ĥpeyatąhą pte' co'nala ku'pi ną e'l he' šlušlu'ta wąži' o'p'a hą'tąhąš he' miyekte lo'. C'e mao'pi ną c'eška'-ot'ą'kaya kį hehą'yą wama'ksapi ną tohą'l ta'ku ini'cakiżapi c'ą'šna oma'kiyaka po', — eya' šk'e'ᵉ. 17. Heyį' ną k'ig.la' yųk'ą' wana' wi' k'u'ciyela ĥcehą'l wiyo'ĥpeyatąhą pte' co'nala ku'pi ną e'l he' šlušlu'ta wą o'p'a šk'e'ᵉ. Mi'yog.las'į hiyu'yapi s'e wiya'kpakpayela ku' c'ąke' ece'la k'uwa'pi ną e'ktepi šk'e'ᵉ. 18. Ną hehą'l e'l e'm.niciyį ną c'e'yapi ną

---

[1] Their promise to the buffalo-calf boy who married into this human tribe prompts them to walk deliberately into camp, though they know it is to their death.
[2] k'ohą', meantime, is the usual Teton word. k'oye'hą is Yankton.
[3] g.na'yąpiśni, they did not fool him, would be the literal meaning; but not so here. It means, "they couldn't dissuade him from his intention to go away."

14

cut off his head, including his chest down to the widest part; and placed it in the holy tipi which the Pawnees maintained; and always treated it with reverence. When food was scarce, and the people suffered, they would immediately sprinkle blue-earth over the head and pray to it, and the buffalo always arrived, they say.

41. A Woman Becomes a Horse.

1. Among the Kiowa a young man was married to a beautiful girl, and they lived contentedly and now had two children. Then one day, the people were travelling, moving to a new camp. As they travelled westward, the girl's puppy disappeared, so she turned her horse, for she was riding, and went back looking for him, and didn't return, as if temporarily delayed; but she never did come back. 2. They looked everywhere for her, and her husband especially, who went wailing about in his search, but did not find her; at last all the people joined in the hunt with him, but it was all in vain. Now a whole year had passed, and the following summer; and now it was fall, so by then they all gave up, and became reconciled to the loss. About that time, a young man went hunting and in two days he returned. 3. He brought home much meat, and invited all the old men to a feast[1] and while they were eating he talked in this wise,

p‘a' kį c‘eśka'-ot‘ą`kaya kį ao'p‘eya waksa' icu'pi ną P‘ala'ni t‘i'pi kį e'l t‘i'pi wą wak‘ą' g.le'pi c‘ąke' e'l e'g.nakapi ną o'hįni wak‘ą'yą awą'yakapi śk‘e’ᵉ. Tohą'l wo'yute wani'cį ną wi'cakiżapi c‘ą wą'cak pte-p‘a' k’ų he' mak‘a't‘o aka'lalapi nąśna c‘e‘kiyapi c‘ą ak‘e' pte' ahi'hųni śk‘e’ᵉ.

41.

1. Wi'ta-Pahatu² oya`te kį e'g.na k‘ośka'laka wą wik‘o'śkalaka wą li'la wį'yą waśte' c‘a yu'zį ną kic‘i' tąyą' ų' ną wana' cį'ca' nų'papi kį lehą'l to'hųwel ąpe'tu wą e'l oya'te kį ig.la'ka a'ya śk‘e’ᵉ. Yųk‘ą' wiyo'ĥpeyatakiya a'ye e'yaś wik‘o'śkalaka k’ų he' śuĥpa'la wą kit‘ą'įśni c‘ąke' śųk-’a'kąyąka' c‘ąke' kawį'gį ną he'ktakiya oki'le-iya`ya yųk‘ą' i'ĥąhą³ s'e g.li'śni ną he'c‘ena to'k‘aĥ’ą śk‘e’ᵉ. 2. C‘ąke' li'la ole'pi ną hįg.na'ku kį iyo'tą c‘e'yaya oki'le k‘e'yaś iye'yeśni kį ų' hąke'ya oya'te kį a'taya oki'cilepi k‘e'yaś itu'ya śk‘e’ᵉ. Ec‘e'l wana' wani'yetu wążi' są'p‘atąhą b.loke'tu ną ak‘e' ptąye'tu kį ekta' iya'ya c‘ąke' wana'ś iye'nayapika hą'l k‘ośka'laka wą waye'-i ną nų'pac‘ą hą'l g.li' śk‘e’ᵉ. 3. Li'la t‘alo' tąyą' ag.li' c‘ąke' wic‘a'ĥcala wic‘a'kic‘o ną wo'l-wic‘ak‘iyį ną le'c‘el wo'wic‘akiyaka śk‘e’ᵉ, — Ĥta'l-ehą'⁴

---

[1] A successful hunter, if he was self-respecting, gave a feast to the old men on his return. It was due to the old men, for they also had given feasts to old men in their time. No hunter was urged to do this, but enjoyed doing it.

² *wi'ta-pahatu* is the Dakota name for the Kiowa tribe.

³ *i'ĥąhą*, in fun; not seriously; temporarily.

⁴ *ĥta'l ehą'*, yesterday; *ĥtaye'tu*, evening. *ehą'*, then; but last evening, or yesterday evening is *ĥta'l eha'-ĥtaye`tu*.

"Yesterday, I stood watching a herd of stray horses, and among them was a human being. The moment I saw that, I recalled something, and I will tell you about it. 4. Long ago, you must remember, Walking Bear's[1] wife was lost. I thought to myself, 'If she was lured away[2] by the stray herd, this might be she;' I am merely passing this on to you for what it is worth." When he said this, a crier rode around announcing the news and the men all went out, as for a chase, and came to the stray herd and surrounded them as they drove them on. 5. From all sides, the men charged on them and rounded them into a small area, so that they could not turn anywhere. And among them was a human being; so they declared, "There is no doubt, that is she." And they went directly after her, but she was so very swift that it took them a long time to rope her. 6. She slipped out of the noose as often as she was caught in it; but they persevered until they had her fast; and when they stood there holding her in check, they say a beautiful black colt kept coming very close and then neighing and running back again[3]. 7. They took the woman back to camp, and caused her to see her two children and her husband, but she seemed to ignore them entirely, and

---

šuk-nų'ni opta'ye wą ų'pi c'ąke' ab.le's nawi'c'awažįhą yųk'ą' e'l mak'a' ama'ni wą o'p'a ye lo'. Yųk'ą' wąb.la'kį na he'c'eg.la wawe'-ksuya c'a oc'i'ciyakapikte lo'. 4. Ehą'ni eyaš Mat'o'-Ma'ni[4] t'awi'cu wą to'k'ah'ą k'ų he' tok'a'š šųknų'ni i'nahmapi he'ci he e' se'ce lo', ec'ą'mi ną le' eya' he'c'ekc'ekel ob.la'ke lo', — eya' c'ąke' howo'kawįh ie'yapahapi ną wo'nase-kahya ole'pi yųk'ą' wana' šuk-nų'ni ece' ka'l ų'pi c'ąke' o'kšą ana'pta awi'c'ayapi šk'e'e. 5. O'kšątąhą našlo'k[5] hiyu'pi ną kawi'taya awi'c'ayapi c'ąke' to'k'i ya'pika nų tk'a' šk'e'e. Yųk'ą' wic'a'ša aką'tu wą e'l o'p'a c'ąke', — Ho, eya' tok'e'tuke e'yaš he' e' ye lo', — eya'pi ną a'tayela k'uwa'pi k'e'yaš a'wicak'ehą' lu'zahą c'ąke' t'e'hą-ok'u'wapi ną o'hąketa k'oya'kyapi šk'e'e. 6. K'e'yaš wi'k'ą kį pašlo'šlok iye'ya šką' šk'e'e. He'c'eca e'yaš wana' ki'tąhcį' suta'ya ik'ą't'ųpi ną yuha' na'žįpi c'ąke' c'įcala wą sa'pa li'la wašte' c'a hot'ų't'ų ahi'kawįgahą šk'e'e. 7. Wį'yą k'ų wana' wic'o't'ita ag.li'pi ną c'įca' nų'pa k'ų hena' e'pi ną hįg.na'ku kį k'o' wąwi'c'a-g.lak-k'iyapi k'eš a'tayaš e'l e'wic'awac'įšni, ec'ą'l hot'ų't'ų nąšna

---

[1] Walking-Bear should be "He walks bear-fashion, or after the manner of bears," because [it is said as one word. As two words, with individual accents, it would be, "a bear walks."

[2] He uses the same word in speaking of horses luring away a woman that is used to mean a man luring away a woman.

[3] We have stories of humans mating with animals in the guise of people, and having children that are human in appearance but with an animal's spirit, but this is the only case I know of in which the off-spring has an animal form.

[4] *mat'o'-ma'ni*, as a bear-he walks. See note 1.

[5] *našlo'k*, plus a verb (to start going or coming) means "to dash, to start with instant speed; to rush forward." *na*, with the feet; *šlo'ka*, to slip.

14*

instead she would neigh and try to run away; they therefore held
her securely tied. 8. And when they offered her food, she refused it,
till at last Walking-Bear said, "I want you to know I appreciate
your help, but I see now that things can never be right, so I may
as well give up now." But that statement seemed to mean nothing
at all to his wife, as if she had not heard it; and she disregarded all
her relatives. 9. So Walking-Bear removed the rope that tied her,
and stepped aside; and straightway, as hard as she could, she ran
towards the wild country, neighing like a horse all the while. Her
body was shocking to behold. She was covered with a thick growth
in all the parts where hair could grow on her body. 10. Again they
chased the stray herd and ran them into a bend in the creek, where
they where cornered by a narrow opening, with a high cliff on the
other side. As the men blocked the one exit, the herd ran round and
round in the enclosed area. 11. And a beautiful black horse was in
the herd; so they said if anyone wished to own it, they would all help
him to catch it. But it seemed to feel that they had designs on it. It
was extremely restless and in motion all the time. And then suddenly,
a black bird, the kind that stay in the woods, flew up and sat on the
cliff; and they say that was the black horse which took that form to
escape. 12. And then there was a buckskin whose four limbs and
head were white. When they caught him, they found that the parts
that were white were weathered bone, as of a dead horse. 13. So the
men viewed it with fear. One was a bay and he had horns, they say.

*mani'takiya iya'yįkteħcį c'ąke' kaśka' ece'-naźį śk'e'ᵉ. 8. Nakų'
wo'k'upi k'eś c'į'śni c'ąke' o'hąketa Mat'o'-Ma`ni heya' śk'e'ᵉ, — Ho
po', eya' tąyą' o'mayakiyapi c'a p'iwa'la tk'a' tų'weni tąyą'kteśni
kį t'ąį' c'a wą'cak e'ś ab.lu'śtąkte lo', — eye' c'e'yaś wį'yą kį i'tok'aśni
nakų'ś nak'ų'śni s'e ų' ną taku'wic'aye ų iyu'ha awi'c'aktaśni śk'e'ᵉ.
9. C'ąke' Mat'o'-Ma`ni ik'ą' k'i' ną ħeya'p ina'źį yųk'ą' he'c'ena
to'k'el-oki`hika mani'takiya hot'ų't'ų iya'ya śk'e'ᵉ. Li'la t'ąc'ą' kį
ową'yak-t'eħi`ka śk'e'ᵉ. To'nakiya hį' u'kta iye'c'eca kį hena'kiya
li'la hiśma' śk'e'ᵉ. 10. Ak'e' śųk-nų'ni ośpa'ye kį wic'a'k'uwapi yųk'ą'
wakpa'la-kaħ.mi` wą oci'k'ayela ekta' ona'kip'api ną ak'o'tąhą maya'
kį g.lihe'ya c'ąke' wą'cakiyela og.li'cuwaste` k'e'yaś he'l k'uśe'ya
na'źįpi yųk'ą' kaħmi' kį ekta' oho'm.ni į'yąkapi śk'e'ᵉ. 11. Yųk'ą'
śųk-sa'pa wą li'la waśte' e'l o'p'a c'ąke' tuwa' he' oyu'spa c'į' hą'tąhąś
o'kiyapikta ke'ya'pi yųk'ą' ac'ą'tag.lepi¹ kį slolki'ya śk'e'ᵉ. Ona'tąyą
ų' ną ųg.na'hąla c'ą'-waħpat'ąka wą k'iye'la kįyą' iya'yį ną maya'
kį ekta' i'yotaka yųk'ą' śųk-sa'pa k'ų he' e śk'e'ᵉ. 12. Heħą'l wąźi'
hį'zi c'a oya'ya to'pa kį iyu'ha ska' ną p'a' kį k'o' ska' śk'e'ᵉ. Yųk'ą'
he' i'ś oyu'spapi yųk'ą' leya tohą'hąyą ska' k'ų heħą'hąyą hohu' kį
śe'ca śk'e'ᵉ. 13. C'ąke' wic'a'śa kį iyu'ha ini'hąyą wąya'kapi śk'e'ᵉ.*

---

¹ *ac'ą'tag.lepi*, they had designs on her; *a*, on; *c'ąte'*, heart (mind); *a*, on;
g.le, to set. (In Dakota, the mind, or thinking, is associated closely with the
heart.)

In such odd ways they were marked, these stray horses. 14. In supernatural ways these horses were different, and were unearthly; and yet that woman preferred them. For that reason, the people abandoned her; so she became one with them, and was wild; but that is what she preferred, they say.

42. Fish-Butte.

1. Long ago, when the race was young, the people of the Dakota came together and settled in winter quarters in a bend of the Pawnee River, they say. But it was still warm and pleasant, when a man who never had a home, and lived "between tipis"[1] as a usual thing, decided to fast and seek a vision. 2. The reason was that he had always lived a hard life. He tried as hard as he could to behave in a way to induce kindness in people towards him, and was generous with what he had, and he never told things[2], and yet, whatever the reason, he was always the object of people's dislike. And by now he was weary of it, and wanted supernatural help. He would wail and then stand; and after he had fasted for three days, his prayer was answered. The Great Spirit himself came to him.

·*Wążi' i'ṡ hį'ṡa c'a he'[3] yuk'a' ṡk'e'ᵉ. He'c'ekc'e oṡte'ṡteya ec'e'capi ṡk'e'ᵉ, ṡųk-nų'ni kį hena'. 14. Wak'ą'k'ąyą owo'hįyąsyela to'k'ecape ṡą' wį'yą kį iha'wicakta[4] kį ų' ayu'ṡtąpi c'ąke' i'ṡ-'eya' oṡte'ka c'a wat'o'g.laya ų' k'e'yaṡ ec'e'l-iyo`kip'i ṡk'e'ᵉ.*

42.

1. *Ehą'ni t'oka'-wic'i`c'aǧe c'ų he'hą' Lak'o'ta kį iyu'ha k'iwi'tayapi ną P'ala'ni T'awa'kpa kį op'a'ya kaḣmi' wą e'l wani't'ipi ṡk'e'ᵉ. Wana' wani'yetu-et'i`pi k'e'yaṡ nahą'ḣcį maṡte'ṡte ną oi'yokip'i hą'l wic'a'ṡa wą t'ic'o'la t'iwo'k'it'ahela[5] ece'-ų yuk'ą' he' hąb.le'[6] ṡk'e'ᵉ. 2. Ta'kole'-hąb.le` kį he' iyo'tiye'kiya ų' kį he' ų' ṡk'e'ᵉ. To'k'el- oki`hi ų'ṡiḣ'ą[7] ece'-ų ną ta'ku yuha' c'ą' it'a'wac'į waṡte'[8] ną to'hįni wo'yakeṡni k'e'yaṡ to'k'a he'cįhą wowi'waḣtelaṡni ų' ṡk'e'ᵉ. Wana' ṡehą' t'awa't'elyeṡni kį he' ų' le' hąb.le' ṡk'e'ᵉ. Hąb.le'-c'eyį nąṡna ak'e' he'c'el na'żį ną wana' ya'm.nic'ą wo'teṡni yuk'ą' wac'e'kiye c'ų iye'kicic'etu ṡk'e'ᵉ. Wak'ą' T'ąka kį he e' c'a iye' iyų'k'ala e'l hi'*

---

[1] To stay "between tipis" is to be an outcast; homeless.

[2] Almost the highest recommendation there is, — "not to tell things".

[3] Horns.

[4] *iha'kta*, to be pulled to remain behind, with someone; cf. *haki'kta*, to look back, when going forward; *iha'wakta*, I hate to leave it; I am pulled back by it; *hawe'kta*, I look back; *t'i-i'hakikta*, she hates to leave her home (said of a confirmed stay-at-home).

[5] *t'iwo'k'it'ahela*, to be homeless (between homes; in the spaces separating homes).

[6] *hąb.le'*, to fast, in order to obtain a vision.

[7] *ų'ṡiḣ'ą*, to perform little acts, in an effort to secure kindness.

[8] *t'awa'c'į waṡte'*, to be good in disposition, or mind; i. e., to be generous; *i*, with what one has.

3. "Come now, tell me just how you see me," he said. So the man replied, "You are after the likeness of a fish; but also you come with limbs, like a man's. You have arms and legs. That is how I see you," he said. 4. And he replied, "Now tell me on what account you have trouble." So the man told him. He, perhaps more than others, had a kind heart and always gave what he could to the needy; but he had no home, in spite of the fact that, whenever anyone in pity took him in, he always tried to outdo himself in performing well the things he should do. 5. He always lived in that way, yet he was disliked; and lived abandoned between tipis. All this he told to the Great Spirit. So, he said, he was weary of it all, and wanted to avenge himself; and for that purpose he wanted supernatural aid. And the Fish-God said, "What you ask is fearful, but it must be what you need so I will help you. Go home; and seven days hence, meet me by the river before sunrise. I shall be there." So he said and left the man. 6. Now came the time, and the man met the Fish-God at the water. But not alone. He had secretly invited those who were kind to him, and brought them with him. He did this because he wanted them to be spared. Just as the sky was crimson before the sun appeared, like a fire just out of sight, there was a roaring sound in the water, so they listened, fearing. And the Fish-God with only

śk'e'ᵉ. 3. — Ho' wo', to'k'eĥcį wąma'yalaka he'cįhą ec'e'l oya'ka yo', — eya' c'ąke' eya' he'c'el wąya'ka c'a, — Ho, eya' hoǵą-ou͝'c'aǵe kį og.na' le' yahi' ye lo'. Tk'a' ak'e' wic'a'śa iye'c'el oya'ya niyu'k'e¹ lo'. Hu' ną isto' k'o' niyu'k'e lo'. He'c'el wąc'i'yake lo', — eya' ke'ᵉ. 4. Yųk'ą' heya' ke'ᵉ, — Ho', ta'ku ų' iyo'tiye'yakiya he'cįhą oya'ka yo', — eya' c'ąke' oki'yaka ke'ᵉ. Iye's wau͝'śila ną ta'ku yuha' kį to'hįni wawi'p'ilaśni ną tuwa' ų'śika c'a ta'ku yuha' kį ų' o'kiya ke'ya' oki'yaka ke'ᵉ. Ho, k'e'yaś t'i'pi ni'cį ną he' ų' tuwa' ų'śila ną yuha' c'ą'śna iye's ak'a'wį-ec'ų² s'e ta'ku iyu'ha e'l tąyą' ec'u'wac'į ke'ya' śk'e'ᵉ. 5. O'hįni he'c'el ų' wesą' waĥte'lapiśni ną t'iwo'k'it'ahela iĥpe'yapi ke'ya' Wak'ą'-T'ą͝ka kį oki'yaka ke'ᵉ. C'ąke' wana' śehą' t'awa't'elyeśni c'a wat'o'kic'ųkta c'į' kį ų' wic'o'ĥ'ą wążi' c'į' ke'ya' śk'e'ᵉ. Yųk'ą' Hoǵą'-Wak'ą' kį heya' ke'ᵉ, — Ho', ta'ku wą t'eĥi'ka c'a yala' k'e'yaś eya' he'c'el yac'į'ka c'a o'c'iciyįkte lo'. C'e g.nį' ną letą'hą śako'wįc'ą kį'hą wi' hina'p'eśni ec'e'l m.nia'g.lag.la na'żį yo'. He'l wai'kte lo', — eyį' ną tok'i'yot'ą k'ig.la' śk'e'ᵉ. 6. Wana' iye'hątu c'ąke' wic'a'śa k'ų he' m.niya'ta Hoǵą'-Wak'ą͝ kį wąya'k-ya ke'ᵉ. K'e'yaś iśna'la śni'ⁱ. Naĥma'la to'na ų'śilakapi k'ų hena'la owi'c'aki-yakį ną o'p ya' ke'ᵉ. Hena' ni' ų'pikta c'į' kį he'ų' awi'c'ai śk'e'ᵉ. Wana' ka'k'el wi' hina'p'įkta c'a ekta' iyo'śayela oi'le s'e hą' yųk'ą' m.ni' kį ekta' ta'ku wą ĥmuye'la ec'e'ca c'a naĥ'ų'pi ną wo'k'okip'ek'i-yapi ke'ᵉ. Yųk'ą' hoǵą'-t'ą͝ka wą c'ąk'a'hu kį hehą'yela t'ąį'yą

---

¹ *yuk'ą'*, there exists; there is; *niyu'k'ą*, there is, to you; i. e., you have.
² *ak'a'wį*, over and above; on purpose; *ak'a'wį-eya*͝, to say more than needed; to exaggarate, on purpose; *ak'a'wį-ec'ų*, to overdo, as with a purpose.

his back visible, came towards them and lay on the shore. 7. Immediately he turned and went back, disappearing under the water, and then the man who was so pitiful, went following him, and he too disappeared in the water. His friends were so frightened that they ran crying to camp. They told all they had seen by the water, and inspired a great fear in the people. 8.What happened then was that the man followed the sacred fish into the water, and then realized that he too was in the form of a fish. But he also had arms and legs, so he was partly like a man. He was, in a word, like the sacred fish himself. 9. He swam in the water but he grew taller and larger; this he observed in himself. At last he grew so large that he was frightful to behold. After a time he came out on land but he was enormously large and long. When he was entirely out of the water, he caused his back to bend into what resembled a gigantic hoop or circle, and thus he lay down. His body was so long that in that position he hemmed in the entire tribe. Like a wall running around them he was. And where the tail and the nose came together was the only passage possible. 10. The people saw it, this huge mountain which came and enclosed them, and a great terror gripped them so that they ran wildly about. But there was no escape. But only the few friends I mentioned were aware of the opening, having been previously informed, so they kept their minds clear and ran in that direction

---

t'ahe'nakiya u' ną o'huta kį e'l hiyų'ka ke'ᵉ. 7. He'c'ena ak'e' ig.lu'-hom.ni ną m.ni' kį ekta' mahe'l t'ąį'sniyela k'ig.la' yųk'ą' he'c'ena wic'a'sa wą ų'sika c'ų he' iha'kap iya'yį ną i's-'eya' m.ni' kį ekta' a't'ąįsniyą iya'ya ke'ᵉ. He'c'ena t'ak'o'laku k'ų iyu'ha yus'į'yayapi ną oya'te t'i'pi kį ekta'kiya c'e ya į'yąkapi ke'ᵉ. He'c'i ta'ku wąya'kapi k'ų a'taya oya'kapi c'ąke' wayu's'įyeyapi-t'ą'ka sk'e'ᵉ. 8. Yųk'ą' leya wic'a'sa wą m.ni-ma'hel hogą'-wak'ą kį iha'kap iya'ye c'ų he' to'k'i ak'i' c'ąke' hehą'l ai'c'ib.leza yųk'ą' i's-'eya' hogą'-oų'c'aġe wą yuha' sk'e'ᵉ. Tk'a i's-'eya' hu' ną isto' k'o' yųk'ą' c'ąke' hąke' wic'a'sa s'e le'c'eca sk'e'ᵉ. Hogą'-wak'ą` k'ų iye'c'eca ke'ᵉ. 9. M.nima'hel nųwą' ų' k'e'yas są'p hą'skį ną t'ą'ka a'ya c'a ai'c'ib.leza ke'ᵉ. Ną o'hąketa li'la t'ą'ka c'ąke' wo'k'okip'e ke'ᵉ, owa'yake kį ekta'. Tohą'tu yųk'ą' o'hutata g.licu' k'e'yas wo'winihąyą t'ą'ka ną hą'ska ke'ᵉ. Wana' mak'a'-pu`za kį ekta' ec'a'c'a-hiyu` k'ų hą' c'ąk'a'hu kį naka's'į-ic'iyį ną mime'ya c'ąg.le'ska s'e iyų'ka ke'ᵉ. T'ąc'ą'-hą`ska c'ąke' he'c'el iyų'ka yųk'ą' le wic'o't'i-t'ą'ka k'ų he' a'taya ao'g.lut'eya hpa'ya ke'ᵉ. Oka'wįh ac'ų'kaskapi s'e hą' ke'ᵉ, ną tukte'l site' kį p'a' kį kic'i' e'c'ip'a yųk'ą' he'l ece'la t'iyo'pya hą' ke'ᵉ. 10. He'c'ena oya'te kį iyu'ha wąya'kapi ną he' wą t'ą'ka it'a'woksą wic'a'hiyųka c'ąke' wo'nihiciye hiya'g.lepi ną ona'tąyą ų'pi k'e'yas oi'yaye wani'ca ke'ᵉ. Ho tk'a' t'ak'o'laku co'nala ke'p'e' c'ų hena'la eya' he'c'el ehą'tąhą owi'c'akiyaka c'ąke' wą'cakiyela t'iyo'pya he' c'ų he'c'etkiya wac'į'-ksapya¹ į'yąkapi ną nii'c'iyapi sk'e'ᵉ. Ho',

---

¹ *wac'į'-ksa`pa*, to be wise in the mind; i. e., to have presence of mind; *ya*, in that manner.

and escaped to safety. So they were all the Dakotas who were saved. And all the others died of fear[1] and great woe fell on them. Some died from that fright, actually. 11. The great fish crushed them with his weight and then straightened his body out and rolled over and annihilated them. Having thus put an end to the people, he stretched out his body and then began to crawl towards the wild country. Selecting a pleasant open plain, he lay down and soon became rock, they say. 12. That is how in the early times many Dakotas died a pitiful death, and only those were spared who had been kind to that poor and homeless man. From that time on, the Dakota people began to expand in earnest, they say. 13. And they say that is when the Dakota people learned to be kind to each other. That is why when anyone is homeless and poor in a Dakota village, someone is always sure to take him in. Even today, nobody in the Dakota country suffers in this way; nobody is entirely homeless. Now-a-days, that hill of rock in the form of a fish is called Fish-Butte and lies somewhere, they say. I myself have never seen it; but some there are, here and there, who have, and they tell this story about it.

43. Bewitched by the Buffalo.

1. This is a tale of the Crow Indians, which the Dakotas often relate.

---

c'ǫke' hena'la Lak'o'ta kį ni'pi nǫ ųma'pi kį iyu'ha t'ǫsa'ksak t'a'pi nǫ wo't'eȟi ahį'ȟpayapi śk'e'ᵉ. Etǫ' he'c'ena t'a'pi śk'e'ᵉ, t'ǫsa'k t'a'pi nǫ. 11. To'na ni' ų'pi k'ų hena' iyu'ha hoǧǫ-t'ǫ'ka kį awi'c'ag.laskici nǫ hehǫ'l nao'wot'ǫic'iyį nǫ ikpa'ptǫ c'ǫke' iyu'ha wic'a'kte śk'e'ᵉ. Ho he'c'el wahǫ'kyį nǫ hehǫ'l nai'c'iowot'ǫ nǫ ȟeya'takiya ya' śk'e'ᵉ. Ka'l ob.la'ye-owa'śtecaka yųk'ǫ' e'l iyu'kį nǫ oȟ'ǫ'k'oya į'yǫ-ica`ǧa śk'e'ᵉ. 12. He'c'el ų' Lak'o'ta kį o'ta ų'śiya t'a'pi nǫ to'na waȟpa'nica nǫ t'i'pi ni'ca wǫ o'kiyapi k'ų hena'la ni'pi c'ǫke' hetǫ' nakeś a'wicak'eya Lak'o'ta-oya`te kį ic'a'ǧapi śk'e'ᵉ. 13. Yųk'ǫ' hetǫ'hǫ Lak'o'ta kį ų'śikic'ilapi-woųspe kį le' u' śk'e'ᵉ. He' ų' tuwa' t'iwo'k'it'ahela ų' nǫ ų'śika c'ǫ ų'śilapi nǫ tukte'l icu'pi nǫ yuha'pi s'a'ᵃ. C'ǫke' lehǫ'tu k'e'yaś Lak'o'ta-oya`te kį e'g.na tuwe'ni he'c'el iyo'liye'kiyeśni'ᵉ; tuwe'na t'iwo'k'it'ahela ų'śni'ⁱ. Wana l'ehǫ'l paha'-kaȟya įyǫ' wǫ t'ǫ'ka c'a hoǧǫ' s'e yǫka' c'ǫke' he' Hoǧǫ'-Paha` eci'yapi c'a tukte' ekta' yǫka' śk'e'ᵉ. Miye' tų'weni wǫb.la'keśni k'e'yaś wǫźi'kźi wǫya'kapi nǫ ų' le' wo'yakapi kį oya'kapi śk'e'ᵉ.

43.

1. Lak'o'ta kį wic'o'oyake kį le' K'ǫǧi'-wic'a`śa t'a'wapi c'a oya'kapi s'a'ᵃ.

---

[1] "To die of fear" is literal for an idiom meaning to be "scared stiff" and lie as if dead.

A youth from the Crow camp once went on a trip away from home, and lay down to rest on the side of a brown-earth cliff, near the bank of the Elkhorn River. 2. And he saw there, standing in the water below, a buffalo. This he watched a long time. But it puzzled him because at times it did not look like a buffalo[1]. Therefore he sat watching to see when it would change its position. He waited so long, in vain, that finally he took stones and hurled them at the animal, hitting him in the middle of his back each time. This had no effect on him. Not at all frightened, the buffalo stood till the young man worked loose a part of the rock imbedded in the cliff, and started it down hill. It came bounding down and hit the buffalo with a thud. This time, he disappeared suddenly in the water. 3. At once the young man started for his home, and on the next day, the tribe broke camp and began the march to a new camp-site. It chanced that they crossed the stream at the very spot where the young man had seen the buffalo. He himself followed in the line, on horseback, at the very end; so he was the last to cross. When he was about half-way across, his horse suddenly stood still. So he called out to his friends. "Hey, friends, I can go no further. Come and help me!" he called. As the water was shallow, the young men all turned without difficulty, and came back, carrying their spears, intending to fight whatever was detaining the young man who called for help. But the water rose in a great tide, as if something

To'hą K'ąǵi'-wic'a`ŝa-k'oŝka`laka wą t'iya'tąhą oma'ni-iya`yį̨ ną manį'l maya' wą a'taya mak'a'-ǵi c'a e'l asni'kiya-iyų`ka ŝk'e'᷉. Yųk'ą' he' maya' kį He'-C'įŝka'yapi-Wakpa` kį aǵ.la'ǵ.la yąka' ŝk'e'᷉. 2. He'c'el ḣpa'yahą yųk'ą' ųǵ.na' k'u`ta m.ni' kį c'op'a' le'c'e t'at'ą'ka wą na'ẑįhą c'ąke' t'e'hą-wąya`k yaka'hą ke'᷉. Tohą'lŝna t'at'ą'ka ŝ'e le'c'eca ną ak'e'ŝna he'c'aŝni ŝ'e le'c'eca c'ąke' ŝkąŝką'kta-ap'e yąka'hą ke'᷉. T'e'hą-yąke' c'e'yaŝ he'c'ena na'ẑį c'ąke' ḣąke'ya į'yą icu' ną ų' k'įį' c'ą iye'na c'ąk'a'hu-c'oka`ya ece'-ap'a` ke'᷉. K'e'yaŝ he'c'ena ŝkąŝką'ŝni'᷉. I'yą ų' k'įį' kį hena' i'tok'aŝni c'ąke' he'c'etu k'eŝ maya' kį t'ahe'piya mak'a' kį t'ą'kaya nao'ŝpį ną ao'-ǵ.miǵ.meya ke'᷉. C'ąke' k'u'takiya kapsi'psil yį' ną t'at'ą'ka k'ų c'ąk'a'hu kį c'oka'yela buya'[2] ap'a' ke'᷉. Yųk'ą' nake' ŝką'-hiǵ.nį ną he'c'ena a't'ąįŝni ke'᷉. 3. He'c'ena k'oŝka'laka kį t'iya'takiya k'iǵ.nį' ną ihį'hąni kį e'l iǵ.la'kapi ną a'ya c'ąke' eha'kela ŝųk-'a'kąyąk ec'e'l ya' yųk'ą' wakpa' kį e'l t'at'ą'ka wą ḣta'l-'ehą' wąya'ke c'ų he'tulaḣcį iyu'weǵapi ke'᷉. C'ąke' ųma'pi kį iyu'ha e'yaya c'a ec'e'l ya' yųk'ą' c'oka'ya wana' ye' cį wale'hąl t'aŝų'ke kį ową'ẑilaḣcį ina'ẑį c'ąke', — K'ola`, hiyu' po'. To'k'a-ib.la`b.leŝni ye, — eya' ke'᷉. M.ni' kį k'a'zela c'ąke' t'ak'o'laku kį iyu'ha wahu'k'eza ǵ.luha'pi ną he' ta'ku c'a ani'ca he'cįhą t'akpe'-ku`pi ke'᷉. Aǵ.na' m.ni' k'ų

---

[1] The spirit of the mad buffalo, an evil spirit.
[2] *bu,* the sound made by striking a drum, or something that gives a low, dull sound, a thud; *buya,* such a sound accompanying an act.

were forcing it to pile up, and completely immersed the young man
who promptly disappeared from view, horse and all. 4. The people
came to land just across the river where they made camp. Then
they hunted for him, and gave up after a time, and wailed for him,
as for one dead. Now, a man in the company regarded himself
as with power. He said, "I can find him; and if I do, I want
one of his younger sisters for my wife." 5. That was all right, they
said; if he found the lost man, he might as well have them both.
He was now about to hunt him, so everyone came out to sit on the
river bank and watch. The man walked on the water's surface, and
ever so often he peered down in as if he actually was seeing through
the stream. "At noon, go home; and come again, later," he said.
So at noon, everyone went to the camp, and after their noon meal
hour, they came out again to watch. He continued to look along the
stream in this manner until the evening. 6. Next morning when
they came out to watch again, he said to them, "Over yonder is a
cliff of brown-earth; and at its base lies the lost horse. And further
on, where you see the, cliff, there is a whirl-pool, and in it lies our
man. He was dead when I reached him, but he has come back to
life. So I placed him on the hillside and came home." As soon as he
announced this, all the people hurried to the place he had indicated,
and found first the horse and then the man, precisely as he had
said. So they took the young man home. 7. But there was still
something wrong with him. So they conferred about what might

ta'ku paa't'aṡ au' s'e wąka'l hiyu' ną k'oṡka'laka k'ų ṡų'kak'ą'-
iyo`was'įyą mahe'l iya'ya ke'ᵉ. 4. He'c'ena oya'te kį iyu'weħ ina'z̧ipi
ną e'na e't'ipi ke'ᵉ. He'c'ųpi ną li'la ole'pi k'eyaṡ a'wicak'eya'-
tok'aħ'ą c'ąke' hąke'ya iye'nayąpi ną ee' li'la waṡi'g.lapi ke'ᵉ.
Yųk'ą' wic'a'ṡa wą wak'ą'-ig.la`wa c'a oya'te kį he'l ų' yųk'ą' he' e
c'a leya' ke'ᵉ, — Miye' iye'waya owa'kihi ye lo'. Tk'a iye'waya
hą'tąhąṡ t'ąkṡi'tku kį ųma' b.lu'z̧ikte lo', — eya' ke'ᵉ. 5. Yųk'ą'
he'c'etulapi ną iye'ya hą'tąhąṡ nąkų' t'ąkṡi'tku kį nųp'į' wic'a'yuze
c'e'yaṡ he'c'etu keya'pi'ⁱ. Wana' ole'kta c'ąke' oya'te kį a'taya m.ni'-
yo'huta kį ekta' wawą'yak-ahi`yotake'ᵉ. Yųk'ą' m.ni' kį ali' oma'ni ną
tohą'tu c'ą ak'e' m.ni' kį kaħlo'k ta'ku wąya'ke se'ṡna li'la e'tųwąhe'ᵉ.
— Ho, wi' c'oka' hiya'ye, g.la'pi ną ec'a'ṡ ak'e' u' po', — eya' c'ąke'
oya'te kį wi' c'oka' hiya'ya c'a t'iya'ta k'i'pi ną wo'tapi ną ak'e'
wawą'yak-hi`pi'ⁱ. C'ąke' m.ni' kį op'a'ya ole'he c'e'yaṡ he'c'enaṡ
ak'e' ħtaye'tu'ᵘ. 6. Hį'hąna c'a ak'e' m.niya'ta hi'yotakapi yųk'ą'
leya' ke'ᵉ, — Ka'k'iya ka mak'a'-ǧi maya' kį he'l oħla't'e wic'a'ṡa
wą ųko'lepi k'ų he' t'aṡų'ke kį ħpa'ye lo'. Ną ak'o'wap'a, ka maya' kį
he'l wam.ni'yom.ni c'a he'l i'ṡ wic'a'ṡa kį iye' yųke' lo'. T'a' hąl e'l
wai' k'e'yaṡ kini' c'a paha'-hepi`ya e'waųpi ną le' wag.li' ye lo', —
eya' c'ąke' he'c'enaħcį oya'te kį a'taya k'e' c'ų he'c'iya ica'k'oyela
e'huni ną wic'a'ṡa kį ag.li'pi ṡk'e'ᵉ. 7. K'e'yaṡ he'c'ena to'k'eca c'ąke'
to'k'el ec'ų'pi-waṡte`ka he'çihą he' ak'i'yapi ṡk'e'ᵉ. Hąke'ya ini'kica-

be the best thing to do for him. At last, they made a sweat lodge and placed him in it for a bath. After that, they made a suitable preparation, and then suddenly exploded some gun-powder in front of his face. And they say it was the shock from that explosion which at last restored him to his right mind.

44. Owl's Eyes.

1. A Pawnee man and his wife went out to hunt deer and were camped out by themselves, away from the tribe. And it happened that while the man was walking abroad, hunting, a war party raided his camp, stole his horses and demolished everything; and his wife was gone. 2. Immediately he gave some bear cries, and braced himself to look for his wife. He found and followed the trail left by the raiders, along the sandy loam of the creek. In all those tracks, he saw all men's foot-prints, and among them, only one woman's. He was certain, now, that his wife was with the men, and he determined to find her. 3. At evening he came upon a place beside a creek where the party had stopped in the woods to build a fire; he therefore sat down on the opposite shore to wait. Soon his wife herself came down to the stream after water for the camp; so he called out to her very softly like this, "It is I who have arrived. Let us start home at once." And she replied, "I must take this water back to the camp first; and then I will go with you. Wait for me there." 4. And right there this woman proved herself a very stupid person. When she took the water back she said, "I have just seen my husband.

ǵapi nǫ e'l e'g.nakapi nǫ oha'kap ta'ku oya's'į yuwį'yeyapi nǫ hehǫ'l wakta'śniħca hǫ'l ite' kį c'aħli' ona'p'opyapi śk'e'ᵉ. Yųk'ǫ' hetǫ' yuś'į'yeyapi kį ų' kawa'c'į-ksa`papi k'e'yapiⁱ.

44.

1. P'ala'ni-wic'a`śa wǫ t'awi'cu kic'i' t'a'ħca-k'ute`-ipi nǫ manį'l wic'o't'i kį i't'ehǫyǫ t'į'pi śk'e'ᵉ. Yųk'ǫ' wic'a'śa kį oma'ni-iya`ya hǫ'l to'k'iyatǫhǫ t'o'ka ahi'ħųni nǫ t'į' k'ų a'taya ik'į'nicapi nǫ t'aśų'ke kį iyu'ha mawi'c'anųpi nǫ t'awi'cu kį to'k'aħ'ǫ ke'ᵉ. 2.He'c'ena wic'a'śa k'ų ħna'ħna nǫ t'awi'cu oki'lekta c'a iya'ya ke'ᵉ. T'o'ka kį oye' k'ig.la'pi c'a wic'i'hakap wakpa'la-op'a`ya c'asmu' kį ec'e'l ya'hǫ ke'ᵉ. Wi'c'a'śa-oye` ece' nǫ wǫżi'la wį'yǫ-oye` c'ǫke' wana'ś t'awi'cu k'ų ak'i'yag.lapi kį slolya' c'ǫke' g.liyo'ya ke'ᵉ. 3. Ħtaye'tu c'ǫke' c'ama'hel wakpa'la ik'iyela e'yotaki nǫ c'et'i'pi c'a maya'-ųma` kį ec'i'yatǫhǫ waa'p'e yǫka'hǫ ke'ᵉ. Ic'ų'hǫ t'awi'cu k'ų he e' c'a m.ni' hiyo'u c'ǫke' tok'e'cela-ho`yek'iyį nǫ, — Le' miye' c'a wahi' ye lo'. G.licu' wo', ųk'i'yag.nįkte, — eya' yųk'ǫ' wį'yǫ kį i'ś, — Hį'yǫka', t'o'wa'ś m.ni' kį le' ak'i'ħpewayį nǫ hehǫ'l wahi'yukte. Iya'makip'e', — eya' ke'ᵉ. 4. Ho, nǫ he'tu c'a wį'yǫ kį le' li'la witko' c'a ikpa'zo śk'e'ᵉ. M.ni' kį ak'i' nǫ, — Mihį'g.na kį le'c'iya m.ni-a'g.lag.la

He is sitting down there on the river bank". So the raiders rose and came and surrounded him, and took him to their camp. Then they put out his eyes, and went away, leaving him tied and blind. 5. There he lay, helpless, and unable to walk or to see; so he rolled and cried out in his distress. Then, from somewhere, an owl came to him, and said, "How is it that you lie here thus?" In reply the man told his experiences. And the owl then spoke and said, "Very well. Will you wait here? Presently the news of your plight shall be taken to your home." He turned and delegated another owl to carry the news; so he flew away at once. Meantime the remainder of the owls set to work, and in some mysterious manner they put a pair of owls' eyes in the place of the ruined ones. Then the man had no further trouble seeing. The owl's eyes did for him. 6. At that point, the warriors from the Pawnee tribe came to the rescue, and found him there. So they proceeded from there on, to follow the enemy and avenge the harm they had done; and the man went with them. They soon reached them and killed all of them, and only the woman was alive. They said then, "To be sure, through Pawnee kinship, she is some relation to us all. But because she has used her husband so poorly, let us give her back to him. Let her be. He shall himself deal with her as pleases him." 7. So the man whose eyes had been put out, took and set the woman at a place apart, the woman who had assisted the enemy in harming him. Then he collected a considerable amount of firewood, tied his wife on to the pile, and setting fire to it all, he left her there. So the woman received what she was looking for when she was so cruel to her husband. 8. That man lived to a ripe old age. But the owls had said

---

yǫka′hǫ c̓a lec̓a′la wǫb.la′ke c̓ų, — eya′ c̓a he′c̓e wic̓a′sa ki̯ iyu′ha ina′z̧i̯pi nǫ ao′g.lut̓eyapi nǫ yǫka′pi ki̯ ekta′ ak̓i′pi sk̓e′ᵉ. Suta′ya p̓aḱta′pi nǫ hehǫ′l ista′ ki̯ nųp̓i̯′ pakpa′pi nǫ iḱpe′ya k̓ig.la′pi sk̓e′ᵉ. 5. C̓ǫke′ to′k̓a-ig.lu′skesni ki̯ ų paptǫ′ptǫyǫ iḱpe′ic̓iya c̓e′yahǫ ke′ᵉ. Yųk̓ǫ′ hi̯hǫ′ wǫ to′k̓iyatǫhǫ hihų′ni nǫ heya′ ke′ᵉ, — To′k̓a yųk̓ǫ′ le′c̓el nųka′ huwo′? — Heya′ c̓ǫke′ oki′yaka ke′ᵉ. Yųk̓ǫ′ — Ec̓a he′na yǫka′ yo′. To′ksa′ oya′k-ya̓pikte lo′ — eyi̯′ nǫ hi̯hǫ′-t̓okeca wǫ hosi′ye-si c̓ǫke′ tok̓i′yot̓ǫ ki̯yǫ′ iya′ya ke′ᵉ. K̓ohǫ′ hi̯hǫ′-ųma̓pi ki̯ li′la skǫ′pi nǫ hi̯hǫ′ ista′ k̓eya′ e′l o′kicistǫpi c̓ǫke′ hena′ ų′ to′k̓asniyǫ wawǫ′yaka sk̓e′ᵉ. 6. Hehǫ′tu hǫl wana′ t̓iya′ta ot̓ǫ′i̯ hųse wic̓o′t̓i ki̯ etǫ′hǫ zuya′ ahi′ nǫ wic̓a′sa ki̯ o′p hetǫ′ iya′ya ke′ᵉ. T̓o′ka k̓eya′ sica′ya ec̓a′kicųpi k̓ų hena′ e′wic̓akig.leǧapi nǫ iyu′hala wic̓a′ktepi sk̓e′ᵉ. Wi̯′yǫ k̓ų hece′la oka′ptapi yųk̓ǫ′, — Ho, eya′ P̓ala′ni-ota̓kuye ki̯ ec̓i′yatǫhǫ wi̯′yǫ ki̯ le′ iyu′ha wo′wahi-c̓ų ųki′yuhapi k̓e′yas hi̯g.na′ku ki̯ t̓eḧi′yela oki′ḱǫ ki̯ ų′ ųki′c̓upi-kte lo′. It̓o′ iye′ to′k̓el c̓i̯′ ki̯hǫ ec̓e′l ec̓a′kic̓ųkta c̓a, — eya′pi ke′ᵉ. 7. C̓ǫke′ wic̓a′sa ki̯ wi̯′yǫ wǫ t̓eḧi′ya ec̓a′kicų nǫ ec̓e′l ista′ iyo′tiye′-kiye c̓ų he′ icu′ nǫ ka′l e′g.le ke′ᵉ. Nǫ c̓ǫ-pa′hi nǫ e′l ayu′skiskiti̯ nǫ ile′ya c̓ǫke′ he′c̓el c̓i̯′ka oḱǫ′ c̓a ec̓e′l ak̓i′p̓a sk̓e′ᵉ. 8. It̓a′hena

to him, "See to it that you never enter a sweat lodge while the sweating rite is in progress." When he was now a very old man, he thought to himself, "Yes; but that was such a long time ago; it can not hold now." And he entered a sweatlodge while the rite was going on. Immediately both his eyes, the ones the owls supplied him, popped, from the heat; and this time he was blind forever. This is a fact!

45. Standing Rock Legend.

1. The rock that stands upright became so in the following manner. In the early beginnings of the people, a certain young man wanted a beautiful young girl for his wife. But she did not care for him, and so she wept continually over the matter. After a time, the young man becoming discouraged, got together practically all the horses there were, and offered them for the girl. 2. The young girl's male relatives, (i. e., cousins and brothers), wished very much to own the horses and they all joined together in urging her to accept the man. So, because of deference towards her male relatives, the girl at last declared her willingness to marry the man. So everyone was very happy. 3. But some days, shortly before the date of the marriage, the girl disappeared; so they all looked for her but she was absolutely gone. Her relatives and all the riders in the tribe joined together in looking for her. The mother of the missing girl

wic‘a'śa kį he' wani'yetu o'ta ni' śk‘e’ᵉ. Ho k‘e'yaś hįhą' kį ehą'ni heya'pi’ⁱ: — Ini'kaǵapi kį etą' ḣeya'p ec‘ų'¹ wo', — eya'pe śą wana' wic‘a'ḣcala k‘ụhą' he'c‘a wą e'l t‘ima' i' ną, — Etą'ś he' ehą'niḣcį heya'pi k‘ụ, — ec‘į' tk‘a'ś ka'k‘el-ok‘a'te cį ekta' t‘ima' i'yotake cį he'c‘ena iśta' nųp‘į' nap‘o'pa c‘ąke' hetą'ḣą tųwe'śni ną ec‘e'l t‘a' śk‘e’ᵉ. Le' wo'wicak‘e ye lo'!

45.

1. I'yą woslą'l he' cį he' le'c‘el ụ' he'c‘eca śk‘e’ᵉ. Ehą'ni wic‘a'ni k‘ụ he'hą' k‘ośka'laka wą wic‘į'cala wą li'la wį'yą waśte' c‘a yu'za c‘į' ke’ᵉ. K‘e'yaś iye' wica'laśni ną c‘e'yahą ke’ᵉ. Hąke'ya wic‘a'śa kį wac‘i' yeye'śni² kį ụ' śų'kak‘ą' wic‘a'yuha kį iyu'ha wi'taya iwi'c‘acu ną ụ' wic‘į'cala kį op‘e't‘ų śk‘e’ᵉ. 2. Yųk‘ą' wic‘į'cala kį t‘ib.lo'ku ną'iś śic‘e'śitku kį hena' śų'kak‘ą' kį wic‘a'yuhapikta c‘į'pi kį u' hįg.na'yeśi i'yopaśtakapi ke’ᵉ. Hena' oho'wic‘akila kį ụ' iyo'wįic’iya c‘ąke' iyu'ha c‘ąte' waśte'pi śk‘e’ᵉ. 3. Wana' yu'zįkta ik‘i'yela yųk‘ą' wic‘į'cala kį to'kel iya'ya c‘ąke' li'la ole'pi k‘e'yaś a'tayaś to'k‘aḣ'ą śk‘e’ᵉ. T‘i'takuye ną eya' wic‘o't‘i kį e'l to'na śųk-’a'kąyąka‘pi kį hena'

---

¹ *ḣeya'p ec‘ų'*, do, away from here; stay away; get out; don't come here, or go there.

² *wac‘į*, mind; *yeya'*, to send. This is generally in the negative, as in the text, and means, "to become discouraged; lose hope in." *wac‘į' yewa'yeśni*, I can no longer stand it.

was especially diligent in her search and often would be gone days at a time, during which she roamed weeping over the land. 4. One day when she was again walking about, when the sun was low, she looked towards the west and saw, outlined against the sunset, a small hill on top of which sat a woman, in the correct sitting posture for a woman[1]. The light in her eyes was so bright that it was difficult for her to see. Yet for all that, she knew at once that that woman was her daughter. And, sitting beside her, was the little puppy also facing the same direction. 5. The woman wept and stroked her daughter's head and shoulders in affection, and then she invited her to go home with her. But when the girl tried to stand, she could not move; so her mother felt of her legs, and already they were turned into rock. There the woman sat, holding her daughter in her arms, and wept continually, and felt of her body from time to time. Each time she found that more and more it was turning into stone. 6. At last both the girl and her little pet were turned into rock, they say. This happened a very long time ago, in fact before anyone's memory. It was only recently, yesterday you might say, that the stone was brought into the agency and set up

---

iyu'ha ole'pi ke'ᵉ. Tuwa' iyo'tą li'la wic'į'cala kį ole' k'ų he' iye' hų'ku kį he e' śk'e'ᵉ. To'nac'ąc'ą g.li'śni c'e'ya oma'ni ke'ᵉ. 4. Ak'e' wana' he'c'el c'e'ya oma'nihą yųk'ą' wi' k'u'ciyela hą'l wiyo'ĥpeyatakiya e'tųwą yųk'ą' wi' ai'yopteya paha' wą aką'l wi'yą wą wi'yą-nawį'ĥ² yąka' ke'ᵉ. K'e'yaś iśta' kį wi' iyo'śniźa c'ąke' tą-wą'yakeśni'ⁱ. He'c'eca k'e'yaś wana' he' c'ųwi'tku k'ų e' c'a slolye'ᵉ. Śų'kala wą yuha' yųk'ą' he e' c'a isa'k'ip i'ś-'eya' ak'o'ketkiya e'tųwą yąke'la'ᵃ³. 5. E'l i' ną c'e'yaya c'ųwi'tku kį p'a' ną hiye'te k'o' yusto'sto ną g.le-a'p'e c'ąke' wana' ina'źįkta yųk'ą' oki'hiśni c'ąke' hų'ku kį hu' kį oyu't'ą yųk'ą' wana'ś hehą'yą a'taya į'yą-ic'aǵe'ᵉ. C'ąke' e'na c'ųwi'tku kį p'o'skil g.lu's yąkį' ną c'e'yahį ną ak'e'śna hu' kį yut'ą' c'ą są'p wąka'takiya į'yą-ic'aĥ a'ye'ᵉ. 6. O'hąketa wic'į'cala k'ų he' śųĥpa'lala wą g.luha' i' k'ų kic'i' a'taya į'yąpi ke'ya'pi'ⁱ. Le' į'śe' li'la ehą'ni he'c'etu c'a lehą'l ni' ų'pi kį tuwe'ni he' slolya'piśni śk'e'ᵉ. Lec'a'la, ĥta'l ehą'kel⁴ į'yą k'ų he' owo'wic'ak'uta⁵ ak'i'pi ną he'l aki'c'ita he'hą' t'i'pi c'a ik'i'yela į'yąśa'-zizi⁶ ų' ag.le'-hą` wą ki'caǵapi ną ekta' aką'l e'g.lepi'ᵉ. Owo'wic'ak'u kį he' etą'hą c'aś'-

---

[1] The correct posture of a woman is to sit with both legs flexed to the right. No woman ever sits cross-legged. Even little girls are corrected, if they do.

² *wį'yą-nawįĥ; wį'yą*, woman; *na*, with the foot; *wįĥ*, from *wį'ǵa*, bent sharply. This means assuming a woman's sitting posture.

³ *yąke'la*, it, the little thing, also sat, (looking the other way); *la*, indicates the puppy is likeable.

⁴ *ĥta'l-ehą'*, yesterday; *kel*, in a manner of speaking, as it were.

⁵ *owo'wic'ak'uta*, at the agency; in the place where they give out food.

⁶ *į'yąśa'-zizi*, tan brick; *i'yą*, stone; *śa*, red. All brick is called *į'yąśa'*. But if it is tan brick, it is further described as *zizi'*, yellow; yellow red-stone.

at the fort[1] and the government disbursing station took its name from the image, and became Standing Rock. Even today, anyone who goes there may see the stone.

46. The Friendship Song.

1. Two men who bore the friend relationship[2] to each other, made a covenant between them one day. They composed a song which they called the friendship song, and they said that only they two might sing it. It was understood that whenever and wherever one of them heard the song it would mean that the other was in great trouble. 2. Thus the one who heard it was immediately to know that here was a situation calling for aid to his friend. One time there was a warparty and these two friends were in it. Always, wherever they went, they went together. At a late hour, when it was dark, they stopped for the night and one of the friends was sent to a lake near by to get water for the camp. So he took a pail and started off. As it was very dark, he had to feel his way along with his feet. 3. Now he reached the bank and tried to dip out a pailful of water, but the water proved to be too shallow; so that he gradually waded towards the centre of the lake, testing the depth as he went, and at last he took up water where it was somewhat deeper; and just then he noticed some black objects here and there, in the lake. 4. But just he as decided that they were large rocks, he heard a

t'ų'pi c'a ļ'yǫ Wosla'l Hǫ' eci'yapi⁾ⁱ. Lehǫ'tu kį tuwa' c'į' hǫ'tǫhǫṡ ekta' yį' nǫ į'yǫ kį he' iṡta' ų' wǫya'ka oki'hi⁾ⁱ.

46.

1. *Wic'a'ṡa nų'p k'ola'kic'iyapi yųk'ǫ' le'c'el wi'wahokic'iyapi ṡk'e⁾ᵉ. Olo'wǫ wǫ iye' ka'ǵapi nǫ he' Kola'kic'iyapi-Olo'wǫ c'a iye'pi kį nųp'į'la³ ahi'yayapikta ke'ya'pi ṡk'e⁾ᵉ. Tohǫ'tuke c'e'yaṡ ųma' ta'ku t'ehi'ka wǫżi' e'l na'żį hǫ'tǫhǫṡ olo'wǫ kį he' ahi'yayįkta ke'ya'pi ṡk'e⁾ᵉ. 2. He'c'el ųma' kį nah'ų' kįhǫ wǫ'cak t'ak'o'laku kį ana'kikṡį-kta wǫ he'c'el slolki'yapi ṡk'e⁾ᵉ. Yųk'ǫ' to'huwel ozu'ye wǫ e'l nųp'į' o'p'api ṡk'e⁾ᵉ. O'hįni to'k'iya ya'pi c'ǫ nųp'į' ece'-op'api c'ǫke' wana' ak'e' ħtaye'tu hǫ'l e't'ipi c'a e'l ų'pi yųk'ǫ' ųma' b.leya'ta m.ni' hiyo'yeṡipi c'ǫke' c'e'ǵa yuha' nǫ li'la oi'yokpaza c'ǫke' nat'ǫ't'ǫkel iwa'ṡteg.la⁴ ya'hǫ ṡk'e⁾ᵉ. 3. Wana' b.le' kį e'l ihų'ni nǫ c'e'ǵa kį m.ni' kį ekta' ipa'g.mųk ożu'la icu'-wac'į k'eṡ k'a'zela c'ǫke' sǫ'p c'oka'takiya c'op'a' iyu't'a ya'hį nǫ hǫke'ya wana' aṡme'laka c'a e'l m.ni' icu' kį ic'ų'hǫ b.le' kį e'l ena'na ta'ku k'eya' sapsa'pya hiye'ya c'a wǫya'ka ṡk'e⁾ᵉ. 4. K'e'yaṡ hena' į'yǫ-t'ǫka ke'c'į' ħcehǫ'l wic'a'ho wǫ*

[1] Fort Yates, North Dakota.
[2] The friend- or *k'ola'*-relationship, assumed once, could never be broken. A man must put himself out, risk his life, do anything, for his friend.
[3] *nųp'į'*, both; *nųp'į'la*, only the two of them.
[4] *iwa'ṡtela*, gently; softly; slowly; sometimes *iwa'ṡteg.la*. There is no corresponding form for the latter, in Yankton.

human voice, so he listened again, and heard a man groaning somewhere. He went towards the sound hurriedly, and on arriving, he felt all around, and there lay a man, alive, but with his entire scalp peeled off so that it hung in front of his eyes. 5. So he hoisted him onto his back, and, standing in the water, holding him thus, he sang the friendship song. Back at camp, they heard him and his friend said, "That means my friend has met with trouble. For that is the song which we agreed to sing, if either of us ever met with disaster." So saying, he ran to him, with his weapons in hand. 6. And there was his friend, coming home with something on his back; so he went to him and. "Friend what is the matter?" he asked. So he told him. Then they straightway took the sick man home, the one whose scalp was loosened; and he told that those were all Dakotas who had been killed, and that he alone was left. 7. Next morning, they went to look at them and found they were all *Hu'kpap'aya;*[1] but their bodies were so bloated that it was difficult to recognize them. These had at first been cornered by the enemy who later threw them into the lake, thinking they had killed all of them. One survived but they did not know it. From then on, it is said, nobody ever drank from that lake again.

47. The Lovers.

1. The Dakota learned this story from the Cheyenne tribe among whom it is said to have happened, and they relate it frequently.

naĥ'ų' c'ąke' p'iya'-ana`ġoptą yųk'ą' wic'a'ša wą to'k'i c'ąya'ka šk'e'ᵉ. Ina'ĥni ekta'kiya yį' ną e'l ihų'ni ną yut'ą't'ą yųk'ą' wic'a'ša wą nata' kį a'taya ona'šloka c'a išta' kį aka'ĥpeya hiyu' k'e'yaš ni' ĥpa'ya šk'e'ᵉ. 5. C'ąke' g.liya'ĥpeic'iyį ną olo'wą k'ų he' ahi'yaya m.nic'o'p k'į' na'žį šk'e'ᵉ. Yųk'ą' t'iya'ta naĥ'ų'pi c'ąke' t'ak'o'laku k'ų heya' šk'e'ᵉ, — K'ola' ta'ku t'eĥi'ka slolye' lo'. Toĥą'l he'c'etu c'ą' olo'wą kį he' ųka'hiyayapikta ke'ya'-iwa`houkic'iyapi k'ų, — eyį' ną he'c'ena wi'p'e g.luha' ekta'kiya į'yąka šk'e'ᵉ. 6. Yųk'ą' t'ak'o'laku k'ų he' ta'ku k'į ną ku'ĥą c'a e'l ihų'ni ną, — K'ola', to'k'a huwo'? — eya' šk'e'ᵉ. C'ąke' oki'yaka šk'e'ᵉ. He'c'ena wic'a'ša wą nata' šloka'he ų he' t'iya'ta ak'i'pi yųk'ą' hena'keĥci Lak'o'tapi c'a wic'a'ktepi ną išna'la oka'ptapi ke'ya' šk'e'ᵉ. 7. Iĥį'ĥąna c'ąke' e'wąwic'ayakapi yųk'ą' hena' Hų'kpap'ayapi c'a naka'poyela ec'e'capi c'ąke' oi'yekiye-ši`capi šk'e'ᵉ. Hena' t'o'ka kį na'žįwic'ayapi ną iyu'ha wic'a'ktepi ke'c'į'pi ną b.le' kį ekta' oi'ĥpewic'ayapi šk'e'ᵉ. Wąži' ni' k'e'yaš slolya'pišni'ⁱ. Hetą' to'hųweni b.le' kį he' e'l tuwe'ni m.niya'tkešni šk'e'ᵉ.

47.

1. *Le' wo'yakapi kį Lak'o'ta kį oya'kapi s'a k'e'yaš Šahi'yelatąhą ag.li'pi ke'ya'pi'ⁱ.*

---

[1] *Hų'kpap'aya,* a band of the Teton Sioux.

The whole tribe was living in one place when the crier went out from the council tent, making this official annoucement as he rode along, 2. "Hear ye, and take warning! The magistrates have decreed it. From this place, the tribe is to separate into two groups. Tomorrow, you are to break up the camp and go away from each other in two directions. All summer long, the time is to be spent by both groups in hunting and the chase; and then, in the fall, you are to meet here again. From here, a suitable place for winter quarters will be found." 3. Now it happened that there was a certain young man and a certain young woman who were greatly affected by this news. This young man had been courting the girl, until, by this time, there was a great love between them. And it happened that the tribe's separating into two groups made it necessary for them also to part. One of them, the woman, belonged in the section that was going towards the Rocky mountains[1]. 4. As for the young man, he must go towards the Missouri, for his people belonged in the group assigned to hunt in that direction. Now the people were slowly moving away in two great paths, in opposite directions; but the young man sat on the edge of a bluff near by, holding his horses by a rope; and dreaded to leave with his people. He had two horses[2]. One which he rode and one which he led, as a spare one, by a rope. As he sat there, he felt as though he must die of grief.

Oya'te kį a'taya wi'tayela t'i'pi yųk'ą' e'yapaha wą howo'kawįh hiya'yį ną t'i'piyo'k'iheya kį etą'hą wo'yak hiya'ya šk'e'e, 2. — Ho', nah'ų' po'. Waki'c'ųza kį he'c'el eya'pe lo'. Letą'hą oya'te kį nų'pakiya k'iyu'špa iya'yapikte lo'. Hį'hąna kįhą ig.la'kapi ną letą'hą t'ok'ą'l ya'pikte lo'. B.loke'tu a'taya wak'u'wapi ną t'alo' m.nayą'pi ną ptąye'tu kįhą le'l ak'e' k'iwi'tayįkte lo'. Ną letą'hą tukte'l wani't'ipikta he'cįhą yasu'pikte lo', — eya' hiya'ya šk'e'e. 3. Ho, yųk'ą' he'-oya`te kį e'l wik'o'škalaka wą k'oška'laka wą kic'i' le wae'yapi kį ų' li'la iwa'tok'iyapi³ šk'e'e. K'oška'laka kį he' wik'o'škalaka kį oyu'špahį ną wana' li'la anu'k'atąhą i'c'iyokip'ipi hą'tu šk'e'e. Yųk'ą' le oya'te k'iyu'špapikte cį e'l ųma' Heska' kį he'c'etkiya ya'pikte cį e'l o'p'a šk'e'e. Wį'yą kį e' c'a hųka'ke kį he'c'iyatąhą o'p'api kį ų'. 4. K'oška'laka kį i'š m.ni'šošetakiya⁴ a'yįkte cį he'c'iyatąhą o'p'a šk'e'e. Wana' ig.la'kapi ną ot'ą'kt'ąkaya c'ąku'-kah a'ya šk'e'e. K'e'yaš k'oška'laka k'ų maya'-ap'a`žeže šųk-ka'ška yuha' yeka'pįhca hpa'yahą šk'e'e. Sų'kak'ą' kį nų'p wic'a'yuha šk'e'e. Ųma' aką'yąkį ną ųma' i'š kaška' yuha' c'a. He'c'el yąka'he c'ų he'c'eya' li'la iyo'kišica ų' t'eki'nica šk'e'e. 5. Oya'te ok'i'se ka

[1] The Rockies were called the White Mountains.
[2] Every man, while travelling, liked to have more than one horse; it was a sign of respectability, beside being a measure of safety.
[3] *iwa'tok'iya*, to be exercised over; to be much concerned by; *i*, by; *wa*, thing (?); *to'k'iya*, somewhere.
[4] *m.ni'šoše*, roiled, turbid water; The Missouri; *takiya*, towards, in the direction of.

15

5. The people going towards the Rockies had, somewhere among them, a young girl who also was very heavy of heart. That evening when this group stopped for the night and camp was being made, the girl became very ill. So her parents brought in the most skilful of medicine men who took turns doctoring her; but she seemed to grow worse; until it was evident, after two days' march, that she was about to die. 6. Meantime the young man, her young man, must have joined this group without her knowledge, for he was coming with the crowd, not able to withstand the pull to join this rather than his own section of the tribe, now well on towards the Missouri. They say he said, "I wish I could see that young woman." and the reply was, "Why, say! that is the one who, they tell, is very ill because she can not see you!" — 7. "Well, in that case, won't you please speak for me. I want the chance to see her," he said. In due time, he came to the tipi where she was and was politely ushered inside. When he entered, the sick girl looked at him and said, "Come over here." So he went to the place of honor of the tipi where she was lying, and sat down beside her. She took his hand in hers and said, 8. "If you came long before this, why didn't you come directly to me? I am sick because of you, and I could have been well long ago. But now, I am on the way to die. Take this, instead of me, and remember me some days." Saying that, she gave him a very beautiful pair of moccasins which she herself had embroidered with porcupine quills. And the young man, caring nothing for the

Ḣeska'takiya a'ye c'ų he'l tukte'l wik'o'śkalaka k'ų he' o'p'a k'e'yaś i'ś-'eya' li'la c'ąte' śi'ca śk'e'ᵉ. He'-ḣtaye`tu kį wana' e't'ipi ną t'ica'- gahąpi yųk'ą' ųg.na' wį'yą k'ų li'la waya'zą c'ąke' huka'ke kį wayų'- p'ika ece' wic'a'kic'opi c'a p'ik'i'yapi k'e'yaś są'p e'ś śica'ya ną hetą' wana' inų'pa-et'ipi yųk'ą' t'i'kte cį og.na' iya'ya śk'e'ᵉ. 6. K'ohą' k'ośka'laka t'awake¹ cų naḣma' oya'te ya'pi kį o'p'eya ya' śk'e'ᵉ. O'kini'ś he'c'etkiya li'la waś'a'kya iyu'tą kį ų, huka'ke kį wana'ś m.ni'śoseta ihų'nipi nac'e'ce c'e'yaś. Yųk'ą', — Eśa' wik'o'śkalaka kį he' wąb.la'ke śni, — eya' yųk'ą', — Wą, he'ś he' wąni'yakeśni kį ų' li'la k'u'źa² śk'į' ną oya'kapi k'ų, — eya'pi ke'ᵉ. 7. C'ąke', — Ec'a omi'ciyakapi ye'. Wąb.la'kįkte lo', — eya' ke'ᵉ. Wana' iye'hątu c'a e'l hi' yųk'ą' yuo'nihąyą t'ima' e'yayapi ke'ᵉ. Ka'k'el-t'ima` hiyu' tk'a' he'c'ena wį'yą k'ų ayu'ta ną, — Le'c'i hiyu' we, — eya' c'ąke' c'atku'ta ḣpa'ya c'a isa'k'ip i'yotaka yųk'ą' nape' e'l oyu'spį ną heya' ke'ᵉ, 8. — Eḣą'ni yahi' he'cįhą wą'cag.na le'l a'tayela ya'u śni. Niye' ų' le' wama'yazą c'a he'c'e eḣą'ni ama'kisnikta-iye`c'etu tk'a' ye'. Tk'a' wana' mat'i'kte cį og.na' iya'ya c'a miye' e'ek'iya le' icu' ną ų' mi'ksuya', — eyį' ną hą'pa wą li'la yup'i'yela iye' he'

---

¹ *t'a'waka*, hers, as it were.

² *k'u'źa*, to be ill. A Teton word, used principally by the Og.lala, and Rosebud Dakota. The rest of the Teton, as well as the Yankton, say, *waya'zą*, to be ill; *yazą'*, it hurts; *maya'zą*, it hurts me; I have a pain.

others who sat in the tipi looking at him, broke down and wept. 9. He came away from there, and that evening the news went about that the young woman had died, and then it was that he came face to face with a great sorrow. He roamed about over the hills and did not return to the camp. After two days, the young woman's body was laid away in a tipi[1], and from there the tribe moved on to another camp ground. But the mother and father remained behind and spent the time weeping over their loss. 10. When the sun was low, the man said to his wife, "Come, now, it is enough. Let us start out along the trail towards the new camp," and so the woman was just getting to her feet, when they heard someone weeping. It proved to be the dead girl's two brothers[2] who had returned to conduct their father and mother to the new camp, which they reached by sundown. 11. As for the young man, he must have been staying near by, instead of going away with the tribe, for in the evening he came weeping to the tipi in which the young woman lay. He carried a sorrow as bitter as if he had lost his wife.

---

ipa't'a c'a k'u' śk'e'ᵉ. Yuk'ą' k'ośka'laka ki e'l yąka'pi ną wąya'kapi k'e'yaś a'tayaś i'tok'aśni c'e'ya śk'e'ᵉ. 9. Ĥeya'p k'ig.ni' ną he'- ĥtaye'tu yuk'ą' wana' wik'o'śkalaka k'u he' t'a' ke'ya'pi c'ąke' wo't'e- ĥika wą ak'i'p'a śk'e'ᵉ. Paha' ki ec'e'kc'e iśna'la oma'ni ną wic'o't'ita ku'śni śk'e'ᵉ. Nu'pac'ą yuk'ą' wik'o'śkalaka k'u t'iyo'kit'i³ e'upapi ną etą'ĥą oya'te ki ig.la'kapi ną mak'o'c'e-t'okeca wą ekta' e't'ipi śk'e'ᵉ. K'e'yaś hu'ku ną atku'ku ki ot'i'wota ki e'na yąka'pi ną c'e'yahąpi śk'e'ᵉ. 10. Wana' wi' k'u'ciyela c'ąke', — Ho, wana' eya'ś he'c'etu we lo'. Iya'yapi ki ec'e'l c'ąku' ki' og.na' uyi'kte lo', — wic'a' ki eya' c'ąke' t'awi'cu ki ina'źi ĥcehą'l tuwa' c'e'ya-naĥ'u'pi, yu- k'ą' t'e' c'u haka'taku nu'p k'ośka'lakapi yuk'ą' hena' e'pi c'a ic'i'paś g.li'pi ną wic'a'hiyohipi⁴ ke'ya'pi c'ąke' o'p iya'yapi ną wi' maĥe'l iya'ye ĥcehą'l wic'o't'ita k'i'pi śk'e'ᵉ. 11. K'ośka'laka k'u i'ś leyalaka hehą'huniyą ot'i'wota ki e'l u' ĥuśe ĥtaye'tu yuk'ą' c'e'ya wak'e'ya ki e'l hi' ke'ᵉ. T'awi'cu t'a' iye'c'el t'eĥi' ak'i'p'a śk'e'ᵉ.

---

[1] Only very specially favored people were "caused to live in their own tipi." It meant that the burial scaffold was erected and the dead bound thereon, and a completely equipped tipi was built over it. Then the doorway was carefully fastened and the base weighted down with heavy logs to insure its security during storms. A tipi on a lonely prairie, with no smoke coming out, and no sign of life about, was avoided as the abode of a ghost.

[2] These might be her father's brother's sons; or her mother's sister's sons; or her father's male parallel or cross cousins' sons; or her mother's female parallel or cross cousins' sons. Or the girl's own brothers; but that is the least likely; for then they would probably wait behind until their parents were ready to go on.

[3] *t'iyo'kit'i*, living in her own tipi. This means, in this restricted sense, that she was laid away inside a tipi; a great honor; *t'i*, her home; *o*, in; *ki*, her; *t'i*, she lives.

[4] *hiyo*, followed by any of the directional verbs, means to come or go to get something and return with it; to go after.

15*

12. He found that the door had been securely fastened and laced, but he worked at it, untying it wherever it was tied, until at last he entered the tipi, thinking thus to himself, "I shall spend at least one night here with her[1] and when morning comes, then I will leave and go on to the camp." 13. He ceased weeping, and sat quietly under the scaffold which held the body of his love. Suddenly, the woman who was lying above him said, "Make a fire, and undo my wrappings!" and the young man fainted from fright. After a time, regaining consciousness, he uttered some bear-cries[2] to make himself brave. And again the woman said, "Make a fire, and take me down. I have come back to life, and I lie here living," and once again, as completely as before, the young man fainted away from fright. 14. After a while, he felt as though whistles (as of steam) charged out of his ears, and then he came to his senses once more. "Is what you just said the truth?" he asked and she said, "I say I have returned to life. Make a fire and take me down." 15. So he went from one tipi site to another, feeling about for wood, and gathered and brought it in. He built a fire and when it was large enough to warm the place he unwrapped the covers from her. Over everything, a smoked tipi had been wrapped. This he removed and

---

12. *T‘iyo'pa ki suta'ya iya'kaškapi nạ pazu̧'tapi k’e'yaš yuška'hi nạ t‘ima' iya'yi nạ — It‘o' le'l hạhe'pi wạži' e'cuḣci'š ama'yạpa nạ hehạ'l c‘aku' ki̧' ot‘a'p m.ni̧'kte, — ec‘i̧' šk‘e’ᵉ. 13. Yaštạ'³ nạ wic‘a't‘a wạ ḣpa'ye c’u̧ oḣla't‘e yạka'hạ yu̧k‘ạ' ug.na' leya' ke’ᵉ, — Ic‘e't‘i nạ mayu'žužu', — eya' c‘ạke' k‘oška'laka k‘u̧ t‘ạsa'k t‘ạ' ke’ᵉ. I't‘ehạ yu̧k‘ạ' wac‘i̧'-ksa`pa c‘ạke' ḣna'ḣna ke’ᵉ. Aḱ‘e wi̧'yạ k‘u̧, — C‘et‘i' nạ mayu'ḣpa'. Le' waki'ni c‘a ni' mu̧ke', — eya' c‘ạke' p‘iya'- t‘ạsa`k t‘a' ke’ᵉ. 14. I'tohạtu nac‘e'ca hạ'l nu̧'ge ki e'l ši'yot‘ạka oya'žopi s’e nasli' nạ wac‘i̧'ksa`pa c‘ạke', — A'wicak‘eya ta'keha huwo'? — eya' yu̧k‘ạ' — Waki'ni c‘e ep‘e'. Ic‘e't‘i nạ mayu'ḣpa'⁴, — eya' ke’ᵉ. 15. C‘ạke' ot‘i'wota ki iya'za yut‘ạ't‘ạ c‘ạpa'hi nạ ag.li' ke’ᵉ. Ḣe'c‘u̧ nạ hehạ'l c‘et‘i' nạ wana' iyo'k‘ata c‘ạke' yužu'žu nạ wizi' wạ t‘ạ'ka akạ'tạhạ ope'm.nipi c‘a he' icu' nạ mak‘a'ta o'zạt‘u̧⁵ nạ šina'-

---

[1] In spite of all the stories about ghosts, and the natural fear of them, the Dakota seem not to fear death, when their relatives are involved. I know of many instances of parents who have spent the entire night at their child's grave, in a cemetery.

[2] Bear-cries are a sort of guttural utterance, made by a man in times of stress, to raise his spirits, and in times of sorrow, to keep from tears. This man did not mind staying by the dead, while everything was as it should be; but when the unnatural took place, i. e., when the dead spoke, then he fainted.

[3] *yaštạ'*, to stop with the mouth; i. e., to stop weeping.

[4] *ḣpa*, to come down; to fall, (always with an instrumental: to cause to fall, by means of;) *ma*, me; *yu*, with the hands; *ḣpa*, down. This is the imperative, "take me down."

[5] *o'zạ*, a sheet, hung, like a curtain, as a protection or to conceal something. He brings the tent down, letting it hang from the scaffold, in such a manner that he can make the girl's bed against it, for protection.

made a sort of partition wall[1], or screen, reaching to the ground. Then he made a bed of the several fur robes he found, and then, taking the girl in his arms, he laid her down on the bed. 16. When she was lying there, she said, "Get my bag and open it. You will find in it several packages of medicine (grass-root). Find one that has a blue cover and give me some of the contents." He did as she had instructed him. She ate it, and gave a great deep sigh and then said, "Now, have no fear of me. I am really alive. Now, get the bag I used for a pillow. In it you will find a cake of pemmican." He found it as she had said. 17. He gave her to eat and ate some himself. And stayed with her till morning. Then he went out and made a travois, using a single pole on each side[2]. He placed her thereon, and started towards the tribal camp, on the trail they had made in moving. When they had travelled a long time, two men came in sight. As the young man walked, he tried to recognize them, and saw at last that they were the girl's brothers coming back again. 18. "Both my brothers-in-law are coming back this way, weeping for you," he told the girl, and at once she became very much agitated, and said, "Stop a little while. I have something to tell you before they get here. It is very evident that you are sincere towards me. That is why I have returned, that I may be your wife;

---

hiśma' to'nakel[3] *nakų' ope'm.nipi c'ąke' hena' k'u'ya owį'śt'ų ną hehą'l wį'yą kį icu' ną k'u'ta e'ųpa ke'ᵉ. 16. K'ų'l iyų'kį ną wį'yą kį heya' ke'ᵉ, — Wo'p'iye mit'awa kį he' yuśkį' ną p'eżu'ta owa'p'ahte to'na he'l ų' c'e wążi' t'oya'pi k'ų he' etą' mak'u', — eya' c'ąke' ec'ų' yųk'ą' yu'tį ną c'uwi' oki'niya ną, — Ho, wak'o'kip'eśni', he'c'eya' wani' ye', — eya' ke'ᵉ. — Ho, hehą'l p'ą' wą iwa'pahį k'ų he' icu'; he'l wasna' wą mahe'l ų' we', — eya' c'ąke' icu' ną yub.le'ca yųk'ą' wasna' wą iye'ya ke'ᵉ. 17. He'c'eś wo'k'u ną i'ś-'eya' wo'tį ną he'na kic'i' ayą'pa ną ihį'hąna yųk'ą' hupa'wążila*[4] *wą ka'ģį ną e'l wį'yą k'ų e'g.nakį ną yuha' c'ąku' kį' ot'a'p ya'hą yųk'ą' t'e'hą wana' ya'pi k'ų lehą'l wic'a'śa nų'p he'ktakiya u'hąpi c'ąke' iye'wic'a-kiye-wac'į yųk'ą' k'iye'la u'pi kį e'l wį'yą kį haka'taku*[5] *k'ų hena' e'pi c'a ak'e' u'pi'ᵉ. 18. — Tąhą' hena' e'pi c'a ak'e' he'ktakiya c'e'ya u'pe lo', — eya' yųk'ą' he'c'ena wį'yą k'ų li'la nihį'ciya leya' ke'ᵉ, — T'o'wa'ś e'na ina'żį'; wo'c'iciyakįkte, — eya' ke'ᵉ. — Miye' e'tkiya li'la wica'yak'a c'a wana' at'ą'į ye'. He' ų'hca c'a le' wag.li' ye', ų'k'ų'kta*

---

[1] Screen, against which a bed is made.
[2] The single-pole travois is a make-shift, the usual travois being made by half of the tipi poles tied on either side of the horse, and all the bundles and bags laid on the carrying platform behind.
[3] *to'nakel*, several; a fair number.
[4] *hupa'-wążi`kżila* is more usual. It means one pole on each side. This is the emergency type.
[5] *haka'taku*, her relatives, which include her brothers, parallel male cousins, and cross male cousins. A relationship requiring the utmost regard and respect, and avoidance to a degree.

but we must always live in mutual kindness. If we do, then we shall
reach the end together. 19. They must erect a tipi inside the camp
circle, and there for four days you and I will live alone together.
On the fourth day, in the morning, I will have something to tell the
people. That is what I want you to tell my elder brothers[1]. For a
while, I want nobody to touch me," she said. 20. When the brothers
were a short distance off, the young man went forward to meet
them, and said, "My brothers-in-law, it is your younger sister that
has come back to life, and I am bringing her with me. But first she
wants me to tell you something." So saying, he gave the instructions
she had just spoken. 21. Both the elder brothers, very greatly
amazed, said, "We will go back to camp and tell what we know,"
and turning about, they hurried away. On arriving there, they
related everything and the whole tribe was thrown into awe and fear
over it. They set about at once to build the tipi and make the
arrangements exactly as the young woman had specified, and soon
everything was in readiness for the marriage. 22. When the young
lovers arrived, it was understood that nobody should touch the
girl even to greet or help her, except her own husband, and so the
people, even the girl's close relations, stood afar off, watching. The

---

c'a ų'. Ho tk'a' o'hįni ų'śiųkic'ilakte'[2]. *He'c'el ųk'ų' hą'tąhąś ece'la
oi'hąke kį ekta' sak'i'p ųki'hųnikte'. 19. T'i'pi wąźi' c'oka'p
it'i'cagapi ną he'l ųki'śnala ya'm.nic'ą ųyą'kįkte'. Ici'topac'ą kįhą
hį'hąna-ec'i'yatąhą oya'te kį wo'wic'awakiyakįkte'*[3]. *C'a he'c'el t'ib.lo'
owi'c'akiyaka'. T'o'wa'ś tuwe'ni oma'yut'ąkteśni ye', — eya' ke'ᵉ.
20. Wana' t'ib.lo'ku kį k'iye'la u'pi c'ąke' k'ośka'laka k'ų itko'p
wic'a'yį ną — T'ąhą`, nit'ą'kśilapi k'ų kini' c'a awa'ku we lo'. Tk'a'
t'oke'ya ta'ku wąźi' nah'ų'nic'iyapikta c'į' c'a oya'k-maśi ye lo', —
eyį' ną wae'ye c'ų hena' ec'e'l oya'ka ke'ᵉ. 21. C'ąke' t'ib.lo'ku k'ų
nųp'į' li'la yuś'į'yayapi ną, — Wą'cag.na he'ktakiya ųg.la'pi ną
oya'te kį ekta' hośi'ųk'ipikte lo', — eya'pi ną iya'yapi ke'ᵉ. K'ihų'nipi
ną a'taya oya'kapi c'ąke' wic'o't'i k'ų ĥmų' ś'e wo'winihą ų' wak'o'-
kip'api ke'ᵉ. C'oka'p t'ica'gapi ną to'k'el eye' c'ų ec'e'l ta'ku oya'ś'į
yuwi'yeyapi c'a wana' hįg.na't'ųkte c'ų iye'hątu śk'e'ᵉ. 22. Wana'
k'ośka'laka kį wį'yą wą t'a' tk'a' k'ų he' ag.li' k'e'yaś ehą'tą — Tuwe'ni
oyu't'ąkteśni ye lo', — eya'pi kį he' o'wącaya ot'ą'į c'ąke' nape' eśa'
yu'zapi*[4]-*śni, ną hįg.na'ku kį ece'la e'l ų'ⁿ. T'i'takuye*[5] *ną hųka'ke kį
e'pika ye'ś k'o' i't'ehąyą wąya'k na'źįpi'*[i]. *Hųka'ke k'ų eha'ś yuś'-*

---

[1] The man becomes her spokesman, because he is to be her husband, and she
is spared talking directly to her brothers, where a certain avoidance is due.
[2] *ų'śiųkic'ilakte*, we shall be kind to each other.
[3] *wowic'awakiyakįkte*, I have something to tell them. *wa*, thing; *oya'ka*, to
tell; *wic'a*, them; *wa*, I; *ki*, dative sign; *kte*, future, sometimes indicating
intent or purpose.
[4] *nape' yu'za*, to take hold of the hand; i. e., to shake hands.
[5] *t'i'takuye*, immediate relatives; *t'i*, in the home; *taku'ya*, to have for a
relation.

mother and father were too astounded to realize what had happened for some time. Four whole days the young couple lived there
alone together, and people bringing them food left it outside the
door and nobody entered. 23. After four days, the young woman
said, "Now, will you ask my father and mother and my elder
brothers all to come here ?" So the husband went outside and said
to his brothers-in-law[1], "Brothers-in-law, you and your father and
your mother are all to come in now. It is your sister's wish." In due
time they all entered the bride's tipi and with great happiness they
met the girl. 24. These people were filled with joy over the fact that
a dead person should have taken up life again and come back to
them. And this was the way the young woman talked to them:
"Now, it is a proven fact that this young man's love for me is
genuine. He showed it in the days when I was still alive; and at my
death, too, he showed it. His sorrow over my going was sincere, and
for that reason I have been instructed to return that I may marry
him. 25. But there is one rule that we must observe. It is this:
Neither of us must ever scold or be unkind to the other. If we
show only kindness to each other all our lives, then at the end we
shall arrive full of years, together. And if we do so, then we shall
have built a great lesson for the tribe, so that hereafter, when men
and women take each other in marriage, they will be kind to each
other." 26. Now, that was the lesson which the young woman

---

*i'yayapi u̧' ta'ku to'k'a ki̧ t'e'hą-slolyapiśni'ⁱ. To'pac'ą a'taya he'l
iśna'lahci̧ t'i'pi ną wo'wic'ak'upe'ś k'o' t'iyo'pa ki̧ it'ą'kal e'g.lepi
ną tuwe'ni t'ima'hel iya'yeśni'ⁱ. 23. Wana' to'pac'ą ki̧ he' są'p-'iya̧`ya
yu̧k'ą' — Ho, wana' ina', ate', ną t'ib.lo' k'o' t'ima' u'pikte', — eya'
c'ąke' wic'a'kic'okta c'a ina'p'i̧ ną, — T'ąhą`, niye'pi ną niya'te²,
nihu̧' k'o' wana' yau'pikte lo'. Nit'ą'kśila he'c'el eye' lo', — eya' ke'ᵉ.
24. He'c'eś t'ima' hi'pi ną li'la wi'yuśkiyą wąki'c'iyakapi, ną
kit'a'pi yu̧k'ą' ak'e' ki'cig.lipi c'ąke' he' u̧' c'ąte' waśte'pi'ⁱ. Ho
yu̧k'ą' le'c'el wo'g.laka śk'e'ᵉ, — Wana' k'ośka'laka ki̧ le' miye' e'l
wica'k'e ci̧ t'ai̧' ye'! Ni' wau̧' k'u̧ hehą'ni he' a't'ai̧ ną mat'a' yu̧k'ą'
są'p a't'ai̧ ye'. E'l wau̧'kteśni yu̧k'ą' he'c'eya' c'ąte' śi'ca c'ąke' he' u̧'
kuma'śipi ną kic'i̧' u̧ma'śipe'. 25. Tk'a' wo'wasukiye wąźi'la
aho'u̧p'apikte'. Le e' ye': Tu̧'weni iyo'p'eu̧kic'iyapikteśni, ną
o'hi̧ni u̧'śiu̧kic'ilapikte'. Tohą'-u̧ni̧`pi k'e'yaś hehą' wo'wau̧śila ece'
u̧ki'c'iyuhapi hą'tąhą̧ś oi'hąke ki̧ ekta' sak'i'p u̧ki'pikta ke'ya'pe'.
He'c'el ec'u̧'k'u̧pi hą'tąhą̧ś wo'u̧spe wą oya'te ki̧ wic'a'u̧kicagapikta
c'a heya'pe'. Ki̧hą wic'a'śa ną wi'yą tohą'l kic'i̧'yuzapi c'ą'śna
iye'c'el i'ś-'eya' u̧'śikic'ilapikte', — eya' ke'ᵉ. 26. Ho he' wo'u̧spe c'a*

---

[1] When the girl wants her relatives, the husband can only talk to her brothers,
which he does; and they convey the invitation to the parents. If the girl
herself invited them, she would address her parents directly, charging them
to bring her brothers in.
[2] It is correct etiquette, in speaking to one person of another, always to
bring in, somehow, the kinship term existing between them.

brought back with her from spiritland and gave to the people. And so, from then on, whenever two people lived together in kindness towards each other and made their marriage a peaceful one, then it was said they were sure to live to a ripe old age together[1].

48. A Double-Face Steals a Child.

1. A young man who was living inside the camp circle as a son-in-law, came home from the hunt one evening and was very tired; but at the time, a little boy, two years old or a little past that, was whining and pouting over something, and the noise he was making irritated the father who said, 2. "Hey, send this boy outside, and let him continue there if he wants to," so his wife took the child by the arm, "Owl-maker[2], throw this one into your ear; he doesn't mind!" she said, sending him out of the door. He went crying around the tipi and then stopped. 3. All evening he didn't return, but they supposed him to have gone to his grandmother's tipi[3], so they didn't look for him, for he often stayed there a long time. Next day the mother went to her parents' home and they said nobody had been there; so she tried at the home of her husband's parents, but they also said he was not there. 4. Then they looked

wik'o'škalaka kį yuha' wana'ġiyatąhą[4] g.li' c'ąke' hetą'hą oya'te kį aho'p'api šk'e'ᵉ. He' ų' tuwa' nų'p ų'šikic'ilapi ną oki'c'iyuze waśte' wąži' ka'ġapi c'ą'śna nųp'į' sak'i'p ką'-iya`g.leya tąyą' ų'pi šk'e'ᵉ.

48.

1. K'oška'laka wą t'ic'o'kap wic'a'woħa-t'i yųk'ą' waye'-i ną wana' ħtaye'tu hą'l watu'k'a-g.li k'e'yaš ec'ą'l hokši'lala wą wani'yetu nų'p są'p-iya`yela c'a waka'kišyahą c'ąke' c'e'yahe cį c'ąti'yokšicį ną heya' šk'e'ᵉ, 2. — He'! Le' eša' t'ąka'l yu's iye'yi ye', ekta' heya'hįkte, — eya' c'ąke' t'awi'cu kį isto' e'l yu'zį ną, — Hįhą'-kaġa, le' nų'ġe oka'ħ'ol iye'ya', ece'š wana'ħ'ušni ye! — eyį' ną t'ąka'takiya yuce'k-cek iye'ya yųk'ą' he'c'enaħcį t'ia'ohom.ni c'e'ya iya'ya-hot'ąį ną hehą'yą aya'štą šk'e'ᵉ. 3. Ħtaye'tu a'taya g.li'šni k'e'yaš k'ų'šitku t'i'pi kį ekta' ų' se'ca c'ąke' iki'g.nipišni šk'e'ᵉ; he'c'i t'e'ħąhą ų' s'a c'ąke' he' ų'. Ihį'hąna c'ąke' wį'yą kį hų'ku t'i'pi kį e'l t'ima' iya'ya yųk'ą' tuwe'ni hi'šni ke'ya'pi c'ąke' ak'e'š hįg.na'ku kį he' hų'ku kį t'i' kį ekta' e'yokas'į k'e'yaš nakų' he'l i'šni ke'ya'pi šk'e'ᵉ. 4. Hetą' nake'š

---

[1] There are several cases where people lived in perfect harmony and died, nearly at the same time.
[2] To impersonate, act like, make oneself appear like something else, is to "make" whatever that is. In this instance, one who appears owl-like is referred to.
[3] This is the child's maternal grandmother whose tipi is near that of his parents. We know this, because the father is described at the beginning as living in the son-in-law state.
[4] wana'ġi, ghost; wana'ġiyatąhą, from ghost-land.

for the child seriously; the parents in tears, looking frantically everywhere. The entire tribe helped to hunt, and some went to the river in case he might have strayed there; and they went out to the holes and caves in the wild country, but all this they did in vain. 5. And then a young man, one of the sort that are rovers in the night, said this, "Night before last, I was passing in front of that tipi inside the circle, when a child came out crying, and someone rose out of the woodpile and took him and went with him towards the rear of the camp-circle." 6. At once they looked in all the tipis, entering one after another, but they could not find him. Meantime some boys and young men were stationed out in the country, far from the camp, where they were letting the horses graze. From this group a boy and young man were out hunting rabbits when they saw a being, covered with hair, and two horrible faces, one in the back of his head. 7. While they stood looking, they observed that he sat holding on one arm of a little naked boy who was crying; and by way of soothing him, the monster was stroking him under the arm with a bunch of wild rosebush stalks; with each stroke the child cried louder. He must have also whipped him with a lash across his body for there were ridges which indicated that; and by long crying the child's voice was strained. 8. When they realized this, they ran away. On arriving at the temporary camp where the rest

wica'k'eya k'oška'laka k'u t'awi'cu kic'i' c'e'ya hokši'-oki'lepi šk'e'ᵉ. C'ąke' wic'o't'i ki a'taya ole'-owic'akiyapi ną m.niya'ta k'o' wak'ą'heža ki ole'pi k'e'yaš iye'yapišni šk'e'ᵉ. Naku' mani'l wašu' hiye'ye ci ekta'kta k'o' ole'pi k'e'yaš itu'ya-hec'uhąpi šk'e'ᵉ. 5. Yuk'ą'- k'oška'laka wą hąo'manipi s'a ki he'c'a c'a leya' šk'e'ᵉ, — Hąhe'pi- ak'o'tąhą k'u he' ehą' t'i'pi wą c'oka'p he' ci he' ik'ą'ye wag.li'yaku k̇cehą'l wak'ą'heža wą c'e'yaya t'ąka'l hina'p'a yuk'ą' tuwa' c'u̇k'i ki etą'hą iya'yi ną icu' ną hola'zatakiya ak'i'yag.le lo', — eya' šk'e'ᵉ. 6. He'c'ena wic'o't'i ki a'taya t'i'yohila t'ima'hel iya'ya ole'pi k'e'yaš tuwe'ni iye'yapišni šk'e'ᵉ. Ic'u̇'hą hokši'la ną k'oška'laka k'eya' mani'l šuk-yu'ha yąka'pi yuk'ą' etą' k'oška'laka wą hokši'la ki wąži' kic'i' mašti'cala k'ute' oma'nihąpi yuk'ą' ta'ku wą a'taya hišma'¹ c'ą anu'k'atąhą ite'-kit'u c'a li'la wo'k'okip'eya wąya'kapi šk'e'ᵉ. 7. Ab.le's na'žipi yuk'ą' hokši'lala wą hac'o'c'ola c'a isto' sani' yu's yąki' ną c'e'ya c'ą kig.na'ka² ke'yi' ną uži'žitka hu' to'na u̇' a'-oškokpa ki hena' iyu'mama icu' ną li'la są'p yuc'e'ya šk'e'ᵉ. Naku' t'ąc'ą'-g.lakikiyą kasa'ka huše b.lob.lo'yela hiyu'ya c'ąke' c'e'yapi u̇' wana' ho' kagi'tela šk'e'ᵉ. 8. He'c'el wąya'kapi ną li'la nap'a'pi šk'e'ᵉ. Ųma' ki ekta' wic'a'g.lipi ną oya'kapi c'ąke' he'c'ena

---

¹ *hišma'*, furry; with thick, long fur. *hi*, hair; *šma*, deep; *wašma'*, deep snow; *wo'k̇ešma*, tall weeds *(wok̇a* hollow place).

² *kig.na'*, to soothe, as a whimpering or crying child. *ka*, by way of; as it were. *ke'yi' ną*, he said, and. It means, "It must have been *his* way of soothing the child;" "He must call that soothing the crying child."

remained, they told what they had seen. At once everyone jumped
on his horse, and the race towards the tribal camp was on. On
arriving there they said, "Somehow[1], there sits a man below a
cliff in the wild country, and he is a fearful being; he is treating
a child in a cruel way. It has evidently been going on for sometime,
judging by the child's strained voice," they said. 9. So as many
of the people as could must go to the scene, they decreed, and the
entire tribe went. Guns, knives, bow-and-arrows, axes, and everything else with which they could fight, all these they took. 10. They
stopped near the scene, and picked their two best runners; these
two were commissioned to go on. And they were ordered to kill the
man, regardless of what he might be. So they advanced cautiously
along the creek, spying about from time to time, and once again the
monster was coming, holding the child dangling from his hand.
11. "'Owl-Maker, take this one and throw him into your ears,' is
what they said to me, and so I took him," he sang and meantime
he struck the child in the face, at each step. So the two waited in
the thick grass for him, and when he was passing close by, they shot
and killed him; and as he fell, one of them ran past him, catching
the child as he ran. At once the people all came on and took axes
and pounded the owl-maker to a pulp. They built two fires over him,
one after the other, and burned him thoroughly, reducing even the
bones to ashes, before they left him. 12. And they say that little

*iyu'ha śųk-ʾa'ką iye'icʾiyapi ną wicʾoʾtʾitakiya bu'wicʾahįg.la śkʾeʾᵉ.
Kʾiʾpi ną oya'kapi ną — Toʾkʾeśkʾe manįʾl maya' wą oħlaʾtʾe wicʾaʾśa
wą woʾkʾokipʾeka cʾa wakʾąʾhezala wą tʾeħiʾya kʾuwa' ye lo', cʾa wana'
tʾeʾhą-hecʾųwelakʾa ho' kagi'tela ye lo', — eya'pi śkʾeʾᵉ. 9. Cʾąke'
oya'te kį etą' toʾna oki'hipi kʾų iyu'ha ekta' ya'pikta ke'ya'pi yųkʾą'
oya'te kį icaʾkʾoyela iya'yapi śkʾeʾᵉ. Ma'za wakʾą', mi'la, wąhįʾkpe,
nazų'spe ną taʾku ųʾ watʾoʾkyepʾica² kʾų oya'sʾį yuha' ya'pi śkʾeʾᵉ.
10. Kʾiye'la ina'zipi ną hehąʾl kʾośkaʾlaka nųʾp li'la lu'zahąpi cʾąke'
hena'yos ekta' yewiʾcʾaśipi śkʾeʾᵉ. He' taʾku-wicʾaʾśa heʾcįhą kteʾpikta
cʾa ųʾ. Cʾąke' wana' wakpaʾla wą kʾaʾpi kʾų he' opʾaʾya aoʾkasʾį ya'hąpi
yųkʾą' wana' akʾeʾ hoksiʾcala wą hacʾoʾcʾola yuha' ną koʾskos uʾhą
śkʾeʾᵉ. 11. — Hįhąʾ-kaʾga, le' icu' ną nųʾge okaʾħʾol iyeʾyaʾ, eya'pi cʾa
iwaʾcu we', — eya'-lowąʾ ną kʾohąʾ hoksiʾcala kį ite' og.naʾg.na
apʾaʾ śkʾeʾᵉ, cʾa' e'g.le cʾą iyeʾna. Cʾąke' woʾħeśma kį eʾl iyaʾpʾepi ną
wana' leʾcʾeg.la hiyaʾya tkʾaʾś katʾiʾyeʾyapi ną g.liħpaʾye cį icʾųʾhą
ųma' įʾyąkį ną wakʾąʾhezala kʾų he' yukʾaʾp icu' ną yuha' iyoʾpteya
iyaʾya śkʾeʾᵉ. Heʾcʾena oya'te kį aʾtaya ahiʾyu ną hįhąʾ-kaʾga kʾų
kaħuʾħųgapi śkʾeʾᵉ. Nųʾpa-akʾiʾg.le acʾeʾtʾipi ną huhu' kʾoʾya cʾaħoʾl-
kaħ³ iħpeʾyapi śkʾeʾᵉ. 12. Yųkʾą' hoksiʾcalala kʾų he' tʾa' nų sʾe niʾla*

---

[1] *toʾkʾeʾśkʾe*, which is translated as "somehow," means "by some means, or
in some manner that is not obvious".

[2] *watʾoʾkya*, to cause death to an enemy. *pʾica*, suitable for.

[3] In good Dakota, I believe this noun would not be abbreviated. *cʾaħoʾta-
kaħ*, reduced to ashes.

boy came very seriously near to dying, but at last he got well. When he grew up, he was very powerful supernaturally, which fact was demonstrated in many ways. And he lived a very long life, and at last he died of old age. Somewhere the butte where this happened is situated, and this incident has given it its name, so that the people call it Owl-Maker Butte, they say. This happened long ago; this is not a myth.

49. The Warriors who Became Snakes.

1. Out of the Winnebago tribe five men went to war; and travelled far without meeting anyone. Their reserve of food was gone, and they were very hungry when what I am about to relate took place. They turned about and were coming home; camping near a butte, beside a lake. 2. Along the water they saw a buffalo-bull grazing, so they selected the one from their number whom they considered their best marksman and asked him to shoot it. Accordingly, while they stood watching, he crept up on the animal, and when near enough, he aimed his gun at it. Just as he prepared to fire, the tail of the buffalo appeared as something else. 3. On closer observation, he saw, not a tail but a rattle snake in place of the tail. At once he was disturbed, and was reluctant to fire, but recalling how hungry they all were he said to himself, "It will be all right, for I shall cut off the tail and remove it; and the body part we shall eat." 4. Then he fired and hit it at the first try, so the others were very happy

---

*šk'e'ᵉ. Ic'a'ǧį ną li'la wak'ą' c'a a't'ąįyą ų' ke'ya'pi*ˣⁱ*. Ną li'la wani'-yetu o'ta ni' ų' ną kąį't'a¹ šk'e'ᵉ. To'k'iyap paha' wą e'l le' he'c'ųpi c'a mak'o'c'ażeyal-yapi ną Hįhą'-Ka`ǧa-Paha`, eci'yapi šk'e'ᵉ. Le' ehą'ni he·c'etu šk'e'ᵉ; le' ohų'kakąšni šk'e' lo'.*

49.

1. *Hot'ą'ke-oya`te kį etą'hą k'oška'laka za'ptą zuya' i'pi ną t'e'hąl ihų'nipi k'e'yaš ta'kuni ata'yapišni ec'e'l ųwe'ya hena'kicilapi c'ąke' li'la loc'į'pi hą'l le ta'ku wą ob.la'kįkte cį le' he'c'etu šk'e'ᵉ. Kawį'ǧapi ną t'iya'takiya ku'pi ną b.le' wą ȟe-o'ȟlat'e yąka' c'ąke' e'l ag.li't'ipi šk'e'ᵉ. 2. Yuk'ą' m.ni-a'g.lag.la t'at'ą'ka wą ų'hą c'ąke' wąya'kapi ną iye'pi kį etą'hą wąži' li'la wątą'yeya c'ąke' he' i'ki-m.napike cį ų' g.laȟni'ǧapi ną t'at'ą'-ka kį he' o-ši'pi šk'e'ᵉ.C'ąke' wana' wąya'k na'žipi kį ec'e'l e'tkiya slohą' yį' ną wana' ik'ą'yela ihų'ni k'uhą' ma'zawak'ą' apa'ha yu'za šk'e'ᵉ. Wana' ut'į'kta hą'l ųg.na' site' kį t'o'keca-hig.la šk'e'ᵉ. 3. Tąyą' ab.le'za yuk'ą' t'asį'tašni², e'e' site'ȟla c'a wąya'ka šk'e'ᵉ. He'c'ena iyo'kip'išni ną k'ute'-kapi k'e'yaš li'la loc'į'pi k'u he' kiksu'yį ną t'ąma'hel leya' šk'e'ᵉ, — To'kša' ec'a'š site' kį hehą'yą waksa' iȟpe'wayį, ną ųma' kį hehą'yela ųyu'tapikte lo', — eya' šk'e'ᵉ. 4. Hehą'l k'ute' ną wą'cag.na kte'*

---

¹ *kąį't'a*, to die of old age.
² *site'* is a noun which becomes *sįta'*, with the prefix *t'a*.

and came, and, being evidently almost starved to death, they promptly cut the meat apart; and meantime the marksman cut off the tail, and threw it away. Now they roasted the meat, and also ate the raw liver[1] and were very much occupied in that way. But one who had gone scouting into the hills had not yet returned; so four men were doing all this. 5. Their hunger satisfied, they lay about in a leisurely fashion when one suddenly made the *hna'pi*[2] sound and said, "Alas, my comrades, something dreadful is happening to me!" when they looked, they saw him to be gradually turning into a snake, from the feet upward, so that by now, he was a man only as far as his head. 6. So they were greatly excited and frightened about it when another exclaimed, "I too am getting like that." So they all stopped to examine themselves, and lo! they were all snakes. In all their terror over themselves, they saw the one who had gone to scout, as he came into view on his return. So they called frantically to him to hurry. 7. "Return home at once! Something horrifying is happening to us, and you must take a message for us!" So he ran unbelieveably fast and came to them, but already they were snakes, like a pile in constant motion they crawled over one another[3]. 8. "Friend, no matter how hungry, don't eat this meat, but rather

---

c'ąke' ųma'pi kį li'la wi'yuśkįyą hiyu'pi ną he'c'eya' aki'h'ąt'a nųs'e ni'pi c'ąke' wą'cak p'a'l iyą'kapi[4] *k'e'yaś k'ohą' wao'ke ų he' śįte' kį hehą'yą waksa' ihpe'ya śk'e'*[e]. *Wana' wac'e'ųpapi ną waśpą'śni*[5] *k'o' yu'tapi ną li'la śką'pi śk'e'*[e]. *K'e'yaś wąźi' paha'ta tųwe'ya-iya`ya c'ąke' e'l o'p'aśni c'a le' to'plala*[6] *le'c'ųhąpi śk'e'*[e]. *5. Wana' wi'p'ipi c'ąke' tok'e' ec'a'c'a k'u'l hpa'yahąpi yųk'ą' wąźi' hna'hna ną,* — *Hehehe', k'ola`pila, t'ehi'ya to'k'eca ama'u we lo'!* — *eya' c'ąke' wąya'kapi yųk'ą' wąka'takiya zuze'ca a'ya c'a wana' p'a' kį hehą'yela wic'a'śa śk'e'*[e]. *6. C'ąke' ini'hįciyapi kį wale'hąl ak'e' wąźi',* — *Mi'ś-'eya' hema'c'eca ye lo'!* — *eya' c'ąke' iyu'ha ai'c'i-b.lezapi yųk'ą' iyu'ha zuze'capi śk'e'*[e]. *Wo'nihįciye yuha'pi kį ec'ą'l tųwe'ya k'ų he' wana' ku' hųśe o't'ąįyą g.liya'hą c'ąke' śica'wac'į kipą' ų'pi śk'e'*[e]. *7.* — *G.licu' wo'+!* *Ot'e'hiya toų'k'ecapi c'a takų'l iwa'hoųniyąpikte ina'hni yo'+!* — *eya' pą'pi c'ąke' wak'ą'yą į'yąkį ną g.lihų'ni k'e'yaś wana'ś iyu'ha zuze'capi c'a itu'śniyąyą hpa'yapi śk'e'*[e]. *8. Yųk'ą',* — *K'ola`, tok'e'hcį loya'c'į k'e'yaś t'alo' kį letą'ni*

---

[1] The liver, the kidney, the omasum, and a certain kind of fat, somewhere near the sternum, were eaten raw, when the beef was freshly killed.

[2] *hna'pi*, the bear-cry; see Page 228, Note 2.

[3] *itu'-śniyą`yą* means "to be in a constant stir, in vain," *itu'*, to no purpose. A pile of snakes, crawling over and under each other in ceaseless activity is what the word means here.

[4] *iyą'ka*, when following a verb of action, means "they fell instantly into the activity". Here, they proceeded at once to butcher the animal.

[5] *waśpą'śni*, uncooked things. The parts that used to be eaten raw, when an animal was freshly killed.

[6] *to'pa*, four; *to'plala*, only four.

go home as quickly as possible. And on your way, you will find a stray horse[1]; take him and ride him in your effort to get home. And tell this: that if our relations should wish to visit us, this is the order in which we will come out to greet them. But be sure that the sick bring offerings," they said. 9. So, after weeping there for a time, he left them behind with a sad heart and coming home he entered a creek bed, and there was a stray horse all by itself, a white, beautiful horse, so he caught it and rode it home. 10. Arrived at home, he related everything; so there was general mourning as for the dead, and soon after, the entire tribe travelled towards the scene. And on the last stop before reaching it, they paused to make some offerings. 11. When they finished this, they went on, stopping below the butte, where the one who first brought back the message now acted as crier for them, "Listen, Thunder-Sounds, I have come with all your relatives!" Immediately four very large snakes came, side by side, and lay near the people. 12. And their interpreter said further, "They told me that they would come to you in this order, in case you visited them, and they have now done it. The one lying towards the sunset is Thunder-Sounds. And that one next to him is Blue-Bird; and the third to them is He-Stands-Holy; and

---

yu'teŝni e' e' li'la k'ig.la' yo'. Nạ t'ahe'na ŝụk-'i'yeyapi² wą olu'spikta c'e he' akạ'yạkį³ nạ k'ihụ'niwac'į yo'. Nạ oya'ka yo', taku'wic'aụyạpi kį ụg.na' wạụ'yak-'upikta hạ'tạhạŝ le'c'el ak'e' i'c'ipaĥlalya ụhi'yụ-kapikte lo'. Tk'a' to'na waya'zạpi kį hena' wo'ụye aụ'pikte lo', — eya'pi ŝk'e'ᵉ. 9. C'ạke' e'na c'e'yahį nạ ụ'yạ⁴ wic'a'g.licu nạ c'ạte' ŝi'ceĥca ku'hạ yụk'ạ' wakpa'la wą e'l g.liyu'weje ĥcehạ'l ŝụ'kak'ạ' wą ska' owạ'yak-waŝte` c'a iŝna'la ụ'hạ c'ạke' oyu'spį nạ akạ'yak k'ig.la' ŝk'e'ᵉ. 10. T'iya'ta g.li' nạ wo'yaka c'ạke' li'la waŝi'g.lapi nạ i'yec'ala wic'o't'i kį he' a'taya ig.la'kapi nạ k'e' c'ụ he'c'etkiya a'ya ŝk'e'ᵉ. Nạ wana' ik'ạ'yela e't'ipi yụk'ạ' he'l waụ'yạpi ka'ġapi ŝk'e'ᵉ. 11. Ig.lu'ŝtạpi c'ạke' yuha' ya'pi nạ paha'-t'ạka k'ụ he' oĥla't'e e'nażį nạ wạżi' waho'ŝi-g.li k'ụ he e' c'a ho'yeyį nạ heya' ŝk'e'ᵉ, — Ho, wo'! Wakį`yạ-Hot'ụ`, nita'kuye kį oya's'į o'p wahi' ye lo'! — eya' yụk'ạ' he'c'ena zuze'ca to'p li'la t'ạkį'kįyạpi c'a i'c'ipaĥlalya u'pi nạ k'iye'la ahi'yụka ŝk'e'ᵉ. 12. Yụk'ạ' iye'skake⁵ c'ụ he' ak'e' leya' ŝk'e'ᵉ, — Ho tohạ'l ekta' wic'a'yahipi kįhạ le'c'eĥcį hiyụ'kapikta ke'ya'pi k'ụ ec'ụ'pe lo'. Wi' mahe'l iya'ye cị ec'i'yatạhạ ĥpa'ye cị he' Wakį'yạ Hot'ụ' e' ye lo'. Nạ i'yok'iheya ĥpa'ye cị he' i'ŝ Zitka'la T'o' e' ye lo'; nạ wic'i'ciyam.ni kį he' i'ŝ Wak'ạ'yạ Na'żį e' ye lo';

---

[1] Already touched with the miraculous, they become] gifted with omniscience.
² *ŝụk*, horse; *iye'yapi*, they find it; a found horse; a stray.
³ *akạ'yạka*, to ride; *akạl*, on; *yạka'*, to sit.
⁴ *ụ'yạ*, leaving them behind.
⁵ *iye'ska*, interpreter. *ia'*, speak; to talk; *ska*, white; clear (?); *ŝai'yela*, The Red-speech people; (The Cheyennes, whose speech was unintelligible). Sometimes *h* is inserted- *ŝahi'yela*.

the one on the other end is High-Star," so he named them in turn.
13. The relatives of each took their places in front of their own, now
transformed into snakes, and laid their gifts before them; and there
was much wailing, and though they were snakes, snakes must cry
too, for tears came into their eyes, they say. 14. After this wailing,
the snakes crawled away, towards the hillside where great rocks
jutted out, making holes, caves and crevices, into which they
entered, as into their homes. 15. Then the entire butte shook and
quaked. All the snakes of the world must live inside there, and must
have stirred about in concert at a signal. Years ago, when the
people lived farther to the south, this was their great, awe-inspiring
legend. Possibly here and there I have been inaccurate; but this
is close enough; they tell it in about this way, regularly.

50. She-who-Dwells-in-the-Rocks.

1. That one they called the Rock-dweller[1] was a *M.nik'ą' Wo'žu*
woman who was married to an *Og.la'la* man, after he had long been
buying her. 2. But he was very cruel, and kept guard over her always;
whenever he was going away he blackened the soles of her moccasins, and when he returned, he examined them for indications that
she had been away from home; and when he found such indications
by an erasure of the black, he whipped her; so that her lot was a

---

*ną ųma'-ihą̀keya k̄pa'ye ci he' Wic'a'k̄pi Wąka'tuya e' ye lo', —
eya'ya c'aže'wic'ayata šk'e'*. 13. C'ąke' t'i'takuye k'ų ec'e'kc'e wic'i't'o-
kapkap ina'žįpi ną wau'yąpi ahi'pi k'ų hena' wic'i't'okap e'g.nakapi
ną li'la wic'a'c'eya yuk'ą' zuze'cape šą' i'š-'eya' c'e'yapelak'a išta'-
m.nihąpi au'pi šk'e'*. 14. Aya'štąpi yuk'ą' hehą'l paha'-hepi`ya i̧'yą
ina'hahayela hiye'yi̧ ną e'l ena'nakiya wašų' t'ąki̧'ki̧yą yuk'ą'
he'tkiya g.la'pi ną t'ima' k'ig.la'pi šk'e'*. 15. Yuk'ą' hehą'l paha'
ki̧ he' a'taya huhu'zahą šk'e'*. He'c'iya zuze'ca mak'a' aką'l u̧'pi ki̧
iyu'ha t'i'pi hu̧še wi'tayela ški̧'ciyapi yuk'ą' paha' ki̧ škąšką' šk'e'*.
Ehą'ni ito'kah oya'te u̧'pi k'ų he'c'iya e'g.na wo'yakapi wo'winihąhce
c'i̧ le' yuha'pi šk'e'*. Eya' tukte'ktel b.lašna' nac'e'ca tk'a' eya'š
wale'c'elya ece'-oya`kapi š'a ye lo'.*

50.

*1. Igu'ǧa Ot'i' Wi̧ eci'yapi ki̧ he' M.nik'ą' Wo'žu-wi̧yą c'a Og.la'latą
wic'a'ša wą c'i̧'hą c'ąke' hig.na'yi̧ ną kic'i' u̧' šk'e'*. 2. K'e'yaš li'la
awą'yaki̧ ną to'k'iya yi̧'kta c'ą' iye'na² sic'u'ha ki̧ a'l-'ataya c'ahli'
iki̧'ciu̧ ną tohą'l g.li' c'ą'šna wi'yu̧ k'ų he' wąg.la'ki̧ ną tukte'l at'ą'i̧šni
c'ą he' to'k'i i' ke'yi̧' ną kaska'ksaka c'ąke' li'la t'ehi'ya u̧' šk'e'*.*

---

[1] This is a well-known character, and her experience is told, with variations,
among all bands, including the Yankton.
² *iye'na*, each time. *(to'na*, as often as, is understood in this sentence).
Ideally, it should read, *to'na to'k'iya yi̧'kta c'a iye'na* as often as he was
going away, so often he painted her soles.

sad one. 3. Because she wept so often her eyes were swollen and hidden by the swelling. Once again the man was away, when the mother of the man's mother (i. e., his maternal grandmother) who lived behind the camp circle said to her daughter-in-law (i. e., the wife of her grandson.) 4. "Daughter-in-law, try to be brave; you shall go home," she said. "No matter how badly my grandson treats you, say nothing; but meantime, get ready some moccasins and food. When you complete this, you shall go." 5. From that time, the woman's courage rose; so, they lived on, and one day, her husband's grandmother came to her again and said, "Now, daughter-in-law, you shall start; beware about looking back." 6. Her husband was walking across the camp, so they stood watching him, and soon he entered a big tent where they were playing a gambling game. 7. "There, daughter-in-law, he is going to gamble; when he is so occupied he stays away long, as you know. Go; over here, along the short branch of the creek, I have hung your rawhide bag on that oak tree." 8. So the woman went indoors, and took some little things she wished to keep, and went outside, and glanced a few final times towards the gambling tipi across the camp-circle; assuring herself that her husband was there for at least some time, she started run-

3. C'e'ye s'a kį ų' wana' ista' kį na'tąisnisniyą¹ po' sk'e'ᵉ. Yųk'ą' ak'e' wic'a'sa kį oma'ni·iya`ya hą'l hų'ku kį he' są'p'a-hų`kula² wą hola'zata t'i' yųk'ą' he' e c'a t'ako'sku³ kį e'l hi' ną heya' sk'e'ᵉ, 4. — T'ako's, c'ąte'-t'is kic'ų';⁴ yag.nį'kte', — eya' ke'ᵉ. — Tok'e'hci ta'ko'za sica'ya nic'u'wa k'e'yas ta'keyesni ną e' e' k'ohą' hą'pa ųwe'ya k'o' ka'ga'; he' lustą' kįhą ila'nįkte', — eya' sk'e'ᵉ. 5. C'ąke' hetą' nake's ki'tąla są'p c'ąto'kihi⁵ c'ąke' he'c'el ų'hąpi yųk'ą' wana' tohą'tuka wą ak'e' hįg.na'ku k'ų'sitkula k'ų he' wi'yą kį e'l i' ną, — Iho', t'ako's, wana' ila'nįkte', ųg.na' haye'kta kį, — eya' sk'e'ᵉ. 6. Yųk'ą' hįg.na'ku kį ka'k'ena hosą'p'atakiya ya'hą c'ąke' awą'yak na'zipi ną t'i'pi wą t'ą'ka c'a e'l k'ąsu'k'ute`pi yųk'ą' he'l t'ima' iya'ya c'ąke' hehą'tu sk'e'ᵉ. 7. — Iho', t'akos, k'ąsu'-k'uteya c'e; he'c'ų c'ą'sna t'e'hąhą g.li'sni k'ų; iya'ya'. Le'c'iya wakpa'la-opahci⁶ wą hiyu'ye cį he'l it'u'hu-c'ą wą he' c'ų he'l wizi'p'ą wą otke'c'ic'iye'⁷ — eya' ke'ᵉ. 8. C'ąke' wi'yą k'ų t'i'l k'ig.nį' ną taku'ku-cikcik'ala iki'kcu ną ina'p'į ną eha'keke hosą'p'atakiya e'tųwe c'e'yas hįg.na'ku k'ų ec'a'c'as t'ima'hel i'yotaka c'ąke' he'c'enahci heya'takiya į'yąkį

---

¹ I. e., closed; out of sight, from weeping. *tąį'*, to show; *na*, of itself.
² *są'p'a-hųku*, the mother beyond his mother; hence, his grandmother.
³ Her daughter-in-law. A greatgrandmother uses the same kinship term for her grand-child's spouse, as her son or daughter does.
⁴ *kic'ų*, to make an effort to be patient; kind; good; "try to be stout-hearted; brave."
⁵ *c'ąte'*, heart; *oki'hi*, to be able; "to have the heart to bear a thing; to make oneself equal to an occasion requiring courage, or some such quality."
⁶ *opa'hci*, a blind or false stream, running out of the main current, and then stopping. The appendix is an excellent example of *opa'hci*.
⁷ "I will hang it up for you" (on my initiative) 2nd dative.

ning away from camp, toward the place the old woman had suggested;
and there she found her, already waiting. 9. "Now, daughter-in-law,
keep generally towards that constellation known as Man-being-
Carried[1]; hide during the day and travel only by night; in three or
four days you should be home," she said. 10. Then she embraced
the young woman, over and over again, and, "My daughter-in-law,
how much I love her, alas!" she said and wept. 11. Then she went
towards her tipi; so the young woman started northward. After
travelling sometime, she began to think of, and pity herself, and
then she wept. "I who was always so timid; can this be I, suffering
so?" she thought, and ran and cried at the same time; and now it
was dawn, so she settled down to hide in the thick woods. 12. She
changed to dry moccasins, and ate her pounded dried meat; and
then she slept. When night came on, she travelled again. For three
days that was her program. 13. Again it was night, very dark, as
she was coming to a deep creek. She was groping along and
feeling her way with her feet. 14. At last she entered into the creek
bed, down the steep banks. But her feet were so wet that she
stopped in a clump of bushes, and, sitting under them, she was
taking off her moccasins to change to others, when she heard some
kind of voice, echoing down the entire creek. 15. "*Hį! Hį! Hį!*"
it said; and she thought, "Even if it should kill me, what of that?
I barely live on, anyway!" and she sat with her blanket pulled up

*ną it'u'hu-c'ą wą k'e' c'ų he'l i' yųk'ą' k'ų'ku-winų'ħcala k'ų t'ani'š[2]
ekta' na'žį ke'ᵉ. 9. — Iho', t'akoš, ka'kiya k'a wic'a'ħpi k'eya' Wic'a'
Ak'i'yuhapi eci'yapi kį he'c'etkiya ece' g.la'; ą'pa c'ą'šna ina'ħmį
ną hąhe'pi c'ą' ece'la g.la'; ya'm.nic'ą nąi'š to'pac'ą kį hehą'l-tuktel
yak'i'hųnikte' — eya' ke'ᵉ. 10. Heyį' ną hehą'l wik'o'škalaka kį
p'o'skiskil oyu'spį ną — Mit'a'koš wašte' wakila k'ų — eyį' ną c'e'ya
ke'ᵉ. 11. He'c'ena aya'štą ną t'iya'takiya k'ig.la' c'ąke' i'š wana'
wazi'yatakiya g.la' ke'ᵉ. O'tohąyą g.nį' ną hehą'l awa'ic'ic'į c'ąke'
c'e'ya ke'ᵉ. — C'ąlwą'k'a ima't'e c'ų, miye'šni s'e iyo'tiye'wakiye', —
ec'į' ną c'e'yaya į'yąkį ną wana' ąpa kab.le's ahi' c'ąke' c'ą-o't'eħika
wą ekta' mahe'l ina'ħma-yąka'hą ke'ᵉ. 12. Hą'pa-puspu'za kic'ų'
ną waka'p'api g.lu'tį ną ištį'ma ke'ᵉ. Wana' oi'yokpas ahi' c'ąke'
ak'e' iya'ya ke'ᵉ. Ya'm.nic'ą he'c'el ece'-ec'ų' ke'ᵉ. 13. Wana' ak'e'
hąhe'pi yųk'ą' li'la oi'yokpaza c'ąke' ku' k'e'yaš li'la wakpa'la wą
mahe'tuya e'tkiya ku' ną ta'kuni wąya'kešni c'ąke' nat'ą't'ą ece'-ku
ke'ᵉ. 14. O'hąketa wakpa'la kį ekta' g.liyo'ħpaya ke'ᵉ. K'e'yaš li'la si'
kį spa'ya c'ąke' t'o' k'e'yaš c'ą-pa'm.na wą oħla'te i'yotakį ną hą'pa
t'o'keca kic'ų'kta c'a hą'pa g.lušlo'kahą yųk'ą' ec'ą'l ta'ku wą wakpa'la
kį yai'yowasya hot'ų' u' ke'ᵉ. 15. -Hį', Hį', Hį',- eya'ya u' c'ąke'
lec'į' ke'ᵉ, — Naku' makte' k'e'yaš etą'š to'k'aka; le' iyu's'oya-wąų`*

---

[1] Man-being-Carried is the Big Dipper; the four stars being the four carriers,
holding the four corners of a blanket in which the one carried, lies.
[2] *t'ąni'*, old; *t'ąni'š*, allready, long before time.

over her head when that being arrived, and went around her and
said, 16. "Young girl, how does it happen you travel like this ?" So
she replied, telling him all things. 17. "A man with whom I lived
treated me cruelly; I am therefore going to my own people," she
said. 18. "Very well; of course, I am not what I used to be, anymore,
but so that when you get back to your people, you may be useful to us,
it shall be thus until you get home, that nobody shall be able to see
you," he said. "Thank you[1]," the young woman answered. 19. Somehow, from that time on, she felt braver; so that she ventured to travel
during the day too. 20. But from then on, something came over her,
and she lost her eagerness to reach her people. She climbed to the
top of a hill, and finding many flat rocks about, she sat down on one
of them, and looked about over the pleasant country. 21. Just then
now one drop of water, and now another, came down; so she
entered into a cave in the rocks, for shelter; and very soon, it was
raining very hard. 22. It was dark in the room. The cave seemed
like a room, with perpendicular walls of rock, so she carried in
sage-brush, and spread it for a bed, and there she lay down to sleep.
23. Her old mother-in-law had given her a small ax, so she used it
to cut the sage. 24. She stayed there all day, and then when the sun

---

*kį̇, — ecʻį̇' ną pʻa'mehel yąka'hą yųkʻą' hihʻų'ni ną oa'kawįġį ną heya'
keʼᵉ, 16. — Wicʻįcala, toʻkʻeśkʻe le' oma'yani huwo'? — eya' cʻąke'
ecʻe'l oki'yaka keʼᵉ. 17. — Wicʻa'śa wą kicʻi' wau̜' kʻe'yaś li'la tʻehi'ya
makʻu'wa cʻa le' tʻiya'takiya mitʻa'oyate kį̇ ekta' wicʻa'wag le', — eya'
keʼᵉ. 18. — Ha'.o, Le' oʻḣ'ą-emacʻetukeśni tkʻa' oya'te tʻi'pi kį̇ ekta'
yakʻi' kį̇hą wo'wanicʻįyekta cʻa toʻkśa' tuwe'ni wąni'yakeśni ece'-
yag.nį̇'² ną ecʻe'l yakʻi'hųnikte lo', — eya' cʻąke' — Pʻila'mayaye', —
eya' keʼᵉ. 19. Yųkʻą' hetą'hą yacʻą'te-tʻįze śʼe-leʻcʻeca cʻąke' ą'pa kʻeś
kʻo' ku' keʼᵉ. 20. Kʼe'yaś hetą'hą toʻkʻeca tʻau̜'śni ną tʻiya'ta kʻi-iʻnahni
kʻu̜ he' aki'sniʸⁱ. Paha' wą ekta' iya'hį̇ ną heʻcʻi į̇'yą-b.laskaˋska o'ta
cʻąke' wążi' akąʼl i'yotakį̇ ną oi'yokipʻila³ oʻkśąkśą e'tu̜wą yąka'hą
keʼᵉ. 21. Ḣcehą'l m.ni' hįhą'hą⁴ cʻąke' oḣloʻka wą iġu'ġa kį̇ eʼl hą' cʻa
ekta' tʻiyo'napʻe kį̇ lehą'l li'la maġa'żu keʼᵉ. 22. Tʻii'yokpaza keʼᵉ.
Iġu'ġa kį̇ g.lihe'heya⁵ tʻi'pi śʼe hą' cʻąke' pʻeżi'-śaśa kaśla' ną owį̇'śtʻu̜
ną eʼl iyu̜'kį̇ ną iśtį̇'ma keʼᵉ. 23. Kʻu̜'ku-winu̜'ḣcala kʻu̜ he' nazu̜'spe-
cikʼala wą kʼu' cʻąke' he' u' pʻeżi' kį̇ kaśla'ʼᵃ. 24. He'l ąpe'tu a'taya
iśtį̇'mahį̇ ną wi' iya'ya yųkʻą' śuk-ma'nitu-tʻąˋka⁶ wą tʻima' g.licu'*

---

[1] There is no word for "please". The particle, *ye*, at the close of a request,
signifies a petition; but even without it, the tone of voice in which a request
is spoken, is the determining factor. But there is a "thank you", literally,
"you cause me to regard it well, or good".
[2] *ece'*, followed by a verb of action, means "to do always, without variation."
[3] Reckoning the scene or prospect a pleasant one, she sat looking around.
la, to regard, consider.
[4] *hįhą'*, to fall as rain.
[5] *g.lihe'ya*, perpendicular.
[6] *śuk-ma'nitu-tʻąka* a large dog of the wilderness, the name for wolf.

16

set, a wolf entered, and sprang lightly over her legs as she slept, and went farther into the cave. 25. Her young ones were in there, the woman inferred, by the whining of cubs which came forth. 26. She stayed where she was, regardless of it, and when morning came, the wolf came back out, once again jumping over her legs. 27. But the strange thing was that it didn't so much as growl at her. The sun was high now, so she sat outdoors, looking down on the valley, where there appeared black spots here and there. She guessed those might be where butchering had been done; so she went to investigate and found that she was right; some buffalo hoofs lay about, so she carried them on her back and came home. She cut them apart and ate the fat that lay between the bones of the feet; and broke the long bones, and ate the marrow. 28. And then she saw a pack of wolves surrounding and driving a herd of buffalo along, by hiding around and then suddenly appearing, causing the buffalo to run. Then, of a sudden, as one might snap a twig in two,[1] they all charged the herd and killed one calf, and soon, another; and only calves they picked out and killed; all this, while she sat watching. 29. She came to them, and they stopped and scattered, so she butchered one of the calves and put the meat on her back and took it home; as it was now warm summer time, she cut the meat into thin layers for preserving and spread it over the flat rocks to dry. 30. At first she would take the dried meat and pound it, uncooked, into her rawhide

---

ną wį'yą wą k̯pa'ye c̓ų he' hu' kį apsi'l mahe'tuk̯cį k̓ig.la' ke̓ᵉ.
25. He'c̓iya mahe'l c̓įca' k̯pa'yapi hųse'ca ekta' šųk̯pa'la zą'kząkapi ke̓ᵉ. 26. K̓e'yaš he'c̓ena k̯pa'yį ną ayą'pa yųk̯ą' ak̓e' šųk-ma'nitu kį ina'p̓įkta yųk̯ą' si' kį apsi'l iya'ya ke̓ᵉ. 27. Ke'yaš to'kel i'š kik̯lo' eša'-šni̓ⁱ. Wana' wi' wąk̓atuya c̓a huk̓u'takiya e'tųwą yąka'hą yųk̯ą' ta'ku sapsa'pya hiye'ya c̓ąke' hena' owa'p̓ate² ke̓c̓į' kį ų' e'tkiya ya'hą yųk̯ą' hena' he'c̓a c̓ąke' t̓asi'ha ece' hiye'ya c̓a k̓į' ag.li' ną t̓asi'ha-oka`za-šį kį hena' špą'šni k̓e'yaš yu'tį ną t̓ac̓u'pa³ kį hena' kaksį' ną yu'ta ke̓ᵉ. 28. Yųk̯ą' ųg.na' šųk-ma'nitu ece' pte' opta'ye wą ao'kas̓į awi'c̓aupi ną ųg.na' c̓ą yuksa'pi s̓e našlo'k hiyu'pi ną ptehį'cala wą kte' ik̯pe'yapi ną ak̓e' wąži' kte'pi ną he'c̓a ece' kak̯ni'k̯ wic̓a'kte ahi'yayapi c̓ąke' ina'žį ną e'tkiya ya'hą ke̓ᵉ. 29. E'l ihų'ni yųk̯ą' ayu'štąpi ną kaa'beya iya'yapi c̓ąke' wąži' p̓a'tį ną t̓alo' kį k̓į' ag.li' ną wana' mašte' c̓ąke' t̓alo' zizi'pyela⁴ kab.la'⁵ ną į'yą-b.laska`ska kį ec̓e'kce ayu'b.laya pusya' ke̓ᵉ. 30. T̓oka' ekta' pa'pa-puza kį wizi'p̓ą og.la'p̓į ną t̓ac̓u'pa

---

[1] Another favorite simile indicating the lightning speed of an act.
[2] Butchering place. *p̓a'ta*, to butcher; *o*, in; *wa*, things.
[3] *c̓upe'*, long bones, containing marrow; also the marrow. Terminal *e* changes to *a*, with *t̓a*-prefix.
[4] *zizi'pela*, to be thin in texture.
[5] *kab.la'* to flatten out; to jerk, as beef, into very thin sheets of meat for drying.

container, mixing marrow-fat with it; and this she ate. But once
the notion came to her that she could have fire, and then she worked
on that. She took red grass, and the downy part of *nape'-oi'lekiyapi* (they cause it to burn in their hands; a kind of plant); this
latter she rolled into a ball, and placed it with some very fine twigs;
and there she held two transparent stones which she struck against
each other until she made a spark; then she carefully and hurriedly
blew on it and caused it to ignite. 31. From then on she had fire;
so she cooked and ate her meat like a human being. 32. Things were
so much improved that she guarded her fire always to keep it alive;
but one day a rain came and extinguished it, so from then on she
was without fire again. 33. The cubs were now large, so whenever
she sat outdoors, they would come out and sit around her. 34. When
she ate, she cut up pieces of meat for them and they ate. 35. The
mother returned, ever so often, but her coming did not frighten the
woman at all; rather she lived with the wolf as she might live with
a dog. 36. The *tⁱi'psila*[1] were now ripe, and grew thick on the hillside,
so she sharpened a digging stick and was out getting them when the
wolf came to her and said, "Grandmother, tomorrow you shall see some
human beings." 37. And the thought came to her, "How contentedly
I have lived here, alas!" and it saddened her. 38. Next morning the
wolf spoke again, "Grandmother, I must leave before they arrive.

*ica'hiya yu'tahą yųk'ą' ųg.na' c'etⁱi'kta-awa`cį c'ąke' p'eżi'-śaśa` ną
nape' oi'lekiyapi²-p'ąśp'ążela k'ų he'c'a yup'ą'p'ą ną c'ą-sa'kala
k'o' e'g.nakį ną e'l į'yą-żążą`la nų'p i'c'icatohą yųk'ą' p'eśn'iża
kai'le c'ąke' śica'wac'į po'ħ śką' ną woi'le ke'ᵉ. 31. Hetą'hą p'e'ta
yuha' c'ąke' t'alo' kį śpąyį' naśna wic'a'śa iye'c'el wo'ta ke'ᵉ. 32. Li'la
nake'ś tąyą' c'ąke' p'eta kį to'k'el sni'kteśni kį he'c'el awą'yaka yųk'ą'
to'hųwel maġa'żu ną ki'casni³ c'ąke' ak'e' p'el-c'o'la iħpe'ya ke'ᵉ.
33. Śųk-c'į'ca k'ų hena' wana' t'ąkį'kįyąpi c'ąke' tohą'l t'ąka'l yąka'
c'ą'śna o'kśą i'ś-'eya' yąka'pila ke'ᵉ. 34. Tohą'l wo'ta c'ą t'alo' hąke'
wawi'c'akiśpuśpu c'ą yu'tapila'ᵃ. 35. Hų'kupi kį g.li' k'eś a'tayaś
k'oki'p'eśni, śų'ka ś'e kic'į' tⁱi' ke'ᵉ. 36. Yųk'ą' wana' hepi'ya
tⁱi'psila kį o'ta ną waśte'śte c'ąke' hų'p'e wą kap'e'sto ną wawo'ptahą
yųk'ą' ųg.na' śųk-ma'nitu-t'ą`ka k'ų he' e'l hi' ną — Ųcì', hį'hąna kįhą
wic'a'śa aką'tula wąwi'c'alakįkte', — eya' ke'ᵉ. 37. C'ąke' — Tąye'ħciś
waų' k'ų', ak'e' wic'a'śa-śica k'ų e'l o'p'a se'cê, — ec'į' ną c'ąte' śi'ca
ke'ᵉ. 38. Hį'hąna yųk'ą' ak'e' śųk-ma'nitu k'ų he' hi' ną heya' ke',
— Ųcì', wana' hihų'nipiśnihą ib.la'm.nįkte'. C'e ec'a'ś t'iya'ta yak'ⁱi'*

[1] *tⁱi'psila*, a bulbous plant that grows wild on hillsides, which was a staple
food in the old days. In its fresh state it does not taste unlike raw sweet
potato.
[2] *nape' oi'lekiyapi*, They cause it to burn in their hand. (This is a plant, the
fruit of which turns into downy tufts. It is used medicinally. The name
must refer to the part the down played in starting fire.)
[3] *ki'casni*, it extinguished it, hers; 1st dative.

16*

So remember, when you get home, hurry matters on my account."
39. By afternoon, she saw two men come into sight, over on the
second hill from her. 40. "Even though they should be enemies, and
should kill me, what of that?" she thought as she walked about
finding *t'i'psila;* and then, they must have been coming nearer in
an effort to recognize her, for they shouted, "Are you a Dakota?"
So she would answer them, but the words stuck in her throat and
she could not utter them; this happened unexpectedly; so they came
on close, and on recognizing her, they wailed over her. 41. They
wished to take her with them but she refused. So, "The people will
arrive tomorrow," they said and went away without her. 42. The
next day, the people came by, and her aunt was in the company, so
she took her and returned with her. 43. Thus it was one complete
time (half-year), that she lived alone, and now she had returned to
be among people again. But this was a fragment of her own band[1],
so the man she was hiding from was not here. 44. The people now
had a buffalo hunt so she said to her aunt, "Aunt, I want a collection
made of all the fat that the people can spare"; so, when her aunt
reported it, two young men took a hair-less buffalo-robe, and
walked about the circle for contributions; and they took the resulting pile of fat to the young woman, so she asked them to empty it
all at a place away from, but within sight of, the camp. 45. Then she
went out and stood by the pile, and gave out a peculiar call, and

*kįhą maki'yuinahni' — eyį' ną c'įca' o'p tok'i'yot'ą iya'ya ke'ᵉ. 39.
Yuk'ą' wana' wi'c'o'kąhiya'ya² są'p-'iya'ya hą'l paha'-ici'nupa kį
he'c'iya wic'a'śa nų'p t'ąį'yą ahi'yokas'įhąpi c'ąke' wąwi'c'ayak
yąk'a ke'ᵉ. 40. — Naku' ka'na³ t'o'kapi ną makte'pi k'e'yaś etą'ś
to'k'aka, — ec'į'c'į t'i'psila ole' oma'nihą yuk'ą' hehą' iye'kiyewac'į
t'ahe'nakiya u'pelak'a, — Nila'k'ota huwo'? — eya'-houyapi c'ąke'
awi'c'ayuptįkte śą' u'c'ųnica-hįg.la c'ąke' he'c'ena u'pi ną k'iye'la
yuk'ą' iye'kiyapi ną g.luha'ha c'e'yapi⁴ ke'ᵉ. 41. Ag.la'pikta yuk'ą'
c'į'śni c'ąke' — Ec'a, hį'hąna kįhą oya'te kį ahi'hųnikte lo', — eya'pi ną
u'yą k'ig.la'pi'ⁱ. 42. Ihį'hąna yuk'ą' oya'te kį e'l hina'żįpi yuk'ą'
t'ųwį'cu wą e'l o'p'a c'ąke' iki'kcu ną g.lok'i' ke'ᵉ. 43. He'c'eś o'maka⁵
wążi' wahe'c'elya mani'l iśna'la u' k'u ak'e' oya'te e'g.na k'ig.la'
ke'ᵉ. K'e'yaś hena' iye' t'ao'yate kį hąke'pi c'ąke' wic'a'śa wą ina'hme-
k'iyį ną he'c'el oma'ni k'u he' e'l o'p'aśni ke'ᵉ. 44. Wana' wana'sapi
yuk'ą' — T'ųwį', waśį' m.nama'k'iyapikte' — eya' c'ąke' oya'ka c'a
k'ośka'laka nų'p pteha'śla⁶ wą yuha'pi ną howo'kawįh waśį' m.nayą'
oma'nipi ną kak'i'pi yuk'ą' t'io't'ąiyą e'kala-wic'aśi ke'ᵉ. 45. He'c'u
ną ekta' ina'żį ną to'k'eśk'e pą'pą ną hehą'l Lak'o'l-iya' — Iho', to'k'i*

---

[1] That means this was part of the Planters-Near-the-Water band of Tetons.
² *wi,* sun; *c'oka',* central; middle; *hiya'ya,* to be going by; i. e., high noon.
³ *kana',* those yonder.
⁴ They wept over her, as their own, a custom, persisting to this day.
⁵ *o'mak'a,* variously used to mean one season, or else one half-year.
⁶ A buffalo hide from which the hair has been removed.

then, in the Dakota tongue, "All right, now; where have you
gone ?" And all the wolves in the world, sprang up from somewhere
as though they had been sitting there waiting for the signal; and
promptly ate everything up. 46. "She dreams the wolf-dream"[1],
they said of her. Soon after, she asked that a tipi be erected for
her; it was done, and there she impersonated that being with the
transparent eyes[2] which first came to her, right in the sight of all
the people; so they decided that her supernatural powers were
limitless. 47. And, they say, that being which first came to her was
what is known as Double-face[3]. 48. In the mystery act, they would
bind her tightly into a buffalo fur hide, and place a mirror outside,
but corresponding to her forehead, and then, lying inside the bundle,
she would be able to look about outside without the slightest difficulty; so whenever anything was lost she would use this devise for
her eyes, and find it easily, they say. 49. And whenever she doctored
the sick, she was always successful, but, they say, in time she
abandoned this practice. 50. She was pregnant when she left, so
now she gave birth to a baby, a girl; she was the child of the man who
had maltreated her so. 51. When that girl was now a very old woman,
she once came to our home, and spent the night there. She occupied
the space on the left of the fireplace[4], and when we were all in bed
for the night, she told this story, so I myself heard it from her lips.

---

*ila'lapi he? — eya' yuk'ą' šuk-ma'nitu eya'pila ki oya's'i tukte'l
wakta' yąke' s'e ahi'huni ną wašį' ki a'taya tepya' iye'yapi šk'e'ᵉ.
46. — Šuk-ma'nitu-ihą`bla eya'pi šk'e'ᵉ. Ak'e' i'yec'ala manį'l t'ica'ħ-
wic'aši ną he'l išta' żążą' wą t'oka'ħci e'l hi' k'ų he'c'a-kaġa c'ąke' oya'te
ki hehą'l iyo'tą wak'ą'yawa`pi šk'e'ᵉ. 47. Yuk'ą' he ta'ku wą e'l hi'
ną o'kiye c'ų he' Anų'k-Ite` eya'pi ki he'c'a šk'e'ᵉ. 48 .Ptehį'šma wą
a'taya oyu'skiskitapi[5] ną p'aħte' ki ai'yopteya mi'yog.las'i wą
ik'o'yakyapi c'ą`sna mahe'l ħpa'ya k'eš heta'ħą t'ok'asniyą wawą'-
yaka c'ąke' tohą'l ta'ku wążi' to'k'aħ'ą c'ą'sna he' išta'-yį nąsna
to'k'asniyą iye'ya šk'e'ᵉ. 49. Naku' wap'i'ya c'ą' oya's'i oki'hi s'a
k'e'yaš wap'i'ye c'ų he' hąke'ya ayu'štą šk'e'ᵉ. 50. Ig.lu'š'aka hą'l he'
g.licu' c'ąke' wic'į'cala wą yuha' ke'ᵉ. He' le wic'a'ša wą šica'ya
k'uwa' k'ų he' c'įca' c'a. 51. He' wic'į'cala ki wana' winų'ħcala hą'l
ųt'i'pi e'l hi' ną t'isą'p ħpa'ya yuk'ą' ųki'yųkapi ki oha'kap le'
oya'ka c'a miye' i'yatayela nawa'ħ'ų*ᵘ.*

---

[1] To dream of some animal, is, of course, to have a vision of an animal and
derive power through it. This woman was said to derive supernatural
power through the wolf-spirit.
[2] The text does not say "transparent eyes" when this being is first introduced.
Evidently it was omitted by narrator.
[3] The only case I have, where the Double-face is represented as being a
friend to man.
[4] This is a space I referred to under Note 2 of page 185, where casual callers,
relatives, and chance visitors sat or slept if they had to pass the night.
[5] *oyu'skiskitapi*, they bound her tightly in, and wound a rope many times
around her, like a mummy.

51. A Bad Deed.

1. This is the tale of a tragic deed that was committed within the Dakota tribal circle. There was a Dakota woman who had two daughters with whom she lived. A young man came and married both the sisters, so his tipi was placed inside the circle, where he lived as a son-in-law. Immediately behind his tipi, the three uncles of the sisters, lived side by side, in the tribal ring of dwellings. They all lived in harmony together there. 2. Now, this young man who married the sisters, went every evening to the council tent which stood in the centre of the circle and returned at a very late hour. 3. It happened that one day the elder of his wives talked thus to her husband, "When you are away at the council tent someone comes in and lies with my younger sister, on the opposite side of our tipi. And when it is almost time for your return, a young man goes out." 4. And the husband said, "I will go to the council tipi again tonight. But I will return early. When I get to the doorway, I will stop and clear my voice. When I do so, you must answer me by clearing your throat also, if he is inside again. That shall be the sign." So the two of them had an understanding of what to do. 5. According to the plan, he went as usual to the council tent, but returned soon after, and, stopping outside, he cleared his throat. And his elder wife cleared her throat also. Thus he knew that a man was with his younger wife. 6. He took his knife out of its scabbard,

---

1. *Lakʻoʻta-hocʻoka¹ kị itʻiʼmahel wicʻoʼḱʻą wą woʼtʻeḣika ecʻųʼpi cʻa heʼ leʼ eʼᵉ. Wį̣ʼyą wą cʻųwį̣ʼtku nų̨ʼpa cʻa oʼp tʻiʼ yųkʻąʼ kʻoṡkaʼlaka wą toʼkʻiyatąhą hiʼ ną nų̨pʻį̣ʼ wicʻaʼyuzį̣ ną cʻokaʼp wicʻaʼwoḣa tʻi ṡkʻeʼᵉ. Tʻawaʼkʻeya kį̣ ilaʼzatalaḣcį̣ hoʻcʻoka kį̣ ahą́keya tʻawiʼcu kį̣ lekṡiʼtku yaʼm.ni iʼṡ-ʼeyaʼ tʻiʼpi ną oyaʼṡʼį̣ heʼl cʻąlwaʼṡteya ų̨ʼpi ṡkʻeʼᵉ.*
2. *Yųkʻąʼ le wicʻoʼwe-wicʻaʼyuze cʻų̨ leʼ hąheʼpi cʻąʼṡna tʻiʼpiyoʼkʻiheya kį̣ ektaʼ iʼ ną hą̨ʼ² tʻeʼhą cʻąʼ g.liʼ ṡʼa ṡkʻeʼᵉ.* 3. *Tʻawiʼcu-tʻokaʼpʻa kį̣ heʼ naḣmaʼla woʼkiyakį̣ ną — Tohąʼl tʻiʼpiyoʼkʻiheya kį̣ ektaʼ yaų̨ʼ cʻąʼṡna tuwaʼ leʼl tʻimaʼ hiʼ ną hosąʼpʻatąhą mitʻąʼ tʻoʼwąke kį̣ eʼl kicʻiʼ yųkį̣ʼ ną wanaʼ yag.liʼkta ikʻiʼyela cʻąʼ wicʻaʼṡa wą inaʼpʻe cʻų̨, — eyaʼ ṡkʻeʼᵉ.* 4. *Cʻąkeʼ, — Hąheʼpi kį̣ leʼ akʻeʼ hoʻcʻokata m.nį̣ʼkta tkʻaʼ ecʻaʼla wag.liʼyakukte loʼ. Tʻiyoʼpa kį̣ eʼl wakuʼ kį̣hą ecʻaʼṡ hoʼpʻimici- yį̣kta cʻe heḣąʼtu kį̣hą niʼṡ-ʼeyaʼ hoʼpʻiciya yoʼ, eʼl ų̨ʼ hą̨ʼtahą̨ṡ. Heʼcʻel isloʼlwayį̣kte, — eyaʼ cʻąkeʼ heʼcʻel nų̨pʻį̣ʼ iwaʼktaya ų̨ʼpi ṡkʻeʼᵉ.* 5. *Wanaʼ eyaʼpi kʻų̨ og.naʼyą hoʻcʻokata iʼ ną iʼyecʻala akʻeʼ g.liʼ ną tʻąkaʼl hoʼpʻiciya keʼᵉ. Heʼcʻena tʻawiʼcu-tʻokaʼpʻa kʻų̨ iʼṡ-ʼeyaʼ hoʼpʻiciya cʻąkeʼ wanaʼ kʻoṡkaʼlaka kʻų̨ akʻeʼ tʻawiʼcu-hakaʼkta kį̣ kicʻiʼ yųkaʼ cʻa slolyeʼᵉ.* 6. *Cʻąkeʼ miʼla wą g.luǧuʼkį̣ ną wį̣ʼyeya*

---

¹ The area enclosed by the Dakota tribe; the heart of the tribe; where everything tribal belongs.
² *hą,* night; from *hąheʼpi.*

and stood in readiness as a young man rushed out from the tipi. As he came past, the husband caught hold of him and at once dug his knife into his rival's abdomen, tearing a great gash across it. 7. Straightway the intestines dropped out, unwinding themselves, and the wounded man died instantly. The angry husband picked up the body of the dead man and threw it against the side of his tipi, letting it slide down to the ground. Then he withdrew to one side. 8. His two wives burst into tears, but he took out his arrows and said, "No! Don't you dare to weep! On your account, I have done horribly for myself, and if you start to weep, I will kill you both!" 9. As he stood watching them every instant, his wives did not dare to cry; his mother-in-law did not weep either. The slain man was one whose father was dead, and whose grandfather kept him as his own son. And the grandfather was the eldest of the wives' three uncles! Secretly, all unknown to the family, for nobody knew how long, those two had been intimate, — the boy and his young aunt. 10. It was he whom his uncle now had killed in the dark, by ripping his body open with a knife. When this became plain, an unspeakable horror fell upon them all. Straightway, that very night, the man and his two wives and his mother-in-law fled from the tribe. 11. Planning to get away when the camp was asleep, they quietly prepared in the dark, and, when nobody knew about it, they left. For two whole days, aimlessly; not knowing to

na'žį hą'l k'oška'laka wą t'ąka'takiya našlo'k g.licuⁿᵘ. O'pta iya'ye-wac'į tk'a's yu'ziyąˋkį ną mi'la k'ų ų' t'ezi' c'ap'į' ną g.lakį'yą yub.la's ahi'yuᵘ. 7. Wą'cak šupe' kį kag.la' hįḣpa'yį ną wic'a'ša wą c'ap'a'pi k'ų he'na t'a' iya'yeˋᵉ. Li'la wic'a'ša wą hįg.na'yąpi k'ų he' c'ąze' kį ų' t'e' c'e'yaš kat'a'ku-yuhaˋ¹ icu' ną t'it'a'hepiya kaḣ'o'l yeya' c'ąke' o'slohį ną mak'a'ta g.liḣpa'yeˋᵉ. He'c'ų ną ḣeya'p k'ina'žįˋⁱ. 8. T'awi'cu kį nųp'į' c'e'ya iya'yapi k'e'yaš wąhį'kpe iki'kcu ną, — C'e'yapišni yo', Niye'pi ų' wo't'iḣi ami'g.luḣpe² lo'. Yac'e'yapi kįhą nųp'į' c'ikte'pikte lo', — eyeˋᵉ. 9. Heyį' ną awi'c'ayuta na'žį c'ąke' to'k'a-c'eyaˋpišniˋⁱ. T'awi'cu kį e'pi k'e'yaš c'e'yapišni ną naku' k'ų'ku kį c'e'yešniˋⁱ. Yųk'ą' k'oška'laka wą kte'pi kį he' wab.le'nica c'a t'ųka'šitku g.luha' k'e'yaš c'įca' iye'c'el g.luha' šk'eˋᵉ. Ną he t'ųka'šitku k'u he' le wį'yą nų'p hįg.na't'ųpi k'ų he' leksi'tkupi t'oka'p'a kį e' šk'eˋᵉ. C'a ehą'k'ų tuwe'ni oslo'lyešni he'c'el tohą'yą wį'yą kį he' t'oška'ku kic'į' naḣma'-šką k'e'yaš nake's at'ą'į'ⁱ. 10. He oi'yokpaza hą'l wic'a'ša wą nawi'zi ną t'ųška'ku kikte' ną t'ezi'-yub.laˋzeˋᵉ. Nake's ta'ku to'k'ų k'ų wąg.la'ka yųk'ą' li'la t'eḣi' kį waya'keˋᵉ. He'c'ena hą' t'ahe'na wic'a'ša kį t'awi'cu nųp'į', ną k'ų'ku kį hena'keca ig.la'kapi ną wic'o't'ⁱ kį etą'hą nap'a'pⁱⁱ. 11. Wic'į'štįma hą'l nap'e'-wac'įpi kį he'ų' oi'yokpaza-ig.la'kapi ną

---

¹ kat'a'ku-yuhaˋ, to take up into the arms for carrying; yuha', to hold.
² ami'g.luḣpa, I have brought down upon myself; I have caused to fall on me.

whom to fly for safety, the fugitives travelled, and the second evening saw them at last making camp. 12. The man shot a buffalo so at least they had plenty of meat. At least, though they were sorrowful, they were not starving. While they were in flight, a snow storm was raging, making it difficult if not altogether impossible, for anyone to follow them. Therefore they had no fear from that quarter. 13. They made their third camp now. In a protected spot, in a bend of the wood where it was pleasant, they placed their tent; and while the women prepared supper at home, the husband went out and cut green tree bark for the horses. This he fed to them. 14. Now the sun had set, and the wives had supper ready; so the man went inside and sat down; and when they placed his food before him, he ate. As he sat there, he heard someone stamping his feet, as people do to get rid of the snow on their moccasins before entering a tipi. At once, instinctively he reached for his gun. 15. A man entered. Then more followed him, one after another until they filled the opposite half of the tipi, where they sat down. "Well, how good this is! Come, (to his wives), put on plenty of food to cook that our guests may eat!" he said. So his two wives hurried about preparing supper for the visitors. Soon it was ready and placed before them, — plenty of excellent food it was. 16. An entire warparty had walked in on them. They were Crows, and there were five of them. When they finished their supper, the war leader began to speak. 17. "When you first began to make camp, and when you

---

tuwe'ni slolye'šni iya'yapi⁼ⁱ. Nų́'pac'ą to'k'iya ya' t'ąį́šni oma'nipi ną ici'nųpa-ħtaye`tu yųk'ą' nake's e't'ipi⁼ⁱ. 12. Wic'a'sa kį pte' wą o' c'ąke' e'cuħci's t'alo' tąyą' yuha'pi c'a tok'e'ħcį c'ąte' ši'capi k'e'yaš e's it'o' aki'ħ'ąpišni⁼ⁱ. Ag.na' wa'p'ipika, hiyu'pi k'ų he'ħą' ec'ą'l li'la ica'm.na c'ąke' to'k'eniš tuwa' at'a'p awi'c'aukta-iye`c'etušni c'ąke' he'c'iyatąhą e'k'eš wak'o'kip'apišni⁼ⁱ. 13. Wana' ici'yam.ni-et'ipi⁼ⁱ. C'ą o'ta ną kaħ.mi'-ob.lula wą e'l wana' t'iki'c'ağapi ną wį'yą kį wo'hąpi c'a k'ohą' hįg.na'kupi kį c'ąya'ħ'u kaħ.la'yahe'ᵉ. Eya'šna he'c'a ų' šuk-wo`k'u c'ąke' he'ų' he'c'ųhe'ᵉ. 14. Wana' wi' iya'ya yųk'ą' wo'hą yuštą'pi c'ąke' wic'a'ša k'ų t'ima' g.li'yotakį ną wo'k'upi c'ąke' wo'tahe'ᵉ. Wo'l-yąke` c'ų, ųg.na' tuwa' t'ąka'l wa'-naki`skis¹ mak'a' naħta'ħtak² u' c'ąke' wą'cak ma'zak'ą' iya'kiħpaye'ᵉ. 15. Wic'a'ša wą t'i'l hiyu'⁼ᵘ. Ną ak'e' o'wec'įhą³ etą' ahi'yu ną hosą'p'atąhą t'i' ot'i's ahi'yotake'ᵉ. — Hųhi', tąyą' ye lo'. Ho, o'ta e'l iyo'ħpeya po'. T'it'o'k'ą hi'pi c'a wo'tapikte, — eya' c'ąke' t'awi'cu k'ų ina'ħni-wo`hapi⁼ⁱ. Wana' yuštą'pi k'e'l wo'wic'ak'upi⁼ⁱ, wo'yute waště'šteħca ece'. 16. He' ozu'ye c'a a'taya hi'yotakapi⁼ⁱ. K'ąǵi'-Wic'a'šapi c'a za'ptąpi⁼ⁱ. Wana' wo'l-yuštąpi yųk'ą' kic'i'za-it'ą'c'ą

---

¹ *wa*, snow; *kį'za*, to squeak; causing the snow to squeak under foot, with every step.
² *naħta'ka*, to kick; stamp.
³ *o'wec'įhą*, in file formation; one behind the other.

stood in the bend of the wood to cut green bark for the horses, we were watching you from the end of yonder cliff. We know that you are the only man in this camp and that there are three women. If I had wanted to, we could have killed you then, and these women we would have taken captive. But I had a special reason for coming here this way instead." Thus the war lord spoke. 18. Then he added, "When man meets man, when they visit one another, they fill the pipe for a smoke together!" And the Dakota replied, "You are right. But first won't you hear my story? When I finish it, then I shall be glad to hear what you will say about it. 19. I have done a tragic deed, and therefore, with these two women, I roam about, a fugitive. The two women are my wives, and the third is their mother whom her daughters keep with them because she has no husband, and that is why she is here with them. 20. I have committed murder. There was a boy, he was a nephew to these women. But alas, one of them was secretly intimate with him and so I killed him. I killed him first, and afterwards I knew it was he! Immediately, while the tribe slept, we broke camp and stole away. A great blizzard came up meantime so we do not know whether they are trying to follow us. 21. It is impossible for me to remain in the tribe, so I must

---

ki̧ wo'g.lake'ᵉ, 17. — T'oka'-ahi̧'yat'ipi nǫ ka ipa'ksǫ ki̧ he'c'iya c'ǫya'k'u yaka'k̇layahe c'ṳ he'hǫ' maya'tǫhǫ ao'nicas'i̧ ṳk̇pa'yape lo'. Nǫ le'l niṡna'la wic'a' yaṳ' nǫ wi̧'yǫ ya'm.ni o'p yaṳ' c'a a'taya slol'ṳ'yǫpe lo'. Wac'i̧ka yṳkǫ'ṡ he'hǫ'nik̇ci̧ ṳni'ktepi nǫ wi̧'yǫ ki̧ lena' iyu'ha waya'ka wic'ṳyuzapikta¹ tk'a'ᵃ. Ho tk'a' ec'a'kel² ec'a'muṡni e'e' le'l le'c'el wahi' ye lo'. — He'cel it'ǫ'c'ǫ ki̧ eye'ᵉ. 18. Ak'e' heye'ᵉ, — He'c'a³ wic'a'ṡa c'a wic'a'ṡa wǫẑi' e'l hi' c'ǫ oki'pagi⁴ nǫ kic'i̧' c'ǫnṳ'pe ṳṡto³, — eya' yṳk'ǫ' Lak'o'ta ki̧ ayu'pti̧ nǫ, — Wica'yak'e lo'. Tk'a' it'o'wa'ṡ wo'wag.lakikte lo'. Ab.la'ṡtǫ kihǫ hehǫ'l ta'kehikta he'cihǫ nawa'k'ukte lo'. 19. — T'ek̇i'ya wae'c'amṳ nǫ ṳ' le'cel wi̧'yǫ nṳ'p o'p nap'a'-oma'wani ye lo'. Lena'yos wic'a'b.luẑi nǫ ṳma' ki̧ he' i'ṡ hṳ'kupi k'e'yaṡ t'ǫṡna'ṳ c'a g.luha'pi nǫ ec'e'l k'o u' we lo'. 20. — T'i wic'a'wakte⁵ ye lo'. Hokṡi'la wǫ lena' wi̧'yǫ ki̧ t'oksa'yapi k'e'yaṡ ṳma' nak̇ma'la kic'i̧' ṡkǫ' c'ǫke' wakte' nǫ oha'kap he e' ki̧ wǫ-b.la'ke lo'. He'c'ena wic'i̧'ṡtima hǫ'l ṳki'g.lakapi nǫ naṳ'p'ape lo'. Ec'ǫ'l iwo'b.lu-t'ǫka c'a oye' ot'a'ṳp'apiṡni nac'e'ce lo'. 21. Wana'

---

¹ *waya'ka yu'za*, to take; lay hold on, as captives.

² *ec'a'kel*, purposely; with a definite reason.

³ *he'c'a*, and, *ṳṡto*, belong together. It is elegant and formal speech. It gives a sentence this force: "Don't you know, it used to be the custom to do so and so? Have you forgot it, or isn't it being done now?" These are not the words, but that is the spirit. It indicates a subtle reprimand, pointing out where the one addressed is remiss, especially as regards social duties.

⁴ *opa'ği*, to fill a pipe.

⁵ *t'i wic'a'kte*, to commit murder; *t'i*, home; *wic'a*, them, or someone; *kte*, he kills. To kill in the tribe, on home territory, is a crime against tribal government; is, in fact, murder. Killing an enemy, anywhere, is different altogether.

roam about in this way, I have decided; and if death overtakes us out here, what of that? I think to myself. 22. That is why I can not fill a pipe for you. Among us Dakota, a murderer's hand is bad. So won't you just blend the tobacco yourself and smoke, my friend? And then, if you kill me, that will be well. But grant me this, that you spare these women. Take them home with you and be kind to them. That is all," he said. 23. And the war leader conferred with his comrades in the Crow tongue and then, turning to the Dakota once more, this is what he told him, "Now, this is what we have to say about your story. Recently, only six days ago, in truth, my wife died. And when I first laid eyes on this young woman who is your younger wife, I saw a great resemblence to my wife in her appearance. 24. Because a great sorrow came over me when I saw her, this is what I want to say to you. If it is agreeable to you, you will all go home with us to Crow land, and you will stay and make your permanent home there." 25. The Dakota laid this invitation before his two wives who found it agreeable to accept. So he told the war chief that his wives were both glad to go and that they said, "Even if we die there, it will be well." 26. The war chief was very happy that his plan was to be accepted. "We will rest here four days," he said, "during which time, a sweatlodge will be prepared for you and you shall be purified. Then, you shall discard the clothing you now wear and put something different, something unpolluted, on your body. And after that, you shall take us to the

oya'te e'g.na waų'kta owa'kihiśni kį ų' manį'l ųk'ų'pi ną to'k'el uł'a'pike c'e'yaś he'c'etu-ųlape lo'. 22. He' ų' le' oc'i'cipagikta owa'kihiśni ye lo'. Lak'o'ta kį tuwa' t'i wic'a'kte c'ą he' nape' śi'ce-ųyawape lo'. C'a niye'ka k'eś ica'hit'ųpi ną c'ąnų'papo', k'ola`. Ną hehą'l maya'ktekta hą'tąhąś he'c'etu we lo'. Tk'a' eya'ś wį'yą kį lena' ni' awi'c'ag.lapi ną ų'śiwic'ala po'. Ho, hena'la ye lo'. — eye"ᵉ. 23. Yųk'ą' zuya'-it'ą'c'ą k'ų he' K'ąǵi'-wic'a`śa-ia` o'p'a kį hena' wo'wic'akiyakahį ną i'ś-'eya' itko'p ta'keyapi yųk'ą' hehą'l ak'e' Lak'o'tiya leye"ᵉ, — Ho, wo'lake cį ų' le'c'el ųke'yapikte lo'. Lec'a'la, śa'kpec'ąla k'ų he'hą' wį'yą wą¹ maki'ťe lo'. Yųk'ą' le wik'o'śkalaka wą lu'ze cį le' li'la iye'c'eca wąya'k ihe'wayį ną he' ų' le' wau' we lo'. 24. Li'la c'ąte' śi'ca-mahįg.la c'ąke' he' ų' le'c'el ep'į'kte lo'. It'o' he'c'el iyo'nicip'ipi kįhą iyu'ha K'ąǵi'-wic'a-śata ųg.la'pi ną hec'i'yani iyą'upikte lo', — eye"ᵉ. 25. C'ąke' Lak'o'ta kį t'awi'cu nųp'į' owi'c'akiyaka yųk'ą' iyo'kip'ipi kį ų' zuya'-it'ą'cą kį oki'yakį ną — Nakų' he'c'iyani uł'a'pi k'e'yaś he'c'etu we', — eya'pi c'a k'o' oki'yaka ke'ᵉ. 26. Yųk'ą' it'ą'c'ą kį li'la c'ąte' waśte' ną, — Ho, le'na it'o' asni'ųkiyapikte lo'. Ną k'ohą' ini'kaǵapi ną e'l nig.lu'skakte lo'. He' yuśtą'pi kįhą haya'pi t'okt'o'keca nų' ną letą'hą he'ktakiya ųka'yalapi ną śųk-ma'ųnupikte lo', — eye"ᵉ. —

---

¹ A woman of mine died. (He probably had other wives.)

Dakota camp where we will steal some horses. When we return here, then we shall go on to Crow-land." 27. When the murderer had been cleansed and new clothing put on him, they went forth until they neared the Dakota camp. Here the women with the baggage were left in care of one Crow, and the rest went on. This place where the women waited was just far enough to the camp so that the warriors could reach it without too much trouble, and yet it was sufficiently remote, for safety. 28. "Now, this is the place. Here is where I lived only recently. And yonder live the fathers[1] of him whom I killed," he said. Somewhat back of the camp circle, there was a new burial scaffold that had not been there before. He concluded that it was the grave of his victim, his nephew whom he had slain. He evidently took his horse with him, for near by, there lay a dead horse. 29. By this time, they were convinced that he was telling them the truth in all respects. Now, "There and there and there they possess swift running horses," he told the Crows. So they distributed themselves about, in such a manner that they might attack the herds of the various families he had pointed out, at about the same time. And they succeeded in bringing away many beautiful horses. 30. They fled with their stolen horses to the place where the women waited.

Ną ųg.li'pi kį hehą'l wana' K'ągi'-wic'aśata ųg.la'pikte lo', — eye'ᵉ. 27. Wana' yuska'pi ną haya'pi t'o'keca ų' yųk'ą' hehą'l wana' ya'pi ną Lak'o'ta t'i'pi kį k'iye'la he'l wį'yą kį wak'ị'² yuha' yąka'pi ną e'l K'ągi'-Wic'a`śa kį wąźi' awą'wic'ayakįkta c'a e'wic'ag.nakapi ną hetą'hą iśna'la iya'yapi'ⁱ. Hetą' Lak'o'ta t'i'pi kį oi'huni-waśte` k'e'yaś ak'e' eya'ś kai'yuzeya c'ąke' wo'k'okip'e-c'ola yąka'pi'ⁱ. 28. — Ho, le'tu we lo'. le'tu c'a he lec'a'la s'e wat'i' tk'a'ᵒ³. Ną ka'ki ka wak'e'ya kį hena' hokśi'la wą wakte' k'ų he' atku'kupi c'a t'i'pe lo', — eye'ᵉ. Hola'zata wato'hąyąkel he'l lec'a'la wic'a'ag.nakapi⁴ wą e'g.lepi c'a wąya'ke'ᵉ. He' wana' t'ųśka'ku⁵ wą kikte' k'ų e'-iteka⁶ c'a slolye'ᵉ; naku'ś śų'kak'ą' g.luha' iya'yelak'a ħpa'ye cį ik'i'yela śų'kak'ą' wą t'a' c'a yųke'ᵉ. 29. Wale'hąl he'c'eya' owo't'ąla wo'g.lake cį tąyą' iye'kiyapi'ⁱ. — Ho, ka'l ną ka'l ną ka'l śuk-lu'zahą wic'a'yuhape lo', — eya'-oya`ka c'ąke' ec'e'kc'e ina'źipi ną wi'tayela cą yuksa'pi s'e iya'yapi ną śų'kak'ą' waśte'śte o'ta awi'c'ag.liyacupi'ⁱ⁷. 30. Wic'a'-yuha li'la g.licu'pi ną wį'yą k'eya' waa'p'e yąka'pi k'ų he'c'i g.lihų-

---

[1] I think this should be "grandfathers", since the three brothers that lived side by side back of this man and his two wives, were fathers to the dead father of the boy just murdered. That dead father was the son of the eldest of these three brothers, who were uncles to the two women, the wives.

[2] *wak'ị*, luggage; baggage; *wa*, things; *k'ị*, to carry on the back.

[3] *tk'a*, at the end of a statement denotes that a thing is no longer so. "Here I lived only recently but (I do no longer)."

[4] *wic'a'ag.nakapi*, burial scaffold; *wic'a*, them; *a*, on; *g.nakapi*, they place.

[5] *t'ųśka'ku*, his nephew; cf. *t'ośka'ku* — her nephew.

[6] *iteka*, evidently; on the face of it; it appears.

[7] Correct Dakota would be *awi'c'ag.liyakupi;* but the way it is used here is heard often.

There they stopped to eat hurriedly, and then, changing their footwear, they went on at the same rate until they came to the camp site from which they had started together. 31. From there they began their flight homeward in earnest and kept going until they reached the land of the Crow Indians. The war leader told his people in careful detail how it came about that he brought these Dakota home; and they realized the situation. "Nobody is to regard them as captives in any sense, and nobody is to do them any harm," he told the people. 32. Accordingly, the people treated them with the highest deference and respect; and that Dakota, who had married sisters so that they bore the *t'e'ya*[1] relation to each other, took his younger wife and gave her to the war chief to be his wife. It was the woman whom the war chief had admired, seeing a close resemblence between her and the wife he had just lost. It was because of this likeness that he refrained from killing the Dakota family in the first place. 33. Thus it happened that the young woman who by her folly had brought disaster on her husband and sister and mother, was now the very means whereby their lives were spared. 34. The war leader took the Dakota into relationship, and they accepted

nipi'[i]. *Ina'ḣni-wo'tapi ną hą'pa t'o'keca oki'hąpi*[2] *ną he'c'ena ak'e' li'la g.licu'pi ną ḣtaye'tu hą'l ka'l et'ipi yuk'ą' e'l t'oka' K'ągi'- wi'ca`sa ki hi'pi k'ų he'c'iya k'iyų'kapi'*[i]. *31. Hį'hąna c'ąke' he'c'ena ta'ku ap'e'sni g.la'pi ną ec'e'l K'ągi'-Wic'a`sata k'ihų'nipi'*[i]. *Yuk'ą' zuya'-it'a`c'ą k'ų he' le'c'el oya'te ki wo'wic'akiyake'*[e], — *Tuwe'na lena' Lak'o'ta ki waya'kape ec'ą'wic'akiktesni ye lo'. Ną tuwe'ni ksu'yewic'ayiktesni*[3] *ye lo', — eyį' ną to'k'esk'e hena' o'p g.li' ki k'o' iyo'kawiḣ oya'ke'*[e]. *32. C'ąke' oya'te ki li'la yuo'nihąyą wic'a'- k'uwapi ną Lak'o'ta wą wic'o'we*[4] *wic'a'yuze c'ų he' t'awi'cu-haka`kta ki zuya'-it'ą`c'ą k'ų he' k'u' c'ąke' yu'ze*[e]. *He e' c'a t'awi'cu wą t'a' yuk'ą' iya'c'į*[5] *ną ų' wic'a'ktesni k'ų he' e*[e]. *33. He'c'es iye' t'o'ḣ'ą ų' wo'sice ahi'yag.lepi k'ų ak'e' iye' ų' ni'pi'*[i]. *34. Zuya'-i'tą`c'ą ki Lak'o'ta ki k'ola'ya ka'ga*[6] *c'ąke' iyu'ha pta'ya tak'ukic'iya ų'pi ną*

[1] When two women were the wives of one man, they generally called each other sister, unless they were natural cross-cousins. But they were said "to have each other for a *t'e'ya.*"

[2] *ohą'*, to put on the feet; literally, to stand in; *ki*, dative.

[3] Nobody shall harm them; shall cause them hurt. (The direct command, and the future tense are identical.)

[4] *wic'o'we*, the same family; the same stock; sisters; brothers; *wica'*, human; *owe'*, make; kind; variety.

[5] *iyac'į*, to compare a person to one dead, whom he resembles. To adopt someone to take the place of one gone; to whom the one in the adoptive position shows every consideration and affection due the one gone. (More properly, the term is *wal-i'yac'į*. But sometimes *wal* is omitted, as in this case.) A ceremony goes with this custom.

[6] *k'ola'ya-ka'ga*, to make or bind a friendship pact, in which the participants pledge life-long loyalty. The wives of one become the sisters-in-law of the other; the children of one feel just as free to ask favors of one as the other. The bond is closer and is obliged to be respected more religiously than that between natural brothers.

each other as friends in the kinship sense. So the families of the two men lived together in a happy group and were as closely related as if they were natural relatives. And that was how, after a time, the children, and the children's children, though they were Dakota, grew up as Crow Indians; and there they multiplied, and there they died. 35. From the very beginnings of people, the Dakota had always kept their tribal unity, and they had lived in a group. To be sure, now and again someone from an enemy tribe came in and made his home there and adopted the Dakota as his own people. But never, till now, did any Dakota separate himself from other Dakota to adopt another tribe and feel content to live and die there. After this, however, it happened that some Dakota did, at one time or other, live abroad. 36. This story they say comes from very far back in the history of the people.

52. A Man Kills his Friend.

1. Once, two young men who had always been great friends[1] went together to war. When they were out in the wild country they killed a buffalo and were rich in meat. Then one of them began building a shelter for himself away from his friend, who was puzzled by his act. 2. "Why, friend, how is it that you are doing this? I

ec'e'l sǫ'p-c'įcapi kį Lak'o'tapi k'e'yaš K'ǫǵi'-wic'a'ša iye'c'el ic'a'ǵapi'ⁱ. sǫ'p'a ig.klu'otapi k'e'yaš ekta'na ų'pi nǫ he'c'iyana t'a'pi'ⁱ. 35. Oya'te wic'i'c'aǵa hǫ'tǫ² Lak'o'ta kį wi'tayela ų'pi nǫ iye' t'ąka'tąhǫ t'o'ka wažį'kži Lak'o'tata hių'pi k'e'yaš to'hįni Lak'o'ta kį iye' lehǫ'yak iya'yapišni yųk'ǫ' nake'š le'c'etu k'ų hetǫ'hǫ he'c'ųpi nǫ hetǫ'hǫ Lak'o'ta i'š-'eya' c'į'pi c'ǫ' t'o'ka-oya'te wąžį' ekta' i'pi ke'ya'-pi'ⁱ. 36. Le' wo'yakapi kį li'la ehǫ'ni ke'ya'pi'ⁱ.

52.

1. K'oška'laka nų'p k'ola'kic'iyapi nǫ li'la t'eki'c'iḣilapi yųk'ǫ' heni'yos³ nųp'į'la zuya' iya'yapi šk'e'ᵉ. Manį'l i'pi hǫ'l t'at'ǫ'ka wą ata'yapi c'ąke' o'pi nǫ t'alo' o'ta yuha'pi yųk'ǫ' ųma' lehǫ'yak wak'e'yahǫ c'ąke' t'ak'o'laku k'ų ta'kowe kį' oka'ḣnigešni⁴ šk'e'ᵉ. 2. — Wǫ, k'ola`, le' ųki'šnala kį, to'k'ešk'e ta'ku to'k'anų⁵ huwo'?

---

[1] This is the friendship pact which was very binding; already discussed.
[2] *hǫ'tǫ*, ever since.
[3] *heni'yos* or *hena'yos* (Yankton, *hena'os*) those two.
[4] *oka'ḣnigešni*, he does not understand; *o*, in; *kaḣ.ni'ǵa*, to choose; select; *šni*, not.
[5] *ta'ku to'k'anų he?* What are you doing? *to'k'ų*, to do, occurs only after *ta'ku*, what; and in the positive, only in questions. Generally, *ta'ku* is shortened to *ta'k; ta'k to'k'amų he?* What am I doing? *ta'k to'k'anų he?* What are you doing? When this form occurs in a declarative sentence, it must always be in the negative; *ta'k to'k'amų šni*, I am doing nothing; *ta'k to'k'anų šni*, You are doing nothing. The ordinary word for to do is *ec'ų'*; *ec'a'mų*, I do; *ec'a'nų*, thou doest; *ec'ų'ųk'ų*, or *ec'ų'k'ų*, we two do.

supposed we would camp together." — "No, it pleases me that we should live in separate tipis," he replied. "Very well, then," the other answered and coming to the fire he sat and roasted some meat for himself. 3. And then the one building a tipi, called over, "Say, friend, are you able to bite into that piece of entrail you ate[1] ?" he asked, so his friend said "Yes." Soon after, a sound, as of pounding, came to him, so he stood up and tiptoed to his friend's tipi and looked in secretly; and there sat his friend, in the centre of the room, sharpening his leg. 4. "O, horrors! I see now, he pretended to question me but really he was trying to find out just where I was, whether in my tipi! Something does ail my friend; what is it ?" He thought along these lines, very unhappily. Sometime later, the other called again and said, "Friend, let us play on a swing; the evening is so pleasant." So the second one replied to that, "*Hoh!* how silly; we are not children!" and he refused; but after much urging he finally consented to play. 5. Now he knew things were wrong, so he set his head-ornament up on a peg in his tipi and addressed it thus, "Now then, my head-ornament, I am depending on you. Whenever he speaks, answer for me." And then he ran away. 6. He was travelling rapidly and the other was not following him; so he thought, "Well, at least little head-ornament[2] is standing

---

Sak'i'p ut'i'kte se'ce u, — eya' yuk'ą', — Hiya`, k'inu'k'ą ut'i'kte c'į he'c'el iyo'makip'i ye lo', — eya' c'ąke' — Ohą', — eyį' ną p'e'ta wą e'l g.li'yotakį ną ini'la wac'e'upahą šk'e'ᵉ. 3. Yuk'ą' ka' t'ika'ge c'u he'c'iyatąhą ho'uyį ną, — K'ola`, t'ašu'pa wą ya'te u he' lahlo'ke so? — eya' c'ąke', — Hą', — eya' šk'e'ᵉ. I'yec'ala ta'ku to'to hįg.lá' c'ąke' ana'slal e'tkiya yį' ną ao'kas'į yuk'ą' t'ak'o'laku wą išna'la e't'i k'u he e' c'a t'ic'o'kap yąkį' ną hug.la'p'estohą³ šk'e'ᵉ. 4. C'ąke', — Huhi! Ehą'kec'u wi'mayuh-kuzį⁴ ną i'še' t'ima'hel maka' he'cįhą he' slolye'wac'į heye' lo'! K'ola' to'k'eca huwó? — ec'į'c'į ic'ą'tešiceńca šk'e'ᵉ. Ak'e' i'tohątu yuk'ą' ho'uyį ną, — K'ola`, ho'hotela-ukic'ukte lo', htao'waštecaka c'a, — eya' c'ąke', — Hoh, it'o' he' ta'ku-houˋksika⁵ c'a! — eyį' ną wica'lašni k'e'yaš li'la oka'kišya c'ąke' hąke'ya iyo'wįyą šk'e'ᵉ. 5. Ną wana' tąyą'šni kį slolya' c'ąke' wap'e'g.nake wą yuha' c'a he' e'na pasla'l e'g.le ną leci'ya šk'e'ᵉ, — Iho', wap'e'- g.nake, wac'į'c'iye⁶ lo'. Ta'keya c'ą' iye'na miye'kahya ayu'pta yo', — eci'yį ną li'la nahma'-g.licu` šk'e'ᵉ. 6. T'e'hąl ku' k'e'yaš iha'kap

---

[1] "Did you make a hole in that entrail, with your teeth ? Could you break into it ?" In other words, was it tender ? But that wasn't really his chief interest.

[2] He personifies his head-ornament still further, having already addressed it as a human being, by leaving off the article, *kį.*

[3] *hug.la'p'estohą,* he was sharpening his leg to a point; *hu,* leg; *ka,* by the ax; by striking; *p'e'sto,* pointed, sharp; *hą,* continuative.

[4] *iyu'ga,* to question; *wa,* something; *kuza,* to pretend.

[5] *ta'ku-houksika c'a!* An idiomatic expression, meaning, "as if we were children! How childish!"

[6] *wac'į'ya,* to depend upon; rely on, have faith in; *wac'į',* mind; thought; *ya,* to use for.

his ground on my behalf!'' But when he was nearing the tribal camp, the man came behind, pursuing him; and so, when he was all but on him, he climbed a tree and sat high in its branches. 7. Sensing that his friend was no longer himself, and that he had designs on his life, he determined to kill him in self-defense, and sat ready to shoot. And the friend came to the foot of his tree, and kicked the base several times, jarring the whole tree. 8. Again he kicked, with even greater force, and his foot was caught in a crack and held fast there. Because he kicked a spot rather high on the side of the trunk, he was now lying with his head down, so his friend climbed down and jumping over his body, he landed clear of it, and then shot an arrow which transfixed him to the tree. And so he died. 9. From there he came on homeward, weeping, and arrived at the tribal encampment; but instead of entering the circle, he sat down, off by himself, at some distance away. Soon a man came to him. ''Why do you sit here like this?'' he asked. ''Alas, what do you ask? Go back and relate this. And whatever they wish to do with me, tell them to hasten with it. For I have killed my friend, and have come home.'' he replied. 10. So he went to the council-tipi and told it, and soon four men came out of that gathering, for the purpose of questioning him officially. To these he told his experience in detail. When he finished, they said this to him, ''Now at last you know. Your friend was of the type that are marked[1] to be bad, and so you have been warned, countless

---

uśni c'ąke' — *Eya'ś wap'e'g.nakela k'uśe'ya nami'ciżị ye lo',* — *eya' śk'e'ᵉ. Wana' t'i'k'iyela ku' hą'l ila'zatąhą k'uwa' au' ną waśte'ya kig.le'gịkta c'ąke' c'ą' wą ali' yị' ną wąka'ta i'yotaka śk'e'ᵉ.* 7. *Wana'ś t'ak'o'laku k'ų li'la t'o'keca ną kte-wa'c'ị kị slolki'ya c'ąke' nai'c'iżị ų' hihų'ni kịhą k'ute'kta c'a wị'yeya yąka' śk'e'ᵉ. Yųk'ą' c'ą' kị e'l hina'żị ną hu'te kị nahta'ĥtakị ną c'ą' kị a'l-'ataya² nao'tątą iye'ya śk'e'ᵉ.* 8. *Ak'e' li'la nahta'ka yųk'ą' si' kị oko' wą e'l nao'tą iye'ya c'ąke' to'k'a-ikï'kcuśni śk'e'ᵉ. C'ą ki' t'ahe'piya wąka'tuya nahta'ka c'ąke' he'c'iyani si' kị ik'o'yake cị ų' p'a' ǵe'ǵeya ĥpa'ya c'ąke' t'ak'o'laku tk'ą' k'ų he' huk'u'takiya ku' ną ĥpa'ye cị e'l g.liĥų'niśni ec'e'l iwą'kap k'iyo'psicị ną c'ą' kị e'l oka'tą o' ną kte' śk'e'ᵉ.* 9. *Hetą' c'e'ya ku'hị ną wic'o't'ita g.li' k'e'yaś ho'c'okata ku'śni manị'l yąka'hą c'ąke' wic'a'śa wą ekta' i' ną,* — *To'k'a c'a le'c'el ĥeya'ta nąka'hą huwo'?* — *eya' yųk'ą',* — *Hehehe', ta'ku yak'e' lo'³. G.nị' ną oya'ka yo'. Ną to'k'el ec'a'maųpikta he'cịhą yui'nahni-wic'aśi yo'. K'ola' le' we'kte ną wag.li' ye lo',* — *eya' śk'e'ᵉ.* 10. *C'ąke' t'iyo't'ipi kị ekta' hośi'-i yųk'ą' ec'i'yatąhą wic'a'śa to'p hi'pi ną iyo'kawiĥ og.la'kśipi c'ąke' ec'ų' śk'e'ᵉ. Ig.lu'śtą yųk'ą',* — *Ho, wana' nake'ś slolya'ye lo'. Nit'a'k'ola kị he' ec'a'kel-śicapi k'ų he'c'a c'a o'ta-*

---

[1] *to be ec'a'-*anything, is to be that, congenitally; as though destined to be that way; *ec'a'kel* means purposely.
² *a'taya*, all, entire, is reduplicated *a'l-'ataya*.
³ *hehehe', ta'ku yak'e' lo'!* Alas, something you mean! An idiom, equivalent to ''Alas, you do not know the half of what you speak!''

times. Yet you always shielded him and refused to listen. Quite by yourself you have now discovered the truth, and seen it with your eyes. It is all right. Come, reënter the camp circle." When they said this, he was able to go home once more.

53. The Gift of the Horse.

1. One winter the people lived without want, on the Powder River where buffaloes were abundant, and everyone was happy; and then, now that spring was here, about the time of the Sore Eyes Moon[1] (March), the cry went forth from the council tipi that the people were to move about, visiting other parts. So everyone broke camp, and soon they were gone. 2. Only one man and his wife were left behind. The reason was that they owned one horse, a mare that was not much good, and with it they could not hope to keep up to the pace of the tribe, and hence they stayed behind. 3. They went from camp-site to camp-site, picking up what they found, of discarded bone[2], or bits of meat; and to the south, there was a lake, so they walked around it, gathering wood. And then the man ascended a hill, and sat down to rest and view the surrounding country, when he saw something come up over the horizon, in the

---

oni`ciyakapi k'eṡ iya'kiyį³ nq̇ nawi'c'ayak'uṡni k'ų̇. Wana' niye'c'įka iṡta' ų' wq̇la'ke lo'. To'k'aṡni ye lo'. Ho'c'okata ku' wo', — eya'pi c'q̇ke' ekta' k'i' ṡk'e'ᵉ.

53.

1. C'aḣli'-Wakpa` kį e'l oya'te kį wani't'ipi nq̇ pte' o'ta c'q̇ke' wani'yetu a'taya tuwe'ni aki'ḣ'q̇sni c'a oi'yokip'iya wic'o't'i nq̇ wana' we'tu a'ya c'q̇ke', iṡta' wic'a'yazq̇-wi kį wahe'hq̇tu⁴ se'ca t'i'pi-iyo'k'i- heya kį etq̇' e'yapahapi nq̇ mak'o'c'e t'okt'o'keca iya'za oi'g.lakekta ke'ya'pi ṡk'e'ᵉ. C'q̇ke' iyu'ha ig.la'kapi nq̇ tok'i'yot'q̇ e'yaya ṡk'e'ᵉ. 2. Yų̇k'q̇' wic'a'ṡa wq̇ t'awi'cu kic'i'la ot'i'weta kį e'na yq̇ka'pi ṡk'e'ᵉ. Ta'kowe' he'c'ų̇pi kį he' ṡų̇k-wi'yela wq̇zi'la li'la ṡi'cela c'a yuha'pi nq̇ he' ų̇' to'k'ani oi'g.lake kį e'l o'p'apiṡni c'q̇ke' owq̇żila yq̇ka'pi ṡk'e'ᵉ. 3. Ot'i'weta kį ec'e'l hohu' nq̇i'ṡ t'alo'-oṡpu`la nq̇i'ṡ c'q̇ eṡa'ṡa e'na ayu'ṡtq̇pi kį hena' pahi'pi nq̇ nakų̇' wi' c'oka' hiya'ye cį hec'i'- yot'q̇ b.le' wq̇ yq̇ka' c'q̇ke' o'huta-ag.la`g.la c'q̇pa'hipi ṡk'e'ᵉ. Nq̇ wic'a'ṡa k'ų̇ he' paha' wq̇ akq̇'l asni'kiya-iyotakį nq̇ wa'k'ilk'il yq̇ka'hq̇ yų̇k'q̇' wi' hina'p'e cį og.na' ta'ku wq̇ hina'p'į nq̇ t'ahe'nakiya

---

[1] In that part of the country, the sun shining very brightly while the snow is yet on the ground causes snowblindness. March is given its name for this reason.

[2] Discarded bone, if still green, can be pounded and boiled, and the grease that rises to the top is skimmed off to be used later in pemmican, and other rich dishes.

[3] *iki'ya*, to defend; take up the cause of; *i*, mouth; words; *ki*, dative, on behalf of; *ya*, to use.

[4] *wahe'hq̇tu*, about that time.

spot where the sun rises, and advance towards his direction. 4. When it was near enough to be observed, it proved to be a beautiful black-spotted horse which was coming for a drink in the lake. After drinking, he stopped under a tree, and stood rubbing against it, and then he lay down and rolled, and then he rose and went back the way he came. 5. And then, a tiny grey bird[1] flew to the man and sitting down near him he said to him, "I bring you a horse[2]. Go home and make a braided rawhide rope, and apply this medicine to it. And hang it, in the form of a noose, from that tree where he always rubs himself. And when his head becomes caught in the rope, chew this root, and apply it on yourself, and catch him. And rub some of this medicine on the mare which you already have." 6. So the man went home and carried out the orders in detail. Now the black-spotted horse was again coming, so he caught him and blew some of the medicine on his nose, which made the horse stand still and permit himself to be held. He stared at the man every second and yet he did not try to get away, so the man stroked him and took him home. 7. Again the little grey bird talked to him. "The days of your hardship in the tribe are now over. By and by this black-spotted horse is going to sire many horses; he will thus multiply himself, but

---

u'hą šk'e'ᵉ. 4. Ki'ye'la u' yųk'ą' šų'kak'ą' wą sa'pa-g.leška` c'a li'la wašte' m.ni' kį e'l hiyu' šk'e'ᵉ. M.niya'tkį ną hehą'l c'ą' wą e'l ina'žį ną ikpa'wazahį ną hehą'l k'u'l iyų'kį ną ica'ptąptą-kic'ų ną hehą'l ak'e' ina'žį ną u' k'ų hec'i'yot'ą k'ig.la' šk'e'ᵉ. 5. Yųk'ą' wa'hpahotela wą kįyą' u' ną wic'a'ša wą yąke' c'ų ik'i'yela i'yotakela ną wo'kiyaka šk'e'ᵉ, — Šų'ka wak'ą' c'ica'hi ye lo'. G.ni' ną wi'k'ą sų'pi wąži' ka'gį ną p'ežu'ta kį le' ių' wo'. Ną c'ą' kį ka'l eya'šna ikpa'waza c'e he'l wi'k'ą kį c'ąg.le'ška kahya otke'ya yo'. Ną ec'a'š p'a' ik'o'yake cihą p'ežu'ta kį le' yat'a't'a³ ii'c'ių ną e'l u' ną oyu'spa yo'. Ną p'ežu'ta kį letą' nakų' šųk-wi'yela wą luha' kį he' ių' wo', — eya' šk'e'ᵉ. 6. C'ąke' wic'a'ša kį t'iya'ta k'i' ną ec'e'hcį ec'ų' šk'e'ᵉ. Ną wana' ak'e' šų'kak'ą' wą sa'pa-g.leška` c'a wašte' k'ų he' u' c'ąke' oyu'spį ną p'e'zu'ta kį etą' p'ute' kį apo'hpogą ną ową'ži na'žį c'ąke' wi'k'ą kį yu'ziyąka šk'e'ᵉ. Ayu'ta ų'-selya naki'cip'ešni c'ąke' yusto'sto ną t'iya'ta ak'i' šk'e'ᵉ. 7. Yųk'ą' wa'hpahotela k'ų he' ak'e' hi' ną leya' šk'e'ᵉ, — Oya'te e'g.na iyo'tiye'yakiye c'ų wana' hena'la ye lo'. To'kša' g.leška'-sapa kį le' c'ica' o'takta tk'a' anų'k'atąhą wai'c'ahyįkte⁴

---

[1] A bird resembling the common prairie blackbird, and with the same habits of staying around buffaloes and cows, but with a grey instead of a black coat.

[2] The bird uses the uncontracted term for horse, *šų'ka wak'ą'*, mysterious dog. In songs, and formal speech and religious language of the old days, this form was always used when the horse was spoken of with the respect due it.

[3] *yat'a'*, to chew; *t'a*, packed tight; compressed; *ya*, with the mouth.

[4] *wai'c'ah-ya*, to cause things to grow; *ic'a'ga*, to develop; grow.

17

on both sides[1]," he told him. 8. So he allowed the horse to stay with
the mare he already owned, and the following summer, there was
a colt, as beautiful as, and marked exactly like, the black-spotted
horse. It was a male. 9. Another year and then a female colt was
born. Again the following summer a male was born. So from that
horse which the bird had brought him, the man owned three horses,
exactly alike, possessing inconceivable speed. 10. In the tribe they
became famous, and the man who owned them was now far different
from that poor man he used to be; now his name was held high in
the tribe. 11. During the night he used to picket these horses in
front of his door; and one night, someone crept up to them, planning
evil against them; but that first black-spotted horse spoke, "Wake
up, and come out. Someone approaches with the intention of causing
our death." He said this while neighing[2] and his master heard it and
came outside. 12. And this is what he said, "I do not keep these

---

*lo', — eya' šk'e'ᵉ. 8. C'ǫke' wana' šuk-sa'pa kį yuha' c'a šuk-wiⁿyelawa
ehǫ'tǫ³-yuha`pi k'u he' kic'i' u' yuk'ǫ' b.loke'tu kį ekta' c'įca'la wǫ
i's-'eya' sa'pa-g.leška c'a li'la wašte' t'u' šk'e'ᵉ. He' b.loka' šk'e'ᵉ.
9. Ak'e' wani'yetu wǫži' yuk'ǫ' hehǫ'l wi'yela wǫ t'u' šk'e'ᵉ. Ak'e'
bloke'tu sǫp'a yuk'ǫ' hehǫ'l b.loka' wǫ t'u' šk'e'ᵉ. Wana' šuk-sa'pa-
g.leška` wǫ kahi'pi k'u hetǫ'hǫ šu'kak'ǫ' ya'm.ni a'k'iyec'ecapi c'a,
wo'c'et'ug.laya⁴ c'a' icu'pi ece' ic'a'ǵapi šk'e'ᵉ. 10. Wana' hena' oya'te
e'l u'pi c'ǫke' li'la ok'i't'ǫiyǫ u'pi nǫ u' wic'a'ša wǫ wic'a'yuha k'u
he' ehǫ'ni u'šiya u' k'u e'šni s'e lehǫ'l li'la wic'o't'i kį e'l wǫka'tuya
u' šk'e'ᵉ. 11. Hǫhe'pi c'ǫ' t'i'-t'iyopa kį o'štǫ hena' kaška' wic'a'kig.le
s'a yuk'ǫ' hǫhe'pi wǫ e'l tuwa' šil-wi'yukcǫ u' t'ewi'c'aye-wac'į slohǫ'
e'tkiya wic'a'u yuk'ǫ' šuk-b.lo'ka wǫ t'oka'-yuha` k'u he e' c'a, —
Kikta' nǫ hina'p'a yo'. Tuwa' t'eu'yǫpikta c'a u' we lo', — eya'-
hot'u yuk'ǫ' wic'a'ša kį naḣ'u' nǫ hina'p'a šk'e'ᵉ. 12. Nǫ leya' šk'e'ᵉ,*

---

[1] This has been explained to me, because I did not get the meaning, that
the black horse was destined to sire a breed through both a male and a
female line.

[2] The Dakotas sometimes hear things in the utterances of animals. Once,
a man heard a person wailing, far, far away; and stood listening intently,
wondering who was dead, and what it was all about. He thought he
understood the words, telling who had died and the
details of the death. Then he found that he was listening to a common
fly, which, very near his ear, was trying to free itself. All the same, in due
time the message came that so and so had died, and that a friend of the
dead man had gone about wailing, using the words he had heard. Old
people used to say the wolves told the future, when they howled at night.
Anyone, with or without supernatural power, can understand the meadowlark. Its song is not indicative of impending evil; only amusing, and a
welcome note of spring.

[3] *ehǫ'tǫ*, plus a verb, means that that thing was already being done; *ehǫ'tǫ-
yuha`pi*, they had it already, before something else happened.

[4] *wo'c'et'ug.laya*, unbelieveably; incredibly; *c'et'u'g.la*, to disbelieve; *c'et'u-
wag.la* st. person.

horses in order that you shall insult me through them. I keep them for the sole purpose of bringing good to the tribe, and in that spirit, I lend them to you to hunt meat for your children, as you know; you have also used them freely in war and, as a result, have achieved glory. These horses stand here to serve. 13. Yet when I tied them for the night and then came in to rest, someone sneaked up on them, causing them to run home. You see then it is useless to do anything to them secretly." That man understood the speech of his horses, they say. And then the first horse spoke this way; so his master announced it. 14. "In order that you in this tribe might be fortunate in all things, I and my young have multiplied; and from that, you have benefited in the past; yet now, because an evil thing has entered the tribe, this source of good shall stop. You must go back to your former state when things were hard for you, all because that one who tried to kill us has by his act brought it upon the entire tribe." 15. In that way he spoke, so his owner told the people. The horses now lost their power to run as of old, and no more colts were born, until at last that entire breed became extinct. In that way, this tribe which was so fortunate, took a backward step to their former state of hardships. 16. That man who owned them and permitted the tribe to rely on them was named *"Tąyą'-ma'ni-ų'"* (He always walks guardedly — i. e., free of pitfalls.) He was

---

— *Šų'ka wak'ą' kį lena' ai'mayaȟaȟapikta¹ c'a wic'a'b.luhašni ye lo'.* *Niye'š oya'te kį ini'waštepikta ų' lena' wic'a'b.luha c'aš ų' waya'-k'uwapi c'ą nic'į'ca wo'tapi k'ų; ną nakų'š ozu'ye c'ą wic'a'nųpi² ną ų' wic'o'ȟ'ą wašte'šte slolya'yapi k'ų. Šų'ka wak'ą' kį lena' wo'wac'į-yepi c'a na'žįpe lo'. 13. Tk'a' e'wic'awakaškį ną wag.li'mųka yųk'ą' oi'yokpaza hą'l tuwa' ana'wic'aslate e'yaš t'i'yanakitąpe lo'. C'a naȟma'la e'l ta'ku oe'c'ųšice lo', — eya' šk'e'ᵉ. Wic'a'ša kį he' šų'kak'ą' kį ia'-nawi`c'aȟ'ų šk'e'ᵉ. C'ąke' šų'kak'ą' -t'oka`heya k'ų he' le'c'el wo'kiyaka ke'yį' ną yao't'ąį šk'e'ᵉ, 14. — Oya'te kį le' e'l ta'ku iyu'ha og.na' tąyą' yaų'pikta c'a mic'į'ca o'p mig.lu'ota ną ų' ini'waštepi k'ų, wic'o'ȟ'ą ši'ca wą e'l hiyu' c'a wana' hehą'yelakte lo'. C'a ak'e' šica'ya yaų'pikta tk'a' he tuwa' t'eų'ye-wac'į'pi kį he' e' c'a oya'te wawi'c'akiyušice lo'. — eya' šk'e'ᵉ. 15. Hec'į'yot'ą wo'g.laka c'ąke' t'i'ȟįyetku³ kį ec'e'l oya'te kį owi'cakiyaka šk'e'ᵉ. Hehą'yela lu'zahąpi k'ų aki'snipi ną kic'i't'ųpišni c'ąke' hąke'ya he'-ošpaye k'ų ata'kunipišni šk'e'ᵉ. He'c'eš oya'te wą tąyą' ų'pi k'ų, ak'e' ehą'nı iyo'tiye'kiyapi k'ų he'c'iya k'ina'žįpi šk'e'ᵉ. 16. Wic'a'ša wą hena' wic'a'yuha ną ų' oya'te wac'į'yąpi k'ų he' Tąyą'-Ma'ni-Ų' eci'yapi*

---

¹ *ai'mayaȟaȟapikta*, you will insult me on them, i. e., through them as a medium; *iȟa'ȟa*, to ridicule; insult; mock.

² *wic'a'nųpi*, you use them; *ų*, he uses; *mų*, I use; *nų*, thou usest. *ųk'ų'*, we two use.

³ *t'i'ȟįyetku*, his master; his owner; said of a pet; or a domestic animal. I am not sure whether the first *i* is nasalized.

17*

pitied and caused to have good fortune himself; had he so wished, he might have enjoyed it alone; but that was not what he wanted. He caused all the tribe to share in it; and then, regretful fact, one, through jealousy perhaps, brought ill-fortune on them all.

54. Old Woman's Lake.

1. Old Woman's Lake lies up in the Grandmother's[1] country, they say. This is how it got its name. It is a large lake with a thickly wooded island in its midst. And long ago, some Santee were travelling along the shore of it. 2. And last of the whole procession was an old woman who had two black dogs carrying her goods on a dog-travois. But the poor old thing was slow, and the people always left her far behind. 3. And once they were stopping for the night, but she failed to arrive, so they rather waited around for her, but finally it was bed time and she had not come. They thought she was only temporarily lost, and looked; but they failed to find her,

---

śk'e'ᵉ. Ų'śilapi ną wa'p'iyapi² c'a c'į'ka hą'tąhąś iśna'la iwa'śte-ic'iya oki'hi k'e'yaś he'c'el c'į'śni ną oya'te a'taya i'yoważa-wic'ak'iya³ yųk'ą' eha'kal e'ś wążi' wo'winawizi se'ca ų' oya'te wawi'c'akiyuśica śk'e'ᵉ.

54.

1. Waką'ką⁴ T'ab.le' eci'yapi kį he' Ųci'yapi⁵-T'ama`k'oc'e kį ekta' yąka' śk'e'ᵉ. Yųk'ą' ka'k'el ų' he' b.le' kį he'c'el c'aże' śk'e'ᵉ. B.le' kį he' li'la t'ą'ka c'a c'oka'ta wi'taya wą yąka' yųk'ą' he' a'taya li'la c'ų'śoke śk'e'ᵉ. Ehą'ni b.le' kį he' ag.la'g.la ig.la'ka a'ya śk'e'ᵉ, Isą'yat'i-oya`tepi c'a. 2. Yųk'ą' oi'c'imani kį ihą'kelice cį ekta' winų'-ñcala wą sų'ka nu'p sapsa'papi c'a wak'į'wic'ak'iyį ną ec'e'l ya'hela śk'e'ᵉ. K'e'yaś śika hų'kelaśni⁶ kį u' li'la t'e'hąl he'kta ece'-mani śk'e'ᵉ. 3. Yųk'ą' ñtaye'tu-et'ipi k'e'yaś ihų'niśni c'ąke' ap'e'kel⁷ yąka'pi ną he'c'ena i'śni ec'e'l wic'i'yųka śk'e'ᵉ. Yųk'ą' i'ñąhą s'e to'k'ah'ą c'a ole'pi k'e'yaś to'hųweni iye'yapiśni ec'e'l hąke'ya

---

[1] This means Canada. The name Grandmother's land has remained since the people knew that Queen Victoria was the sovereign of that land. Grandfather's land is the United States. The Indian agents in charge of the various reservations, being subordinates of the great man in Washington, are called fathers.

[2] *wa'p'i*, lucky; *yapi*, they caused him, i. e., the supernatural powers gave him good fortune.

[3] *i'yoważa*, to have a right to (a thing); *wic'ak'iya*, he caused them to.

[4] *waką'ką*, an old woman. Santee word principally; *wa*, thing; *ką*, aged; full of years.

[5] *ųci'yapi*, they have her for a grandmother; i. e., Queen Victoria.

[6] *hų'keśni*, not strong; not fleet-footed; feeble; The *la* is again an enlisting of sympathy for the old woman.

[7] Kind of waiting for her, *ap'e'kel;* kel indicates that they were not seriously waiting, not "we shall not sleep until she comes," but just keeping her in mind, while they went through the business of living..

till at last they gave up trying. 4. In after years a man was travelling by himself and was passing near that lake when he saw a woman and two dogs emerge from the woods on the island and roam about. 5. He told this; and a long time after, another man saw exactly the same thing. But this was all so long after the time the old woman had disappeared that they judged she must have been dead those many years; but, even today, if someone chances to pass that way alone, he sees the old woman and her two dogs; till the people have decided that the ghosts of the woman and her dogs remain on that island. So they call the lake, "Old Woman's Lake," they say.

55. A Woman Joins her Lover in Death.

1. There was a big hill, a butte, where years ago a warparty was held at bay till all the members died; and none escaped, they say. And it was there that the people stopped, on a journey, and stood looking for a suitable place to make camp, when this, which I am about to relate, took place. 2. At the foot of that butte, there was already a camp; and this group came to it and stopped, when a woman, her shawl pulled up over her head, started to sing. "There was a man I loved, alas. Can it be that I shall see him again, my own ?" With such words she stood on the hilltop, singing. 3. As

---

iye′nayapi šk‘e’ᵉ. 4. It‘a′hena wic‘a′ša wą išna′la b.le′ kį he′l ik‘i′yela hiya′ya hą′l wi′taya kį ekta′ c‘ų′šoke k‘ų etą′hą wį′yą wą šų′ka nų′p o′p oma′nihą c‘a wąya′ka šk‘e’ᵉ. 5. Oya′kį ną etą′ ak‘e′ t‘e′hą yųk‘ą′ wic‘a′ša-t‘okeca wą ec‘e′ḣcį wąya′ka šk‘e’ᵉ. K‘e′yaš i′še′ li′la lena′ i′t‘ehą c‘a wana′š ehą′ni winų′ḣcala k‘ų he′ t‘a′-iye`c‘etu k‘e′yaš, lehą′tuka ye′š tuwa′ he′l k‘ąye′la išna′la hiya′ya c‘ą′šna wį′yą kį he′ šų′ka nų′p o′p wąya′kapi š’a c‘ąke′ he′ ų′ he′ nagi′ kį e′e ke′ya′pi ną ų′ b.le′ kį he′ Waką′ką T‘ab.le′ eya′-c‘aže`yatapi šk‘e’ᵉ.

55.

1. Paha′ wa′ t‘ą′ka, he′l ehą′ni ozu′ye wą iya′yewic‘ayapi ną ao′-g.lut‘ewic‘ayapi c‘ąke′ wąži′ni ni′šni iyu′haḣcį he′na t‘a′pi šk‘e’ᵉ. Yųk‘ą′ he′tu c‘a oya′te kį ig.la′ka a′yį ną ową′k-iwą`yak e′nažį c‘ąke′ ḣmu′ š’e le′c‘eca yųk‘ą′ ec‘ą′l le ob.la′kįkte cį le′ he′c‘etu šk‘e’ᵉ. 2. He′-paha` kį oḣla′t‘e ehą′tą-wic‘o′t‘i c‘ąke′ haka′p lena′ ig.la′ka e′nažį ḣcehą′l ųg.na′ wį′yą wą šina′ p‘a′mahel ic‘o′mį ną olo′wą wą yawą′kal e′yayį ną — Eca¹ wic‘a′ša wą t‘ewa′ḣila k‘ų, leya wąwe′g.lakįkta hųše !, — eya′-wo′c‘ažeyalya² lową′ paha′-aką′l na′žį šk‘e’ᵉ. 3. Oya′te

---

¹ *eca* . . . . *hųše!* These two words, enclosing a song, are characteristic. They mean something like, "O, can it be that I am to see him whom I love! O, Is it really so ?"

² *wo′c‘ažeyate,* the words of a song; *wa,* thing; *o,* in which; *c‘aže′yata,* a name is called. This is derived from the custom of naming a man, to sing his praises, in song; *wo′c‘ažeyal-ya,* she uses, for the words of the song, such a sentiment as quoted.

the tribe fixed their attention singly on her, she started taking dancing steps backwards, and allowed herself to fall headlong over the cliff, landing, all bruised and broken, among the rocks below. She was dead. 4. So they took up her body and carried it to her tipi, but her husband, evidently jealous, did not so much as weep a tear; but said, instead, "No, do not bring her here. Take her back, she has announced that she loved him; so let her rot with him!" so they could not enter her tipi with her body. 5. Instead they took it back and left it where she fell. And they came away. So there, with him, who from all appearances was her lover, she mingled her bones, and they together in time became as dust, just as she desired in her song. 6. Then a crier went around announcing a removal of the camp. It was according to the magistrates' decision. They said, "There is no other way; we cannot stay here. We must move from this spot where such a foul deed has taken place." So, in spite of the fact that camp had just been made, they all packed in haste and moved away that same evening.

56. How Bear Woman Got her Name.

1. On a summer day when the sun came beating down hot, the people arrived at a certain spot near the edge of the wood and there they pitched their camp. Then everyone, men, women and children even, all turned their entire attention to gathering the wild fruits which were ripe and abundant in that wood. 2. They worked

---

kį' a'taya ekta' e'tųwąpi ñcehą'l ųži'hektakta wac'i'c'i hiya'yį ną maya' kį ekta' ohį'ñpayeic'iyį ną oñla't'e igu'ga o'ta c'ąke' he'c'iya kañle'ñlel g.liñpa'ya c'a t'a' šk'e'ᵉ. 4. C'ąke' t'ąc'ą' kį icu'pi ną t'i' kį ekta' ak'i'pi yuk'ą' hįg.na'ku kį a'tayaš c'e'yešni ec'ą'l nawi'zi c'ąke' heya' šk'e'ᵉ, — Hiya`, le'l au'pišni lo'. Ekta' a'ya po', he' t'eñi'la ke'ya' c'a kic'i' k'eš ata'kunikteṧni ye lo', — eya' c'ąke' t'i' kį e'l a'yapišni šk'e'ᵉ. 5. E' e' he'ktakiya a'yapi ną he'l hįñpa'ya c'ąke' e'l ak'e' e'ųpapi šk'e'ᵉ. He'c'ųpi ną iñpe'ya g.licu'pi c'ąke' he'na t'awi'c'aša se'ce ų kic'i' hohu' ic'i'cahiya ata'kuniṧni ške'ᵉ, he'c'el c'į ke'ya'-lową` k'ų og.na'yą'ᵠ. 6. Hehą'l e'yapaha wą hiya'yį ną ig.la'k-wic'aṧi šk'e'ᵉ. Waki'c'ųza kį hena' e'pi c'a iyu'kcąpi kį og.na'yą. Heya'pi šk'e'ᵉ: — Ho, tako'm.ni¹ le'na t'i-p'i'cašni ye lo'. Le'l wic'o'ñ'ą ši'ca wą yąka' c'a ųki'g.lakapikte lo', — eya'pi c'ąke' ki'tąñcį'š e'wic'ot'i ną t'ig.la'ñ k'o' yuštą'pi k'ų iyu'ha ig.la'kapi ną ñtaye'tu-hąke`yela a'taya to'k'el iya'yapi šk'e'ᵉ.

56.

1. B.loke'tu-mašte`-t'ą`ka hą'l oya'te kį c'ą-a'g.lag.la e't'ipi ke'ᵉ. He'c'ena wic'a'ṧa, wį'yą ną wak'ą'heža ye'š k'o' iyu'ha wat'o'keca li'la o'ta c'ąke' wo'špi iyą'kapi ke'ᵉ. 2. Li'lakel šką'pi yuk'ą' ųg.na'-

¹ tako'm.ni, at all costs; at all events; anyway.

very energetically, when, all of a sudden, they heard the shouts of
a man who did not work with them, but sat on top of a hill, looking
about. He called out, saying, "Watch out, workers! There is a bear
returning into the wood!" His warning shouts echoed and reёchoed
through the length of the wood and everyone hearing it rushed
madly out towards safety. 3. Now there was in the company an old
woman who was working with the others, trying to provide for
herself against the future. When she heard the warning, she too
rushed out of the wood, running as hard as it was possible for her.
But the bear soon caught up with her, and holding his paw flattened
out, he struck her such a blow on her cheek that she fell right over.
4. Luckily she was not hurt. The bear ran past her and caught up
with another woman, also running to safety. He struck her somewhere and knocked her over, face to the ground. At once he stopped
and tried to turn her over, but she bent her body double and held
her hands tightly over her abdomen, the position she was in as she
fell. While falling, she caught hold of her knife-case which she was
wearing in her belt, and her hand was on the knife handle, so she
drew it out, and thrust the knife behind her, wildly. 5. When she
did so, she felt something soft and cushion-like, into which her
knife went for a moment. Again she reached her knife back and
again she thrust it into the same substance but by then she had cut
and torn off the flank of the bear. He gave up now, and started off
elsewhere. 6. The woman, unhurt, stood up, and looked around for

---

hạla wic'a'śa wą wo'waśi ec'ų'śni paha'-aką'l wa'k'il-yạka'hą yųk'ą'
he e' c'a pạ'-houya ke'ᵉ. — Wo'śpi kị wakta' po'+! Mat'o' wą c'aya'ta-
kiya g.le' lo'+ — eya' wakta'wic'aya c'ạke' c'ą' kị yai'yowasyela
t'ạị' c'a iyu'ha nak'ų'pi kị ų' keya'takiya nii'c'iye-wa'cị naki'p'api
ke'ᵉ. 3. K'e'yaś le wo'śpipi kị e'g.na winų'ḣcala wą, he'c'ake c'e'yaś
i'ś-'eya' ic'i'ksapa¹ c'a wak'ạ'yạ śkạ' ke'ᵉ. Yųk'ą' he' e c'a ka'k'el-
wic'a'śa wą pạ' k'ų he'c'ena ḣeya'takiya tohạ'yạ-oki'ḣika į'yạka ke'ᵉ.
K'e'yaś tako'm.ni mat'o' kị i't'ap ahi'kig.legị nạ nape' b.laska'ya
g.lu'zị nạ ok'o'kip'eya winų'ḣcala k'ų ap'a' c'ạke' kawạ'ka ke'ᵉ.
4. Iśni'ś ksu'yeyelaśni, he'c'ena iyo'pteya iya'yị nạ wị'yạ wą he' i'ś-
'eya' naki'p'a c'a į'yạka yųk'ą' el ihų'ni nạ ak'e' he' ap'į' nạ kawạ'ka
ke'ᵉ, ite' og.na'laḣcị ap'į nạ. He'c'ena itų'kap yuptạ'ye-wac'į k'e'yaś
yukśa'la ig.lo'nica nạ nape'-nup'į ų' t'ezi' g.lu's ų' ke'ᵉ, he'c'el
g.liḣpa'ya c'a ec'e'na. Mi'la wą mi'yoźuha og.na' mig.na'ka c'ạke'
iki'kcu nạ tok'i'yot'ạ t'ạị'śni k'e'yaś he'ktakiya mi'la kị pazo iye'ya
ke'ᵉ. 5. He'c'ų yųk'ą' ta'ku wą p'ạśp'ą'źela c'a c'ap'a' ke'ᵉ. Ak'e'
he'ktakiya mi'la k'ų yeyi' nạ p'ạśye'la c'ap'a' yųk'ą' mat'o' kị e' c'a
oyu't'e kị waśpa' ahi'yu ke'ᵉ. Hehạ'yela mat'o' k'ų ayu'śtạ nạ ka'k'ena
iya'ya ke'ᵉ. 6. C'ạke' wị'yạ kị a'taya ksu'yeyeśni c'a ina'źị nạ o'kśạ

---

¹ *ic'i'ksapa*, to be wise on one's own behalf. To be foresighted, for one's own
good; to be provident.

the bear, just disappearing in a little hollow in the ground. The spectators who had stood afar off watching the encounter, now came up to the bear and saw that he had fallen dead. 7. From then on, because of such a brave deed by which the woman saved her own life, she was known as Bear Woman, and her former name was no longer used.

57. A Ghost Story.

1. A large war party came to a place which had formerly been used by other war parties as a place to spend the night; and finding a grass hut in good repair they prepared to stop for the night when one of their number objected, saying, 2. "Let us go a little farther, and stop at another place. This is the spot where they tell that a strange somebody comes and scares away all who try to stop here, so that they have to move on." But another one answered thus, "That may be so when there are only a few in the group. But look at our number!" 3. And then another one spoke up, "Well, I agree with the first speaker and think we should follow his suggestion. You know, whatever anyone says, that ghosts are odd folk and they are certainly to be feared and reckoned with. How much better, then, not to tempt disaster, but to go on just a little farther where we may rest and spend the night in peace. All too soon we shall reach the region where danger lurks on every side, and then sleep will be out of the question. We are on a long errand and we better rest while we may." 4. Then another one spoke and

---

e'tųwą yųk'ą' ośko'kpa wą ekta' mat'o' ki̧ iyo'ĥpaya c'a wąya'ka ke'ᵉ. Wawą'yaka ki̧ kai'yuzeya na'ži̧pi c'ąke' wana' mat'o' ki̧ iha'kap i̧'yąkapi yųk'ą' he'c'i mahe'l t'a g.liĥpa'ya śk'e'ᵉ. 7. Hetą'hą wi̧'yą ki̧ he' ohi'tike ci̧ u̧' nii'c'iya c'ąke' c'aźe' ki̧ iĥpe'yi̧ ną Mat'o'-Wi̧'yą eci'yapi ke'ᵉ.

57.

1. Zuya' k'eya' wic'o'tapi c'a ozu'ye-ot'i̧'weta wą e'l ina'ži̧pi ke'ᵉ; yųk'ą' e'l p'eži'-wok'eya wą tąyą'kel hą' c'ąke' e'na ĥpà'yapikta yųk'ą' waži' wica'laśni ną heya' ke'ᵉ, 2. — Wą, ak'o'wap'a uki'yųkapikte lo'. Le'tu c'a he' tuwa' iyu̧'k-wac'i̧pi c'ą'śna ta'ku wą u' nąśna yuś'i̧'yewic'aya c'ą' naki'p'api keya'pi k'u̧, — eya' yųk'ą' waži' i's heya' ke'ᵉ, — Hoĥ, eya' c'i̧' co'napila hą'l he'c'etu nac'e'ce lo', tk'a le' wiu̧'c'otapi ki̧! — eya' ke'ᵉ. 3. Ak'e' waži' — Wą t'oke'ya-eye ci̧ he'c'etu we lo'. Wą'cak e'ś he'c'el ec'u̧'k'u̧pi-wastè'ke. Tako'm.ni wana'ği ki̧ ośte'pika c'a wo'k'okip'epe lo'. Wą'cak e'ś nap'e'ceśni ak'o'wap'a u̧yą'pi ną he'c'i u̧ki'śti̧mapi-wastè'ke. To'kśa' wana' ec'a'laĥci̧ ok'o'p'e ki̧ ekta' u̧ki'yayapi ki̧hą hehą'yą iśti̧'me-p'icakteśni ye lo'. Wą, t'e'hąl u̧yą'pi c'a u̧ko'kihipi ki̧ e'l e'cuĥci's asni'u̧kiyapikte lo', — eya' ke'ᵉ. 4. Yųk'ą' waži' ak'e', — Hoĥ, i's e'ktą'¹. Le' wau̧'tu-

¹ *i's e'ktą'*, an idiom, something like, "Oh, what's the use?"

answered, "What is the use ? We are tired and want to sleep. It is absurd for us to move now and travel again!" and the others in the party felt as he did; so they settled for the night there. 5. They reinforced the lodge in the faulty spots by adding blankets to it, and then made a fire in the centre and were sitting about comfortably. It was now dark. And then, they heard someone coming up the river. First they thought he sang, but after a time, they were sure he was weeping and wailing as he came towards them. 6. "There now, what did we tell you!" said the man who first raised the objection to that place and suggested moving on. But the answer from another one was, "Well, he might not come here, after all, you know." Just the same, by tacit agreement, they put out the fire at once and sat in the dark. 7. "If that should be a human being, he may not come here if he does not see any light," they said. But he did arrive, and angrily, "Move on from here, will you ? Why pick this place as though there were no other spot in the world ?" he called out, and the warriors sat still, and without saying a word. 8. He stood outside the lodge when he said that, and whenever anyone in the group whispered the slightest word to his neighbor, the ghost would come and strike the lodge, directly outside the place where the speaker sat. The uncanny way he knew where to strike greatly frightened the men, and each time they moved a little from the outer edge of the room towards the center until they found themselves sitting in a tight huddle in the very

---

k'api c'a ųki'štįmapikte cį. It'o' wo'wihaya ak'e' ųki'g.lakapi ną są'p ųyą'piktelak'a! — *eya' ke'e. Yųk'ą' ųma'pi kį he'c'etu keya'pi c'ąke' wana' e'na hpa'yapikta og.na'yą ig.lu'wiyeyapi ke'e.* 5. *Wo'- k'eya kį ena'na ohlo'ka c'ąke' ec'e'kc'e šina' aka'hpapi ną t'ima' c'et'i'pi ną wana' yup'i'yela yąka'pi ke'e. Wana' oi'yokpaza c'ąke' he'c'el yąka'pi'i. Yųk'ą' ųg.na'hąla tuwa' wakpo'p'aya u' c'a ho'na- h'ųpi'i. T'oke'ya lową' ną hąke'ya ak'e' c'e'ya u' ną i'c'ilową u'u.* 6. — *Iho'! eya'š hep'e' c'ų!* — *wąži' t'oka' ig.la'kiktehcį k'ų he' eya' ke'e. Yųk'ą' ųma' kį wąži'* — *Ho, į'še' le'l u'šni nac'e'ce lo',* — *eya' ke'e. K'e'yaš ini'la p'elsni'yąpi ną oi'yokpasya yąka'pi ke'e.* 7. — *Le' wic'a'ša c'a u' hą'tąhąš ižą'žą wąya'kešni kįhą iyo'pteya iya'yįkte lo',* — *eya'pi ke'e. Ho, k'e'yaš a'tayelaš u' ną li'la c'ąze'ka ke'e.* — *Letą' iya'yapi ye', wą. E'ktą' le'tulahciš, ową'ka wani'ce š'e,* — *eya' c'ąke' zuya'-wic'a'ša kį ta'kuni eye'šni ini'lahcį yąka'pi ke'e.* 8. *T'ąka'l na'ži ną heyį' ną tohą'l t'ima' yąka'pi kį wąži' tok'e'cela tuwa' oži'-wokiyaka c'ą'šna wana'gi kį hiyu' ną he' tuwe' c'a ia' he'cįhą yąke' cį ila'zatalahcį wo'k'eya kį ahi'ap'a ke'e. To'k'eškc'e slolya' t'ąį'šni, a'tayela ece'-ahi'ap'e cį ų' li'la wic'a'ša kį iyu'ha k'oki'p'a it'a'pi[1] ną to'na-hec'ų c'ą iye'na są'p t'ic'o'katakiya i'yotak u'pi c'ąke' hąke'ya t'ic'o'kayela wi'taya yuska'pi š'e yąka'pi ke'e.* 9. *Hą-*

---

[1] *k'oki'p'a it'a'pi*, they dreaded it very, very much; *it'a'pi*, they are dead by it, literally.

middle of the lodge. 9. At last they were sitting so very close together that they could feel each other's breath. Then someone came along from one to the other of them, in order, whispering something to each. When he came to Male Bear, he invited him to go outdoors. Nobody accepted the invitation, and the warriors were all nearly dead with fright as they sat there. 10. And then, of a sudden, an idea came to Male Bear. He thought, "Ah, this must certainly be the ghost himself who has come in unnoticed, and is trying hard to persuade somebody to go outside with him. What was it my uncles taught me? O yes; never, in an emergency to forget my weapon." With that, he grabbed his gun with a mighty effort, and tried to utter the bear-cry, but when his voice sounded, it came out as a weak cry of fear. Nevertheless, he fired off the gun; and so suddenly, that Eagle-Bear who sat nearest the door, ducked and threw himself down in fear, thinking he had been hit. 11. But at least the shot was effective, for the ghost was so frightened that he ran off crying, to nobody knows where, and did not return any more to disturb them.

58. Two Enemy Scouts Make an Agreement.

1. An Og.lala war party stopped for the night; so one of their number ascended a butte near by, in order to scout. At the time, a thunder storm came up, causing the man to seek shelter in a deep

ke'ya kic'i'pat'a nuse'kse yąka'pi kį ų' niya' iyo'hikic'iyapi¹ ke'ᵉ. Ho yųk'ą' hehą'l tuwa' ag.la'g.la wąźi'kźila oźi' awi'c'au ke'ᵉ. Mat'o'-B.loka` ehą'hi yųk'ą' t'ąka'l yea'p'e ke'ᵉ. Heya' au' nac'e'ce c'e'yaś tuwe'ni iyo'kiciwįyeśni ną zuya'-wic'a`śapi k'ų iyu'ha t'ąsa'k t'a'pi c'a c'ą' se'kse ̗yąka'pi ke'ᵉ. 10. Ųg.na'hąla hehą'l wo'wiyukcą wą e'l hi' ke'ᵉ. — Eh! Le' wana'ǵi kį e' c'a oslo'l-ųyąpiśni hą'l t'ima' hiyu' ną t'ąka'l ye-a'wic'ap'ehe se'ce lô. Ta'ku wąś lekśi' oma'kiyakapi k'ų. Ohą́, ta'ku wo't'ehika c'ą' wi'p'e kį aki'ktuźeśni maśipi k'ų, — ec'į' ną he'c'ena śkį'ciya-hįg.la ma'za wak'ą' iya'kiḱpaya ke'ᵉ. Ną ḱina'ḱina-wac'į k'e'yaś t'e'hą ho' e'nap'eyeśni ną o'hąketa tok'e'cela ho'-c'ąc'ą`yela ho't'ąį ke'ᵉ. He'c'eca k'e'yaś ma'zak'ą' kį uki't'a ke'ᵉ; ųg.na'hąla wakta'piśni hą'l ec'ų' c'ąke' Wąb.li'-Mat'o` t'iyo'pa kį ec'i'yatąhą yąka' c'ąke' o'pi ke'c'į' ną p'ama'g.le iḱpe'ic'iya ke'ᵉ. 11. Ho, k'e'yaś t'o' ma'zawak'ą' k'ų wawo'kihi c'ąke' wana'ǵi k'ų yuś'į'yeya c'a c'e'ya į'yąk k'ig.nį' ną tok'i'yot'ą iya'ya t'ąį'śni ke'ᵉ. Ną hehą'yela naǵi' yewi'c'ayeśni ke'ᵉ.

58.

1. *Og.la'la k'eya' zuya' ya'pi yųk'ą' ka'l e'yųka c'ąke' etą' wąźi' tųwe'yakta c'a paha' wą ekta' iya'hą ke'ᵉ. Yųk'ą' ec'ą'l wakį'yą uki'ya c'ąke' he'l oḱlo'ka wą mahe'tuya hą' c'a ekta' iya'ya ke'ᵉ. Li'la*

¹ *iyo'hiya,* to reach onto; they reached each other with their breaths, so huddled were they.

cavern in the rocks. It was very dark within, so he felt about, and grasped the hand of a man! 2. So the two sat, holding unto each other all night, and when morning came, and it was pleasant outside, they came back out; and the other was a Crow Indian who also came there to scout for his war party, also stationed near by. But he feared the thunder beings and hid. This he made clear to the Dakota by signs. 3. He said the plan was to attack the Dakota that morning at a certain open meadow near; and that he would be riding a spotted horse and would wear his warbonnet. So the Dakota also informed him about himself, that he would ride a white horse and would also wear his warbonnet. 4. Then they exchanged presents. This they did that their friends should not doubt their story. When the morning came, the two parties approached each other on that meadow already indicated, and stood ready to charge; and then they began to fight. 5. And it happened that these two who had already talked together, attacked each other, while still seated on their horses. In such a manner did they fight that the others stopped to watch them. They soon worsted each other so that one was dead and the other taking his last breath. So then the spectators took up the fight, but at that moment, a Crow Indian walked along the line, saying something with great earnestness; and then his men stepped back, withdrew a distance, and an interpreter said, 6. "It is enough; you all have a fair cause for relating war deeds when you return[1]." So, though they had already wounded one another

oi'yokpaza c'ąke' yut'ą't'ą ya'hą yųk'ą' wic'a'śa wą nape' e'l oyu'spa ke'ᵉ. 2. C'ąke' he'c'el kic'i'yus yąka'hąpi ną wana' ą'pa ną t'ąka'l owa'śtecaka c'ąke' k'ina'p'api yųk'ą' he' K'ąǵi'-wic'a'śa c'a i'ś-'eya' ozu'ye wą etą' tųwe'ya-i k'e'yaś wakį'yą k'owi'c'akip'į¹ ną ų' oȟlo'ka ona'p'a śk'e'ᵉ. He'c'el wi yut'a oki'yaka ke'ᵉ. 3. He'-hįhąni kį tukte'l k'iye'la mak'o'b.laye c'a e'l lak'o'ta kį t'awi'c'a-kpapikta ke'ya'-wiyut'a ke'ᵉ. Śųk-g.le'śka wą aką'yąkį ną wap'a'hakit'ųkta ke'ya'-wiyut'a c'ąke' Lak'o'ta kį i'ś-'eya' ska' wą aką'yąkį ną i'ś-'eya' wap'a'ha-kit'ųkta ke'ya' śk'e'ᵉ. 4. Hehą'l anų'k ta'ku kic'i'c'upi śk'e'ᵉ. He'c'el c'et'ų'wic'ag.lapikteśni c'a. Wana' hį'hąna yųk'ą' mak'o'c'e wą k'a'pi k'ų he'tu c'a anų'k'atąhą u'pi ną paǵe'ya na'żįpi c'ąke' hehą'l wana' t'aki'c'ikpapi śk'e'ᵉ. 5. Yųk'ą' le nų'p ehą'ni-wi'wahokic'iyapi k'ų hena'yos wąka'tąhąla iya'kic'iȟpayapi ną kic'i'zapi c'ąke' k'ohą' ųma'pi kį wąwi'c'ayak na'żįpi śk'e'ᵉ. Wana' kic'i'ktepi c'a ųma' t'į' ną ųma' i'ś eha'keke-niya̧ śk'e'ᵉ. C'ąke' wa-wą'yak na'żįpi k'ų hena' nake'ś wana' i'ś eha'kela t'aki'c'ikpapi yųk'ą' ec'ą'l K'ąǵi'-wic'a'śa wą li'klila ta'keyaya ag.la'g.la u' yųk'ą' t'aho'kśila kį iyu'ha kaȟe'yawap'aya ak'i'nażį yųk'ą' iye'ska wą c'oka'ta hiyu' nę leya' ke'ᵉ, 6. — Ho, eya'ś wana' he'c'etu ke'ye' lo'. Le'c'eg.la c'aś ų' anų'k wakte'-oya̧'g.lakapikte lo', — eya' ke'ᵉ. C'ąke'

---

[1] They would have this overwhelming demonstration of bravery to take home, and be proud of. It was so complete that further fighting would have been anti-climactic. And both war parties had equal reason for claiming victory.

here and there, they stopped fighting and went home. That is the only time opposing sides agreed to give up, without killing each other, it is said.

59. Crow-Dakota Woman.

1. In past times, the Dakota used to say to a child that cried and gave trouble, "Beware! Owl-maker[1], come and throw this one into your ear; he is crying too much!" and then the child would get quiet. 2. Doubtless nobody ever saw the Owl-maker; but it was said that he possessed enormous ears which he could open out and throw in anyone he pleased and then close them, so that there was no way to escape. 3. And once, in winter camp, a child was crying so that the sound echoed throughout the entire camp. It was a little girl only four years old, whose mother had died and whose father had married again, this time to a cold woman lacking in kindly qualities. She hated this child which was not her own, and scolded her whenever she cried. 4. Again she must have asked for something, the poor child, and was crying for it, when, "Owl-maker, take this one; she cries too much!" the woman said and threw her outside. At once, as if gagged, she stopped her crying. She did not return, but the woman said no doubt she would come back, in time, and did not look for her; but she was really lost, and never returned there. 5. The whole tribe hated the woman for this; and the father whose child had disappeared went about always with a heavy heart till at

---

wana' ena'na oya'ząkic'iyapi k'e'yaš hehą'yela sa'p ta'kuni to'k'ųšni ak'i'yag.la šk'e'ᵉ. He'hą' ece'la he'c'ehči anų'k'atąhą kic'i'žiktešni-g.luštą`pi ną wat'o'kyešni ena'kiyapi ną t'iya'takiya k'ig.la'pi šk'e'ᵉ.

59.

1. Ehą'ni Lak'o'ta ki wak'ą'heža wąži' wana'h'ųšni nąi'š waka'ki-šya c'ą'šna — Yu! Hįhą'-ka`ga, u' ną le' nų'ge oka'h'ol iye'ya', ec'e'š li'la c'e'ye s'a ye! — eya'pi c'ą nąke' ini'la i'yotakapi s'a'ᵃ. 2. Hįhą'-ka`ga eya'pi ki he' tuwe'ni to'hųweni wąya'kešni nac'e'ce'ᵉ; k'e'yaš he' tuwe' ki nų'ge t'ąkt'ą'ka c'a g.lub.la'yį nąšna tuwa' c'į'ka c'ą ekta' oka'h'ol iye'yį ną nų'ge ki ayu'g.muza c'ą to'k'a-g.licušni ke'ya'pi s'a'ᵃ. 3. Yųk'ą' tų'wel wani't'ipi hą'l wak'ą'hežala wą c'e'yahą yųk'ą' wic'o't'i ki a'taya yai'yowas'yela ho't'ąi šk'e'ᵉ. He' wani'yetu to'pala c'a hų'ku t'a' yųk'ą' atku'ku ki wi'yą-hįyą`zeca wą yu'za ke'ᵉ. Yųk'ą' wic'i'calala ki ec'a' ina'yešni c'ąke' li'la wahte'lašni ną c'e'ya c'ą i'yoktekteka ke'ᵉ. 4. Ak'e' he' ta'ku la'la ną heya'hą yųk'ą', — Hįyą'-ka`ga, le' icu' na; ece'š c'e'ye s'a ye, — eyi' ną t'ąka'l yu's iye'ya ke'ᵉ. He'c'ena i'-og.mus yu'zapi s'e aya'štą ke'ᵉ. To'k'iya'ya t'ąi'šni k'e'yaš to'kša' ku'kta ke'yį' ną ole'šni c'ąke' he'c'ena g.li'šni ną ec'a'c'a-tok'ah'ą šk'e'ᵉ. 5. C'ąke' oya'te ki a'taya wi'yą k'ų he' i'wahtelapišni šk'e'ᵉ. Ną wic'a'ša ki i'š c'įca' wą kit'ą-

last he died of sorrow. What happened was that a Crow-Indian
scout was lying in hiding near by when the little girl was sent out.
And she appeared to be about the size of a little girl he had lost, and
because of whose death he now came to war. So he took this child
and returned to Crow-land with it. 6. There the man formally
adopted the child in place of the lost one, and lavished much
affection on her. So she grew up there and spoke Crow, like a Crow
woman. But the other people sometimes ridiculed her. And after
her marriage her sisters-in-law and her mother-in-law[1] continually
referred to her as "that Dakota woman" in an unkind tone. 7. She
grew tired of this, and when her foster-father died, she said to
herself. "Now that the one who befriended me is gone, I shall be
more like a captive than ever. I believe I'll go home." So one day
when there was an uproar over something in camp, she took the
opportunity to run away. Her father had often told her where he got
her, and in what direction her people lived. So, without any idea of
where it was, she travelled in what she considered the right direction.
"All my life I have had a hard lot; so it is just as well; what matter
even if I should fall by the way?" she mused as she travelled.
8. But after an uneventful journey, she came upon a camp. She had
not eaten for days and was so weak that she walked straight towards
the camp. She did not know what people these were, but did not
stop to consider whether they were friends or enemies. And some men
on horseback came to meet her, and spoke to her in Dakota. 9. She

išni k'ų he' ic'ą'tešica ece'-ų ną o'hąketa t'a' šk'e'ᵉ. Leya t'i'pi ki
he'l it'ą'kal K'ąǧi'-wic'a`ša wą tųwe'ya-hi ną ina'ḥma-ḥpa`yahe
ḥcehą'l wic'i'calala ki t'ąka'l iye'yapi ke'ᵉ. Yųk'ą' he' he'c'eya'
wic'i'cala wą wahe'c'etu c'a kit'a' c'ąke' he ų' zuya' hi'ⁿⁱ, yųk'ą' li'la
iye'c'eca c'ąke' K'ąǧi'-wic'a`šata ak'i' šk'e'ᵉ. 6. He'c'i k'i' ki ekta'
wic'i'cala k'ų he' wal-i'yac'i ną li'la t'eḥi'la šk'e'ᵉ. C'ąke' he'c'iyani
ų' ną hąke'ya K'ąǧi'-wic'a`ša ų' ną he'c'a-wiyą iye'c'el ic'a'ǧa
šk'e'ᵉ. K'e'yaš oya'te-ųma`pi ki etą' i'ḥapi s'a ke'ᵉ. Ną hig.na't'ų ki
hehą'yą šce'p'ąku ną k'ų'ku ki hena' o'hįni — Lak'o'ta-wiyą ki, —
eya'-k'uwa`pi ke'ᵉ. 7. O'hąketa wana' heki'yapi ki iwa'tuk'a ną ag.na'
ate'ye c'ų he' t'a' c'ąke', — Hece'laš ų'šimala k'ų wana' t'a' c'a hehą'l
iyo'tą waya'ka wau̯'kte. It'o' wag.la' kê, — ec'i' ną ąpe'tu wą e'l ta'ku
iki'k'opi tk'a'š ic'i'g.nuniyą g.licu' ke'ᵉ. K'e'yaš atku'ku k'ų to'k'iyatąhą ag.li' ki o'ta-oki`yaka c'ąke' to'k'iya ya' t'ąi'šni k'e'yaš eya'
ai'yoptaye s'e ece' ku' ną, — Tohą'tą ki iyo'tiye'wakiya c'a eya'š
he'c'etu'ᵘ, naku' c'ąku og.na' mųke' c'e'yaš he' to'k'aka, — ec'i'c'i
ku' ke'ᵉ. 8. K'e'yaš taku'nikel ak'i'p'ašni ec'e'l wic'o't'i wą e'l ku
ke'ᵉ. K'e'yaš t'e'hą wo'tešni c'ąke' loc'i' ki ų' a'tayela e'l ya' ke'ᵉ.
Hena' ta'ku-oya`tepi ki slolye'šni k'e'yaš he'c'ų ke'ᵉ. Yųk'ą' šųk-`a'kąyąka k'eya' itko'p u'pi ną ao'kawiǧapi ną lak'o'l-ia` ok'i'yapi šk'e'ᵉ.

[1] Now and then there was a mean mother-in-law, as in this case; and especially so here, because the girl was not a Crow.

had no idea what they were saying, for she did not know the language. And the men thought she was an enemy woman, so they caused her to walk ahead and marched her to the centre, and she dropped to the ground repeatedly from weakness, as she advanced. When she stopped all the people came around to look at her. And then one old woman lifted up her voice and wept, and said, "This is my niece Badger Woman's child; the child who disappeared many years ago. She does not miss one line of her mother's features; there is no doubt that this is she!" 10. And then she told the assembly the story I told you at the beginning. How, on the death of her mother, her father had remarried, taking a cold, cruel woman who maltreated her and sent her out to the Owl-maker; and how the father finally died of grief over the child's disappearance. 11. When it became plain that this was a Dakota woman, the people wailed over her and gave her so many presents that all in a day she became rich. She soon spoke Dakota and married the son of a chief. 12. Now, then, this young man she married was one who was very fearful of war, and had an uncontrollable dread whenever he went on the warpath. But one day when they were going again, the woman said to her husband, "Let me go with you. I understand they are going to Crow-land, and it is just possible that I can help you." So he took her with him; and during a dark night they stood waiting when, sure enough, a man was coming towards them. He

---

9. *Iye'skaśni c'ąke' ta'ku k'a'pi t'ąį'śni ke'ᵉ. I'ś k'ośka'laka kį t'o'ka-wiyą ke'c'į'pi ną ho'c'okatakiya pasi' ag.la'pi c'ąke' kasa'psapyela iħpa'ya yį' ną c'oka'ta ina'żį c'ąke' oya'te kį a'taya wąya'k-ʾahi` ke'ᵉ. Yųk'ą' winų'ħcala wą e'l u' ną c'e'yaya iya'yį ną heya' ke'ᵉ: — Mit'o'żą Hoka'wį c'ųwį'tku wą t'ąį'śni k'ų he' le' e' ye'. Hų'ku kį g.lug.na'yeśni¹ kį ų' tako'm.ni he' e' ye', — eya' ke'ᵉ. 10. Heyį' ną le t'oka' ekta' wo'b.lake c'ų he'c'eħcį oya'ka ke'ᵉ. Hų'ku t'a' yųk'ą' wį'yą-hįyą`zeca wą ina'ye e'yaś li'la k'iyu'śe ną t'ąka'l iye'ya yųk'ą' t'ąį'śni ną ec'e'l atku'ku kį iyo'kiśica-t'e c'ų hena' oya'ka ke'ᵉ. 11. C'ąke' ehą'kec'ų Lak'o'ta-wįyą kį slolya'pi ną g.luha'ha c'e'yapi ną li'la wak'u'pi c'ąke' ąpe'tu-ħąke'yela wi'żica ke'ᵉ. Ec'a'la ħcį lak'o'ta-iį ną wic'a'śa it'ą'c'ą-c'įca` wą hįg.na'yą śk'e'ᵉ. 12. Ho, yųk'ą' i'ś tuwa'wapike ħcį², k'ośka'laka wą hįg.na'ye c'ų he' li'la ozu'ye ekta' c'ąl-wą'k'a³ ke'ᵉ. K'e'yaś zuya'pikta yųk'ą', — It'o', ųyį'kte. K'ągį'-wic'a'śata a'yįkta ke'ya'pi c'a tok'a'ś o'c'iciya owa'-kihikte se'ce, — eya' ke'ᵉ, wį'yą kį. C'ąke' wana' kic'i' zuya' i' ną oi'yokpaza hą'l ina'żįpi yųk'ą' he'c'ecakte c'ų, wic'a'śa wą t'ahe'nakiya u' c'a wąya'kapi ke'ᵉ. C'ąpa'm.na wą ao'hom.ni hiyu' ną wąwi'c'ayak*

---

¹ *g.lug.na'yeśni* literally means "she does not miss or let anything of her own, get by;" meaning "to resemble a relative in every feature."

² *i'ś tuwa'wapike ħcį*, an idiom, "here was someone just as involved, in his way," as in the case under discussion.

³ *c'ąte'*, heart; *wą'k'ala*, weak; that is, to be faint-hearted in times of danger.

Deloria, Dakota Texts 271

stepped around the bushes and saw them at once. Instinctively he reached for his knife when the woman rushed up to him and addressed him in Crow. 13. For an instant this disarmed him, and he stopped short; but in that instant the woman's husband went around him and killed him. And from that day on, this young man began to be very successful in battle so that many songs were composed in his honor. 14. This woman who from her youth on had known only hardship and was even obliged to grow up in an alien tribe, and speak an alien tongue, did thus turn her griefs to account by making a man out of her husband. From then on, only after she was a woman grown, she knew what it was to live a happy life, and so she lived till the end.

60. A Woman Kills her Husband's Slayer.

1. A man and his wife camped out alone while he was deer-hunting, and each day he would bring home some game, and then go off again, while his wife busied herself preparing the meat for preserving. He had just left her with more meat to care for, and gone away; so she was preparing it. But it was getting dark now; so she was covering things up and leaving them for the night, when she heard her husband unloading something, perhaps a deer that fell to the ground with a thud, on the other side of the tipi. 2. "Well, he must be home already," she thought and went around the tipi and saw him unloading so much fresh meat that she hastened to help him and chatted over nothing as she worked, but he said never

ihe'ya ke'ᵉ. He'c'ena mi'la iya'kiḣpaya tk'a's wį'yą k'ų he' K'ągi'wic'a`sa-ia` ok'i'ya ke'ᵉ. 13. He'c'ų kį ų ų'c'ųnilya¹ c'ąke' pat'a'k ina'ži c'a ec'e'l laza'tąhą wį'yą kį hįg.na'ku k'ų he' hiyu' ną kte' śk'e'ᵉ. Ho, hetą' nake's wat'o'kya-wo`hitikį ną g.li' c'ąke' li'la ki'cilowąpi śk'e'ᵉ. 14. Wį'yą wą ci'k'ala hą'tą iyo'tiye'kiyį ną oya'te-t'okeca ekta' k'o' ic'a'ġe c'e'yas t'ok-'į' ną ec'e'l hįg.na'ku kį g.luwi'c'aśa ną hetą'hą wį'yą-t'ąka hą'l nake's c'ąl-wa'śteya ų' ną ec'e'l t'a' śk'e'ᵉ.

60.

1. Wic'a'śa wą t'awi'cu kic'i'la manį'l t'a'te-t'ipi yųk'ą' t'alo' ag.li' nąśna ak'e' iya'ya c'ą k'ohą' t'awi'cu kį waka'b.lahą ke'ᵉ. Ak'e' wana' tok'i'yot'ą iya'ye c'e'yas he'c'eya' t'alo' o'ta ag.li' ną iya'ya c'ąke' t'awi'cu kį hena' k'ic'ą'yąhą ke'ᵉ. K'e'yaś wana' ḣtai'yakpaza c'ąke' ec'e'kc'e aka'ḣpa e'g.nakahe c'ų lehą'l wana' ak'e' hįg.na'ku k'ų g.li'yelak'a t'ia'k'otąhą ta'ku sliye'la g.liḣpe'ya ke'ᵉ. 2. — Hinų́, tų'weni g.li' hųśê, — ec'į' ną t'ia'ohom.ni iya'ya yųk'ą' t'alo' ośų'kyela yuḣpa'hą c'ąke' o'kiya iyą'kį ną wo'kiyak śką' k'e'yaś ayu'pteśni ke'ᵉ.

¹ *ų'c'ųnica*, to be stage-struck; to be frozen on the spot from fright; or from some strong emotional conflict within; *ų'c'ų*, (?); *nica*, to lack.

a word. "Something must be disturbing him; he never was like this before. He always came home in such gay spirits," she thought; yet dreading to question him and perhaps irritate him further, she refrained from saying anything. 3. Moreover, she could not see his face; for it was now dark. So, pretending she did not realize that he was not feeling like himself, she took off his moccasins, and was inwardly shocked to find the big toe missing on one foot. She gave him food which he ate hurriedly; and on finishing, he slid the dish at her without a single word. So she wiped her dish and set it away, talking all the while; and then she went outside. 4. Out there she took up the task of arranging the new meat for the night, when she heard him snoring, evidently having lain down as soon as she went out. So she tiptoed in and looked at him, stretched out flat on his back, asleep. She knew now, of course, that this was not her husband, so she hastily sharpened a knife in secret and entered the tipi with it. She pretended to put the room in order, and worked with something for a minute, but that did not disturb him; so then she placed the knife against the farther side of his throat in an upright position, and quickly drew it towards her, cutting him deeply. In his sleep, he choked and gasped and then that was all. 5. Her heart beat furiously as she started out in the darkness of night and arrived breathless at the tribal camp. Immediately

— *To'k'eśk'e ta'ku iyo'kip'iśni se'ce le'. Tų'weniś le'c'ecaśni k'ų.
Tohą'l ku' c'ą'ś wo'g.lag.lak wi'hahaya¹ g.liyą'ke s'a k'ų, — eci̧'
k'e'yaś ak'e'ś wi'yų̀ a'ye ci̧hą sa'p iyo'kip'iśniyi̧kta-k'oki̧'p'a
c'ąke' hehą'yela ta'keyeśni ke'ᵉ. 3. Naku̧' ite' wąya'ka-oki'hiśni'ⁱ, ec'i̧'
wana' oi'yokpaza c'ąke' he' ų'. He'c'etu k'eś e'ekeśni² ki̧ ab.le'ześni-kųs
hą'pa ki'ciyuślokahą yųk'ą' si-sa'ni sip'a'hųka³ wani'ca c'ąke' hehą'l
iyo'tą nihi̧'ciya ke'ᵉ. Wo'k'u yųk'ą' śica'wac'i̧-woti̧` ną ta'ku eye'śni
wakśi'ca ki̧ paslo'hą iye'kcic'iya c'ąke' wo'g.lag.lak kpak'i̧'ti̧⁴ ną
mahe'l iye'kiyi̧ ną t'ąka'l ina'p'eᵉ. 4. He'c'iya ak'e' t'alo' ki̧ ec'e'kc'e
e'g.nakahą yųk'ą' le'na wana' i̧yų'ka hųse i't'ap go'pahą c'ąke' nasla'-
slal yi̧' ną ao'kas'i̧ yųk'ą' itų'kapyela k̀pa'yi̧ ną li'la iśti̧'ma ke'ᵉ.
He'c'ena wana'ś he' hi̧g.na'ku ki̧ e'śni c'a slolki'ya c'ąke' i'nak̀ma s'e
mi'la wą og.li'kiyi̧ ną yuha' t'ima' iya'yi̧ ną wap'i'kiye-kųs ta'ku
ok'u'wa k'e'yaś ec'a'c'aś-iśti̧'ma⁵ c'ąke' lote' i'sap ag.le' yu'zi̧ ną
waksa' ahi'yu ke'ᵉ. He'c'ena ų'śti̧ma-ona`g.log.lo ną hehą'yą ta'ku-
niśni'ⁱ. 5. He'c'ų ną hehą'l li'la c'ąte' iya'p'a c'ąke' ina'p'i̧ ną
wic'o't'itakiya hąhe'pi-oi`yokpaze c'e'yaś i̧'yąkahi̧ ną niya'śniśni⁶*

---

¹ *wi'haha*, to be pleasant; cheerful is the best meaning; *wi'mahaha*, I am cheerful.

² *e'ekeśni*, rather not himself; to be out of sorts.

³ *sip'a'*, foot-head; toes; *-hųka*, the big toe, cf. *nap'a'hųka*, the thumb; *nąpe'*, hand; *hųka'*, the eldest; or leader; an elder relative.

⁴ *pak'i̧'ta*, to wipe; *kpa*, one's own.

⁵ *ec'a'c'a*, before a verb, means to do thoroughly what the verb indicates. "He was in deep slumber. There was no doubting he was asleep."

⁶ *niya'śni*, he does not breathe; *niya'śniśni*, all out of breath, (adverb).

several men hurried out to the place in the wilderness where her
tipi was, and on arriving, they lighted the tipi, and found a Crow
Indian with ugly features, lying dead; there was great confusion for
a few minutes while they all scrambled over the order of counting
coup[1]. 6. When morning came, they looked about and found the
woman's husband lying dead a little distance away. As he was
coming home with his day's killing the Crow evidently had slain
him, taken his clothes and was wearing them. The woman he tried
to trick tricked him and thus he lay, pitiable, in death.

61. Gartersnake-Earring-Wearers.

1. Some men were on a hunting trip, and out there they were
roasting some of the meat when one of them took a piece of the
aorta and fastened it to his ear in the style of an earring while he
waited for his meat to cook. Later he forgot to remove it, and went
to bed with it still in his ear. During his sleep, something moving on
his neck wakened him so that he sat up quickly; and it was now
dawn. 2. He looked down at his neck and saw a snake dangling in
front of him, and wriggling; so he gave some bear-cries and sprang
to his feet and ran frantically about. It was so tightly fastened to
him that when one man came and got the snake by the tail and
pulled on it, he could not get it off, so firmly was it biting the man's
ear; but then he gave an extra hard pull and at last it came off, the

*k'ihų'ni šk'e'ᵉ. C'ake' wic'a'ša to'na wą'cak manį'l t'i' k'ų he'c'etkiya
natą'pi ną e'l ihų'nipi ną ao'žąžąyapi yųk'ą' K'ąǧi'-wic'a'ša c'a
ite' ki šilye'la t'a' ḣpa'ya c'ake' t'ok-ʾa'k'inicapi² šk'e'ᵉ. 6. wana' ą'pa
a'ya c'a t'iwo'kšą atų'wąpi yųk'ą' wį'yą ki hiġ.na'ku k'ų he' k'iye'la
t'a' ḣpa'ya ke'ᵉ. Ku' hą'l iya'ḣpayį ną kte' ną t'aha'yapi ki ų' ną
wa'g.li g.li' ke'ya'pi'ⁱ. Wį'yą wą g.na'yewac'į k'e'yaš iye' eha' g.na'yą
c'ake' ų'šiya ḣpa'ya šk'e'ᵉ.*

61.

*1. Wic'a'ša k'eya' wana'se-ipi ną ekta'na wac'e'ųpaḣąpi yųk'ą'
wąži' t'ac'ą'ta³-ką' wą nų'ǵe e'l owi'-kaḣya iye'kiyi ną wac'e'ųpaḣą
yųk'ą' e'ktuža c'ake' he'c'ena ištį'mi na hąhe'pi ki ekta' oi'kpaǵuǵa
yųk'ą' ta'ku wą t'ahu' ki e'l ošką'šką š'e le'c'eca c'a i'yotak hiya'ya
yųk'ą' wana' ą'pa kab.le's ahi' ke'ᵉ. 2. C'ake' t'ahu' ki e'l e'tųwą yųk'ą'
wag.le'za wą ite' ki it'o'kap oka'koskozį nąško'škopa c'ake' ḣna'ḣna
ina'žį ną yukšą'kšą į'yąka ke'ᵉ. Suta'ya ik'o'yaka c'ake' wąži' hiyu'
ną zuze'ca ki site' e'l oyu'spį ną yuti'ktitą k'e'yaš li'la waš'a'kya
yaḣta'ka c'ake' li'la šehąs a'wicak'eya yuti'tą yųk'ą' t'aką' k'ų hee*

---

[1] The woman actually killed the enemy; but it was for the ones coming after,
to strike coup. Only a limited number of coups are counted, with the first
carrying the highest honor, and so on down. It is no wonder that everyone
tried at once to get to the dead Crow:
[2] *ak'i'nica*, to dispute over; *awa'k'inica*, I disputed with him over.
[3] *c'ate'*, heart; *t'ac'ą'ta*, ruminant's heart. Terminal *e* changed to *a* after *t'a* prefix.

18

artery with which the man had played before retiring. 3. From that time on, the clan to which this man belonged were called, "Those-who-wear-gartersnakes-for-earrings." *(Wag.le'za owį')* That is sometimes the way a clan came by its name, — by one of its members having something unusual happen to him; and that accounts for some seemingly absurd names.

62. *Owner-of-White-Buffaloes-Woman.*

1. Long ago, there was a girl who owned a doll and named it, "Owner-of-White-Buffaloes-Woman;"[1] and she loved it very much. Her parents humored her affection for the doll, and they too called it by name, and had pretty things made for it in imitation of women's belongings. 2. Whenever a buffalo was killed, they would lay aside the choice portions saying, "Owner-of-White-Buffaloes-Woman shall have this for her dinner," and they treated the doll like a child-beloved. They always did this, up to the time when the daughter came to woman's estate; but even then, and perhaps even more, she loved her doll and paid no attention to the young men who courted her. 3. She had no self-consciousness in the presence of the opposite sex, instead she concentrated on the doll, causing it to have even horses, and in time, she gave things away at the give-away dances, in the doll's name; then the singers would laud that name. But this girl was very beautiful; and there was a certain brave young man in the tribe who was regarded highly, and he wanted to

---

c'a yuślo'k ahi'yu śk'e'ᵉ. 3. C'ąke' hetą'hą t'iyo'śpaye kį he' wag.le'za owį'[2] ewi'c'akiyapi śk'e'ᵉ. He'c'el t'iyo'śpaye wąźi' e'l tuwa' takų'l ak'i'p'a c'ą'śna ų' ic'a'źewic'ayatapi kį ec'i'yatąhą ų' ośte'śteya-c'aźe`kit'ųpi kį he'c'etu śk'e'ᵉ.

62.

1. Wic'į'cala wą ehą'ni hok'si'cala wą yuha' yųk'ą' Ptesą' Yuha'wį eya'-c'aśkit'ų ną li'la t'eħi'la ke'ᵉ. C'ąke' huka'ke kį o'kiyapi ną i'ś-'eya' wic'a'śa iye'cel c'aźe'yal wo'yuha yuha'k'iyapi ną ta'ku waśte'śte ki'caǵapi ke'ᵉ. 2. Ptekte'pi c'ą'śna o'waśteke cį hena' ħeya'p e'g.nakapi ną, — Ptesą' Yuha'wį hena' yu'tįkte, — eya'pi ną hokśi'-c'ąlki`yapi s'e k'uwa'pi śk'e'ᵉ. He'c'el ece'-ec'ų'pi ną hąke'ya wana'ś wic'į'cala k'ų he' wik'o'śkalaka į'śkokeca k'e'yaś hehą'iyag.leya, e'ś iyo'tą, li'la hokśi'cala kį t'eħi'la ną ok'i'yapi kį k'o' e'l e'wac'įśni śk'e'ᵉ. 3. A'taya scu'śni ną ec'ą'l eś hokśi'l-ka`ǵapila kį he' śų'kak'ą' k'o' yuha'k'iyį ną o'hąketa k'o' otu'ħ'ąk'iya c'ąke' wic'a'śa s'e ki'cilowąhąpi śk'e'ᵉ. He'c'eca k'e'yaś li'la wį'yą waśte' c'ąke' k'ośka'-laka wą wo'im.naka c'a ohi'tiki ną ok'i't'ąįyą ų' yųk'ą' op'e't'ų

---

[1] To name a child "Owner-of-White-Buffaloes" is to aim at the highest, for white buffaloes were so scarce that they were valued very greatly.

[2] *owį'*, to wear on the ears, as earrings; *owa'wį, ųko'wį*, I, we two, wear as earrings.

marry her; giving presents for her until they gave her to him.
4. Now that she was married, people supposed that she would
abandon her worship of the doll, and devote herself to her home,
but she doted on the doll even harder, and ever so often, though she
knew it was not so, she would say, "My daughter is crying! And how
I love her, too!" and she would pet it, taking it in her arms and
crooning over it. 5. Even when she went to bed, she placed the doll
between herself and her husband, and soothed it as one would a
child. And it came about that in time this girl changed; her eyes
grew staring and unnatural, and she became very thin. So she never
did a bit of work, nor could she. Therefore, whenever her husband
brought home game, he always took it directly to his mother-in-law's
tipi to be cared for and prepared. There they would cook it and
then at meal time the mother would call to her daughter who lived
in the tipi next door and could hear her through the skin walls, and
say, "Mother of Owner-of-White-Buffaloes-Woman, this meat is
now cooked." Then the young woman would call back, "All right,"
and then she and her husband would come into her mother's lodge to
eat their meal. 6. But one evening when they came in like that and
were seated ready for their supper, the young woman said that her
doll in the other tipi was calling "Mother," and crying, and she
sprang to her feet and rushed out of the room, falling and staggering
through the doorway, and entered her own tipi; and there they
say she was found later, dead.

---

*c'ąke' k'u'pi śk'e'ᵉ. 4. Wana' wik'o'śkalaka kį hįg.na't'ų c'ąke'
hokśi'l-ka`ǵapi kį iħpe'yįkta ke'c'į'pi yųk'ą' ec'ą'l eś sa'p t'eħi'la ną
ųg.na'hąśna c'e'ya ke'yį' ną i'ħąl-eya` c'a slol-i'c'iye c'e'yaś, —
Mic'ųkśi'+, c'e'ye le'+, t'ewa'ħila k'u+! — eya'ya alo'ksohą icu'
nąśna kilo'wą śk'e'ᵉ. 5. Naku' iyų'kapi c'ą'śna hįg.na'ku kic'i'
ħpa'ya k'eś c'oka'ya ece'-ųpį ną wic'a'śa se'śna kig.na' śk'e'ᵉ.
Yųk'ą' hąke'ya iśta' kį li'la nag.le'g.les¹ a'yį ną sa'p t'ama'heca²
a'ya śk'e'ᵉ. C'ąke' ta'ku wo'waśi wąźi'caka ye'ś ec'ų'śni ną nakų'
oki'hiśni śk'e'ᵉ. He' ų' tohą'l k'ośka'laka kį wa'g.li gli'³ c'ą'śna k'ų'ku
t'i' kį ekta' a'tayela e'iħpeya c'ą he'l iħ'ą'pi ną wana' wo'tapi-iye`hątu
c'ą le'c'eg.lala t'ių'ma kį e'l wik'o'śkalaka kį yąka' c'ąke' t'io'ǵeya
hų'ku kį kipą' ke'ᵉ, — Ptesą` Yuha'wį hųku'+, wana' t'alo' kį le'
śpą' ye', — eya' c'ą — Ohą', — eyį' ną hįg.na'ku kic'i' wo'l-hi`yota-
kapi ke'ᵉ. 6. Yųk'ą' to'hųwel ħtaye'tu hą'l he'c'eħcį hi'yotakapi
ħcehą'l hokśi'l-ka`ǵapi kį t'ių'mata c'e'yį ną Ina' eya' ke'yį' ną
ħilħi'cahą⁴ yuka' k'ina'p'į ną t'ių'ma kį ekta' k'ig.la' yųk'ą' ekta'na
t'a' ħpa'ya c'a iye'yapi śk'e'ᵉ.*

---

¹ *nag.le'g.leza*, to appear striped; glary, with pronounced colors; *na*, of its
    own accord; from within; like a crazed person, whose eyes are staring.
² *t'ama'heca*, to be thin; lean; especially to the point of looking sick.
³ *wa'g.li*, an adverb, meaning returning from the hunt with success; *g.li*, to
    return home; *wa'g.li g.li*, to bring something home.
⁴ *ħica'hą*, to trip, and fall.

18*

63. A Man who Profited by Returning Dead Bodies of Enemies.

1. Crow Indians invaded a *Hų́'kpap'aya* camp; so the men jumped on their horses and chased them. But it was a very warm day and soon the horses gave out and perspired so that the riders turned about and gave up the raiders, content to bring in as hostages the women whom they found stationed some distance out with extra supplies (horses, and food). 2. Only a few Dakota whose horses were good enough to warrant it, went on, and soon they ambushed a man and his son in a clump of wood. When their fate was obvious, the man stepped out and called to them, "I am perfectly willing to die; it is what I was looking for. But this young boy does not know about such things, and therefore I beg of you to let him live. This is Brown-Blanket speaking!" this he said in the Crow tongue . 3. There was only one of the Dakota who understood Crow, and he shouted back, "Very well, send him over here." Instantly the boy ran out of the wood and directly towards the Dakota; but before he reached them, he was shot; and that turned the father into a bear[1] so that he ran out, leaves rustling after him, and charged at them till they surrounded and killed him too. 4. What came out later about this incident was that this man who knew the Crow tongue, was in business for himself[2]. Whenever Crow Indians were killed, he made note of it, and the following winter, he took their bodies to their people and received always

---

1. *K'ą́ǵi'-wic'a`śa k'eya' to'hųwel Hų́'kpap'aya t'i'pi ki e'l natą, ahi'yu c'ąke' wic'a' ki śųk-ʾa'ką iye'ic'iyapi ną wic'a'k'uwapi śk'eʾe. K'e'yaś li'la ok'a'ta c'ąke' ec'a'lahci śų'kak'ą' ki t'em.ni't'api ki ų' nam.ni'pi ną he'l k'iye'la wį'yą k'eya' iwa'g.lam.na wic'a'kiciyuha yąka'pi c'a hena' e' k'eś waya'ka wic'a'yuzapi ną natą' ahi' k'ų hena' e' awi'c'ayuśtąpi śk'eʾe. 2. K'e'yaś Lak'o'ta co'nala śųk-lu'zahą yuha'pi ki hena'la he'c'ena wic'a'k'uwapi ną ka'l K'ą́ǵi'-wic'a`śa wą c'ica' wą hokśi'lahca[3] c'a kic'i' c'ąya'l iya'yewic'ayapi ną ana'pta nawi- c'ąźipi keʾe. Yųk'ą' wic'a'śa ki ho'uyį ną, — Miye' he'c'a owa'le c'a mat'į'kte cį he'c'etuwala tk'a' hokśi'la ki le' ta'kuni he'c'el slolye'śni ki he' ų' nimi'cic'iyapi wacį' ye lo'. T'aśi'na Ǵi' le' miye' ye lo'! — eya' K'ą́ǵi'-wic'a`śa-ia` ho'uya keʾe. 3. Yųk'ą' Lak'o'ta ki wązi'la iya'-nah'ų` c'ąke', — Ho, hiyu'ya yo'! — eya'-ayu`pta keʾe. Heye' c'ų he'c'ena hok'si'la ki c'ąma'hetąhą į'yąk hiyu' ną Lak'o'ta na'źipi ki ana'wic'atąla k'e'yaś hihų'niśnihą kat'a' yeya'pi c'ąke' atku'ku k'ų yuma't'opi ki ų' c'ą' yusna'pi s'e iha'kap hina'p'į ną u' c'ąke' ao'g.lut'eyapi ną kte'pi śk'eʾe. 4. Yųk'ą' leyalaka le wic'a'śa wą K'ą́ǵi'-wic'a`śa-iye` c'ų he' eya'śna K'ą́ǵi'wic'a`śa wąźi' Lak'o'tata e'ktepi c'ą'śna t'ąc'ą' ki t'iya'ta wic'a'kicicak'i c'ą li'la tątą'yą*

---

[1] To be made into a bear, is to be incited to raging anger.
[2] This is rare — for a Dakota to be in business for himself in any way.
[3] Very much of a boy; a lad too young for warfare.

very valuable gifts in return. That was why, for selfish reasons, he wanted the boy killed, and ordered him out without consulting the others, who, in their ignorance of motives, killed him. 5. Sometime later he took several bodies to Crow-land and restored them to their relatives who, in their great grief, gave lavishly to him. But in the tribe lived a cousin of the boy victim, who knew what he had done, and was angrily waiting for a chance to get him; but he was unaware of this as he went on with his activities. 6. The people now sat in a great circle, and feasted and he was among them as guest of honor, when the cousin came up behind him, and with one forceful blow on the head, knocked him cold. 7. But in all the excitement and confusion of receiving their dead, nobody took notice of him, so he lay unconscious there for some time, and when he came to, he got up, and without visiting in the camp as was his custom, he went directly off from the tribe. He came home to Dakota-land without stopping, and never again did he venture to go visiting to Crow-land, or try to return any more dead bodies.

64. A Pouting Girl Finds a Husband.

1. A young woman whose feelings were hurt to such an extent that she pouted[1] and nobody could appease her, worried her father so much by her actions, that he finally went to a son of his younger

wak'u'pi c'ąke' he'c'ų s'a c'a ak'e' he' hoksi'la kį kte'pikta c'į' ną Lak'o'ta-uma`pi kį ta'ku k'a'pi kį slolya'pisni ec'e'l iye' hiyu'si ną ų' kte'pi sk'e'e. 5. Wana' ak'e' i't'ęhą yųk'ą' k'ągi'-wic'a`sa to'nakel wic'a'ktepi k'ų iyu'ha huhu' kį wic'a'kicicak'i ną c'aże'yal owi'c'aki-yakahą c'ą iwi'c'akikcupi ną c'ąte' si'capi kį ų' li'la o'l-'ota wak'u'hąpi yųk'ą' leya tąyą' ec'ų'sni k'ų ehą'ni ot'ą'į c'as hoksi'la k'ų he' t'ąhą'-sitku[2] wą li'la c'ąze' ną iya'p'e yesą' slolye'sni he'c'ųhą sk'e'e. 6. Wana' yumi'meya e'yotaki ną wo'tapi kį e'l o'p'eya yuo'nihąyą wo'k'upi yųk'ą' ila'zatąhą wic'a'sa wą iya'p'e k'ų he' hiyu' ną p'a' aką'l ap'į' ną sniye'la kat'a' sk'e'e. 7. K'e'yas wic'at'a iwi'c'akikcupi kį he' ų' li'la iki'k'opi ną e'l e'tųwąpisni c'ąke' tohą'yą he'l lipa'yahį ną kini' k'ųhą' tok'i'yot'ą wic'o't'i-eg.na ye'sni, nake' mani'takiya iya'ya sk'e'e. He'c'ena Lak'o'tatakiya g.licu' ną hehą'yela to'hųweni K'ągi'-wic'a`sata ye'sni ną tų'weni wic'at'a wic'a'pahisni sk'e'e.

64.

1. *Wik'o'skalaka wą ta'ku iwa'c'įk'owelak'a li'la yua'sni-p'icasniyą wac'į'ko c'ąke' hąke'ya atku'ku kį sųka'ku c'įca' wą e'l i' ną heya' ke'e, — Wą, c'įks, nit'ą'ksila wana' li'la t'e'hą c'ąte' si'ca ų' c'a*

---

[1] Pouting was indulged in generally by women, when their pride was hurt; and they might not eat, or take an interest in life for indefinite periods. I never saw anyone do this; except children. I think it is out of style for adults now.

[2] His male cross-cousin.

brother and said to him, "Son, I can no longer stand to see your younger sister so unhappy; won't you try somehow to help her to come out of it ?" So the young man went home and related what his father had said. 2. "My father talked to me just now and asked me to look to the fact that my younger sister is pouting; and to think of what could be done to bring her through, so I came home meditating on it," he said; and his wife who was sorry for her sister-in-law, said, "Let us take her with us into the country away from people, and she may forget; meantime, your excuse will be that you are grazing your horses," she suggested. Accordingly, they moved out and camped in a pleasant place where there was nobody about. 3. They used two tipis. The man and his wife lived in one, and the young woman in the other. Now they had lived there several days during which time the girl seemed to be very happy with her sister-in-law, as they together took care of the meat from the game that her brother brought in every day; so things seemed to be going well. 4. Then one morning the girl who was getting on so well, suddenly showed that she was unhappy again, so her sister-in-law said, "Sister-in-law, recently something has displeased you again, it appears. Whatever it is, tell me." And she replied thus, "For two nights in succession now, my brother has been coming to me where I sleep, but I could not say anything, and that is why I am very unhappy," she said. 5. So the wife told her husband when he returned, secretly. And he was very sad and ashamed, and said, "Tell my younger sister that she and you shall sleep with one end of a

---

t‘awa′t‘elwayeśni¹ ye lo′. To′k‘eśk‘ekel yua′sni-wac‘i̧ ye′, — eya′ c‘a̧ke′ k‘i′ na̧ oya′ka ke’ᵉ. 2. — Ate′ lec‘a′la wo′makiyaki̧ na̧ t‘a̧kśi′ wac‘i̧ko ki̧ he′ e′l e′tu̧we-maśi c‘a̧ke′ to′k‘el k̇‘a̧p‘i′ca he′ci̧ha̧ iyu′kca̧ waku′ k‘u̧, — eya′ yu̧k‘a̧′ t‘awi′cu ki̧, śce′p‘a̧ku u̧′śikila c‘a̧ke′, — It‘o′ mani̧′l ȩut‘ipi na̧ kic‘i′la he′c‘iya u̧k‘u̧′pi ki̧ha̧ aki′snikte se′ce, k‘oha̧′ ec‘a′ś śu̧k-wa′yaślayak‘iyi̧kte, — eya′ c‘a̧ke′ wana′ mani̧′l tuwe′ni u̧′śni wa̧ owa′śtecaka c‘a̧ke′ e′l e′t‘ipi ke’ᵉ. 3. T‘i-nu̧′p e′t‘ipi yu̧k‘a̧′ u̧ma′ wik‘o′śkalaka ki̧ t‘i′ śk‘e’ᵉ. Wana′ to′nac‘a̧² t‘i′pi k‘e′yaś wik‘o′śkalaka ki̧ śce′p‘a̧ku kic‘i′ wi′hahayakel ece′-u̧ c‘a̧ke′ k‘oha̧′ t‘ib.lo′ku ki̧ t‘a′ḣca awi′c‘ag.liha̧ c‘a̧ke′ waka′b.lapi na̧ ta̧ya̧′ ya̧ka′pi ke’ᵉ. 4. Yu̧k‘a̧′ to′hu̧wel-hi̧`ha̧naka wa̧ wik‘o′śkalaka ki̧ ta̧ye′ḣci̧ś c‘a̧l-wa′śteya u̧′ se′ce c‘u̧ ak‘e′ ta′ku iyo′yaka c‘a̧ke′ śce′p‘a̧ku ki̧, — Ścep‘a̧`, lec‘a′la ak‘e′ ta′ku iyo′nicip‘iśni iteke′. Ta′ku he′c‘iha̧ oma′kiyaki ye′, — eya′ ke’ᵉ. Yu̧k‘a̧′ ayu′pti̧ na̧ heya′ ke’ᵉ, — Wana′ ha̧he′pi nu̧′powec‘iha̧ mu̧ke′ ci̧ ekta′ t‘ib.lo′ hi′ k‘e′yaś to′k‘ani- ta`kep‘eśni ki̧ u̧′ li′la c‘a̧te′ maśi′ce′, ścep‘a̧`, — eya′ ke’ᵉ. 5. C‘a̧ke′ wi̧′ya̧ ki̧ hi̧g.na′ku g.li′ c‘a oki′yaka ke’ᵉ, naḣma′la. Yu̧k‘a̧′ li′la

---

¹ t‘awa′t‘elya, to feel equal to difficulty; hardship; sorrow. "I do not feel able to stand it", the father says.
² to′nac‘a̧, several days, c‘a̧, a twenty-four hour period; one night and day. c‘a̧ is always an enclitic, added to numbers, as well as to to′na.

rope tied to an arm of each of you. Whoever it is who is troubling her, when he comes in again, she must jerk on the rope. When that happens I will run in from here and find out who this visitor is. — *Hoȟ!* How in the world could I go do such a thing ?'' he added. 6. It was night again, so the two women retired in their respective tipis, with a rope tied to them both; and sometime in the night the girl gave it a few quick jerks. So the woman woke her husband. They had some kindling in readiness which they lighted and ran with it into the other tipi; and there they found a Crow Indian sitting with his arm around the girl's neck; thus they caught him 7. As it was not clear at the moment just what the brother should do with him, he waited while the man, by means of signs, indicated that he had been watching this girl from the bank, and found her very attractive to him and that he wished her for his wife; so, instead of killing him as an enemy, they sat there with him until morning, and at once they broke camp and returned to the tribal encampment. And for a son-in-law, they brought home this handsome Crow Indian. And from then on, this young woman was cured of her pouting.

---

c‘ąte' śi'cį ną iśte'cį ną heya' ke’ᵉ, — T‘ąkśi' oki'yaka yo', wi'k‘ą wążi' ihą'ke anų'k isto' ik‘o'yakya nųka'pikte lo'. Ną he' tuwe' c‘a e'l i' he'cįhą ak‘e' t‘ima' iya'ye cįhą yuti'ktitąkte lo'. To'kśa' he'c‘ų kįhą ekta' ib.la'm.nįkte lo'. Hoȟ, ta'kowe' miye' he'c‘i wai'ktelak‘a, — eya' ke’ᵉ. 6. Wana' hąhe'pi c‘ąke' wį'yą kį nųp‘į' wi'k‘ą ai'yag.laśka ȟpa'yapi yųk‘ą' hąwa'tohąl wik‘o'śkalaka k‘ų wi'k‘ą kį yuti'ktitą c‘ąke' wį'yą kį hįg.na'ku yuȟi'ca ke’ᵉ. Peti'leye¹ wį'yeya g.na'kapi c‘ąke' yui'le icu'pi ną yuha' naślo'k iya'yapi yųk‘ą' K‘ągi'-wic‘a'śa wą wik‘o'śkalaka k‘ų he' p‘o'skil yus' yąka'hą c‘a i'yaślalyapi śk‘e’ᵉ. 7. C‘ąke' t‘ib.lo'ku kį to'k‘el ok‘u'wakta t‘ąį'śni yųk‘ą' wi'yut‘at‘a ną maya'tąhą wį'yą kį he' awą'yak k‘uwa' k‘e'yaś li'la waśte'laka c‘a yu'zįkta c‘į' ke'ya'-wiyu't‘a c‘ąke' kte'śni yuha' ayą'pyapi ną he'c‘ena ig.la'ka g.licu'pi ke’ᵉ. Ną wic‘a'woȟa wą K‘ągi'-wic‘a'śa c‘a ową'yak- waśte agili'pi śk‘e’ᵉ. Yųk‘ą' hetą'hą nake'ś wik‘o'śkalaka wą wac‘i'k‘o k‘ų he' aki'sni ke'ya'pi’ⁱ.

---

¹ This would better be *p‘el-’i'leye*, kindling; *p‘e'ta*, fire; *i'le*, to ignite; *ya*, to cause.

Lightning Source UK Ltd.
Milton Keynes UK
UKHW022003290921
391396UK00010B/443